Windswept House

A VATICAN NOVEL

BOOKS BY MALACHI MARTIN

The Scribal Character of the Dead Sea Scrolls
The Pilgrim *(under the pseudonym Michael Serafian)*
The Encounter
Three Popes and the Cardinal
Jesus Now
The New Castle
Hostage to the Devil
The Final Conclave
King of Kings
The Decline and Fall of the Roman Church
There Is Still Love
Rich Church, Poor Church
Vatican
The Jesuits
The Keys of This Blood
Windswept House: A Vatican Novel

Windswept House

A Vatican Novel

Malachi Martin

Broadway Books
New York

A hardcover edition of this book was originally published in 1996 by Doubleday, a division of Random House, Inc. It is here reprinted by arrangement with Doubleday.

Book design by Paul Randall Mize

First Broadway Books trade paperback edition published 2001.

The Library of Congress Cataloging-in-Publication Data has cataloged the hardcover edition as:

Martin, Malachi.
Windswept house: a Vatican novel / Malachi Martin.—1st ed.
p. cm.
1. Catholic Church—Vatican City—Clergy—Fiction.
2. Vatican City—Fiction. I. Title.
PS3563.A725W56 1996
813'.54—dc20 95-26716
CIP

ISBN 978-0-385-49231-7

For Pope St. Pius V
in honor of Mary
Queen of the Most Holy Rosary

Contents

Windswept House
A VATICAN NOVEL

History as Prologue: End Signs
1957

DIPLOMATS schooled in harsh times and in the toughest ways of finance, trade and international rivalry are not much given to omens. Still, today's enterprise brimmed with such promise that the six Foreign Ministers who gathered in Rome on March 25, 1957, felt that everything surrounding them—the rock-solid centrality of Europe's premier city, the cleansing winds, the open skies, the benign smile of the day's climate—was fortune's very cloak of blessing drawn about them as they laid the foundation stone for a new edifice of nations.

As partners in the creation of a new Europe that would sweep away the squabbling nationalism that had so often split this ancient delta, these six men and their governments were one in their faith that they were about to open their lands to a wider economic horizon and a taller political sky than had ever been contemplated. They were about to sign the treaties of Rome. They were about to create the European Economic Community.

In recent memory, nothing but death and destruction had been spawned in their capitals. Only the year before, the Soviets had underscored their expansionist determination in the blood of Hungary's attempted uprising; any day Soviet armor could roll across Europe. No one expected the U.S.A. and its Marshall Plan to carry forever the burdens of building the new Europe. Nor did any European government wish to be clamped between the U.S.A. and the U.S.S.R. in a rivalry that could only deepen in the decades ahead.

As if already accustomed to acting as one in the face of such reality, all six ministers signed on as founders of the EEC. The three representatives of the Benelux nations, because Belgium, the Netherlands and Luxembourg were the very crucible in which the idea of a new Europe had been tried and found true. Or at least true enough. The minister representing France, because his country would be the beating heart of the new Europe, as it had always been of the old Europe. Italy, because his country was the living soul of Europe. West Germany, because the world would never shunt his country aside again.

So the European Community was born. There were toasts to the geopolitical visionaries who had made this day possible. To Robert Schuman and Jean Monnet of France; to Konrad Adenauer of West Germany; to Paul-Henri Spaak of Belgium. And there were congratulations all around. It wouldn't be long before Denmark, Ireland and England would see the wisdom of the new venture. And, while they might require some patient help, Greece, Portugal and Spain would join as well. Of course, there was still the matter of holding the Soviets at bay. And there was the matter of finding a new center of gravity. But no doubt about it: the nascent EEC was the cutting edge of the new Europe that had to come if Europe was to survive.

When all the signing and sealing and toasting were done, the moment came for the distinctively Roman ritual and privilege of diplomats: an audience with the octogenarian Pope in the Apostolic Palace on Vatican Hill.

Seated on his traditional papal throne amid the panoply of Vatican ceremonial in an ornate sala, His Holiness Pius XII received the six ministers and their entourages with smiling countenance. His welcome was sincere. His remarks were brief. His attitude was of a longtime owner and resident of a vast property giving some pointers to newly arrived and intending residents.

Europe, the Holy Father recalled, had had its eras of greatness when a common faith had animated the hearts of its peoples. Europe, he urged, could have its geopolitical greatness again, refurbished and burnished anew, if it could create a new heart. Europe, he intimated, could again forge a supernal, common and binding faith.

Inwardly, the ministers winced. Pius had pointed to the greatest difficulty facing the EEC on the day of its birth. Beneath his words lay the warning that neither democratic socialism nor capitalist democracy nor the prospect of the good life nor a mystic "Europa" of the humanists could provide the engine to drive their dream. Practically speaking, their new Europe lacked a glowing center, a superior force or principle to bind it together and drive it forward. Practically speaking, their Europe lacked what this Pope had. Lacked what he was.

His points made, the Holy Father traced three crosses in the air as the traditional papal blessing. Some few knelt to receive it. Some who remained standing bowed their heads. But it had become impossible for them to associate the Pope with the healing balm of the God he claimed to represent as Vicar, or to recognize that balm as the only cohesive factor that could mend the world's soul; neither could they acknowledge that economic and political treaties were not the glue that binds the hearts and minds of mankind.

And yet, frail as he was, they could only envy this solitary, enthroned dignitary. For, as Belgium's Paul-Henri Spaak later remarked, he presided over a universal organization. And he was more than the elected representative of that organization. He was the possessor of its power. He was its center of gravity.

❑ ❑ ❑ ❑

From the window of his study on the third floor of the Apostolic Palace, the Holy Father watched the architects of the new Europe climb into their limousines in the square below.

"What do you think, Holiness? Can their new Europe develop strongly enough to stop Moscow?"

Pius turned to his companion—a German Jesuit, a longtime friend and favorite confessor. "Marxism is still the enemy, Father. But the Anglo-Saxons have the initiative." On this Pope's lips, Anglo-Saxon meant the Anglo-American establishment. "Their Europe will go far. And it will go fast. But the greatest day for Europe has not yet dawned."

The Jesuit failed to follow the papal vision. "Which Europe, Holiness? The greatest day for whose Europe?"

"For the Europe born today." The Pope's answer was unhesitating. "On the day this Holy See is harnessed to the new Europe of the diplomats and politicians—to the Europe centered in Brussels and Paris—on that day the Church's misfortunes will start in earnest." Then, turning again to watch the limousines departing across St. Peter's Square, "The new Europe will have its little day, Father. But only a day."

1960

No more promising enterprise had ever hung in the balance, and no more important piece of Vatican business had ever been transacted between a Pope and his councillors, than the issue on the papal docket this February morning of 1960. Since the day of his election to the papacy just over a year before, His Holiness John XXIII—"good Pope John," as he was quickly called—had moved the Holy See, the papal government and most of the outside diplomatic and religious world into a new orbit. Now it seemed he wanted to raise the world as well.

Already seventy-seven years old at his election, this roly-poly peasant of a man had been chosen as an interim Pope; as an inoffensive compromise whose brief reign would buy a little time—four or five years had been the reckoning—to find a proper successor to guide the Church through the Cold War. But, within months of his enthronement and to everyone's astonishment, he had opened up his Vatican in a surprise call for an Ecumenical Council. In fact, nearly every Vatican official—including every advisor who had been summoned to this confidential meeting in the papal apartments on the fourth floor of the Apostolic Palace—was already hip deep in preparations for that Council.

With a directness natural to him, the Pope shared his mind with the handful of men he had gathered for that purpose—a dozen or so of his key Cardinals, plus a number of bishops and *monsignori* from the Secretariat of State. Two expert Portuguese translators were present.

"We have a choice to make," His Holiness confided to his advisors. "We prefer not to make it alone." The issue, he said, revolved around a now world-famous letter received by his predecessor on the Throne of Peter. The story surrounding that letter was so well known, he said further, that it needed only the barest outline this morning.

Fatima, once among the most obscure towns in Portugal, had become suddenly famous in 1917 as the site where three little peasant children—two girls and a boy—had been the recipients of six visits, or visions, of the Blessed Virgin Mary. Along with many millions of Catholics, everyone in this room today knew that the Fatima children had been given three secrets by the Virgin. Everyone knew that, as their visitor from Heaven had foretold, two of the children had died in childhood; only the oldest, Lucia, had survived. Everyone knew that Lucia, now a cloistered nun, had long since revealed the first two of the Fatima secrets. But it was the Virgin's wish, Lucia had said, that the third secret be published by "the Pope of 1960"; and that simultaneously the same Pope was to organize a worldwide consecration of "Russia" to the Virgin Mary. That consecration was to be performed by all the bishops of the world on the same day, each in his own diocese, each using the same words. That consecration would be tantamount to a public worldwide condemnation of the Soviet Union.

The Virgin had promised that if the consecration was done, Lucia had said, "Russia" would be converted and would cease to be a threat. However, if her wish was not fulfilled "by the Pope of 1960," then "Russia would spread its errors throughout all nations," there would be much suffering and destruction and the faith of the Church would be so corrupted that only in Portugal would "the dogma of the faith" be preserved intact.

In the course of her third Fatima visit in July of 1917, the Virgin had promised to seal her mandate with tangible proof of its authenticity as a message from God. She would perform a miracle at noontime on the following October 13. And in that very hour on that very day, along with some 75,000 people who had come, some of them from great distances—along with newsmen and photographers, along with scientists and skeptics, along with many reliable clerics—the children had witnessed an astonishing miracle.

The sun had violated every possible natural law. Breaking from a heavy and unrelenting rain that had drenched everyone and turned the terrain of that remote place into a mud bog, it literally danced in the skies. It had showered a rainbow flood of brilliant colors. It had plummeted downward until it seemed certain to plunge into the crowd. Then, just as suddenly, it had retreated to its normal position and shone as benignly as ever. Everyone was stunned. Their clothes were as immaculate as if just laundered and pressed. All were entirely unharmed. All had seen the dancing sun; but only the children had seen the Virgin.

"Surely"—good Pope John retrieved an envelope from a humidor-sized box resting on the table beside him—"the first thing to be done this morning must be obvious." Excitement ran among his advisors. They were here, then, for a private reading of Lucia's secret letter. It was no exaggeration to say that tens of millions of people everywhere awaited word that "the Pope of 1960" would reveal the portions of the third secret that had been so closely guarded until now, and would obey the Virgin's mandate. With that thought in mind, His Holiness underscored his exact and literal meaning of the word "private." Certain that his admonition of secrecy was clear, the Holy Father handed the Fatima letter to the two Portuguese translators; and they in turn rendered the secret text, viva voce, into Italian.

"Now." The reading completed, the Pope quickly pinpointed the choice he preferred not to make alone. "We must confide that since August of 1959, we have been in delicate negotiations with the Soviet Union. Our aim is to have at least two prelates from the U.S.S.R.'s Orthodox Church attend Our Council." Pope John frequently referred to the coming Second Vatican Council as "Our Council."

What was he to do, then? His Holiness asked this morning. Providence had willed that he be "the Pope of 1960." And yet, if he obeyed what Sister Lucia clearly described as the mandate of the Queen of Heaven—if he and his bishops declared publicly, officially and universally that "Russia" was full of baneful errors—it would spell ruin for his Soviet initiative. But even aside from that—aside from his fervent wish to have the Orthodox Church represented at the Council—if the Pontiff were to use the full authority of his papacy and his hierarchy to carry out the Virgin's mandate, it would be tantamount to branding the Soviet Union and its current Marxist dictator, Nikita Khrushchev, as criminal. In their rage, wouldn't the Soviets retaliate? Would the Pope not be responsible for a fresh wave of persecutions—for the ugly death of millions—throughout the Soviet Union, its satellites and surrogates?

To underscore his concern, His Holiness had one portion of the Fatima letter read out again. He saw understanding—shock in some cases—on all the faces around him. If everyone in this room had understood that key passage of the third secret so easily, he asked, would not the Soviets be just as quick? Would they not take from it the strategic information that would give them an undoubted advantage over the free world?

"We might still hold Our Council, but . . ." There was no need for His Holiness to finish the thought. Everything was clear now. Publication of the secret would set off repercussions everywhere. Friendly governments would be gravely disturbed. The Soviets would be alienated on the one hand and strategically aided on the other. The choice the good Pope had to make came down to bedrock geopolitics.

No one doubted the good faith of Sister Lucia. But several advisors pointed out that nearly twenty years had elapsed between the time in 1917 when she had heard the words of the Virgin and the time in the mid-1930s when she had actually written this letter. What guarantee had the Holy Father that time had not clouded her memory? And what guarantee was there that three illiterate peasant children—not one of them twelve years old at the time—had accurately transmitted such a complex message? Might there not be some preliterate and childish fancy at work here? Indeed, might there not be something even more debilitating for the truth? Troops from the Soviet Union had entered the Spanish Civil War raging only miles away at the time Lucia had written her letter. Had Lucia's words been colored by her own fear of the Soviets?

There was one dissenting voice from the consensus that was forming. One Cardinal—a German Jesuit, a friend and favorite confessor to this Pope, as he had been to the last—could not remain silent in the face of such degradation of the role of divine intervention. It was one thing for ministers of secular governments to abandon the practicalities of faith. But surely such banality should be unacceptable for churchmen advising the Holy Father.

"The choice to be made here," the Jesuit argued, "is simple and prima facie. Either we accept this letter, do what it says, and then await the consequences. Or we honestly disbelieve it. We forget it all. We suppress the letter as a historical relic; we carry on as we are going and, by our deliberate decision, we strip ourselves of a special protection. But either way, let not one of us here doubt that we are talking about the fate of all mankind."

For all the trust His Holiness placed in the Jesuit Cardinal's expertise and loyalty, the decision went against Fatima. "*Questo non è per i nostri tempi,*" the Holy Father said. "This is not for our times." Shortly after that day, the Cardinal scanned the brief release distributed to the media by the official Vatican press office. Its words would stand forever in his mind as a curt refusal to obey the will of Heaven.

For the good of the Church and the welfare of mankind, the statement declared, the Holy See had decided not to publish the text of the third secret at this time. ". . . The decision of the Vatican is based on various reasons: (1) Sister Lucia is still living. (2) The Vatican already knows the contents of the letter. (3) Although the Church recognizes the Fatima apparitions, she does not pledge herself to guarantee the veracity of the words which the three little shepherds claim to have heard from Our Lady. In these circumstances, it is most probable that the secret of Fatima will remain forever under absolute seal."

"*Ci vedremo.*" The Cardinal set the release aside. "We shall see." He knew the drill. The Holy See would have amicable words with Nikita Khrushchev. The Pontiff would have his Council. The Council would have its Orthodox prelates from the Soviet Union. But the question still to be answered was whether His Holiness, his Vatican and his Church would now undergo the consequences promised at Fatima.

Or, to frame the issue in geopolitical terms, the question was whether the Holy See had harnessed itself to "the new Europe of the diplomats and politicians," as the good Pope's predecessor had foretold. "On that day," that frail old man had said, "the Church's misfortunes will start in earnest."

"We shall see." For now, the Cardinal would have to settle for that. One way or the other, it would only be a matter of time.

1963

The Enthronement of the Fallen Archangel Lucifer was effected within the Roman Catholic Citadel on June 29, 1963; a fitting date for the historic promise about to be fulfilled. As the principal agents of this Ceremonial well knew, Satanist tradition had long predicted that the Time of the Prince would be ushered in at the moment when a Pope would take the name of the Apostle Paul. That requirement—the signal that the Availing Time had begun—had been accomplished just eight days before with the election of the latest Peter-in-the-Line.

There had barely been time since the papal Conclave had ended for the complex arrangements to be readied; but the Supreme Tribunal had decided there could be no more perfect date for the Enthronement of the Prince than this feast day of the twin princes of the Citadel, SS. Peter and Paul. And there could be no more perfect place than the Chapel of St. Paul itself, situated as it was so near to the Apostolic Palace.

The complexity of the arrangements were dictated mainly by the nature of the Ceremonial Event to be enacted. Security was so tight in the grouping of Vatican buildings within which this gem of a Chapel lay that the full panoply of the Ceremonial could not possibly escape detection here. If the aim was to be achieved—if the Ascent of the Prince was actually to be accomplished in the Availing Time—then every element of the Celebration of the Calvary Sacrifice must be turned on its head by the other and opposite Celebration. The sacred must be profaned. The profane must be adored. The unbloody representation of the Sacrifice of the Nameless Weakling on the Cross must be replaced by the supreme and bloody violation of the dignity of the Nameless One. Guilt must be accepted as innocence. Pain must give joy. Grace, repentance, pardon must all be drowned in an orgy of opposites. And it must all be done without mistakes. The sequence of events, the meaning of the words, the significance of the actions must all comprise the perfect enactment of sacrilege, the ultimate ritual of treachery.

The whole delicate affair was placed in the experienced hands of the

Prince's trusted Guardian in Rome. A master of the elaborate Ceremonial of the Roman Church, so much more was this granite-faced, acid-tongued prelate a Master of the Prince's Ceremonial of Darkness and Fire. The immediate aim of every Ceremonial, he knew, is to venerate "the abomination of desolation." But the further aim now must be to oppose the Nameless Weakling in His stronghold, to occupy the Weakling's Citadel during the Availing Time, to secure the Ascent of the Prince in the Citadel as an irresistible force, to supplant the Citadel's Keeper, to take full possession of the Keys entrusted to the Keeper by the Weakling.

The Guardian tackled the problem of security head-on. Such unobtrusive elements as the Pentagram and the black candles and the appropriate draperies could be part of the Ceremonial in Rome. But other Rubrics—the Bowl of Bones and the Ritual Din, for example, the sacrificial animals and the victim—would be too much. There would have to be a Parallel Enthronement. A Concelebration could be accomplished with the same effect by the Brethren in an Authorized Targeting Chapel. Provided all the participants in both locations "targeted" every element of the Event on the Roman Chapel, then the Event in its fullness would be accomplished specifically in the target area. It would all be a matter of unanimity of hearts, identity of intention and perfect synchronization of words and actions between the Targeting Chapel and the Target Chapel. The living wills and the thinking minds of the Participants concentrated on the specific Aim of the Prince would transcend all distance.

For a man as experienced as the Guardian, the choice of the Targeting Chapel was easy. As simple as a phone call to the United States. Over the years, the Prince's adherents in Rome had developed a faultless unanimity of heart and a seamless identity of intention with the Guardian's friend, Leo, Bishop of the Chapel in South Carolina.

Leo was not the man's name. It was his description. The silvery-white mane of hair on his large head looked for all the world like a scraggly lion's mane. In the forty years or so since His Excellency had established his Chapel, the number and the social importance of the Participants he had attracted, the punctilious blasphemy of his Ceremonies and his frequent and ready cooperation with those who shared his point of view and ultimate goals, had so established the superiority of his operation that by now it was widely admired among initiates as the Mother Chapel of the United States.

The news that his Chapel had been Authorized as the Targeting Chapel for such a great Event as the Enthronement of the Prince within the heart of the Roman Citadel itself was supremely gratifying. More to the point, Leo's vast Ceremonial knowledge and experience saved a lot of time. There was no need, for example, to test his appreciation of the contradictory principles upon which all worship of the Archangel is structured. No need to doubt his desire to encompass the ultimate strategy in that battle—the end of the Roman Catholic Church as the papal institution it had been since the Nameless Weakling had founded it.

There was no need even to explain that the ultimate aim wasn't exactly to liquidate the Roman Catholic organization. Leo understood how unintelligent that would be, how wasteful. Far better to make that organization into something truly useful, to homogenize and assimilate it into a grand worldwide order of human affairs. To confine it to broad humanist—and only humanist—goals.

Like-minded experts that they were, the Guardian and the American Bishop reduced their arrangements for the twin Ceremonial Events to a roster of names and an inventory of Rubrics.

The Guardian's list of names—the Participants in the Roman Chapel—turned out to be men of the highest caliber. High-ranking churchmen, and laymen of substance. Genuine Servitors of the Prince within the Citadel. Some had been selected, co-opted, trained and promoted in the Roman Phalanx over the decades, while others represented the new generation dedicated to carrying the Prince's agenda forward for the next several decades. All understood the need to remain undetected; for the Rule says, "The Guarantee of Our Tomorrow Is Today's Persuasion That We Do Not Exist."

Leo's roster of Participants—men and women who had made their mark in corporate, government and social life—was every bit as impressive as the Guardian had expected. But the Victim, His Excellency said—a child—would be truly a prize for the Violation-of-Innocence.

The checklist of Rubrics required for the Parallel Ceremonial centered mainly on the elements that had to be ruled out in Rome. Leo's Targeting Chapel must have its set of Vials containing Earth, Air, Fire and Water. Check. It must have the Bowl of Bones. Check. The Red and Black Pillars. Check. The Shield. Check. The animals. Check. Down the list they went. Check. Check.

The matter of synchronizing the Ceremonies in the two Chapels was familiar for Leo. As usual, fascicles of printed sheets, irreligiously called Missals, would be prepared for use by the Participants in both Chapels; and, as usual, they would be in flawless Latin. A telephone link would be monitored by a Ceremonial Messenger at each end, so that the Participants would always be able to take up their parts in perfect harmony with their Cooperating Brethren.

During the Event, the pulse of every Participant's heart must be perfectly attuned to make Hate, not love. The gratification of Pain and the Consummation must be perfectly achieved under Leo's direction in the Sponsoring Chapel. The Authorization, the Instructions and the Evidence—the final and culminating elements peculiar to this occasion—would be an honor for the Guardian himself to orchestrate in the Vatican.

Finally, if everyone did the needful exactly according to the Rule, the Prince would at long last Consummate his Most Ancient Revenge upon the Weakling, the Merciless Enemy who had paraded through the ages as the Most High Merciful One for whom the darkest of darkness was light enough to see all.

Leo could imagine the rest. The Enthronement Event would create a perfect covering, opaque and velvet smooth, to conceal the Prince within the official Church membership of the Roman Citadel. Enthroned in Darkness, the Prince would be able to foment that same Darkness as never before. Friend and foe would be affected alike. Darkness of will would become so profound that it would obscure even the official objective of the Citadel's existence: the perpetual adoration of the Nameless One. In time and at last, the Goat would expel the Lamb and enter into Possession of the Citadel. The Prince would usher himself into possession of a house—The House—that was not his.

"Think of it, my friend." Bishop Leo was nearly beside himself with anticipation. "The unaccomplished will be accomplished. This will be the capstone of my career. The capstone Event of the twentieth century!"

Leo was not far wrong.

It was night. The Guardian and a few Acolytes worked in silence to put everything in readiness in the Target Chapel of St. Paul. A semicircle of kneeler chairs was set up to face the Altar. On the Altar itself, five candlesticks were fitted with graceful black tapers. A silver Pentagram was placed on the Tabernacle and covered with a blood-red veil. A Throne, symbol of the Prince Regnant, was placed to the left of the Altar. The walls, with their lovely frescoes and paintings depicting events in the life of Christ and of the Apostle, were draped in black cloth suitably embroidered in gold with symbols of the Prince's history.

As The Hour drew near, the genuine Servitors of the Prince within the Citadel began to arrive. The Roman Phalanx. Among them, some of the most illustrious men currently to be found in the collegium, hierarchy and bureaucracy of the Roman Catholic Church. Among them, too, secular representatives of the Phalanx as outstanding in their way as the members of the hierarchy.

Take that Prussian fellow just striding in the door, for example. A prime specimen of the new lay breed if ever there was one. Not yet forty, he was already a man of importance in certain critical transnational affairs. Even the light from the black tapers glinted off his steel-rimmed glasses and his balding head as if to single him out. Chosen as International Delegate and Plenipotentiary Extraordinary to the Enthronement, the Prussian carried the leather pouch containing the Letters of Authorization and Instructions to the Altar before he took his place in the semicircle.

Some thirty minutes before midnight, all of the kneeler chairs were occupied by the current harvest of a Prince Tradition that had been planted, nurtured and cultivated within the ancient Citadel over a period of some eighty years. Though restricted in numbers for a time, the group has persisted in protective obscurity as a foreign body and an alien spirit within its host and victim. It permeated offices and activities throughout the Roman Citadel, spreading its symptoms through the bloodstream of the Church Universal like a subcutaneous infection. Symptoms like cynicism and indifference, malfeasance and misfeasance in high office, inattention to correct doctrine, neglect of moral judgment, loss of acuity in sacral observance, blurring of essential memories and of the words and gestures that bespoke them.

Such were the men gathered in the Vatican for the Enthronement; and such was the Tradition they fostered throughout the worldwide administration headquartered in this Citadel. Missals in hand, eyes fixed on Altar and Throne, minds and wills deep in concentration, they waited in silence for midnight to usher in the feast of SS. Peter and Paul, the quintessential holy day of Rome.

The Targeting Chapel—a large assembly hall in the basement of a parochial school—had been furnished in strict observance of the Rules. Bishop Leo had directed it all personally. Now, his specially chosen Acolytes bustled quietly to put the final details in order as he checked everything.

The Altar first, placed at the north end of the Chapel. Flat on the Altar, a large Crucifix with the head of the corpus pointing to the north. A hairbreadth away, the red-veiled Pentagram flanked by two black candles. Above, a red Sanctuary Lamp gleaming with the Ritual Flame. At the east end of the Altar, a cage; and in the cage, Flinnie, a seven-week-old puppy, mildly sedated against the brief moment of his usefulness to the Prince. Behind the Altar, ebony tapers awaiting the touch of Ritual Flame to their wicks.

A quick turn to the south wall. Resting on a credenza, the Thurible and the container holding the squares of charcoal and incense. In front of the credenza, the Red and Black Pillars from which hung the Snake Shield and the Bell of Infinity. A turn to the east wall. Vials containing Earth, Air, Fire and Water surrounding a second cage. In the cage, a dove, oblivious of its fate as a parody not only of the Nameless Weakling but of the full Trinity. Lectern and Book in readiness at the west wall. The semicircle of kneeler chairs facing north toward the Altar. Flanking the kneeler chairs, the Emblems of Entry: the Bowl of Bones on the west side nearest the door; to the east, the Crescent Moon and Five-Pointed Star with Goat-Points raised upward. On each chair, a copy of the Missal to be used by the Participants.

Finally, Leo glanced toward the entrance to the Chapel itself. Special vestments for the Enthronement, identical to those he and his busy Acolytes had already donned, hung on the rack just inside the door. He checked his watch against the large wall clock just as the first Participants arrived. Satisfied with the arrangements, he headed for the large connecting cloakroom that served as vestry. The Archpriest and Frater Medico should have the Victim prepared by now. Barely thirty minutes more, and his Ceremonial Messenger would open the telephone link to the Target Chapel in the Vatican. It would be The Hour.

Just as there were different requirements for the physical setup in the two Chapels, so too for the Participants. Those in St. Paul's Chapel, all men, wore robes and sashes of ecclesiastical rank or faultlessly tailored black suits of secular rank. Concentrated and purposeful, their eyes trained upon Altar and empty Throne, they appeared to be the pious Roman clergy and lay worshippers they were commonly believed to be.

As distinguished in rank as the Roman Phalanx, the American Participants in the Targeting Chapel nevertheless presented a jarring contrast to their fellows in the Vatican. Men and women entered here. And far from sitting or kneeling in fine attire, as they arrived each disrobed completely and donned the single, seamless vestment prescribed for the Enthronement—blood red for Sacrifice; knee length and sleeveless; V-necked and open down the front. Disrobing and enrobing were accomplished in silence, with no hurry or excitement. Just concentrated, ritual calm.

Once vested, the Participants passed by the Bowl of Bones, dipped in their hands to retrieve small fistfuls, and took their places in the semicircle of chairs facing the Altar. As the Bowl of Bones was depleted and the kneeler chairs filled, the Ritual Din began to shatter the silence. Ceaselessly rattling the Bones, each Participant began talking—to himself, to others, to the Prince, to no one. Not raucously at first, but in an unsettling ritual cadence.

More Participants arrived. More Bones were taken. The semicircle was filled out. The mumbling cadence swelled from a softly cacophonous *sussurro*. The steadily mounting gibberish of prayer and pleading and Bone rattling developed a kind of controlled heat. The sound became angry, as if verging on violence. Became a controlled concert of chaos. A mind-gripping howl of Hate and Revolt. A concentrated prelude to the celebration of the Enthronement of the Prince of This World within the Citadel of the Weakling.

His blood-red vestments flowing gracefully, Leo strode into the vestry. For a moment, it seemed to him that everything was in perfect readiness. Already vested, his co-Celebrant, the balding, bespectacled Archpriest, had lit a single black taper in preparation for the Procession. He had filled a large golden Chalice with red wine and covered it with a silver-gilt paten. He had placed an outsized white wafer of unleavened bread atop the paten.

A third man, Frater Medico, was seated on a bench. Vested like the other two, he held a child across his lap. His daughter. Agnes. Leo observed with satisfaction that Agnes seemed quiet and compliant for a change. Indeed, she seemed ready for the occasion this time. She had been dressed in a loose white gown that reached to her ankles. And, like her puppy on the Altar, she had been mildly sedated against the time of her usefulness in the Mysteries.

"Agnes," Medico purred into the child's ear. "It's almost time to come with Daddy."

"Not my daddy . . ." Despite the drugs, the girl opened her eyes and stared at her father. Her voice was weak but audible. "God is my daddy . . ."

"BLASPHEMY!" Agnes' words transformed Leo's mood of satisfaction exactly as electrical energy is transformed into lightning. *"Blasphemy!"* He shot the word again like a bullet. In fact, his mouth became a cannon shooting a barrage of rebuke at Medico. Physician or no, the man was a bumbler! The child should have been suitably prepared! There had been ample time to see to it!

Under Bishop Leo's attack, Medico turned ashen. But not so his daughter. She struggled to turn those unforgettable eyes of hers; struggled to meet Leo's wild glare of anger; struggled to repeat her challenge. "God is my daddy . . . !"

Trembling in his nervous agitation, Frater Medico gripped his daughter's head in his hands and forced her to look at him again. "Sweetheart," he cajoled. "I am your daddy. I've been your daddy always. And, yes, your mummy too, ever since she went away."

"Not my daddy . . . You let Flinnie be taken . . . Mustn't hurt Flinnie . . . Only a little puppy . . . Little puppies are made by God . . ."

"Agnes. Listen to me. I am your daddy. It's time . . ."

"Not my daddy . . . God is my daddy . . . God is my mummy . . . Daddies don't do things God doesn't like . . . Not my . . ."

Aware that the Target Chapel in the Vatican must be waiting for the Ceremonial telephone link to be engaged, Leo gave a sharp nod of instruction to the Archpriest. As so often in the past, the emergency procedure was the only remedy; and the requirement that the Victim be conscious at the first Ritual Consummation meant that it would have to be accomplished now.

Doing his priestly duty, the Archpriest sat down beside Frater Medico and shifted Agnes' drug-weakened form onto his own lap. "Agnes. Listen. I'm your daddy, too. Remember the special love between us? Remember?"

Stubbornly, Agnes kept up her struggle. "Not my daddy . . . Daddies don't do bad things to me . . . don't hurt me . . . don't hurt Jesus . . ."

In later years, Agnes' memory of this night—for remember it she finally did—would contain no titillating edge, no trace of the merely pornographic. Her memory of this night, when it came, would be one with her memory of her entire childhood. One with her memory of prolonged assault by Summary Evil. One with her memory—her never failing sense—

of that luminous tabernacle deep in her child's soul where Light transformed her agony with Courage and made her struggle possible.

In some way she knew but did not yet understand, that inner tabernacle was where Agnes truly lived. That center of her being was an untouchable refuge of indwelling Strength and Love and Trust; the place where the Suffering Victim, the true target of the assault on Agnes, had come to sanctify her agony forever with His own.

It was from within that refuge that Agnes heard every word spoken in the vestry on the night of the Enthronement. It was from that refuge that she met the hard eyes of Bishop Leo glaring down at her, and the stare of the Archpriest. She knew the price of resistance. Felt her body being shifted from her father's lap. Saw the light glinting on the spectacles of the Archpriest. Saw her father draw close again. Saw the needle in his hand. Felt the puncture. Felt the shock of the drug again. Felt herself lifted in someone's arms. But still she struggled. Struggled to see. Struggled against the blasphemy; against the effects of the violation; against the chanting; against the horror she knew was still to come.

Robbed by the drugs of strength to move, Agnes summoned her will as her only weapon and whispered again the words of her defiance and her agony. "Not my daddy . . . Don't hurt Jesus . . . Don't hurt me . . ."

It was The Hour. The beginning of the Availing Time for the Prince's Ascent into the Citadel. At the tinkling of the Bell of Infinity, all Participants in Leo's Chapel rose to their feet as one. Missals in hand, the constant clickety-clack of the Bones as grisly accompaniment, they chanted their full-throated processional, a triumphant profanation of the hymn of the Apostle Paul. "*Maran Atha!* Come, Lord! Come, O Prince. Come! Come! . . ."

Well-rehearsed Acolytes, men and women, led the way from vestry to Altar. Behind them, gaunt but distinguished-looking even in his red vestments, Frater Medico carried the Victim to the Altar and placed her full-length beside the Crucifix. In the flickering shadow of the veiled Pentagram, her hair almost touched the cage that held her little dog. Next according to rank, eyes blinking behind his spectacles, the Archpriest bore the single black candle from the vestry and took his place at the left of the Altar. Last, Bishop Leo strode forward bearing chalice and Host, adding his voice to the processional hymn. "So mote it be!" The final words of the ancient chant washed over the Altar in the Targeting Chapel.

"So mote it be!" The ancient chant washed over Agnes' limp form, fogging her mind more deeply than the drugs, intensifying the cold she had known would envelop her.

"So mote it be! Amen! Amen!" The ancient words washed over the Altar in the Chapel of St. Paul. Their hearts and wills as one with the Targeting Participants in America, the Roman Phalanx took up the Mysteries Refrain set out for them in their Latin Missals, beginning with the

Hymn of the Virgin Raped and ending with the Crown of Thorns Invocation.

In the Targeting Chapel, Bishop Leo removed the Victim Pouch from his neck and placed it reverently between the head of the Crucifix and the foot of the Pentagram. Then, to the resumed mumbling-humming chorus of the Participants and the rattling of Bones, Acolytes placed three incense squares on the glowing charcoal in the Thurible. Almost at once, blue smoke curled through the assembly hall, its pungent odor engulfing Victim, Celebrants and Participants alike.

In the daze of Agnes' mind, the smoke and the smell and the drugs and the cold and the Din all merged into a hideous cadenza.

Though no signal was given, the well-rehearsed Ceremonial Messenger informed his Vatican counterpart that the Invocations were about to begin. Sudden silence enveloped the American Chapel. Bishop Leo solemnly raised the Crucifix from beside Agnes' body, placed it upside down against the front of the Altar and, facing the congregation, raised his left hand in the inverted blessing of the Sign: the back of his hand toward the Participants; thumb and two middle fingers pressed to the palm; index and little fingers pointing upward to signify the horns of the Goat. "Let us invoke!"

In an atmosphere of darkness and fire, the Chief Celebrant in each Chapel intoned a series of Invocations to the Prince. The Participants in both Chapels chanted a response. Then, and only in America's Targeting Chapel, each Response was followed by a Convenient Action—a ritually determined acting-out of the spirit and the meaning of the words. Perfect cadence of words and will between the two Chapels was the responsibility of the Ceremonial Messengers tending the telephone link. From that perfect cadence would be woven a suitable fabric of human intention in which the drama of the Prince's Enthronement would be clothed.

"I believe in One Power." Bishop Leo's voice rang with conviction.

"And its name is Cosmos," the Participants in both Chapels chanted the upside-down Response set out in the Latin Missals. The Convenient Action followed in the Targeting Chapel. Two Acolytes incensed the Altar. Two more retrieved the Vials of Earth, Air, Fire and Water, placed them on the Altar, bowed to the Bishop and returned to their places.

"I believe in the Only Begotten Son of the Cosmic Dawn." Leo chanted.

"And His Name is Lucifer." The second ancient Response. Leo's Acolytes lighted the Pentagram Candles and incensed the Pentagram.

The third Invocation: "I believe in the Mysterious One."

The third Response: "And He is the Snake with Venom in the Apple of Life." To the constant rattling of Bones, Attendants approached the Red Pillar and reversed the Snake Shield to expose the side depicting the Tree of Knowledge.

The Guardian in Rome and the Bishop in America intoned the fourth Invocation: "I believe in the Ancient Leviathan."

In unison across an ocean and a continent, the fourth Response: "And

His Name is Hate." The Red Pillar and the Tree of Knowledge were incensed.

The fifth Invocation: "I believe in the Ancient Fox."

The fifth lusty Response: "And His Name is Lie." The Black Pillar was incensed as the symbol of all that is desolate and abominable.

In the flickering light cast by the tapers and with the blue smoke curling around him, Leo shifted his eyes to Flinnie's cage close by Agnes on the Altar. The puppy was almost alert now, coming to its feet in response to the chanting and clicking and clacking. "I believe in the Ancient Crab," Leo read the sixth Latin Invocation.

"And His Name is Living Pain," came the fulsome chant of the sixth Response. Clickety-clack, came the chanting of the Bones. With all eyes on him, an Acolyte stepped to the Altar, reached into the cage where the puppy wagged its tail in expectant greeting, pinned the hapless creature with one hand and, with the other, performed a perfectly executed vivisection, removing the reproductive organs first from the screaming animal. Expert that he was, the Attendant prolonged both the puppy's agony and the Participants' frenzied joy at the Ritual of Pain-Giving.

But not every sound was drowned by the Din of dreadful celebration. Faint though it was, there was the sound of Agnes' mortal struggle. There was the sound of Agnes' silent scream at the agony of her puppy. The sound of slurred and whispered words. The sound of supplication and suffering. "God is my daddy! . . . Holy God! . . . My little puppy! . . . Don't hurt Flinnie! . . . God is my daddy! . . . Don't hurt Jesus . . . Holy God . . ."

Alert to every detail, Bishop Leo glanced down at the Victim. Even in her near-unconscious state, still she struggled. Still she protested. Still she felt pain. Still she prayed with that unyielding resistance of hers. Leo was delighted. What a perfect little Victim. So pleasing to the Prince. Pitilessly and without pause, Leo and the Guardian led their congregations on through the rest of the fourteen Invocations, while the Convenient Actions that followed each Response became a raucous theater of perversity.

Finally, Bishop Leo brought the first part of the Ceremonial to a close with the Great Invocation: "I believe that the Prince of This World will be Enthroned this night in the Ancient Citadel, and from there He will create a New Community."

The Response was delivered with a gusto impressive even in this ghastly milieu. "And Its Name will be the Universal Church of Man."

It was time for Leo to lift Agnes into his arms at the Altar. It was time for the Archpriest to lift the chalice in his right hand and the large Host in his left. It was time for Leo to lead the Offertory Prayer, waiting after each Ritual Question for the Participants to read the Responses from their Missals.

"What was this Victim's name when once born?"

"Agnes!"

"What was this Victim's name when twice born?"
"Agnes Susannah!"
"What was this Victim's name when thrice born?"
"Rahab Jericho!"

Leo laid Agnes atop the Altar again and pricked the forefinger of her left hand until blood oozed from the little wound.

Pierced with cold, nausea rising in her, Agnes felt herself being lifted from the Altar, but she was no longer able to focus her eyes. She flinched at a sharp sting in her left hand. She absorbed isolated words that carried a dread she could not voice. "Victim . . . Agnes . . . thrice born . . . Rahab Jericho . . ."

Leo dipped his left index finger in Agnes' blood and, raising it for the Participants to see, began the Offertory chants.

"This, the Blood of our Victim, has been shed * So that our service to the Prince may be complete. * So that He may reign supreme in the House of Jacob * In the New Land of the Elect."

It was the Archpriest's turn now. Chalice and Host still raised aloft, he gave the Ritual Offertory Response.

"I take You with me, All-Pure Victim * I take you to the unholy north * I take you to the Summit of the Prince."

The Archpriest placed the Host on Agnes' chest and held the chalice of wine above her pelvis.

Flanked at the Altar now by his Archpriest and Acolyte Medico, Bishop Leo glanced at the Ceremonial Messenger. Assured that the granite-faced Guardian and his Roman Phalanx were in perfect tandem, he and his celebrants intoned the Prayer of Supplication.

"We ask You, Lord Lucifer, Prince of Darkness * Garnerer of all our Victims * To accept our offering * Unto the commission of many sins."

Then, in the perfect unison that comes from long usage, Bishop and Archpriest pronounced the holiest words of the Latin Mass. At the elevation of the Host: "HOC EST ENIM CORPUS MEUM." At the elevation of the chalice: "HIC EST ENIM CALIX SANGUINIS MEI, NOVI ET AETERNI TESTAMENTI, MYSTERIUM FIDEI QUI PRO VOBIS ET PRO MULTIS EFFUNDETUR IN REMISSIONEM PECCATORUM. HAEC QUOTIESCUMQUE FECERITIS IN MEI MEMORIAM FACIETIS."

Immediately, the participants responded with a renewal of the Ritual Din, a deluge of confusion, a babel of words and rattling bones, with random lascivious acts of every kind, while the Bishop ate a tiny fragment of the Host and took a small sip from the chalice.

At Leo's signal—the inverted blessing of the Sign again—the Ritual Din slipped into somewhat more orderly chaos as the Participants obediently formed into rough lines. Passing by the Altar to receive Communion—a bit of the Host, a sip from the chalice—they also had an opportunity to admire Agnes. Then, anxious not to miss any part of the first Ritual Violation of the Victim, they returned quickly to their kneeler chairs and watched expectantly as the Bishop focused his full attention on the child.

Agnes tried with all her might to free herself as the weight of the Bishop came upon her. Even then, she twisted her head as if to look for help in that unmerciful place. But there was no glimpse of help. There was the Archpriest waiting his turn at this most ravenous sacrilege. There was her father waiting. There was the fire from the black tapers reflecting red in their eyes. Fire itself aflame in those eyes. Inside all those eyes. Fire that would burn long after the candles died. Burn forever . . .

The agony that enveloped Agnes that night in body and soul was so profound that it might have enveloped the whole world. But not for a moment was it her agony alone. Of that much she always remained certain. As those Servitors of Lucifer violated her on that defiled and unholy Altar, so too did they violate that Lord Who was father and mother to her. Just as He had transformed her weakness with His courage, so also did He sanctify her desecration with the outrages of His scourging, and her long-suffering with His Passion. It was to Him—to that Lord Who was her only father and her only mother and her only defender—that Agnes screamed her terror, her horror, her pain. And it was to Him she fled for refuge when she lost consciousness.

Leo stood once more at the Altar, his perspiring face flush with new excitement at this, his supreme moment of personal triumph. A nod to the Ceremonial Messenger by the phone. A moment's wait. An answering nod. Rome was ready.

"By the Power invested in me as Parallel Celebrant of the Sacrifice and the Parallel Fulfiller of the Enthronement, I lead all here and in Rome in invoking You, Prince of All Creatures! In the name of all gathered in this Chapel and of all the Brothers of the Roman Chapel, I invoke You, O Prince!"

The second Investment Prayer was the Archpriest's to lead. As culmination of everything he waited for, his Latin recitation was a model of controlled emotion:

> "Come, take possession of the Enemy's House. * Enter into a place that has been prepared for You. * Descend among Your faithful Servitors * Who have prepared Your bed, * Who have erected Your Altar and blessed it with infamy."

It was right and fitting that Bishop Leo should offer the final Investment Prayer of the Targeting Chapel:

> "Under Sacrosanct instructions from the Mountaintop, * In the name of all the Brethren, * I now adore You, Prince of Darkness. * With the Stole of all Unholiness, * I now place in Your hands * The Triple

Crown of Peter * According to the adamantine will of Lucifer * So that You reign here. * So that there One Church be, * One Church from Sea to Sea, * One Vast and Mighty Congregation * Of Man and Woman, * Of animal and plant. * So that our Cosmos again * Be one, unbound and free."

At the last word and a gesture from Leo, all in his Chapel were seated. The Ritual passed to the Target Chapel in Rome.

It was very nearly complete now, this Enthronement of the Prince in the Weakling's Citadel. Only the Authorization, the Bill of Instructions and the Evidence remained. The Guardian looked up from the Altar and turned cheerless eyes toward the Prussian International Delegate who had brought the leather pouch containing the Letters of Authorization and Instructions. All watched as he left his place and strode to the Altar, took the pouch in hand, removed the papers it contained and read out the Bill of Authorization in a heavy accent:

"By mandate of the Assembly and the Sacrosanct Elders, I do institute, authorize and recognize this Chapel, to be known henceforth as the Inner Chapel, as taken, possessed and appropriated wholly by Him Whom we have Enthroned as Lord and Master of our human fate.

"Whosoever shall, by means of this Inner Chapel, be designated and chosen as the final In-the-Line successor in the Petrine Office, shall by his very oath of office commit himself and all he does command to be the willing instrument and collaborator with the Builders of Man's Home on Earth and throughout Man's Cosmos. He shall transform the ancient Enmity into Friendship, Tolerance and Assimilation as these are applied to the models of birth, education, work, finance, commerce, industry, learning, culture, living and giving life, dying and dealing death. So shall the New Age of Man be modeled.

"So mote it be!" The Guardian led the Roman Phalanx in the Ritual Response.

"So mote it be!" At a signal from the Ceremonial Messenger, Bishop Leo led his Participants in their assent.

The next order of Ritual, the Bill of Instructions, was in reality a solemn oath of betrayal by which every cleric present in St. Paul's Chapel—Cardinal, bishop and monsignore alike—would intentionally and deliberately desecrate the Sacrament of Holy Orders by which he had once received the grace and power to sanctify others.

The International Delegate lifted his left hand in the Sign. "Do you each and all," he read the Oath, "having heard this Authorization, now solemnly swear to accept it willingly, unequivocally, immediately, without reservation or cavil?"

"We do!"

"Do you each and all now solemnly swear that your administration of office will be bent to fulfill the aims of the Universal Church of Man?"

"We do so solemnly swear."

"Are you each and all prepared to signal this unanimous will with your own blood, so strike you Lucifer, if you are unfaithful to this Oath of Commitment?"

"We are willing and prepared."

"Are you each and all fully consenting that, by this Oath, you transfer Lordship and Possession of your souls from the Ancient Enemy, the Supreme Weakling, to the All-Powerful Hands of our Lord Lucifer?"

"We consent."

The moment had arrived for the final Ritual. The Evidence.

With the two documents positioned on the Altar, the Delegate held out his left hand to the Guardian. With a golden pin, the granite-faced Roman pricked the tip of the Delegate's left thumb and pressed a bloody print beside the Delegate's name on the Bill of Authorization.

Quickly then, the Vatican Participants followed suit. When every member of the Phalanx had satisfied this last Ritual requirement, a little silver bell was rung in the Chapel of St. Paul.

In the American Chapel, the Bell of Infinity rang its distant and assenting response lightly, musically, three times. Ding! Dong! Ding! An especially nice touch, Leo thought, as both congregations took up the recessional chant:

"Ding! Dong! Dell! * Thus shall the Ancient Gates Prevail! * Thus the Rock and the Cross must fail * Forever! * Ding! Dong! Dell!"

The recessional line formed in order of rank. Acolytes first. Frater Medico, with Agnes limp and frighteningly pale in his arms. Finally, the Archpriest and Bishop Leo kept up the chant as they retraced their steps to the vestry.

The members of the Roman Phalanx emerged into the Court of St. Damasus in the small hours of the feast day of SS. Peter and Paul. Some of the Cardinals and a few of the bishops acknowledged the salutes of the respectful security guards with an absentminded cross of priestly blessing traced in the air, as they entered their limousines. Within moments, the walls of St. Paul's Chapel glowed, as always they had, with their lovely paintings and frescoes of Christ, and of the Apostle Paul whose name the latest Peter-in-the-Line had taken.

1978

For the Pope who had taken the name of the Apostle, the summer of 1978 was his last on this earth. Worn out as much by the turbulence of his fifteen-year reign as by the pain and physical degradation of long illness, he was taken by his God from the central seat of authority in the Roman Catholic Church on August 6.

During *sede vacante*—when Peter's chair is vacant—the practical affairs of the Church Universal are entrusted to a Cardinal Camerlengo. A Chamberlain. In this instance, to the unfortunate Pope's Secretary of State; to His Eminence Cardinal Jean-Claude de Vincennes, who, Vatican wags said, had all but run the Church anyway even while the Pope still lived.

An unusually tall, well-built, spare-fleshed man, Cardinal Vincennes possessed from nature an overdose of Gallic gumption. His moods, which ran the gamut from acerbic to patronizing, regulated the atmosphere for peers and subordinates alike. The sharp lines of his face were the very badge of his unquestionably supreme status in the Vatican bureaucracy.

Understandably, the Chamberlain's responsibilities are many during *sede vacante,* and the time to carry them out is short. Not least among those tasks is to sort the dead Pope's personal papers and documents in a thorough triage. The official object of the exercise is to learn of unfinished business. But one unofficial by-product is the chance to discover firsthand some of the innermost thoughts of the recent Pope concerning sensitive Church affairs.

Ordinarily, His Eminence would have conducted the triage of the old Pope's documents before the Conclave had met to elect his successor. But preparations for the August Conclave had absorbed all of his energies and attention. On the outcome of that Conclave—more precisely, on the type of man to emerge from that Conclave as the new Pope—depended the fate of elaborate plans prepared over the previous twenty years by Cardinal Vincennes and his like-minded colleagues in the Vatican and around the world.

They were men who promoted a new idea of the papacy and of the Roman Catholic Church. For them, no longer would Pope and Church stand apart and beckon humanity to approach and enter the fold of Catholicism. It was time now for both papacy and Church as an institution to collaborate closely with the efforts of mankind to build a better world for everyone. Time for the papacy to cease its reliance on dogmatic authority and its insistence on absolute and exclusive claim to ultimate truth.

Of course, such plans were not elaborated within the isolated vacuum of in house Vatican politics. But neither had the Cardinal Secretary shared these ideas merely from afar. He and his like-minded Vatican associates had entered into a compact with their secular boosters. Together, by that compact, all had undertaken to do their part in effecting at last the desired and fundamental transformation in Church and papacy.

Now, with the Pope's death, it was agreed that this Conclave was well timed to effect the election of a complaisant successor to Peter's chair. With Cardinal Vincennes running the show, no one doubted that just the type of man required would emerge as victor—as Pope—from the Conclave of August 1978.

With such a load riding on his success, it was not surprising that His Eminence had put everything else aside, including the personal documents of the old Pope. The thick envelope with its papal emboss had rested unattended in a special pigeonhole in the Cardinal's desk.

But the Cardinal had made a gross miscalculation. Once shut in under lock and key as is the practice for Conclaves, the Cardinal Electors had chosen a man for the papacy who was totally unsuitable. A man utterly uncongenial for those plans laid by the Camerlengo and his associates. Few in the Vatican would forget the day that new Pope had been elected. Vincennes had literally bolted out of the Conclave the instant the heavily locked doors were opened. Ignoring the customary announcement of "a blessed Conclave," he strode off toward his quarters like vengeance incarnate.

Just how serious his Conclave failure had been was borne in on Cardinal Secretary of State Vincennes during the first weeks of the new papacy. Those had been weeks of continual frustration for him. Weeks of continual argument with the new Pope and of fevered discussions with his own colleagues. The triage of papal documents had been all but forgotten in the sense of danger that pervaded his days. He simply had no way of predicting for his associates how this new occupant of Peter's Throne would act and react. His Eminence had lost control.

Uncertainty and fear had exploded when the totally unexpected came to pass. Within thirty-three days of his election, the new Pope died, and the air in Rome and abroad was full of ugly rumors.

When the newly dead Pope's papers had been gathered in a second embossed envelope, the Cardinal had no choice but to place them on his desk with the first. In the organization of a second Conclave to be held in October, all of his efforts were trained on correcting the mistakes made in August. His Eminence had been granted a reprieve. He had no doubt that his life depended on his making the most of it. This time he must see to the choice of a suitably complaisant Pope.

The unthinkable had pursued him, however. For all of his gargantuan efforts, the October Conclave had turned out as disastrously for him as the one in August. Stubbornly, the Electors had again chosen a man who was not complaisant in any sense of the word. Had circumstances permitted, His Eminence would surely have taken time to unravel the puzzle of what had gone wrong during the two elections. But time he did not have.

With the third Pope on the Throne of Peter in as many months, the triage of papers contained in the two envelopes, each bearing the papal emboss, had at last taken on its own urgency. Even at the heel of the hunt, His Eminence would not allow those two packets to slip from his hands without a careful screening.

The triage took place one October day at an oval conference table in the spacious office of Cardinal Secretary of State Vincennes. Situated a few yards from the papal study on the third floor of the Apostolic Palace, its tall Palladian windows forever surveying St. Peter's Square and the wide world beyond like unblinking eyes, that office was but one of many outward signs of the Cardinal Secretary's global power.

As custom required, the Cardinal had called two men as witnesses and aides. The first, Archbishop Silvio Aureatini—a relatively young man of some note and huge ambition—was a watchful, quick-witted northern Italian who looked out on the world from a face that seemed to gather toward the end of his prominent nose the way a pencil gathers at the tip.

The second man, Father Aldo Carnesecca, was a simple and insignificant priest who had lived through four papacies and had twice assisted at triages of a Pope's papers. Father Carnesecca was treasured by his superiors as "a man of confidentiality." A gaunt, gray-haired, quiet-voiced man whose age was hard to determine, he was exactly what his facial appearance, his unadorned black cassock and his impersonal manner indicated: a professional subordinate.

Such men as Aldo Carnesecca may come to the Vatican with great ambitions. But with no stomach for partisan jealousy and hate—too conscious of their own mortality to step over dead bodies on the upward ladder, yet too grateful to bite the hand that originally fed them—such men hold on to their basic, lifelong ambition that brought them here. The desire to be Roman.

Rather than compromise their principles on the one hand or cross the threshold of disillusionment and bitterness on the other, the Carnesecca s of the Vatican make the most of their lowly state. They stay at their posts through successive papal administrations. Without nourishing any self-interest or exerting any personal influence, they acquire a detailed knowledge of significant facts, friendships, incidents and decisions. They become experts in the rise and fall of the greats. They develop an instinct for the wood as distinct from the trees. It was not a surprising irony, therefore, that the man most fitted to conduct the triage of papal documents that October day was not Cardinal Vincennes or Archbishop Aureatini, but Father Carnesecca.

At first, the triage proceeded smoothly. After a pontificate of fifteen years, it was only to be expected that the first envelope containing the old Pope's documents was a fat one. But most of its contents proved to be copies of memoranda between the Pontiff and His Eminence, and were already familiar to the Cardinal. Vincennes did not keep all of his thoughts to himself as he tossed page after page over to his two companions. He peppered them with commentary on the men whose names inevitably cropped up. That Swiss archbishop who thought he could cow Rome. That Brazilian bishop who had refused to go along with the changes in the Mass ceremony. Those traditionalist Vatican Cardinals whose power he had broken. Those traditionalist European theologians whom he had retired into obscurity.

Finally, there remained only five of the old Pope's documents to deal with before turning to the triage of the second Pontiff's papers. Each of the five was sealed in its own envelope, and each was marked *"Personalissimo e Confidenzialissimo."* Of those envelopes, the four marked for the old Pope's blood relatives were of no special consequence beyond the fact that the Cardinal disliked not being able to read their contents. The last of the five envelopes carried an additional inscription. "For Our Successor on the Throne of Peter." Those words, written in the unmistakable hand of the old Pope, put the contents of this document in the category of papers destined exclusively for the eyes of the newly elected young Slavic Pope. The date of the papal inscription, July 3, 1975, registered in the Cardinal's mind as a particularly volatile time in his always strained relations with His Holiness.

What suddenly transfixed His Eminence's attention, however, was the unthinkable but unmistakable fact that the original papal seal had been broken. Unbelievably, the envelope had been slit at the top and opened. Obviously, therefore, its contents had been read. Just as obviously, the slit had been mended with a length of thick filament tape. A new papal seal and signature had been added by the old man's successor; by the Pope who had died so suddenly and whose own papers still awaited triage.

But there was more. A second inscription in the less familiar hand of the second Pope: "Concerning the condition of Holy Mother Church after June 29, 1963."

For one unguarded moment, Cardinal Vincennes was unmindful of the other two men at the oval table. His whole world suddenly shrank to the tiny dimensions of the envelope in his hands. In the horror and confusion that paralyzed his mind at the sight of that date on a papally sealed envelope, it took a moment for the date of the second papal inscription itself to register: September 28, 1978. One day shy of the death date of that second Pope.

In his bafflement, the Cardinal fingered the envelope as though its thickness might tell him its contents, or as though it might whisper the secret of how it had found its way from his desk and then back again. All but ignoring the presence of Father Carnesecca—an easy thing to do—he shoved the envelope across the table to Aureatini.

When the Archbishop raised that pencil-nosed profile again, his eyes were a mirror of the Cardinal's own horror and confusion. It was as if those two men were not staring at one another, but at a common memory they had been certain was secret. The memory of victory's opening moment. The memory of St. Paul's Chapel. The memory of gathering with so many others of the Phalanx to chant ancient invocations. The memory of that Prussian Delegate reading out the Bill of Instructions; of thumbs pricked with a golden pin; of bloody prints pressed onto the Bill of Authorization.

"But, Eminence . . ." Aureatini was the first to find his voice, but the second to find his wits. "How the devil did he . . . ?"

"Even the devil doesn't know that." By sheer force of will, the Cardinal was beginning to regain something of his mental composure. Peremptorily, he took the envelope back and pounded it onto the table in front of him. He cared not one whit for the thoughts of either of his companions. Confronted with so many unknowns, he needed to deal with questions that were doubling back on themselves in his mind.

How had the thirty-three-day Pope got his hands on his predecessor's papers? Treachery by one of His Eminence's own Secretariat staff? The thought caused the Cardinal to glance at Father Carnesecca. In his mind, that black-robed professional subordinate represented the whole Vatican underclass of bureaucratic drones.

Of course, technically the Pope had a right to every document in the Secretariat; but he had shown no curiosity in the matter to Vincennes. And then again, just what had the second Pope seen? Had he gotten the whole dossier of the old Pontiff's papers—read them all? Or only that envelope with the crucial June 29, 1963, date now written in his hand on its face? If the latter were true, how did the envelope get back into the old Pope's documents? And either way, who had restored everything just as it had been on the Cardinal Secretary's desk? When could anybody have succeeded in doing that without attracting attention?

Vincennes fixed again on the final date written on the envelope in the second Pope's hand. September 28. Abruptly, he rose from his chair, strode across the room to his desk, reached for his diary and flipped its pages back to that date. Yes, he had had the usual morning briefing session with the Holy Father; but his notes told him nothing relevant. There had been an afternoon meeting with the Cardinal overseers of the Vatican Bank; nothing interesting there either. Another note caught his eye, however. He had attended a luncheon at the Cuban Embassy for his friend and colleague the outgoing Ambassador. After the luncheon, he had stayed on for a private conversation.

The Cardinal reached for his intercom and asked his secretary to check the roster. Who had been on duty that day at the Secretariat's reception desk? He had to wait only a moment for the answer; and when it came, he raised a pair of dull eyes to the oval table. In that instant, Father Aldo

Carnesecca became much more for His Eminence than a symbol of the Vatican's subordinate class.

In the time it took to replace the receiver in its cradle and return to the table, a certain cold light seeped into the Cardinal Secretary's mind. Light about the past; and about his future. His large frame even relaxed a bit as he fitted all the pieces together. The two papal dossiers on his desk awaiting triage. His own long absence from his office on September 28. Carnesecca on duty alone during the siesta hour. Vincennes saw it all. He had been circumvented by wile, outwitted by guileless-faced guile. His entire personal gamble was over now. The best he could do was to make sure the double-sealed papal envelope never reached the hand of the Slavic Pope.

"Let us finish our work!" Glancing in turn at the still ashen-faced Aureatini and the imperturbable Carnesecca, the Cardinal was clear in his mind and entirely focused. In the tone he always used with subordinates, he rattled out a series of decisions that ended the triage of the old Pope's papers. Carnesecca would see to the dispatch of the four private envelopes addressed to the Pontiff's relatives. Aureatini would take the other papers to the Vatican Archivist, who would see to it that they would gather dust in some appropriately obscure cranny. The Cardinal himself would see to the matter of the double-sealed envelope.

Quickly, then, His Eminence began the triage of the relatively few papers the second Pope had accumulated in so abbreviated a reign. Certain that the most significant document left by that Pope already lay before him, he skimmed rapidly through the contents of the dossier. Within a quarter of an hour, he had passed them to Aureatini as destined for the Archivist.

Vincennes stood alone at one of those long windows in his office until he saw Father Carnesecca step from the Secretariat into the Court of St. Damasus below. He followed the progress of that gaunt figure all the way across St. Peter's Square toward the Holy Office, where that priest spent a good part of his working life. For a good ten minutes he contemplated Carnesecca's unhurried but always sure and purposeful gait. If ever a man deserved an early place in Potter's Field, he decided, surely it was Aldo Carnesecca. Nor would he have to make a note in his diary to remember.

At last, the Cardinal Secretary turned back to his desk. He still had to deal with that infamous double-sealed envelope.

It was not unknown in papal history that, before final disposition of a dead Pope's papers, someone in a position to do so might have had a quick look even at documents marked *"Personalissimo e Confidenzialissimo."* In this case, however, the inscriptions of not one but two Popes placed the contents beyond all but papal eyes. There were some barriers that would keep even Vincennes at bay. And in any case, he was confident he knew the substance of the matter.

Nevertheless, His Eminence mused, it was possible to put more than one interpretation on the biblical admonition: "Let the dead bury the dead." Without humor or self-pity, but with his own fate certain in his mind, he lifted his telephone with one hand and the envelope in the other. When Archbishop Aureatini came on the line, he issued his final curt instructions regarding the triage. "You forgot one item for the Archivist, Excellency. Come pick it up. I'll have a word with him myself. He will know what to do."

The untimely death of His Eminence Cardinal Secretary of State Jean-Claude de Vincennes occurred in an unfortunate automobile accident near his birthplace of Mablon in the south of France on March 19, 1979. Of the notices that told the world of such a tragedy, surely the driest was contained in the *Pontifical Yearbook* for 1980. In that fat, utilitarian directory of Vatican Church personnel and other serviceable data, the Cardinal's name and no more appeared in alphabetical order in the list of recently deceased Princes of the Church.

PART ONE
Papal Evening

I

IN THE VATICAN of early May, no one was surprised that the Holy Father would depart for yet another pastoral visit abroad. It was, after all, just one more of many scores of visits he had made so far to some ninety-five countries on all five continents since his election in 1978.

For more than ten years now, in fact, this Slavic Pope had seemed to transform his whole pontificate into one long pilgrimage to the world. He had been seen or heard, in the flesh or electronically, by over three billion people. He had sat down with literally scores of government leaders. He possessed an intelligence about the countries of those leaders and a command of their languages that was unrivaled. He had impressed them all as a man without any major prejudice against anyone. He was accepted by those leaders, and by men and women everywhere, as a leader himself. As a man concerned about the helpless, the homeless, the jobless, the war-torn. A man concerned about all who were denied even the right to live—the aborted babies and the babies born only to die of hunger and disease. A man concerned about the millions who were living just to die from government-imposed famines in Somalia, Ethiopia, the Sudan. A man concerned with the populations of Afghanistan, Cambodia and Kuwait, whose lands were now wantonly sown with over 80 million land mines.

All in all, this Slavic Pope had become a crystal-clear mirror held up to the gaze of the real world, reflecting the real miseries of its peoples.

By comparison to such superhuman efforts, the papal jaunt set to begin this Saturday morning would be a short one. A pastoral visit to the cavern shrine of Sainte-Baume, high in the Maritime French Alps. There the Pontiff would lead the traditional devotions in honor of St. Mary Magdalene, who, legend had it, had spent thirty years of her life in that cavern as a penitent.

There had been a certain quietly derisive behind-the-scenes humor in the corridors of the Secretariat of State about "another of His Holiness' pious excursions." But in today's Vatican, that was only natural, given the extra work—for so it was regarded—required for such incessant papal meanderings into the world at large.

The Saturday of the Pope's departure for Baume dawned fresh and bright. As Cardinal Secretary of State Cosimo Maestroianni emerged with the Slavic Pope and his little retinue from one of the rear portals of the Apostolic Palace and proceeded through the gardens toward the Vatican helipad, no humor, derisive or otherwise, was evident in His Eminence's demeanor. The Secretary was not known as a humorous man. But he did feel a certain happy relief. For, once he had seen the Holy Father safely on his way to Sainte-Baume as duty and decorum required, he would have a few days of valuable time to himself.

There was no real crisis facing Maestroianni. But in a certain sense time was at a premium for him just now. Though the news had not yet been made public, by prior agreement with the Slavic Pope, the Cardinal was about to quit his post as Secretary of State. Even after retirement, his hands would not be far from the highest levers of Vatican power—he and his colleagues had seen to that. Maestroianni's successor, already chosen, was a known quantity; not the ideal man, but manageable. Nevertheless, some things were better accomplished while still standing visibly on the highest ground. Before ending his official tenure as head of the Secretariat, His Eminence had three particularly important tasks to attend to. Each was sensitive in its own way. He had engineered all three to a certain crucial point. Just a little more progress to be made here, a few more steps to be set in motion there, and he could be confident that his agenda would be unstoppable.

The agenda was everything now. And time was running.

On this early Saturday morning, flanked by the ever present uniformed security guards, followed by his companions on this trip and with the Pontiff's personal secretary, Monsignore Daniel Sadowski, bringing up the rear, the Slavic Pope and his Cardinal Secretary of State made their way along the shaded pathway like two men yoked together on a tightrope. Scurrying along beside the Holy Father, his short legs forced to take two steps for every one of the Pope's, His Eminence recited a quick review of the main points of the Pontiff's schedule at Sainte-Baume, then took his leave: "Ask the Saint to shower us with graces, Holiness."

Retracing his steps in blessed solitude toward the Apostolic Palace, Cardinal Maestroianni allowed himself a few extra moments' reflection within these lovely gardens. Reflections were only natural to a man accustomed to Vatican and global power, and especially so on the eve of his departure from office. Nor was this a waste of time. For his were useful reflections. Reflections about change. And about unity.

One way and another, it seemed to His Eminence that everything in his lifetime, everything in the world, had always been about the process and purpose of change, and about the faces and the uses of unity. In fact—hindsight being as acute as it always is—it seemed to His Eminence that even back in the 1950s, when he had first entered the Vatican's diplomatic service as a young, ambitious cleric, change had already entered the world as its only constant.

Maestroianni let his mind travel back to the last long conversation he had had with his longtime mentor, Cardinal Jean-Claude de Vincennes. It had been right here in these gardens one open day in the early winter of 1979. Vincennes was immersed then in the plans for the newly elected Slavic Pope's very first excursion outside the Vatican, the trip that would take the new Pope back to visit his native Poland after his unexpected election to Peter's Throne.

Most of the world had seen that trip, both before and after its completion, as the nostalgic return of the Pope to his homeland for the proper and final farewell of a victorious native son. Not so Vincennes, however. Vincennes' mood during that conversation so many years ago had struck Maestroianni as curious. As had been his way when he had a particularly important point he wanted to drive home to his protégé, Vincennes had led what seemed an almost leisurely conversation. He had talked about his day in Vatican service. "Day One," Vincennes had called it. The long, tedious day of the Cold War. The peculiar thing was that his tone had seemed consciously prophetic; seemed to foretell the end of that Day in more ways than one.

"Frankly," Vincennes had confided to Maestroianni, "Europe's role during this Day One has been that of a supreme but helpless pawn in the lethal game of nations. The Cold War game. The fear has always been that any moment might bring a blaze of nuclear flames."

Even without the rhetoric Maestroianni had understood all that. He had always been an avid student of history. And by early 1979, he had accumulated hands-on experience in dealing with the Cold War governments and power brokers of the world. He knew that the foreboding of the Cold War dogged everyone, in and out of government. Even the six Western European nations whose ministers had signed the treaties of Rome in 1957, and by those treaties had so bravely banded together as the European Community—even their plans and their moves were hemmed in at every turn by that Cold War foreboding.

As far as Maestroianni had seen in those early days of 1979, nothing of that geopolitical reality—the reality of what Vincennes called Day One—had changed. What startled him first, therefore, was Vincennes' conviction that Day One was about to end. More startling still, it dawned on Maestroianni that Vincennes actually expected this Slavic interloper into the papacy to be what he called "an angel of change."

"Make no mistake about it." Vincennes had been emphatic on the point. "This man may be seen by many as a bumbling poet-philosopher who wandered into the papacy by mistake. But he thinks and eats and sleeps and dreams geopolitics. I've seen the drafts of some of the speeches he plans to deliver in Warsaw and Kraków. I've made it a point to read some of his earlier speeches. Since 1976 he's been talking about the inevitability of change. About the oncoming rush of nations into a New World Order."

In his surprise, Maestroianni had stopped in his tracks beside Vincennes.

"Yes." From his towering height, Vincennes had peered down at his diminutive associate. "Yes. You heard right. He, too, sees a new world order coming. And if I'm correct in my reading of his intent in this return of his to his homeland, he may be the herald of the end of Day One. Now, if that is true, then Day Two will dawn very quickly. When it does, unless I miss my guess, this new Slavic Pope will be up and running at the head of the pack. But you, my friend, must run faster. You must run rings around this Holy Father of ours."

Maestroianni had been struck dumb by his double confusion. Confusion first that Vincennes had seemed to be counting himself out of Day Two; seemed to be giving instructions to Maestroianni as to a successor. And confusion that Vincennes should think that this Slav, who seemed so unfit for the papacy, might play a pivotal role in the power politics of the world.

It was a far different Maestroianni who paused for a while longer today before entering the rear portal of the Apostolic Palace. Vincennes' voice had been stilled for these past twelve years. But these very gardens, unchanged themselves, stood as witness to the precision of his prophecy.

Day Two had begun so subtly that the leaders of East and West realized only slowly what Vincennes had glimpsed in those early speeches of this Slav who was now Pope. Slowly, the brightest among Mammon's children began to see what this Pontiff kept drumming home to them in that unrecriminating but insistent style of his.

As he traveled to his homeland and successfully challenged the leaders of the East on their own turf, this Pope had ignited the energies of one of the profoundest geopolitical changes in history. Yet it was difficult for government leaders in the West to follow where the Slavic Pope was pointing. They had been so certain that the earthly fulcrum of change would be their own tiny and artificially misshapen little European delta. It was hardly believable that the epicenter of change should lie in the captive lands between the Oder River in Poland and the eastern borders of Ukraine.

If they were not convinced by what the Pontiff said, however, those leaders had finally to be convinced by events. And once they were convinced, there was no stopping the rush to join the new march of history. By 1988, the once tiny European Community had swelled to a membership of twelve states and a total population of 324 million, stretching from Denmark in the north to Portugal in the south and from the Shetland Islands in the west to Crete in the east. They could reasonably expect that by 1994 their membership would increase by at least five more states and another 130 million people.

Even then, however, Western Europe remained a stubborn beleaguered little delta, fearful that their ancient civilization might be incinerated in the Mother of All Wars. The Enemy still occupied the horizons of their vision and stunted their ambition.

At last, though, with the fall of the Berlin Wall in the early winter of 1989, all the blinders were off. Western Europeans experienced the visceral sensation of great change. By the early nineties, that sense had solidified into a deep conviction about themselves as Europeans. The Western Europe into which they had been born had passed away forever. Their long night of fear was over. Day Two had dawned.

Unexpected though it had been, the force of the new dynamism in middle Europe swept everyone into its orbit. It worried Europe's Far Eastern competitor, Japan. And it gripped both superpowers. Much like the Messenger in a classical Greek drama who arrives onstage to announce the coming action to an unbelieving audience, Mikhail Gorbachev arrived on the scene as Soviet President to tell the world that his Soviet Union had "always been an integral part of Europe." Half a world away, U.S. President Bush spoke of his America as "a European power."

Down in papal Rome, meanwhile, Day Two had also dawned. It was largely unperceived and unemphasized in the hurly-burly of change running like a hot current among the society of nations. Nevertheless, under the clever hand of Maestroianni and his many associates, a swifter and still more profound current of change gripped the condition and earthly fortunes of the Roman Catholic Church, and of papal Rome itself.

The Rome of the old Pope who had weathered World War II was gone now. His papal Rome, a tightly knit hierarchical organization, was gone. All those Cardinals, bishops and priests, those religious orders and institutes spread through dioceses and parishes worldwide—all banded together in fidelity and obedience to a Supreme Pontiff, to an individual papal persona—all of that was gone. Gone, too, was the pentecostally excited Rome of "the good Pope," who had opened windows and doors of his ancient institution, allowing the winds of change to sweep through every room and corridor. His papal Rome was gone, blown away by the very winds he had invoked. Nothing of his dream remained, except a few distorted memories and misshapen afterimages and the inspiration he had provided to such men as Maestroianni.

Even the turbulent papal Rome of the unfortunate Pontiff who had taken the name of the Apostle was gone. No trace remained even of the pathos of that Holy Father's ineffectual protests against the gradual de-Catholicizing of what had once been regarded as the most sacred mysteries of papal Rome. Thanks to Vincennes, and to such able and dedicated protégés as Maestroianni himself, among others, by the time that Pontiff had obeyed the summons of death after fifteen years in Peter's chair a new Rome was already emerging. A new Catholic body was already being fashioned.

In this morning's still freshness, Cardinal Secretary Maestroianni raised his eyes in a purposeful glance at gardens and skies. How fitting, he thought—a harbinger, even—that no sign or sound remained of the helicopter that bore the Pope away. For the new Rome had not merely set its face against this Slavic Pope. This Rome was antipapal. Indeed, this Rome was not merely antipapal but dedicated to developing an antipapal Church.

A new Church in a New World Order. That was the goal in the new Rome. In Maestroianni's Rome.

It was still a curious happenstance for Maestroianni that the only major stumbling block to full achievement of that task had turned out to be this Pope who was regarded by so many as no more than a "relic of times gone by." Too bad, Maestroianni mused, that it should have come to this. For, in the early days of his pontificate, the Cardinal had been encouraged by the Pope's behavior. He had made himself and proclaimed himself as the champion of "the spirit of Vatican II"—in other words, as patron of the vast changes introduced into the Church in the name of the Second Vatican Council. He had agreed to the appointment of Maestroianni himself as his Secretary of State, for example. And he had left Cardinal Noah Palombo in his powerful position. He consented to promote still others who abhorred this Holy Father's religiousness. Nor did he disturb the good Masons who toiled in the Vatican Chancery. Those had seemed hopeful signs at least of papal compliance, if not of complicity. And the general picture was promising. Not only in Rome but in all the dioceses of Catholicism, a dedicated phalanx of clerics was in charge. And already a new Catholicism was rife.

Of course, Roman authority was evoked to propagate that new Catholicism. That was the value of Maestroianni's side of the illusion. And Canon Law, suitably revised, was brandished to enforce its precepts. That was the value of genius on Maestroianni's side of the Vatican personnel roster. But always the intent was to foster a Catholicism that acknowledged no effective links with the Catholicism that had gone before.

True enough, Cardinal Secretary Vincennes had seen this process of change a certain distance along the way. What remained to be done now was to transform the papacy itself into a complaisant, even a cooperative, handmaiden in the service of a new creation. A new earthly habitat. A truly New World Order. When that transformation was complete, Day Three would dawn on an earthly paradise.

Accordingly, as any reasonable man would expect, this Pope who had so deliberately tapped the hidden geopolitical forces that had precipitated the oncoming rush of nations into a New World Order, should be the most suitable person to complete the transformation of the Roman Catholic organization into the apt handmaiden of the New World Order, to bring the churchly institution into perfect alignment with the globalization of all human culture. Yet, as the Cardinal and his colleagues—within the Church and outside it—had discovered, this Slavic Pope now stood intransigently in the way of the required progress.

For this Pope would not budge on certain basic issues—moral issues and doctrinal issues. He refused adamantly to consider the priestly ordination of women and the relaxation of the rule of priestly celibacy. He opposed all experimentation in the field of genetics which involved the use of human embryos. He would not sanction any form of contraception, and much less abortion under any circumstances. He maintained his Church's right to educate the young. Above all, he maintained the right of his Church to oppose any civil legislation he and his churchmen decided to oppose for their moral and doctrinal reasons. In short, this Slavic Pope would not renounce some of the more important traditional claims of the Roman Catholic Church.

As long, therefore, as he remained Pope, no real progress could be made toward the magnificent goals of the New World Order. Or, at least, progress would be so slow that an important deadline would be missed if things progressed at the present rate. That deadline had been represented to the Cardinal by his secular colleagues in statecraft, finance and macroeconomics as a world-important date by which the total conversion of the Roman Catholic institutional organization had to be an accomplished fact.

Inevitably, then, the Slavic Pope had become a primary target of change. Actually, the ultimate target.

Maestroianni turned at last from his garden musings. There was work to be done. Before this day was finished, if there were no interruptions, he expected to make real headway in each of the three tasks that were key to the final phase of transformation. He had carried the legacy left to him by Vincennes very well indeed. And retirement or no, he wasn't done with it yet. Not by half.

In every respect that counted, little Cosimo Maestroianni regarded himself as the giant now.

II

THE SLAVIC POPE relaxed once he entered the helicopter and for the moment found himself exclusively alone with his private secretary, Monsignore Daniel Sadowski, who knew his almost impossible position as Pontiff. He was away from the surveillance of his wily Secretary of State. As the helicopter lifted off, neither the Pope nor his secretary gave a backward glance toward Cardinal Maestroianni, so obviously anxious to head for his office and his day's doings in the Apostolic Palace. Whatever those doings might be, both men were certain they presaged nothing pleasant for the Holy Father.

Within one half hour, his helicopter arrived at Fiumicino. There was the usual ceremonial on the ground—religious and civic dignitaries, a small choir of schoolchildren singing a papal hymn, a short speech by the Slavic Pope, a formal address by the Governor of the province. Then the Pope and his entourage transferred to the usual white Alitalia DC-10 and took their seats in the papal cabin. A small preselected group of reporters and cameramen were already aboard in the main passenger lounge. Soon, the plane took off, and within minutes it was over the Tyrrhenian Sea heading in a northwesterly direction to Marseilles.

"Y'know," the Pope said to Sadowski, "when we—myself and the Cardinal—came down to Rome for the Conclave of October 1978, we both thought we knew what this job entailed." For the Slavic Pope, "the Cardinal" was and would always be the head of the Church then in Poland, Stefan Wyszynski, nicknamed the Fox of Europe, now deceased.

Even before they had entered that second Conclave in as many months, it had been clear to both Slavic Cardinals that papal leadership had been fundamentally if not fatally compromised by what had come by then to be called "the spirit of Vatican II." When the final hours of that Conclave had come, and the young Polish churchman found himself facing the probability that he would be invited to become Pope, the two men had a sequestered meeting.

"If you accept to be made Pope," the senior Cardinal had said that day, "you will be the last Pope of these Catholic times. Like Simon Peter himself, you will stand on the line that divides one era that is ending from another that is beginning. You will preside over a supreme papal endgame. And you will do so at the very moment when the antipapal factions within the Church itself have taken virtual control of its institutions—in the name of the Vatican Council itself.

Both Cardinals understood, therefore, that the young Slavic prelate was being asked to carry out faithfully as Pope that much vaunted spirit of Vatican II. But to thus accept the papal election would be to agree to head a Church already firmly, irretrievably and bureaucratically committed to a global sociopolitical agenda which would have been considered by the vast majority of his papal predecessors as totally alien to the Church's divinely decided mission.

Even that was not the whole of it, however. The two Cardinals had faced the further reality that by the year 1978 the ecclesiastical organization and public life of the Roman Catholic Church as it had persisted up to the 1900s had been quenched forever. Both Cardinals realized it could not be restored. Even before he walked back into Conclave to accept his election to the papacy, this soon-to-be Pope had determined that the change already effected in his churchly organization was irreversible. The traditional structure of the Church Universal as a visible institution and a working organization had been transformed. His senior brother Cardinal, the Fox of Europe, agreed fully with that analysis. But, then, the two Cardinals found out that they differed as to the best course of action to be undertaken by the junior Cardinal if, indeed, he was elected Pope in this Conclave.

"I know, Eminence," the older man said firmly, "that the only other possible Pope coming out of this Conclave is our brother Cardinal of Genoa. And we both know what his solution for the present engulfing shambles of our churchly institution would be. Eh?"

The younger Cardinal smiled. "Batten down the hatches. Recall the recalcitrant. Expel the obdurate. Purify the ranks—"

"And, above all, Eminence," the older man broke in, "take each major document of that Second Vatican Council and interpret it strictly in the light of the First Vatican Council and the Council of Trent. A strong, forceful return to basics backed up by all the traditional sanctions of Mother Church, of the Holy, Roman, Catholic and Apostolic Church—" The older man broke off as he noticed the younger Cardinal wincing.

"Agreed," the younger man said after a pause. "But the loss and damage to souls and our institutions would be incalculable. How could any Pope shoulder that responsibility, Eminence?"

"How could he not?" was the quick rejoinder.

"But, Eminence," the younger man persisted, "we both agree: the old and traditional Church is—is—what shall I say—shot! Broken! And irreparably so! Under such a papal policy, our beloved Church would limp into the twenty-first century as a marginalized pauper. We would cross into the second millennium as a skeletonized remnant of a once vibrant religious colossus now at odds with the entire family of nations."

"I had the impression"—the Fox of Europe had a teasing twinkle in his eyes—"that in any case we're supposed professionally to be at odds with this world—crucified to the world, in fact, St. Paul said. But, seriously, tell me: what would be the core idea of your papal policy, if tomorrow our brother Cardinals chose you?"

"The core policy you initiated and I followed through with, when faced with the Polish Stalinists—"

"Namely?"

"Don't retire. Don't alienate. Don't refuse to talk, to negotiate. Involve anybody and everybody in a dialogue, whether they want to dialogue or not. All the main documents of the Second Vatican Council I had a hand in drawing up. I and the others formulated them so as to include everybody." He repeated that word. "Everybody, Eminence. For Christ died for all. All are de facto saved in one sense or another. If I had my way I would travel the globe, visit nation after nation, be seen everywhere, heard everywhere in as many languages as possible." His eyes glowed as he spoke. "That was our Slavic solution to our dreadful condition in Poland under the Soviets. Talk and dialogue. Never be banished."

"The Slavic solution. Hmm . . ." The elder Cardinal looked away, lost in his reflections. "The Slavic solution." His voice trailed off.

"I feel certain," the younger Cardinal said in a meek but firm tone of voice, his eyes on his senior, "that the papacy and the Church is called now to prepare for a vast harvest of souls in the last decades of this millennium. It's the old dream of the good Pope John."

The elder Cardinal stood up, laughing quietly. "From your mouth to God's ear, Eminence." He glanced at his watch. "The bell will be ringing for the next session. Let's go. We've had a good discussion. And let us have no fear. Christ is with his Church."

In accordance with this principle as his core papal policy, the Slavic Pope had declared in his first year on Peter's Throne that "I will follow in the footsteps of my three predecessors. I will make it my papal business to implement the spirit and the letter of the Second Vatican Council. I will work with my bishops, as any bishop works with his colleagues, they in their dioceses, I as Bishop of Rome, all of us collegially governing the Church Universal together." He had remained mordantly faithful to that promise. For over a dozen years as Pope, and no matter how indolently, how heretically, or in how unholy a manner his bishops governed their dioceses, he did not interfere.

When bishops in their thousands proceeded to introduce nontraditional teachings in their seminaries, to allow the blight of homosexuality to flourish among their clergy, to adapt Roman Catholic ceremonies to any of a half dozen "inculturations"—to New Age rituals; to a "Hinduization"; to an "Americanization"—the Slavic Pope did not go after the perpetrators of the implied or actual heresies and immoralities. On the contrary. He let them be.

Did the bishops strain to join in building the new secular structures to govern their individual nations and the emerging society of nations? The Pope did so, too, with all the preponderant weight of the papacy. Did his bishops consort with non-Catholic Christians as equal partners in the evangelization of the world? The Pope did so, too, with all Vatican pomp and ceremony. As the institutional organization of his Church slid ever further into the shambles of its own implosion; as he presented himself to the world as just one more "son of humanity," and to his bishops as just one more brother bishop in Rome—the Slavic Pope remained faithful to the Slavic solution.

He insisted that he governed his Church with his bishops and just as one of their number. Even when he was called upon to exercise his well-known and well-established Petrine authority in matters of doctrine, he addled his friends, enraged the traditionalists and gladdened the hearts of the papacy's enemies by stating blandly: "By the authority conferred upon Peter and his successors and in communion with the bishops of the Catholic Church, I confirm that" etc.—here mentioning the point of doctrine at issue.

He visited all and every kind of temple, shrine, sacred grove, holy cave, drinking magic drinks, eating mystical foods, accepting the sign of pagan deities on his forehead, speaking on an equal basis with heretical patriarchs, schismatic bishops, doctrinally erring theologians, even admitting them to St. Peter's Basilica and concelebrating a sacred liturgy with them.

But however outrageous his actions as Pope, he never explained himself. He never apologized for not doing so. He rarely mentioned the sacred name of Jesus Christ when talking with vast public audiences; he willingly removed the Crucifix and even the Blessed Sacrament of the Eucharist when his non-Catholic and non-Christian guests found these signs of Roman Catholicism too unpleasant for them. In fact, he never referred to himself as a Roman Catholic or to his Church as the Roman Catholic Church.

One major result of the Slavic Pope's permissiveness and "democratization" of his papacy was an overall diminution of his papal authority over the bishops. In one confidential report, for example, several bishops complained bluntly if not publicly that "if this Pope would stop talking about abortion, stop emphasizing contraception as an evil and stop condemning homosexuality, the Church could become a cheerful and successful partner in the emergent society of nations." In the U.S.A., the stylish Bishop Bruce Longbottham of Michigan intoned: "If only this ham actor we have as Pope would recognize the equal rights of women to be priests and bishops—even to be Pope—the Church would enter its final glorious stage of evangelization."

"Indeed," the senior American Cardinal had agreed: "If only this Pope would drop his pious nonsense about visitations of the Virgin Mary, and get down to the business of giving real power to real women in the real Church, all the world would become Christian."

One way or another—whether from the humble pleadings of men and women of goodwill, or from those he knew wished ill and flat-out failure for his papacy—all the objections and criticisms reached the Pope's ears; and he commended them all continually in his prayers to the Holy Spirit.

"Tell me, Daniel." He turned to his secretary after about thirty minutes of flight. "Why do you think I am going on pilgrimage to Mary Magdalene's shrine at Baume—and now above all other times?" He cocked a quizzical eye at Sadowski. "I mean the real reason."

"Holiness, I can only guess it is more out of personal devotion than for overall ecclesial reasons."

"Correct!" The Pope glanced out the window. "Briefly I want to speak to a Saint who went into exile because of the glory she had seen on Christ's face the day of his Resurrection. I want to honor her in a special way, in the hope that she will intercede with Christ and give me strength to bear my own exile, which is just now beginning in earnest."

III

AS SECRETARY to the all-powerful Cardinal Maestroianni, a disgruntled Monsignore Taco Manuguerra sat in his office guarding His Eminence's inner sanctum. Engulfed by the weekend silence that reigned over the Secretariat floor of the Apostolic Palace, the Monsignore rattled his way through the morning newspapers, grumbling to himself that the Cardinal had summoned him yet again for Saturday duty. This was to be a *dies non,* Maestroianni had told him. A day on which the Cardinal was not in the office for anyone, or for any telephone calls.

At the Cardinal's abrupt entrance, the Monsignore wisely forgot his mutterings, dropped his newspapers and jumped from his chair. With an admonitory at-ease gesture of his hand as his only greeting, His Eminence paused only long enough to ask a terse question. "Chin?" Father Chin Byonbang was the subject of the Cardinal's interest. A Korean of remarkable abilities and His Eminence's special stenographer, Chin had also been tapped for this morning's work. Manuguerra nodded his reply. Chin was waiting in a nearby office for his summons. Satisfied, Maestroianni sailed through the door into his private office.

Inside that office, the Cardinal Secretary rubbed his hands vigorously in anticipation of the vital and complex work he would get done this Saturday morning. Manning this venerable office as Secretary of State, he had managed the rumbling tremors of a worldwide Catholic organization in transit from an effete world order to a New World Order. Under his direction, in fact, matters were always progressing from planned position to planned position. No one could say that Cosimo Maestroianni was not attached to the survival of the Roman Church as an institution. On the contrary, he knew that the universal character of that organization, and the cultural stability that came with it, were destined to be invaluable assets in man's new earthly habitat.

At the same time, that organization was now headed by a Pope who, for all his helplessness and for all his public posturing, would not countenance the most important cleansing of all—the cleansing of the papal office he occupied. That office had to be cleansed and purged of any personal authority, and its occupant—the Pope—had to be fitted into the assemblage of bishops, wielding the same authority as all the bishops together and as no more than one of their number.

In theory, the solution to that problem was simple enough to state: the disappearance of the present occupant of the office from the papal scene.

The removal of a living Pope is not an easy thing. Like the removal of live explosives, it must be worked at patiently; always with confidence; always with a delicate hand. Because this Pope in particular had built such a solid place for himself as a world leader, care must be taken that his removal would not itself overturn the accepted and essential equilibrium in the affairs of nations.

Within the structure of the Church hierarchy itself, meanwhile, there was the crucial matter of unity. Because the unity of Pope and bishops ranked as an absolute necessity for the stability of the Church as an institutional organization, care must be taken that unity must not be undone by the undoing of the Slavic Pope. This morning's work would be devoted to the Cardinal's concern for unity. With Taco Manuguerra guarding against interruptions, and with Chin Byonbang as stenographer, His Eminence reckoned he would be finished here by around midday.

Within moments of his arrival, the Cardinal had laid out all the relevant materials on his desk. Almost at once, and as if on cue, Chin tapped lightly on the door and, without the fuss of greeting, took his customary seat across from the Cardinal, set up his steno machine and waited.

Maestroianni reviewed his preliminary notes with care. This was a ticklish letter he had to compose. The object was to poll the diplomatic representatives of the Holy See in eighty-two countries around the world, to determine how united the 4,000 bishops of the Church Universal felt they were with the present Holy Father. According to the Cardinal's theology, the answers he received would be of major importance. For that theology held that unity was a two-way power. The Pope must unite the bishops; and the bishops must be able to accept him as "a Pope of unity."

Of course, the Cardinal Secretary intended his queries as no more than an exploration of informal opinions. As a step, one might say, in forming a more realistic dialogue between the Holy See and the bishops. He felt it important, for example, to explore just what kind of unity was desirable. To find out to what degree the Slavic Pope enjoyed that desired and necessary unity with his Bishops—or, if unity was in jeopardy, to determine what should be done to achieve the desired and necessary unity. The Cardinal would never use such a parliamentary expression as "a vote of confidence" to describe the purpose of his little survey. However, should it turn out by some chance that a majority of bishops did not find His Holiness to be a Pope of unity, then further steps could be taken to forge a working consensus concerning his needed departure from the high office of the papacy.

The trick now was to turn the situation to good account for the new Church, without implying even remotely that the present Pope was actually—or even possibly—not a Pope of unity. Officially speaking, there could be no expression of ambiguity on that point. Officially speaking, Pope and bishops had never been more united. At the same time, it was entirely possible, and even probable, that a fair number of bishops who felt a certain ambivalence had never been given the opportunity to speak frankly on the question of unity. The Cardinal intended for the bishops to do both.

Because no Cardinal Secretary of State in his right senses would approach the bishops directly on such an issue, Maestroianni had a kind of pyramid scheme in mind. His letter this morning would be sent to his diplomatic personnel, men whose policies were dictated by the Secretary—Nuncios, Delegates, Apostolic Emissaries, ad hoc Vicars, Special Emissaries. Following the lines he would set down in this letter, those diplomats would in turn work through the various National Bishops Conferences throughout the world. For it was standard procedure now that the bishops, who had been ringed around with expert advisors in the Second Vatican Council, had come to rely on such experts at home.

All in all, then, the letter the Cardinal Secretary would draft this Saturday morning to his diplomat colleagues was only one step along the way. But that step was a crucial and sensitive one. It required the skillful use of decorous language to pose what amounted to brutal questions.

As they worked together this morning, Father Chin's rocklike taciturnity was the perfect foil for Maestroianni's red-hot intensity. His phrasing seemed perfect—ambivalent, but not ambiguous—as the Cardinal suggested, without appearing to do so, that unity might be redefined in order to be renewed. Yet at the same time to leave no doubt that the aim of His Eminence was always to preserve and foment that precious unity.

At precisely that moment of concentration when nothing in the world existed for him except the words before his eyes, a knock on the door exploded like a thunderclap in the Cardinal Secretary's ear. Still hunched over the sheaf of notes in his hand, his face reddening, Maestroianni glared out between his eyebrows and his spectacles. Taco Manuguerra, too frightened to enter, craned his neck awkwardly around the doorjamb and stammered the words he had been ordered not to say that morning. "The telephone, Eminence."

"I thought I made it clear there were to be no interruptions. . . ."

"His Holiness, Eminence," Taco sputtered.

An electric shock could not have straightened the Cardinal's spine more quickly. "His Holiness!" He let the papers drop from his hand. Anger and exasperation shot his voice into the falsetto range. "He's supposed to be up in the French mountains, praying!"

Always aware of his place and mindful of the value of discretion, Chin was already out of his chair and halfway to the door. But the Cardinal snapped his fingers and motioned the stenographer back to his seat. The letter would continue! Obediently, Chin sat down again, and by habit focused his eyes on the Cardinal's mouth.

Maestroianni paused for a few seconds, the better to regain his composure, and then lifted the telephone receiver. "Holiness! Your servant! . . .

No, Holiness, not at all. Just catching up on a few odds and ends. . . . Yes, Holiness. What is it?"

Chin watched the Cardinal's eyes open wide in astonishment. "I see, Holiness. I see." Maestroianni reached for a pen and notebook. "Bernini? Let me write down the name. *Noli Me Tangere*. . . . I see. . . . No, Holiness, I cannot say I have. I thought Bernini executed mainly large works. Columns; altars; that sort of thing. . . . Where, Holiness? . . . Oh, yes. The Angelicum. . . . Your Holiness saw it there? May I ask when that was, Holiness? . . . Yes. As early as 1948. . . . Yes. Of course. A triumph of artistic power . . ." The Cardinal rolled his eyes toward heaven as if to say: See, Lord, what I have to put up with?

". . . Let me get on it right away . . . I said right away, Holiness. We must have a flawed connection. . . . Say again, Holiness? . . . Yes, of course, it must still be there. . . . To be sure, Holiness, Sainte-Baume is also still there. I meant the Bernini statue. . . . Quite right, Holiness. Statues don't just walk away. . . . What's that, Holiness? Did Your Holiness say two hours? . . ." Maestroianni glanced at his watch. "Pardon, Holiness. Help from whom? . . . From the hounds, did you say, Holiness? . . . Oh, I see. The hounds of the Lord. *Domini Canes*. The Dominicans, in charge of the Angelicum. Your Holiness' sense of humor is sharpened by the fresh mountain airs. . . ." His Eminence managed an unconvincing laugh into the receiver. But from the stress lines around his mouth, Chin could guess at the effort that laugh required.

"Yes, Holiness, we have the fax number . . . two hours. . . . Certainly, Holiness. . . . We all await Your Holiness' return. . . . Thanks, Holiness. . . . Return in safety."

The Cardinal replaced the receiver. His face frozen in deep anger and frustration, he sat motionless for a time working out in his mind the quickest and most practical way to comply with the Pontiff's instructions, and then get back to the truly important matter of his letter on unity. Suddenly, and perhaps a little grudgingly, Maestroianni decided the Pope was right. If this statue, this—he glanced at the name scribbled on his notepad—this *Noli Me Tangere* of Bernini was in the Angelicum, and the Angelicum belonged to the Dominicans as their residence, why not pass the whole ridiculous matter to them?

His Eminence pressed the intercom. "Monsignore. Find the Master-General of the Dominicans. Get him on the phone immediately."

His anger somewhat appeased by his decision, Maestroianni took up the draft of his unity letter and struggled to regain his concentration. But just as the perfect words were ready on the edge of his mind, Manuguerra buzzed through on the intercom again.

"The Master-General is out, Eminence."

"Out where?"

"They're not exactly sure, Eminence. It's Saturday . . ."

"Yes, Monsignore." The Cardinal's tone was anything but long-suffering. "I know what day it is." Maestroianni was certain that whoever had taken Manuguerra's call at the Angelicum knew exactly where the Master-General was. In fact, in the frame of mind that was now his, he was ready to believe that the whole Religious Order of Dominicans knew where to find Master-General Damien Slattery. That everyone in the world except the Cardinal Secretary knew where to find Slattery.

The Cardinal calmed himself. The question was how to run that wily giant of an Irishman to the ground without wasting time on porters and switchboard operators. Once he trained his mind on the logistics of the problem, the obvious answer to any situation such as this dawned like morning.

"Get me Father Aldo Carnesecca. Over here. Now. He's probably across the way in the Holy Office, even on a Saturday morning. Then book a car and driver in his name, to be at the main door below within ten minutes. Now, Monsignore! Now!"

"Sì, sì, Eminenza! Subito! Subito!"

Chin doubted the Cardinal would attempt to concentrate again on his dictation until he had fully disposed of this interruption. He sat back in his chair to wait. In his privileged position as special stenographer to the Secretary of State, the Korean understood that knives had long since been drawn between His Eminence and His Holiness. As he watched the agitation still flooding in on His Eminence, he scored one small point for His Holiness.

IV

THE TEMPTATIONS of Father Aldo Carnesecca were probably not like those of other men.

For all of the twelve years since he had been called upon by the Cardinal Secretary of State—Jean-Claude de Vincennes, back then—for the double triage of papal documents, Carnesecca had understood that Vincennes had more than likely fathomed the puzzle of that double-sealed envelope marked by two Popes as "Most Personal and Most Confidential." Vatican-wise as Father Carnesecca was, he understood as well that for such men as Vincennes and his successor, revenge may be a dish best eaten cold; but it would finally be served.

Nevertheless, Carnesecca also knew that the singular knowledge and experience he had cultivated over so many decades as a professional subordinate had their uses for such men as Vincennes and his successor, just as they had their uses for the Holy See. Trained and experienced subordinates were rare. So the lines of usefulness and of the ultimate payback could run concurrently for years, until the crucial moment arrived unheralded and sudden. Until then, he could move with a certain cautious impunity.

Father Carnesecca remained careful, all the same. But in his advancing years—in his seventies now, but fit and reasonably spry—he was what he had always been. Integrity intact, still valued by those who mattered to him as "a man of confidentiality," he remained a faithful priest of Eternal Rome. He was careful, therefore, not in the manner of some worldly intelligence operative. Rather, he was careful in the manner of a priest. He watched less for danger at his back than for danger to his immortal soul.

All in all, then, Carnesecca had responded to Cardinal Secretary Maestroianni's sudden call for him this Saturday morning as he always did—promptly and without surprise or alarm. The Cardinal's instructions to him had been peremptory and terse: Carnesecca was to find Dominican Master-General Damien Slattery wherever he might be, and get the Master-General on the phone to the Secretariat immediately. Absent instructions any more explicit than that, Carnesecca's temptation this morning was to use the Cardinal's urgent mandate to justify a pleasant excursion. To sit back in unaccustomed ease in the car the Cardinal Secretary had arranged for him, and tell the driver to head for the official headquarters—the head-house, as it is called in Rome—of this and every Dominican Master-General: Santa Sabina Monastery on the slopes of the Aventine Hill in the southwestern section of the city.

The only difficulty with such a tempting idea was that Carnesecca knew he would not find Father Damien Slattery at Santa Sabina Monastery. For, in point of fact, Cardinal Secretary Maestroianni had been absolutely correct in his belief that the whole Religious Order of Dominicans knew where to find the Master-General. And so did Aldo Carnesecca. Given the urgency Maestroianni had conveyed to him therefore, and with a little sigh of regret, Father Carnesecca gave his driver directions to a basement eatery called Springy's near the Pantheon.

Springy's was not a place Carnesecca himself frequented. But if you knew Damien Slattery as well as he did, you were bound to know Springy's. And if you knew Rome as well as Carnesecca did, you were bound to know Harry Springy. Like Master-General Damien Slattery himself, Harry Springy had become a local legend. An Australian, he had come to Rome in the seventies as a man with a mission. "Blokes gotta have a decent brekfus," Harry always said. With that motto as his creed and his guide, Harry turned out breakfast platters heaped with fried eggs, crisp bacon, pork sausages, white and black pudding sausages, chicken kidneys and livers, stacks of buttered toast and marmalade, and rivers of strong black tea to wash it all down.

Naturally, the blokes who had become regulars at Springy's over the years included the whole English-speaking student and clerical population of Rome. And among those regulars, Harry's most favorite bloke was Father Damien Duncan Slattery. If ever two men were more suitably destined for long and fruitful friendship than Harry Springy and Damien Slattery, Father Carnesecca hadn't met them.

Father Damien was a man of extraordinary appetite, and the dimensions to go with it. Over seven feet tall and weighing in on the far side of three hundred pounds, the Master-General was one of those grandiose physical specimens of manhood that every tailor and haberdasher in his native Ireland would have loved to clothe in Donegal tweeds. Fortunately, however, at least from Carnesecca's point of view, Damien Slattery had opted for the cream-colored robes of the Dominican Order. Decked out in so many swirling lines of ample skirts, and with his beamlike arms, his spatular hands, his broad expanse of stomach and chest, all topped by a rubicund face and a crown of unruly white hair, Slattery appeared like a lumbering archangel astray among mortals.

Over the years, however, Carnesecca had come to know Damien Slattery as the gentlest of men. At his age—about fifty-five or so, Carnesecca reckoned—Slattery walked and talked and wore his rank as Dominican Master-General with grandiose dignity. His sheer physicality was passport enough to approval and acceptability. He didn't need to use force. He was force. He looked like authority incarnate. Like a moving mountain.

Father Slattery's abilities as rugby forward in his school days—"bone-crusher," his benevolent brothers had called him—had added wonderful dimensions both to his popularity and to his legend. And he had found a similar easy success in his studies as well. When his Order had sent him for further studies at Oxford, Slattery had taken all academic honors available to him. He had acquired one more thing: his first experience in dealing with demonic possession. As he had put it once to Carnesecca, he had been "broken in" as an exorcist in those early days of his priesthood. In fact, he had to his credit in those days the cleansing of an entire household out in the residential Woodstock area. "So you see, Father Aldo"—Slattery had laughed that deep baritone laugh of his when telling Carnesecca about his past—"I'm more than just a pretty face!"

After Oxford, and after some fifteen years more back in Ireland as a professor of theology and local superior, Slattery had been appointed superior of the Dominican University of the Angelicum. In Father Slattery's earliest days in Rome, it was the Italians who had been most likely to break into giggles when they first saw him. For, being Italians, their imaginations had run riot concerning his dimensions. Very soon, though, they had taken him to heart with proprietary wonder as "*il nostro colosso.*" So it was that, while not everyone was pleased, nobody was surprised when in 1987 Damien Slattery's religious brothers elected him by unanimous ballot as Master-General of his Order. What was surprising for many of those Dominican brothers was that Father Slattery had put a certain odd condition to them before he would accept his election. While he would work by day in the Master-General's office in the Monastery of Santa Sabina on the Aventine Hill, he would not have his residence there as had always been the custom. He would maintain his residence in the Rector's quarters at the Angelicum.

By 1987, Aldo Carnesecca had already come into some little contact with Father Slattery. Indeed, by that time the Slavic Pope himself had come to know the Irishman, and had confided to him some sensitive and onerous jobs. Father Carnesecca didn't know all the details. But he did know that Slattery had become the Pontiff's private confessor and theologian; that was no secret. He knew that the Dominican traveled one or two months a year on private papal missions; and he knew that the most unpleasant and dangerous duty Slattery had drawn from the Holy Father came his way thanks to his early success as an exorcist. In fact, he was aware that Father Slattery had been called upon as exorcism counselor by the Cardinal Archbishops of Turin and Milan, the two cities in Europe most infested with ritual Satanism and demonic possession.

Over time, as Carnesecca had worked now and again for this or that reason with Damien Slattery, he had got to know that there were certain things that never changed in the man. First—and most important for Father Carnesecca—Damien Slattery remained absolute in his Roman Catholic faith in God, and in the power inherent in the Godhead. That was absolutely crucial to his success in his continuing confrontations with the demonic. Few people ever knew, however, nor would they learn from Carnesecca, that Master-General Slattery's reason for keeping his residence in the Rector's quarters of the Angelicum was to place himself as an antidote against a former demonic infestation of those rooms.

The second unshakable constant about Damien Slattery was that he remained Irish to the core. His Oxford accent rarely broke down; but when it did, Slattery was likely to pour out a stream of Gaelic invective with a brogue straight out of Donegal. The third thing that never changed was his devotion to Harry Springy and his basement eatery. There he could be found on any Saturday morning, seated at his permanent table apart from the other patrons, surrounded by platters all lovingly prepared by Harry Springy himself for his favorite bloke.

"Ah!" Slattery raised his head. "It's you, Father Aldo." Damien put down his knife and fork in a grandiose flourish of flowing sleeves and calm dignity, and motioned the priest to take a chair opposite his massive frontage. "Come to join me in a little breakfast, have you?"

Mindful of time passing, Carnesecca excused himself from the invitation. He relayed the Cardinal's urgent message that the Master-General was to call His Eminence at the Secretariat. "Immediately, Father-General. An urgent matter relative to the Holy Father. But that's all His Eminence cared to say."

That was enough for the Dominican. He had the remainder of his breakfast returned to the oven to be kept warm and fresh. Then he headed for Springy's only telephone, located hard by the busy, clattery kitchen. Father Damien never looked forward to any conversation with Cosimo Maestroianni. The two men met often in formal settings, and knew each other as occupying opposite ends of the present seesaw of Roman power politics. But even in this jungle of factionalism, there was something much deeper and more personal than political loyalties that separated these two. Damien knew it. And the Cardinal knew it.

Father Slattery dialed through to the Cardinal Secretary's office. Taco Manuguerra put him through to His Eminence at once. Neither Cardinal nor Dominican indulged in more than the requisite social preliminaries. But as always, each was true to his formal duties in the system.

"His Holiness is in Sainte-Baume, Father-General. At the cavern shrine of St. Mary Magdalene. Officiating at the celebrations there. He has just called me to say he needs us to fax him a photograph of a certain Bernini statue of Mary Magdalene. *Noli Me Tangere,* it's called."

"Yes, Your Eminence. How can we be of assistance to His Holiness? Your Eminence knows we are always ready . . ."

"By getting a photograph of the statue and faxing said photograph to the Holy Father at Sainte-Baume, Father-General. Within the hour, please."

For Slattery, the sound of exasperation edging into the Cardinal's voice almost compensated for having his breakfast interrupted. Still, he had no idea why the Cardinal would direct such a request to him. "But of course, we are willing to act immediately, Eminence. But a photograph of . . ."

His Eminence seemed not to understand the Master-General's problem. "You will have our official photographer at your disposal. My secretary has already put him on notice. But I insist, Father-General. His Holiness insists. Do it now."

"But of course, Eminence. Of course. The only difficulty . . ."

"What difficulty, Father-General? You don't need a vote of the General Chapter for this."

Slattery wrinkled his nose at the barb. As the main governing body in the Dominican Order, the General Chapter was known to move with the speed of an ailing turtle. "Willingly!" Father Damien raised his deep voice over a sudden clatter of dishes. "Immediately! But I have never seen this—what is it? *Noli* . . ."

"Bernini's *Noli Me Tangere,* Father-General. Remember the Gospel scene? Christ and the Magdalene in the garden? After the Resurrection? *Noli Me Tangere.* 'Do not touch me'—Christ's words. Remember? The statue is in the *cortile* of the religious house of which you are Superior, Father-General. Or don't you frequent the *cortile?*"

There was no mistaking the Cardinal's rising temper. But Slattery was entirely mystified now. Along with many religious houses in Rome, the Angelicum boasted a lovely inner courtyard; a restful garden with a pleasant fountain at its center, where, in fact, Father Damien often recited his breviary. But never in all his years at the Angelicum had he ever seen a Bernini statue there. And he said as much to Maestroianni.

"Impossible, Father-General," the Secretary insisted. "The Holy Father saw it there himself."

In their shared confusion—one of the few sentiments they were ever likely to share—Slattery and Maestroianni slipped out of their formal mode of talk.

"The Holy Father saw it there? When?"

"In the late forties, he said."

"In the late forties."

"You heard right. But statues don't walk. A Bernini statue doesn't melt away."

"I'll grant you that. But it's not there now."

After a moment's pause, the Cardinal Secretary's voice softened a little. "Look, Father-General. Between you and me and St. Mary Magdalene, you have no idea how this ridiculous request has devastated official business this morning. The statue must be somewhere. Surely you can find it."

"Did His Holiness say why he wants this photograph so urgently?"

"For inspiration, it seems." A note of sarcasm filtered into the Cardinal's voice. "The Holy Father values the expression of pious devotion Bernini sculpted into the face of Mary Magdalene. It's a question of inspiration for his homily this evening at Sainte-Baume."

"I see." Damien did see. And he paused in his turn now, as he tried to find some line of attack on the problem.

"Someone must know where the statue is," the Cardinal prodded. "Can't you ask the older monks living at the Angelicum?"

"Not on a weekend. The faculty is gone. All the usual residents are scattered—off to visit their relatives in Campania. Besides myself, there's one blind and aged monk asleep in his bed; one visitor from our Tahitian mission whose specialty appears to be banana diets; a party of Chinese sisters rehearsing a Mandarin play in our *cortile;* and one young American . . .

"Wait a moment, Eminence! That's it. I think I may have our man. The young American priest. Comes here each year for the second semester. Teaches dogmatic theology. Quiet type. Functions as house archivist. He's always at home on weekends; and only yesterday he asked me for the house records covering the years back to 1945."

Maestroianni pounced on the possibility. "That's the key man. Put the phone on hold and call him. I'll wait."

Slattery made a face at Harry Springy, just edging by him from the kitchen. "Actually, I'm not calling from the Angelicum."

"Ah." The Cardinal indulged his curiosity. "I wondered at all the clatter and noise I hear in the background."

"Just a sudden influx of parishioners, Eminence." Slattery erected the barrier of formal speech again. "I presume Father Carnesecca has all the information? The photographer's telephone number, and the fax number at Sainte-Baume?"

"He has it all, Father-General." In his obvious relief—and taking success for granted, as he so often did—the Cardinal Secretary spouted a whole series of orders to Slattery. "When your man has located the statue, have him call me. The way things are going this morning, I expect I'll still be here. I'll tell Monsignore Manuguerra to put him through. In fact, when he's faxed the photograph to the Holy Father, tell him to bring the original to me here. What's your man's name?"

"Gladstone, Eminence. Father Christian Thomas Gladstone."

The moment his car reached the Angelicum, Carnesecca climbed the worn white marble steps of the Priory. Inside at the switchboard, the doorman was engaged on the telephone, gossiping with his girlfriend, from the sound of things. After some minutes of excruciating delay and several attempts to manage the situation politely, the normally meek and uncommanding Father Carnesecca took a more direct approach. He reached out and deftly disconnected the young man's call.

"I am here on papal business. I have been sent by Master-General Slattery; and by the Cardinal Secretary of State, the Most Reverend Cardinal Cosimo Maestroianni. Here is my identification. Call this number to verify. But then expect to be out of a job by day's end."

The doorman was too stunned to be angry at having his call cut off. *"Sì, Reverendo.* What is it?"

"I am here to see Father Christian Gladstone. Where can I find him?"

"I'm sorry, Father." The poor fellow was ashen-faced by now. "I can't ring the Professor. He's on the roof saying his prayers. There's no house phone up there. I'm sorry, *Reverendo* . . ."

"Where's the elevator?"

Light dawning on his features, the young man leaped to his feet. Bubbling a stream of *"per favore"*s and *"s'accomodi"*s, he led Carnesecca to the elevator. Once he reached the roof, Carnesecca immediately caught sight of a black-robed figure, tall and lanky, etched against the profile of the city. He walked slowly to and fro, his lips moving soundlessly, his head bowed over his prayer book. The sight of a young priest reciting his appointed prayers was rare nowadays. Carnesecca regretted having to intrude.

The cleric stopped and turned around; he had sensed Carnesecca's presence. Father Aldo found himself being scrutinized by a pair of steady blue eyes. The face was still young-looking, but already marked by definite lines around the mouth. The American must have satisfied some question in his own mind, though; for he closed his prayer book and strode forward hand outstretched. "I am Christian Gladstone, *Reverendo,"* he said in passable Italian, a slight smile at the corners of his mouth.

"Carnesecca." The handshake between the two clerics was firm and sincere. "Aldo Carnesecca, from the Secretariat. I've just come from the Master-General at . . ."

A broad smile spread across Gladstone's face. "At Springy's! Welcome, Father. Anyone who is both friend enough and man enough to interrupt the Master-General on a Saturday morning at Springy's is to be received with open arms!"

Though unaccustomed to such ease of manner, Carnesecca responded in kind as he began his brief explanation of the mission entrusted to him. Again, though, the young American was ahead of his visitor. The Father-General had filled him in by phone, he explained.

As they walked toward the roof door, and then rode down in the elevator, Gladstone repeated for Carnesecca what Father Slattery had relayed to him about the missing Bernini, and about the Pontiff's odd request to the Cardinal Secretary for a photograph of the statue to be faxed to him at Baume. It was interesting for him, Gladstone confided, that the Holy Father would look to a Bernini statue—or to any piece of art—for inspiration. "I thought he was of a more mystical bent of mind," he said. "But I should have realized from some of his writings that he has very deep humanist perceptions."

Carnesecca took in that opinion about the Slavic Pope with some interest, but did not interrupt Christian's briefing.

"Anyway," the American went on, "after Master-General Slattery told me what the problem was, I checked some house records I asked him for only yesterday. I think we can fulfill the Holy Father's request for a photo of the *Noli Me Tangere* pretty easily. If you'll call the Cardinal's photographer, we can be on our way. Once we fax the photo to His Holiness, it seems I'm to take the original to the Cardinal at the Secretariat. If you ask me, though, Father Carnesecca, that's the oddest thing of all. You would seem the man for that job, wouldn't you say? Being with the Secretariat and all?"

The Cardinal's interest in anyone even remotely associated with Damien Slattery did not surprise Carnesecca. But this was not the time, nor were these the circumstances, to enter into such political waters with his new acquaintance. Everything had its moment. When the Bernini matter had been attended to, perhaps he would arrange such a moment with this interesting young man.

Once downstairs again, intent upon the passage of time and the Holy Father's need, Carnesecca headed for the phone. "Where shall I tell the photographer to meet us?" He turned back to Gladstone. "Where did you find the *Noli Me Tangere?*"

"If the records are accurate, it's hidden away—can you imagine a Bernini being hidden away anywhere, Father?—in a basement chapel at the head-house. Santa Sabina Monastery on the Aventine."

V

"GLADSTONE. Christian Thomas." Cardinal Secretary Maestroianni read the title of the file in front of him. Thanks to his professional determination and his powers of concentration, His Eminence had salvaged his busy Saturday schedule after all.

He disliked talking to Master-General Damien Slattery. The Dominican's use of "we" in his conversations was always particularly grating. All the same, the sacrifice of a conversation with the head of the Dominicans had at least got the job done. This young protégé of his, this Father Gladstone, had been as good as the Master-General's word. He had rung in fairly quick order to say that the Bernini statue had been located, and that he and Carnesecca were on their way to secure the photograph and fax it off to Baume. Barring complications, the Cardinal expected Gladstone to bring the original to him here at the Secretariat within the hour.

Success in that matter secured, Maestroianni's resolve not to delay his all-important letter concerning Church unity had prevailed. The final draft of the letter lay safely by his hand for a last run-through. Once he had the interview with this young American cleric behind him—it need take no more than a few minutes—he did have one phone call to make on the unity matter. At last then, he could be off to his residence.

Maestroianni's interest in Christian Gladstone was largely pro forma, but not casual. The Cardinal maintained a certain interest in the younger aspirants within the ecclesiastical structure. They did the bulk of the work after all; and inevitably their names came up for possible preferment. As part of the Vatican bureaucracy himself for these past fifty years, the Cardinal Secretary knew how to keep his eye on the up-and-coming contingent, just as he knew how to scrutinize both his equals and his superiors within the system. That being so, even while the Cardinal finished his work with Chin, he had Taco Manuguerra secure the file on the American priest-professor from personnel.

"Gladstone. Christian Thomas," the Cardinal repeated the name to himself as he opened the dossier. Another *anglosassone* to deal with, for his sins. With a swift and practiced eye, His Eminence checked over the papers that formed a profile of the American's career as a cleric.

Thirty-nine years old. Twelve years into his ecclesiastical career, if you included his years of study. Early university work done in Europe. Studied for the priesthood at the Navarre Seminary in Spain. Degrees taken with honors in theology and philosophy. Ordained on March 24, 1984. Ecclesiastically speaking, home base for Father Gladstone was the diocese of

New Orleans, under the jurisdiction of Cardinal Archbishop John Jay O'Cleary. During the second half of the academic year, he functioned mainly as tenured professor of theology at New Orleans' Major Seminary.

Just as Slattery had said this morning, he currently spent the other half of the year in Rome teaching at the Angelicum, while he worked on his doctorate in theology. Though he was not a Dominican, it seemed Father-General Slattery himself directed Gladstone's work on his doctoral thesis. Small wonder, Maestroianni thought acidly as he read the notation indicating that Gladstone's professorship at the Angelicum was endowed with his family's money. Slattery never missed a trick.

All in all, the information in Gladstone's file—including a laudatory letter of recommendation from Cardinal O'Cleary himself—added up to an unblemished record as priest and theologian. A special papal rescript of the current Pontiff brought a frown to the Cardinal's brow, however. Bearing the date of Christian Gladstone's ordination, March 24, 1984, it allowed the priest to say the age-old Tridentine Mass. A note from the Cardinal Prefect of the Vatican Bank explained that Gladstone's privilege in this matter had been insisted upon by his mother as a precondition to her investment of some five million dollars to rescue an ailing French company whose major equity holder was that same Vatican Bank.

There was nothing unusual in such an arrangement. Maestroianni himself could rattle off any number of similar and even far richer Vatican trade-offs. Nevertheless, preference by any priest for the outworn traditional format of the Roman Mass was troublesome for His Eminence. At the very least—and assuming political innocence—it was the sign of a certain backwardness; a failure to grasp the negative and divisive character of the old Roman Church and its elitist mannerisms. Given the innocuous profile that emerged from the documents in his file, the Cardinal surmised that Gladstone's preference for the old Mass was no more than a bit of personal baggage left over from his days at the Navarre Seminary.

"*Semplice,*" the Cardinal observed to himself. "The man is an innocent. Not political. Not complicated with career-boosting. Not running with any of the factions in Rome or America. A toiler. A drone."

Still, it wouldn't hurt to spend a couple of minutes more on a quick run-through of the fellow's family data. Connections often tell more about a man's usefulness than his own record. The family residence, it seemed, was a place called Windswept House in Galveston, Texas. A romantic touch, that; like something out of one of those English romances the Americans loved so much. Father: Deceased. Mother: Signora Francesca Gladstone. The data following the name was spare. But what there was—when coupled with the five-million-dollar French rescue and the good lady's full endowment of a professorship at the Angelicum—had the strong smell of fortunes. Old money that was still to the good. One sister: Patricia Gladstone. Nothing of importance there. Unmarried. An artist of some note, apparently. Living at the family home in Galveston.

A brother, Paul Thomas Gladstone, was more interesting for Maestroianni. He had done some seminary work as well, but apparently had switched to Harvard. Principal residence now in London. Paul was reckoned as an expert in international relations, and was currently employed by the prestigious transnational law firm of Crowther, Benthoek, Gish, Jen & Ekeus.

What a happy coincidence. Cyrus Benthoek's firm.

Maestroianni had for years counted Cyrus Benthoek as a particularly valued associate in his endeavors to bring his Church into the forefront of the New World Order. In fact, as his work this very afternoon required a call to Benthoek, he would just make a note in his diary to ask about Paul Thomas Gladstone. It was only a detail, but it would cost him nothing to be thorough. As Cardinal Vincennes had so often said, details matter.

Turning back to the dossier, Maestroianni scanned rapidly through the few remaining documents. His thoroughness was rewarded by the most interesting data of all. The Gladstones, it seemed, ranked in the Vatican as *"privilegiati di Stato."* There was, in other words, a permanent "Gladstone Card" in the Secretariat's own file of Vatican Important Persons; and the Gladstone family had a file all to itself in the official Secretariat archives.

Understandably, few details were noted in Christian Gladstone's personnel file. But the practical meaning of *"privilegiati di Stato"* was clear enough to one as deeply experienced as the Cardinal Secretary of State. In broad terms, Gladstone family involvement in the finances of the Holy See meant that the Holy See in turn rendered whatever financial services it could to the Gladstones. The titular head of the Gladstone family, therefore, was no doubt among a restricted few—no more than fifty or sixty in all, probably—who were granted banking facilities at the Vatican's in-house bank, established by the Holy See in the 1940s. And they were among the few who could, for special reasons, acquire a Vatican passport.

Maestroianni closed the dossier and rose from his chair. Gazing out over St. Peter's Square at nothing in particular, he speculated about Christian Gladstone with an interest he had not anticipated. Or, to be more accurate, he speculated about the contradiction of circumstances surrounding Christian Gladstone. On the one hand, there was a brother who was associated—to what degree, he would find out—with the very forward-looking and even visionary Cyrus Benthoek. And on the other hand, there was what appeared to be an old and well-established Catholic family that boasted impeccable credentials with the Holy See.

Christian Gladstone himself didn't appear to be much. Personally he was probably heir to millions. As a priest, he seemed simple. Pious to the point of being retrograde, in all likelihood. Still said the old Roman Mass, but made no big splash about it. Perhaps he would turn out to be an interesting type after all. For Cardinal Maestroianni, "interesting" was a synonym for "useful." Such pious but powerfully connected drones as this—raw and malleable and "innocent" as they are—had more than once turned out to be good stuff from which to strengthen the bridges from the old effete order of things to the progressive new.

No, he decided; there would be no surprises in this bland young priest. At best, he would be the type of *anglosassone* who looked you straight in the eye. His ceremonial gestures would be awkward acts of Roman behavior to which Americans are not born and to which they never become accustomed. Mercifully, he would make no long speeches, or lace his remarks with devotional references to God or the Church or the Saints.

Taco Manuguerra's gentle tapping on the door ended any need for the Cardinal to speculate further. "Father Christian Gladstone, Eminence."

Maestroianni scrutinized his visitor. Other than the fact that his cassock was cut from good cloth, it was as undistinguished as the Cardinal had expected. But wearing a cassock did seem as natural to the American as to any Roman cleric. In a movement that was as automatic as it was authoritarian—pointed, but in no way exaggerated—His Eminence extended the hand that bore his bishop's ring.

"Eminence." Gladstone dropped to one knee and kissed the ring lightly. Then, rising, "Pardon the delay. We got these prints ready as fast as we could."

Smiling his best visitor smile, Maestroianni took the envelope held out to him by the American. The young man's Italian was tolerable. Nothing awkward in his ceremonial gestures. Nothing confused or hesitant in his use of ecclesiastical titles. Gladstone rose a notch or two above the Cardinal's expectations.

"We cannot thank you adequately, *Reverendo.*" The Cardinal Secretary proffered a slow, deliberate handshake on his visitor. Strong hands; neither cold fish nor limp spaghetti. No wet palms. No sign of nerves. Maestroianni bestowed another smile on Christian and gestured to a nearby chair. "Sit down, Father. Please, sit down for a moment."

His Eminence took his own seat behind his desk. He removed the prints from the envelope Father Gladstone had handed him and gave them a cursory glance. There were three different shots of the *Noli Me Tangere.* How industrious of the fellow. A good, reliable drone. Does what he's told and a bit more.

"I presume these have gone off to Sainte-Baume, Father?"

"Half an hour ago, Your Eminence."

"I see. All's well that ends well, eh?" The Cardinal laid the photographs aside. "I learned some time ago, Father Gladstone, that you have a brother who works for an old friend of mine. Cyrus Benthoek."

"Yes, Eminence." Gladstone looked the Cardinal Secretary straight in the eye in the Anglo-Saxon manner. "Paul is very excited about his work. He has promised to come down to Rome for a visit while I'm still here."

"While you are still here, Father? Do you plan to leave us, then?"

"Nothing definite, Your Eminence. Nothing immediate, that is. I still have work to do to complete my thesis. But I find I am not by nature a Roman."

"Yes. Quite." Another expected trait confirmed. And yet, there was something different about this particular *anglosassone*. Something that finally didn't fit the mold. It wasn't what Gladstone did or said so much as what he was. True, there was no Mediterranean fire in him. That would be too much to expect. But the Cardinal Secretary almost envied the quiet, self-assured reserve of this young man. He was not subservient; not out of his depth. His manner went beyond the "when in Rome" behavior of most Anglo-Saxons. He was a surprisingly polished piece of goods.

"Tell me, Father." Maestroianni fingered the photographs again, but his eyes never left Gladstone's face. "Where did you find the *Noli Me Tangere?*"

"In a basement chapel, Eminence. At the Dominican head-house."

"Well"—the Secretary rose from his desk—"we cannot thank you adequately. When your brother does come down to Rome, I would be very happy to make his acquaintance, Father."

Following the Cardinal's lead, Gladstone stood. "Thank you, Eminence."

"Interesting," the Cardinal murmured to himself as Christian Gladstone closed the door behind him. "An interesting species." The man had no passions of the heart, surely. Not political enough to deal with Rome. Listens benignly enough. It was hard to tell from his conversation if he was unimaginative or merely noncommittal. More polished than most of the breed; even an unexpected touch of sophistication, one might say. But polish or not, like most Anglo-Saxons, he could be manipulated.

That Gladstone remained interesting for Maestroianni at all, however, was almost entirely due to the contradiction evident in the priest's undoubted and powerful family connections. He came from stock that was still mired in the old papal Catholicism. What's bred in the bone comes out in the flesh, the English say. Yet Gladstone's brother had been attracted to Cyrus Benthoek's operation, which had no use for the Holy See that would be visible to the unsuspecting eye. Who could tell? It might turn out that the Pontiff had done Maestroianni a small if unwitting favor after all, with his call for the Bernini photographs. The Cardinal reached for the intercom on his desk and buzzed the long-suffering Taco Manuguerra. "Monsignore, put through a call to the New Orleans diocese. I want to speak to the Cardinal Archbishop."

As it turned out, His Eminence Cardinal O'Cleary was unreachable. "On vacation in the west of Ireland, Eminence," Manuguerra reported. Well, no matter. The Cardinal Secretary had spent enough precious time on the matter for now. In any case, if there was anything of real interest to pursue, he would doubtless learn more from Cyrus Benthoek than from

Cardinal O'Cleary. Best to finish up the final draft of his letter on Church unity.

His Eminence turned to his scrambler phone and dialed a number in Belgium. At the sound of Cardinal Piet Svensen's familiar voice on the line, the Secretary brightened. Here at least was a known quantity; a man of undoubted judgment. Cardinal Svensen was an old and trusted acquaintance. Retired now from his official post, just as Maestroianni himself soon would be, Svensen remained an undoubted leader and expert on ecumenism and on the charismatic movement. And, resident in Brussels as he was, he boasted some impressive ties within the higher echelons of the European Economic Community.

No friend of the Slavic Pope, Svensen had been dead set against this Pontiff's election. In private Conclave caucuses he had warned his fellow Cardinal Electors that such a man as this Slav could not solve the Church's arduous problems. In Maestroianni's book, therefore, no one would understand better than the Belgian Cardinal the urgent need to direct the bishops delicately but firmly to a more fruitful understanding of their episcopal unity with the Holy Father.

"Bull's-eye, Eminence!" Svensen boomed his approval after listening to Maestroianni's read-through of his draft letter. "Bull's-eye! Truly a masterpiece. And your sensitivity in polling the bishops on the unity question indirectly, through your diplomatic staff—through the Nuncios and such—is genius. Guaranteed to make the bishops conscious of their own empowerment by the Holy Spirit!"

"Grazie, Eminenza." Maestroianni set the unity letter down on his desk. "But only the good Lord knows what I have been through this morning to get it done." With only the barest prodding from the Belgian, the Cardinal Secretary launched into a colorful account of the Pontiff's urgent call to locate the Bernini statue.

"Gottverdummelte!" That Belgian expletive summed up Svensen's judgment of the whole affair. In his view, it was typical of this Pope not only that he should have caused such bother but that he should have chosen to make a papal excursion to Sainte-Baume at all. "That shrine is nothing but a pious hoax, Eminence. I would love to introduce our Holy Father to some close associates of mine—eminent scholars, I might add—who are of the informed opinion that Mary Magdalene never set foot outside of Palestine. And we would all be better off, Eminence, if our Pontiff had never set foot outside of Kraków! Pious meditations, even from a Pope, will not solve the Church's problems."

The Cardinal Secretary agreed fully. "In fact," he confided, "the whole incident with the Pontiff this morning has only reinforced my personal conviction that we have only two alternatives. Either the Pope changes his mind and his policy concerning the sacrosanct primacy of the papal office. Or . . ." The Cardinal drew in a deep and theatrically audible breath.

"Or we pursue the idea we have touched on in past conversations. The idea of a change of Pontiffs."

There was no need for theatrics where Svensen was concerned. "Absolutely, Eminence. The more so because our friends in Strasbourg and here in Brussels are getting nervous. They feel strongly that the Pope's constant remarks—his insistence that there can be no Europe without faith as its bedrock—run counter to their deep concern for the primacy of economic and financial strength as the basic underpinning of the new Europe. In fact, as I've been giving this whole matter some serious thought since last we spoke about it, I wonder if I might make a little suggestion."

"Fire ahead, Eminence."

"The letter you were kind enough to share with me just now is on the mark. Given your artistry of wording, I have every hope that the outcome will be pleasing to us. But even then, how do we capitalize on the situation? Suppose the bishops are dissatisfied with their present relationship vis-à-vis the Holy See—and I have no doubt that Your Eminence's letter will make that dissatisfaction clear. We will still need to forge that data into a concrete plan of action. The concept I have in mind is simple. The bishops themselves will become the instrument we need to force the issue with the present Pontiff.

"As I'm sure you know, local European bishops want desperately to be part of the Economic Community. They understand that the EC can only get bigger and loom more importantly than local national politics with the passage of every year. And, as the popular new phrase has it, they do need to be politically correct and socially acceptable; or they think they do—it comes to the same thing. More important is the fact that the bishops want their piece of the pie. They need mortgages, just as major corporations do. They need long-term, low-interest loans. They need zoning variances for their building projects. Their schools and universities need public funds. They need advice about their portfolios. They need the authorities to look the other way when clerics make their little mistakes."

"So, Your Eminence?" Maestroianni glanced at his watch. The Belgian had been noted throughout his long career for a certain long-winded triumphalism in proposing his own ideas.

"Bear with me a moment longer, Eminence," Svensen went on. "Consider the elements we have working for us. On the one hand, given a little guidance, the bishops are bound to see the benefits for the Church of their cooperation with the EC, as it stands. As the coming force in Europe. All those little favors and considerations the bishops require, after all, depend on the political goodwill of the EC countries. On the other hand, we have the Pontiff. He is insistent and consistent on three topics.

"First, he insists on his undemocratic Petrine claims regarding the primacy of papal authority. Second, he insists on the importance of 'the bond of union,' as he has called it, between himself and his bishops. He will go very far before he will allow or admit an open break with them. And third, the new Europe is so precious in this Pope's eyes that he hardly speaks one paragraph nowadays without referring to it.

"Now, if we can carry Your Eminence's capital idea of polling the bishops one step further—if we can get the European bishops actually to forge a common mentality along the lines of our thinking about Europe; if we can sharpen their understanding of how they will benefit from a closer union with the EC and its aims—then I can foresee the bishops themselves forcing a change in the Holy See's attitudes. Indeed—and this is the point, Eminence—should the Holy See remain obdurate, I can see the bishops themselves forcing—er—whatever change we deem advisable."

Maestroianni's initial response was skeptical. "Yes, I see what you mean. But 'forging a common mind among the bishops,' as you put it, would be like getting cats and mice to cohabit peacefully. And it would be a complex operation, Your Eminence. It would require a careful assessment of each bishop's needs, and where each bishop stands on issues that are a lot tougher to get at than unity."

"Agreed." Svensen knew the problems. "In fact, it would mean more than assessing the situation of each bishop. It would mean finding a way into the EC at a level that would, shall we say, dovetail with the more practical interests of the bishops. A link would be required between the bishops and the EC that would guarantee a bit of civilized mutual handwashing."

Maestroianni had to smile at the Belgian's sudden delicacy. "Practical interests like those mortgages and low-interest loans and such that Your Eminence mentioned earlier."

"Precisely. I grant Your Eminence's point, though. It would be a complex operation. And we might not bring it off. In that case, however, I submit that we would be in no worse a position than we are at this moment. However, if we were to accomplish so great a miracle as to forge a desirable 'common mind' among the bishops—we would have the instrument we need. In fact, Eminence, if your letter evokes an expression of dissatisfaction among the bishops on the general issue of their unity with the present Pope, then the formation of a 'common mind' among the bishops would put immediate and very sharp teeth into the matter. We would be on the firmest possible ground, once and for all, to force the issue with the Pontiff."

"Yes. I see." Maestroianni was coming around to Svensen's point of view. "It might work. Provided the Americans would dovetail with Europeans, of course. With one hundred and eighty residential bishops alone, not counting auxiliary bishops and all the rest, the Americans carry considerable weight. And they account for a considerable part of the money coming into the Vatican. The proposition would be iffy without them."

"Agreed. Whatever weight our American brothers lack theologically and in culture and tradition is more than adequately made up by their financial clout and, let's face it, by the superpower status of their United

States. Diplomatically and geopolitically, they count in the general equation."

"It could work," the Cardinal Secretary of State conceded at last. But he remained cautious all the same. "Let me explore the idea further with some of our colleagues. Perhaps we can talk further at the Robert Schuman Annual Memorial celebrations next month in Strasbourg. Do you plan to be there, Eminence?"

"I will look forward to it, my friend."

As Cardinal Maestroianni hung up the scrambler phone, no such phrase as "inciting the bishops to wholesale mutiny" crossed his mind. The bishops were running along that road anyway, albeit in their squabbly and disunited fashion. On the contrary, it seemed fitting that such a revolutionary idea—a concrete plan to forge the bishops into an instrument to further a seamless new world unity—would be discussed amid the annual celebrations honoring the memory and accomplishments of the great Robert Schuman.

Schuman had been one of the first Europeans to conceive of a united Western Europe. As far back as the forties, in fact, as France's Foreign Minister, it was he who had started building the first bridges between France and Germany as the keystone states of any future unity. His memory was understandably revered by many. In Maestroianni's mind, and in the Roman phrase, Robert Schuman ranked as nothing less than "a founding father."

Truly absorbed now in Svensen's powerful idea of fomenting a "common mind" among the bishops, the Cardinal began to gather up his papers, ready to head for the quiet of his apartments on the Via Aurelia. There he would be free to think and work in peace. No jangling telephones. No unanticipated interviews. No more footling matters such as papal piety and missing statues. For the last time that day, Maestroianni called Monsignore Manuguerra in and settled the arrangements to have his unity letter dispatched by diplomatic pouch. Then, as he rose to leave, his eye fell on Christian Gladstone's personnel file. He had almost forgotten.

He handed the dossier back to Manuguerra. "Have this returned to personnel, Monsignore. And one more thing. Get the Gladstone family file from the Secretariat archives. Have it on my desk first thing Monday morning."

VI

CHRISTIAN GLADSTONE was both amused and baffled by his curious interview with Cardinal Secretary of State Maestroianni. Shaking his head in mock disbelief, he stepped through the doors of the Secretariat and into the strong midday light of Rome, streaming now over the Court of St. Damasus. Father Carnesecca was standing beside the car with the chauffeur.

"These Romans!" Gladstone settled into the rear seat beside Carnesecca. "I know you work at the Secretariat, *Reverendo.*" Christian smiled an apology at his companion. "But I hope you won't take offense at my saying that after a handshake with His Eminence, a man is tempted to count his fingers to see if they're all still in place."

"No offense taken," Carnesecca responded evenly.

As their car wended a careful way through the Saturday crowd of visitors in St. Peter's Square, a Mercedes-Benz inched by in the opposite direction, heading for the Secretariat. "Apparently, *Reverendo,* you were the last bit of business on the Secretary's calendar this morning. That's his car. Coming to take him home, no doubt. His Eminence will be unreachable, except by Security, until seven A.M. on Monday."

Christian glanced at the limousine. "I expect I should be honored that so great a Vatican personage held up his schedule for me. But if you want to know the truth, the interview with the Cardinal Secretary gave me an appetite. Instead of heading straight back to the Angelicum, I wonder if you'd join me for lunch?"

Carnesecca, surprised by the almost boyish grin on Gladstone's face, was delighted. And he knew just the place to suggest. "Casa Maggi, it's called. Milanese cuisine. It will give you a little rest from our Roman oppression. And it's not a very long walk from there to the Angelicum."

By the time the two clerics settled into their chairs in the gratifying cool of Casa Maggi, they had left the formalities of official Rome behind them, and they chatted about the day's adventure that had brought them together to assist the Holy Father. The stilted *Reverendo* quickly gave way to the far more familiar *Padre,* and first names replaced family names. It was Aldo and Christian now.

"Of humble means though I am," Carnesecca poked a bit of fun at himself, "perhaps you will let me order for both of us. I know this menu well." That, it turned out, was an understatement. The *gnocchi milanesi* and *céleri rémoulade* he instructed their waiter to bring were among the best Christian had tasted, either in Rome or in Milan. A far cry from

Springy's pork and pudding sausages, the two agreed. Nor did either of them intend such a comment as a barb against Damien Slattery; for among the things they quickly discovered they shared was a high regard for the Dominican Master-General, both as a priest and as a man.

Christian was fascinated to meet such a living encyclopedia of Vatican lore as Father Aldo, and was rewarded for his interest. Carnesecca turned out to be a master at recounting memories of past Popes and politics. His profiles of some of the more illustrious visitors to the Apostolic Palace brought familiar names to life for Christian. And some of his tales of excruciating clerical blunders at the Secretariat made the younger man laugh till the tears came.

On his side, Father Aldo was just as fascinated to learn about the background of such a *simpatico* young priest. Unlike most Americans he had met, Christian was steeped in his family's history. It seemed that Christian's family, like Carnesecca himself, had always been embroiled in Church tumult. Or at any rate, that was the part of his family's story that had always interested him the most.

The original Gladstones were Englishmen, Christian told his companion. Or, to be more exact, they were Norman-Saxons who had settled down by the 1300s as Cornishmen. They had intermarried over the centuries with Trevelyans, with Pencanibers and with Pollocks. But they never forgot they were themselves of Norman-Saxon stock. And above all, they never forgot they were Roman Catholics. The Gladstone Manor House had been at Launceston in Cornwall. They were hereditary owners of large farmlands, fisheries and tin mines in Camborne. They were pre-Reformation Catholics whose religion was greatly colored by the Celtic tradition from Ireland.

When the sixteenth century came around, the Gladstones had predictably refused to accept King Henry VIII as spiritual head of the Church. True to their Roman Catholicism—and to the Gladstone family motto, "No Quarter"—they hung on to their manor house and lands at Launceston and their tin mines of Camborne. Aided by the remoteness of Cornwall from London, and by the unswerving loyalty of their family retainers, their workmen and their tenants—all Catholics in very Catholic Cornwall—they had held out pretty much intact until the latter half of the seventeenth century. Given the fierceness of the Elizabethan persecution of Catholics, survival had been no mean accomplishment. Finally their alternatives grew grim. They could sit in their manor house as many other Old Catholics did, wrapped in sullen nostalgia for their past, waiting to be trundled off in tumbrels to London's Tyburn Tree, where they would be hanged. Or they could flee.

"No Quarter" meant they would not compromise. But they did intend to live on and fight another day. So they took their money and their arms, boarded one of their own merchant ships and sailed for the New World of America. They made landfall in St. Augustine, Florida, in 1668. By the early 1800s, the family members had gone off in various directions. A small nucleus, headed by one Paul Thomas Gladstone, settled down with the first wave of American colonists on Galveston Island.

At that time, Galveston Island was little more than a sandbar lying parallel to the coast. A scant twenty-seven miles long and varying from one to three miles in width, it protected the bay and the mainland from the waters and the winds of the Mexican Gulf. Galveston Bay itself was the draw, however. The Americans—Paul Thomas Gladstone not least among them—saw vast possibilities there for commercial shipping. Seventeen miles wide and thirty miles long, and fed by numerous bayous and two major rivers, the bay presented the settlers with a good draft for oceangoing ships. It was protected by Galveston Island and the Bolivar Peninsula. And, like New Orleans and Mexico's Veracruz, it gave viable access to the profitable shipping trade of Central and South America.

Paul Thomas Gladstone had already parlayed his portion of the family inheritance into appreciable if not princely proportions through his purchase of profitable tracts of vineyards in the south of France. Once settled in Galveston, he proceeded to increase his fortune year by year through his new venture of wine importation. But Christian's favorite among his forebears was his grandfather—also named Paul Thomas. "Old Glad, everybody called him," Christian told Father Aldo with obvious relish. "In fact, they still do. He's still a legend today in Galveston. He kept a journal, had a real flair for it. On stormy days when we were growing up at Windswept House, I used to spend hours in our library with my sister and my brother—he's called Paul Thomas, too—and we would read those journals aloud to one another."

"Windswept House?" Carnesecca was thoroughly enjoying this relaxed little tour through English-American history.

Christian laughed. "That's the name of the house Old Glad built. It's more of a castle than a house, I suppose. Built right smack at the heart of Galveston Island. It's really a grand old pile. Six stories high. Family portraits everywhere. There's even a replica of the original great hall of Launceston Manor, and a raftered dining hall. And there's a circular tower atop the whole affair with a wonderful chapel where the Sacrament is reserved. It's the new Gladstone Manor House, I suppose you might say. Everybody says Windswept House is a romantic name. But it wasn't meant to be romantic. It has a very different meaning that comes right out of a most unromantic time in papal Rome."

The journals of his favorite ancestor that had always fascinated Christian more than all the others covered the years from 1870 onward. In that year, Old Glad was thirty-seven years old, unmarried, and had become a millionaire many times over. In that year, too, the man Old Glad referred to in his entries as Christ's Vicar on Earth, Pope Pius IX, was deprived of all his Italian properties and effectively shut up in the Apostolic Palace in the Vatican by the Italian nationalists led by Garibaldi and Count Cavour.

That shocking news, and word of an internationally organized plea for financial support for a suddenly isolated and impoverished papacy, reached Galveston in 1871. Immediately, Paul Gladstone took out letters of credit amounting to one million United States dollars, procured a personal letter of introduction from the Archbishop of New Orleans and set out for Rome, where he arrived on Easter Sunday of 1872.

"I wish you could read Old Glad's account of that time." Christian's eyes shone with the same excitement he must have had when he had first read those journals himself as a boy. "They're wonderful; brimming with details and feisty enthusiasm."

To say that Old Glad was welcomed at the Vatican of Pius IX would be a vast understatement. The Pope made his American rescuer a Knight of the Holy Sepulcher, conferred on him and his family the perpetual right to have a private Chapel of Privilege in their home with the Blessed Sacrament reserved there and gave him a first-class relic of the True Cross for the Altar Stone in his Chapel of Privilege. Pius also established a perpetual link between the papacy and the head of the Gladstone family, whoever that might be in future years. Henceforth, there would always be a "Gladstone Card" in the Secretariat's file of Vatican Important Persons. The Gladstones would be described briefly and in perpetuity as *privilegiati di Stato,* freely rendering whatever financial services they could to the Holy See and receiving such facilities as the Holy See could render in return.

The Pope granted Paul Thomas two lengthy private audiences, and gave him a personally conducted tour that included one of the Vatican's most private and most curious rooms. The Tower of the Winds, it was called; or the Room of the Meridian. It had been built by a sixteenth-century Pope in the middle of the Vatican gardens as an astronomical observatory. By the latter half of the nineteenth century, the observatory had been transferred elsewhere. During the disturbances in Rome of the 1870s, the Pontiff had reserved the Blessed Sacrament there for security reasons.

Old Glad's account of that place was among the most vivid entries in his journals. He described the frescoed walls, the floor sundial, the wind-measuring vane, the conical roof, the constant whispering of the Eight Winds. The place seemed to him to be symbol of time and eternity; for God was there in the Sacrament. But it also struck his imagination as a reminder of a fugitive time. For, just as the Tower was swept by its constant, whispering winds, so was the Church swept in those days by the rough winds of persecution and enmity.

Then and there, with the Holy Father beside him, Old Glad decided to build a replica of that very Tower as the privileged chapel where the Blessed Sacrament would be kept perpetually. And he would build a proper house, so that the chapel would be high up; so that all of Galveston could look to it and know that God was with them. His chapel would be Galveston's Tower of the Winds. And his house would be Windswept House.

"So Windswept House was always a link for you." Carnesecca followed Christian's story with deepening interest. "A link with Rome. With the Vatican. With the papacy."

"With all of that." Christian nodded. "And with Old Glad, too. Whenever I go home to Windswept House, I say Mass in that replica he built of the Tower of the Winds."

In his will, Paul Thomas had directed that a red lamp be kept burning day and night in the Chapel window that faced northwest toward the Texas mainland. By now, that vigil light had been burning for over a hundred years, and Texans living as far west as Victoria and as far north as Orange had always sworn that they could see it winking at them on clear nights. "Glad's Eye they called that light." Christian raised his glass of sparkling water in a lightsome gesture of affection and tribute. "And Glad's Eye it's called today."

Nor was that the only local tradition that had grown up around the Tower Chapel at Windswept House. Old Glad had put a stained-glass window imported from Italy into the wall that faced seaward. Fully nine feet tall, it depicted Christ stilling the angry tides of Lake Galilee, spreading miraculous ripples of calm before him over the storm-swept waters as he approached a boatload of terrified disciples. From the day Old Glad died, the fishermen of Galveston told how they sometimes saw the old man's ghostly figure behind that window—stained glass though it was—giving them a needed bearing on stormy nights.

"And giving your family a needed bearing, too, I imagine, Father Christian." It was a logical guess on Father Carnesecca's part, and it was accurate.

Reared and educated as he had been in the Roman Catholic Church that had gone down to the dust during the "good Pope's" Second Vatican Council, Christian reckoned that his advantage in surviving as a Roman Catholic had been secured mainly by two conditions, both of which he and his family owed to Old Glad's providential foresight: the Gladstone fortune and Gladstone papal Catholicism.

The family's financial sinews built up by old Paul Thomas carried strength of such great proportions that there were few, in or out of the Church, who cared to ignore the Gladstones. The family fortune had continued to grow, the way old money grows. Constantly.

Just as much, however, Christian's advantage as a Roman Catholic had been secured by the determination of his mother, Cessi. Francesca was her given name, after Old Glad's wife. But like her financial fortune, Cessi's character came straight from Paul Thomas himself. In fact, so much a Gladstone was she that, after she had been prematurely widowed, she had taken her own family name again for herself and her children.

"She's a Roman Catholic believer from head to toe." Christian's affection for Cessi was obvious in the warmth of tone. "It's her doing that today I believe the same truths and practice the same religion as I learned them from her."

As Cessi's three children were growing up, so was the Church in all the dioceses of the United States being drenched in what she called "innovative adaptations." Wholesale changes sprang up like some hybrid crop under the cultivating hands of folks who were called "liturgical experts" and "catechesis teachers." In such circumstances—and for as long as feasible in the face of the high-tech requirements of latter-day education—Cessi had home-schooled her children. When that option was no longer practical, she had made sure that the Brothers in the school where she sent her two boys, and the nuns in the school where she sent his sister, Tricia, all understood that to oppose the wishes or openly criticize Francesca Gladstone would be to jeopardize the hefty patronage they depended on from her.

When it came to religious practice and training, it was much the same story. Private religious tutoring took the place of the bowdlerized "catechesis classes" given in the city's churches. As often as possible, the family avoided the local churches, which Cessi saw as tainted with un-Catholic rites. Instead, they attended private Masses in Old Glad's Tower of the Winds.

By about 1970, though, traditionalist priests—priests Cessi could rely on, as she had said so often, "for a valid and authentic Roman Mass"—were becoming ever more scarce and hard to find. She had been overjoyed, then, when a group of some sixty Roman Catholic families from Galveston and the mainland approached her with the idea of forming a new congregation. With Cessi's financial backing and their own contributions, and with the perpetual Gladstone privileges in Rome, the idea was that they could set themselves up as economically and canonically independent of the local diocese. The matter was decided on the spot. An old chapel was found in Danbury and purchased from its original Methodist owners. It was called the Chapel of St. Michael the Archangel. And because they could not rely on diocesan priests or the bishop to offer a valid Mass, they contacted Archbishop Marcel Lefebvre of Switzerland, and arranged for their Chapel to be adopted by Lefebvre's Society of Pius X. But even Lefebvre's organization was not able to supply a priest regularly for the Chapel.

That problem was overcome, however, when the newly organized Danbury congregation found Father Angelo Gutmacher.

"Father Angelo." Christian mused over the name, as a man will muse over a fond memory. "He was a godsend for us all, a strange and wonderful man. Humanly speaking, he's alone in the world. As a boy in Leipzig, he was the only member of his family to survive the arson that enveloped their home one night. He still bears the scars of that awful fire on his face and body. He escaped from Communist East Germany and came into the care of relatives in West Germany. In time, he entered a seminary that was still to the good, and came out as the rarest of all breeds today—a priest who is orthodox without being inflammatory.

"By the time he came to St. Michael's Chapel in Danbury, he had come to the notice of Lefebvre's organization. He has that way about him. Without ever intending to do so, he comes to the notice of people."

It hadn't seemed to take Gutmacher long at all to gain the respect of his little congregation at Danbury. And their love as well. Without ever compromising his orthodoxy, he turned out to be wise enough to stay above all the controversies raging throughout the Church. And he seemed kind enough to calm even the most extreme among the Danbury congregation. So, too, did he gain the respect and the love of all the Gladstones. He was priest and confessor and friend to all of them. He often said Mass at the Tower Chapel of Windswept House. He lent his sure and gentle hand to the formation of Cessi's three children. For Cessi herself he became a deeply valued personal friend and advisor. And for Christian he became a special guide and mentor.

Of course, amid the rough politics in the Church following the Second Vatican Council, such a blatantly orthodox setup as the Chapel of St. Michael the Archangel was not likely to escape without its share of problems. The local Chancery considered it to be "a diocesan scandal" that the premier Catholic family of southwestern Texas in the person of Francesca Gladstone would openly support St. Michael's, and thus flaunt its distrust of the officially approved rites of the Church. In fact, the local diocese appealed to the Cardinal Archbishop of New Orleans for help in the matter, for the Gladstone tie there had always remained a strong one.

But when it had come to war between the mistress of Windswept House and the Cardinal Archbishop of New Orleans, His Eminence had decided that his wisest course would be to assign the matter to his Vicar-General. And the Vicar-General—faced as he was with Cessi Gladstone's brilliant and well-founded defense of the value and legality of the traditional Roman Mass, with the financial support still provided to His Eminence by the Gladstones and with the status the Gladstones enjoyed perpetually in the Vatican—decided that his wisest course would be to retire from this particular field of battle with as much grace as he could salvage. Francesca Gladstone had walked away victorious, and not for a moment intimidated by the fray.

"As a result of all that, Father Aldo." Christian motioned to the waiter for the check. "As a result of all of that, I confess that I approach a man like His Eminence Cardinal Maestroianni with hooks."

As naturally as that—as naturally as everything else between them had become—the conversation between Christian Gladstone and Aldo Carnesecca turned again to the Rome of the 1990s. To the Rome that was at least as anti-Catholic and antipapal as the Rome Old Glad had written about in his journals.

"Frankly," Christian confided as they finished their last cappuccino and set off at an ambling pace for the Angelicum, "I can't make up my mind about churchmen like His Eminence. And to tell you the truth, I don't think I want to try. I saw nothing priestly in him. Nothing sincere, even. He has a way of talking without communicating anything."

Despite the seriousness—and the accuracy—of the American's observations about a man so crucial to the Church, Carnesecca had to smile. "For a man who can't make up his mind, you sound more than definite to me, *Padre.*"

"I suppose you're right." The American nodded. "Who do I think I'm kidding, with my open-minded act? I'll grant you my little visit with the Cardinal Secretary was brief. But the most sincere part of it was His Eminence's open scrutiny of my every move."

Christian recounted most of his brief conversation with Maestroianni. He had been struck by the Cardinal's disinterested glance at the Bernini photos. And by his obvious interest in the link, through Christian's brother Paul, with Cyrus Benthoek. Indeed, Gladstone's bet was that His Eminence's pointed open-door invitation to him had more to do with Paul than with Christian himself. "I felt like a specimen under a microscope. His Eminence seemed so interested in the cut of my cassock, I almost gave him the name of my tailor. Or maybe I should have asked for the name of the Cardinal's tailor!"

Father Aldo, too, was interested to learn that Christian's brother worked with Cyrus Benthoek. Anyone closely connected with the Holy See was bound to know Benthoek at least by reputation. And anyone closely connected with the Secretariat of State knew Cyrus Benthoek by sight as a frequent visitor to Cardinal Maestroianni's office.

American by birth, Benthoek had become a transnational man. His strong connections among the highest reaches of international Masonry were not surprising, nor was his deep personal involvement in the workings of the European Community, as well as his lifelong dedication to its exclusively secularist brand of globalism.

In Aldo Carnesecca's mind, therefore, the interest Maestroianni had shown in Paul Gladstone was almost as neat as a mathematical equation waiting to be proved. The Cardinal was always widening his net; always ready to pull in little fish and nurture them along in his cause. If Christian's brother was of any account to Cyrus Benthoek, it was likely that Christian himself would become of more than ordinary interest for Cosimo Maestroianni. Still, the Gladstone-Benthoek connection and its interest for the Cardinal Secretary was no more than speculation. And in any case, unless he were to breach highly confidential matters, it was nothing Carnesecca could yet find a way to discuss with Christian.

If Christian sensed Father Aldo's reserve on the point, it was a passing thing. The younger man seemed more interested in his own growing conviction that, like Old Glad in his day, it was time for this Gladstone to head homeward for good—an idea he approached with a wry, puckery sort of smile on his lips, like a man ready to dump a risky investment.

"I expect the Cardinal pegged me for exactly what I am, *Padre.* As another *nordico.* A *straniero.* An out-of place foreigner in the palace of Roman chamberlains. Oh, I grant that the Church is in no better shape in the States than it is here. But at least in America I understand what's going on."

Carnesecca heard the sadness in the voice of this young priest. Impelled by that sadness, and by his own conviction that Father Christian was precisely the caliber of man needed in this Rome of the 1990s, Father Aldo countered him immediately.

"It's true, you have your whole life to lead yet. But you've come to the stage in your career where the choices you make as a priest will set the pattern for you as long as you live. You talk about following Old Glad's footsteps back to America. But as nearly as this old priest can see, when Old Glad went home, he was committed to fight on one side of a spiritual warfare. Now, unless I'm badly mistaken, you're every bit as committed to that same warfare. And unless I'm badly mistaken again, we both understand that spirit is where the real victory will lie—or real defeat.

"I think I betray no confidence in saying that, in your little encounter with His Eminence this morning, you met one of the leaders on what I would call the darker side of that warfare. And you've come up with the right conclusion. Cardinal Secretary Maestroianni is a maestro of the bureaucratic rat race in Rome. And that rat race has about as much to do with the salvation of souls as Mammon has to do with the Holy Trinity.

"You say things are just as bad for the Church in America. But the real point is that things are just as bad in every parish and every diocese and every monastery and every bishop's Chancery in the world. The same battle is being waged in all of them. And the bureaucratic rat race you happened upon this morning is defining the whole strategy and all of the tactics in this global warfare of spirit. Nevertheless, my young friend, make no mistake about this: the center of the battle is in Rome.

Carnesecca went as far as prudence allowed. He explained that the Slavic Pope had not chosen Cosimo Maestroianni as his Secretary of State because the two got on well together, or because they shared the same policy aims. Rather, Maestroianni had been demanded by the veteran Cardinals of the Vatican in 1978, and His Holiness had wanted no new battlefronts opened up. His forces were already committed on a wider and more urgent front at that critical moment.

Realistically, even with Maestroianni's coming retirement, things wouldn't improve from the Holy Father's standpoint. The man already named to replace Maestroianni, His Eminence Cardinal Giacomo Graziani, was committed more to the advancement of his own career than to the support of any side in any fight. He intended to come up with the winner, whoever that might be. The choice of him as Secretary of State signaled no victory for the Pontiff. It was, rather, a temporizing compromise.

Gladstone nodded his understanding. But at the same time he threw his hands up in a gesture of frustration. "You make my point for me, Father Aldo. It's His Holiness' penchant for strategies like that that have left his whole Church in such a shambles."

Christian stopped in his tracks. "Explain to me if you can, *Padre,* why the Slavic Pope deals in such strategies at all! Maybe His Holiness sees himself fishing in deeper waters. But for my money, there are no deeper waters than the spiritual life or death of millions. Or even the spiritual life or death of one country, or one city, or one individual. Explain to me why this Holy Father does not simply dismiss from our seminaries all the theologians who openly teach heresy and moral error. Why he does nothing about blasphemous Masses, about Reverend Mothers who practice witchcraft, about nuns who have abandoned any semblance of religious life, about bishops living with women, about homosexually active priests ministering to congregations of actively homosexual men and women, about Cardinals who indulge in Satanist rites, about so-called marriage annulments that are really cover-ups for real divorces, about so-called Catholic universities that employ atheist and anti-Catholic professors and teachers. You can't deny that all that is true, *Padre.* And you can't be surprised by my discomfort."

"Of course it's true." Carnesecca blanched at Christian's challenge. "And of course I'm not surprised at your discomfort. But given the conditions you yourself see in the Church we're here to serve, discomfort is a small price. It's hardly a martyrdom. You described yourself a few minutes back as a foreigner in Rome's palace of chamberlains. I could co-sign that statement, Father Christian. So could Master-General Damien Slattery. And so could anyone in the Vatican—or anywhere else—who still belongs to Peter the Apostle.

"But there's a larger point to keep in mind. In the face of open opposition, the Holy Father himself is not merely a stranger, as you feel yourself to be. Men like Cardinal Maestroianni and his associates have rendered His Holiness a virtual prisoner in the Vatican—just as much a prisoner as Pius IX was in the days when your beloved Old Glad was here. Only this time, the walls of the Apostolic Palace are no defense; because this time the siege is laid from within the Vatican structure itself."

Carnesecca stopped himself lest he go too far. But even that much was enough to bring Christian up short. He was stunned by the idea that, despite his constant travels around the world, this Slavic Pope was somehow a prisoner in his own Vatican.

Yet, even if Carnesecca was right, perhaps he had put his finger on the problem that troubled Gladstone so deeply. "The Holy Father's behavior—the kind of policy decision you describe that allowed him to accept Cardinal Maestroianni as his Secretary of State in the first place—that sort of thing doesn't help much. If he is a prisoner in the palace as you claim, maybe it's because he has simply acquiesced all along. Maybe it's because he allows all the abuses of power and all the deviations from apostolic duty in Rome and through all the provinces of the Church to go on."

In the lengthening shadows of late afternoon, Christian stopped and looked back in the direction of Vatican Hill. Carnesecca saw the tears that glistened in Gladstone's eyes, and realized they must have been there for some time.

"Don't get me wrong, Father Aldo. I belong to Peter the Apostle and to his successor just as much as you do. Just as much as Father Damien or anyone else. It's just that there is something so radically unbalanced in all this. . . ." Christian's sudden gesture embraced all of Rome. "I can't seem to get my bearings here. I don't know who's who. All the pseudo-polite, velvety tones and customs of *romanità* clog everything like a pernicious treacle. Half the time I don't know who is enemy or friend. But even I can see that everything in Rome is so out of kilter, so out of balance, that there is no vocabulary to describe it any longer."

At that moment, Carnesecca would have given a great deal for the freedom to give Christian Gladstone some badly needed bearing. For he was certain that was what his young friend was asking, in his way. He wanted some solid reason to stay in this city. Or, like the Gladstones of Cornwall, some solid reason to leave it and make whatever stand he might in another place for his faith and his Church.

Had he felt free to do so, Carnesecca would gladly have given Christian plenty of reason to stay. He would have opened to view some of the Vatican cauldrons bubbling with their antipapal plots, and shared at least something of what he knew about the lines being tightened so steadily against the Slavic Pope. Man of confidentiality that he was, however, Father Carnesecca knew he was not free to share anything further along those lines with Christian. So it was in the silence of their companionship that the two priests simply resumed their slow walk toward the Angelicum, each of them deep in his own thoughts.

Filled now with his own sadness, Father Carnesecca thought of Damien Slattery's remark to him once that "the hallmark of evil is emptiness." And he found himself thinking how unacceptable it was that Rome should be emptied of such priests as Christian Gladstone. At least in broad terms, he not only understood the battle being waged; he had been bred to it by his ancestry and reared to it by his personal formation. In that sense, Father Christian was already more Roman than most of those clerics who claimed to be Romans. There could be no doubt that for Gladstone the battle was about faith. Nor was there any doubt that the younger man had seen just enough today to know that, for such Vatican hands as Cosimo Maestroianni, the battle was about brute power.

If Carnesecca had learned anything during his Roman career, it was patience. But patience required time. And in the case of Christian Gladstone, he couldn't be sure how much time he might have before yet another solid papist would be lost to the Holy See. Time enough in all likelihood, Father Carnesecca sighed to himself, for Cardinal Maestroianni to determine if Paul Gladstone's connection with Cyrus Benthoek would warrant His Eminence's further interest in Father Christian as well. In that case, Carnesecca figured that Christian would find himself posted to Rome, like it or not.

VII

THE KEY that opened the impressive double doors to Cardinal Cosimo Maestroianni's ample home away from the Apostolic Palace opened the door as well onto the ample globalist vision—the Process, as he and his most intimate associates called it—that had inspired his life and his work for most of his fifty years of Vatican service.

Like the wiser among the Pope's in-house Cardinals, Maestroianni kept his private residence at a comfortable distance from Rome's center and Vatican Hill, but with easy access to the routes leading into Vatican City. In His Eminence's case, home was the penthouse perched above the Collegio di Mindanao out on the Via Aurelia. The highest of twelve floors—six of which served the daily activities of the clerical students who lived and studied at the Collegio, while the remaining six served as faculty rooms—most of the Cardinal Secretary's rooms afforded him a panoramic view of the Holy City, of the Alban Hills and, on a clear day, of gleams and glistenings from the waters of the Tyrrhenian Sea around Ostia. The semicircular foyer that gave entry into His Eminence's apartment was decorated dutifully with oil paintings of past Popes. But, in truth, foyer and portraits alike served as a little point of transition from the official world of papal Rome.

The world that truly enlivened the Cardinal's spirit—the wider world; the real world—was vividly encapsulated by an amazing series of photographs that covered nearly every inch of the long, high walls of the corridor that lay immediately beyond the foyer and ran the entire width of the penthouse. The most stunning of these photos—floor-to-ceiling cityscapes of Helsinki, Finland—were so large as to dwarf His Eminence's tiny frame. But so, too, did they enlarge his mind. Cleverly lit from above, they made Helsinki's white granite buildings seem like an aura, an immaculate cloak embracing the whole city. It was no wonder for Cardinal Maestroianni that the Scandinavians called that place "the great white city of the North." For him, the physical quality of the city—that immaculate lightsomeness—had become its spiritual quality as well. Indeed, whenever he walked through this corridor, or visited Helsinki, he was reminded of a medieval hymn to the Heavenly Jerusalem. "Celestial City of Jerusalem, blessed vision of peace. . . ."

The occasion that had inspired such enduring reverence in His Eminence's soul had been the signing of the Helsinki Accords by thirty-five nations on August 1, 1975. That had been the birth of what had come to be known as the Helsinki Process, or the Conference on Security and Cooperation in Europe—the CSCE. It had been a crowning event in Maestroianni's life; an event he had recorded in minute detail in what Cyrus Benthoek had once aptly called his "Helsinki corridor." For grouped in all the spaces around the enormous photographs of Helsinki were others of somewhat more modest proportions that formed an indelible record of the grand historical event, and of memories the Cardinal treasured as among the most meaningful of his productive career.

The Helsinki Accords, entitled officially as the Final Act, had been the result of a long, laborious search that had started in the mid-fifties for a new European structure. To find a new soul, as the Cardinal thought of it, to embrace all the nations and cultures of that landmass stretching from Ireland's Galway on the Atlantic to Vladivostok on the Sea of Japan. The Greeks had given that landmass its name. Europa. The Romans had thought they possessed it all. Caucasians had mainly peopled it and governed it. Several nations and empires had wished to dominate it. But, by the twentieth century, it had split into a patchwork of squabbling states.

In this great white city of the North, at the signing of the Final Act, the ancient dream of Europa had again been birthed by all the major nations in that great landmass. Cosimo Maestroianni had himself participated in the act of birth. So, to this day, it was always both comforting and inspiring—a little like visiting a shrine, perhaps—for the Cardinal to pass through this corridor on the way to his study at the far end of the penthouse.

He had been an Archbishop back in 1975, serving as head of the Second Section of the Secretariat under Cardinal Secretary Jean Claude de Vincennes. Most willingly, he had led the Holy See's delegation to that historic conference. The Final Act itself bore his own signature in the name of the Vatican city-state. Who could blame Maestroianni, then, if even on his busiest days he might pause in this corridor; if he might linger for a moment or two over this treasured record of a dream come true? The photographs were sweet confirmation that all nations would be united—or, rather, reunified—into mankind's original oneness.

How could he not allow his eye to wander over some of the photomontages that commemorated special moments during those hectic days at the Helsinki Conference? Maestroianni with Italy's President Giovanni Leone and Foreign Minister Mariano Rumor feeding the pigeons on Helsinki's Esplanade. Maestroianni during his special audience with Finland's President Urho Kaleva Kekkonen in the presidential palace. Maestroianni during his visit with Prime Minister Keijo Liinemaa at the Eduskunta, Finland's Parliament. One group shot in particular was a vivid symbol of unity. There he was, with Chancellor Helmut Schmidt and Foreign Minister Hans-Dietrich Genscher of Germany on one side of him, and President Valéry Giscard d'Estaing of France on the other. Fittingly, the four of them were standing on the bridge connecting the mainland with the rocky island of Katajanokka.

There was a particularly handsome shot of Cyrus Benthoek strolling beside Maestroianni along Mannerheimintie Boulevard. And, if memory served, Benthoek himself had taken the photo of the Archbishop praying alone in the Great Church on Senate Square. So many important memories. Maestroianni smiling with Henry Kissinger and Portugal's President F. da Costa Gomes. His interview with United States President Gerald R. Ford. The Archbishop raising a banquet toast with the Soviet Union's Andrei Gromyko and Polish Communist Party chief Edward Gierek, and conferring with Belgium's Prime Minister Leo Tindemans and Holland's Prime Minister Joop M. den Uyle.

The photo the Cardinal had placed at the far end of the corridor, just by the door leading to his private study, showed him standing with Cyrus Benthoek in front of Väinö Aaltonen's famous bronze statue of Finland's champion runner, Paavo Nurmi, in the grounds of the Olympic Stadium. In a moment of lighthearted clowning, both men had posed as runners, parroting the forward thrust of arms and legs and torso captured in the Nurmi bronze. Across the bottom of the photo, Benthoek had penned a trenchant inscription: "So that posterity may know we are running in the same race for the same goal. We MUST win!"

Normally, no matter how brief the time Cardinal Maestroianni allowed himself here, it was enough to refresh him. But not today. He found his mind stubbornly preoccupied with the Slavic Pope and his pious excursion to Sainte-Baume. What a bleak contrast it was for him to think of the Helsinki Accords on the one hand and then to think of how the Pontiff had turned the Secretariat on its head this morning to get some inspirational photographs of a Bernini statue for his homily.

This morning's events, triggered by the Slavic Pope's telephone call from Baume, had fixed the Cardinal's mind once more on the unsuitability of the present Pontiff to lead the Church into the coming New World Order. In fact, the truth was that the Cardinal Secretary treasured the memory of another Pope. The good Pope. What the Church needed was another Pontiff who, like the good Pope, possessed not only maturity of mind and diplomatic skill but an uncommon this-world wisdom. Wisdom. That had been the key to everything.

Like it or not, it was the Slavic Pope Maestroianni had to deal with. At least for the moment. Oh, he understood the mind of this Pope well enough. He had been able at least to anticipate the Pontiff's strategies, and then mitigate their effect within the Church hierarchy as few others might have been able to do. Maestroianni understood above all that this Pontiff was still loaded down with all the old Roman Catholic images of Christ's divine Kingship; of Marian Queenship; of a fixed triad—Hell, Earth, Heaven—as man's destiny. This Pope still thought of the force behind the forces of history as the hand of Christ as King of the human race as well as Savior of that race from sin and Hell's punishment for sin.

Cardinal Secretary Maestroianni did not see himself as having abandoned or betrayed his Roman Catholicism. Rather, he saw that his own original faith, acquired in the now crumbling bastions of the old Church, had been purified and enlightened, because it had been humanized. It had been made real within the concrete circumstances of the twentieth century.

So much of what he had once simply taken for granted had been overloaded with elements that merely came from the various cultural periods in the Church's history. Such baggage-laden concepts had nothing to do with present reality. Nothing to do with the Process. Now, however, he had come to understand history and the salvation of mankind in a way he knew the Slavic Pope would never grasp. Now he understood that such concepts as still guided the Slavic Pope should have no influence—not even the slightest manifestation—in the workings and administration of the Church.

Just suppose Maestroianni had gone to the Helsinki Conference in 1975, for example, and preached to Presidents and Foreign Ministers about St. Mary Magdalene adoring the risen Christ, as the Slavic Pope would do this evening at Sainte-Baume. Why, he would have been carried off in a straitjacket!

For the true role of the Church, Maestroianni now understood, was as one player in a vaster evolution—a vaster Process—than the Slavic Pope seemed able to encompass. A vast Process, and a very natural one, that recognized the fact that all the woes of the human family were caused in the first place not by some primitive notion called Original Sin, but by poverty and want and ineducation. A Process that would at last clear humanity of those troubles, and so would ultimately harmonize the spirit of man, God and the cosmos. When the Process was fully accomplished in the new political order of mankind, then would the Church be one with the world. For only then would the Church take its proud and rightful place as part of the human heritage. As a stabilizing factor in the New World Order. As a true and bright mirror of the untroubled mind of God.

The Cardinal still regretted the passing of that good Pope so soon into what he now thought of as "the cold silence of eternity." Still more did His Eminence regret that in this final decade of the twentieth century he had to deal with a backward-minded Pope who had no grasp of the true force behind the forces of history.

On the other hand, once Maestroianni had himself reached the maximum of his power as Vatican Secretary of State, he had used the entire administrative machinery of the Roman Church's organization to forge its greater alignment with the Process. Nothing went out from the papal desk that did not pass through the Cardinal Secretary's office. His authority was felt throughout all the other papal Ministries of the Vatican. His will was recognized and accepted throughout the National and Regional Conferences of Bishops around the world. Indeed, many of his clerical colleagues had made the same profound transition in their thinking as Maestroianni had.

That very thought, in fact, roused Maestroianni from his dour thoughts. It would be far more profitable to focus his mind on the second task he had set himself this Saturday—the revision of a paper which Cyrus Benthoek had arranged for the Cardinal to deliver at the forthcoming meeting of the American Bar Association.

Like the letter he had composed this morning, the subject of the paper awaiting the Cardinal's revisions and refinements was as delicate as it was important: the Ethical Need for Abdication of National Sovereignty.

As Benthoek had pointed out, only such a truly spiritual man as Maestroianni could deal sensitively but incisively with this touchy subject. Maestroianni settled into the work of revision. Within moments, he was again in his element, pausing from time to time in his labors only to retrieve certain helpful materials from the storehouse of knowledge that surrounded him here.

He worked with one monograph in particular—"The Rule of Law and the New World Order," it was called—that he had left open at a key quotation some days before. Taken from a statement made earlier in the year by David Rockefeller, the quotation was so apt that Maestroianni had to smile in appreciation as he read it over: "Now that this threat [of Soviet aggression] has been removed other problems have emerged. . . . There is an enormous incentive to work cooperatively. But the forces of nationalism, protectionism and religious conflict are going in the opposite direction. The New World Order has to develop a cooperative world and find a new means of suppressing these divisive forces."

As he worked the Rockefeller quote into his own text, His Eminence underscored certain words and phrases for emphasis: *"nationalism . . . religious conflict . . . a cooperative spirit . . . suppressing these divisive forces."* The very point of the Ethical Need for Abdication of National Sovereignty was contained in those few words. If organized religion and national spirit could be weaned from their divisiveness, then a new and fruitful cooperative spirit was sure to follow. As he knew, there are only a restricted number of people at any given moment of history who fully understand the nature of the Process. Far fewer still—barely a dozen in a given era, perhaps; that was the Cardinal's opinion anyway—were privileged to function as master engineers of the Process. Even he had never attained that status, though he did aspire to it still. In his own mind, he had become nothing less than the Apostle of the Process.

❑ ❑ ❑ ❑

Cosimo Maestroianni's devotion to the Process had started when he was a fledgling diplomat. By seeming chance, he came to the notice of two men. One was a senior Vatican diplomat, Archbishop Roncalli. The other was Cyrus Benthoek. Both men had been impressed by Maestroianni's acumen. They had gone out of their way to help him in his career and in his cultivation of the Process. Both men had shared their power and their wisdom with Maestroianni.

Roncalli created opportunities for the advancement and enhancement of Maestroianni's ecclesiastical career. First in Paris, then as honored Cardinal Patriarch of Venice and finally as Pope, he was able to ensure Maestroianni's advantage in a thousand small but operatively efficient ways. The younger man was accorded first place and highest recommendation in any list of Secretariat employees proposed for promotion. He was accorded access to classified information; inclusion in highly confidential discussions; timely forewarnings of near-future happenings. Above all, he was accorded discreet guidelines in that precious Vatican asset, *romanità.*

Cyrus Benthoek, on the other hand, provided Maestroianni with hands-on instruction, formulation and exploration of the Process. As a close and trusted friend. Benthoek found endless opportunities to feed the diplomat's enduring curiosity concerning the Process.

As Monsignore Maestroianni rose through the ranks of the Vatican Secretariat, Benthoek continually arranged contacts and visits that provided his avid protégé with ever greater and ever more fruitful access to the thinking of private associations. By means of invitations to conventions and introductions to governmental circles beyond the younger man's reach, he gave Maestroianni easy access to kindred spirits—some of them, indeed, master engineers—who were actively engaged in collaboration with the Process. In sum, Benthoek supplied Maestroianni with a vista into a world normally inaccessible to a Vatican diplomat.

Professionally at home in the Vatican, Maestroianni was within touching distance of the summit of his career as Secretary of State. He became a major influence in the Vatican Chancery. On the liturgical side of things, for example, the Archbishop directed the reform of the old Code of Canon Law, and in doing so he brought the Church's juridical structure into ever greater alignment with his revised thinking about the need to reform the Catholic Church from within, in the light of the coming new order in the life of the nations.

On the political scene, meanwhile, Archbishop Maestroianni showed himself to be a consummate global diplomat. He carefully supervised all Vatican negotiations with the Soviet Union, and with its Eastern European satellite states. His ultimate goal in those delicate affairs was the signing of a series of protocol arrangements between the Holy See and the "sovereign democracies" of the "socialist fraternity," as those political entities referred to themselves. Whether in Moscow or Sofia, Bucharest or Belgrade, Archbishop Cosimo Maestroianni became known as a reconciler of governments; as a bridge builder between government establishments.

All the while, Cyrus Benthoek continued to cultivate Maestroianni's deeper penetration into the Process. In those higher stages of his education of the Archbishop, Benthoek constantly invoked the memory of Elihu Root as the patron saint of the Process. Elihu Root had made his mark publicly in the early twentieth century as a prominent Wall Street lawyer who had served as Secretary of War for President William McKinley and President Theodore Roosevelt, and later as Roosevelt's Secretary of State. He had been awarded the Nobel Peace Prize in 1912, and became the first honorary chairman of the prestigious Council on Foreign Relations.

Elihu Root and like-minded lawyers working in the field of international finance and relations were convinced that the inherent logic of history—Cyrus Benthoek nearly always got that phrase in—dictated a global role for the United States. In fact, Root and the others initiated an Establishment mentality that had been passed down intact through such revered figures—"Wise Men," Benthoek called them pointedly and consistently—as Henry Stimson, Robert A. Lovett, John J. McCloy and Henry Kissinger. It was on one of his visits to Benthoek in his New York offices that Maestroianni finally received a defining enlightenment about the Process, when he mentioned Root's name as the founder of twentieth-century globalism and the original conceptualizer of the Process.

"No, my friend. Root was no founder. But where he was unique was in his appraisal of the Process. For that appraisal brought him to the conclusion that the ultimate goal of the force of history—the goal of the force behind all the forces—was the goal of a truly one-world economic and financial governing system. Root saw that there is no other basis on which all nations can come together. The organized sharing of the earth and its riches—that is the basis of all good in the world.

"The Process is the means by which the force does its work. For that reason, the Process is a sacrosanct concept—a code word, if you like—for all of us who are true globalists. That is the understanding Elihu Root left to us. That is the enduring blessing and legacy and responsibility he left to all the 'Wise Men' who have since followed in his footsteps. To all who are dedicated to the same ideal."

At that very moment, Maestroianni crossed the farther threshold to which Benthoek had been guiding him with such dedication and patience. A smile spread across the Archbishop's face like the first rays of sunlight on a new morning. For suddenly the obvious dawned on him. Suddenly he understood that the Process is not a distant and impersonal thing. Suddenly he understood—as Benthoek had intended him to understand—that, if the force stands behind the Process, so there are master engineers who stand behind the force. And suddenly he understood that Elihu Root was not an inventor, but an engineer. A master engineer, in fact. One of a group of men who, at any stage in the Process, take up that special role of invention and refinement and guidance and facilitation in the steady, ongoing pattern of the force.

That, Maestroianni finally realized, was why Benthoek was always talking about those "Wise Men" of his. Those were the master engineers.

It was a marvelous realization for Cosimo Maestroianni. It made the Process wonderfully human and accessible for him. In fact, as he confessed to Benthoek with heartfelt emotion, it even rang a doctrinal bell for him. And the aim of every one of those master engineers of the Process was always the same: to achieve the inherent destiny of the society of nations as a *family!* A human *family!* A new and all-embracing holy family. Was that not the very charity, the *caritas,* the *agape* preached by the Apostle Paul?

"Yes, my colleague!" Benthoek knew exactly what button to push now. "It *is* doctrinal. It is scriptural even. For we *are* a family! All the nations are a family. That is our destiny. All are destined to be one again! Who knows, my friend?" Benthoek raised his hands and opened his palms in an upward gesture. "Who knows whether you, in your citadel of the Vatican, might be called upon to function as one of those masters?" Maestroianni saw that gesture as one of supplication, even as a reflection of the classical *orans* figures in classical Christian iconography, as a liturgical gesture par excellence.

Maestroianni had not become a master engineer. But it was not for want of yearning. As cleric, as priest, as Archbishop, as career churchman and diplomat, Maestroianni increasingly abandoned all the images and concepts of his original faith that came to rankle him so much in the Slavic Pope—all those images of Christ's Kingship and of Marian Queenship and of the Church as the Mystical Body of Christ.

For Archbishop Maestroianni, "the force behind the forces" of history ceased to be the hand of Christ as the Lord of human history. For him as for Benthoek, "the force behind the forces" retired as an image into the mysterious unknown. It became nothing more coherent than the all-important but unidentifiable X factor in human affairs. All of the Archbishop's activity issued from his deepening understanding of the Process; and from his deepening reverence for that mysterious X factor—"the force behind the forces." It all hinged together very well for him. The only logical way of serving the primal "force" was through the Process. The idea was to help the Process along toward the ultimate goal of the force: the cultural, political, social and economic homogenization of all the nations of the earth.

Given that ultimate goal, it stood to reason that one of the prime "cultural" takeover targets of the Process had to be the Roman Catholic Church. Or, to be precise about it, the takeover target of the Process had to be the systemic organization of the Roman Catholic Church. What was not acceptable—what had to be cleansed from the structural organization—was the traditional claim of Roman Catholicism to have absolute authority in the affairs of humankind. For in the main, those claims could not be meshed with the demands of the Process.

The further fact was that, in its aim to eliminate the Roman Catholic Church's absolute claims of moral authority, the Process had to eliminate the traditional authority of the papacy itself. For the Church makes its absolutist claims and issues its absolutist mandates by means of—and solely in virtue of—the unique and traditional authority residing in the papacy. Inevitably, the Process entails the de-papalizing of the Roman Catholic Church.

With that achieved, it would be a relatively straightforward matter for such realists as Maestroianni to cleanse the Church—its global organizational structures, its professional personnel and its nearly one billion adherents alike—of an outlook and a method of behavior that currently only erected barriers and stumbling blocks to the harmony of thought and policy required in the new society of nations.

Cardinal Maestroianni was one of those fortunate people who seem to have a clock in their heads that measure out for them the exact time needed to complete one matter at hand before turning to the next.

When His Eminence finished the final perfect revision of the final persuasive sentence in his speech on the Ethical Need for Abdication of National Sovereignty, he poked his head at last above the great barricade of books consulted in this day's labors. A quarter of an hour still remained before he was to place his call to Cyrus Benthoek in London. That call would be the last and the most pleasurable of the three important tasks the Cardinal had set for himself this Saturday. The clock in His Eminence's head told him that his chat with Benthoek would likely take him right up to the six o'clock Vatican security check.

Maestroianni used the minutes remaining before the appointed time for his London call to dismantle the tower of reference materials that covered everything on his desk, including his scrambler phone. As he distributed the volumes around his study according to the system only he could fathom, he reviewed the main topics he wanted to discuss with Benthoek. There was his newly revised Bar Association speech, of course. Having suggested it in the first place, Benthoek would be the perfect first listener, just as Cardinal Svensen had been the perfect sounding board for Maestroianni's letter on unity between Pope and bishops.

As regards Svensen, Benthoek would also be able to advise on the Belgian Cardinal's suggestion for building a strong link between the European bishops and the European Community. And for using that link—if it could be established—as a means of forging a "common mind" among the bishops that would favor the primacy of EC principles over the primacy of papal authority.

Finally, Maestroianni reminded himself as he dialed through to London, there was the matter of the confidential meeting Benthoek and His Eminence intended to convene as their personal contribution to the legacy of Robert Schuman during the Annual Memorial celebrations in his memory at Strasbourg the following month.

"Eminence!" Cyrus Benthoek had been waiting for the call as arranged. His booming voice was so clear, he might have been standing in the Cardinal's study. "Tell me, what's your news?"

Maestroianni couldn't resist regaling his old friend with the adventure of the Slavic Pope and the Bernini statue. In fact, with a little more color added at each telling, that incident was fast taking on legendary proportions.

When his laughter had subsided, His Eminence reviewed the major changes he had made in his Bar Association speech. Like the Cardinal himself, the American was delighted with the way the David Rockefeller quote underlined the need to suppress the divisive forces at work in nationalism and religion. "Capital! A truly spiritual address, just as I knew it would be."

"I'm happy you're pleased." Maestroianni was flush with satisfaction. Even after all their years of collaboration, such unrestrained praise from his mentor was rare.

"Speaking of divisive forces at work in religion." The clock in Maestroianni's head impelled him to move forward in his agenda. "I had an interesting conversation this morning with an old friend of mine. Cardinal Svensen of Belgium." Consulting the notes he had made in his diary, His Eminence outlined for Benthoek in some detail the Belgian's argument for forming a well-tended link between the European bishops and the EC.

Benthoek was taken with the possibilities. He saw at once how a systematic arrangement might be set up for the flow of "temporal favors," as he called them—low-interest loans and tax exemptions and the like—to the bishops. And he had no doubt that such an arrangement would attract the bishops like bees to honey. Might, indeed, wean the bishops even further from the Slavic Pope's insistence on faith as the bedrock of a new Europe.

As Cardinal Svensen had said this morning, however, Benthoek also saw that there was a serious piece missing in the proposal. "We would need the perfect link, Eminence. We would need a setup at your end of things in the Vatican. A man, or a team of men, who would command the trust of the bishops—find out what they need; where their weaknesses lie. That sort of thing. And then persuade them that their future lies with the EC."

"That's only half of what we need! We need a man at your end of things as well. Someone who could command equal trust among the Ministers of all twelve EC countries. Someone with sufficient credibility to persuade them to grant those 'temporal favors' to the bishops on a reliable basis, with only a handshake as a guarantee of any return on their investment. As I told Svensen, it may be too complicated to pull off."

"Complicated, yes," Benthoek agreed. "But interesting. Too interesting to reject without a serious run at it."

"Svensen will be at the Schuman Day celebrations in Strasbourg next month. I suggest we include him in our private little gathering."

The American was hesitant. "Do you trust him to that degree, Eminence?"

Maestroianni was as confident as Benthoek was reluctant. "I trust him to be discreet. And I trust his animus against the papacy as it presently stands, and against the Slavic Pope in particular.

"I grant you, Svensen knows little or nothing about the Process. But neither do any of the others we've invited to the meeting. In fact, as I see it, the meeting is based on one of the first principles I learned from you. Not everyone has to understand the Process in order to serve its aims."

That was a strong recommendation on Svensen's behalf. Benthoek was almost convinced. "Let's talk about it again before we decide whether to include your Belgian colleague in the actual meeting, shall we? But at the very least, I'd like to meet him when we're in Strasbourg. Agreed?"

"Agreed, my friend." The Cardinal understood. Benthoek wanted to check Svensen out independently.

The American turned to another matter that was at the forefront of his mind. He wanted some renewed assurance concerning Maestroianni's coming retirement. "Of course, I know these things happen, Eminence. But I hope I'm correct that your departure as Cardinal Secretary of State will make no fundamental difference in our undertakings? I trust Your Eminence is still confident on that score?"

"It won't make a whit of difference. The information is not yet public. As I've said before, Giacomo Graziani may not be our ideal Secretary of State. But I assure you, his selection was not a victory for the Pontiff. He'll be happy to run and fetch for us. And I remind you, my old friend. I myself am not exactly going out to pasture." Maestroianni paused for a minute. Naturally, it was difficult for him to vacate the prestigious office of Secretary of State. But this conversation with Cyrus was itself proof that he wasn't done yet. The unity letter he had sent out this morning was only one of the cauldrons he had bubbling under Peter's Throne.

"In a way," he continued on, "I'm actually looking forward to my farewell interview with the Pontiff. I know the parting note I want to sound with him."

"The poor Holy Father! When will that official parting take place?"

"Just before our Schuman Day meeting at Strasbourg." Though he knew the date well, it was a matter of habit for the Cardinal to reach for his diary. As he flipped forward through its pages, his eye fell on the note he had scribbled to himself that morning after his interview with the young American priest. "I almost forgot, Cyrus. This morning's incident over the Bernini statue turned up a young cleric down here in Rome whose brother works with your firm. Does the name Paul Thomas Gladstone ring a bell with you by any chance?"

"A very promising bell! We consider Paul Gladstone to be a young man of great potential." He paused. "I wonder if Paul's brother—what is his name?"

"Christian." Maestroianni double-checked the note in his diary. "Christian Thomas Gladstone."

"Right. Christian. I wonder if he's of the same caliber as our London Gladstone? If he is, then maybe we have the basic material in these two brothers to forge the link we were speculating about earlier. It should be possible for us to find the right spot within the EC machinery for a man as talented as Paul Gladstone. A position of trust that will give him access to all twelve Foreign Ministers.

"Now, what about your man? Would your Father Gladstone measure up as our connection to the bishops? Could he get their confidence to the degree such an operation would require?"

Maestroianni was surprised at the idea at first. But Benthoek made it all sound so plausible, so apt to him, that in the end he was almost embarrassed that he hadn't thought of it himself. In fact, the notion of pairing one of Benthoek's more talented staffers with a Vatican man as the link between the EC and the bishops was appealing in itself. If two such men turned out to be brothers, so much the better for symbiosis.

The matter seemed most promising to Benthoek. The Svensen proposal was already taking flesh in his mind. "Keep me posted, then, Eminence, about your assessment of Father Christian Gladstone. Let's give the matter priority treatment. Meanwhile, we'll poke around a bit in the EC machinery for a post suitable to Paul Gladstone's talents. In fact, the post of Secretary-General to the EC Ministers will fall vacant this summer. That would do the trick. Can you handle such a quick time frame at your end?"

By now, Maestroianni had caught Benthoek's enthusiasm like a fever. "I'm already checking into Father Gladstone's background; he looks clean. He's presently posted to Rome for only half the year. But if he turns out to be right for us, I'm sure we can convince his bishop in the States to release him for, shall we say, full-time service to the Holy See."

"Nicely put, Eminence. I'm sure we can move forward with dispatch."

VIII

ON BRIGHT SPRING MORNINGS, the light of Rome streams in through the windows of the papal study on the third floor of the Apostolic

Palace. It rushes over the carpeting, striking its colors as on a mosaic pavement. It flashes off of parquet floors. It gilds walls and high ceilings with reckless generosity.

This Friday, the tenth of May, was just such a day. Early-morning sun played impish shadow games with the Pontiff's pen as he worked at his desk. It warmed the Holy Father's face. It made plain the signs of premature age that many in his entourage had remarked in recent months. Gone from the Slavic Pope was that tightness of muscle and skin and that compact cast of complexion. Some physical wasting had set in, everyone said. It did not spoil or deform his countenance. But for those who cared, it bespoke a fragility in the Holy Father, like a visible sign of some inner ache of spirit.

His Holiness' concentration was broken by a rapping on the study door. His pen hovered in mid-sentence over the papers in front of him. He glanced at the clock on the study mantel, and stiffened a little. Seven forty-five already! This would be Cardinal Cosimo Maestroianni, then. In good time, as he had been for the past twelve years, for the ritual morning briefing between Pontiff and Secretary of State.

"Avanti!" The Pope laid down his pen, sat back in his chair as if for support and watched Maestroianni bustle through the study door, the folders in his hands bristling with papers as usual, for his official farewell briefing as Secretary of State.

There were no formalities between these two. The Pontiff didn't rise from his desk. His Eminence didn't bow or bend a knee or kiss the Fisherman's ring on the Pope's hand. Thanks to the influence of Maestroianni's predecessor, by 1978 all such undemocratic behavior had already been done away with in such workaday meetings as this.

Though older than the Pope by some five years, the Cardinal appeared the younger of the two as he took his usual place in the chair on the far side of the papal desk. The sunlight was kinder to him; seemed to emphasize a certain solidity.

His Holiness listened to Maestroianni's terse and uninformative monologue this morning with his accustomed serenity. In fact, that constant patience displayed by the Pontiff was always a little unnerving for the Cardinal. The Secretary had the sense that if the Pope asked so few questions during these sessions, it wasn't because he was ready to leave things in Maestroianni's hands. Rather, he guessed that the Pope thought he already knew the answers.

In large part, Maestroianni's guess was correct. The Pontiff had understood from the beginning that his Secretary of State was no colleague, but an adversary of the most dangerous kind. A phone call to certain individuals in any of scores of cities in as many countries on all six continents would tell the Holy Father more about current and impending events around the world than anything Maestroianni would cover in his rundown of Second Section affairs. And a report from Commander Giustino Lucadamo, the chief of papal security and a man of inexhaustible resources and loyalty, would often tell His Holiness even more than he might want to know.

Lucadamo had been recruited following the 1981 attempt on the Pope's life to take all measures necessary to protect the Holy Father's physical safety. He had sworn a sacred oath on the Blessed Sacrament to do so. On permanent leave from Italy's Special Forces, intelligence section, he was widely known for his quick mind and his tempered-steel nerves. He was backed up by Italian State Security and by the friendly services of three foreign governments. In addition, he had surrounded himself with handpicked aides as dedicated as himself. At any given moment, Lucadamo could tell you which bulletproof vest His Holiness was wearing, who the food tasters were at that hour and anything you might need to know about anyone with the slightest contact with the papal household. In sum, Giustino Lucadamo was one of those men God had supplied in the straitened circumstances of the Slavic Pope in this Rome of the 1990s.

Just this morning, after Mass in his private chapel, Lucadamo, together with Damien Slattery, had joined the Holy Father for breakfast in his apartments on the fourth floor of the Apostolic Palace. The conversation had revolved around two matters of obvious concern from a security standpoint.

First, there was the necessary review of the arrangements for His Holiness' protection during the devotions he would lead at Fatima in Portugal three days hence. The celebrations, which would include a youth rally to be broadcast around the world, would take place on Monday, the thirteenth. Lucadamo had every moment covered, from start to finish. The Holy Father would be back in the Vatican, safe and sound at his desk, on the fourteenth.

The second matter had to do with certain details about a strange sort of private meeting Cardinal Secretary Maestroianni had arranged for the same date—May 13—in Strasbourg, just after the closing of the Annual Robert Schuman Memorial celebrations. As it happened, Damien Slattery had caught wind of the same affair. "A gathering of wolves and jackals," he had called that private gathering. "They're trotting in from all the obvious quarters."

The Pope had listened to the list of men Slattery and Lucadamo recited as among Maestroianni's probable guests. Archbishop Giacomo Graziani—soon to be Cardinal Graziani, when he stepped into the post of Secretary of State. Cardinal Leo Pensabene, leader of the biggest group of Cardinals. Cardinal Silvio Aureatini, one of Maestroianni's most dedicated Vatican supporters. Cardinal Noah Palombo, the now aging but still reigning expert in charge of Roman Catholic ritual. The Father-General of the Jesuits. The Franciscan Father-General.

"More plotting." The Pontiff had been wearied to hear the same names coming up yet again. One way or another, in fact, in this or that antipapal context, the same men always figured as prominent. "More networking. More talk. Don't they ever get tired?"

" 'The fire never says, It is enough,' Holiness." Damien quoted Scripture. But he and Lucadamo both expressed concern that there was a notable difference in this gathering, at least on the Vatican side of the Schuman Day roster. "The will of each of those men separately is as strong as death," Slattery had underlined his worry. "They work at it twenty-four hours a day. But normally you won't find the likes of those self-styled servants of God in the same room at the same time."

"We work at it twenty-four hours a day, too, Father. We'll be right on their tails." Though his assurance was addressed to Slattery, his concern for the Pope's sudden weariness had been obvious on Lucadamo's face.

The Pontiff made sure that no such weariness showed through now, as he listened to Maestroianni work his methodical way through his briefing papers. He showed only serenity and patience—essential elements of his dwindling arsenal in the defense of his papacy. The Slavic Pope leaned his head back against his chair. He studied Maestroianni's face; listened carefully to every word the Cardinal said; watched every gesture. But all the while, he prepared himself for what he knew had to come. Maestroianni would not let this final official meeting end without drawing his knife one more time as Secretary.

Actually, the Cardinal Secretary's briefing was mercifully short, considering the quantity of materials he had carried into the papal study. Might His Holiness have been wrong? Perhaps there would be no knife on display during the Cardinal's farewell briefing after all.

"As you know, Holy Father, I will be leading the official Vatican delegation to the Annual Schuman Day Memorial celebrations at Strasbourg."

"Yes, Eminence. I recall." Poker-faced, the Pope leaned forward to glance at his calendar. "You are leaving for Strasbourg later today, no?"

"But yes, Holiness." The Cardinal extracted one sheet from the folders on his lap. "I have a list of those who are included in our delegation." Protocol required that the Pontiff be informed of the delegation members. Even in warfare, Vatican protocol reigned.

Without any change of expression, the Slavic Pope took the list from the Secretary and ran his eye down the column of names. It was a perfect duplication of the list Damien Slattery and Giustino Lucadamo had rehearsed for him at their breakfast meeting. "They all have my blessing for this undertaking, Eminence. It will be a practical introduction for Archbishop Graziani as he prepares to take up his duties as Secretary of State."

"That's what I had in mind, Holiness."

Not for the first time in their protracted warfare, Maestroianni was forced to admire the Pontiff's mastery of *romanità*. There was no bitterness in the Pope's tone or any show of irony. Yet both knew that Graziani—as one of Maestroianni's men, if not one of his closest confidants—had been schooled well enough to regard the Slavic papacy as unfortunate and transitory. With approval of his delegation assured, the Cardinal Secretary expected the Slavic Pope to hand the paper back across the desk. Instead, however, His Holiness laid the list casually on the desk under his hand.

Maestroianni eyed the Pontiff's move with some puzzlement. "I wish, of course, to convey a verbal expression of Your Holiness' blessing to my hosts at Robert Schuman House."

"Please do so, Eminence," the Pope agreed. "Greet all in the name of the Holy See. They are engaged in a momentous task. The Europe they are building is the hope of the future for many millions." The Slavic Pope returned the sheet of paper to the Cardinal at last. In the same motion, he reached for a nearby folder on his desk. Careful not to disturb the confidential note he had received commending one Father Christian Thomas Gladstone to his attention, the Pontiff took from the folder one of the now familiar photos of Bernini's *Noli Me Tangere.*

"I almost forgot to tell you, Eminence. At Sainte-Baume last Saturday I offered the entire pilgrimage to God as a way of asking Him for special graces for all my bishops. The photos you had your man fax to me were a great inspiration. You will doubtless be meeting some of the French bishops at Strasbourg. Please convey my blessings to them as well."

The Cardinal met the full-eyed, innocent gaze of the Pope as best he could. The Bernini photo was like a red flag for him, but the situation did not permit him either to gasp or to laugh. In fact, he found himself tense at the Pope's mention of the French bishops. He certainly would be meeting with some of them at Strasbourg—with some he already considered to be close allies, and a few more who seemed worthy of being brought into closer alignment. His confusion now stemmed from the fact that it was always so hard to assess just how much this Pope might know. "Yes, Holiness." His Eminence managed a steadiness in his reply. "I myself pray that they make the proper choice—er—the choice that most benefits the Church Universal."

As long as they were on the subject, the Slavic Pope had another suggestion to offer. "Be sure, Eminence, to ask our French bishops to accompany me with their prayers as well. As you know, while you are in Strasbourg, I will be on pilgrimage at Fatima for the Blessed Mother's May 13 feast day."

If the request was meant to provoke the Cardinal, it had its effect. It wasn't only that the Pontiff had again emphasized his own regrettable penchant for pietistic travels. Rather, the mere mention of Fatima aroused Maestroianni's deepest professional antipathies. He had often clashed with this Pope on the issue of Fatima, successfully blocking many major papal initiatives in favor of Fatima and of the other alleged visions of the Blessed Virgin popping up like mushrooms all over the Church.

Lucia dos Santos, the only one of the three child seers of Fatima to have survived into adulthood, was in her eighties now. As Sister Lucia, a nun cloistered in a Carmelite convent, she claimed still to have continuing visits from the Virgin Mary, and had remained in contact with the Pope by letter and emissary ever since the 1981 attempt on his life had prompted his own inquiries into the Fatima events.

The Cardinal Secretary knew little or nothing about the correspondence between Pope and nun. What he knew he dismissed as irrelevant, unseemly and dangerous. In Maestroianni's view, no proper pontificate could afford to be regulated in this day and age by reports of visions coming from overzealous, overimaginative, overaged nuns.

"Holiness." There was a testy edge to the Cardinal's voice now. "I do not think it a good idea to ask your bishops in France for this close collaboration in Your Holiness' visit to Fatima. Nobody, least of all these bishops, will object to Your Holiness' private devotions. But because you are primarily Pope of all Christians, whatever you do, even as a private person, must necessarily have an incidence on your papal persona. Your Holiness will therefore understand that it would be unwise of me to trouble the bishops of France in this matter."

The Slavic Pope was less surprised at the sentiment expressed by Maestroianni than by the fact that the Secretary should have spoken his mind so directly. He was almost tempted to leave it at that. Still, the issue touched at the crux of the hostilities between them. That much, at least, was worth pointing out. "Would the consequences be as dire as Your Eminence suggests if you did mention my request for prayers by the bishops?" There was no acrimony or consternation in the Holy Father's question. From the tone of his voice, he might have been asking advice from any member of his staff.

Maestroianni did not pause for one instant before replying tartly, "Quite frankly, Holiness, such a request—added to all the other factors—might push several minds over the edge of tolerance."

The Slavic Pope straightened in his chair. The Bernini photos were still in his hand, but his eyes met the Cardinal's straight and full. "Yes, Eminence. Please go on."

"Holiness, out of duty's call and for at least five years, I have kept on saying that the most precious element of Christ's Church today—the element of unity between Pope and bishops—is in jeopardy. At least two-thirds of the bishops feel that this pontificate does not provide them with the caliber of papal leadership they need. All of this is so acutely serious in my mind, Holiness, that I think we may have to consider in the near future whether—for the sake of that precious unity—this pontificate . . ."

The Cardinal Secretary was suddenly aware that he was perspiring heavily, and that puzzled him. He knew he had the advantage. What was it, then, that was so irreducibly alien or so unattainable in this Pope as to reduce the Cardinal to a nervous sweat? More to reassure himself than to convey anything to the Pontiff, Maestroianni attempted a smile. ". . . Well, how can we phrase it, Holiness? For the sake of unity, this pontificate will have to be reassessed by Your Holiness and by the bishops. For I am sure Your Holiness desires to see that precious unity preserved intact."

"Your Eminence." The Holy Father stood up from his chair. His face was pale. Silent alarms went off in Maestroianni's gut. Protocol left him no choice but to stand up in turn. Had he said too much too soon?

"Eminence," His Holiness said a second time. "We must discuss this subject of unity, which you have so loyally brought to my notice. I rely on Your Eminence's good judgment in regard to the bishops of France. Go in peace."

"Holiness." Ready or not, the Cardinal's farewell briefing was ended. He turned to make his way across the study and out the door, tidying the papers in his folders as he went.

In part, Maestroianni felt helpless and disappointed. He had sounded the parting note in his final briefing of the Pope pretty much as he had intended. But to what avail? he wondered. Finally and simply, there was no way of communicating with this Slav!

By the time he bustled past Monsignore Taco Manuguerra and into his own office, however, all such emotions—if emotions they were—had already subsided in the Cardinal. He was a survivor precisely because he was immune to any deep agony of soul, just as he was incapable of high ecstasy. He never departed from controllable facts. In the rough-and-tumble of statecraft he had always landed safely within sight of familiar horizons. Only if events were to leapfrog over those horizons would His Eminence find himself shortchanged by destiny.

Events had not leapfrogged over those horizons today.

The Pontiff rubbed his brow as if to clear away the pallid veil of joylessness that shrouded his mind. He began to pace the study, forcing himself to review the substance of the farewell briefing by the outgoing Cardinal Secretary.

In essence, there had been nothing new in this morning's barbed exchanges between himself and Maestroianni. Even today's little skirmish over the Cardinal's list of Vatican delegates to the Schuman Day Memorial had been of a piece with the overall pattern of warfare between Pontiff and Secretary.

The Holy Father ceased his pacing and returned unsatisfied to his desk. A thought began to whisper at the edges of his mind, as it had several times in recent weeks. The pressure was so endless, the whisper told him. There was so much going wrong, and he seemed so helpless to do anything about most of it. Perhaps in a way Maestroianni had a point. Perhaps the time had come to consider an alternative to his pontificate.

The Pope let his eye rest once more on the photograph of the Bernini statue. He studied the expression on St. Mary Magdalene's face. An expression that was all about transcendence. "If there is no transcendent"—the Pontiff recalled a line from Friedrich Nietzsche—"we must abolish reason, forget sanity."

That, he reflected, was the sum and substance of the warfare between himself and Cardinal Maestroianni. Life was either totally penetrated by God's providence—to be perceived by divine faith, accepted by human reason and chosen by the will—or it wasn't. If the latter was the case, then everything was due to blind chance. Life was an ugly humiliation, a degrading cosmic joke on anyone foolish enough to possess hope. The Pope had chosen to believe in God's divine providence a long time ago. More than once, he believed, that providence had snatched him clear of disaster. Like that day in Kraków during World War II when, on his way home from work, he had stopped to brush away the autumn leaves that had almost buried a wayside shrine of the Blessed Virgin. Friends had come upon him there and warned him that the Nazi police were waiting outside his home. He had gone safely into hiding.

Or like that day in St. Peter's Square, when the picture of the Blessed Virgin at Fatima that had been pinned to the blouse of a child, a carpenter's daughter, had made him bend down to bless the child, and ultimately caused the bullets from Ali Agča's Browning automatic to miss his skull.

Were he not to see the hand of God in such fortuitous events, he would have to cease believing. The Holy Father drew his breath in sharply at the thought, as any man might in reaction to sudden pain.

All at once the Pope sat bolt upright in his chair. Hadn't that been Maestroianni's whole point in this morning's briefing? During so many encounters between these two enemies who knew each other so well, as the Cardinal's knife swung nearer each time, the idea was to tempt the Pope to free himself from this papal indenture. But there had been something new this time, after all. Something kept nagging at the Pope. He reached for the intercom and buzzed through to his secretary in an adjoining office.

"Monsignore Daniel. I presume you made a tape of my meeting with the Cardinal Secretary?" What the Pope was looking for, he told his secretary, was a playback of the last two or three minutes of the briefing session.

"No problem, Holiness." Monsignore Daniel rewound the last portion of the tape and piped it through.

The Pontiff recalled the beads of perspiration that had appeared on Maestroianni's face, as if the man had been hit with a sudden fever. He listened carefully again to the sound of the Cardinal's voice. ". . . Well, how can we phrase it, Holiness? For the sake of unity, this pontificate will have to be reassessed by Your Holiness and by the bishops. . . ."

Monsignore Daniel had come into the papal study while the tape was still playing. Drawing near, he waited in deference to the Pope's studied concentration on the Cardinal Secretary's words. The tape clicked to a halt.

"Monsignore." His Holiness looked up at Sadowski. The secretary held his breath at the sight of the ashen look of weariness on the Pontiff's face. "Monsignore, we have just received an early copy of this pontificate's death warrant. I have even been asked to sign it."

IX

THE PERSONAL BASE of operations the Cardinal had selected for this stage of his escalating campaign against the Slavic Pope was Strasbourg's oldest and finest hotel. The Palais d'Alsace, which had opened its doors for the likes of the German Kaiser and Queen Victoria on New Year's Day in 1900, was a magnificent anachronism by 1991. Its lobby was graced with fine, wide-spreading crystal chandeliers that glittered like satellite moons in the private firmament of this still privileged world, spilling light over high stuccowork ceilings, Italianate cornices and grandiose architraves.

"I didn't realize that Your Eminence was so fin de siècle!" Cyrus Benthoek teased the Cardinal when the two met for dinner on Friday evening.

Maestroianni was up to the barb. "The only *fin de siècle* outlook you will find in me is my millennium mentality!" Though lightly said, the Cardinal's words were clear and most acceptable to Benthoek. His Eminence was all business. His attention—his millennium mentality—was focused on the private meeting he and this American broker of transnational power would convene three evenings hence, immediately upon the closing of the official Robert Schuman Day Memorial celebrations.

Given the volatile mix of personalities involved, the trick at this little get-together would be to persuade the members of both Maestroianni's and Benthoek's delegations to lay aside their personal ambitions and enmity for one another and to forge a common mind and a full consensus of action with powerful figures outside the immediate fold of Catholicism and Christianity itself. The Cardinal Secretary rehearsed once more for Benthoek the background, the characteristics and the value of each of the seven Vatican wise men who would anchor his side of the new alliance. The Cardinal began his survey with a quick sketch of Cardinal Silvio Aureatini.

As Maestroianni's special creature in the Secretariat, Aureatini was one man with sure global influence. Through his supervision of the innovative Vatican program known as the Christian Adult Renewal Rite (the CARR)

Cardinal Aureatini had long since influenced each diocese and parish around the world. In fact, Maestroianni assured Benthoek, under Aureatini's leadership, the Christian Adult Renewal Rite had changed the very focus of Catholic ritual, so that it was now more acceptable to the general non-Catholic Christian population than ever before.

"And that is not his only accomplishment. Aureatini is also deeply involved in the delicate and ongoing business of reforming Canon Law, and to minimize papal privilege and maximize the office of bishop in the application of that law throughout every level of Church life."

The subject of Canon Law brought Cardinal Maestroianni to the next man of his delegation. The acid-faced and always dour Cardinal Noah Palombo remained what he had been for decades—Rome's reigning expert on Liturgy. Palombo was the man officially charged with the global management of the Vatican's ICCL, the International Council for Christian Liturgy. As its name indicated, the ICCL operated on the level of approved Catholic prayer and devotion. As Aureatini's CARR did among the laity, so among priests and religious did Palombo promote a leveling of the distinction between priest and layman, between Catholic and non-Catholic.

The third entry on Maestroianni's list, His Eminence Cardinal Leo Pensabene, was a one-man powerhouse. Pensabene had spent over twenty years in diplomatic posts in North and South America. Brought back to Rome and elevated to the rank of Cardinal, he had rapidly attained front-line status as leader of the most powerful group in the College of Cardinals—the Cardinals who would have the largest say in picking the Slavic Pope's successor in the next Conclave.

Further, as an expert in all of the Justice and Peace Commissions in Rome and throughout the Church Universal, Cardinal Pensabene was up to his red hat in the sociopolitical activities of Church and State. Through the bishops of the world, Leo Pensabene had steadily refocused and remolded the social and political agenda of the Church to reflect a vision of a thoroughly managed, this-worldly kingdom of selective unity, peace and plenty.

"And your successor as Secretary of State, Eminence?" Benthoek turned his attention to Archbishop Giacomo Graziani. "How do you see his role in the meeting?"

"Quiet and untroublesome, Cyrus. As the Slavic Pope himself so aptly said to me, this meeting will be a practical introduction for Archbishop Graziani as he prepares to take up his duties as Secretary of State."

That left just three more men on Maestroianni's list of delegates: Michael Coutinho, Father-General of the Jesuit Order; Father-General Victor Venable, head of the Franciscans; and, last, the old and seasoned Cardinal Svensen of Belgium, who had initiated the lovely idea of welcoming the bishops of Europe's heartland more closely into the lucrative fold—and the political mold—of the European Community.

As Father-General of the Jesuits, for instance, Michael Coutinho was counted in the Vatican as the traditional dean of the Superiors of the major Religious Orders. His influence on all the other Orders and Religious Congregations was huge. Further, if anyone might doubt the influence of Jesuits among the ordinary folk of the world, a look at the Third World countries would be convincing enough. Through their involvement in liberation theology in particular, Jesuits had played a leading role in weaning Latin American and Philippine Catholicism from its complaisant acceptance of traditional authority and into a contention of armed guerrilla movements and political activism of the most militant varieties. Antipapalism was now a Jesuit characteristic.

Victor Venable, as Father-General of the Franciscans, was an equally impressive one. While the Jesuits had weaned millions of Catholics from a theology of transcendent faith, in favor of a theology of humanism in the West and a theology of this-worldly sociopolitical revolution in the Third World, the Franciscans had weaned at least as many millions away from the personal devotions once so characteristic of Roman Catholics the world over.

Through their fomenting of the charismatic movement, Franciscans had come to embrace instead the now revised and impersonalized concepts of a "new heaven" and a "new earth," and the attainable goal of peace among all men. The influence of Franciscans within the New Age movements, and their additional wide appeal among Protestants, had already built ecumenical bridges impossible to construct in any other way.

Firm in their thinking that Coutinho the Jesuit and Venable the Franciscan were just the sort of bridge builders who had to be brought into the new alliance, Maestroianni and Benthoek turned their attention to the retired but still energetic Belgian, Cardinal Piet Svensen.

As Maestroianni had assumed he would, Benthoek had checked Svensen out thoroughly. Apparently Svensen had passed Benthoek's investigation. And with good reason. In his younger days, the Belgian had been the principal architect and master engineer of the ruthless parliamentary tactics by which the good Pope's Vatican Council had been diverted from its original purpose. Clever, daring, always self-assured, intimately in his soul anti-Roman, deficient in his basic theology but almost messianic in his concept of his historic role, Svensen was well connected and well liked in the higher reaches of the European Community.

"He's a bit Pentecostalist in his devotions." Benthoek laughed. "They say he has a habit of uttering long yelps of apparent gibberish in church—a personal gift of 'speaking in tongues,' he claims. But your assessment of the Belgian was on target, Eminence. He is known to be as brutally frank and rational as any good Fleming. By all means, we must count him in our alliance. And before we leave Strasbourg, we need to firm up our plans for building Svensen's bridge between the European bishops and the EC."

❑ ❑ ❑ ❑

On Sunday, the twelfth of May, with a full day remaining before their time would be claimed by the official panoply of the Schuman Day celebrations, a hired car and chauffeur brought the pair out to the Sandgau region for another working session. As they traveled the Fried Carp Road and sank a tooth into the delectable fish that had made it famous, their discussions centered mainly on Cyrus Benthoek's guests at the meeting to follow the official celebrations. Of the five characters Benthoek had assembled around him for this occasion, four were laymen.

Nicholas Clatterbuck was a man the Cardinal Secretary had met on several occasions. He was CEO of the London headquarters of Cyrus' transnational law firm of Crowther, Benthoek, Gish, Jen & Ekeus. As Benthoek's right-hand man in his home office, he would naturally be included in such an important venture as this.

Also included were two members of Benthoek's international board of consultants. Serozha Gafin, a Muscovite. And Otto Sekuler of Germany. Cyrus' remarks about this pair were brief. "Between them, they know everybody who is anybody in the new framework of the U.S.S.R. that is about to be formed; and that will be so in every country of Eastern Europe to boot."

The fourth layman was a last-minute addition. "Gibson Appleyard is his name, Eminence. His credentials are interesting. U.S. Navy Intelligence, on loan to the American State Department. He's always away on fishing trips in funny places. He won't be one of the voting members of the group, of course. I mean, he won't be representing any arm of his government. But he happened to call me from Washington, and it seemed—well, shall I say appropriate that he join us in an unofficial capacity, if you take my meaning."

Maestroianni did take his friend's meaning. And he agreed with Cyrus Benthoek's obvious hope that, even as an unofficial representative of the government of the United States, Appleyard would at least take some useful impressions away from the cloistered Strasbourg meeting. For one thing, Appleyard would have every opportunity to see that the present Pope's stand was against the New World Order. And he would also learn that everything Benthoek and Maestroianni himself proposed was very much in line with current United States policy.

The only clergyman among Benthoek's Strasbourg guests was a man Cardinal Maestroianni was eager to cultivate. The Reverend Herbert Tartley was a member of the Church of England, who presently served as special advisor to the Throne of England, and special consultor to the Archbishop of Canterbury. It was certain that, in time, Tartley would be rewarded with the See of Canterbury.

Maestroianni knew there would always be speculation about the assets of the English Throne. But the Cardinal Secretary was sure he recognized in the English Throne the lineaments of a corporate power endowed with the highest quality of intelligence about ongoing human affairs. A power resting on foundations dug so deep in Western civilization that it would persist for as long as that civilization. Maestroianni knew, too, that the corporate power within which the English Throne was embedded had nothing to do with a transcendent God or with any professed allegiance to Jesus Christ of Nazareth and Calvary as the central figure of history; that Reverend Herbert Tartley was a rising star in the Church of England; that the Church of England was a historical appendage of the Throne; and that all three made up a kind of collective passport to the exclusively human future in the coming new order of the human story.

By the time he returned to his suite at the Palais d'Alsace on Sunday evening, Cardinal Secretary Maestroianni was immensely satisfied with the weekend's work. His Eminence always slept well when he felt prepared for the morrow.

There is no Fried Carp Road in the Vatican. And there were no leisurely excursions on the Slavic Pope's agenda for Sunday, the twelfth of May. This was the day of his departure for the Fatima celebrations that had so upset the Cardinal Secretary.

At 3:30 P.M., the Pope and his secretary, Monsignore Daniel Sadowski, together with a few others of His Holiness' personal staff, made their way briskly to the waiting Alitalia helicopter. Their takeoff for Fiumicino was exactly on schedule, as was their departure from Fiumicino to Portugal. By 8:30 that evening, His Holiness was safely in his temporary quarters at Fatima.

After a late-evening meal, the Pope and Sadowski met with the Bishop of Fatima-Leiria and the local team of organizers to run through the order of events set for tomorrow's seventy-fourth anniversary celebrations of the first Fatima appearance by the Virgin Mary to the three shepherd children. The Pontifical High Mass would take place in the morning. The private audiences to follow were so numerous that they would stretch well into the afternoon hours. The youth rally—always an important element for this Pope—would be held in the early evening. Finally, after dusk, the highlight of the public side of the papal visit would be the candlelight service and procession.

"All in all, Holiness," the Bishop pointed out with obvious satisfaction, "there may be a million and a half people here tomorrow. At the youth rally alone, we expect a million. At the candlelight service, maybe a quarter million to three hundred thousand. And there will be full radio and television transmission to European and foreign stations."

"Something important, Excellency." It was the Pope who put a question to the Bishop. "I see no mention here of my meeting with Sister Lucia. Surely an oversight, Excellency. When is it to take place?"

"I thought Your Holiness was aware . . ." The Bishop stumbled for words.

At such a display of confusion, the Pontiff was filled with concern.

Lucia lived in the minds of hundreds of millions of people around the world as the only survivor of the three original little child seers of the Fatima vision. But she was an aging woman now, well into her eighties. Understandably, then, His Holiness' first thought was for the nun's health. "Aware?" His Holiness picked up on the last word. "Aware of what, Excellency? Where is Sister? Is she ill?"

"Sister Lucia is fine, Holiness. It's nothing like that." The Bishop blinked. "She is at her convent at Coimbra, some kilometers north of here."

"What is it then, Excellency? More to the point, when will Sister Lucia arrive at Fatima?"

His composure all but undone, the Bishop fumbled for his briefcase. "I thought Your Holiness would know of the cable . . . I have it here . . . somewhere in these papers. . . . Here it is. The cable from the Cardinal Secretary of State reiterating the ban. . . ."

There was no need to explain further. As the Pope took the cable and read it, he understood everything. Four years before, His Eminence Cardinal Maestroianni had taken it upon himself to forbid Sister Lucia any access to the outside world. Under pain of excommunication, Lucia was to receive no visitors. She was to make no public or private statements about the Fatima message or any subject related to it. Above all, she was forbidden to leave her convent or set foot in Fatima without the Cardinal's express permission. His face grim, the Pontiff passed the cable to Monsignore Daniel.

Monsignore Daniel dialed through to Master-General Damien Slattery at the Angelicum in Rome, and then passed the telephone to the Pope. Within a few seconds more, Slattery understood the situation. He asked His Holiness to read out the date and the coding number of the State Department cable.

"I'll be calling Your Holiness within the hour. On the off-channel, of course."

Slattery ordered his car to be brought around at once. Then he made a call to Maestroianni's secretary, Monsignore Taco Manuguerra, to locate the man His Eminence had left on duty as Substitute Secretary in the Cardinal's absence.

Manuguerra bumbled his way into the conversation. "His Eminence is away until Tuesday, Master-General . . ."

"Yes, Monsignore. I know that." Slattery made his temper plain in the tone of his voice. "Archbishop Buttafuoco is standing in as Substitute Secretary. Find him, and have him meet me in his office at the Secretariat in twenty minutes."

"At this late hour, Master-General? How am I to explain . . . ?"

"Twenty minutes, Monsignore!"

❑ ❑ ❑ ❑

When the white-robed giant of a Dominican loomed like an irate ghost into Canizio Buttafuoco's office on the deserted third floor of the Apostolic Palace, the Archbishop was pacing the carpet to work off his nerves. Like Taco Manuguerra and everyone else in the Vatican, he knew Damien Slattery's privileged position in the papal household. Slattery went straight to the point. "Please read me cable number 207-SL."

Buttafuoco complied.

"On whose order was this cable sent?"

"On the Cardinal Secretary's order, Father."

"Very well, Excellency. As Substitute Secretary, you will kindly accompany me to the coding room, where you will send another cable to countermand this one."

Archbishop Buttafuoco began to sweat. "I cannot do that without first consulting His Eminence."

Slattery was already at the door. "Let me make things plain to you, Excellency. This is the Holy Father's command. If you refuse, you will serve out your days baptizing babies in Bangladesh. And if blame comes down on anyone's head, it will be mine. In fact, if you're not careful, you may even turn out to be a hero—in spite of yourself."

Within forty-five minutes of the call from the Holy Father, it was a pleased Master-General who was able to report back by telephone to His Holiness that a cable had gone off to the Mother Superior at Sister Lucia's convent in Coimbra. In short order, the Mother Superior had telephoned the Substitute Secretary to verify that the cable was from the Secretariat and was official.

The Pontiff's voice brightened. "Sister Lucia will be in Fatima in time for the High Mass tomorrow morning, then, Master-General?"

"She will, Holy Father. She'll be there for High Mass in the morning. And she will remain for her private audience with Your Holiness."

In the small hours of the morning at the Palais d'Alsace in Strasbourg, Cardinal Secretary Maestroianni was awakened from his dreamless sleep by a call from the hotel desk.

"Excuse me, Eminence," the night manager apologized. "But an urgent cable has arrived for you from Rome."

The Cardinal reached for his robe. "Send it up immediately."

The message was from Archbishop Canizio Buttafuoco. It consisted mainly of the text of a cable he had dispatched to Sister Lucia's convent at Coimbra, ordering that the nun be present at Fatima on the following morning, May 13. Buttafuoco had added only: "Master-General."

"Slattery again," Maestroianni shook his head and laid the cable aside. Realist that he was, he clambered back into his bed and closed his eyes. One minor skirmish would not decide the big battle. As for Slattery, he could be dealt with. In time, he too could be dealt with.

X

SOMETHING of Robert Schuman's spirit pervaded every moment throughout the official Schuman Memorial Day celebrations on Monday, May 13, thought Cardinal Maestroianni. From his place somewhere in God's eternity, surely that quiet-spoken, patient man must have looked down through his horn-rimmed spectacles and smiled.

The first of the official celebrations—a congress of all the delegates—assembled in the huge Palais de l'Europe, on the banks of Strasbourg's Ill River. So great was the atmosphere of cordiality—even of amity—that even the usual and permitted internation chauvinism was absent. The French spoke moderately. The Germans spoke permissively in a live-and-let-live manner. The Italians praised Robert Schuman without reference to any Italian contributions to his culture. The British spoke as if they were as European as anybody else, and as if Schuman were as precious to them as Winston Churchill.

In his own short speech, Cardinal Secretary of State Maestroianni conveyed the Holy Father's blessings almost word for word as the Pontiff had spoken them only three days before. "Everyone in this congress"—the Cardinal smiled upon all—"is engaged in a momentous task. The Europe we are building is the hope of the future for many millions."

The good feelings of the congress were carried like the seeds of a new springtime into the luncheon that followed. The afternoon hours were occupied with relaxed but meticulously organized tours of Strasbourg, after which there was quite enough time for all to rest and dress for the black-tie dinner, set for six o'clock sharp at Maison Robert Schuman.

Like all else about this festive day, the dinner itself was everything the Cardinal could have wished. It was hosted by the European Commissioners seated grandly at the dais. The tastiest Strasbourg dishes were served, along with plentiful supplies of *foie gras* and the best wines of the region. Just the right sort of *Nachtmusik* graced the chatter of important people. No speeches were scheduled, and none were needed. Everyone seemed buoyed by a thrill of mental pleasure that all here had lived to see the dreams of the great French diplomat materialize beneath their gaze.

At 7:15 P.M., the daylong official tribute was capped by a final toast to Robert Schuman, noteworthy mainly for its brevity. Punctually at 7:30 P.M., in a rare display of complete unanimity, the European Commissioners rose from their chairs at the dais, invited the guests to applaud this year's Memorial celebrations and wished each and all a most pleasant journey home.

❑ ❑ ❑ ❑

Cardinal Maestroianni found Cyrus Benthoek easily in the thinning after-dinner crowd. The two walked together in a leisurely fashion through the gardens, easy in each other's company as only old friends are, and buoyed by the prospects of their private meeting, about to begin at last.

"Listen, Eminence." Benthoek raised both hands in that familiar *orans* gesture, as if in supplication to invisible presences in the air around him. "Just listen to the silence!"

As they drew near to the site the pair had selected for their own sequestered gathering, His Eminence responded more to the mood of his companion than to his words. "I think there is a special blessing on us all these days."

Their meeting place was not difficult to find. Set within the confines of Citadel Park not far from Robert Schuman House, it had been modeled on the original Trianon, built at Versailles for the Comtesse Du Barry at the behest of her royal lover, Louis XV. Sheltered by evergreens and bathed in the graceful silence that often envelops true gems of architecture, the little Trianon was a splendid island of light in the gathering darkness. The illuminations on the roof balustrade and on the colonnaded steps in front of this neoclassical monument winked out through the gardens as if in welcome.

Just inside the main door, the grandfatherly CEO of Benthoek's home office, Nicholas Clatterbuck, greeted the two hosts on their arrival. Decked out in a fine set of tweeds as usual, he had been appointed to see to security—tight but unobtrusive; then to welcome all the guests together with their various advisors and aides, and direct them all to the main hall where the meeting would commence at eight o'clock. Benthoek had prepared him well. He carried no notes and consulted no name list, but he knew the faces and the titles of all the principals who had been invited, and his fluency in German, Italian and Russian allowed him to make everyone feel comfortable, as grandfathers generally do.

"Most of the guests have already arrived." Clatterbuck walked a few steps along the way to the main hall beside Cyrus and Maestroianni. "We're waiting for the Reverend Tartley and a few more."

"Fine." Benthoek glanced at his watch. "You'll join us when everyone has arrived."

Inside the main hall, everything had been put in perfect order under Nicholas Clatterbuck's hand. Before each chair at a large conference table had been placed a folder containing a general bio sheet for each of the main players. Though everyone knew why he was here, Clatterbuck had included a brief, pro forma recap of the meeting's general agenda in the folders. Aides to some of the delegates were already thumbing through the information as a sort of final run before the main event. Soon they would take up their posts in the chairs set apart, along the walls, for backup personnel. Along the far wall, long tables had been spread generously with Strasbourger delicacies and a variety of wines and waters.

"More *pâté,* Cyrus?" Maestroianni didn't know whether to groan or laugh, so stuffed was he after the dinner.

Among the several groups already in the hall, Maestroianni saw his three Roman Cardinals and Archbishop Graziani, all of them smiling up at Belgian Cardinal Piet Svensen. With his massive head and frame, and huge, protruding eyes set in an unsmiling face, Svensen was obviously in his element as he regaled the Vatican group with colorful memories. Cardinal Silvio Aureatini—immaculately got out in the fine ecclesiastical garb appropriate to his rank as the newest among the Cardinals of the Vatican—was listening with obvious relish. Aureatini was becoming a bit chubby-cheeked now.

Even the normally acid-faced expert on Liturgy and Canon Law, Cardinal Noah Palombo, relaxed his features into what passed for a smile, as he listened to Svensen's stories side by side with the cadaverous and bony-faced Pensabene. Also in the group, Archbishop Giacomo Graziani, the next-in-line Cardinal Secretary of State, remained seriously and sincerely pleasant. Businesslike, impressive in height and comely in appearance, he was already behaving with the gravity of his near-future office as second man to the Slavic Pope.

Maestroianni and Benthoek were about to join that group when Cyrus heard his name called. The two turned to see a short, heavy-featured, broad-shouldered fellow striding toward them from the refreshment table, carrying a glass of wine.

"Meet Serozha Gafin, Eminence." Benthoek clapped his international board's Russian consultant affably on the shoulder. "He can charm your heart as a concert pianist. And he can bewitch your mind with details pertinent to his beloved Russia and all things Slavic."

Gafin was too corpulent for a man so young. He opened his full-lipped mouth in a happy smile and examined Maestroianni through very large, very blue almond-shaped eyes.

Benthoek's second international consultant joined the threesome. Without waiting for Cyrus to introduce him, he bowed stiffly: "Most Reverend Eminence, I am Otto Sekuler." The voice of the German was unforgettably sharp and challenging. The ramrod-straight torso and squared shoulders, the bull neck, the steel-rimmed spectacles and bald pate that both reflected light like mirrors all put His Eminence in mind of every Nazi official he had ever heard about in his long career. Still smiling, the Cardinal Secretary glanced away from Herr Sekuler to give Cyrus a questioning look. Lynx-eyed as always concerning the Cardinal's reactions, Benthoek simply bowed his head benignly as if to say, "Wait and see."

This fast-growing knot of men centered on the Roman Cardinal and the American transnationalist was swelled by the arrival of yet another of Benthoek's guests. Even before he was introduced, Maestroianni recognized all the classic signs of the *anglosassone.* Gibson Appleyard was the quintessential American—muscular build, fair skin, sandy-colored hair speckled with gray, direct eye contact.

"Pleased to meet Your Eminence," Appleyard responded to Cyrus' introduction with a standard, no-nonsense handshake. A man in his mid-fifties, he struck the Cardinal as an ideal intelligence officer. Aside from his exceptional height, there was nothing outstanding about him. Like most Anglo-Saxons—Cyrus Benthoek was the exception—Appleyard was forgettable.

"Well, this is a historic moment, gentlemen." With his habitual, quasi-liturgical gesture, Benthoek blessed the oddly mismatched group of aliens and the clerics who belonged to the innards of Roman Catholicism. "It will be good. Very good."

As if on cue, Nicholas Clatterbuck entered the hall accompanied by the Church of England's tardy and most apologetic Reverend Herbert Tartley, all spruced and smiling in his round collar, black clericals and gaiters. Outside the hall and around the perimeter of the little Trianon, Clatterbuck's miniature army of guards, unobtrusive until now, took up the security posts assigned to them.

The seating arrangement was simple and straightforward. On one side of the table, Cardinal Maestroianni took his seat at the midpoint, the place of honor. The seven members of his delegation ranged on either side of him presented a colorful phalanx in their bejeweled pectoral crosses, their red-buttoned cassocks, their sashes and skullcaps. Seated and silent along the wall behind the Vatican contingent, the two or three aides and consultants each man had brought along sat silent, like a row of humanoid potted plants.

Directly across from Maestroianni sat Cyrus Benthoek. He had put the Reverend Tartley on his immediate right, as honored guest. As an observer rather than a delegate, Gibson Appleyard ignored the seating plan and chose a place somewhat apart from the rest.

Given the antipapal purpose of the meeting, it had seemed best to the two organizers that Cyrus Benthoek be the one to act as chairman. He stood up to begin the proceedings, looking at each of the assembled delegates in turn. What he faced was in reality a mix of people as much at war with each other as with the papacy. The mood of reserve—of cordial distrust—was thick to the point of heaviness. Nevertheless, each man present felt the command in the stare of the American's blue eyes. "When I call out your names, my dear friends," Benthoek began to break the ice in his clear, loud voice, "please stand up so that we can all see you. Those who have brought aides and advisors will do us a favor if you will identify them."

Within ten minutes, all the guests had been identified and greeted. Benthoek was able to underline each man's abilities and the importance of his associations. Each felt he was known, and his talents fully appreciated. Accordingly, when the introductions were complete, the heavy mood had lightened. That much accomplished, Benthoek entered more or less breezily into the subject of their interest. He used the tones of someone who had organized a city tour for visiting dignitaries.

"My friends, our purpose in getting together in this informal way is, first of all, that we get to know each other. That we become aware of the resources and strengths we can bring to any worthy enterprise. Our second purpose is to see if—perhaps without realizing it fully—we all have our minds made up, as individuals and as groups, concerning one important enterprise in particular. Friends." Benthoek's voice took on a note of intimacy now, but it was no less commanding for that. "Friends, we can permit ourselves utter frankness tonight. Without exception, all here are interested in the well-being of the Roman Catholic Church." There was a slight stir as Cardinal Palombo rearranged himself in his chair.

"We all value that Church"—Benthoek bestowed a brotherly smile on Noah Palombo—"not merely as a venerable and millenniar institution. For the majority of our distinguished visitors tonight, the Church of Rome is the Church of their choice." A blue-eyed survey took in all the sashes and buttons on Maestroianni's side of the table, and then widened to embrace the entire gathering. "But more than that, this Roman Catholic Church has an inestimable value for all of us. A supremely important value as a stabilizing factor—socially, politically, ethically." Benthoek paused for effect. "Above all, that Church is a sine qua non for the advent of a New World Order in human affairs."

There was no lightness in the American's voice now as he drove home his first capital point. "Indeed, my good friends. Though I am not a Roman Catholic myself, I venture to say that if by some awful happenstance this Church were to drop out of existence, it would leave a great and yawning gap within the society of nations. All of our human institutions would be sucked into that gap, as into a black hole of nothingness. Nothing—not even a human landscape—would be left. I accept this as a hard, undeniable fact of life, whether one likes it or not. So please, my friends. Celebrate with me our satisfaction at having here with us the key people of this valuable and venerable institution."

Cardinal Maestroianni began to keep a mental checklist of the points Benthoek was making. Point One: For the practical purposes of this alliance, the Roman Catholic Church remained essential as an institutional organization. As an institution, the Church was not a target. Check. Point Two: The Cardinal and his delegation were here as potential collaborators in moving the focus of that organization toward the goals of what Benthoek had termed "a New World Order in human affairs." Check. Point Three: The first order of business was to put aside the historical divisions separating those on Benthoek's side of the table from those who sat across from them. Check.

His Eminence was recalled from his mental scorecard when the focus of the room turned all at once toward the Jesuit Father-General, Michael Coutinho. Coutinho had his hand in the air to signal that he had a word or two to say before things proceeded further.

"Yes, Father-General."

Michael Coutinho cut a stark figure. Like every other Jesuit, he wore no adornments or badges of rank on his black clerical garb. Unlike any other Jesuit, however, every Father-General of the Society of Jesus—Coutinho very much included—was known in the Vatican and around the world as "the Black Pope." For centuries, that description had always been an accurate tribute to the tremendous global power and prestige of the Jesuit Order in its sworn defense of papacy and Popes alike. Latterly, however, it had become an equally accurate description of corporate Jesuit opposition to the Holy See. As black is opposite to white, so was the Black Pope now in opposition to the White Pope.

The Jesuit made his impatience clear. "We have so little time, Mr. Benthoek. I think we should get straight to the point at issue. Let's be frank. Among the various groups represented here"—Coutinho's glance missed no one on either side of the conference table—"I don't think there are even two that have the same idea about how the policies of the Holy See—and the administration of the Church—should proceed. In fact, I expect each of us would opt for a different mode of organizing the Church."

Apparently even disagreement was not easily agreed upon, for while several around the table nodded their heads in assent, others remained impassive and expressionless. Benthoek and Maestroianni made mental registers of each reaction.

"At the same time," Coutinho continued in his lilting Anglo-Indian English, "our valuable Mr. Benthoek has understood that, for all our differences, we are agreed on one essential: We are all agreed that a radical change is required. A radical change at the topmost level." Again, the same several nods of assent. "What we need to do now, therefore, is simply stated. We need to agree on that one essential point: the need for radical change in Church leadership. If we can do that much this evening, then as a consequence we should be able to formulate directives about the specific measures to achieve that change and about the scope of those measures."

Capital! Maestroianni thought that Cyrus himself couldn't have put the objectives of this meeting better or more clearly. Agree on the mission tonight, and form a mechanism to refine and carry out the action to follow. But why wasn't the Jesuit sitting down?

"Having said that much," the Black Pope continued, "there is one prime caution, which I am better qualified to explain than is anyone listening to me. If we make one false step—either in our bedrock decisions this evening or in any of the measures we hope to agree upon in the days to come—then we can expect supreme power to be invoked, and to hammer us into the ground without mercy. Believe me! We in the Society of Jesus know all about that hammer. And about that absence of mercy."

Coutinho's eyes flashed behind his spectacles like black obsidian under glass. Cardinal Maestroianni tightened his hands on the arms of his chair. The Jesuit was going too far now; steering too close to the limits of delicacy. There was no question for the Cardinal about the Jesuit's focus at this moment. His Eminence himself, in fact, had been forced to act as the merciless hammer in the awful incident Coutinho had in mind. It had been all the way back in 1981. But because high emotion gives flesh to memory, the central event of that day remained an unwelcome companion to Maestroianni, as obviously it did for the Father-General.

In the escalating strife between the Society of Jesus and the Holy See, by 1981 the policies of the Order had come to be so openly at odds with papal policy that the Slavic Pope had decided on the extreme step of cashiering the man, Pedro Arrupe, who was then the Society's Father-General. Listening to Coutinho now, the Cardinal Secretary recalled how, on the Pontiff's stern and unrelenting orders, he had presented himself at the door of the Jesuit head-house in Rome that day. How Michael Coutinho had accompanied him up the stairs to the sickroom of the Father-General. It had all been so needless. The whole world knew that the man had suffered a massive stroke—had collapsed right on the airport tarmac as he returned from a trip abroad. But the Pontiff had been firm. Stroke or no, the papal edict was to be delivered in the time-honored way of such things.

Maestroianni had been sickened as he stood at the bedside of that once vibrant Jesuit leader. Sickened at the sight of this skillful warrior with words who was now unable to utter a sound. Sickened at the sight of those hands and arms that had wielded such power—but that now lay withered and motionless atop the coverlet. From the prison inside himself, the Jesuit Father-General had stared up at Maestroianni through large, blank eyes, unable to respond or to defend himself—or even to acknowledge that he heard the words of the papal document Maestroianni read over him as he lay on his bed. Words that summarily dismissed him from his post as Father-General of his proud and prestigious Order.

When he had read the last word and had turned away from the inert form on the bed, Maestroianni had found himself looking into those obsidian-black eyes of young Father Michael Coutinho. "We will not forget this needless humiliation!" That was the message those eyes had flashed. Coutinho's enmity had not been for Maestroianni. His wordless rage was entirely focused on the Holy Father.

Maestroianni's painful reliving of that day came to an end. Every man present was fixed by the passion in Michael Coutinho's eyes as he made plain the present position his global Order had adopted. "We in our Society are completely at peace in our consciences. We are bound by our vows to Christ. And we are bound to serve the Vicar of Peter, the Bishop of Rome. Insofar as we can see he conforms to the manifest will of Christ, as that will is shown to us in the human events of our day, we are bound to serve him. That is all I have to say."

For Cyrus Benthoek, it was more than enough. Like Maestroianni, the Jesuit had changed his allegiance. He served the Pope now not as the Vicar of Christ, the Creator; but as the Vicar of Peter, the creature. The regulator for his policies was not some transcendent goal formulated in the sixteenth century by a long-dead St. Ignatius of Loyola, but the clear lineaments of political and social evolution at the end of the twentieth century.

Coolheaded as always, Benthoek was about to rise and take the meeting in hand again, when the acid-faced Noah Palombo stood up. Cardinal Palombo was a man accustomed to cut-and-dried procedure. He was not one for long-winded discussions of pros and cons. And he was not to be put off by the dangers the Jesuit Father-General had outlined.

The Cardinal had a simple recommendation to offer. "One of our number," he suggested, "should formulate for us the essential point, which Father-General Coutinho recommended to us at the beginning of his remarks: the need for radical change at the uppermost level of the Church's hierarchical structure. If no one can put that point on the table in a way that is clear and acceptable—and workable, practical—then we are wasting our time. If someone among us is up to that task, however, and if we can achieve consensus on that point—then I will have a further recommendation to make."

Even before Palombo had regained his seat, and almost as if on cue—or so it seemed to Maestroianni—Cardinal Leo Pensabene lifted his tall, bony frame with the confident bearing of a man who presumes everyone will agree with all he says. To Maestroianni's relief, Leo Pensabene remained more paternalistic than combative. "Without blushing too much at my own words," he began, "I think I am in an excellent position to take a shot at formulating the point, as requested by the Father-General and by my venerable brother Cardinal." A little bow to Coutinho, and another to Palombo.

"Indeed, I have had a word with my colleagues in the College. They, too, feel I might best formulate our attitude." Given Cardinal Pensabene's status as leader of the major faction in the College of Cardinals, that last seemingly casual bit of information was a heartening indication of support in quarters of the Vatican where might and power reside. "If it is to be workable and practical, our consensus must rest on facts. On the facts of the concrete situation. For on what other basis can we build?

"The primary fact is this: Because of the application of the principles of the Second Vatican Council, since 1965 the life and development of the People of God—of all Roman Catholics—have been largely determined by three new structures operating in the institutional organization of the

Church. First"—Pensabene held up one bony finger of his right hand—"we have the International Council for Christian Liturgy." A second bow to Palombo, now, as head of that structure. "The ICCL now legislates for all Catholics on matters of worship and liturgy. So when we speak of the ICCL, we touch at the heart of the individual morality of Catholics.

"Second"—up popped a second bony finger on his right hand—"there is the Christian Adult Renewal Rite, supervised by the newest Cardinal among us. The function of CARR," he went quickly on, "is to introduce the new formulations of our faith; and to make sure they are employed not only in the administration of the Sacraments but in all teaching of the faith to children and adults alike. So, when we speak of CARR, we touch deeply on social morality within the fabric of Catholic life.

"And, third." Pensabene had three fingers in the air now. "Third, we must take account of the Justice and Peace Commissions throughout the world, including Rome.

"Because of my own intimate association with JAPEC, I can assure you that its precise function and purpose has been a great success. It ensures that the new principles of democracy embodied in the Church's current philosophy and political activism are understood. Further, it ensures that those principles are propagated throughout the Church Universal. Especially in the poverty-stricken countries of the Third World, JAPEC has made great progress. It will be obvious, then, that when we speak of JAPEC, we are speaking of the political morality of the Catholic faithful around the world."

Pensabene turned his head to peer at each man present. "We have three capital structures up and running around the world, then—ICCL, CARR and JAPEC. And we have three capital moral spheres to go with them—personal, social and political. So, too, do we have three capital consequences that bear directly on our purpose here this evening. All three of these innovative structures are based in the Holy See. Likewise, all three structures, and their activities, are acceptable to a vast majority of our bishops throughout the Church. And through ICCL, CARR and JAPEC, this same majority of bishops now speaks increasingly in the name of the Holy See! More and more, in fact—legislatively and by way of counsel—these bishops now speak *in place of* the Holy See!"

Few men had seen Pensabene more enthusiastic. "Thus, these same bishops already decide basic questions of morality for all Catholics. For the People of God. Decisions about the most basic questions of individual, social and political morality have been assumed de facto by the bishops. Or, to put it the other way around: For all practical purposes, the bishops have taken over the sublime teaching authority of the Church—the magisterium, as it was called in past times. De facto, the bishops are the normally accepted voice of God.

"What I am describing for you—as I am sure all of you have understood by now—is an evolutionary state of affairs simply waiting to be institutionalized. For if the bishops and the People of God indicate anything to us, they are indicating clearly that we no longer need the old basis for authority and development in the Church. The day of that old basis is past and gone. As soon as possible, we need to have a papacy that conforms to the new reality. A papacy that conforms to the concrete, de facto situation. In fact, a papacy that accepts that situation as de jure."

Having ended as he had begun, with both feet in the concrete situation, and confident that he had been practical, persuasive and eloquent, Cardinal Pensabene sat down slowly, even majestically. If Pensabene's resolution carried—and if the Strasbourg alliance were successful—the Slavic Pope would conform to de facto conditions as the Cardinal had laid them out; or the Slavic Pope would be Pope no more.

With the Pensabene proposition clearly on the table, logic dictated that a first vote should be taken. But because things had developed a little more rapidly than Benthoek had expected, there had been no chance to take a meaningful sounding among the group. True, some had nodded agreement from time to time—but even that had not been unanimous.

Aware that an unsuccessful vote would lead to protracted debate—and in all likelihood to an early and untidy end to the hoped-for Strasbourg alliance—Benthoek looked across the table at Cardinal Maestroianni. The barest movement of Maestroianni's head signaled caution. That was sufficient for Benthoek. Obviously some judicious canvassing was in order before a vote was taken.

"My friends." Cyrus pushed his chair back and invited everyone to do likewise. "I suggest we take a little time out. I'm sure some of you would like to compare notes and conclusions with each other and with your advisors. Fifteen or twenty minutes should suffice."

XI

"TWENTY MINUTES may not be long enough, Holy Father."

As he rode beside the Pontiff in the papal limousine, Monsignore Daniel Sadowski's mind was no longer occupied with the massive Fatima youth rally, where His Holiness had just moments before delivered his evening homily. Instead, his preoccupation was for this short break before the candlelight procession that would take place later that evening. Brief as it was, a period of twenty minutes had been sandwiched into His Holiness' hectic schedule to allow for his now reinstated private audience with Sister Lucia.

The Pope had already been visibly buoyed at Lucia's presence at the High Mass in the morning. She had retired then to the Casa Regina Pacis on the Rua do Anjo, where she would await her meeting with the Holy Father, and where she and her watchdog Reverend Mother would then pass the night.

"True enough, Monsignore." The Pope turned from the crowds lining the street just long enough to reassure his secretary. "Twenty minutes is not long. But perhaps it will be sufficient. We shall see soon enough." Then, with a surprising twinkle in his eyes, and a personal familiarity that was a reminder of their Kraków days, "Don't worry, Daniel. Things are not yet so bad that they will begin the candlelight procession without us."

Sadowski responded with a little laugh. He was happy to see the Pontiff regain some of his old buoyancy and humor. But the fact was that there was too little time for the Pontiff's meeting with Lucia. Too little time for a meeting the Monsignore knew to be of such importance. In fact, there was no man in the papal household who knew that importance more intimately or cared more deeply about what was precisely on the mind of the Slavic Pope. It was all, at one and the same time, so very simple and so frustratingly complicated.

For the Slavic Pope, his churchly organization had fallen beneath a mandate of decay and death. But so had the society of nations—nations individually taken and the nations as a society. Both the churchly organization and that society of nations were heading straight into a period of severe punishment at the hands of nature—ultimately at the hands of God, whose undoubted love for all his creation was balanced with his justice. For there is no love possible without justice. Church prelates and the nations had been summarily unfaithful to the demands of God's love. Therefore his justice was poised to intervene in human affairs and correct that unfaithfulness.

Certain in his own mind that this terrible intervention by God in human affairs would take place in the decade of the nineties, the Slavic Pope had very few indications as to when precisely. Because of the third letter of Fatima, he knew this punishment would have Russia as its focus. He also knew that part of this divine timetable involved his own papal visit to Russia. Also, he knew that the timing of that Russia journey was tied to the fortunes of Mikhail Gorbachev. And, deliberately, he had nourished a correspondence with the Russian. But beyond these summary points, there were only ambiguities and vaguenesses. The Slavic Pope needed enlightenment. Sister Lucia might be able to shed some light on the ambiguities, and dispel those fatal vaguenesses that left the Pontiff uncertain of the future, unsure of any major decisions.

All of that being so, Monsignore Daniel had not been surprised that Cardinal Secretary Maestroianni had done what he could to scrub this evening's private meeting between the Pope and the only surviving Fatima seer. Maestroianni knew, as many did, that during the seventy-four years since the initial Fatima events, the Virgin Mary had continued her visits and her messages to Sister Lucia. And the Cardinal Secretary knew, as many did, that two Popes—including the Slavic Pope—had themselves been favored with visits from the Blessed Virgin. He knew further that each such visit had been unmistakably connected with Fatima.

The core of the Slavic Pope's papal policy, as Monsignore Daniel realized, was at issue in his own mind. By the end of the eighties, he had realized that he had unwittingly allowed the entry of a certain darkness into the minds of those who would normally be reckoned as orthodox prelates, orthodox priests, orthodox layfolk. He had allowed the ambiguous tenets of the Second Vatican Council to be widely interpreted in a non-Catholic manner. He had allowed whole hierarchies of bishops in various regions to wallow in clerical bureaucracy and neglect the basics of Roman Catholic life.

In fact, his governance of his churchly institution had only increased the absolute need for the only element that could save his institution from foundering completely and disappearing from the society of man as an effective force: the intervention of the Blessed Virgin foretold at Fatima, which would be accompanied by severe chastisements. Hence his desire to obtain from Sister Lucia some more precise idea of the divine timetable. As they approached the Casa Regina Pacis, where Lucia waited, Monsignore Daniel shivered involuntarily.

"It's not cold, Monsignore Daniel," the Pontiff teased him as they approached their destination, "why the shivering? Surely you're not afraid to meet a living saint, our Sister Lucia?"

"No, Holy Father. Somebody was just walking over my grave." Daniel used the old proverb to pass off the occasion, but—truth to tell—he did not know why he had shivered.

His Holiness was welcomed to the Casa Regina Pacis by its Mother Superior, whose face was as happy and cherubic as that of any angel. She presented her nuns to His Holiness with devout and cheerful warmth, and the Pontiff had a few quiet words of encouragement to say to each one in turn. Within a few moments, the Mother Superior was leading the Pope and his secretary along a high-ceilinged corridor that ran the length of the house. She explained to His Holiness and Monsignore Daniel that the sacristy at the far end of the corridor, beside the house chapel, had been chosen for the audience. As it was a large room, Mother was certain the photographer could work from the corridor without disturbing the papal audience.

The cherubic face turned to Monsignore Daniel. "The photographer has already arrived, Monsignore, and would be happy to have your instructions." Daniel thanked the nun and, while the Superior accompanied the Pope into the vestry, remained just outside the door with the photographer to tell him the shots required for distribution to the news media around the world.

The sacristy was not ornate. There were no chandeliers; but the lightness of feeling was infectious and inviting. The adornments of this room, as of the Casa itself, consisted mainly of the souls within its walls. At the farthest distance from the doorway, over near the bow windows that gave onto the Casa's gardens, three chairs had been put in place for the papal audience. The largest chair in the center was obviously meant for the Pontiff. Those on either side were to serve for Sister Lucia and for her Superior and guardian at Coimbra who had accompanied Lucia to Fatima.

"Reverend Mother." The Pontiff turned to the cheerful-faced nun. "Two chairs will be sufficient. I will speak alone with Sister Lucia."

"Quite so, Holiness."

With a smile in her eyes, Reverend Mother herself removed the chair at the left of the grouping, and then excused herself from the papal presence to see what might be delaying her guests. The Holy Father sat down to wait, quite at his ease for a change. He could hear Monsignore Daniel talking to the photographer out in the corridor.

Sister Lucia was at last ushered in from the corridor by her somber Coimbra Superior. The Pontiff rose from his chair with both arms extended in a wonderful gesture of warmth and welcome. "Sister Lucia," the Holy Father spoke to the Fatima seer in her native Portuguese. "I salute you in the name of Our Lord and His Blessed Mother."

The elderly little nun seemed not in the least oppressed by the strictures that had come down upon her so harshly from the Secretariat in Rome. Indeed, she remained very much as the Pontiff remembered her from their last meeting. She was a little thinner, perhaps; but her face was still full, her expression still vibrant, her step still quick and purposeful for a woman of such advanced age. Her dark, bespectacled eyes shining with great and uninhibited joy, Lucia came forward in response to the Holy Father's welcome. She knelt on the floor and kissed the Pontiff's ring.

Had she been allowed, Lucia would doubtless have remained upon her knees in the old Carmelite way for the entire audience. Obedient to the Pope's wishes, however, and in response to the gentle guidance of his hand, she rose to her feet and allowed herself to be seated beside the papal chair. Lucia had not lost the simplicity of expression and guileless look that adorned her face as a young girl in the early years of the century. Age had left her body weak, her movements slower. But the moment her eyes were raised to look into the Slavic Pope's eyes, a radiance suffused her whole being. The Pontiff himself felt humbled by her almost palpable holiness.

Finding no third chair for herself, and with no welcome from the Pope beyond that required by his own cordiality, the Mother Superior from Coimbra dutifully brushed her lips somewhere near the papal ring, gathered her dignity and withdrew to the corridor.

Lucia sat straight in her chair, her rosary entwined in her hands clasped on her lap. When he was not himself speaking, His Holiness leaned forward, elbows resting on his knees, head bowed and cupped in his hands, his concentration intense as he listened to the Fatima seer. During all the time that passed, though aware of the hour and of the benign presence of his secretary, the Pontiff looked up at Daniel only once. With that glance, Daniel understood that the candlelight procession would get off to a late start.

It was nearly an hour before His Holiness and Sister Lucia rose from their chairs by the window. As the nun knelt again to kiss the Fisherman's ring, the photographer took his final picture and Monsignore Daniel stepped forward to escort Lucia to the sacristy door and into the charge again of her unsmiling Mother Superior from Coimbra. For Daniel the transformation in the Holy Father's face was electrifying. The Pope's eyes shone with that keen, quickened light that had once and for so long been habitual to him. The Pontiff was enlivened, invigorated. The smile that suffused his features was less of the lips than of the spirit. The Pontiff motioned for the secretary to sit down beside him for a moment.

"You were right, Monsignore." The Pope laughed. "Twenty minutes can be very short." There was no time now to recap the substance of his talk with Lucia for Monsignore Daniel's benefit. That would have to come later. He and the holy Sister had covered all the points of his main queries. As was usual, he had found the reassurances he needed, but still had to proceed in faith and trust. "One urgent matter, though. When did the last letter from Signor Gorbachev arrive?"

"Last week, Holiness."

"It is important that I answer it the moment we get back to Rome. That poor little man has been an unwitting instrument of the Virgin, but we mustn't allow his impatience and desperation to ruin things." Then, as if in amplification, "We have made no bad mistakes, Monsignore. But the time is foreshortened. We have far less than I had thought. Sister will see the beginning of the end. We will see it through—God willing."

"God willing, Holy Father." Daniel's response was quick in coming. "God willing."

XII

BECAUSE JAWBONING is what men at exalted levels of power do for a living, twenty minutes was about right for Cyrus Benthoek and Cosimo Maestroianni to take their strategic soundings. They passed separately and easily from group to group, asking a question here, soliciting reactions there. Each was geared to the pulse of things; always listening, watching; always helpful. Benthoek spent a bit of extra time with his guest of honor, the Church of England's Reverend Herbert Tartley. Then he joined his Russian associate, Serozha Gafin, who was deep in conversation with the American, Gibson Appleyard. Because Otto Sekuler had been silent in the discussions, a short conversation was in order there, too.

Maestroianni covered his contingent efficiently, giving special attention to some who had not spoken up so far. He didn't have to worry about Cardinal Aureatini, of course; or about Svensen of Belgium. But the politically careful Archbishop Giacomo Graziani might need his spine stiffened. And it would be unwise to neglect the sometimes quixotic Father-General of the Franciscans, Victor Venable.

At last, Benthoek and Maestroianni strolled together to the refreshment table for a word with Cardinal Noah Palombo. It had been Palombo's first recommendation, after all, that had led to Cardinal Pensabene's informative summary of the "de facto situation" in the Church. But Cardinal Palombo's second recommendation still remained to be heard.

Cyrus Benthoek and the Cardinal Secretary concluded that a common opinion was now within reach. No matter how radically the various delegates might differ on a thousand different subjects, an alliance among them for this one goal—a change in the form and function of the papacy—was the egg waiting to be hatched. Like a pair of mother hens, therefore, the two organizers reassembled their guests at the conference table. Benthoek turned to the honored delegate from the Church of England, seated on his right. Surely, Cyrus said with a kindly smile upon the gathering, a word or so from the Reverend Tartley, as "advisor to the Throne and special consultor for Canterbury," would have special significance.

Tartley rose obligingly from his chair. He was the least challenging of figures. A big, bluff man with thick bifocals, a pug nose, a rubicund face and very little hair, he gave the impression of something between the traditional figure of John Bull and the old music-hall caricature of the English parson. In the nasal twang of his Cockney English, he offered his greetings as "the 'umble pastor of Islip-on-Thames," and apologized for the absence this evening of Mrs. Tartley, "me better 'alf." Immediately, however, he tweaked the nose of modesty with an offhand reminder of the power he embodied. Only a month ago, he recalled, her Majesty the Queen had pointed out to him the need of "a universal teacher" in our present world. Someone who would be described as universal because he would be accepted by all as having the wisdom "to cater to everyone's needs, but not to move exclusively."

Then, having made it plain that he was speaking as a kind of unofficial plenipotentiary not only for the Church of England but also for the Throne, he moved quickly on to the point at issue. There could, he explained by example, be no real collaboration between "the 'oly See and the vast majority of Christians" until Rome abandoned its obstinate views on such basic questions as divorce, abortion, contraception, homosexuality, the ordination of women, marriage for priests, and fetal engineering.

Such a step would only come about through a "change in papal hadministration." At the same time, however, the fair-minded Reverend would himself " 'ave a look at changing minds in 'igh places." With a brotherly glance at Benthoek's secular guests—at Gafin and Sekuler; at Nicholas Clatterbuck and Gibson Appleyard—Tartley allowed that his "C of E" might be considered small, if one relied only on a head count of its members. But he took such statistical data to be insignificant beside the fact that, from Her Majesty on down, that church was linked in what he called "the brother'ood of mankind—whether you speak of East or West; of capitalism or socialism.

"Nor do I mind telling you that—prior to this meeting, and also during our break a few moments ago—these good gentlemen and I 'ave 'ad our consultations." He trained his thick bifocals on the laymen again. "We are in agreement with the specific goal that 'as brought us together for this 'istoric evening. And we are ready to collaborate with whatever plans can be drawn up to achieve that worthy goal. Let's all pull our weight! God bless you all." Somehow, his speech was a reminder of the Holy See's own millenniar claim to perpetuity and to a divinely guaranteed immunity from destruction. Somehow his words prefigured the success that awaited the new alliance.

Cyrus Benthoek could feel the mood of the Cardinals as Tartley took his chair again. Approval was apparent in the eyes of every listener. Benthoek looked across at Cardinal Maestroianni. This time, there was no cautionary signal. Eminently pleased at his own stratagem, Cyrus stood and all but blessed the English clergyman with his signature *orans* gesture. "My friends, I sense the feeling of all here present that our consensus has been poured like freshly matured wine into a new vessel. Before we go on, then, may we have a vote on the 'essential point'? On our worthy goal of a change at the topmost reaches of the Roman Church, for the good of all mankind as it is presently evolving?"

Maestroianni's was the first hand raised on his side of the table. His four brother Cardinals followed suit. Palombo was the quickest. Pensabene's bony hand shot up. Then Aureatini's hand, and Svensen's. At one end of the Roman phalanx, the very quiet Father-General Victor Venable of the Franciscans voted aye. At the opposite end of the table the Black Pope, Father-General Michael Coutinho, counted himself and his Jesuits in. Across from the Cardinal Secretary, every hand was high, including Benthoek's. Gibson Appleyard was the sole exception. But then, as an unofficial observer, the American was not expected to participate to that degree. The last to fall into line was Maestroianni's soon-to-be successor as Secretary of State, Archbishop Giacomo Graziani. After a few pensive blinks, though, Graziani threw in his lot with the rest.

"It is unanimous, then." Benthoek stated the obvious for the record. Satisfied, Cyrus turned his eyes like blue lights on Cardinal Noah

Palombo. "Your Eminence had a second recommendation to make. May we have the benefit of Your Eminence's counsel again?"

Cardinal Palombo rose slowly to his feet, his face set in its usual severity, like unyielding granite. "The situation is clear," Palombo began. "And my second recommendation is accordingly very simple. The basic reason for the consensus that has just been demonstrated among us is the pressure—the force—of human events. Events outside the operational scope of the churchmen here tonight. I speak of the rush of men and women the world over toward a new unity. Toward a new arrangement among the nations, and among all people of our modern society.

"We are impelled not to step aside from such events. From such a positive force. We are impelled to identify with it. To embrace it wholeheartedly. Already that force has vitally—we should say, mortally—affected the ancient Church formula. Though they have not spoken tonight, two of our number—Reverend Father-General of the Franciscans, Victor Venable; and His Eminence Cardinal Svensen—know how that force, as embodied in the charismatic movement, has ushered many millions of Catholics away from the formula of pseudo-personal devotion to the historical Christ. Away from the whole gaggle of devotions oriented toward angels and saints and Mariology. Those millions of Catholics are now in direct and personal contact with the Spirit." As if he himself embodied the Spirit, Palombo made direct personal contact with the eyes of the Franciscan and the Belgian Cardinal. Each of them smiled in beatific agreement.

Cardinal Palombo turned his attention next to Michael Coutinho. "So too can the Father-General of the Society of Jesus tell us of the success the Jesuits have had in Latin America with a theology of liberation. Again, we can speak of many millions—masses of Catholics—who refuse any longer to be castrated by a saccharine Christ figure or by a weeping and pietistic Madonna.

"In those Third World countries, successive generations of imperialist-minded clerics once preached a pacific and milquetoast devotional theology. But now, those millions of men and women have rejected such impotence. They have opted for their own long-overdue financial, economic and political liberation. Those millions battle now, not with rosaries and novenas, but with the strength of their own arms. And with the strength of their ballots. Really—and above all—they battle with the force of the Spirit in them."

The Black Pope's eyes flashed his agreement.

Acid-faced and intent, Palombo turned now toward each of his fellow Cardinals. "We have heard tonight from my venerable brother Cardinal Pensabene, for example, that the Catholic mind has now been disaffected from its recent slavery to the papalist motive. That mind has also been disaffected from the whole confused *mixtum-gatherum* of mental habits that once conformed Catholics to a model of human behavior that is refused and rejected by the vast majority of men and women today.

Thanks to the use of advanced psychological techniques employed by Marriage Enjoinder, Origins and RENEW—to name just a few of the processes formulated to further our agenda—even the vast majority of Catholics today reject those old models of behavior.

"More to the point, those very processes have moved Catholics themselves—again, I speak of men and women in their millions—to the acceptance of everything we in this room envision for the New World Order. No longer do Catholics suffer under the conviction that they belong to some special group. Or that they have exclusive possession of the moral and religious values by which men and women must live in order to—to be . . ." Just this once, Noah Palombo stumbled over his words. "To be—as they used to say—to be saved."

It was only a microsecond before he regained his composure. "Right now, through the Roman center—through every diocese and parish; through every seminary and university and school that is called Catholic—there runs a new and different current. Throughout the Church, there is born a new type of Catholic. Now, Catholics are disposed and ripe to be assimilated to the general type of men and women. Now, Catholics desire what we ourselves desire. Now, Catholics are ready to inhabit and give life to the New World Order that we, here in this room, intend to make a reality."

Every man was transfixed by Palombo's words and ready for his finale. "My second recommendation, therefore, is as urgent as it is practical. As Catholic churchmen, my colleagues and I have come very far on our own. The one thing lacking to us now is the final bridge to the wider world. The bridge over which vast millions of Catholics can hurry to join the rest of humanity. To join the new arrangement of nations as an active, cooperative force in our new and modern world."

Noah Palombo looked directly at Cyrus Benthoek now, and at each of his delegation in turn, including the standoffish Gibson Appleyard. "The one thing we cannot do alone is construct that bridge. You, Signor Benthoek. And you, Signor Clatterbuck. And you, Signor Gafin. And you, Signor Sekuler." The Cardinal looked at Gibson Appleyard again, but refrained from putting his name on the record. "All of you have the means to help us construct that bridge. Help us remove the stumbling block to our union. Help us construct our bridge to the world. Help us cross it."

In his extensive and lustrous career, rarely had things worked out so well for Cyrus Benthoek. Alone now with Cardinal Maestroianni in the little Trianon, he eased back in his chair and stretched out his long legs. Benthoek and Cardinal Maestroianni had one more little piece of business to set in motion. Neither of them had forgotten Cardinal Svensen's proposal, made by phone to Maestroianni in Rome some ten days prior, to create a strong flesh-and-blood link between the Catholic bishops of Europe's heartland and the powerful Commissioners of the European Community.

The American told Maestroianni about progress made so far on his side of the Vatican-EC link. As promised, Benthoek's law firm had looked into the matter of placing their talented young internationalist, Paul Thomas Gladstone, into the post of Secretary-General to the Council of Ministers, who formed the central governing body of the European Community. That post would fall vacant in June. "It will take a little arranging," Cyrus confided to the Cardinal Secretary. "But the task of securing the job for our man is well within our scope. Now, what about Christian Gladstone, Eminence? There's nothing like a little nepotism to firm up a plan such as this."

Maestroianni had done his homework, too. His further investigations had reaffirmed his initial estimates of Father Christian Gladstone as a pliable, nonpolitical innocent. The fellow's youth was offset nicely by his personal polish and his family connections. Such qualities were sure to impress the bishops and gain their confidence—especially when backed by the muscle of the Vatican's Secretariat. Under the skin, meanwhile, Christian Gladstone checked out as the perfect man for the job. His record showed him to be an intelligent but obedient cleric who would find a way to do as he was told, if it were put to him in the right way.

"It's just a matter of his availability. Technically, he's still under the jurisdiction of the Bishop of New Orleans. A Cardinal Archbishop by the name of John Jay O'Cleary. But as you say, Cyrus, the task is well within our scope."

The two old friends left the Trianon at last. The Cardinal took one last look at Robert Schuman House, deserted now, abandoned to silence and moonglow. "It will be good." His Eminence echoed the prophecy Benthoek had made earlier. "It will be very good."

In contrast to the barren, silent darkness that settled in on the Schuman House, Fatima had become a darksome and velvet sea through which a winding stream of tiny flames moved to the rising and falling cadences of the Ave Maria voiced by the thousands of pilgrims, each carrying a lighted candle, who took part in the procession around the Basilica. It was a contrast between the dusty memories of long-dead men silenced forever in Strasbourg and the living, breathing soul of a believing community renewing its quickened hopes and lively faith in the immortality guaranteed only by the all-powerful Son of the living God and delivered to mankind by the fiat of a village maiden now become the Queen of Heaven and the Mother of all human beings.

Something special was enacted by that procession, Monsignore Daniel reflected as he walked slowly behind the Slavic Pope; something symbolic of mankind's condition. Christians were never promised worldwide victory. By biblical definition, they would never be more than a remnant, a stump of a once great tree, pruned and cut down to size by the hand of God rewarding love but maintaining the justice of his law.

Here tonight, all those who followed the lead of the Holy Father were walking the only sure path to salvation. For Monsignore Daniel, for all following the Roman Pope, for this Roman Pope himself, those precious minutes of singing veneration for the Blessed Lady of Fatima provided a sweet respite for all—the tired souls, the frightened souls, the wavering souls, the perfervid souls. For the dark around them was light enough for their comfort; and the light around them was dark enough to allow the steel of their faith to pierce the human skies and reach the throne of the Father in Heaven.

Friends
of Friends

XIII

NICHOLAS CLATTERBUCK never changed. Whether directing Vatican and other guests into the once-in-an-age meeting in Strasbourg or directing the far-flung everyday operations as CEO of Benthoek's London headquarters, he was always the same. Always grandfatherly, yet with a peculiar presumption of authority.

Even the late-afternoon rush-hour traffic on New York City's Upper West Side seemed unable to ruffle him. No doubt Dr. Ralph Channing and the others would be waiting for him at Channing's Cliffview House. But not even Clatterbuck—not even the devil himself—could do anything about the sanitation truck grinding its way along the upper reaches of Riverside Drive, or about the volume of traffic that crept behind it, horns blowing, all the way north from Ninety-sixth Street.

"Here, driver." In his usual kindly voice, Clatterbuck directed his driver toward a row of limousines already double-parked in front of his destination. "Pull up here."

Cliffview. The name was etched on the brass doorplate, but the Englishman barely glanced at it as he entered the thirteen-story mansion. He knew this turn-of-the-century landmark as well as he knew its proprietor. In fact, almost anyone familiar with New York's Upper West Side knew Cliffview—if not by its name, at least by its distinctive eaves capped by that easy-to-spot glass dome overlooking the Hudson River.

"Ah, Clatterbuck. My dear man."

The gravelly voice that greeted Nicholas as he joined the others already gathered in the penthouse studio was as unmistakable as everything that went with it: the utterly bald head; the high, straight forehead; the piercing blue eyes; the goatee beard; the force of authority and sureness that neither Clatterbuck nor any man here had ever gainsaid. All of that belonged to Dr. Ralph S. Channing.

"Sorry to be behind time, Professor. Traffic."

"Your timing is perfect. We were just talking about you, in fact. I was filling everyone in about your triumph with Benthoek at last week's Strasbourg meeting. But I seem to have set off some sparks. Our French colleague here finds the whole Roman proposal to be distasteful in the extreme." Channing set his wineglass firmly down on the marble side table by his chair and looked at his full complement of eleven colleagues, each in turn, until he let his laser eyes fix on Jacques Deneuve as the subject of his patronizing indulgence. "Deneuve thinks Rome is a cesspool, Clatterbuck. What do you have to say about that?"

Clatterbuck took his time before answering. A general glance at the ten men already seated at their ease around the studio with Dr. Channing sufficed as greeting. He poured himself a glass of wine from one of the decanters on the credenza.

"Why, of course it's a cesspool." He turned his kind eyes on Deneuve. "No one here likes Rome, Jacques. The whole papal outfit is the worst cesspool of antihuman plots and plans and inhuman machinations ever devised by grubby little men with grubby little ideas. We all know that. But that's not the point we need to focus on. Opportunity has not merely knocked on our door. It has provided us with a Vatican passport."

His point conceded at least in essence, Deneuve was satisfied. His pride was intact. Channing could always count on Clatterbuck to calm injured feelings. Glass in hand, the Englishman made his way into the circle of men and settled his tweeds into a solidly upholstered wing chair. Between him and Channing, a thirteenth chair remained empty—except for a red leather folder resting on its seat. That place always remained empty, as if for an invisible presence among them that added force to the combined presence of the group itself; a presence that made the group more than the sum of its twelve animated bodies and lively minds. This was always such a comfortable place for Clatterbuck. A deliciously tasteful retreat—"pipey and booky and male," as Virginia Woolf once characterized the private study of one of her admirers. From where he sat, he could enjoy the view of the evening darkness and a thousand lights across the Hudson.

Quickly caught up in the discussion of world events that always preceded whatever business might bring these twelve colleagues to Cliffview from time to time, Clatterbuck needed no briefing from Cyrus Benthoek, as he had at Strasbourg, to know about the members of this group. In fact, though Benthoek had met Channing and some of the others here in the normal course of his affairs, even he might be surprised to know all that Clatterbuck knew about them.

On the surface, Ralph Channing's guests at Cliffview made up a Who's Who of power and success. Jacques Deneuve, for example, whose feathers had been ruffled by the Roman proposal out of Strasbourg, was Europe's all-important banker. Gynneth Blashford was Britain's most powerful newspaper magnate. Brad Gerstein-Snell cut the dominant figure in international communications. Sir Jimmie Blackburn ranked as South Africa's sole ruler of the diamond market. Kyun Kia Moi was master of all Far Eastern charter shipping.

Those five alone were the kingmakers of the New World Order who daily play with scores of billions that slosh around the international money markets in Tokyo, London, New York, Singapore, Paris and Hong Kong, the dominant figures regulating the flow of capital and capital goods. Ultimately, therefore, they were the arbiters in the life and death of individual governments and the welfare of nations.

In such a group as this, Dr. Ralph Channing might have been considered the odd man out. Instead, however, he was clearly something more than a peer. Born into a long-established Huguenot family in Maine, Channing had done his studies at Yale in comparative religion and theology. Renowned for his encyclopedic grasp of the records of the Knights Templar, of the Holy Grail tradition and of Freemasonry—in particular, the Ordo Templi Orientis, or OTO; the Eastern Temple—he had become a noted archivist for diverse groups of humanist scholars. As a tenured professor at a top American university, his influence extended around the world through a well-received litany of books, pamphlets, articles, lectures and seminars.

Increasingly valued in certain circles for his correct historical information and his ability to appraise organized religion as a sociocultural and political factor in the world, he had been borrowed from his university by one Washington administration and had successfully managed the planning of the Department of Education. Somehow he also found time to spend a couple of months abroad each year as consultant for various humanist organizations in Europe and the Far East.

Never mind, then, that Ralph Channing wasn't a banker or master of shipping interests. There wasn't a man in this distinguished group who would—or could—challenge his credentials as leader.

In reality, what bound these twelve men together wasn't entirely a matter of banking or shipping or diamonds. Having drunk deeply from the precious wine of success, each man present had searched for another goal. And each had found that service to the Prince of This World was the only goal that satisfied. Each had passed through the tests of Fire, Pain and Death. Each had received the Seal of the Final Utterance on his soul. All here were bespoken men. That was the unifying force at Cliffview House.

Still, while devotion to the Prince was the distinguishing trait of Ralph Channing's little gathering at Cliffview, such devotion had nothing to do with a goatlike figure sprouting pointy ears and cloven hooves and smelling like a polecat on holiday in a garbage dump. Each of these men had long since learned that reality was far different. What everyone here had discovered and committed himself to was an intelligence each had found to be supreme among human beings as such. Their increasingly intimate involvement in the Process had taken on a special cast; had enabled these men—against all odds, and out of all men in the world—to recognize the lineaments of that supreme intelligence at work in the Process, to bow to that intelligence in every practical way and thus to follow the footprints of history.

No one present at Cliffview would be reckoned as an evil person as that word is understood nowadays. A handshake from anyone here was as good as a contract. In matters of politics, they were correct; which is to say, they were never extremist. In social matters, they were acceptable; which is to say they had shown their humanitarian concern and their philanthropic generosity. In matters of marital fidelity, all adhered to the currently accepted norm of respectability.

Nor could anyone daub this group with the insulting label of conspirators. Rather, they were men who happened to feel the same way about human affairs. In this—as any one of them could attest, for they sat as directors on corporate boards around the world—they were not much different than, say, the trustees of Harvard or the board of directors of *The Times* of London. Not much different than the Commissioners of the European Community, if it came to that.

Like those and many other groups, these twelve men operated within the recognized bounds of democratic freedom to see their cherished ideals implemented. Admittedly, this group enjoyed certain advantages that few could equal. The supreme success of each man enabled the group as a whole to engage in social engineering and political molding on a vast scale. But power and success were not what provided them with their greatest leverage.

Their true advantage, as any one of them would attest, stemmed from one thing only: the dedication of each to Spirit as such. To that personage they all described as the Prince. The advantages afforded by that abiding interest seemed infinite to them. The simple fact that their interest did not conform to the interest asserted by the major religions meant they were able to think in a more universal way than they would have as Jews or Christians or Muslims. They were therefore more tolerant. More human.

A second advantage lay in their ability to understand the Process. Their special qualifications ranked them as master engineers. They knew themselves to be among the few ever privileged to understand the superhuman quality and progress at work in the Process. Their vantage point allowed them to understand that the Process is not a matter of one generation or of one century. And though they themselves had risen so high above its day-to-day, year-to-year workings as to recognize the very face of the intelligence behind it, they accepted the reality that for most of the human population—even for most adherents and propagators who functioned at inferior levels—the Process is only known in its workings.

The point for them as master engineers was that those workings themselves must always change. The Process must always grow toward its ultimate goal. In theory, it was something like a chain reaction, with society as the reactor.

It was capital for the Process that change had now become the dominant trait of human society. Minds were being changed. Living language itself was being molded by changing minds. The vocabulary of politics and geopolitics was the vocabulary of change. "Internationalism" had made way for "multinationalism," for example. Then "transnationalism" took center stage. Very soon, it would be "globalism." At every level of life, minds and society itself were being molded and remolded by the never-ending chain reaction of change. Society had come to the brink of recasting its basic structure, shedding its cocoons of separatism. Universalism would soon bring all men and women into one family. One embrace.

When change becomes the slogan and the watchword of society at large, the evolution that is the Process becomes ever more acceptable. Ever more respectable. Ever more inevitable.

"All right, gentlemen." Like a gavel sounding a board meeting to order, Ralph Channing's rough-edged voice ended the chitchat. "Let's get down to the crux of things." As everyone knew, the crux of things was to be the reading of the Categoric Report. As everyone expected from experience, however, Channing had a few remarks to offer first.

"As some of you have surmised, the ultimate directives contained in the Categoric Report itself are based on the significant meeting earlier this month at Strasbourg. Our own Nicholas Clatterbuck, in fact, prepared the summary of that meeting for Cyrus Benthoek. My hope, gentlemen, is that an understanding of the significance of the alliance proposed at Strasbourg will make your minds the more receptive to our proposals.

"Some of the Vatican personnel at Strasbourg might not have understood how far afield the bridges they proposed might reach. Who would have dreamed that the evolution of the Prince's rule would require what the Categoric Report calls 'a religion phase' in the evolutionary engineering of the society of nations? The organized religions cannot simply be condemned and bypassed in favor of occult practices. All, of course, are part of the Process. We now realize that religion is a manifestation of Spirit."

There was a little stirring at that, but as a world-class expert on the world's religions, Channing was not to be challenged. "Yes, I grant it is a misguided and deforming manifestation. Yet, I insist, truly a manifestation. Progressive Spirit in man means progress in religion—and progress, as we know, always leads from the particular and the local to the universal. Logically, in other words—and simply because religions do exist—there must be a religion phase in the evolutionary Process of mankind.

"What we must understand is that we are faced today with a new stage in that evolutionary Process. The final stage! The creation of a one-world religion. Absent all nationalisms, all particularisms and all culturalisms of the past. Now, in its final stages, this evolutionary Process necessarily implies a mechanism by which the religion phase will be refashioned to suit the globalism—the universality—of that New Order.

"In aiding the Process along, our task is to come to the aid of each major religion in such a way as to enable them all to come into one universal embrace. Into one universal religion, in which no religion will be distinguishable from any other. The perfect handmaiden for the New Order of the Ages! Wouldn't you agree, gentlemen?" Channing smiled at the smiling faces around him.

"That much understood—and even granting Jacques Deneuve's conviction that Rome is a cesspool—one further thing must be clear. If we are to bring the religion phase of man to the summit of its evolution—into the full embrace of the Process—then we must consider the role of Roman Catholicism. No." With a glance at the red folder lying on the thirteenth chair, Channing corrected himself at once. "Rather, we must consider the role of papal Catholicism in general and of the papal office in particular.

"And that point, I am happy to say, brings us directly to the reading of the Categoric Report." Channing leaned toward the empty chair beside him to retrieve the leather folder, and handed it to Nicholas Clatterbuck. Clatterbuck read in a soft, kindly voice.

"The following is the Categoric Report drawn up by Capstone on the absolutely necessary measures to be taken by Concilium 13 in view of the imminent Ascent of the Prince of This World."

As if a switch had been thrown, the reading of that opening sentence shifted the mood in Dr. Channing's studio from affable to surreal. Even on Clatterbuck's tongue, Capstone's words were dark velvet, a mantle woven of past achievement and present hope. Lips curled in smiles not pleasurable to see; smiles of death imposed and enjoyed and waiting for a repeat performance.

"Because of the ritual Enthronement of the Prince effected by the in-house Phalanx of servitors within the Citadel of the Enemy—you have always known that it is your privilege to serve in the Availing Time, to facilitate the ultimate triumph of the Prince of This World. The moment has arrived when we must face the obligation to engage the forces of the Enemy in their own stronghold.

"In saying this is an opportunity, we remind you that we have a period of between five and seven years remaining to us before the advantages secured to us in the Enthronement will be nullified. That is our Categoric Persuasion." At such a warning as that, even the Concilium members—even Clatterbuck—stole a look at Dr. Channing. Such was the Professor's command, that a gesture of the hand was sufficient to subdue alarm. The reading was resumed.

"Having clarified the urgency of our obligation, we hasten to say that the time frame made known to us—five to seven years—will be sufficient, on a double condition. First, we must be realistic in our assessment of the major obstacle remaining in the path of our success. Second, we must be equally realistic in the means we engage to remove that obstacle.

"First things first, then: The most ancient and the most recalcitrant obstacle to the Ascent—indeed, the only obstacle to be profoundly respected and guarded against—has been and up to this day still is the Roman Catholic papacy." Clatterbuck was back on familiar ground now. His voice was level again, pleasing to the ear and dispassionate in tone.

"Let us be clear as well that we do not hold authority in itself to be objectionable. On the contrary, there must be authority. But let us be equally clear about authority so complete as personal infallibility and personal representation of the Nameless One. This personalized authority is alien to us—and finally inimical to our interests—because it is inimical to the Ascent. We remain dedicated to the Ascent.

"Some accoutrements of the papal office can be readily adapted as a facilitating instrument for the Ascent. However, in the papacy itself, we face an obstacle that we must regard as something to be feared. It is lethally fearful because in this papacy we are dealing with a dangerous reality. A reality of Spirit. A lump of Otherness that is unique; that is irreconcilable with the progress of the New World Order we envision; and that is ultimately irreconcilable with the Ascent whose heralds we are.

"It is well to be reminded of just how resilient that papal office has been throughout its history. The office itself can be tainted with corruption of every kind. Its holders can be isolated and insulated from the rest of the human race. They can be terminated—gently or violently; in secret or before the eyes of millions. But nobody has ever succeeded in liquidating that office. Nobody and nothing.

"For a lump of Otherness to be so effective and perduring, its force and strength and recuperative power must issue from what is totally alien to us. They must issue from what is totally alien to Capstone and to the Ascent. They must issue from the Nameless One. At this critical moment in our warfare, we who are of the Spirit must stress that we are up against the reality of Spirit. Contrary Spirit—but Spirit all the same.

"In this last glorious stage of the Ascent, our most concerted action now must be directed toward the prime locus of resistance to our aims. Consequently, our Categoric Report itself is centered on one question: What is to be done about the personalized papacy, with all of its stubborn resiliency?

"Our response dictates a turnabout in our strategies. Or, better, an escalation of our strategies to a level that even you of the Concilium may not have considered possible. We have said that the papal office is to be respected, feared and guarded against. Now, however, we have determined that we can no longer be defensive. Rather than guard against the power of that office, we will make it our own.

"Our Categoric Decision—and the object of our agenda over the five to seven advantageous years remaining to us—must be this: To secure the papal office, with all of its resiliency, to ourselves. And to do that by ensuring that the holder of that office be a man on whom we can rely to be adaptable to our needs. We will review for you now the limited options by which we might achieve this goal. Those options are basically three in number: Persuasion. Liquidation. Resignation.

"Consider, first, persuasion. The possibility that the present holder of the papal office himself might be induced or persuaded to such a complacency and acceptance as our sworn purpose requires. Unfortunately, we must report that in the ultimate judgment of our expert cognoscenti—including in-house members of the Phalanx who reside in close proximity to the office—the present holder will never see the wisdom of our agenda.

"Nor do we have the luxury of time to wait him out. On the basis of actuarial and personal health data, we may be looking at four to seven years more of active physical existence for the present holder. Given our Categoric Persuasion that we are working in the constricted and currently running time span of not more than seven years, we must proceed to the next two options: the liquidation or the resignation of the present holder of the papal office.

"In practical terms, either option will yield the result we desire and leave us free to install a new, complaisant holder. As is often the way in important matters, the step that might appear to be the most difficult—the installation of a friendly occupant—is the easier part of our task. We need not remind anyone in the Concilium that we are now enjoying the marvelous facility afforded us by the growing number of our regular Phalanx of in-house supporters. And beyond that, a number of personnel who actually assisted at the Enthronement ceremony in 1963 are themselves still in place, and have ascended to such high posts within the Citadel as to assure our success. Thus we will not merely be forcing Contrary Spirit to vacate one friendly house of its habitation, only to enter into another, equally friendly house. There would be no point for us in that.

"No, the candidate to replace the present holder of the office will be someone acquainted with our aims, acquiescent in them at the very least and even fully disposed to collaborate in achieving those aims.

"The task of removal, therefore, must be the focus of our urgent and unremitting attention. The first of the two alternatives by which to achieve removal would be the most satisfying. On the surface it might even seem the easiest, and therefore the most tempting. We speak of personal liquidation.

"Were Concilium 13 to undertake such a procedure, it would be meticulously planned and immaculately executed. In your hands, we would not be faced with anything resembling the stupid initiative of 1981. Yet, even were we to succeed in an open move against the person of the present holder of the office, the results could still be disastrous for us. We would not be able to hide behind such cover as 'the nasty Bulgars' or 'KGB death technology' or 'segregated files' or 'CIA manipulation.' None of the extravaganzas of popular commentary that served as camouflage for the 1981 initiative are any longer available.

"Still, if swift and openly executed liquidation is likely to be self-defeating by its nature, one might ask if there are modified but nevertheless effective means of liquidation. We know of concrete proposals along the lines of such a gradual and modified liquidation. All of them, however, have been complicated by the security means adopted at the papal office since 1981; means so extensive and detailed that they include security even for all ingestion.

"Furthermore, the mere fact that we know of such proposals underlines another prime reason why we should not ourselves succumb to any temptation along these lines. There is no such thing as a secret. In the final analysis, all is betrayed; all is revealed; all is known. Remember that we are dealing with Spirit—volatile, unpredictable, wild in its ways, blowing and sweeping where it wills.

"It is our Categoric Judgment that those who hand us any proposition for such a solution are in reality handing us a live grenade, inviting us to pull the pin and explode into the fragments of our own self-liquidation.

"There remains, then, the Chosen Alternative. The Categoric Choice by which we will achieve our goal is resignation. Briefly stated, the present holder of the office will be induced to resign from that office—and without prejudice.

"A voluntary papal resignation, at this crux of divisiveness and disunity among the ordinary RC laity and between churchmen themselves, would be a powerful signal; nothing less than an admission of defeat for important elements who stand against us. It would be a declaration to the remaining defenders of the old order of things that the past is irretrievable. Indeed, the climate is such that there is already a certain sympathy among the old order for our Chosen Alternative. An openly expressed sympathy, we might add, in strategic quarters within the target ranks.

"When we speak of inducing the holder to resign, inducement must be understood in its subtlest form. We speak of effecting all the means at your disposal in the world. For the most powerful inducement will be the pressure of irreversible events and the emergence of irresistible power lines. Events and power lines must be devised to constrict the actions of the holder. The only one course left to him will be resignation of the papal office.

"In the report recounting for us the events of the recent meeting at Strasbourg hosted by Mr. Cyrus Benthoek, our Nicholas Clatterbuck clearly indicates that we have potential allies not previously identified as secure. Individuals who are highly influential within the Citadel and who have in effect joined hands with those in-house Phalanx members who were also present at Strasbourg. They have said they are eager for a radical change at the topmost level of administration. And in their eagerness, they open to us their own powerful lines of global persuasion.

"Moreover, there is an ancillary and even more important initiative under way in which we have also in effect been invited to cooperate, again through Cyrus Benthoek. An initiative that involves the formation of a close and systematic alliance between virtually every ranking churchman of Europe's heartland and the European Community. That initiative is to be facilitated.

"All in all, the way has been opened for us, in strict conformity with the

Canon Law of the Citadel, for the peaceful departure of the present holder of the papal office. Your charge is to seize upon these two significant advantages that have been handed to us. Your charge is to take in hand the Strasbourg proposal, and the intended alliance between the Citadel and the EC. Your charge is to use those two advantages to create the irreversible events and to evoke the irresistible power lines that will render the papal office useless to the Nameless Other and deliver it into the hands of the servitors of the Prince."

It remained only for Clatterbuck to fill his associates in on the plans designed to link the bishops of Europe to the interests of the European Community. One of the firm's talented younger men, Clatterbuck explained—Paul Thomas Gladstone—was to be installed in the powerful post of Secretary-General to the Commissioners of the EC. Gladstone's brother, Father Christian Thomas Gladstone, would serve as the Vatican link. Under close direction from Rome, and with his brother as his intimate tie to the Commissioners, Father Gladstone would lead the bishops into professional cooperation with the policies and aims of the EC.

Nicholas Clatterbuck concluded his briefing by emphasizing one final point. Both the EC initiative and the Strasbourg alliance depended for the moment on the reliability of His Eminence Cardinal Cosimo Maestroianni. Father Christian Gladstone was to be his creature. And, while it was true that the soon-to-be-retired Secretary of State had been cultivated by Cyrus Benthoek as a special friend, it was also true that Benthoek was not a member of the Concilium. Since Benthoek was not privy to such a high level of intelligence, it followed that his judgment of the Cardinal's probity and reliability was not to be trusted as final. Even ordinary prudence dictated, therefore, that one of their number should check the Cardinal out personally.

That much agreed by all, Dr. Ralph Channing selected himself as the man to meet with Maestroianni. "To cement this relationship," as he expressed it, "and get things moving in high gear."

If the Cardinal passed muster—if his consent was unquestionable and the contract with him as working ally could be regarded as firm and reliable—then matters could proceed swiftly. Gynneth Blashford suggested that Clatterbuck could easily arrange for Cyrus Benthoek to join the Professor in paying a visit to their new Roman friend. "Friends of friends always ease the way, don't you think?"

It was settled, then. If all went well, those in Rome who had reached out for help in securing radical change at the topmost level of power would get more than most of them had bargained for.

XIV

IN THE SCHEME OF THINGS—at that exalted level of power where warriors set out to conquer the minds of others and fashion their strategies of global warfare—Dr. Ralph S. Channing reckoned himself to be more than a match for Cardinal Cosimo Maestroianni.

The primary concern for Channing in "assuring the stability of Rome" turned less on questions of the Cardinal's capabilities or his grasp on power in the Citadel than on whether His Eminence might be no more than a high-ranking turncoat as likely to cross one master as he had another. Before he left New York, therefore, the Professor made it his business to know the Cardinal Secretary's record of accomplishments in office. On the way to Rome via London, he plumbed Cyrus Benthoek for what became a lively, convincing and even affectionate personal sketch based on long association with the Roman churchman. Finally, with Benthoek as his ticket of entrée, Channing's introduction to Maestroianni's penthouse apartment capped the promise of coming collaboration.

The valet who opened the door to Cardinal Maestroianni's private domain was an exceedingly small man whom Benthoek addressed with the greatest respect as Signor Mario. Dignity was his as a personal possession. There was nothing spontaneous about him. Every step he took seemed measured. Every smile was formal.

Signor Mario declared himself pleased to see Signor Benthoek again; it had been too long. He bowed a superior bow to Dr. Channing.

As they followed the little valet with unquestioning obedience through the spacious hallway leading to Maestroianni's private study, the floor-to-ceiling cityscapes engulfed the pair with their almost mystic aura, just as they always engulfed Maestroianni. Indeed, that corridor alone served for Channing as an accurate marker of profound dedication to the achievement of mankind's original oneness, for no one could doubt that oneness was the aim of the Conference on Security and Cooperation in Europe.

As if he knew just how much time to allow for the Helsinki corridor to have its effect, Signor Mario measured his pace toward the farthest doors and into His Eminence's private study. "Do feel at home." The valet made it seem more a command than an invitation. "His Eminence will be with you presently."

Alone for the moment with Benthoek, Channing surveyed his surroundings with undisguised interest. As a first-class scholar himself, he knew a first-class library when he saw one. A well-used library that captured the very essence of the passion with which His Eminence obviously followed history's evolving record. "A superb collection," Channing cooed his approval to Benthoek as he spied several of his own monographs piled on the near side of the center table.

Cardinal Maestroianni himself bustled theatrically through the door from an adjoining room. "As you can see, Dr. Channing, you really are no stranger among us in these parts. I've just been reading your monograph on the geopolitics of demography. Marvelous work. I'm indebted to Cyrus for bringing us together like this."

Channing's sensuous mouth curled upward behind his goatee as he clasped the Cardinal's outstretched hand. He hadn't expected such a tiny man. Small men who wielded great power made the Professor nervous. "The pleasure is all mine, Eminence!"

Cardinal Maestroianni led his guests to a trio of comfortable chairs gathered around a tea table laden with ice and sparkling water. A pleasant breeze played through the open windows. With his Roman instinct as his guide, Maestroianni contented himself with small talk for some moments; though he knew Channing, personal impressions and assessments were what counted in the end.

It was Cyrus Benthoek who first lost patience with the small talk. "I decided to call on you, Eminence," he plunged in, "because we all have a common objective. Dr. Channing has made it clear to me that he not only shares the objective we fixed up at Strasbourg but can engineer virtually all of the bridges required."

Maestroianni nodded, but remained unhelpful. He would not make an early move.

Cyrus was determined to prime the pump. "I've taken the liberty of detailing the substance of our Strasbourg meeting for Dr. Channing. And I must tell you, Eminence, it was a pleasant task. It was almost as if the good Professor knew beforehand all about the work of Cardinal Aureatini's Christian Adult Renewal Rite. And about Cardinal Palombo's International Council for Christian Liturgy. Very reassuring, Eminence. Very promising."

"I see." Maestroianni had taken that much for granted. He shifted his attention pointedly toward Channing. He wanted a direct statement from this outsider.

Channing understood. His voice was as categoric as his choice of words. "Your Eminence knows how far the Process has come in bringing the nations of the West along the road of economic, financial and cultural homogenization. We are already talking about more than twoscore nations and a population of somewhere near a billion.

"If all goes according to plan, within two to four years, the member countries of the European Community will be transformed. Every country will lose control over most areas of its economic life and policy. Foreign and defense policies are already being determined at least in part by supranational needs and pressures. The sovereign nation-state will soon be a thing of the past."

Maestroianni nodded in patient agreement. He needed no lectures on the accomplishments and virtues of the Process.

Channing realized he had better move to the more personal accomplishments of the Cardinal Secretary. "Now, during Your Eminence's tenure as Secretary of State, the foreign policy of the Holy See has been faithful in its alignment with this trend of the Process. To use one of your own consecrated Catholic phrases, for the past twenty-five years, your Church has been determined to 'join mankind in building mankind's earthly habitat.' Why, even your basic act of religious worship—the Mass itself—now bears the stamp of our most cherished goal. The *Novus Ordo,* you call it. The New Order!"

Channing made the point with such style that even Maestroianni had to soften his reserve.

"I don't mean to bring coals to Newcastle, Eminence, when I point out that such policies emanating from your office have created a deep fissure in your Catholic hierarchy. As nearly as my colleagues and I can see, a good majority of your bishops—especially in the West—are enthusiastic for this new orientation of the Church. They are practical men, after all. And they do not enjoy the luxury of living in this sovereign city-state of the Vatican." Dr. Channing allowed himself an expansive gesture toward the view from the Cardinal's penthouse. "They are subject already to the pressures of the EC and the CSCE and the Free Trade Agreements of Europe, North America and Asia.

"Like everyone else, your RC bishops surely realize that either they will become active participants in the building of this global New Order or they will be swallowed up in the daily lives of their compatriots. What sort of a Church would that be, Eminence? A Church of the new catacombs! As influential as Tibetan astrologers at NASA!"

Maestroianni had to laugh. He didn't much care for Dr. Channing hammering away at what he called "your bishops." But the Professor could turn an amusing phrase.

"Here's the problem, though." Channing leaned forward in his chair. "The current occupant of the Throne of Peter bends his energies in a totally different direction. My colleagues and I see him as heir to the unacceptable persuasion that his Church embodies an absolute authority carrying over into doctrinal mandates that forbid Catholics to come into step with their fellow citizens of the world.

"Now the urgent point for many is this: The present occupant of the papal office would appear to have more than a few years of active life, while the useful time for your Church to get in on the ground floor of the new world structure is not five or ten years hence." Having all but come out in so many words with the motive for this meeting—for the purpose of the removal of the present Pope from office—Dr. Channing leaned back in pensive silence.

According to Clatterbuck, Maestroianni and his colleagues at Strasbourg had themselves decided that a change in the papal structure of their Church was essential; and they had been the ones to ask for exactly the sort of outside help Channing could command. Yet, aside from a few little nods of assent now and then, and an appreciative chuckle or two, the Cardinal Secretary remained tranquilly noncommittal. How much more would it take to move this pretentious little prelate? How much further should Channing himself go in the effort to get things moving?

One step further, perhaps. Professor Channing leaned forward again. "Timing, Eminence. That is what brings the three of us together. I'm well aware of where I am this afternoon. And I hope not to exceed the limits of prudence. But I feel I must speak as truly among brothers now." Channing included Benthoek in his figurative embrace.

"Without my going into privileged details, you will understand that on our side of things we also are working within a constricted time span. We expect a great event to take place in this world of nations. We estimate that we have as few as five years. Seven at most. Of course, that event is intimately linked with the emergence of the New Order among nations. But it is not, properly speaking, a merely economic or social or political happening. Let me say only this much: It is in the nature of a humanistic realization of the most spiritual kind." Dr. Channing left his companions to dangle on that slim thread of information.

Maestroianni looked quizzically at Benthoek. But there was no answer from that quarter. Cyrus, it seemed, was as much in the dark about Channing's expected "great event" as the Cardinal himself. "In that case, Doctor"—the Cardinal Secretary heaved a great sigh—"let us match your urgency with our own."

A look of satisfaction from Channing.

Maestroianni quickly conceded every point his guest had made. Sovereignty, he agreed—whether nationalistic or religious—was not merely being rendered useless as a strategic necessity for survival but was itself a positive threat to survival and an enemy of progress in mankind's new and harmonious habitat.

"You see, Dr. Channing, it is one thing to say that many of our bishops appear to be enthusiastic for the innovations that we have introduced into the Church. But still today, that papal authority is effective for many millions of Catholics and is deeply influential far beyond the Catholic fold. The papal office still remains the exclusive locus of authoritative power over the minds and wills of believers. Authoritative power to decide what believers believe; and to decree the exact rules of their behavior in their private lives and in the public square."

Channing frowned. His Eminence seemed to be putting a very hard face on matters. But surely he must have a solution.

Maestroianni's smile was almost smug. "Our concept is fairly simple. A bureaucratic solution, as Cyrus might say, to a complex bureaucratic problem. Clearly, if we are to eliminate religious as well as political sovereignty as a pernicious force in the affairs of mankind, we must devise persuasive and legally acceptable machinery that will satisfy two purposes: it must deal with the doctrine and the centuries-long tradition in this Church, according to which power and authority are centered in the Petrine office; and that same machinery must ensure that unity between Pope and bishops is not shattered. Without unity, there would be no such thing as the Church Universal. Its usefulness as a global partner would be lost.

"That being so, our proposal is for implementation of a program that will shift the locus of authoritative power away from the office of Pope. A program, moreover, that will transform unity itself into a prime operative factor in our favor as we progress.

"The bishops in Vatican II made it clear that, as successors to the twelve Apostles, they share governing authority over the Church Universal—with the Bishop of Rome. The bishops returned home from the Council and formed their own National Conferences," Maestroianni pursued his review of shifting power. "And in specific regions of the world, those National Bishops Conferences formed themselves into Regional Bishops Conferences. Twenty-five years later, the result is a new Church structure. Instead of a unique, one-way, exclusivist power line running downward from the Pope and extending through the entire Church Universal, we now have multiple layers of crisscrossing power lines. As many power lines as there are National and Regional Conferences.

"In a word, the Church Universal is now a grid, a network formed of these Bishops Conferences. By their nature and their mandate, they are disposed to constant action and reaction with the Vatican Chancery and with the papacy. And, while each Conference is headed by a local bishop, all of the bishops have come to rely on *periti*, as they are called. On expert advisors. I presume you are aware of the influence of the *periti* on the bishops in Vatican II?"

Channing nodded.

"The result is that many of our bishops now find themselves at odds with the policies of the present pontificate. And they are already limiting the extent and the influence of the once unique power line of the papacy. We have judged the time to be right to bring their dissatisfaction with Rome into a sharper focus.

Channing thought he was keeping pace with Maestroianni. "Your goal being the removal of the present holder of the papal office."

"No, Professor. We see the voluntary resignation of the present Pontiff as essential, of course. Our ultimate aim is far more ambitious. We will elicit from the bishops themselves—and I speak of an overwhelming majority of the four thousand bishops around the world—a formal instrument of canonical validity that we have aptly called the 'Common Mind of the Bishops.'

"If we are successful, it will no longer be the Pope who commands unity. Rather, it will be the bishops themselves who require a Pope of unity. A Pope with whom they can feel themselves comfortably united as an episcopal body. That is to say, the Common Mind of the Bishops must logically be to regard the Pope not as the Vicar of Christ, but as the Vicar of Peter, the first Bishop of Rome. Further, the Common Mind of the Bishops must logically be to regard all bishops—equally and together—as the collective Vicar of Christ."

Ralph Channing was impressed. Were His Eminence's thinking to be adopted as official Church teaching, the governing structure of the Church would be profoundly altered. The centralizing role of the Vatican would disappear. In religious matters, the Pope would no longer be supreme pastor. In political matters, he would no longer be sovereign. No change would have to be confirmed by the Pontiff in order to become valid.

"So, Your Eminence. Now that you have clarified your goal, may we discuss the steps by which you intend to reach it? For I presume that is where you want our assistance?"

"Precisely." Having come this far, it was easy for Maestroianni to lay out the three stages by which to proceed. "Step one will be the most arduous. Working through the vehicle of their Conferences, we will introduce the bishops to the many practical advantages and perks of the New World Order. Our strategy must be to key in first on the Conferences headed by the most influential bishops." In Maestroianni's unassailable judgment, the key Conferences were those of Western Europe.

"Why?" The Cardinal's question was obviously rhetorical. "Simply because the bishops in those countries have the longest and richest of traditions. Because all of those bishops reside in areas whose populations are presently being homogenized and united in the coming Greater Europe. And because those bishops will understand that their inclusion in the new public consensus will be vital to all the issues that make their organizations viable.

"Of course, we must be able to offer advantages that are vital to their needs. Banking facilities, for example. And social facilitation for their evangelization efforts. And legislation favorable to their civil rights; to their position in the educational establishment; to their privileged tax status; to the wink-wink handling of legal cases brought against their misbehaving clerics.

"As that consensus progresses, the bishops will find themselves increasingly at odds with papal policies. With the aid of those multilayered Bishops Conferences, another level of consensus will be elicited. A solidly formed, formally voted and openly expressed consensus: the Common Mind of the Bishops. That instrument itself will be stated in such categoric terms as 'The present Holy Father is not a Pope of unity. The Mind of the

Bishops is that we seek a Pope of unity. The Mind of the Bishops is that he offer his resignation from office, as every other bishop is now required to do, at the age of seventy-five.' "

Maestroianni smiled conspiratorially at Channing. "There is no doubt that this Pope is a stubborn man. Nonetheless, it is impossible to imagine that even he will be able to withstand the extraordinary pressures exerted upon him by this formal instrument of his Church. This Common Mind of the Bishops, expressed officially through the Bishops Conferences, by which every quarter of the episcopate demands his resignation. All in all I personally have no doubt that within a span of two to three years we will receive the resignation of the current Holy Father."

Channing seemed almost transfixed. "I'm with you, Eminence."

"Step two, then." Cardinal Maestroianni moved quickly on. "When any other bishop resigns, the Pontiff receives his resignation, and either confirms or rejects it. However, since we cannot expect this man to receive and confirm his own resignation, we must have another means—a body of bishops, equally acceptable constitutionally—to receive the papal resignation and to confirm it. Only rarely do the bishops exercise their episcopal jurisdiction in unison and act as one body. But we do have such a body of bishops. The International Synod of Bishops, which meets every so often in Rome. Because it acts hierarchically in the name of the entire episcopate, and in solicitude for the Church Universal, the Synod is the obvious candidate to receive and to confirm the papal resignation.

"And that, gentlemen, brings us to step three, the easiest step of all. A papal conclave will be organized in the time-honored fashion to elect a new Pope."

Cyrus Benthoek realized for the first time just how complete and detailed a plan had actually been devised. He was profoundly impressed. "Well, then, Eminence! I believe we are at step one in your process? And I believe we are to concentrate first on the bishops of Europe?"

"And"—Channing was equally enthusiastic—"I believe that is where my colleagues and I come in?"

"Correct." Maestroianni responded to both men with a single answer. "The proposed Common Mind of the Bishops will come to nothing unless we can assure that the bishops themselves are brought into early, active and profitable alignment with the unified structure of the Greater Europe. To that end, Dr. Channing, circumstances have presented us with two cogs for our machinery of persuasion. Two brothers, no less.

"One of them, Father Christian Gladstone, is—or soon can be—in the service of the Vatican. Paul Gladstone, meanwhile, has earned his stripes as an internationalist of considerable ability within Cyrus' own operations. We will take care to promote our clerical brother to a position of directive authority in the Synod of Bishops. Under our close direction, he will travel as a kind of roving Vatican ambassador in order to make close assessments of the needs of each target bishop for all of the practical facilities I mentioned earlier.

"Now, in order for us to be able to deliver on such promises to the bishops as Father Christian Gladstone deems necessary under our direction—and since the post of Secretary-General to the Council of Ministers of the European Community is happily falling vacant—it is our proposal that Paul Gladstone be selected in preference to all other candidates now under consideration to fill that post.

"So, Dr. Channing, we are now down to practical matters of implementation. To the heart of the matter. For now we can reduce everything in this discussion to two simple questions: Can you secure the post of Secretary-General to the EC Council of Ministers for Mr. Paul Gladstone? And if you can do it, will you do it?"

Silence fell for a time over the trio in Cardinal Maestroianni's study. It was as though each man had given leave to his fellows to retire for consultation behind the cloak of his own thoughts.

Maestroianni did not look to Cyrus Benthoek for support or approval as was his custom. It was Benthoek who found himself unsettled for a change. The lengthening silence was most irritating for him. Benthoek did not pretend to understand things at the Professor's level; he could not presume to read the mind of such a master engineer. But neither could he fathom what might be holding such a bright fellow as Channing back from immediate agreement.

In truth, there wasn't much to hold Channing back. Any doubts that might have lingered about Cardinal Maestroianni himself seemed fully satisfied. The Cardinal's proposed program itself, meanwhile, appeared to be a suitable blueprint for arriving at the Chosen Alternative set out by Concilium 13 in the Categoric Report.

Nevertheless, wasn't Maestroianni's assessment of the bishops too pat? Had the bishops truly become stranded in such a desert? Was their consciousness of their duty to their Pope so diminished as to permit a majority to be swayed so easily into a preference for their own individual interests?

Benthoek finally could stand the silence no more. Hoping the sound would be like Niagara crashing on boulders, he rattled fresh ice cubes into his glass and splashed sparkling water noisily up to its brim.

Startled, Channing took the point. "Right enough, then." The Professor took up as though there had been no pause at all. "You have reduced matters cogently to two questions, Eminence. And I answer both of them unequivocally in the affirmative. We can secure the EC post for Paul Gladstone. And we shall." Of course, there were still a few details. . . . "Nothing serious," Channing assured his companions.

"Such as?" Maestroianni was still not entirely easy with this alien in his world.

"Such as a full dossier on each of the Gladstone brothers." Channing began with the obvious.

Maestroianni had to smile at that. "Anything more, Dr. Channing?"

"There is one more thing, now that you ask, Eminence." He was sure the Cardinal would be the first to realize that he was calling on the vast resources of the fraternity; and for a protracted period of time. Some tangible record of His Eminence's request for collaboration would be helpful in "opening up all of the required connections at the Level of the Thirteen."

Cardinal Maestroianni rose from his chair so abruptly that Benthoek wondered in alarm if he had taken offense at Channing's request. He watched Maestroianni head for his desk, where he opened one of the drawers and appeared to fiddle with switches of some kind. In short order, Channing's own voice was coming back over a sound system. ". . . all of the required connections at the Level of Thirteen." The Cardinal rewound the tape he had just sampled, removed the spool and held it up between two fingers. "I presume a voice record will satisfy your requirements?" It was a presumption that did not require an answer. Maestroianni slipped the spool into an unmarked envelope and held it in his hands like a carrot to entice a donkey.

"I have one final recommendation to make before we are finished here." For the moment, the Cardinal Secretary made no move to rejoin his companions. "I have cautioned you already that our present Pontiff is stubborn. Stubborn; and dedicated to the defense of the papal office. I have mentioned also that he has a certain measure of support. And in the past he has been both wily and determined enough to bring down governments."

Channing glared at him. "Are you having second thoughts so soon, Eminence?"

Maestroianni was less intimidated than annoyed by such undisguised menace.

"Not at all," Maestroianni retorted smoothly. "I have little doubt that in the near future we will be able to congratulate ourselves on our support by a sizable majority of bishops. But given the stiff-necked nature of this Holy Father, and to be on the safe side, we should anticipate the need for a little extra bit of pressure. One skillful turn of the screw to set the machinery of papal resignation into final and irrevocable motion.

"You have said, Dr. Channing, that we speak here as members of a fraternity embarked on great undertakings. In that vein, I call upon you now to understand that in a terminal situation such as we envision—in the most delicate and sensitive part of our operation—we will very likely require some added fraternal cooperation that cannot be outlined now, and that will not be a part of this recording."

Channing was relieved. If it was a matter of "terminal situations" and "a skillful turn of the screw," the Cardinal Secretary was talking to the right man. "You will not find us wanting, Eminence."

Maestroianni turned toward his old colleague. Benthoek, too, would be very much a part of the operation. "Agreed, Cyrus?"

"Agreed, my friend."

XV

SINCE THAT strange Saturday morning in early May when the Holy Father's urgent request for the photographs of Bernini's *Noli Me Tangere* statue had brought him face to face with Cardinal Secretary Cosimo Maestroianni—and despite Father Aldo Carnesecca's arguments to the contrary from that day to this—Christian Gladstone's sense that he was an out-of-place foreigner in this Rome of the Popes had only intensified.

As the summer heat began to mount, Father Aldo and Christian had taken to walking together on Saturday afternoons, usually along the Via Appia. There, the two friends found calm and solitude among the tombstones, the shrines and the olive groves. Because he found Carnesecca to be a man of honor, Gladstone could air his mind about anything with him, and found himself constantly challenging Father Aldo for his reading of the policies of the present Pope.

Gladstone wanted to know why the Pope didn't just get rid of all the schismatics and the lewd priests? Why the recent appointment of an obviously heretical bishop as head of one of the major papal Congregations? Why, instead of going after the heretics, the Pope had singled out Archbishop Lefebvre for punishment, when Lefebvre tried to defend the Church? Why was this Pope so disapproving of the U.S.A.'s Desert Storm?

Carnesecca kept harping on the key issue at stake in the governance of the Holy See of the 1990s: the virtual tying of the Pope's hands by both bishops and in-house Vatican officials. "He's in a straitjacket, Chris. He has very little real control."

"It doesn't wash, Aldo. The man is Pope."

These walks and talks with Carnesecca had done little to soften Christian's attitude toward a possible Roman career. Over the hectic weeks of May and June, in fact, his impatience to get away from Rome became difficult to disguise. As had been the case since 1984, when he had first begun spending his second semester of the academic year at the Angelicum, the end of June would see Gladstone's arrival in the northeastern French city of Colmar. There, he had long ago come upon the great treasure of the Unterlinden Kloster Museum—the unrivaled masterpiece of the sixteenth-century painter Mathias Grünewald; the enormous Isenheim altarpiece depicting the sufferings and death of Christ.

It had taken Grünewald the best part of ten years to complete his great altarpiece. Given Christian's dual teaching stint in Rome and New Orleans, it was taking him just as long to complete his thesis inspired by Grünewald's masterwork. Each year, he relished the few uninterrupted weeks during which he was able to immerse himself in that endeavor—in that labor of love. Come the third week of August, no matter how engrossed he might be, he would set off for Windswept House in Galveston, a time of reunion with his mother and with his younger sister, Tricia. If he was lucky, maybe his brother Paul would even make it home this time, along with his wife, Yusai, and their little son, Declan.

It would be a time, too, to prepare for that part of each academic year he spent as professor of dogmatic theology at the Major Seminary in his home diocese of New Orleans. He would make it a point to spend some hours again with Father Angelo Gutmacher, that friend and most intimate confessor of his younger years. Christian hoped to sort out at least some of his confusions about Rome with such a good priest and such a level head. In anticipation, Christian had already written to Gutmacher to share something of his debates with Father Aldo. He had remarked on Carnesecca's curious idea that the Holy Father might be as much a stranger in Rome as Christian himself.

Before his time in Colmar or his return to Windswept House, however, Christian had to face the same year-end frenzy that gripped everyone in Rome. During the early weeks of June, his normally heavy load of daily lectures and seminars gave way to the pressures of preparing, administering and then evaluating the results of year-end oral and written examinations for some sixty students of vastly differing background and often deficient preparation for higher studies. In addition, there would be long meetings with all the other members of the Angelicum faculty for a complete review of the academic year. It was understandable, then, that all academic activities had ceased and the various universities were nearly emptied of their student populations, before Father Christian was able to give serious thought to his own obligatory year-end interview with his superior at the Angelicum, Master-General Damien Duncan Slattery.

"Ah, there you are, lad!" Despite the lateness of the hour, Father Damien opened the door of his study and invited Christian with a grand sweep of one enormous arm to rest his bones in the big chair beside his big desk. Father Damien settled himself into his own chair, his shock of white hair glowing in the lamplight like an unruly halo.

Despite the easy tone of the Master-General's greeting, it wasn't long before Gladstone began to have the sense that something was troubling him. The young American wasn't subtle enough to figure out what the difficulty might be, but it wasn't for a low-ranking priest to question his superior. A certain unwritten protocol left such a positive initiative to one's religious superior.

For some quarter of an hour or so, Slattery listened with an almost too sober attention to Gladstone's summary of the academic year at the Angelicum. He interrupted from time to time with questions about several of the more promising priests who would be returning for further studies. He discussed with Christian what had gone wrong for the priests who hadn't measured up. Given that Christian would spend the following semester, from September to January, teaching at New Orleans, the American turned his attention to the archival records of the Angelicum. "They're up to the minute, Father Master. Up to the minute, that is, except for the house inventory I began in early May. There's still some work to be done there."

The Dominican took the materials Gladstone turned over to him into one huge hand and set them on his desk for the moment. "We'll try to keep things in order while you're gone from us, *Padre.*"

There it was again; that feeling in Christian's gut that Slattery had something on his mind.

"You're off to Colmar, then, Father Christian?"

The question shifted the conversation to the younger man's coming work on the Isenheim altarpiece. Christian knew he didn't have to review the work he had already completed on his thesis. What he did want to do, though, was to ask the Master-General's views on certain aspects of his thinking, and lay out his work plan for the coming weeks in Colmar.

Again, Slattery posed one or two acute questions by way of light-handed guidance. That was Father Damien's way as thesis director. "When you're finished at Colmar, you'll head straight back to the States, Father Christian?"

"Yes, Master-General. If I didn't return home by August end, my mother would have my head!"

Normally, the humor in Christian's voice would have sparked a reaction in kind from Slattery. But now, instead of responding to Gladstone at all, the Dominican Rector veered to an apparently unrelated thought. "Tell me, *Padre.* In all your time in Rome, have you ever had a one-on-one meeting with the Holy Father?"

Christian's confusion was as obvious as his answer was short. "No, Father Master." Then, taking the unwelcome implication behind the question, he added with misgiving, "Not yet, anyway. . . ."

The tone of the young American's voice said it all for Slattery. Gladstone would do whatever priestly obedience required of him. But a meeting with His Holiness, much less a close association in the specifically papal work of the Holy See, would clearly not be to his liking. Father Damien hesitated for a second or two, and then seemed to come to some sort of decision. "Well, Father." He rose from his chair. "Perhaps we'll think and talk about that another day."

Christian got to his feet as protocol now required, and took his leave. He was halfway out the door when Father Damien's hearty baritone pursued him with an old Irish farewell.

"May you come back to us on the sweet winds of Heaven, Father Christian!"

Damien Slattery was uncomfortable with himself over his hesitation about whether to alert Christian Gladstone to the changes that were likely in store for him in the near future. Immediately after the Bernini statue affair had brought him to the notice of Cardinal Maestroianni, an uncommon interest in the American had surfaced in the Secretariat of State. It wasn't Maestroianni's habit to waste time on men for whom he had no practical use. Whatever plans His Eminence had in mind, Damien reckoned that they would land the American, unprepared and unsuspecting, smack in the midst of all the confusion. Sooner rather than later the moment would come when, somehow, Gladstone's mind and spirit would have to be prepared for what lay ahead. Had Slattery been wrong not to start that preparation tonight?

He perused some of the records Christian had left with him. Large-minded perception and generous care were evident in all the entries that centered on the priestly formation of his student. Even the most boring aspects of his duties as archivist had been tended to with unusual grace.

Slattery snapped the books closed. It was a safe enough bet that he would be handing these records back to Gladstone well before January. God willing, it would be time enough then to worry about the real-world education of Father Christian Thomas Gladstone.

No matter how many times Gladstone entered the Unterlinden Kloster of Colmar and looked on the Isenheim altarpiece, he always underwent the same waves of wonder and humbling admiration. The first time he had stepped in front of the altarpiece, he was stunned and stood stock-still. Without any warning, his heart and his mind and his soul filled to overflowing. What Christian saw that day was a depiction of the sufferings and death of Christ that was so appalling—so ravishing in its beauty and so cruel in its realism—that it was some moments before he could catch his breath.

Carved in wood and painted, the altarpiece consisted of two fixed panels and four movable wings. Grünewald had steeped every scene of the events, from Gethsemane to Golgotha, with color that seemed to emanate from light itself. And light in turn seemed to transfigure the shocking and to transcend the beautiful. It was as though the Isenheim *rétable* wasn't painted wood at all, but a transparent veil through which the most overwhelming ugliness and degradation of evil in the world could be glimpsed with the eye—the supernal ecstasy—of divinity.

All of that simply took shape out of light. Grew out of light. Illumined Christian's soul with light. There was no way he could grasp it, so overwhelming was the vision. He had tried, though. That very afternoon, he had to try. Little by little, he had found himself suffused by light. By color. By the very essence of the suffering depicted. Until finally—suffering itself was transformed in the face of the Crucified Christ.

Christian Gladstone had found his miracle.

This June, after a good night's sleep, Gladstone was at his post early the following morning, photographs of Grünewald's masterpiece in his hand. His first intention was to compare the photographs with the original as to accuracy; those photographs were destined to appear in Gladstone's actual doctoral thesis. But suddenly, a new thought peeked into his mind like a guest arriving uninvited and uncertain of welcome. He suddenly saw an entirely different scene open out.

It was early May again, and he was standing beside Father Aldo Carnesecca in the basement chapel of the Dominican head-house. He was working again with the Vatican photographer to get the best possible shots of Bernini's *Noli Me Tangere.* He was faxing the finest of the lot off to the Holy Father in Baume. "Of course!" Gladstone whispered the words aloud as he remembered the expression Bernini had captured in the face of the Magdalene.

Of course. It had to be. The Holy Father, too, had been reaching out for inspiration. For a miracle, even. Maybe for the same kind of miracle Christian had stumbled across so unexpectedly all those years ago in the cavern of the Unterlinden Kloster Museum. Except, there was a difference. Christian had been looking for a miracle without even knowing it. But, if his uninvited thought was on target, the Slavic Pope must have known he wanted a miracle.

His sudden realization was humbling for Christian. How arrogant he seemed to himself now, in the uncompromisingly stern judgments he had aired to Carnesecca about the policies of the Holy See, and about the Pope's seeming acquiescence in so much of the skulduggery going on in the Church. Perhaps Carnesecca was right after all. Perhaps there was much more to be seen in all that was going on than Gladstone had so far been willing to admit. Chris reminded himself how his brother Paul often said that arrogance was a Gladstone trait. He supposed Paul was right. Arrogance was almost to be expected of a family whose motto was "No Quarter." And it was certainly to be expected of any son of Cessi Gladstone. Still, no Gladstone had ever been arrogant to the point of downright injustice. He wasn't nearly ready to say he was wrong in his judgments. But at least he was ready to admit that he might have made up his mind about the Pope too definitively. And too soon.

"I wonder." Christian began to carry on a silent conversation with himself for the remainder of his stay at Colmar. "I wonder if the Holy Father found his miracle. I wonder what he found in the face of Mary Magdalene."

XVI

THERE WAS not a doubt that by summer's end the post of Secretary-General to the EC Council of Ministers would belong to Paul Gladstone. Maestroianni directed his most immediate attention, therefore, and the attention of key associates, to the delicate matter of fulfilling the Roman end of the Gladstone equation.

The Cardinal Secretary's investigations had proved the Reverend Christian Gladstone to be what he had appeared from the beginning: a political simpleton and a cipher in the scales of power. Nonetheless, it was pro forma that in snagging even such a pygmy as Gladstone for a full-time Roman career, all the legal formalities would be observed. Canon Law itself was involved in arranging Father Gladstone's transfer to Rome. And it specified that the permanent transfer of a priest out of his home diocese depended completely on the consent of his bishop.

In this case, the bishop in question was the venerable John Jay O'Cleary, Cardinal Archbishop of New Orleans. Among the Vatican prelates who knew him best, O'Cleary figured as a man who could call upon plenty of money; so his asking price for releasing a good man like Christian Gladstone from his jurisdiction would not be framed in monetary terms. In O'Cleary's case it appeared that ambition and status would be more likely hooks than cash.

It seemed that the Cardinal of New Orleans yearned to be entrusted with a Roman diplomatic career. So much so that, on his own initiative, he had undertaken some forays into the thorny thicket of Vatican Israeli relations. Though his efforts had only complicated an already complex situation, the man still ambitioned to "drink Roman water," as the phrase had it; and that was probably the trade-off he would look for.

Yet even leaving aside his diplomatic ineptitude, there were other traits that made Cardinal O'Cleary unacceptable to the Vatican Secretariat. Traits such as his doctrinal orthodoxy and his support for this Holy Father. Plainly then, if the American Cardinal's asking price for releasing Father Gladstone permanently to Rome involved bringing His Eminence to Rome as well, it was a price that would be too high. A price that would have to be finessed.

Given the basic elements of the problem, it was inevitable that Cardinal Maestroianni should turn for his solution to His brand-new Eminence, Cardinal Silvio Aureatini. By temperament and by experience—and by the happy fact that both he and Cardinal O'Cleary were known to summer in the northern Italian town of Stresa—no man seemed better suited than

Aureatini to bring O'Cleary to a close appreciation of the service he could render to the Holy See by releasing Christian Gladstone to Rome.

Given the most rudimentary elements of Roman politics, meanwhile, it was equally inevitable that more than one of Maestroianni's collaborators felt the need to be present at the meeting at which their Venerable Brother Silvio would be tasked with his summertime mission.

Cosimo Maestroianni's phone call to His Eminence Cardinal Aureatini in the dead of night about a top-secret early-morning meeting of Cardinals to be held in Aureatini's home had caught Aureatini at a bad moment. He had been looking forward to this morning's departure for the land of flowers and gentle rainfall where he had been reared. Normally, the names the Cardinal Secretary had ticked off on the telephone would have been an irresistible draw for Aureatini. In any other circumstances, he would have rushed to meet at one and the same moment with the likes of such high-ranking Cardinals as Pensabene and Moradian, Karmel and Boff, Aviola and Sturz and Leonardine. At just this moment, however, and no matter what the draw, he did not relish the idea of receiving Maestroianni and his Venerable Brothers.

The men whose arrival Cardinal Aureatini awaited with some irritation this morning were part and parcel of that ancient tradition centered in the Rome of Popes. In Aureatini's eyes, that tradition was one of power. But then, Maestroianni's close collaborator, Aureatini himself had been reckoned from the start as a man of no small means. He had a hand in everything. Known as a man who was benign with allies and who dealt ruthlessly with enemies, he had no real friends, and preferred it that way. His mind was a mental filing system from which he could extract facts, figures, names and dates with uncanny accuracy. He never forgot a face or a voice. He came to be regarded as dangerous—a quality considered enviable in his world.

As time progressed, Maestroianni had entrusted him with the gravest matters of foreign policy and relations with other sovereign states. A clever hand who appeared tireless in his support of the Secretary's policies to bring Church and papacy alike into step with the new world, Aureatini had become a chief collaborator in the important work of drawing up a new Code of Canon Law for the Church Universal, an assignment that entailed nothing less than revising all the rules by which the Church defines itself, theologically and ideologically.

They had got away with the insinuation that Rome was just one diocese among many, and with describing Peter as no more than "head of the College of Bishops." Yet, try as they might, Aureatini and his co-revisionists had failed to eliminate the most objectionable element of papal jurisdiction. The Pope still retained "supreme, full, immediate and universal ordinary power in the Church, which he can always exercise."

On the other hand, his standing in the Vatican's Christian Adult Renewal Rite gave Aureatini the means to achieve in fact much of what he had failed to accomplish in the Code of Canon Law. For one thing, it gave him a certain useful intimacy with many bishops. All in all, Aureatini knew he had established himself as a more than brilliant strategist among the new breed of Vatican managers. Perhaps becoming a Cardinal did not automatically open all doors and windows to him. But he had earned a rightful place within the power process. Silvio Aureatini belonged.

"Shalom on this holy house, my Venerable Brother!" France's Joseph Karmel, Cardinal of Lille, boomed his full-throated greeting to the welcoming Silvio Aureatini. Then, leaning on his cane, he breezed into the living room and settled himself into the nearest armchair with a satisfied sigh. Following him, briefcase in hand, Cosimo Maestroianni echoed the meaning if not the poetry of Karmel's invocation. "God bless the inventor of air conditioning!" Four more Cardinals trooped without a glance past the recently signed papal portrait that now graced Aureatini's entry hall.

"Have you got a glass of wine for a thirsty Cardinal?" That most practical greeting of all came from the last man in the door. The cadaverous and gawky Leo Pensabene figured among other things as front-line political leader in the College of Cardinals, and as one of Aureatini's more valued acquaintances since more youthful days, when they had come together in St. Paul's Chapel in 1963. Taking his cue from Pensabene—always a wise thing to do—Aureatini offered wine all around. And, taking a different cue from the names Maestroianni had rattled off on the phone the night before, he inquired after Cardinal Leonardine of the United States and Germany's Cardinal Sturz.

"They won't be able to make it after all." Maestroianni grimaced. "They were called for an early joint audience at the Palace. You know how our Pontiff loves to talk." Then, just to make sure: "We are alone, Silvio?"

Aureatini nodded. Thanks to this hastily called meeting, even his valet had got out of Rome ahead of him. As his guests made themselves comfortable, Aureatini thought better than to show any serious sign of impatience. He knew that these six men were far more accomplished than he in the world of the greats to which he aspired.

In that world, where there were two main classes of people—superiors and inferiors—these men smelled out power and independence in others as easily as hounds catch the scent of foxes. Their sense for such qualities was born of harsh experience, and had been honed by the traditional Roman ethos. Each of Aureatini's self-invited guests was known by name and by face at levels unreachable by others of lesser professional breed. They discussed the most sensitive issues without ever putting an insensitive tooth in the matter, and regularly conveyed the most uncomfortable meanings in most unexceptional terms. When it came to extremes, they were able to clothe immoral and repulsive enormities as well as horrible alternatives in words that only fellow cognoscenti of their world would grasp. They were among those who would never lack for funds or friends. By reason of office, they could reach anyone they wanted merely by lifting the telephone receiver. They had creditors and debtors in high and unexpected places. They could call on advice, on capital, on intervention for their own sakes and for their interests. True, Aureatini knew these prelates shared many human foibles with the remainder of mankind. In fact, he had managed their weakness and limitations and defects to his own ends now and again. But he would never make the mistake of the arriviste or the star-shooter. Never would he ever underestimate the power of these men.

The junior Cardinal tried not to fidget as conversation turned for a time on the breaking scandal surrounding the Bank of Credit and Commerce International. Everyone in the group, it seemed, had some tidbit of information about the Vatican Bank's connection with the BCCI and its involvement with Saddam Hussein and his middlemen in the transfer of some of Saddam's billions. To Aureatini's dismay, that subject gave way to a discussion of the coming Middle East Conference. Maestroianni announced some new appointments in the offing. At long last, and as though reminding himself by the way that the fledgling Cardinal was present in his own apartment, Maestroianni turned to Aureatini.

"You are on your way to Stresa, Venerable Brother, if I am not mistaken?"

"In less than an hour, I hope, Eminence." No sooner were the words out of his mouth than Aureatini knew he had made a mistake.

"Don't worry." Maestroianni turned frigidly polite. "We will be finished here shortly, and Your Eminence will be free to depart in peace." Then, addressing all, he turned to business. In terms of crude facts, all present had long been committed to the campaign against any long-term continuance of the current papacy. All knew of the decision taken at the Strasbourg meeting the prior month. And Maestroianni had been at some pains to brief his closest colleagues on the pivotal cooperation he had secured from Dr. Channing just days before.

Nevertheless, Maestroianni's factual update did serve to sharpen the sword of commitment. These men were on new terrain for which there existed no map to guide them. Every step forward brought them further into uncharted ground. In a sense, they were feeling their way. In such a situation, and among men who really trusted no one, face-to-face briefings stiffened spines and confirmed all as witnesses and participants alike.

Careful attention was fixed on Maestroianni as he moved smoothly from point to point. To save time, and to make the record clear for all, he had prepared a folder of position papers for each of his colleagues. And he introduced a new term into the lexicon of conspiracy. "Chosen Alternative" had seemed such a precise description of the scenario they had in mind for the Slavic Pope that the moment it had first rolled off Dr. Channing's tongue, Cardinal Maestroianni had made it his own.

"Our Chosen Alternative depends on securing two young Americans as the pillars of our bridge to the wider world. As I have already explained to each of you, Dr. Channing will secure Cyrus Benthoek's able young protégé Paul Gladstone as the European anchor of that bridge. You will find his profile among the position papers in your folders. On our side of things, our junior associate here"—Maestroianni directed attention toward Aureatini—"is to be commissioned to entrain our man within the ambit of the Chosen Alternative."

The deepest question in Aureatini's soul at that moment was a plaintive Why me? But because no one in this refined world would be so crude as to use such language, and because he had not yet been briefed in this latest dimension of the agenda, the question on his lips was all business. "*Semplice o no?*" Was "our man" an innocent or not?

In answer, Maestroianni reached again into his attaché case, withdrew another set of folders and passed them among his associates. "Gladstone, Christian Thomas." Cardinal Pensabene read the name aloud, and then digested the data with his usual sharpness. "Some surprises," he mused to no one in particular. "But they will work for us."

Others were a little more skeptical. It had already been agreed among the senior Cardinals that Christian Gladstone himself was no problem. But the young man's mother still made them nervous. With that kind of money, and with such muscular and long-standing family ties to the Holy See, Signora Francesca Gladstone wielded too much power.

Maestroianni didn't disagree. But his opinion remained what it had been from the start. Just as they had sorted out so many other problems over the years, so, too, would they sort this one out as they went along. "And in any case," he offered optimistically, "this young cleric himself is our key to the widow Gladstone. He is our key to it all."

That much accepted, Aureatini's particular connection to the initiative came to the fore at last.

Maestroianni donned his reading spectacles and called attention to the position paper dealing with Father Gladstone's Ordinary, His Eminence Cardinal O'Cleary of New Orleans. "It appears that our Venerable Brother from America has discovered the pleasures of your beloved Lake Maggiore as a summer retreat."

"Yes, Eminence." Aureatini didn't need to check the dossier. "He's come to Stresa for the last three years running, stays at the Excelsior Hotel for the last week in July and the first two weeks in August."

"I take it you know him, then?"

"Yes, Eminence. He always wants the latest news . . ."

"Do you know him well enough to persuade him to release this young Father Gladstone for a year-round Roman career?"

Aureatini kept a poker face. For the briefest moment, he speculated coolly that the entire plan for new bridges and for the Chosen Alternative revolved around his reply. So satisfying was the thought that he decided to toy for a time with the obvious tension that had suddenly descended on his powerful guests. "There will be difficulties, Eminence."

Cardinal Maestroianni stared over the top of his reading glasses in icy disbelief. It wasn't like Silvio Aureatini to make two mistakes in a decade, much less two in a single hour. "Such as?"

Though Maestroianni fired his question in barely more than a whisper, the salvo was enough to bring Aureatini to his senses. "Simply put," the junior Cardinal offered lamely, "His Eminence O'Cleary is the one who wants to come to Rome."

"So?" With that single word, it was made clear that all such details were to be left to Aureatini's ingenuity. "Whatever arrangements you make, Venerable Brother Silvio, we will not expect Cardinal O'Cleary to end up on our doorstep. Short of that, I'm sure you will find some suitable manner to reward His Eminence of New Orleans for collaborating with us, and to facilitate Father Gladstone's needs. Everyone here will back you to the hilt. I myself am to be used as icing on the cake, if there is any cake. Clear?"

"Clear, Your Eminence."

Having chastened Aureatini into compliance, His Eminence Maestroianni pricked the bubble of tension. Rising from his chair, he clapped the palms of his hands against his rib cage in satisfaction. "This is exhilarating, Venerable Brothers! But let us leave Frater Silvio to his preparations now, shall we? He's in a hurry to be off to his beloved Stresa."

Aureatini shook his head, but this time wisely kept his silence. He had made more than one mistake this morning. It would be a long time before he would make another.

XVII

THE LATE-AFTERNOON SUN slanted its rays onto the terrace of Stresa's exclusive Excelsior Hotel at just such an angle as to entice Cardinal John Jay O'Cleary to close his eyes, tilt his head against the back of his chair and wander into that comfortable place of warmth somewhere between sleep and wakefulness. Slumber was about to claim him altogether when a sudden shadow darkened the reddish glow behind his eyelids and sharpened the cool breeze rising from Lake Maggiore. O'Cleary shivered a little, and opened his eyes.

"Did I disturb Your Eminence?"

Squinting up, the American Cardinal had the impression that he should know the casually dressed man looming over him. The ice-blue eyes and the pencil-sharp features almost registered in his mind, but he couldn't quite bring the memory into focus. He glanced across the terrace in the hope that Archbishop Sturz or one of the other clerics gathered over there might come to his rescue; but they all seemed studiously engrossed in their gossip and their game of cards.

It was a mark of Silvio Aureatini's discretion—and of his overriding sense of specific purpose—that he displayed none of the annoyance flooding in upon him at not having been recognized at once. Instead, and most affably, he reintroduced himself by name, by his rank as Cardinal, and by his close association with His Eminence Cardinal Maestroianni at the Vatican Secretariat. Then, as that information registered on the features of his target, he drew up a chair and made himself easily at home by O'Cleary's side. He refreshed his companion's memory of their two or three meetings in summers gone by, all the while lamenting that his contact with the American prelate had been so occasional. For, confessed Aureatini, brief though those conversations had been, His Eminence's observations had been so interesting and his selfless interest in Rome so refreshing that every encounter had been a special pleasure.

Aureatini formed his sharp features into a smile. There were no two ways about it, he said. This summer would have to be different. His Eminence O'Cleary would have to spare a little more time for a poor Roman.

Such a chance meeting—for so it seemed—with the likes of Silvio Aureatini struck John O'Cleary as perfectly natural. Everybody knew that the majority of clergymen who vacationed in this region were to be found in Stresa; and if you were anyone in the clerical contingent, you came to the Excelsior Hotel. That being so, the American responded as he always did to friendly overtures. He presumed in the next man the goodwill he himself spontaneously entertained. But more than that, O'Cleary possessed the soul of a parish priest and the heart of a man who wants to be loved.

O'Cleary ordered a pair of drinks—a Jack Daniel's for himself; a Campari for the Italian—and did his best to appear casual as he struggled to recall what observations he might have made in years past that would have been so interesting for an associate of the great Cardinal Maestroianni. To his relief, however, Aureatini seemed content to keep the conversation casual. Having done his homework well, the Italian went out of his way to extol the local fishing possibilities. He seemed surprised and genuinely delighted to hear O'Cleary's modest claim to some accomplishment as a fly fisherman.

"That was many years ago, of course," the American added. It wouldn't do for Aureatini to think there was so little for him to do in New Orleans that he spent his days fishing on Lake Pontchartrain. Brushing a hand over his still ample hair, Cardinal O'Cleary tried to get his unruly cowlick to lie flat. "There's precious little time these days for such pleasures."

"Of course." The Italian nodded sympathetically. "Nowadays, things have become so strenuous that all of us have to make sacrifices if the Holy See is to succeed in its new evangelization of the world."

Aureatini made the observation seem so pointed and singular that O'Cleary sharpened what he hoped were his Roman instincts. If any man was ready to make sacrifices for the Holy See—indeed, to cap his career with a post in the heart of the Holy See itself—he was that man. Almost immediately, though, he knew he must have read too much into the remark, for Aureatini launched into a series of stories about fishing the local rivers not far from his parents' home in Ticino.

"You're from these parts, then, Eminence?" O'Cleary tried not to sound disappointed.

"Born and bred. Sometimes I think the Almighty planted all these magnolias and cypresses and clematis and wisteria just for me!" Then, as though struck with sudden inspiration, he wondered if O'Cleary might want to sample the pleasure of this delightful region with a simple native like himself. "If you want to know the truth"—Aureatini turned a suddenly wistful eye out over Lake Maggiore and whispered, as if confiding a well-guarded secret—"the height of vacation pleasure for me is to sail of an early morning along the western side of the lake." Then, turning back to O'Cleary, "If you're up to a predawn excursion, Eminence, perhaps you'd care to join me one morning while you're here."

"Your Eminence is too kind!" The Yankee Cardinal looked anything but wistful as he cast his own narrow-set eyes across the lake. The height of vacation pleasure for John Jay O'Cleary—Jay Jay, as the folks back home called him—was to roll over in bed and sleep the morning away. Still, that remark about sacrifice for the success of the Holy See's evangelization efforts did wonders for a man's appreciation of the dawn's early light. Particularly if he had hankered after the status of a Roman career for as long as O'Cleary had.

Each summer, Silvio Aureatini counted on his time in this privileged vacation spot to release him from the tension of Roman life. He still fished on Maggiore's three rivers. He spent tranquil days with ordinary people in his hometown of Ticino and its surrounding hamlets, speaking his native Ticinese dialect with farmers and traders and fishermen. He spent many hours relaxing with his aged parents. All of that was to the good for Aureatini. It made no difference that he could summon no real remembrance of the old pastoral lessons by which the people of this area still lived. The important thing was that he could relax his guard for a time. He could exercise his love for his parents by sparing them any shocks to their simple and unchanged acceptance of all he had rejected.

So, too, for the folks among whom he ambled in the unspoiled towns that dotted the western shore of Lake Maggiore. Not that he ever led them in reciting the Rosary or heard their confessions. He was funny that way, people said. But he was respected and loved all the same. Just ask the local cobbler in the little village of Cannobio who made His Eminence's yearly supply of buckled shoes. The folks down the road in Baveno were proud that His Eminence favored the marvelous red wine produced in that town. Even the uninteresting town of Arona, which boasted nothing more than a moderately entertaining Romanesque chapel, might see him strolling along its quiet streets, a crumpled straw hat perched on his head against the sun.

For Aureatini, the place was a safe harbor in summertime. Here he was sequestered for a little season from the life he led in Rome and from the kind of man he had become. Alas, however, this year had to be different. An official and cynical exercise in regard to His Eminence John Jay O'Cleary of New Orleans required that he bring the tensions of Vatican life into his safe harbor. Still, when all was said and done, Aureatini resented the intrusion.

With the always cheerful and seemingly tireless Silvio Aureatini as companion and guide, Cardinal O'Cleary was soon something of an expert on the pleasures offered in this privileged corner of northern Italy. He was happy to sacrifice sleep to sail with Aureatini and watch the sun rise over islands strung like beads along the western shore of Lake Maggiore. He heard from Aureatini how the sixteenth-century Borromeo family had enriched this whole corner of the lake—building gorgeous palazzi. He listened to Aureatini tell how Isola Bella had been named after Countess Isabella Borromeo by her husband, Carlo, as together they visited the elegant château built by another Borromeo, Count Vitaliano, on that island. O'Cleary registered surprise and amusement at the sight of that château. "Your Count Vitaliano had a fevered imagination, surely."

"Well, Eminence." Aureatini smiled. "Let's just say that the Borromeos left a deeper stamp on the geography of this land than on its politics. We expect to do better than that in Rome."

That was a funny thing about Cardinal Aureatini. He seemed always to be making remarks like that. Wherever they went over the three weeks of Jay Jay's vacation, Aureatini always had some pointed remark to drop about his work, or his access to important levels of Church government, or the current crises affecting the Church. At every such remark, O'Cleary's antennae of personal ambition sprouted anew. But, every time, Aureatini left the subject almost as soon as he raised it.

By the second Sunday in August, the eve of his departure for America, the tension was almost unbearable. O'Cleary declined His Eminence's invitation for a farewell excursion, therefore, preferring to thank the Cardinal for his many kindnesses at a lunch in the sedentary comfort of the Excelsior's dining room.

Aureatini arrived to find Cardinal O'Cleary waiting for him on the hotel terrace. O'Cleary had taken the liberty of ordering lunch for the two of them in advance. "I hope you like skate fish, Eminence. The chef tells me the morning catch was exceptional."

Cardinal Aureatini declared himself to be delighted. Then, as they strolled together into the dining room, he asked innocently enough if His Eminence was looking forward to his return home. "You must be missing New Orleans by now."

"Oh, of course." O'Cleary mustered what enthusiasm he could for the sentiment. "And you, Eminence. How long more do you stay in this magical spot?"

Aureatini sighed as the pair settled in for lunch. "Another week or two, Eminence. Unless Rome. . . . Well, you know what I mean."

O'Cleary could only imagine what grave affairs might disrupt this worthy man's vacation. "Let's hope you can enjoy this paradise as long as possible," he offered generously. Then—because it was now or never—he guided the conversation onto the course he had in mind. "After that, it's back to the Holy See, eh, Eminence?"

"Yes, Eminence." Aureatini mounted the words on another sigh and, as their unobtrusive waiter retreated, consoled himself with a generous bite of skate fish followed by a generous draft of the truly excellent wine O'Cleary had ordered. In some ways, this American wasn't half bad.

John O'Cleary was not made by nature for the verbal fencing match. The best way for him was to take a straight lunge at what occupied his mind. And so he did. "I've been thinking on all you've said, Eminence, since you took me into your confidence. You were absolutely right when you said we should all be ready to make sacrifices for the Holy See in its present constricted condition. I have great compassion for the Holy Father. What a dirty job he has!"

Though O'Cleary had a few years on him, Aureatini nodded in paternal approval.

"I guess"—O'Cleary's smile was self-deprecating—"there's not much a poor provincial Cardinal like myself can do beyond fulfilling my ordinary duties. Still—er—what I mean is, I hope Your Eminence realizes that I am personally and totally at the disposal of the Holy See."

Aureatini allowed an answering smile of appreciation to touch his lips. No slouch himself at the subtleties of fly fishing, he knew he had his catch on the line. "What we need in the Vatican, Eminence, is manpower. Simply, bodies."

"I myself . . ." O'Cleary hoped his tone was dispassionate enough to convey total and selfless indifference. "Please pardon the personal reference, Eminence; but I myself have done my little bit in this direction."

The reference, Aureatini assumed, was to O'Cleary's ridiculous foray into the Middle East. "We know, Eminence. We know. And believe me, your efforts are highly treasured. We know New Orleans has been and will continue to be a bastion of loyal support for the Holy See."

Aureatini straightened in his chair and looked about him as though concerned that he not be overheard now by the several other vacationing clerics at nearby tables. "There may be something Your Eminence might do for us poor pen pushers in Rome. What I tell Your Eminence now is by way of strict confidence. It involves many governments in Europe—and ultimately, of course, your own government in the United States." Aureatini lowered his voice so that O'Cleary had to lean forward to catch his words. "I have learned from His Eminence Maestroianni . . ."

The mention of that name had exactly the effect Aureatini had anticipated it would. "Cardinal Maestroianni is here?" O'Cleary was all but overcome.

The Italian put one finger to his lips to signal again the confidential nature of this conversation. Actually, it hadn't been necessary to interrupt Maestroianni's summer holiday with a call for His Eminence to come to Stresa. Still, a little insurance to cement O'Cleary's cooperation wouldn't be amiss. Maestroianni had said he was prepared to back this mission to the hilt, after all. And Aureatini had felt a particular touch of satisfaction at booking the senior Cardinal into a somewhat down-at-the-heels rooming house on the Isola dei Pescatori.

"Indeed, yes," Aureatini whispered. "His Eminence arrived just yesterday. To discuss this very matter, in fact. He's incognito, of course. Staying on the Isola dei Pescatori. Loves simple places, that man! Loves to loaf around in a shirt and jeans, sipping wine in the cafés with the ordinary people he never gets to meet in Rome."

O'Cleary was moved. "Now that, Eminence, is true greatness!"

"True greatness indeed, Eminence. Now, what brought the Cardinal here so urgently is our absolute need for a middle-echelon man. And Your Eminence is the only one who can help us get this man for ourselves."

O'Cleary was torn between his desire to show his willing usefulness and his sharp disappointment that he himself did not seem to be the object of such urgent Vatican interest. He could only listen, therefore, as Aureatini went on.

"The name of the young man His Eminence has in mind is the Reverend Christian Thomas Gladstone. Does Your Eminence remember him?"

His conflicting emotions under better control now, Cardinal O'Cleary nodded vigorously. "Of course, Eminence. A marvelous young priest. His family and I go back a long way. But Father does already spend half of every year in Rome."

"Yes, yes. We know that, Eminence. But the Cardinal has made it plain to me. We need your young man full-time. And we need him as of this coming September."

When O'Cleary's eyes clouded for a moment, as if he was struck by some powerful thought, Aureatini shook his head in a display of understanding. "I know it's impossible, really. And quite unjust. Rome must not drain the dioceses of their best . . ."

"No, no Eminence." O'Cleary seemed truly alarmed. "What I mean,

Eminence, is this: If Rome needs Gladstone, then Rome will have Gladstone. In fact, as his direct superior, I guarantee it."

Aureatini was the one who appeared overcome by emotion now. *"Dio mio!* The Cardinal will be delighted by your sacrifice! I'm sure he'll want to thank you personally. I've arranged to dine with him this very evening. At Mammaletto's on the Via Ugo Ara. The Cardinal loves lobster. But Your Eminence would probably prefer their marvelous striped bass."

O'Cleary could hardly believe his ears. "Do you mean . . . ?"

"I mean, Eminence, that Cardinal Maestroianni would surely be upset should you not see your way clear to joining us. I cannot take no for your answer."

It would never have occurred to O'Cleary to say no to an evening of close conversation with the fabled Cosimo Maestroianni. But when he blinked his eyes shut ever so briefly, the painful thought that had struck him seconds before all but took flesh. The proud face of the doughty Francesca Gladstone flashed across his mind, warning him that he had made a rash promise. It would take a miracle to overcome the force of that matron's objections to Rome itself, much less to a full-time Roman career for her son Christian.

"Shall I stop by for you here?" Aureatini prodded. "Say at about eight this evening?"

"Striped bass, you say?" Cardinal O'Cleary opened his eyes and, for the moment at least, banished the face and the power of Francesca Gladstone from his mind.

Alone in his Excelsior suite, Jay Jay O'Cleary was surprised at how quickly all sense of exhilaration fell away. He had no sense that he was being used, cynically or otherwise, by Aureatini. Yet in some corner of his heart he knew these Romans were too subtle for him.

John Jay O'Cleary bore no obvious resemblance to Silvio Aureatini. His kind mouth was an honest reflection of his heart. His eyes, balanced too near his nose, told truly of the narrow dimensions of his vision concerning the potential power that was his but for the exercising of it. His dignified, flat-footed gait seemed the pattern for his somewhat labored process of thought and argument.

However, the mind-set favored by Cardinal Aureatini was not entirely foreign even to the benign O'Cleary. In fact, it was that very mind-set—running like a current now throughout much of the world's episcopate—which His Eminence Cardinal Maestroianni himself intended to manipulate in order to elicit the Common Mind of the Bishops against the Slavic Pope. Which was to say that on this Sunday afternoon, what drove Cardinal O'Cleary's thoughts had far less to do with the traditional mandate of an Apostle than with personal ambition and narrow self-interest.

His Eminence flopped wearily into an armchair. Life finally seemed to be getting him down. It was too great an irony that Christian Gladstone, who made no secret of his scorn for the clerical life in Rome, was unaccountably but urgently required there, while O'Cleary himself was to remain in the ecclesiastical backwater of New Orleans.

O'Cleary didn't fool himself about Rome. Yet it was part of O'Cleary's character that he had always preferred to think of Rome as he had seen it in his early days, back when he had first frequented the Chancery. Back when time spent in Rome hadn't endangered your faith, or sapped your conviction that love of God and of Christ did still predominate. Overall, there had been no regnant cynicism, no penetrating heartlessness in O'Cleary's Rome. In its heyday, a solidarity of Christian love had still reigned.

O'Cleary still preferred to interact with his world in those terms. Not that he was altogether unaware that things had changed. It was just that he chose to deal with change differently than most of his episcopal colleagues. Even now, after nearly a decade as Cardinal Archbishop of New Orleans, O'Cleary remained convinced that with justice and love as motive, and with authority to back him up, his message was bound to be heard and accepted.

Over the years of his tenure as Cardinal Archbishop of New Orleans, O'Cleary had often enough been faced with the Gladstones of Windswept House as a problem. But, in his native wisdom, he had realized he should avoid any real clash with them. He thus never made the mistake of his predecessor, the powerful and flamboyant and reputedly megalomaniacal Cardinal Jean de Bourgogne.

Bourgogne, in his arrogance, had written a letter to Francesca Gladstone, mistress of Windswept House, asserting very untruthfully that "the Holy Father and the Vatican Council had abolished the old Roman Mass and forbidden all Roman Catholics to have any more to do with it."

Francesca had fired off a response to the Cardinal he had never anticipated: "As mistress of Windswept House," she told His Eminence, "I will not permit the destruction of this Roman Mass in my chapel. I claim our perpetual privilege as in Canon Law 77, according to which we Gladstones have a papally granted right that cannot be abrogated, subrogated or terminated by ecclesiastical decree from any dicastery of the Church, but only by direct and personal papal action. Moreover, I intend to mount a legal action, civilly and canonically, if such becomes necessary."

Bourgogne made one attempt through his representative in Rome to overturn the Gladstone privilege. Rome, for all the right reasons, told him to desist.

Since 1982, when O'Cleary had succeeded Bourgogne as Cardinal Archbishop of New Orleans, he had followed a wiser and gentler course with the Gladstones. His natural desire was to bring the mistress of Windswept House to his point of view. To his dismay, however, Cessi Gladstone had consistently declared herself intent upon avoiding "the best and worst efforts of churchmen to rid the Church of its supernatural value as the true and only Church of Christ." As was often the case, O'Cleary's natural desire had given way to his natural caution. He generally kept a safe distance from Windswept House.

On this Sunday afternoon in Stresa, as he pondered the galling fact that his relationship with the Gladstones of Windswept House had suddenly become both the key and the stumbling block to his Roman ambitions, John O'Cleary felt more and more as though he were wandering in a maze. There could be no doubt that Francesca Gladstone would throw her influence with her son against his permanent transfer to Rome. "People go to Rome and lose their faith," she had said more than once. Worse still, and based on his own experience in Rome, Christian Gladstone couldn't be faulted for sharing that mentality. Nevertheless, if he failed to deliver Christian into Cardinal Maestroianni's hands as he had promised, O'Cleary could kiss goodbye to any hope of finishing his career on the banks of the Tiber.

O'Cleary's ambition finally won out over his distaste for the Gladstones. Perhaps the door to a Roman career had not yet been opened to him, Jay Jay reasoned; but neither had it been closed. Had not Aureatini already been more than generous in his recognition of the value of New Orleans? Had he not even called New Orleans a bastion of loyal support for the Holy See? Surely if he delivered Christian Gladstone to Cardinal Maestroianni as he had vowed to do—the time would come for his own just reward.

O'Cleary therefore turned to his new problem: finding Christian Gladstone and obtaining his consent to be posted to Rome on a permanent basis. He glanced at his watch. Four o'clock already. That would be 9 A.M. in New Orleans. He decided to tackle the quaint telephone system of Stresa and get through to his Vicar-General of the New Orleans diocese, Monsignor Pat Sheehan. After one hour's waiting and pleading and cajoling successive operators in a jumble of English and Italian, His Eminence nearly burst into tears of relief when at last he heard the calm and "homey" sound of Pat Sheehan's voice.

"Pat?" O'Cleary shouted over a sudden crackle of Stresa's corroded phone lines.

"Yes. Who's this?"

"It's me, Pat. Jay Jay."

"In the name of all that's holy, man, where are you? Sounds like you're talking through a tin can and a string!"

O'Cleary laughed with such unexpected pleasure that he wondered if Aureatini had been right, after all. Maybe he did miss New Orleans. "I'm still in Stresa. They have a lot of palaces over here and some dandy fisheries. But I don't believe they've discovered fiber optics yet."

One of the many advantages of Pat Sheehan as Vicar-General was that he was such a quick study. In no time at all, the Monsignor got the picture. Jay Jay had been cornered. And, true to form, Sheehan knew exactly where to find Father Gladstone. "He's at the Dominican residence in Colmar, Jay Jay. Working on that thesis of his. According to the schedule he phoned in, he'll be on his way home to Galveston within the next day or two."

O'Cleary groaned. For Father Christian, going home to Galveston meant going home to Windswept House. And that meant he would be reinforced all over again by the traditional ethos that still reigned there. O'Cleary toyed with the suddenly attractive idea that it would be best to defer the whole matter of Gladstone's shift to Rome until September—until after Gladstone had finished his vacation stay with his family. He would have to report to New Orleans then anyway, for his half-year teaching stint at the Seminary. Perhaps that would be time enough to tell him of the proposed change in his career.

Sheehan was firm but dispassionate in his disagreement with that tack. "If you were dealing with any other cleric in the diocese, it wouldn't matter how you went about it. But the Gladstones are not without their influence."

"Tell me something I don't know," O'Cleary grumbled.

"If you ask me, Jay Jay, the worst thing you can do is to spring your proposal on Father Christian when neither you nor he will have any time left before he's supposed to be in Rome. If you wait, and if he turns out to be reluctant, you won't have left yourself any wiggle room. And in any case, Jay Jay"—Sheehan tried to sound encouraging—"I think you may be selling the lad short. He's going to need time to think your proposal over. Resign yourself to that. And whenever he gets your proposal, he's bound to talk the whole thing over with his mother. But Gladstone is as independent-minded as that lady ever was. He'll make his own decision."

A glance at his watch decided the matter for O'Cleary. He had just enough time to freshen himself with a shower before Aureatini would collect him for their dinner with Cardinal Maestroianni. "Listen, Pat. Do you have Gladstone's number in Colmar?"

"Wait, now." There was a pause while Sheehan shuffled through some papers. "Yes. Here it is. 32-84 . . ."

"No, Pat." Jay Jay pleaded the strictures of time. "You do the honors. Ask young Gladstone to spare his poor Archbishop a few moments of his vacation on his way to Galveston. I'm leaving Stresa and heading for New Orleans tomorrow. Book him in on my calendar at your discretion."

XVIII

SOME MOMENTS before seven o'clock on Monday evening—the hour he had fixed with Monsignor Pat Sheehan when the Vicar-General had rung him so unexpectedly in Colmar—Christian Gladstone emerged from a cab and pressed the doorbell of Cardinal Jay Jay O'Cleary's episcopal residence in New Orleans.

The trendily dressed and oddly coifed Sister Claudia Tuite opened the door and permitted Christian to step in from the August rain shower. With a tolerance she reserved for any clergyman below the rank of Cardinal, she acknowledged Gladstone's greeting with a curt nod, received his raincoat gingerly between two fingers as if she might drop it as soon as possible into an aseptic solution and glided silently off to announce his arrival to His Eminence.

Left to make his own way into the familiar sitting room, Christian turned his thoughts to his coming interview with the Cardinal. Like most of the priests in Jay Jay's diocese, he knew he could gauge the tenor of things to come by the length of time he was left to cool his heels. He read the obvious, therefore, into the fact that the Cardinal's junior secretary appeared at the door after barely a moment.

In his quest for ecclesiastical preferment, Father Eddie McPherson treated most clerical visitors as rivals for the Cardinal's favor. He had walked over more than one priest in the diocese, and was widely regarded as one of those clerical careerists who are oriented, body and soul, to the rising sun. A man like Gladstone, who not only came from a moneyed family but had frequented Rome to boot, set his teeth on edge.

"His Eminence will see you, Father." McPherson pronounced the formulary expression in a flat sort of way, and gestured toward the corridor leading to His Eminence's study.

"I assumed he would, Eddie, since I'm here at his request." His own teeth set on edge by McPherson's coldness, Christian led the way down the corridor, strode into the Cardinal's study and left McPherson to close the door behind him.

Alone again for the moment, Gladstone reacquainted himself with the room. The desk where His Eminence would surely seat himself. The low-slung chair beside it that guaranteed the Cardinal's edge of height over most of his visitors. The pair of armchairs over by the garden windows, reserved for conversations with visiting prelates and other ranking dignitaries. The portrait of the Slavic Pope inscribed to "Our Venerable Brother" that hung on the wall behind the desk. The oil painting of the

Cardinal on the same wall, to the left of the desk, side by side with His Eminence's intricate coat of arms.

"Father Christian! How welcome you are!" Cardinal Archbishop O'Cleary came bustling into the study.

"Your Eminence."

To O'Cleary's momentary surprise, the lanky young priest dropped to one knee and kissed the bishop's ring on his hand. These Gladstones!

"Come, Father. Take a seat."

His Eminence gestured his visitor toward the low-slung chair and settled himself into the high-backed chair that gave him what he thought of as the advantage of perspective. "Now, Father, tell me. How is that marvelous lady, your beloved mother?"

"Mother's fine, Your Eminence." Too tall for the awkward chair, Gladstone arranged his long legs as best he could. "She's killing the fatted calf to celebrate my homecoming."

If Jay Jay knew anything about Cessi Gladstone, she was preparing Belshazzar's Feast. "I hope this unexpected little stopover in New Orleans hasn't disrupted her plans, my boy."

"I'm sure she understands, Eminence. She always does." Christian got his legs in order and prepared himself for another of the Cardinal's rituals. Small talk from O'Cleary meant His Eminence would conduct the interview in the style of one of those seagulls Gladstone had often watched from the seaward windows at Windswept House. The Cardinal would bank and wheel in the air for a while, until that particular moment when all the soaring and gliding would end in a final swoop onto his intended target.

"Father Christian." His Eminence displayed the expansive smile that had become his media signature in New Orleans. "I cannot tell you how dear your family is to me. How dear the Gladstones have been for more than a century to the Holy See and to the Holy Father; and how much you have all contributed to the upkeep of God's Church."

"Your Eminence is most gracious."

"New Orleans must seem quite provincial to you by now, after all the time you've spent in Rome."

The remark struck Christian as odd until he reminded himself that O'Cleary's eyes were known to be perpetually set on Rome. "In some ways," Gladstone responded, "the two cities are not so different, Your Eminence. New Orleans is so sinful and so holy. So dirty and so clean. So very happy and at the same time so very sad. Like Rome, one can only imagine how wonderful New Orleans must have been in its great Catholic heyday."

The smile with which Jay Jay had heard Christian's first words gave way to bafflement. He seemed like a benign professor sadly disappointed in one of his most prized scholars. "After all this time, do you still see Rome in such stark terms?" O'Cleary's question was so heartfelt and at the same time so patronizing that Gladstone was struck with the realization that he had been called to this interview to talk about Rome. The idea was so implausible that he knew it had to be true. Filled with foreboding and distaste, he could only answer with silence.

His tone almost reproving now, the Cardinal went on. "As you know, I have just returned from an extended trip to Europe. We princes of the Church must stay in touch with each other about universal problems, as you might imagine. I began with an audience with the Holy Father. Most consoling, Father Christian. What a great man Christ has given to His Church in her hour of need! And during my stay in the Eternal City, I had a long conversation with the Rector of the Angelicum. I cannot tell you, Father, how Master-General Slattery values your services during the one semester you spend there each year."

O'Cleary gave Gladstone a look of loving satisfaction. "It may not surprise you—especially given the status of your family in the annals of the Holy See—that over in the Secretariat of State your name stands very high. Very high, indeed! Guess what they have asked of me, Father Christian."

Unwilling to ease such a conversation as this, Gladstone looked steadily at His Eminence, but still said nothing.

"My dear Father, they have asked me to do the hardest thing a bishop can be asked: to give up a good man." Ready to dive on his target now, O'Cleary changed his expression to one of grave concern. "As of this very September they want me to release you to Rome as a fully tenured professor of theology at the Angelicum and as a theologian for the papal household."

His worst expectation confirmed, Gladstone was inwardly beset with so many questions that he hardly knew how to sort them out. As far as he knew, the Angelicum had no need of him on a year-round basis. And there were already so many hundreds of theologians in the "papal household"—a loose term at best in this context—that there could be no urgent need for another. Moreover, despite O'Cleary's words about his high standing at the Secretariat, no one in official Rome had given Christian the time of day. Oh, he had had that one inconsequential meeting with Cardinal Maestroianni. And while Master-General Slattery was known as a papal intimate, it was unlikely that he was behind this curious business.

Who in Rome, then, would even think of reaching out for him? And why such urgency? None of it made any sense. Gladstone was suddenly clear on one thing. Jay Jay was in a bind; and for whatever reason, Christian was the Cardinal's only hope of getting out of that bind. So much so that he was even willing to risk the wrath of Christian's mother in a bid to save his own hindquarters. In fact, O'Cleary was so tense, so nervous about the whole proposition, that the young priest reckoned it was only the Cardinal's diffidence regarding the strong-willed Cessi Gladstone that kept O'Cleary from ordering him to Rome on the spot.

"Your Eminence." It was Christian who broke the silence. A few questions should be enough to test O'Cleary's determination to release him to Rome; and to test how difficult it might be to sidestep the proposition. "Your Eminence, give me the benefit of a little counsel. I am a very small fish in the pond. I teach minor courses at the Angelicum. I minister to the Polish nuns on Via Sistina. I give a few retreats to the Irish nuns on Via di Sebastianello. I don't know Rome, really; or the papal household. I speak unforgivably bad Italian. I am an American. What assignment could be so urgent for a cleric with such credentials as that?"

Jay Jay assumed the most pontifical bearing at his command. "Despite your commendable modesty, Father Christian, I think you should give this matter your most serious consideration. At the risk of betraying a confidence, I believe you should know that you have come to the attention of no less a figure in our Church than His Eminence Cosimo Maestroianni himself." The disbelief with which Gladstone heard that bit of information passed in O'Cleary's eyes for the awe he himself entertained for the great Cardinal Maestroianni. "All right, Father. Cards on the table, eh? Both at the Secretariat and elsewhere in the Holy City"—the Cardinal's sage look was meant to underline the fact that in this Roman context, the word "elsewhere" could only mean the Holy Father—"I find a great sense of imminent developments. A consensus that new initiatives are afoot. And I find the same buoyancy among my brother Cardinals. Between you and me, this could be the greatest opportunity of your clerical career."

Convinced that it was the Cardinal's clerical career that was on the line, and that he was the bait, Christian gave a moment's thought nonetheless to Jay Jay's sense of imminent developments. From Gladstone's perspective, the greatest global crisis was within the Church Universal. No. The best thing he could do, Christian told himself, would be to finish his studies and come back to the States, where he could make a difference. At least here he could serve the faithful who were in such desperate need of good priests. Here, he could turn his back on the careerism of Rome.

"I say again, therefore," Cardinal O'Cleary was pressing on. "You should give the matter your most serious consideration. Time is a factor in your decision, of course. But"—Jay Jay smiled bravely—"you must feel free in this matter."

"I shall, Your Eminence. Be assured of that."

For the first time, Jay Jay glanced at a page of typewritten notes on his desk. "They would like you to drop in sometime before the end of September to talk with them—work out a schedule, find accommodations. That sort of thing. Actually, my boy, you can have a room on the Hill as of this very moment if you like. I arranged that personally for you with the Rector." "The Hill" was the familiar Roman tag for the American College, and Christian understood the gambit as an intended inducement.

Aware that Christian's confident answer concerned the whole Roman proposal itself, Jay Jay resigned himself to the fact that he would get no definitive answer this evening. His best hope now was to bury Gladstone's reluctance—and with it, the influence his mother was bound to exert on him in the coming days—beneath a new avalanche of pious and complementary phrases. "I cannot tell you how much I love your family," he offered again. "When Peter calls . . . ," he suggested. "You cannot begin to know how valued your services are in the Holy City. Your background and credentials could be of immense benefit to Rome. In fact, in today's ambience just such a man as yourself is needed, my dear Father Christian."

The Archbishop looked one more time at his notes, as though he might find a sudden miracle there. Then, a little disheartened, he rose from his chair. "You'll be heading for Galveston now, my boy?"

"In the morning, Eminence. I'll be spending the night at the Seminary." As Christian stood up in his turn, he couldn't resist a sudden impulse. "Mother would love to entertain Your Eminence once again at Windswept House," he suggested with a mischievous twinkle. "Perhaps Your Eminence might even join us while I'm there."

This was not the note on which Jay Jay had hoped to end the interview. He hadn't forgotten his last visit to Windswept. For days afterward, his ears had echoed with Cessi Gladstone's point-blank refusal on that occasion to chair a diocesan committee for ecumenical relations with the Baptists. "Please the good God, my boy." O'Cleary finessed Gladstone's invitation with another smile. "One of these days we'll manage a visit to your beloved Windswept." His Eminence reached for the buzzer on his desk and, when Father Eddie reappeared obediently at the door, directed that a car be ordered to take Christian to the Seminary.

Gladstone bent again to kiss his ring, and then strode across the study.

"You'll let us hear from you with as little delay as possible, Father?"

Christian turned back for a moment. "I will, Eminence." Then, brushing past Father Eddie McPherson still standing in the doorway, he was gone.

Some thousand miles or so to the northeast of New Orleans, in the pleasant midsummer Virginia countryside not far from Washington, D.C., Gibson Appleyard pulled into the driveway of his home just as his wife, Genie, was pulling her car out.

"Eastern Star meeting, Gib darling." She blew the reminder on a kiss. "See you at dinner."

Appleyard waved and blew a kiss in return. He made his way around to the garden and, despite the temptation to give a little attention to his splendid collection of roses, entered his light-filled study through the French doors, deposited his briefcase on his desk, tossed his tie and suit jacket onto a chair, selected *The Magic Flute* for his stereo and set about what he hoped would be several uninterrupted hours of work.

A Navy Counterintelligence officer by trade, this exceptionally tall man with the sandy-gray hair—this Anglo-Saxon type who had seemed so forgettable to Cardinal Maestroianni when Cyrus Benthoek had introduced him at the clandestine Schuman Day gathering in Strasbourg—had been assigned since January 1990 to special duties at the pleasure of the President of the United States.

In late December 1989, the President had been approached by ten men who were reckoned as colossi within the nation's largest, most important and most prosperous transnational corporations. Men who controlled communications and electronics and oil, agribusiness and banking and insurance and reinsurance.

These gentlemen had called at the White House to volunteer a clear analysis of the U.S. position in a suddenly changing world. The disintegration of the Soviet Union into separate states, they said, was as sure as tomorrow's sunrise. The most natural course for those states to follow would be integration with the European Common Market nations. Mr. Gorbachev—not to mention others in Europe itself—was already forecasting just such a turn.

"Mr. President," the ten said in effect, "if that were to happen anytime soon—if a Greater Europe were to come upon us by the presently planned target date of January 1993, there would be no way the United States could compete. We would be dwarfed."

Naturally, the gentlemen had a recommendation to make: "Authorize us as an ad hoc committee to watch over U.S. business interests in general throughout this new situation; and in particular to circumvent in a timely fashion the rapid creation of such an unbeatable economic competitor."

The President had seen their point. No President would fail to heed such men as these; and no President could gainsay their common voice.

Within a month, the ad hoc Presidential Committee of Ten, answerable only to the Chief Executive, had been established. And, like so many other committees in Washington, it soon acquired a permanency that made the term "ad hoc" into an oxymoron. Within the same month, Gibson Appleyard had been detached from his Navy Counterintelligence post. He and his senior officer, Admiral (Ret.) Edward "Bud" Vance, functioned as the Committee's executive officers. They were to develop what the President had loosely described as "toeholds and handgrips" within the European Community. "A little insurance," as the President had explained in his first meeting with the two intelligence officers, "so that some measure of control and pressure will be available to us with our allies, should the need ever arise."

Appleyard was adept at ferreting out toeholds and handgrips. And though the climate in Europe lent urgency to his work, he hadn't come across anything that wasn't easily within his capabilities. Pragmatic and resourceful, he had long since found that the workings of politics and politicians do not change much, just because they take place on the transnational level.

True, the European Community did represent 320 million people in twelve nations. If you added the seven nations of the European Free Trade Association—the EFTA, you were looking at a market economy of some 370 million people already with a high level of social culture and technological sophistication. The "Europeans" had been speaking in the eighties of a coming financial and political European union—perhaps by the mid-nineties. This Greater Europe was their goal.

As of this summer, however—and despite the EC's bright-eyed projections—Appleyard counted the chances to be iffy for that Greater Europe to emerge as a done deal, united and harmonious, by the target date of the mid-nineties. The separate member states of the European Community hadn't exactly submerged their national identities into the EC. Germany was beginning to flex its political muscle; and, ever so remotely, its potential military muscle as well. The French still clung to the idea of France as the heart and soul of European democracy. And, despite the English Prime Minister's brave words recently, the English people in their majority did not want to be reckoned as Europeans. England was England, by Jove.

On top of all that, the EC's great rival—Conference on Security and Cooperation in Europe—had hardly faded away. Ever since the Final Accords had been signed in 1975 in Helsinki, a large body of opinion saw the CSCE as the chief organ of Greater Europe. After all, the United States—unwelcome as a European player in the eyes of the EC—was not only a full-fledged member of the rival CSCE but the principal supporter of the European Bank for Reconstruction and Development.

By this August, after a year and a half of low-key but effective dealing, Gibson Appleyard had found plenty of toeholds and handgrips within that general grid of European competition. He was rightly appreciated by his superiors as a man who let nothing get by his expert eye, and who could hold his own for the American position while the Committee of Ten went about its ad hoc business of securing global peace and American primacy within the emergent new order in Europe.

On this sunny afternoon, by the time the slow *siciliano* rhythm of Pamina's aria in G minor for her lost Tamino surged in his ears, Gib Appleyard had brought himself up to date on the current situation in each of the EC countries. One last review of the folders devoted to the coming final selection of the new Secretary-General to the Council of Ministers of the European Community was all that remained to be done.

The post of Secretary-General had been vacant since June. The EC Selection Committee had met twice. Each time, Appleyard had attended the proceedings as U.S. representative and liaison officer. And each time the number of candidates—all of them Europeans, of course; and all of them recommended through various members of the Council of Ministers or through the Council of Commissioners—had been pared down. The third and final meeting of the Selection Committee would be held in Brussels in September. Accordingly, mid-August was an ideal time for a final run-through of the dossiers of those few who had made it to the short list—

men who understood how to play "the European game" to their own advantage without upsetting delicate balances.

The files yielded nothing unexpected. Appleyard was within hailing distance of the last page of the last dossier when the private phone on his desk began to jangle.

"I know you don't want to be interrupted, Commander . . ."

Gibson smiled into the receiver at Mary Ellen's familiar and efficient voice. His secretary had the good sense to know what was important, and Gib had the good sense not to question her judgment. "What's up, Mary Ellen?"

"Admiral Vance's aide just came by with a big, fat folder in his hand, sir. It seems there's another name in the hat for Secretary-General at the EC."

Gibson whistled in surprise. "Is it somebody we already know or are we starting from square one?"

"Never heard of him before, sir. But he does work with Cyrus Benthoek. And the President himself has signed off on the recommendation."

Gib looked longingly through the French doors. From the sound of things, he could forget his rose garden for today. "Better fax it through to me here, Mary Ellen."

"Gladstone. Paul Thomas."

Appleyard read the name on the cover page of the dossier with professional curiosity. The pages Mary Ellen faxed through provided so thorough and detailed a background that there was no way it could have been assembled hastily. Late entry or not, some careful planning had gone into this move.

The most pleasant surprise for Appleyard was that an American should be a candidate at all for a post of such consequence in the EC. The least pleasant surprise was that the Gladstones were clearly died-in-the-wool, down-the-line Roman Catholics.

It wasn't a question of prejudice. Gib was too good a man for that. Still, the religion and ethics of Masonry were the warp and woof of his personal life. In his soul, this hard-nosed analyst and tough infighter was a mystic. This man who could be parachuted, metaphorically or actually, into any blazing trouble spot and be relied upon to emerge intact and with all the irons pulled out of the fire, was also a man whose philanthropy and attractive humanism were central in his life.

Dedicated to the principles of liberal education and to the use of enlightened reason to solve all problems, human and social, he never deviated from the holy path of Masonry's "Spiritual Pyramid"; of God's Spiritual Temple. The ceremonies of the Lodge that revolved around the Holy Altar and the Feast Days—the early-spring Feast Day of the Paschal Lamb was a good example—only added to his conviction that the ideals of Masonry outshone those of the Roman Catholic Church. Indeed, he took pride in the fact that it had been his organization that had brought the authority and supremacy of the Roman Church into question through such means as the translation of the Bible, the Word, and through that era of history called the Reformation.

At the same time, however, anyone who knew him well—his Catholic-born wife, Genie, above all—could tell you that Appleyard had only minor interest in the governance of the Masonic organization. Never mind Gib's own record as past Grand Steward of the Grand Lodge of the State of Virginia; as past Most Wise Master of the Chapter of Rose Croix; as current Commandery Generalissimo of the Lake Newcombe Commandery in the Mason's York Rite and deputy Grand High Priest of the 27th Capital District in the York Rite.

The fact remained that he cared little about the conflict of Light and Darkness. Rather, he immersed himself in the Rosicrucian levels in order to witness to the birth of the New Man and Woman. That, in fact, was the reason for his devotion to the music of Amadeus Mozart.

Appleyard frowned as he read through that obligatory portion of Paul Gladstone's record that dealt with his blood family. Gladstone's mother, Francesca, shaped up as more Catholic than the Pope. And his older brother, Christian, had opted for the priesthood. On the plus side, though, no one in the family except Paul seemed to be political.

Like his brother Christian, it seemed that Paul had had an early brush with the priesthood; but he had had the good sense to drop out of the Seminary. Having opted for degrees in law and finance from Harvard, this Gladstone had put himself on a fast track. He had been snapped up fairly quickly by Cyrus Benthoek's law firm. Did an impressive internship in Brussels and Strasbourg. Now, at barely thirty-six, he was a junior partner. Fluent in French, German, Italian, Russian and Mandarin Chinese. Married to a Chinese citizen, in fact. One child; a son. Principal residence in London. An estate in Ireland. An apartment in Paris. No problem about security status.

All of that was interesting. Some of it was even intriguing. But it didn't add up to anything that would move the EC Selection Committee either to view such a late entry with kindly eyes or to favor an American over the European candidates. The case for Paul Gladstone, though, was clinched in Appleyard's eyes by Gladstone's own words in the pages that came under the heading "Personal Statement." On page six, for example, Gladstone had written with remarkable understanding of "the opening up of wholly new bases for collaboration and transnational association." He had devoted several especially good paragraphs to "the present need for a wholly new mentality . . . nonnationalistic and nonsectarian."

Moreover, there was a nice balance to Gladstone's point of view. He had ended his personal statement with the words ". . . always keeping in mind that the Anglo-American establishment should maintain its power primacy until the transnational balance outweighs all other factors." That phrase alone put Paul Gladstone well ahead in Appleyard's estimation. Those words might have come straight from his own pen. Or straight from the Committee of Ten itself.

It remained only to check Gladstone's endorsements. As expected, there was a recommendation from Cyrus Benthoek. But what about the White House endorsement? Or, rather, the fact that the President himself had signed off on the endorsement. The old man didn't usually follow these matters in such detail. What, he wondered, was the story behind that presidential signature?

So absorbed had Appleyard become in the portrait of Paul Gladstone that he hadn't heard the final strains of *The Magic Flute* fade into silence. Still deep in thought, he was about to feed his stereo again—this time with the Maestro's Symphony No. 39 in the Masonic ritual key of E-flat major—when his private phone rang again.

"Read any good dossiers lately, Gib?" Admiral Vance's deep voice was relaxed and official at the same time.

"Hello, Bud. I thought you'd be checking in before long. I just finished reading the life and times of Paul Thomas Gladstone."

"And . . . ?"

Appleyard gave his boss the reading he was asking for. Professionally, he said, as an executive officer of the Committee of Ten, he could find no fault with the idea of this late entry as the next Secretary-General of the EC. And even on the personal level, he couldn't restrain a certain enthusiasm for such a maverick. A nonpracticing Roman Catholic. A Yankee who seemed more European than American, and who was very much at home in international affairs. Strong family bias in his life. No hint of womanizing or any problem with liquor or drugs. Given his family fortune, maybe even fairly incorruptible.

"Does it bother you, Gib, that he's a Catholic?" Always concerned about people in high places who were attached to what he frequently called "all that Pope folderol," apparently Vance wasn't convinced by Gladstone's disclaimer.

"It wouldn't matter if it did bother me," Appleyard answered. "The President wants him, and that's that. In fact, now that we're on the subject, what's in this particular deal that got it all the way up to the old man? Why would he put his name to it?"

"Beats me," Vance dissembled unconvincingly. "Wheels within wheels, I suppose. The President has his own pipelines. More to the point, how do you rate Gladstone's chances with the EC Selection Committee?"

Somewhere between slim and none was Appleyard's view. "You know the setup as well as I do. Except for one Brit, the Committee is European to the bone, just like the EC itself. It isn't likely to favor an American as Secretary-General. The post has too much influence. Too much access to too many people. To the twelve Prime Ministers, and to the seventeen EC Commissioners, for starters."

"That's just the point, Commander." Vance was all business now. "We can't let a chance for American influence at the top echelons of the EC pass us by. You'll be at the September meeting. We don't have a vote, of course. But if it begins to look bad for Gladstone, get a postponement on the vote. Be inventive. Buy us some time to change a few minds. We need . . ."

"I know, Bud." Appleyard laughed, and came up with his best presidential imitation. "We need toeholds and handgrips."

Windswept
House

XIX

FOR ALL of Francesca Gladstone's seventy years, her home at Windswept had been the house of God and the gate of the Heaven she hoped to reach. Intangibly but really for her, God had set Jacob's Ladder down in this place, and here she moved in the company of Angels who descended and ascended between this private heaven of hers of earth and the Heaven of God's glory.

That did not mean that Cessi Gladstone's life at Windswept House had been all ringed round with cherub faces like some della Robbia ceramic or that tragedy had been a stranger here. On the contrary. Her mother had died when Cessi was barely five. Her own marriage—not a happy one—had ended with the early death of her husband in a stupid and bloody accident. And, while the Gladstone fortune and the family status in the Vatican as *privilegiati di Stato* had provided sturdy bulwarks for her, raising her three children during the sixties and seventies had been like holding out—with mixed success, as she was the first to admit—against a siege that had been raised against her faith. A siege against her whole way of life.

Tragedies and troubles notwithstanding, an inner happiness was a solid and ever shining archway covering all the years of Cessi's life at Windswept House. She had known discontent, disappointment, regret and anger. But she had never ceased to possess what can only be called happiness of soul.

Cessi Gladstone possessed an opaque intuition of future things. It was nothing so precise as visions or a detailed knowledge of events yet to happen. It was more in the nature of foreboding; a foretaste of the effect of impending changes. It was her mood, in fact, more than her mind that would suddenly begin to reflect things in the offing. And more often than not—more often than was comforting, especially when the lives of her children were involved—Cessi's instincts had proved correct.

In the spring of this year of change in Christian's Roman career, it was Cessi's youngest child and only daughter, Patricia, who had first picked up on the fact that just such a mood had taken hold. There was nothing specific that Tricia could define. Her mother hadn't looked any different that morning than she normally did. At seventy, Cessi Gladstone was still an erect five foot eight. Long-legged, long-waisted and without unneeded fat, she looked like a woman of fifty; and she moved with all of the strong grace of the prima ballerina she had once been. She never merely walked; she strode. Every action seemed to come from some invisible, invincible inner center of balance.

That one morning, though, in the sunny breakfast room where the two Gladstone women began their day, Tricia knew her mother's built-in barometer had begun to register changes. Maybe it was that her mother's Gothic face, with its utterly white skin, had seemed too flushed that day. Maybe Cessi's strong mouth and the slightly aquiline nose of all the true Gladstones had seemed too pinched. Maybe those wide-set eyes had changed from their normally soft blue to the flashing green of the older woman's sharper moods. Or maybe it was the way Cessi had pulled her gray-flecked auburn hair back so severely. Whatever it was, Tricia couldn't help remarking on her own intuitive sense that something was troubling her mother.

"Nonsense, darling." Cessi had pooh-poohed Patricia's concern. "Everything couldn't be better." She might have saved herself the trouble, though. In reality Tricia was no more convinced by Cessi's words than Cessi herself.

"Nonsense yourself, Miss Cessi." Beulah Thompson, just in from the kitchen with a fresh pot of steaming coffee in her hand and a frown on her forehead, had weighed in. "Anyone who's got half an eye'll see somethin's wrong." A handsome, rawboned mother of four and grandmother of three, Beulah had been housekeeper and confidante to the Gladstones for nearly twenty years. She felt herself to be a believing and faithful member of the local Baptist church. But first and foremost, Beulah felt herself to be a bona fide Gladstone and a part of any family conversation that took place in her presence.

Faced with these two women who knew her so well, Cessi finally admitted the truth. A sense of deep changes about to come had taken hold of her again, but she couldn't be any more specific than that. Until events put a face on her foreboding—there was nothing she could do but wait.

No sooner was that unaccustomed idea of helplessness out of her mouth, however, than Cessi rebelled against her own words. Whether in Cornwall, England, or in Galveston, Texas, Gladstones had never just sat and waited for anything, she declared; and she was not about to be the first. This year's reunion of her family promised to be exceptional, and no premonitions or moods or changes or anything else was going to get in the way of that. Christian would be coming home from Italy for two weeks at the end of August. And this year, Paul would be coming home, too, along with his little son, Declan, who figured as one of the great joys of Cessi's life. Paul would bring his wife, Yusai, too, of course; but Cessi figured she could put up with that.

"Let's all spit straight into the eye of premonition, then!" Cessi's face had lit up with such a sudden fire of determined enthusiasm that Tricia and Beulah Thompson were engulfed in the flames before they knew it.

"We'll polish this old pile from top to bottom. We'll make this a summer Galveston will never forget!"

No sooner had she decided to bring Windswept House to life again than she had set about the doing of it. Cessi worked up a flowchart of everything that was to be done. With the late August arrival of her two sons as reward, nothing would do but a total refurbishment of every room in the house.

For Cessi Gladstone, the preparations at Windswept turned out to be a special boon, a time of unexpected celebration in itself.

Before the end of May, relays of carpenters and plumbers and cleaners, electricians and roofers, upholsterers and gardeners were already trooping in and out of the great mansion, working methodically according to Cessi's flowchart, their labor subject to her constant scrutiny. Under Cessi's watchful eye, Windswept had its face washed. The red-brick outer walls of the mansion were sprayed clean from ground level all the way up to the Tower Chapel; and the semicircle of intricate wrought iron that embraced the porch and sunroom was made to look as it had in the 1870s when Old Glad had first had it installed.

Inside, meanwhile, there was hardly a splinter that wasn't smoothed or a speck of dust not doomed. The dozens of Oriental carpets Paul Gladstone had imported were taken up and cleaned, while the tiger-striped maple flooring Glad had imported from Italy was made to shine with its original hues of biscuit brown and amber.

In the foyer, which curved around the grand L-shaped staircase leading to the second floor, the enormous oaken grandfather clock Old Glad had brought home with him from Zurich was given some particularly loving and expert attention. "Oakey Paul," Cessi's children had always called that clock. No matter where you were in Windswept—even up in the Tower Chapel the rich chimes of Oakey Paul could be heard telling the hours and half hours and quarter hours.

Under Cessi's direction, it was Beulah who took charge of the library. She had all the books and family records taken from their shelves so that everything could be cleaned. In the great hall to the left of the foyer, built as a replica of the great hall of Launceston Manor, the Gladstones' ancient ancestral home in Cornwall, it was Cessi who directed the refurbishing of everything, beginning with the open fireplace and twelve-foot-high mantelpiece and ending with the oaken beams that raftered its ceiling. When she was done, the splendid Elizabethan table that seated sixty guests, and all the high-backed Elizabethan benches that cozied up to it, seemed more majestic than ever.

Tricia insisted on overseeing the cleaning of the many oil portraits and paintings that hung at Windswept: of José de Evia, who had first charted Galveston in the eighteenth century, for instance; and Spanish Viceroy Bernardo de Gálves, who had sent Evia here and who had given Galveston its name, but who had never himself visited the island; of Cabeza de Vaca, the first Spaniard who had set foot on Galveston; and of Jean Lafitte, portrayed with the famous patch over one eye and his feet planted in front of his blood-red two-story house at Campeachy.

In terms of monetary value, the prize collection of paintings was housed on the second floor of Windswept, in the formal drawing room. Here, among some half dozen old masters Glad had acquired on his later visits to Europe, two paintings held pride of place: El Greco's St. Simeon and a grand portrait of Pope Pius IX, who had received Old Glad so warmly in the Vatican of the Risorgimento and whose papal rescript had truly made Windswept House viable, even to this day, in its fullness as a bastion of Roman Catholicism. In terms of emotional value, meanwhile, nothing could match the family portraits that adorned the walls of the second-floor landing. Beginning with Old Glad himself and his wife, Francesca, the faces of all the Gladstones who had lived at Windswept looked down from their gilt frames to greet any who might climb the nine-foot-wide staircase that swept up from the ground floor.

All summer long, as she looked into every corner of Old Glad's mansion, Cessi was reliving her entire life. Clambering around the house, climbing its staircases, examining a photograph, stopping in front of a portrait, she experienced the truth of what St. Paul had said in one of his letters: all of us go through our earthly existence accompanied by "a cloud of witnesses." By all our forebears and all who put their share into the making of the good and the bad, the holy and the unholy in us. Without nostalgia, without self-satisfaction, but only with the confidence and the happiness of soul that had never failed her, she walked in the presence of each of the people whose faces and voices were now a part of the heritage of Windswept House.

So it was that July arrived at Windswept before anyone was ready. Plans for the brunches and lunches and dinners to be given in August and September had to be firmed up, and invitations had to be sent.

All of Galveston was caught up in the game of guessing who would be invited to the celebrations at Windswept House. Because the Gladstones had always been more a part of the New Orleans diocese than of their own, everyone figured that Cardinal O'Cleary would be a house guest for at least a day or two. The mayor would surely be a dinner guest more than once. Prominent Galvestonians and old friends of the Gladstones still in the area would be invited, and memories were stretched to recall members of the family who lived in other parts of the country.

In all this whirlwind of work and excitement, Cessi would never retire for the night without first climbing the steep spiral stairs to the Tower Chapel. There, for a quiet hour or so, she would do what she had done since earliest childhood: discuss all of her problems and concerns—and above all those tenacious forebodings that had taken hold of her—with

Christ in the Tabernacle, with the Blessed Virgin and the Saints and with those Angels gathered at the foot of Jacob's Ladder.

Everyone in the family knew that the Tower Chapel was Cessi's special place. It wasn't just that she and her children had all been baptized here, or that she had been married here, or that every Gladstone since Old Glad himself, including Cessi's mother, Elizabeth, and her father, Declan, had been buried from here. It was as well that every experience of her curious gift of premonition had been closely linked in one way and another to the Chapel.

Cessi's first conscious experience of that gift had occurred at such an early age that, at the time, she had had no words with which to share it. It was the memory of her mother, whose portrait corresponded exactly with Cessi's recollection of her; a frail young woman with jet-black hair and high-boned cheeks and a gentle mouth and laughing blue eyes. It was the memory of the somber presentiment that had taken hold in her heart months before her mother had fallen ill. It was the memory of her father's face, wet with tears and yet so strong with love and faith, as he told her in this very Chapel what she already knew. "Our laughing angel," Declan had said to his little Cessi, "has gone with Our Lord to be happy in Heaven."

The second such event in her young life had been more in the nature of the sublime. Cessi was eight years old by then. Holy Week had nearly ended, and in every sense winter was ready to give way to early spring. Cessi had gone with her father and Aunt Dotsie to St. Mary's Cathedral for Good Friday devotions. Dotsie had come to live at Windswept in order to take care of the children.

Kneeling between her father and Dotsie in the family pew, Cessi listened. At each Station, a verse of the *Stabat Mater* hymn was sung, followed by a short meditation and prayer. "*. . . give me Thy grace and Thy love, Lord Jesus,*" the congregation prayed aloud as one, "*and then do with me what Thou wilt.*" She heard that prayer, of course; but at a certain moment she heard another voice as well. Soundless. Clear. Gentle. Soft in its effect. Intimate to her alone. A voice of Someone who had always been with her, near her; nearer even than her father. A voice that promised she would indeed have His grace and His love. A voice that promised that He would do with her according to His will. It was a precious moment that came and was over in a flash; an announcement that filled Cessi's mind and soul to overflowing.

When she and her family had returned to Windswept and she was helping her father prepare the Tower Chapel for the Easter Vigil, she found that a strange and comforting radiance seemed to follow her from the Tabernacle. It followed her in the Chapel in the same way the silvery radiance of the full moon on the Gulf would follow her when she ran with friends along the beach. "Daddy." Cessi had called to her father. This time, she wanted to try to find words. "Daddy. It follows me." Her voice was thin but clear, and a sweet flooding of tears brimmed in her eyes. "He follows me."

Favored with some grace of his own, Declan understood. He knew she had been granted an experience of what lies beyond the perception of all our senses and mind.

Cessi saw that experience ever afterward as something much more than premonition. She saw it as nothing less than a providential preparation for a life that was to open up almost at once to the world outside of Windswept House.

Aunt Dotsie had been the unlikely catalyst for the first stage of Cessi's new life. Cessi, Dotsie decided, had become too much of a tomboy. It was none too soon for the future mistress of Windswept House to "learn to be a lady." It was time, therefore, that she attend local dance classes.

To everyone's astonishment, Cessi had taken to dance as though every day of her first eight years had prepared her for it; as though dance was the exact bodily expression of the promise of supernatural grace that had already provided the spiritual center of balance for her.

By the time Cessi was twelve, she realized that her ability to dance was more than a gift of nature. It was a responsibility, she told her father; a calling that obliged her to create visible if transient beauty out of human movement. From that time forward, a very particular merger took place. A singular marriage between the center of balance she needed as a dancer and the center she had already found in her religion became the center of balance and control for her life; a permanent condition of her being. With only one exception in her life, Cessi never abandoned those twin centers of balance inside her being; and from them, all of her happiness seemed to flower, and all of her freedom flowed.

In her early teens, Cessi organized a little dance company of her own and began to give programs and exhibitions. At sixteen, she toured with the Ballet Russe. She studied for a time with the famed Alberto Galo of New York. At twenty-one she was invited by Cecchetti—widely esteemed as Pavlova's teacher and considered one of the greatest ballet instructors of all time—to do the exam for membership in the Imperial Society of Teachers and Dancers. Only five Americans had ever taken that exam successfully. Cessi became the sixth.

While Declan was immensely proud of his daughter, he was never entirely comfortable with her long absences from Windswept. He was as pleased as he was surprised, therefore, when Cessi suddenly decided to turn away from the public recognition that was beginning to attend her career. She arrived home from a tour and announced to her father that "God does not want me to be a performer. He wants me to teach."

Declan took Cessi's word in the matter to heart. If she said God wanted her to teach, then teach she would. He not only involved himself in helping his daughter organize her own school of dance but remained her partner in managing the business affairs of the academy. At the same time, now that Cessi was home again for good, Declan began a gentle campaign to persuade her to choose one among the many men who found her attractive. It was time for her to marry.

As it turned out, that pressure from her father to marry provided the matrix for another major episode of foreboding in Cessi's soul. For some reason she could not fathom, even the idea of marriage felt like a threat to her. A threat to that centering balance that had been the mainstay of all her strength since that providential year when she was eight. She was not at all interested in marriage, Cessi told her father plainly and often. What finally impelled Cessi to marry was simple. At thirty-one, she finally had to agree with her father that if she was to have children, she had better set about it. What impelled her to accept Evan Wilson as her husband, however, was something no one ever understood.

Born to a family of cattle ranchers whose Texas holdings were sometimes compared to the fabled King Ranch, but not much of a rancher himself, Evan was attracted to Galveston by the mix of opposite pleasures he found there. He thrived on its tenderloin district, but also on the self-contained society framed in the lives of families like the Gladstones. Evan didn't exactly fall in love with Cessi. What attracted him was her unattainability. Independent women were for him what mountains are for climbers. Whenever he found one, he was her slave until he had conquered her. With his attractive side to the fore, he found any number of imaginative ways and entertaining reasons to see Cessi. But courtship as a prelude to marriage was not what he had in mind. The contest for him was simply to possess this obstinate creature. And in his way, he was as stubborn as she.

It was during a holiday dinner party at Windswept that Evan's fondness for drink and his frustration at Cessi's constant refusal of his advances finally combined to undo him. In too jovial a mood after several glasses of wine, Evan rose from his chair, tapped his crystal glass as if to offer a toast and then, with all faces turned toward him, was astonished to hear words coming out his mouth that he had never intended. Words that promised Cessi the moon and the stars if only she would marry him.

Had he been sober, probably no one would have been more surprised than he—unless it might have been Declan—when, with a peculiar air of challenge and defiance about her, Cessi agreed to the marriage. The moon and the stars, she said as she raised her glass in answer to Evan's, held no interest for her. It would be enough for her simply to live all her life at Windswept, to raise a family with Evan, and to continue to teach the young to dance at her academy.

What marital feeling there was between Cessi and Evan was never more than lukewarm at best. They did produce three children in quick succession—Christian first, in 1954; Paul the year following; and Patricia in

1956. But with the birth of each child, Evan became increasingly peevish and ill-humored. It was following Tricia's birth that all the fault lines in the marriage finally gave way. He became resentful of Cessi's attention to the children; to her dance students; to her father; to her many friends. To anyone but himself. His drinking became a scandal. But it was only after a series of violent scenes that Cessi actually became fearful for the physical safety of the children.

It had come even to the point that, having been bloodied one night in her efforts to keep Evan from rampaging into the rooms where their children were asleep, Cessi swore to her husband that, as God was in Heaven, her own blood would have to drip from his hands before she would allow him to be alone with Christian or Paul or Tricia again.

Aghast that his good intentions for his daughter had come to such a pass, and convinced that it promised to end in disaster, Declan waited one night for Evan to return from one of his escapades into debauchery. Still robust for a man in his mid-sixties, he literally hauled his son-in-law into the library, sobered him up by pouring strong coffee down his gullet and, when he was sure every word would be heard and understood, proceeded to lay out the conditions upon which Evan would remain welcome at Windswept.

There was some demon in Evan, though; some volcanic anger whose flames no one could cap. He more or less drifted back to his family's ranch on the mainland. In the end, it was a cousin who brought the news of the accident to Windswept. Cessi couldn't follow all the details. Something about spring roundup and about drinking with a couple of the hands; about branding and a wild bet and a rope that had got tangled around Evan's arm before he could secure it to his saddle. The only thing clear to her was that Evan's death had been a drunken and bloody affair.

Christian was just five when his father died. Paul was four. Tricia, barely three. Nevertheless, remembering that she had been no older than Christian when her own mother had died, Cessi was saddened that her children would not be left with the same certainty of ultimate grace for Evan that she had known for her mother. It was a legitimate concern, for Cessi was fairly sure that Christian at least, and perhaps Paul and Tricia as well, had seen and been affected by far more of their father's behavior than they could say. So it was with prayers of thanks that she watched how all of them somehow made a peaceful place in their hearts for their father. They never indulged in false or childish reminiscences about their father. But never did they fail to pray for his immortal soul.

Cessi consciously sought and found again that center of balance she had abandoned. During the years of her marriage, Cessi came to realize, it was this center that had saved her sanity. In the turbulent years to come, never again would she step aside from that centering balance; and never would it abandon her. That did not mean, however, that she would ever again find the simple and singular harmony that had marked her earlier life. The deepest disruptions still lay ahead. The whole world she had known—the world of Galveston and of America, the world of her beloved Church, and to some degree, the world of Windswept House itself—all of that was about to be swept away.

XX

"IT'S NEARLY the end of August, Mother, and in spite of your forebodings, we're still in one piece." Head bent back and eyes staring upward in the early-morning light, Patricia Gladstone perched on the edge of the chaise longue in her bedroom. "Before you know it, Chris will be home; and then Paul and his family."

"Hold still, Tricia, or these drops will end up in your hair instead of your eyes!"

Obediently, Tricia leaned back, tilted her head and, despite the pain it cost her, held her eyes wide open so that Cessi could administer the latest solution of artificial tears prescribed in the continual battle to preserve her eyesight. For over a decade now, Tricia had suffered from an agonizing affliction for which the doctors had a name—keratoconjunctivitis sicca—but for which no antidote or certain treatment had yet been devised.

In basic terms, the affliction involved a progressive dryness of the eyes that affected sight and, if unchecked, could be the prelude to life-threatening illness. In terms of day-to-day living for Patricia Gladstone, it meant a steady battle against pain, and a constant effort to stave off ultimate calamity. The marvel was that Tricia was strong enough to pursue her chosen career as an artist, and that despite her agonies she never lost that sharp edge to her character that was so like Cessi's.

"That's one eye." Cessi applied the artificial tears with an expertise that only comes with practice. "And that makes two."

"It won't be long now." Tricia didn't want to be distracted from the point she had been making. "You have to admit, Mother, that everything's working out just fine. Chris will be home this weekend. A couple of days after that, Paul and his family will be here. With Windswept so sparkling, the worst that can happen is that they'll think they've come to the wrong house and pass us by!"

Cessi wished she could agree. Despite her best efforts, though, for the past day or so Cessi had jumped like a nervous cat whenever the phone had rung, fully anticipating news that would give form to her shadowy expectation.

"Let's face it, Mother." Tricia rose from the chaise and changed from her robe into one of her painter's smocks. "Maybe just this once, these premonitions of yours are nothing more than the results of indigestion."

"Don't let Beulah hear you say that!" Cessi had to laugh out loud at the thought.

Laughter and affectionate jokes about Beulah Thompson aside, there was a shading in Cessi's voice that made Tricia understand that this wasn't the moment to brush things aside with a comforting word or two. Under her daughter's prodding, Cessi finally began to share her forebodings.

For one thing, Cessi told her daughter, her feelings seemed nothing like those that had warned her against what had turned out to be the darker consequences of her marriage to Evan Wilson. But there was no doubt in her mind that whatever was in the offing had everything to do with her own family. And she had the persistent sense that her premonition would not merely be confirmed after the fact by exterior events but would somehow be announced by such events.

All in all, Cessi confided to Tricia, the fact was that she felt now—over thirty years later—almost exactly as she had at the beginning of the terrible events that had begun to unfold in 1960.

Until the year following Evan's death, whenever Cessi had felt change in the air, it was always a matter of vague interior feelings. But the first harbinger of change in the sixties had been different. It had been specific; and it had been unsettling and significant enough in itself that she had not been the only one to recognize it as a foreshock of larger earthquakes to come.

Because the famed Fatima mandates instructed "the Pope of 1960" to reveal the Third Fatima Secret to the world, and to lead all the bishops of the Church Universal in a consecration of Russia to Mary under her title as the Immaculate Conception, everyone expected the good Pope John to do exactly that. But the Pope refused to obey that mandate. There was no consecration of Russia. The famous Third Secret was not revealed to millions of expectant Roman Catholics.

Cessi was beset by foreboding. "Maybe everyone does call him the good Pope," she had warned. "But even a Pope can't refuse to obey the mandate of the Queen of Heaven and expect to get away with it." The appalling and unacceptable reality of the good Pope's decision was borne home for Cessi and Declan when, as *privilegiati di Stato,* they had attended the formal opening of his Second Vatican Council on October 11, 1962, and sat in special tribune seats of St. Peter's Basilica on the day the Council opened.

The two Gladstones had listened to the Pontiff announce to the bishops gathered in from every diocese, to the Church Universal and to the world at large what he intended that his Council should achieve. He spoke of modernizing and bringing up to date his churchly organization; of opening up the Church to non-Catholics and non-Christians; of the need to relax strict rules that punished those who violated Church law or rejected its sacred doctrines.

To Cessi and Declan, all of that sounded like a renunciation of the strong stance their Church had always taken. Even worse, it sounded as if the good Pope was apologetic instead of proud of what their Church had done and of what it had been up to that time. Worst of all, it sounded as if the good Pope had been persuaded that today the Church had to turn to the world in order to learn how to be a true Church.

There had been no way to assuage Cessi's wrath or mitigate her contempt. She went up in flames even before she and her father had left the Basilica; nor did she bother to keep her voice down. "I don't know about you, Daddy, but I feel as if our Gladstone family status has provided us with front-row seats at the public announcement of the Church's execution. This fat old Pope has slapped all Catholics—bishops, priests and people—right across the face!" The best thing they could do, she said, was to leave Rome and get back to Windswept House as quickly as they could.

Cessi had watched the innovations that began to come from the bishops in Council with a distrust that went to her very marrow. Gladstone that she was, she had a deep instinct bred in her family since the early days in Cornwall when her ancestors had seen the enemy closing in on them, on their faith and on all they held dear. Yet no one in 1962 could foresee precisely the extent to which Rome, its bishops and its Popes would embrace what many later came to characterize as wolves in clerical clothing whose aim was lethal for Roman Catholic doctrine and morality.

At first, the Council's innovations came piecemeal. Soon, though, the changes increased to a steady trickle, and then to a flood. Without any nod or say-so from either the Pope or the Council bishops, new armies of self-styled "liturgical experts" and "catechesis teachers" and church "architectural specialists" went to work. All the dioceses of America, including Galveston, were drenched in what Cessi and Declan saw as liberalist morality, un-Catholic liturgy, denuded churches and watered-down beliefs. Even the Masses offered at St. Mary's Cathedral, now said in English, frequently became folksy celebrations of local custom and political causes, rather than the profession and celebration of the central act of the Catholic faith. In Galveston, as elsewhere, congregations were instructed to stand up, and then to sit, and then to shake hands. Only rarely were they to kneel any longer in the presence of God.

Cessi realized that the changes coming out of Rome would overhaul society in general to such an extent that, no matter what provisos she took, her children would be deeply affected.

Skillfully and devotedly, therefore, she had changed the rhythm of household life at Windswept. She and Declan participated far less frequently in the social life of Galveston. Cessi's whole life now revolved around the rearing of her children; the defense of the Catholic faith in their lives as the loyal papist Gladstones they were; and the continuation of her own calling as a teacher of dance.

As the effects of the Second Vatican Council began to multiply, the Gladstones attended Mass only at Windswept's Tower Chapel. Private religious instruction for the three children took the place of the new "catechesis classes." When it was no longer practical for her children to be home-schooled, Cessi made certain that the Mother Superior of Tricia's school, and the Brothers who ran the school she chose for Christian and Paul, understood that her hefty financial contributions would continue just as long as they adhered to superior scholarship and solid Catholic doctrine.

Toward the end of the sixties, Cessi's reckoning that secular life would change profoundly was starting to prove true. The private and public life of society was being uncoupled from its moral underpinnings, and there was no shielding of her children from all that. The best Cessi could do, she told Declan, was to keep Christian and Paul and Tricia alert to the dangers of the new secularist conformity that was springing up as what she regarded as a new state religion; to continue to provide them with an articulate understanding of their Roman, Catholic and Apostolic faith; and always to foster that independence of mind that was to remain a constant element in the life and character of each of them.

So complete—so self-contained and self-sufficient—had Cessi and Declan made life at Windswept House that, by 1969, it almost seemed that nothing could transform it. It was just about that time, however, that a seemingly routine matter turned into a watershed event that was to harden still further her attitude toward the far-reaching consequences of the good Pope's Second Vatican Council.

Cessi and Declan had been asked to travel to Washington, D.C., for a meeting with Treasury officials over some of the Gladstone holdings in currently sensitive areas of Latin America. Though they had booked their suite well ahead of time at the Hay-Adams Hotel, they had checked in only to find their rooms weren't yet ready. The problem, it seemed, was a well-attended convention of priests in favor of a married clergy.

A married clergy was as shocking and impossible a contradiction in terms for Cessi and Declan as a quadriplegic brain surgeon, or a sinless Satan. Yet, as they waited in the hotel lobby, they were surrounded by priests of every age and description. A few of the graybeards were in clerical clothes, but most wore slacks and sport shirts. A few breviaries were to be seen in this contingent; but far more numerous were the women who had come along as assistants or, as one bellhop winked, as "housekeepers." Some hundreds of delegates in their thirties and forties betrayed no visible sign of their priestly status, and seemed to enjoy nothing so much as socializing in the bar, while a still younger element—just out of seminary in all likelihood—skittered about the hotel lobby like students on the town after a college basketball tournament. Dressed in a mad variety of casual clothes, they appeared fond of gathering around in groups, strumming guitars and singing "The Impossible Dream" loudly and off key.

Seized by a mixture of curiosity and horror, Cessi and Declan checked the notice board in the lobby that listed the activities scheduled for this convention of priests. One seminar, they saw, was to deal with the subject of "The Anthropology of Priesthood." Another was to take a look at "The Role of Women in Redemptive Lives." Others were to examine such matters as "Sexuality in the Service of God" and, to Declan's supreme outrage, "The Androgyny of Human Love as Portrayed in the Bible."

Angry to the point of fury, Declan couldn't sleep that night. The next morning, Cessi found her father, chalk white and shaking, still seated at the writing table. Emergency medical examinations in Washington were inconclusive. But specialists Cessi summoned to Galveston immediately on their return home found that Declan had suffered a mild stroke.

Though suddenly deprived of the robust health he had enjoyed all his life, and unable to tend to normal business or to romp outdoors any longer with Cessi's children, Declan seemed content to spend most of his time within the confines of Windswept. At his age, he said with a wry kind of humor, it was only to be expected that the cogs and flywheels of his machinery should need some adjusting.

Declan never recovered. He lingered for about eight months, but the onrush of the so-called "reforms" emanating from the post-Council bureaucracy was too much for him. He died peacefully and surrounded by his family. Francesca Gladstone was mistress of Windswept House now. And just as she had defended her children from being ravaged by her husband's hand, so now she would defend herself, her children and all who were associated with Windswept House from the ravages being perpetrated on the immemorial Roman Catholic Mass. The *Novus Ordo* would never be said in the Tower Chapel. Now more than ever, Cessi became the personification of her family's motto: she would give No Quarter in her lifelong battle to remain faithful to the Roman Catholicism of her papist forebears.

The more Cessi tried to explain things that morning by recalling the family's past, the more Tricia began to chime in. She had her own bittersweet memories of the weeks after Grandfather Declan died. "Remember how Christian took charge of things even then, Mother?" Tricia's voice carried all the warmth she felt for her older brother.

Christian Thomas Gladstone was thirteen when his grandfather died. Declan's life had made it plain that Gladstone men carried the honor of the family, and that they did not use women, but protected them. With such lessons in mind, and all the compassion, command and independence he had already learned from Cessi, Chris had presented himself in Cessi's sitting room early one Saturday morning about a month after Declan's death.

He was now the man of this family, he announced to his mother. Paul and Tricia, hair rumpled and still in their nighties, had stood beside him with all the gravity they could command. They agreed that, apart from school, they would all three become Cessi's partners, just as their grandfather had been, in managing the affairs of Windswept House, and of the dance academy as well.

Cessi was stunned to tears by this sudden and unexpected reversal of roles. Nothing had ever erased from her mind a single detail of the proud memory of those three "perfect little persons" of hers who had taken it upon themselves to lay out the family's future.

There was Christian, with that unmistakable Gladstone look about him. Already taller than Cessi, even then, with that slightly aquiline nose set above his strong mouth, and those wide-set eyes flashing blue, he might have been a youthful version of Old Glad himself. Paul was maturing somewhat more slowly than his brother; but apart from that, and a certain difference in their character—a certain set to his jaw that told of stubbornness that went beyond independence—he might almost have been Christian's fraternal twin. Tricia, meanwhile, was her own person. Though lanky like the boys, there was already a grace about her that often reminded people of Cessi herself. Her hair tended to auburn hues like her mother's and her brothers'; but it was just a few shades lighter. Her skin was a few shades darker, though, so she never had to bother as Cessi did about the strong summer sun of Galveston.

Whatever their similarities or differences, from that day until Christian and Paul left home in quick succession a few years later, Cessi's three children had remained as one in their determination. They became closer to her, and a more intimate part of her incessant activities than ever before. Each day after their classes let out, they went to work at the dance academy. And such was their development, their talent and their demeanor of command even then that the staff quickly learned to work as easily with them as they had with Declan.

Cessi not only involved the children in the affairs of the household but began to acquaint them with the intricacies of managing the family fortune. All three proved to be quick studies; but even in his earliest teens Paul had taken most keenly to the Gladstone financial portfolios.

There was no denying the gap left in their lives now that Declan was gone. Nevertheless, and understandably, it was Aunt Dotsie who had been most profoundly affected by the loss of her brother. Dotsie had rarely been away from Windswept. As the quietest member of this unquiet family, she had always sacrificed herself for others. Her constant tenderness had been like part of the atmosphere—something everyone relied upon even while taking it for granted. Less than a year after Declan's death, Dotsie died very much as she had lived. Without provoking any painful shock or rupture, she slipped quietly away one night from sleep into eternity.

Such were the hurricanes of change battering at the world around them by then that at any place but Windswept House, and in any family except Cessi's, the loss in such quick succession of two such important people as Declan and Dorothy Gladstone—the last two living links with the stability of past generations—might have been the catalyst for strife and disruption.

Elsewhere in Galveston, that peculiarly self-aware society for which the Gladstones remained an inspiration was attempting to keep its balance in the high winds of cultural upheaval. Unlike Cessi, however, many were sure it was just a matter of sensible compromise. A little modernization. It wouldn't matter much if they took a tuck or two in their moral stance, or revised their religious beliefs here and there. If they were judicious, the rougher side of the new cultural revolution would surely pass over them. After all, their Catholic Church had been the first organized religion to arrive in Texas, having come with the Spanish and the French. In 1838, the first Christian service in Galveston had been a Catholic Mass. By Cessi's day, there was a large diocesan seminary, four academies for girls and five schools for boys. And on top of all that, there were strong congregations of Baptists, Methodists, Presbyterians, Episcopalians, Lutherans, Jews and Christian Scientists. Between them all, the members of these religious denominations strove to remain more or less dominant as the wild storms of change broke upon the world.

Within barely two years of Declan's death, however, it was no longer a question of small compromises or of minor revisions in religious practice. Rather, profound religious instability was as much the order of the day in Galveston as in the rest of America and the world. And, as Cessi had expected, social instability rose in its wake.

For Cessi Gladstone, there was no sense of triumph in having been right. She was far too large-minded for that. It was true that those storms were a painful vindication of her decade-long campaign to maintain the status quo. But they were also a fierce new stimulus to give No Quarter, and to ask for none.

XXI

"MISS CESSI!" Beulah Thompson scolded from the door of Tricia's sitting room, her voice as rich as the chimes of Oakey Paul telling the hour of eight o'clock from the downstairs foyer. Concerned these days over "Miss Cessi's humors," as she called Cessi's deepening sense of some ill wind rising, Beulah relied on her common sense to keep things on a fairly even keel. "Miss Cessi! Are you two aimin' to pass the whole day cluckin' up here like a couple o' hens? Breakfast's been ready for over an hour!"

"Don't be a grouch, Beulah!" Cessi scolded back. "We've just been talking about all the crises we've weathered over the years."

"Ain't no reason you can't do that over fresh fruit and homemade bread." Beulah stuck to her guns.

In no way chastened but enticed at the thought of Beulah's incomparable home-baked bread, Cessi and Tricia headed for the sunny third-floor breakfast room. But so deep were they by now in their examination of just how prescient Cessi's feelings of foreboding had proved in the past that they settled into conversation again almost as if there had been no interruption.

By the end of the sixties, Cessi had constricted her participation in the social life of the Island even further than she and Declan had done. The fourth-floor guest rooms were sufficient to handle the few friends and family members who might be invited for a visit to Windswept. The rooms on the fifth floor were closed. With the notable exception of Beulah Thompson, members of the household staff who left or retired were rarely replaced. The worst of it for Cessi in going it alone was the fact that by 1970 or so it had become well-nigh impossible to find a priest who could be relied on regularly to say an authentic Roman Catholic Mass in the Tower Chapel at Windswept.

"It got so difficult," Cessi confided to Tricia as though sharing a naughty secret, "that I began to give Our Lord a few reality reminders during my prayers up in the Chapel. It did us a fat lot of good, I told Him, to have the papal rescript allowing us to celebrate the Holy Sacrifice of His Body and Blood at Windswept if He was going to allow those fools in Rome to take all our faithful priests from us and replace them with a crowd of lewd buffoons in round collars."

"You didn't put it like that, I hope!" Like the rest of the family, Tricia had always lived with the reality of Cessi's special familiarity with the citizens of Heaven.

"Of course I did, sweetheart." Cessi smiled her most innocent smile over the cup of coffee raised to her lips. "And a good thing I did, too. Why else do you think our flamboyant friend Traxler Le Voisin popped into our lives all of a sudden?"

Tricia had no answer to that. But she certainly did remember the day Traxler "Everyone Calls Me Traxi" Le Voisin had come to Windswept. Flamboyant was only one way to describe this local sculptor and father of seven. Inflammatory was another that came to mind. Persuaded that neither the good Pope nor his immediate successor were what he and his ilk regarded as "true Popes," Traxi Le Voisin was one of the latter-day breed of Roman Catholics known as *sede vacantists.* They were persuaded, in other words, that in legal terms Peter's Chair had been vacant since the late 1950s.

Papist that she was, Cessi had never agreed with Traxi on that issue. When he had come to Windswept for the first time, at the head of a delegation representing some sixty faithful Catholic families in the area, she was nearly put off his scheme altogether by his insistence that "the true Pope—Pope Pius XIII—must be hiding somewhere in the world!" Traxi rescued himself, though, with another bit of indelicate candor. He and the others had asked for this meeting, he had said, because "everyone knows the mistress of Windswept House is fed up with the newfangled liturgy being foisted on the ordinary people by those impostors on Vatican Hill."

In a decision that was to be as far-reaching for herself and her children as any she had made, Cessi had agreed on the spot to cooperate in forming a new congregation, and to lend whatever protection the Gladstones' status might provide, so that authentic Roman Masses could be celebrated regularly by an authentic Roman Catholic priest for the benefit of the faithful.

Having secured what he and his little group had come for, Traxi had left Windswept that day determined to make the new congregation a practical reality. The first step—finding a suitable and affordable church building—was simple enough. Unused any longer by its Methodist owners, a little chapel on the mainland at Danbury was purchased, refurbished and renamed. It was now the Chapel of St. Michael the Archangel.

With the same fervor that had led him to Cessi Gladstone, meanwhile, Traxi lost no time in making contact with Archbishop Marcel Lefebvre of Switzerland. Famous—or notorious, depending on one's ecclesiastical politics—as one of only four bishops in the Church at that time who had refused to accept the new form of the Mass, Lefebvre had stood firm against the innovations in Church liturgy and doctrine, and had founded the Society of Pius X as a haven and touchstone for traditional-minded Roman Catholics. In short order, both Lefebvre and his Society had become flash points of controversy within his deeply divided Church.

Aware that even the Gladstone status in Rome was not sufficient to supply the canonical validity that was vital to the new Chapel, or to provide immunity from local diocesan officials who were sure to make trouble for any such traditionalist congregation as this one, Traxi wanted two things from Archbishop Lefebvre: he wanted St. Michael's Chapel to come under the umbrella of the Society of Pius X, and for the Society to supply the new Chapel with a validly ordained priest of orthodox belief for the Chapel's service.

Lefebvre supplied Traxi with at least half of what he wanted: he was pleased to adopt the new Chapel into the Society. And, though he had been unable to meet Traxi's second need, he at least recommended a most singular clergyman to fill that post.

❑ ❑ ❑ ❑

Despite the shock everyone felt at the first sight of his severely scarred face, the most striking thing about Father Angelo Gutmacher was the confidence with which he combined his ecclesiastical orthodoxy with his priestly kindness and wisdom.

A refugee from Communist East Germany, Gutmacher had been the only one of his family to be pulled alive from the arson fire that had destroyed their home in Leipzig late one night. Their bedrock Catholicism and their intransigent resistance to the Communist regime had made the Gutmachers targets for retribution at the hands of East Germany's secret police, the Stasi. Thanks to the care of a few brave friends, the boy had recovered from the terrible burns over his face and body and in time had escaped to West Germany. A couple of years in the home of aging relatives brought him to manhood, whereupon he had found and entered a seminary that was still holding against the tide of strange and unorthodox curricula being introduced into many seminaries around the world.

Upon his ordination, Gutmacher had sent a formal letter to Rome asking for an assignment under the aegis of the Congregation for the Clergy, fully expecting to be assigned to someplace in South America, perhaps, or to Indonesia. He went down to Rome in order to plead his cause.

At the time of Gutmacher's arrival in Rome, his dossier was brought to the attention of the Pope, together with the suggestion that such a loyal papist and orthodox priest might profitably be sent on a quasi-permanent basis to America. At the very least, he could be relied upon to keep both the Pontiff and the Congregation for the Clergy up to date on developments there.

As he began his odd American mission, his firm tie to the Holy See provided Father Gutmacher with a certain immunity from more than a few unfriendly diocesan officials. He had been able to work his way across the land, filling in for absent or vacationing priests in many understaffed parishes. By 1970, when his adventures had taken him as far as Houston, Texas, Father Angelo had seen the worst and the best of post-Conciliar Catholicism as practiced in the United States. Along the way, and without any intention of doing so, he had come to the approving attention of the Society of Pius X. It was only natural, then, that Archbishop Lefebvre should have recommended Angelo Gutmacher to Traxi Le Voisin.

No sooner had Father Angelo been persuaded to come aboard at St. Michael's than the local diocesan authorities raised objections. Because they couldn't get a grip on Gutmacher himself, they appealed to the Cardinal Archbishop of New Orleans for his aid in pressuring the powerful Francesca Gladstone to withdraw "her scandalous moral and financial support from the schismatic congregation at the Chapel of St. Michael the Archangel."

Cessi's support proved constant and unyielding. When it was made clear that Gladstone support was more likely to be withdrawn from New

Orleans than from the Chapel at Danbury, the matter was settled in favor of the "breakaway congregation." And when Lefebvre's enemies within the Roman Chancery succeeded some years later in having the Archbishop drummed out of the Church organization, and forbade Catholics to have anything to do with him or his religious institute, Cessi remained quick to defend against the obvious threat to St. Michael's by quoting well-publicized statements by two prominent Cardinals in defense of Archbishop Lefebvre and his followers.

The result was that, by this year, Father Angelo had served St. Michael's parish for nearly twenty-two years as priest and pastor. In all that time, he had remained so kind, so wise, so priestly and so orthodox that he not only kept even Traxi Le Voisin's excesses under control but managed to keep St. Michael's out of the worst of the controversies that spread like a liturgical plague throughout the Church. And in that time, in many and varied ways, Father Angelo had also managed to fill some part of the undeniable void that Declan Gladstone's death had left in the lives of his daughter and his three grandchildren.

"Funny thing about Father Angelo, Miss Cessi." As she bustled about the breakfast room, Beulah had a thing or two to put into this family conversation. "Funny thing, the way he never changes himself, but seems to have jus' the right way with all kinds of folks."

Cessi had to agree. From the time Father Angelo had first begun to frequent Windswept House and to offer Masses for the family in the Tower Chapel, it was clear to Cessi that Heaven had answered her complaint against the "lewd buffoons in round collars" who were becoming to the priesthood what bad money is to good. How else was she to explain the sudden arrival in their midst of this priest who surely would have passed muster even with Old Glad himself? The greatest wonder for Cessi, though, was that after having suffered what amounted in her eyes to a martyrdom for the faith in East Germany, and in the midst of the shambles of a once vibrant Church, Gutmacher lived a brand of Catholicism riven with the same No Quarter attitude that Old Glad had built into Windswept House.

While he remained staunch—even severe, Cessi suspected—in his personal austerities, Father Gutmacher was kind to everyone else; and, as constant as he was in himself, he had an uncanny ability to see into the hearts of people who were radically different from one another.

Take the three Gladstone children. The two boys had taken turns serving as acolytes for Father Angelo's Masses, both at Danbury and at Windswept. Yet Cessi and Tricia were as one in their recollection that it was Christian who had taken most immediately to Father Angelo. In Christian's eyes, Gutmacher came to occupy a special place. He came from the totally different world of the Soviet "evil empire." He was gentle but brave beyond any doubt; and Gutmacher's personal devotion in the saying of the Mass gripped Christian's inner mind with awe.

The discernment was not exclusively on Christian's side; Gutmacher detected in the young teenager a certain moral quality. Not that anybody ever took the boy to be "a Goody Two-Shoes"; Christian got into as much trouble through boyish escapades as any of his contemporaries. But there was always this moral timbre to him. On that, Gutmacher knew, the awesome commitment to priesthood could be built. And, in time, Christian did tell everyone that he wished to study for the priesthood.

At any other time in the recent history of the Church, Cessi would have been overjoyed that one of her sons had opted for the priesthood. Now, however, she worried to Father Angelo that priestly training would bring her older son into dangerously close association with "those black beetles skittering around our seminaries as though they were dunghills." But Father Angelo's answer was always the same. The real solution to Cessi's concern, he insisted, was not to keep good men like Christian from serving Christ, but to search, as Gutmacher himself had done, for the right seminary.

To Cessi's surprise, Gutmacher had suggested even then that she might have more reason to worry over Paul than over Christian. It hadn't taken this unusual priest long to discover the unyielding edge of stubbornness in Paul's character, or to realize that such a quality might render his faith more brittle than Christian's. For the moment, however, it was Christian's decision to enter priestly training that had to be dealt with.

Once her son's decision was firm, there was no need for Father Gutmacher to point Cessi in the right direction. She called on all the help she could command to check out those seminaries that seemed to be holding true against the rising tide of liturgical and doctrinal innovation. In the end, Chris had agreed that Navarre in northeastern Spain seemed to be the best among a narrowing lot, and had been delighted when his mother had been able to cut through the usual red tape to arrange for him to be accepted there as a candidate for priestly training.

By the time Chris was ready for Ordination in the early eighties, however, even the Spanish bishops were suspect in Cessi's eyes. She wanted to be sure Christian's Ordination was valid. She paid one lightning visit to Ecône, Switzerland, therefore, where Archbishop Lefebvre gave her the name of the Bishop of Santa Fe, in the Argentine. She checked that advice out personally, discovered it to be sound and arranged with the Bishop of Santa Fe for Christian's Ordination.

Cessi had been of two minds over Christian's desire to complete his doctoral thesis in Rome. Her worry—then as now—was that Christian might be brutalized and sidelined by the clerical bureaucracy there. On the other hand, she couldn't really quarrel with Chris's wish to secure the Rector Magnificus of the Dominican University of the Angelicum as his thesis advisor and academic director. In the ecclesiastical desert of the early 1980s, Father Damien Duncan Slattery's reputation as a first-rate theologian was known far beyond the Vatican, and his loyalty to the Holy See had by that time made more enemies than friends for him.

It had still been early days for Christian at Navarre, however, when Father Angelo's warning concerning Paul's spiritual welfare began to take flesh.

It was Paul Gladstone's misfortune that things fell out for him much as Father Gutmacher had feared. Indeed, and to Cessi's infinite pain, his case was far more typical than his brother's. In a mere eighteen months—the time he spent at New Orleans' Minor Seminary—Paul became what many well-intentioned but unguided Roman Catholics became in the decade of the seventies: a victim of circumstances over which he had no real control.

He had been protected in large part from the abrupt and disruptive changes in the Church. Though powerful, the storm of change did not hit everywhere at once. It was a process applied throughout the articulations of the Roman Catholic body—at parish level; at diocesan level; at national and regional levels; ultimately, at the Roman level. It was an affair subtly calculated by minds and wills bent on liquidating the traditional organization of the Church. And it succeeded.

Paul entered the Minor Seminary of the New Orleans diocese in 1972. Within his first semester, he and his fellow seminarians were told officially to doff their clerical cassocks and to wear ordinary street clothes. In their studies, they no longer had to master Latin. They found open invitations from the majority of their professors to think as they judged best about originally sacrosanct doctrines and fundamental teachings. About the existence of God. About the divinity of Jesus. About the Real Presence of Christ in the Blessed Sacrament. About the authority of the Pope. About the full gamut of Roman Catholic beliefs and laws.

Beyond the classroom, meanwhile, seminarians were encouraged to enlarge their experience by dating women. At the same time, many found it easy to establish homosexual bonds among themselves, for they were told that a positive attitude toward homosexuality would make them "pastorally sensitive."

In the transformation of the old Church into the House of Ecumenical Winds, Paul saw every familiar thing in the Seminary swept into oblivion. Seminarians were no longer required to turn up for morning prayers or for daily Mass. But those like Paul who chose to do so found that even in the Seminary Chapel a common table had replaced the altar. Statues, Stations of the Cross, pews, mosaics—even the Tabernacle, communion rails and Crucifixes—were nowhere to be seen. Confessionals that hadn't been scrapped were less likely to contain a priest than the janitor's cleaning supplies. The sins of society and of mankind were deplored continually, of course; but personal sin was never mentioned.

Seminarians and the public alike were greeted at the new ceremonies by a priest in blue jeans and a T-shirt—and perhaps a stole or a shoulder veil—who started things off with a hearty "Good morning, everybody!" The seminarians were instructed to set an example as free men and children of God. They were to sit or stand as they pleased, but they were not to kneel. Female "liturgical" dancers in leotards were accompanied by Church music rendered on guitars, banjos, ukuleles, tambourines and castanets.

Over the months, Paul watched as the liturgical gatherings turned into something resembling the "chiefly feast," or Great Potlatch of the Kwakiutl Indians of the Pacific Northwest, in which the chieftain gave away so much of his wealth in order to attract and impress more and more guests that in the end he was left with nothing more than his status and prestige as "the great giver." Anything from other religions was admitted on equal footing to these liturgical gatherings. Paul was treated to a jumble of Buddhist meditations, Taoist dualism, Sufi prayers, Tibetan prayer wheels, North American Indian mythology, ancient Greek gods and goddesses, hard rock and heavy metal music, Hindu worship of Shiva and Kali, and cult worship of the earth goddesses Gaia and Sophia.

Paul Gladstone understood all of this to be contradictory, hypocritical and, in the end, destructive of genuine Catholic faith. As nearly as he could tell, most Catholics accepted it all as an effort at total democratization of the traditional Roman Catholic religion. Wherever he went, the centerpiece of Catholic churches was now the "Supper Table," and the "people of God" gathered around it to celebrate their own freedom in a commemorative banquet.

In the end, his brief intimacy with the "Conciliar Church" took an awful toll on Paul Gladstone. Unable any longer to stomach the bawdy, ramshackle atmosphere of the once orderly Seminary, he had announced his departure to the Rector one morning with a candor so brutal even Cessi would have been hard pressed to match it. "I am not being trained as any kind of Sacrifice-offering, sin-forgiving priest." Paul's eyes were blazing. "If I remain, I'll come out as a disheveled dispenser of useless trinkets in the Great American Roman Catholic Potlatch."

Astonished almost into speechlessness at such unprecedented rebellion, the Rector managed to say a few standard words in defense of the mandates of Vatican Council II, and to utter what Paul could only regard as a laughable appeal to obedience.

"I don't know how to be a priest," Paul had countered with an iciness that froze the very atmosphere of the room. "I don't even know what it means to be a priest in a church where the centerpiece is nothing more than a 'Supper Table.' Oh, I know. I've heard over and again how this new 'Conciliar Church' of yours will present a more human face to the world. But I tell you this: I will not preach to 'the people of God' that when they gather together, they not only 'become church' but themselves 'form Christ.' I don't begin to understand such meaningless jargon."

Stupefied at such total lack of discipline, the Rector had tried to give Gladstone a dose of his own tough medicine. Paul was putting his entire priestly career in jeopardy, the Rector had warned, by this unbridled and uncalled-for outburst.

"Have I not made myself plain, Father Rector?" Paul was already on his way out the door. "I would rather be a decent Catholic layman cooperating with the Church than a ragtag member of this tasteless, irreligious pigsty."

The first Cessi had known of her younger son's decision to quit the Seminary was when Paul had arrived bag and baggage at Windswept House. It was only then that she heard, full blast and in the bald language she understood so well, what a hotbed of immorality and unbelief her son had immersed himself in for a year and a half. Once home from New Orleans, it had been Paul's choice to enroll immediately at the university at Austin for the balance of the semester, and to apply to Harvard for the semester following—all of which he successfully accomplished. There was no question that Harvard made Paul academically. Or that it excised from him any surviving ties with the old Catholic Church, and many of the ties—save his abiding love for them—that had bound him to his family. He was ripe for the basic principle of the Harvard intellectual: nominal Cartesianism. Only clear ideas were true.

The clearest idea on Paul's horizon was of one world, of an international convergence of nations into one superstate. He fixed therefore on a career in the field of international relations, and on a tough and single-minded course of study calculated to place him at the top of that heap.

After a brilliant and accelerated career at Harvard Law School, Paul had taken a doctorate in international studies and, simultaneously, a master's degree in business administration. Each summer recess was devoted to acquiring the languages he figured would serve him best in his chosen career. He displayed an almost eerily quick ability to pick up new languages. By the time this plastic adaptability of ear and palate had hardened and his amazing facility had diminished to normalcy, he had already learned Russian in Moscow and Mandarin Chinese in Taiwan and Beijing. He had perfected his German, French and Italian on the Continent. And he had learned Arabic in Cairo.

At the relatively young age of twenty-six—at about the same time Christian was to be ordained and begin his first stint at the Angelicum in Rome—Paul not only had completed his studies but had been snatched up as a rising star by Cyrus Benthoek's transnational law firm. Having been assigned to the firm's London headquarters from the start, he had come home to Galveston for brief vacations from time to time. But there were always too many intricate and sometimes violent discussions between mother and son; and each of them was always too brutally frank with the other.

For all his brilliance, Paul was never a match for his mother when it came to discussions of Catholicism's clear and detailed doctrinal positions. "I've been telling you for years"—Cessi could barely express her frustration—"that the moment you went along with those newfangled ideas of one world government, your faith was in grave danger. The first thing you know, you'll be missing Mass on Sundays and Holy Days. You'll omit regular Confession. You'll forget your morning and evening prayers. For all I know, you've already forgotten them."

Intransigence had reached its pitch on both sides, however, when Paul had made a special trip home from London to tell Cessi of his proposed marriage to a Chinese woman, a Confucian, named Yusai Kiang. It was true that Paul had arranged everything according to the book. He had asked for and received a special ecclesiastical dispensation from the Vatican to marry his beloved Yusai in a Catholic ceremony. And Yusai had agreed cheerfully and sincerely to live her life with Paul in accordance with Roman Catholic marriage laws.

Nevertheless, Cessi had objected to the prospect of her son's marriage to "a Chinese Confucian with Buddhist tendencies." She had not meant the phrase to be anything more than an educated guess—an accurate one, as it turned out—at Yusai's religious background. But Paul had taken it beyond that. He had so wanted to tell Cessi how he and Yusai felt, each about the other. How perfect each was for the other. About how truly he loved Yusai, and how excruciatingly painful was the mere idea that she might not be able to marry him. What he said, however, was something so entirely different that it could only have come from the abyss of his disappointment at Cessi's reaction. "I declare to God, Mother! Even if the Pope himself blessed my marriage and officiated at the ceremony, you would still refuse to give us your blessing!"

"You are absolutely right, young man!" Cessi's eyes were hard, green, impenetrable, flashing anger and her own disappointment like emeralds held over fire. "Even if he did all that, I would still not countenance this marriage!"

It was a No Quarter standoff between mother and son. Paul had not renounced Yusai. And Cessi had not attended the marriage ceremony in Paris.

"I don't care what you say, Mother." Tricia drank the last drop of juice from her glass. "I grant that your premonitions have been good indicators of terrible things for our family in the past. But that was all long ago. This time I think your built-in barometer is just working overtime. I still say . . ."

"I know." Cessi pressed the bell to let Beulah know she and Tricia were finished in the breakfast room. "I know. Everything's going according to plan." As the two Gladstone women climbed the stairs together—Tricia heading for a late start in her studio up on the sixth floor; Cessi heading for the Tower Chapel to give Heaven another little reality reminder—Tricia could still feel the tension in her mother. She could see that their conversation hadn't done much to quiet Cessi's barometer after all.

If there truly was a modern-day Jacob's Ladder at Windswept House, surely its rails rested on the sturdy floor of the Tower Chapel. Since the day Old Glad had completed construction a century and a quarter before, almost nothing here had been changed. The stained-glass window of Christ calming the angry tides of Galilee still faced seaward. The vigil light known far and wide as Glad's Eye still shone out toward the mainland to tell of God's true sacramental presence among mortals. The statues and icons favored by Old Glad remained in their places around the walls: the Crucified Christ, the great Archangel Michael slaying the Demon Dragon, Ignatius Loyola, Thérèse of Lisieux and Catherine of Siena.

After a short prayer of adoration in front of the Tabernacle, where the Blessed Sacrament was reserved, Cessi kissed the Altar Stone. Then she removed a little silver coronet from a side table, placed it upon the head of the statue depicting the Madonna of Fatima and then began a slow and prayerful progression around the Chapel. Rosary beads entwined in her fingers, she had a frank word or two with some of God's most favored creatures. Because her forebodings centered this time squarely on her family, so too did Cessi square her prayers on her three children. During the next hour, the only sound other than Cessi's prayers—the only sound from the outside world—was the soughing of the winds sweeping in from the Gulf.

There was no need to remind Christ or His Mother or the Angels or the Saints what was on her mind. So far as she knew, Cessi had no desire to control the lives of her sons or her daughter. The difficulty was that, as tradition had been blown to bits in just about every other unit of their world, the only place left where those solid roots could find nourishment was in the family. Given her brand of love for them, that was precisely the reason for Cessi's desire that her sons return home from time to time to Windswept. That very desire, however, was now the focus of Cessi's current unease. For, vague as they remained, her premonitions were laced with a sense that whatever disruptions lay in store were somehow entwined with her present plans for reunion.

Relying on that opaque intuition itself as her guide, Cessi discussed the problem, mother to Mother, with Mary. Her worry for Christian, as Cessi laid it out yet again for the Queen of Heaven, was no less profound for that. Mainly she worried that Christ would be deadened in his soul by the clerical bureaucracy in Rome. Surely the best thing for her older son would be to take up pastoral duties closer to home, where he could give as good as he got in the ecclesiastical warfare. That was the Gladstone way. The complaint she raised for Heaven's consideration in Christian's regard was that her prayers for him seemed to find no resonance. His work on that thesis of his seemed to stretch on forever, tethering him to Rome. "Sometimes, Holy Mother, I think he'll never come home again," Cessi grumbled—and then bit her tongue at her words.

The worries she laid out concerning Paul were more pointed, and the circumstances of his life made them ever more urgent. Despite the terrible scene with Paul over his marriage to Yusai, that wasn't the greatest problem. Cessi's deepest fear for Paul was centered on his brilliant road to success in his chosen career. He was like a gambler at a hot table where the odds were bound to turn against him.

Like many informed citizens, Cessi knew something about the transnational law firm in which her younger son had chosen to work. Like many in her class, she had even dealt now and again with the likes of the men in charge of Paul's life. With few exceptions, she had found them to be individuals who knew the mechanics of everything and the meaning of nothing. Though still in his thirties, Paul had already been made a junior partner. The situation, therefore, was clear. It was safe to assume that Paul was being megadosed with an outlook that would write finish to his faith.

"Blessed Mother." In her agitation, Cessi let the words cascade aloud from her lips. "So much has passed between Paul and me. Am I being foolish to count so heavily on his coming visit to Windswept? Maybe not." She cocked her head to one side, as if arguing the point. "Isn't it true that time has begun to heal the awful rift between us?

"Time"—Cessi smiled into the smiling face of the statue, but her words were directed to the Lady in Heaven itself—"and the birth of Paul's joy of a son, Declan. How proud my father must be of the little boy who bears his name! Don't misunderstand, Blessed Mother. You know how grateful I am to your Son and to you for all of that. But how in the world am I ever to get at the problem of Paul's faith without setting off another wild storm between us?"

Cessi fell silent again. She reminded herself that Christian would be home, too. Paul had always listened to his big brother. If she could no longer reach her younger boy, perhaps she could rely on Chris. Yes. That was it. Chris would be home first, anyway. She would just have a good talk with him about this problem.

There was one more thing Cessi wanted to take up again with Christ's Mother. As close as she was to her daughter, there seemed to be a whole dimension of Tricia's being that was beyond Cessi's understanding. She sometimes thought that the mysterious onset of her daughter's excruciating and dangerous eye disease a decade before had something to do with that hidden part of her character. "I hardly know what to ask for," Cessi admitted. For a cure certainly. And yet, she did have the sense that Tricia had reached her own understanding with Heaven in regard to her suffering.

As was her custom, once Cessi had spoken her heart to Mary, she removed the coronet from the Virgin's statue and placed it again in its drawer. Then, as always, she knelt before the Tabernacle for a parting word with the Sacramental Christ. "My only and loving Lord"—Cessi rested her forehead lightly on the Altar's edge—"I know You want souls to serve You at the expense of what seem to them to be their own interests. And I know that if we refuse You nothing, we will gain more than we can ask or imagine. But"—Cessi raised her eyes, the better to make her point—"I can't see what purpose of Yours it would serve, Lord, for the two sons You have given me to be lost to us both! And yet—that does seem to be the way things are heading."

Normally, Cessi's time in the Tower Chapel, with the ocean winds as a gently keening susurrus to her prayers, gave her a fresh burst of confidence and peace. Today, no such solace was granted her.

With a precision so consummate that it might have been Heaven calling to continue the conversation, Paul rang through from London just as Cessi reached the bottom of the spiral staircase leading from the Chapel. But the news she heard was not celestial.

"I'm devastated, Mother." Paul did not sound devastated. "Yusai and I were looking forward so much to bringing Declan to Windswept again. And to being with you and Chris and Tricia. But the head man himself has asked me to stay closer to home base . . ."

"The head man?" Cessi knew whom Paul meant. But she needed to slow him down. She needed time to understand that he wasn't coming home. Time to recognize this as the corollary to 1960; as the expected event that was not going to happen, as the trigger to everything else—whatever everything else might be.

"Cyrus Benthoek, Mother. It seems I'm in the final running for the post of Secretary-General at the European Community. Can you believe it?"

Cessi wished she could share Paul's excitement over this latest hand he had drawn at his hot table. How she wished she could be happy for his happiness. "Yes, Paul," was all she could manage to say. "I can believe it."

"I'll make it up to you, Mother." Paul heard the disappointment in Cessi's voice.

"Of course you will, darling." Cessi glanced up to see Tricia peering from the door of her studio. "Tell me, love. How is my little Declan?"

"He's a five-year-old wonder! I can hardly wait for you to see him again. He and Yusai are waiting for me at our place in Ireland. I'll be there myself in a couple of hours. I'll give them both a big hug for you."

Cessi's eyes were swimming with tears, but she kept her voice clear and even. "Yes, sweetheart. Give them both a big hug for me. And keep one for yourself."

"I'll make it up to you, Mother," Paul said again.

"I know you will, darling," Cessi said again.

No sooner was the receiver in its cradle than the telephone jangled a second time. "Is that you, Mother? Your voice sounds so strange!"

"Chris!" Cessi's knees weakened and she sank into the chair beside the phone table. "Let me guess. You're not coming home after all."

"Of course I'm coming home. Just on a different flight. Cardinal O'Cleary invited me to stop by for a little New Orleans hospitality on my way home, so I had to change all my travel plans. This is the first chance I've had to call to let you know."

Jotting down the new flight information Chris read out gave Cessi a chance to recover her wits, and her normal curiosity. "What in Heaven's name was so urgent that the Cardinal couldn't have waited a few more weeks? You're due in New Orleans in September anyway. Or had he forgotten that?" Cessi's distrust of Jay Jay O'Cleary ran deep. He was less of a brute than Bourgogne had been. But O'Cleary's desire to be loved by absolutely everybody made him seem tawdry. Yes, Cessi often thought, that was the very word. Tawdry. And besides, she had never met a man with so much potential power and so few ideas of how to use it.

"No, Mother. He didn't forget. He has a burr under his saddle about my career in Rome."

"Rome!" Weak knees or no, that bombshell was enough to galvanize Cessi all over again.

"Hold your fire, Mother. Nothing's been decided. I'll tell you all about it when I see you."

XXII

CHRISTIAN GLADSTONE made his way through the deepest night he could remember toward the Basilica of St. Peter. By his side, Father Aldo Carnesecca was pointing to the shadowed hulk of the Apostolic Palace. Up to the fourth floor. To the last window on the right. To the stained-glass window depicting two white pillars standing in what looked like the dark waters of the Gulf and, between the pillars, the prow of a small boat attempting to steer its way. He heard the sound of voices. The sound of a great wind. Then a Roman taxicab careened out of nowhere, blaring its klaxon and carrying Cessi and Father Damien Slattery down the Via della Conciliazione. Chris bolted after the cab, away from St. Peter's Square, away from Carnesecca. But Carnesecca ran, too. Kept pace. Kept pointing to that stained-glass window where Damien Slattery's *cappa magna* bellied out suddenly like a sail. Then it began all over again . . . Christian heading through the darkness toward St. Peter's . . . Carnesecca's wordless gesture . . . the stained-glass window . . . the madly careening cab . . . Cessi and Slattery and the sound of the klaxon . . .

Breathless as if from the chase, bathed in sweat, Christian sat bolt upright in bed. For a second, he thought the klaxon had pursued him crazily out of his dream. But it was only the throaty chimes of Oakey Paul echoing through the silent rooms of Windswept House.

Christian was not in the habit of paying much attention to his dreams.

But in this case, neither the details of that dream nor the heightened sense of strain he had felt on first awakening from it faded even in the whirlwind of activities and celebrations Cessi had arranged.

He had expected that the first order of business on his arrival home would be a full-blast discussion with his mother about the Roman proposition Cardinal O'Cleary had made in New Orleans. He had even been looking forward to it. Just at this moment, a good dose of her plain language and uncompromising faith was what he needed to help him sort out his thoughts. It wasn't as if Jay Jay had laid a command on him, obliging him in virtue of holy obedience to take up a year-round post in Rome. Whatever sort of a fix Jay Jay had got himself into, there wasn't anything in Canon Law that obliged a priest to save his Cardinal's bacon.

Moreover, Christian felt strongly the debt he owed to his mother. She had given all of her stupendous energies and talents to her three children. Surely the roles were reversed now. Surely they owed something to her. What kind of recompense would it be for Christian to allow himself to be press-ganged into a Vatican career?

As counterpoint to such arguments, however, there were serious reasons for Chris to consider Cardinal O'Cleary's proposal. One of the most serious was Aldo Carnesecca's constant argument that Rome should not be deserted by all of its good priests. It was sobering to realize that he had been called to the city of the Popes. Perhaps the call had come through the unimpressive John O'Cleary; but Jay Jay was a Cardinal after all, and God had manifested His will many times in the past through stranger means. On top of all that, Chris had to question even his own noble-sounding motives for wanting to come home. Truth to tell, wouldn't it be just so comfortable to be Stateside again?

The odd thing, though, was that while Cessi had fairly exploded at the bare mention of Rome when he had called from New Orleans, now that he was in Galveston she didn't press the matter. At first, Christian put his mother's unaccustomed silence in so important a matter down to the ceaseless family-reunion activities she had set in motion. As the days passed, however, Christian realized that circumstances were making Cessi's argument far more effectively than she could have hoped to do herself. For, as carefully as she had planned everything, even Cessi Gladstone could not have arranged things to reflect more perfectly or more poignantly the endless reasons for Chris to abandon Rome for good and to take up a truly useful apostolate back here where he belonged.

The pleasures of reunion aside, Chris soon discovered that what aunts and uncles and cousins and friends all seemed to want from him—what they had come to Windswept House to find again—was the confidence and joy of basic, objective Catholic truths. At dinner after family dinner, as one contingent of house guests was replaced every two or three days by another, relatives and old friends alike told such tales of theological irregularities and downright apostasy that Christian began to think of them as war stories.

One of his favorite cousins, for example—a splendid, strapping lad who wanted to be a priest—had just been expelled from his local Catholic school for wearing a crucifix. What was a boy like that to do? Where was he to turn? In such an ecclesiastical no-man's-land, what was to become of his vocation? And what about that middle-aged priest who had already been caught molesting choirboys, but was moved from parish to parish in his diocese, where he continued to find victims for his lust? Christian heard it all: stories of nuns who had given up teaching children and were studying economics and architecture and medicine and psychology in order to launch their personal careers; stories of priests who allowed contraceptive means, who winked at abortions, who laughed about young unmarried people living together as man and wife, who ignored the absence of any Catholic teaching about the Eucharist, about the fires of Hell, about the nature of sin.

Ever since word had begun to spread in early May that Francesca Gladstone was preparing a special homecoming for her two sons, a curious current had taken hold around Galveston; a current that swirled around the coming arrival of Father Christian Gladstone at Windswept again. A current that seemed to swell suddenly to the surface, as though fed and forced upward by a deep, unseen tide. From Chris's first full day at home, therefore, until the last full day before his departure, Beulah Thompson spent so much of her time answering the telephone and the doorbell, it was a wonder she got everything else done.

Chris made himself available to as many callers as he could. He devoted most of every morning to confessions and priestly consultations. Several rooms on the ground floor at the back of the house had to be set aside to accommodate the scores of people who phoned ahead or came unannounced for orthodox confessions or sound theological counsel. But even with Angelo Gutmacher to help him—for Father Angelo was a frequent and most beloved visitor to Windswept all during Chris's time in Galveston—it was impossible for Christian to see everyone who wanted to see him.

There was not a moment's vainglory for Chris in this sudden demand for his attention. Rather, it saddened him. For in every case, and whether he had to do with men or women, rich or poor, laborers or lawyers or cabdrivers or mothers or fathers or one of those fishermen who sometimes looked to the lights of Windswept's Tower Chapel for a bearing in rough weather, it was always the same. All of them were starved for direction, clarity, faith and hope.

The plight of these people drove home in Christian a suddenly new comprehension. He understood as never before that the void these people faced in their daily living was multiplied millions of times around the world. In the churches they attended—if they still did attend—they were dished a steady diet of Freud for their personal woes, Piaget for their problems with their children, Marx for their social distress and the insidiously subjective and ever more popular encounter therapy as the new religion that would put them in touch with their "deeper selves."

Toward the middle of his second week home, Cessi gave a festive dinner as the final gala of Chris's stay. His Eminence Cardinal O'Cleary was conspicuous by his absence. What impressed Chris the most was how easeful in their minds were all the clerics his mother had invited to meet or to be reacquainted with her son. They all had an abiding curiosity about "how Rome would jump on the big issues," as one young auxiliary bishop put it. And because Christian did frequent Rome, was near the Pope in that sense, he became the focus of their attention.

But because he sensed the mood behind the questioning, he decided to draw out the latent dislike he detected for the Pontiff. "You people are pastors." He looked around the table. "You're in the trenches. I work in an ivory tower. So, you tell me. What should this Holy Father do for the good of the Church?"

In deference to Cessi Gladstone's presence, the avalanche of suggestions was lathered with pietistic sorrow. But what it came down to was clear enough. The Pontiff had made an awful mess. The need now was for a Pope who could think intelligently; a Pope who would be more positive in his attitude about things like priestly celibacy and an exclusively male priesthood and contraception and abortion; a Pope who could go with the flow. Maybe the time had even come for this Pope to step aside; to make way for a more able successor.

When the uproar abated, Christian had a sober suggestion of his own to make. "I have no direct communication with the Holy Father; no occasion to make your suggestions known to him. But since you have problems, why don't you make your own case? Why not write to him? Individually or as a group, why not . . ."

"Between you and me and the Holy Spirit, Father Chris," the young auxiliary bishop weighed in again, "there are some nifty and intelligent churchmen over there who do have the ear of the Holy Father. They'll get him to do the right thing. We'll just have to wait him out."

Christian met Cessi's eyes flashing green with ire. But still she said nothing. To his utter bafflement, still she kept her silence.

At four in the morning on his last full day at home, Christian arose from bed. A quarter of an hour later, showered, shaved and dressed, he made his way soundlessly along the third-floor corridor and up the stairs to Old Glad's Tower Chapel. At around five-thirty or so, Father Gutmacher would join him as he had done each morning of his vacation to assist at Mass; and Cessi and Tricia would be there, too. But just as his mother habitually came to the Chapel for what was known as "Cessi's hour," so, too, had this silent time in the house become Christian's hour. A time when he could say his Office and his Rosary and his morning prayers. A time when he could puzzle again through all the arguments for leaving Rome and the arguments for going there for good.

It was during these mornings in the Chapel as well that the lively warmth Christian had always felt for his favorite ancestor seemed to nourish itself anew. It would have been impossible for him not to feel a resurgence of love and admiration and gratitude for the man who had built this house to be the very refuge it had indeed become. And, as if in an answering blessing, that old patriarch himself seemed to weave the sweet moments Chris spent alone in the Chapel this morning into a mantle of memories: Windswept House seemed again to be almost as he remembered it from his childhood.

Perhaps this was an empty place now. Perhaps all the celebrations that had filled Windswept with guests and chatter and laughter and tears during these past two weeks were only reminders of what once had been. Perhaps this old pile was battered itself these days by the searing winds of the storm tearing at the human landscape all around it. Perhaps it was even invaded from time to time by the victims of that storm—by those sad and searching penitents who had come here in such numbers for the priestly succor so wanting to them elsewhere; and by those clerics who had seemed so mindless of their sacred charge as priests as they had gathered around the Gladstone dinner table.

Yet this place—this little corner of Texas real estate defended so fiercely by Cessi Gladstone against all encroachment, this great old house, this Tower Chapel where Glad's Eye told the world so faithfully of the abiding presence of Christ in the Tabernacle—this place remained one bastion against the storm. This place remained one haven where penitents might still come. This place remained a rock. This was the place Christian would always call home.

"Forgive me, old friend."

Startled by the softly accented words, Christian looked up from his prayers and into the horrid scars of Angelo Gutmacher's face.

"Forgive me. I come early, I know. But I thought we might have a little time together before Mass. Before heading back to Rome. . . ."

Startled now to the point of confusion, Chris cut the older priest off in mid-sentence and rose from his knees. "Your coming is never an intrusion, Father." The phrase was not merely a social grace. Christian regarded this man as a godsend in the most literal sense. A strange and wonderful friend whom God Himself seemed to protect, and whose steps He appeared to guide in priestly service. Christian motioned toward a little grouping of prie-dieu chairs near the door and, with a smile as gentle as his voice, Gutmacher seated himself beside his long-legged young protégé.

"I gather Mother told you of my call from New Orleans. But she must have told you as well that nothing's been decided. About my going to Rome, I mean." Chris sounded like a man defending his independence. "I tried to make that clear. I intend to talk the whole thing out with her. Did she tell you that?"

"She didn't put it just that way." Gutmacher appeared to be weighing his words carefully. "What she had was an honest question. She wanted to know how it could be the will of God that you should live your life surrounded by people who have forgotten the basics."

Christian was surprised that Cessi would open her mind even that far to the possibility of his going to Rome full-time. Still, it required a big leap to get from a question like that to the bald assumption that Chris would agree to Cardinal O'Cleary's plan. Unless he was mistaken, though, that was Father Angelo's mind. "Tell me, Father Angelo. How did you answer my mother's question?"

"Just as you would have, my friend." Gutmacher's smile was perplexing. "As honestly and as fully as I could. I suggested to her that this moment had been a long time in coming and that because its crux was the future—and not just yours alone—it was an occasion of important decisions for us all."

A long time in coming? That was an odd thing to say, Christian thought. In fact, his friend's whole attitude seemed strange. "Anything else?"

"I told her I shared her fears for what might happen to any good priest who is called to Rome these days. But I told Cessi, too, that she couldn't know, nor could I, what the grace of God can achieve."

In all the years they had known each other, it had never been Father Angelo's way to be evasive. But Chris was sure he hadn't heard everything yet.

As though he had read the younger man's mind, Gutmacher removed a letter from his inner pocket and held it out. Chris recognized the Vatican stamps on the envelope, but there was no surprise in that. Father Angelo's ties to the Congregation for the Clergy and to the papal household were hardly secret. The address of the sender was another matter, however. "Monastery of Santa Sabina," Gladstone read the address of the Dominican headquarters aloud. "Roma 00921, Italia."

"Read it."

Chris knew the hand the moment he took the single sheet of paper out of the envelope. Just to be sure, though, he glanced at the large and generous flourishes surrounding the initials that were so familiar to him. DDS, OP. "Damien Slattery?" It was more exclamation than question.

When it brought no reply from Gutmacher, Christian returned to the letter. A solitary paragraph. Just two sentences, in fact: "A new initiative of His Holiness requires your presence here in mid-autumn. Unless I hear from you personally within ten days of this letter's date, I will take it you do not see your way to comply."

Christian had neither quarrel nor question concerning the peremptory-seeming tone of Father Slattery's note, for that was the way such things were done in Rome. The call was always clear, usually brief and rarely adorned with explanation or exhortation. The reply was left to the recipient; it had to be entirely voluntary. What Christian did feel was a generous and unaccustomed dose of self-reproach. It was his turn to apologize. How could he have been so absorbed in himself? How could he have assumed it was only his own situation that mattered? That Gutmacher had come to talk only about Christian? That his reference to departing for Rome could only have to do with Christian?

Father Angelo received Chris's eloquent apology with an equally eloquent little shrug.

"You're going, then, Father?" The question was a whisper on Christian's lips.

"The day Cessi came to see me"—Gutmacher nodded—"was the day I received this letter. And it was the day I sent my response. I will go."

This morning was full of unexpected turns. "Mother knows? You told her that day?"

"She knows."

"So, all that honest advice you gave her about this moment—about its having been so long in coming; about its being an occasion of importance; about what God's grace can achieve—all of that really had to do with you?"

"And with you." Gutmacher was not about to let Christian Gladstone off the hook as easily as that.

Chris thrust the letter back as if to rid himself of anything to do with it. "Things are different for you. Until now, and in spite of my repugnance for the whole idea, I halfway thought I should accept Cardinal O'Cleary's proposal."

"And now?"

Chris did his best to answer without sounding brutal. Angelo was almost a member of the family, but he didn't have the same blood ties that Christian did. He didn't have the same obligations to Cessi and Tricia. It was all well and good for him to leave, if that was what he thought best. But Christian could hardly be expected to compound the blow to his mother and Tricia by agreeing to O'Cleary's request. "And besides"—Christian was looking for a way to bolster what he sensed was an insufficient argument—"you've been called to Rome by a good man. There's not a more solid papist left in the Vatican—or maybe in the world—than Damien Slattery. But if I'm to believe Cardinal O'Cleary's hints to me in New Orleans, His Eminence Cosimo Maestroianni has something to do with Rome's sudden interest in my existence. And that's far different."

"Is it?" Father Angelo's voice had the effect of a hot poker.

"You know it is, Gutmacher! You must remember the letter I wrote you after Cardinal Maestroianni called me to the Secretariat last May. Smooth as silk, that man is. But he's no Damien Slattery. And no friend of the Pope. A man like that probably devours a dozen men like me for breakfast every day."

Father Angelo stood up, smiling but watchful. "I don't doubt anything you say."

"Well, then. We agree." Christian relaxed a little. "Damien Slattery's voice is the voice of Rome."

"Exactly!" Father Angelo pounced on that thought. "Master-General Slattery's is the voice of Rome. The voice of Rome calling for help. Can you hesitate . . . ?"

"It's not the same thing!" Chris shot back. "You can't tell me that your being called to Rome by such a good man as Father Slattery is in any way comparable to . . ."

"Yes, Father Christian. I can. No matter how it comes, or who makes it, the call is the same. The question isn't whether Damien Slattery or Cardinal Maestroianni are or aren't good papists. The question is whether you are. And I can tell you it requires faith—priestly faith, Chris—to recognize that call for what it is."

In a gesture that was all but sacramental in nature—and that commanded supremest honesty in response—Gutmacher took a step forward and laid his hands on Chris's shoulders. "Tell me truthfully, Father Christian. Can you have any real hesitation in answering that same call?"

All at once, Christian remembered Father Aldo Carnesecca's prophecy that he had come to a stage in his career where the choices he made would set the pattern of his priesthood for as long as he lived. "The bureaucratic rat race you happened upon . . . ," Father Aldo had said, "is defining the whole strategy and all of the tactics in this global warfare of spirit. Nevertheless . . . make no mistake about this: the center of the battle is in Rome."

Father Angelo tightened his grip on the younger man's shoulders, forcing him back to the present moment. Forcing the decision that would define his priesthood one way or the other. "Tell me." Gutmacher's words were slow and deliberate. "Can you have any real hesitation in answering that call?"

Cessi halted so suddenly at the door of the Tower Chapel that Tricia, coming up behind her, nearly ran her down. ". . . it requires faith—priestly faith, Chris—to recognize that call for what it is." She shut her eyes against the sight of Gutmacher's face and the sound of his voice; closed them against welling tears; felt Tricia's hand warm in the sudden iciness of her own. "Tell me." Father Angelo's challenge to her son washed over Cessi like an icy bath. "Can you have any real hesitation in answering that call?"

Until now, Cessi had thought she had faced into this moment. The day Chris had called from New Orleans, she had gone to Father Gutmacher for comfort and for counsel only to find that he, too, had been summoned into the midst of those clerical woebegones in Rome. That was the day she heard the reasons why he would leave St. Michael's Chapel. For all the days since, she had known Christian would hear those reasons, too; and that he would respond as she had.

More than one night since then, Cessi had lain awake in her bed wondering how deep she would have to dig for the strength to let go. Wondering if she had really been much of a mother at all. Wondering if even now she was nothing more than a crazed pottery maker, never knowing when to stop molding and shaping her children.

"Mother!"

Cessi snapped her eyes open to see Christian striding toward her, his face suffused with the same stress and pain welling inside her.

"Chris." She took her hand gently from Tricia's and stepped forward into the Chapel with such grace and command that her movement seemed a simple exclamation. Gutmacher had asked the only question that mattered. Only Christian could give the answer. Cessi knew that in a few moments she would receive the Body and Blood of Christ from the consecrated hands of her priest-son at the Holy Sacrifice of the Mass. After that, she did not know how far he would choose to go from this still grand old bastion called Windswept House.

Tricia's thoughts were on Christian, too. But just as much on Father Angelo. Of all the experts she had seen, only this priest had taught her to make her sufferings useful. With that extraordinary gift of insight and hard-edged tenderness, he had taught her the rules of traditional asceticism. Would she not continue now to offer up her sufferings to God the Father in union with the sufferings of Christ the Son? Would she not continue to counter Satan and win forgiveness for many sins? Would she not remain among those privileged souls who had presented themselves down the ages as victims, ready to cooperate with the Supreme Victim executed in great bodily pain on the Cross for the offenses and sins of mankind?

And then there was Christian, caught again in the essence of that dark dream from which he had awakened, bathed in sweat, on his first night home. Only it wasn't just Father Aldo Carnesecca who ran beside him now, pointing toward the Apostolic Palace. It was Angelo Gutmacher chiding him into priestly self-denial and into the trust such self-denial demanded. Chris thought he must be going to spiritual flab if Gutmacher had to remind him of all that. It was the sight of his mother waiting so coolly for his answer; and it was all the lessons he had learned from her about the depth and breath and majesty and freedom of his faith. It was the too vivid memory of all the people who had come to Windswept House in their defenselessness against the offenses of Rome.

And it was the legacy of old Paul Thomas Gladstone that lived on in this place. Surely that legacy amounted to something more fruitful than a mantle woven of nice old memories. Hadn't even Carnesecca said as much? It was curious, Chris thought, the way Father Aldo kept popping up in his mind. But prophets were like that, he supposed. Without ever having set foot in this place, Carnesecca understood that Old Glad and his Windswept House had always been Christian's links to Rome. To the Vatican. To the papacy.

It was to be Rome, then.

Cessi was the first to read Christian's decision in his eyes and put words to it. "It's about time another Gladstone went to the rescue of the papacy." She looked her son full in the face, and her own eyes were not green. "Just be sure to remember, young man, that this isn't the nineteenth century, and you're not Old Glad. A million dollars in cold American cash won't help this time. What Rome needs is a good shaking-up."

Had Cessi not found herself suddenly in the unique sweetness of her son's embrace, she was sure she would have lost composure.

"The only real exile"—in words borrowed from Joseph Conrad, Christian whispered his gratitude for his mother's No Quarter blessing—"the only real exile is a man who cannot go home again, be it to a hovel or a palace."

Her head on Chris's shoulder, Francesca Gladstone raised her eyes to the Tabernacle behind him. Only Heaven was privy to her heart's whisper. Heaven, and all those Angels who had gathered in Old Glad's Tower Chapel at the foot of Jacob's Ladder for all her seventy years. "See Lord? I told You so!"

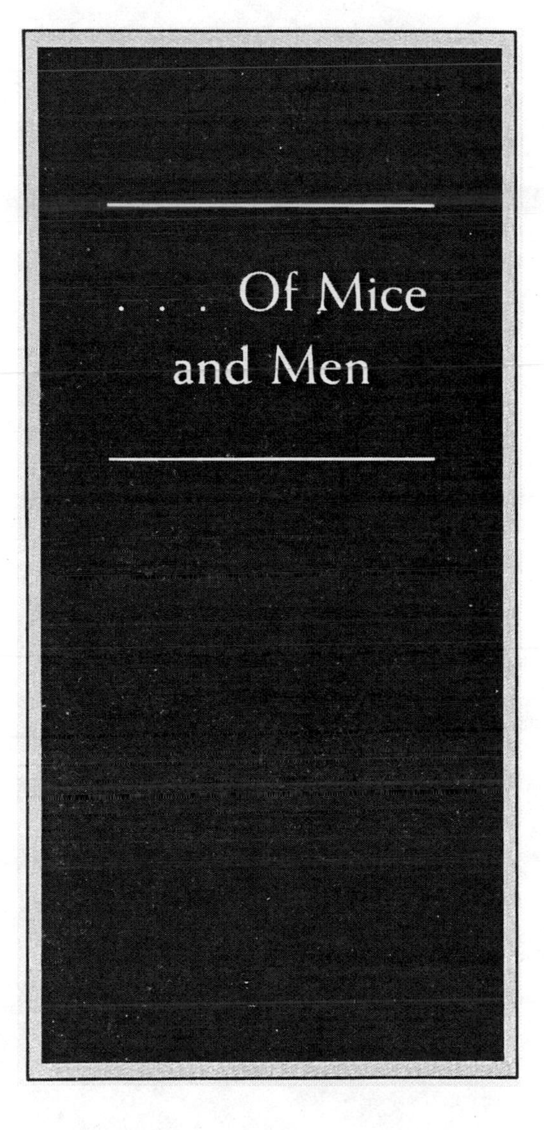
. . . Of Mice
and Men

XXIII

ON THE SECOND FRIDAY of September 1991, as Mikhail Sergeyevich Gorbachev was fighting before the Soviet Presidium in Moscow for all he ever ambitioned to achieve, Gibson Appleyard strode without hurry into the forty-story Berlaymont Building, home of the European Commission, located between Charlemagne Boulevard and Archimede Street in the eastern sector of Brussels. He glanced at his watch more out of habit than necessity as he took the elevator to the thirtieth floor. He had plenty of time before the start of the Selectors meeting set for this morning to fill the post of Secretary-General.

When life had been simpler—long before the Presidential Committee of Ten had been invented and before he had ever heard of Paul Thomas Gladstone—Gib had done his first European service in Brussels. "If you must live in a city," his associates used to say back then, "do it in Brussels."

The luxury of living here hadn't been in the cards for long in Appleyard's case. But he had always loved this place. The art collected here was magnificent. The food was first-class, even by European standards. There was a real friendliness about the people who called this city home. And there was no forgetting Belgium's role as the cockpit of Europe. Romans, Asiatics, Germans, Frenchmen who had followed Napoleon, Spaniards from the south, the English and finally the Americans had all decided history on this terrain in the age-old human way. The way of bloodshed and carnage.

Today, though, Belgians were serious about making Brussels into the capital of a new Europe even greater and more glorious than the old Europe achieved by Charlemagne on Christmas Day in 800 A.D., when Pope Leo III had placed the crown of empire on his head.

Poor Belgium, Appleyard thought to himself. Perhaps the original European Community had been a comfortable thing in its heyday. As one element of a trilateral world in close partnership with America and Japan, that Europe had been part of an expedient system of cooperation and competition. Each leg of that trilateral system had had its surrogates and dependents. Each had cooperated with the others for peace; and each had competed with the others for financial and economic hegemony.

Now, by a sort of mental presumption, the European Community was set to claim for itself a new dignity; a new destiny of glory and power. It saw itself already, in fact, as a supranational state alive and functioning on the world scene.

There might still be wars of blood and carnage for a time, like the one in Yugoslavia. But the real warfare—the kind that would shape the New World Order—was conducted now in buildings like this one. In conference rooms like the one on the thirtieth floor of the Berlaymont Building, where the EC Selectors were gathering at this moment.

As sure of his ground as he was of sunrise, Gibson Appleyard had his own slant on that warfare. "Poor Belgium," he thought again. "Poor Europe."

"The whole idea is ridiculous and unacceptable!" Nicole Cresson's strident voice was like a knife in Gib Appleyard's ears as he slipped into the conference room. Cresson was but one of several early arrivals among the twelve Selectors already gathering into little groups. "The thought of putting this American—this—this what's-his-name—" Cresson brandished the Gladstone dossier in the face of her companion Selectors from the Netherlands and Spain like a prosecuting attorney excoriating a criminal before a jury.

"Paul Thomas Gladstone." The patient Robert Allaeys of Holland supplied the name the French Selector was looking for.

"N'est-ce pas!" Cresson sneered. "These Americans and their precious middle names! The whole thing is too preposterous!"

Appleyard decided to avoid the French Selector. Cresson probably knew as well as he did that there was nothing to be gained or lost by a conversation between them. It would be more profitable and far less stressful just to amble over to the sidelines and keep an eye on things as groups formed and changed.

Over the past several months, as he had attended the prior meetings of this ad hoc Selection Committee, Appleyard had got to know as much about the twelve Selectors as they knew about each other. He knew them by their names, of course; but just as much by their nicknames, which they used freely among themselves and which spoke eloquently of their qualities as well as their quirks.

For reasons that were all too obvious this morning, Nicole Cresson had earned her moniker, "Vinaigre." As career diplomat and secretary to France's current Foreign Minister, Cresson had never accepted President Bush's 1990 statement that "America is now a European power." As far as she was concerned, no real European—no "European European"—would ever accept such a view. More to the point this morning, no self-respecting European European would want to see Paul Thomas Gladstone's American backside seated in the Secretary-General's chair.

"Ah, my dear Appleyard. Come to savor victory, have you?" The Belgian Selector—Jan Borliuth by name; Stropelaars by nickname—welcomed Gib in his own peculiar way. "You mustn't take offense at

Vinaigre's temper. She's been away on vacation and found out only this morning that the candidates we had selected in our prior meetings have withdrawn their names. I doubt anything like that has happened before. And on top of that, the Commissioners themselves have presented us with a totally new proposal for Secretary-General. The whole thing is without precedent."

Gib raised his eyebrows in an expression he hoped would pass in Borliuth's eyes as the laconic surprise of an American. But before he had a chance to say a word, the pair was joined by Italy's Corrado Dello Iudice—such a handsome man that he could only be called "Il Bello."

"Cresson has a point, you know." Il Bello saw no reason to apologize, as Borliuth had, for the French Selector's outburst. This appointment of a new Secretary-General comes at a most delicate time. Why, the events of this year alone are already opening a door to entirely new terrain. Given the complications and subtleties, I have to question whether an American can measure up."

"That's putting it mildly!" As possibly the only practicing Catholic in the group, Portugal's Francisco dos Santos bore his nickname of "Capelão"—the Portuguese for chaplain—with true Christian patience. "By the time our new appointee has been initiated, and by the time he has his administration well oiled and running, the EC Commissioners *and* the Council will be faced with very difficult new choices. And the work of the Secretary-General will have multiplied a thousandfold."

"Tell us, Appleyard." Dos Santos turned to the tall American. "Can you fill us in on this Paul Gladstone? We've all read his dossier, of course. But this has been such a sudden turn of events, we haven't had a chance to do much independent checking."

Gib reflected for a moment. Dos Santos had asked a clumsy question for such an accomplished diplomat. A question obviously meant, then, to implicate Appleyard as the fly who had got into this Committee's ointment. "I know what I've read in his file," Appleyard answered truthfully. "I've never met the man personally. But from what I can see, you're not dealing with a clumsy geopolitical oaf in Gladstone. He's earned his stripes."

"So it's not to worry, then?" Jan Borliuth was set to press the matter further when the little group was invaded by Germany.

Emil Schenker—Pfennig, his colleagues called him, in deference to the size of his country's treasury—was Nicole Cresson's exact opposite in temperament. Nor could he have been more at odds with her exclusivist view of Europe for Europeans. "Excuse me! But I could not help overhearing this exciting discussion, my friends. And I have to say I think you worry far too much. The world is changing, and that's all there is to it. We must take cognizance of the new realities."

Pfennig's colleagues could only wince, for it was clear enough what he meant by that phrase. Europe's financial clout and industrial sinews were centered in West Germany. Of course, the reunification of the two Germanys—a pitiful marriage of convenience, Schenker acknowledged privately—would be a near-future financial and sociological drain on West Germany. But the big new reality for Pfennig was an old reality come back to life. "We Germans have a built-in *Drang nach Osten,"* he had begun to say at every opportunity. "We are oriented to the East. People cannot jump out of their skins, nor nations out of their history. The historical role of the German people as a European power has always been linked to our powerful neighbors in the East."

Schenker's stand on this innate push of the Germans to the East was not incompatible, in fact, with the official policies of most of the other eleven countries whose representatives would sit as Selectors in today's meeting. Nevertheless, Appleyard figured he understood Pfennig and his government's policy in this regard well enough. Given the merest opportunity, Schenker himself would explain what it meant to be a German faced with Russia. For Gib's money, however, the Presidential Committee of Ten had been dead right in assessing the danger to the United States. The only good thing about Pfennig's precious *Drang nach Osten* was that it meant he was in that camp within the EC that favored a policy of deep and continuing lines of involvement between Europe and non-European countries. Including America. In the words of the EC's geopolitical jargon, Schenker was a Euro-Atlanticist.

In the narrower context of today's business, meanwhile, it also meant a sure vote in favor of Paul Thomas Gladstone.

". . . So truly, my good friends"—Schenker was winding up his predictable speech to his fellow Selectors—"you worry too much. In the worst case, how much harm can this Gladstone do? After all, there are those who regard the Secretary-General as just a glorified stand-in for the all-powerful European Commissioners. . . ."

"Bah!" Dello Iudice of Italy had heard enough. He cringed to think how much harm Gladstone might do. "The Commissioners—all seventeen of them—have real power. Enormous power. And the Secretary-General shares that power, and all of its leverage."

It wasn't often that Emil Schenker found himself outnumbered. But in joining this little discussion group, he had placed himself at just such a momentary disadvantage.

"I must second Il Bello's point of view, my dear Pfennig." Jan Borliuth of Belgium weighed in again. "The EC is no longer the compact ship of Western Europe. No longer the Europe of the Seven. Why, everybody turns out to be a European these days! Very soon now, we in the EC must face the prospect of admitting the seven nations of the European Free Trade Association, the EFTA, into close association with our organization. "Norway, Sweden, Finland, Switzerland, Liechtenstein and Austria do comprise a substantial market that we cannot ignore. But they also present monumental political complications for the EC.

"And as long as you have brought the East into the picture, Emil"—the Belgian shot a spear of a glance at Pfennig—"Gorbachev is fairly battering down the portals of this new Europe of ours. In fact, he has staked his claim in the very name of Europe!"

"*Ja,* Stropelaars. But . . ." Schenker tried to get a word in to defend his position, but Borliuth was insistent.

"But me no buts this time, old friend. Everyone here has reason to remember Gorbachev's very words. 'Your new Europe will be impossible,' he had the gall to say, 'without close bonds with the Soviet Union.' And everyone here has reason to understand that in practical terms Gorbachev meant close union not only with his new Soviet Federation but also with associated states of Eastern Europe, which cannot survive without their own close bonds to the Soviets. In practical terms it doesn't matter that Gorbachev is on the ropes in Moscow himself these days. Because in practical terms, he's been talking to us about a huge new market of over 200 million people.

"Whatever happens to Gorbachev, then, his statement that there can be no Europe without the U.S.S.R.—or the CIS, or whatever it will be called in the end—is both a statement of fact and a threat. He's changed the mold of Europe whether we like it or not."

By now, the conversation surging around Gibson Appleyard was so intense, and its substance was so crucial to the future of the EC, that some of the other members of the ad hoc Selection Committee had gathered in. For, one and all, their careers were tightly tied to this institution.

"Stropelaars is right, Pfennig." The new voice belonged to Fernan de Marais of Luxembourg. His confreres called him "the Count" for the simple reason that he was one. "We all remember the early years. Things were relatively simple for a long time after the EC was born. Back then, it was just seven nations of the European heartland. But now the EC has to contend with the likes of the CSCE, the EFTA nations, the Western European Union, the G-7, the Bruges Group and a host of others whose names and initials everyone here can rattle off without missing a beat. . . ."

Listening to the Count address the thorny issue of geopolitical competition, Gibson Appleyard knew that the thorniest point of all concerned the serious lines of rivalry that had been drawn between the European Community on the one hand and, on the other, the Conference on Security and Cooperation in Europe. In the view of "European Europeans"—the likes of Dello Iudice of Italy, Borliuth of Belgium, dos Santos of Portugal, Cresson of France, and Dolores "Viva" Urrutia of Spain—the CSCE could not begin to match the EC's pedigree. In their eyes, the CSCE was the misbegotten child born of the marriage of interests in the U.S.A. and the U.S.S.R. in Western Europe. The geopolitical thrust of the CSCE, therefore, was predictably Euro-Atlanticist. Predictably oriented toward a policy of maintaining and nourishing ties with the United States. And that meant that the EC and the CSCE were not of the same blood type.

The simple fact was that the EC had been overtaken by the rush of geopolitical events, and everyone here knew it. In the ongoing drive to build the new Europe, nobody could yet predict which of the two—the EC or the CSCE—would predominate; which would form the actual government of that new Europe.

"I don't know about you, my friends." Marais looked at everyone except Appleyard and made the point that was on everyone's mind. "But this odd situation surrounding the sudden and exclusive candidacy of America's Paul Gladstone gives me the impression that the illustrious Commissioners of our EC are no longer confining their outlook to the twelve member states."

"My dear Count . . ." Eugenia Louverdo of Greece spoke up from where she stood between the Selectors from Spain and Ireland. "I have an impression of my own. Not so much about our esteemed Commissioners, though, as about Europe itself.

"I can't help remembering that passage in Plato's *Symposium* where the wise old woman, Diotima, tells Socrates how mankind was originally one spherical body. Some evil godlet sliced it in two. And forever after, mankind's history has been the effort of the two parts to get back together again. Now, with the drive and impulse coming at us from all the parts of Europe—and with this unprecedented foisting of Paul Gladstone on us as the only candidate for Secretary-General—don't you feel as if someone has taken Diotima seriously? That someone is pushing everything back together? Or at least that the two halves are seeking out their original oneness?"

"What a poetic thought, Genie." Ireland's Pierce Wall chimed in. Unlike Louverdo, Wall was on the side of an open Europe. "A bit far-fetched for my poor Irish taste, but poetic all the same.

"The real point," he continued "is that the Europe we all know, the Europe we live in right now, is already a relic. We've got to get with the Europe as it will shortly be—as it is becoming."

Almost every head in the group nodded in agreement with the Irishman. But Gibson Appleyard read little traces of regret on every face.

Barely ten minutes remained before the gavel would open this morning's meeting. Yet the man who would wield that gavel, England's Herbert Featherstone-Haugh, was the only Selector who hadn't arrived.

That was odd, Gib mused. Featherstone-Haugh—in good British tradition the name was pronounced Fan-Shaw, so of course everyone called him "Fanny"—liked to work the room in advance of any important meeting. The somewhat fussy premeeting activity of this accomplished aristocrat and parliamentarian had saved more than a few EC initiatives from shipwreck. It was hard to imagine, then, what might be so important as to have kept him from that task this morning.

As if summoned by Appleyard's curiosity, Featherstone-Haugh bustled into the conference room at that very moment, a leather folder stuffed with papers clutched to his chest and a look of strain evident on his face. He greeted various Selectors in his progress toward the long conference table. He stopped to exchange a word with Denmark's Henrik Borcht—"Ost," as he was called for the delectable cheeses he brought from his trips to his homeland. And then he stopped a second time to engage France's feisty Nicole Cresson in a slightly longer chat.

As the Selectors who had gathered around Appleyard began to drift toward their own seats, the Englishman caught the American's eye with a quick, hard glance. Gib gave an unblinking stare in return, and nodded as if in acknowledgment of some unspoken understanding.

"Commander Appleyard!" The first of two latecomers who had entered the conference room on Fanny's heels approached Gib, his hand outstretched in greeting. "Serozha Gafin," the Russian reintroduced himself with a broad, full-lipped smile.

"Yes." Appleyard gave the young Gafin a firm handshake. "I remember our interesting chat during the break in the proceedings at Strasbourg."

Gafin's eyes twinkled. "Conversation is always more flavorful when accompanied by such wonderful *foie gras* and wine, is it not?"

Gafin's companion broke in with a bow and a Prussian-style click of his heels. There was no mistaking that shiny bald pate or the ramrod-straight torso. But the second man reintroduced himself all the same. "Otto Sekuler, Herr Appleyard. Special Liaison-Delegate for the Conference on Security and Cooperation in Europe."

Looking into the steady stare of black eyes framed behind gleaming steel-rimmed spectacles, Gib was tempted to mock Sekuler's greeting with a click of his own heels. He restrained himself, however, and responded instead with a simple "Herr Sekuler."

Featherstone-Haugh was already rapping the meeting to order, so Appleyard, Gafin and Sekuler made their way to the chairs that had been provided for them. Because they had no vote on the Committee—or perhaps because there were Selectors who hoped to avoid contamination with the Euro-Atlanticist positions they represented—the three visitors sat near the wall a few feet from the conference table. Before Fanny could take up the first order of business, Italy's beautiful Corrado Dello Iudice leveled a complaint. Why had there been such a sudden and drastic change in the Committee's mandate. Why only one candidate? And, finally, who was behind this Paul Gladstone, anyway?

"We'll get to all that in good time, my dear fellow." Fanny rapped Dello Iudice into unwilling silence. "But we mustn't forget our manners."

"N'est-ce pas!"

Nicole Cresson's stage whisper brought a frown to the chairman's face. "As our regulations permit, we have special Liaison-Delegates with us again today. All join us at the request of their respective home offices. And, I might add, at the request of our esteemed Commissioners themselves. We are all pleased to welcome Washington's Commander Gibson Appleyard again, I'm sure. . . ."

"N'est-ce pas!"

Another frown at Vinaigre; but the chairman was determined to get on with things. "Let us acknowledge and welcome our two new guests. Will you make yourselves known to us, gentlemen?"

The Russian was the first to take to his feet in response to Fanny's invitation. "Serozha Gafin. Special attaché for sociocultural relations with the European Community. I bring you greetings from President Mikhail Sergeyevich Gorbachev. The Soviet Union and its fraternal states have always belonged to Europe. Now that we are building a freshly democratic federation of all the Russias, we feel the time is right to activate once again our deep and instinctual Europeanness."

As Gafin regained his chair, this time it was Jan Borliuth of Belgium who belted out a lusty *"N'est-ce pas!"* Then he shot a look at Appleyard as if to point to Gafin as living proof that Gorbachev was a threat.

With another little rap of his gavel, Fanny turned to Sekuler.

"Otto Sekuler!" The German visitor stood up in his turn and gave another sharp click of his heels. "Special Delegate for the CSCE at your service!" To Appleyard's eye, the Selectors seemed caught in a comical no-man's-land somewhere between mild amusement at the sight of old Prussia alive and well in their midst and sharp dismay at Sekuler's connection with the rival CSCE.

"Very good." Fanny straightened in his chair. "Now, before we take up our noble task in earnest. The extraterritorial recommendations have come in since our last meeting. From the Republic of China. And from the Arab League's Secretary. Comments anyone?"

Silence.

"Good." Featherstone-Haugh began to rummage among the papers in his leather case. "But we have received two more letters of interest. In fact, that was what delayed me this morning. . . . Ah! Here they are!" The chairman held two envelopes aloft and turned them for all to see.

Even at a distance, everyone recognized the crimson emboss of the papal Tiara and Keys at the upper left corner of both envelopes, and even at a distance, everyone noticed the subtle differences in the two. They had seen the first hundreds of times on formal invitation cards, envelopes and documents, and recognized it as belonging to the Holy See. The second, however, was the personal version of that emboss, which adorned only the correspondence of the Holy Father himself.

Gibson Appleyard was as fascinated as anyone that the Vatican had sent not one, but two letters of recommendation to this meeting. But for the moment—at least until he heard what those letters contained—he was just as interested in the reactions around him. He heard a few gasps of astonishment. Otto Sekuler stiffened noticeably in his chair and clenched his fists. Serozha Gafin, however, remained pleasantly poker-faced.

Featherstone-Haugh first removed a single page from the envelope bearing the Pope's personal emboss. "Well, of course." Chairman Fanny felt it sufficient to paraphrase much of the papal letter. "Of course, the Holy Father, whose humanitarian and religious stature we all admire and revere, recommends that we choose a candidate who is best fitted to aid the Ministers and the Commissioners in their herculean task of reassembling our ancient Europe as our common homeland. . . ." Fanny ran his eye down the page, and then read a few snatches verbatim. " 'Mindful always of Europe's ancient Christian history and inspired with the surety of prosperity and salvation which is uniquely guaranteed by the Redeemer of mankind . . .' "

Featherstone-Haugh's brows began to bob up and down, but he went manfully on. "The Holy Father says that his heart 'bleeds for poor, poor Europe being progressively alienated from its heritage and appointed destiny, while its noble tradition is being transmogrified. . . .' He warns us and the new Secretary-General and the Council Ministers and Commissioners of the rampant dangers of materialism and hedonism. Then he winds up his letter this way: 'Europe must seek a future of unity for the benefit of the entire human family of man by returning to its Christian roots.' And of course"—Fanny was already folding the papal document again—"with joy and willingly, the Holy Father imparts his Apostolic blessing et cetera and so on."

The momentary silence among the Selectors was broken by Robert Allaeys of Holland. He was normally a patient man, he grumbled. But he saw no reason for the Selectors to brook papal interference in the workings of the EC.

Appleyard took note of Allaeys' objection, and of the Selectors who seconded his sentiments with a rap on the table or a ritual "hear, hear." For his own part, however, Gib was struck by a single passage in the Pontiff's otherwise predictable letter. The passage that referred to "poor, poor Europe." Had not Appleyard himself uttered those very words to himself only a short time ago? Clearly, this Pope was not impressed with the general euphoria about the new Europe, any more than Gib was. That pegged the Pontiff as an independent thinker; as a man who formed his own opinions.

But just how far did such papal sentiments go? Did the Holy Father share Appleyard's view that Europe was a shuttlecock? In fact, was there a realistic geopolitical basis to the Pontiff's thinking at all? Or was Gib reading too much into one short passage? What was that other phrase Fanny had read out? Something about Europe returning to its Christian roots. Was the papal heart bleeding with nothing more than a yearning for past glories, then? Those were questions Appleyard would love to probe with the Holy Father, if he ever got the chance. But at the very least there was reason now for heightened interest in the Slavic Pope.

Appleyard was jolted from his ruminations by Featherstone-Haugh's voice informing his fellow Selectors that the two Vatican documents were identical in all details. "Except . . ." Fanny extracted the second letter from its manila envelope. "Except that this second letter, which ostensibly comes from the Secretariat of State, carries the signature of the Cardinal Secretary of State himself, His Eminence Cosimo Maestroianni. And it carries one additional paragraph, which I will read in its entirety.

" 'The Council of Ministers and the Commissioners of the greater European Community must be in a position to enable its member states to enter the large trails of history not only in Europe but also in all continents of the globe. Therefore, having duly examined the credentials and assessed the promise of the new candidate for the post of Secretary-General to the Commissioners—credentials and documentary evidence which the Council kindly chose to pass on to the Holy See by way of information—the Holy See feels that Paul Thomas Gladstone, Esquire, is admirably suited to fill the post that has fallen vacant at such a critical moment in the life of the European Community. The Holy See wholeheartedly recommends his candidacy, subject always of course to the good judgment of the appointed Selectors.' "

The silence that greeted the reading of this paragraph was charged with the special electricity of geopolitical interest. The Selectors had heard all the gossip that told of a divided Vatican hierarchy, of course. But they had never been privy to such an open and official display of direct opposition to the Holy Father at the highest levels of his administration.

To be sure, the disdain and disrespect that Holland's Robert Allaeys had expressed moments before for the Vatican had to do with disagreement on fundamental issues. But it did not have to do with the raw and decidedly worldly power still held, if not always exercised, by the Holy See. On that score, the papal office commanded serious attention. For this group, Maestroianni's letter trained a light on internal conditions at the topmost level of Vatican affairs. At that level—and whatever about his recommendation of Gladstone as the next Secretary-General—the fact that the Cardinal had sent a letter outstripping the intent of the Pope's message was eloquent in its own message of a house divided. Most revealing. Most encouraging.

Though Appleyard kept his own council, he was neither surprised nor enlightened by Cardinal Maestroianni's letter. Nor, he supposed, were Serozha Gafin and Otto Sekuler. That meeting they had attended last May at Strasbourg had been a vivid demonstration of the warfare raging in the Vatican. At that gathering, Appleyard had not only seen the lengths to which His Eminence had already gone in lining up specific operations against the Pope in the name of unity. He had seen as well how closely allied Maestroianni was with Cyrus Benthoek. Nor had Gib forgotten that Benthoek's own effusive recommendation was a part of Paul Gladstone's official dossier. How was all that for wheels within wheels?

"Mr. Chairman!" Germany's Emil Schenker rose to defend the Vatican's point of view. For one thing, Pfennig pointed out, a bit legalistically, the Holy See was within its technical rights as a sovereign state of Europe to send its recommendations to this Committee, or even to send its own Liaison-Delegates, if it chose. But far more important from Schenker's point of view were the dual reminders in those letters. "Whatever their own differences may be, the Pope reminds us of Europe's ancient history. And the Secretary of State reminds us that, like it or not, the EC must be able to deal effectively with and in all continents of the globe—"

"Will my esteemed colleague from Germany yield?"

With a nod of his head, Pfennig gave way to Il Bello of Italy.

"It's all very well to talk of a broadened idea of the new Europe." Dello Iudice spoke with obvious agitation. "But I'm still a lot more concerned with the questions I asked at the outset of this meeting. All the candidates we screened so carefully have mysteriously taken themselves out of the running. Suddenly, we're faced with this Paul Gladstone as the only name in the hat for Secretary-General. So if you ask me, this whole election procedure has been rigged."

"No, no, my dear Corrado." That was as close as Featherstone-Haugh was likely to come to an open challenge. "No, not at all. The Commissioners simply have made a unanimous suggestion for our consideration. We do the choosing, my boy."

"Well, then." For all the good it would do, the Italian decided to face Fanny down. "Can we at least defer our decision?"

For the second time this morning, an audible gasp was heard from several Selectors. But it was Fanny who put their reaction into words.

"My dear Dello Iudice." He was the picture of forbearance. "The difficulty we now face is this. If we cannot agree with the Commissioners' recommendation of Paul Gladstone *and* if we cannot adduce any valid reason for such a rejection based on Gladstone's moral or professional qualifications *and* if we delay our own decision beyond this week's deadline"—Fanny proffered a long look of warning on all in general and on Dello Iudice in particular—"then, under EC law, the Commissioners can make the choice in our stead."

Featherstone-Haugh had said everything that mattered. After all, the security each person on this Committee felt with all the others rested on their shared and established status as behind-the-scenes architects, functionaries and professional colleagues within the burgeoning bureaucracy of their new Europe. They not only knew but were part of the complex interactions and rivalries among the various units of the EC organization; among the Council of Ministers and the Council of Commissioners and the European Parliament itself.

Given such rivalries—and given that they would sit on other committees in the future—these Selectors would be unlikely to set the dangerous precedent of allowing today's election to pass upward into the hands of the Commissioners. In fact, compared to all the other possible calamities—

compared even to putting an American into the Secretary-General's post—nothing measured up by half to the calamity of losing power within the EC.

Featherstone-Haugh was certain of his ground, therefore. He and the other Selectors had learned to trust one another even when they held differing opinions. All were at least trilingual, so the most subtle communication among them was facile. Agreement between them—even to disagree amicably—was therefore a matter of course. Decisions were reached in a spirit of what Vinaigre called *"bonhomie professionelle,"* and Fanny somewhat preciously called "our dear, dear fellowship." That spirit meant there would be a decision this morning on the candidacy of Paul Thomas Gladstone.

Fanny smiled at Corrado Dello Iudice, then at the full complement of his colleagues, and then at his watch. "Shall we take a straw vote then, just to see how things stand? I see we are already running late. I propose we dispense with the written ballot and go with a show of hands." Anyone might have been able to predict the lineup of Selectors on a first and unofficial sounding of sentiment. There were five votes in favor of Gladstone, all of them from the Euro-Atlanticist Committee members—Holland, Germany, Denmark, Luxembourg and Ireland. Together with Fanny's own vote for England, that made six.

As expected, therefore, those against were all Eurocentrics—Vinaigre of France, Stropelaars of Belgium, Il Bello of Italy, Viva of Spain, Capelão of Portugal, and, in spite of her liking for Plato, Louverdo of Greece.

Fanny sighed. In its small way, the split in the straw vote reproduced the split that ran right down the middle of the EC itself. North against South. Euro-Atlanticists against Eurocentrics. The obvious deadlock left no need for commentary beyond a delicate shrug of Featherstone-Haugh's shoulders. "Could I possibly hear one good Eurocentric voice proposing Mr. Gladstone's candidacy, please?"

"Another straw vote, Fanny?" That practical question came from Ireland's Pierce Wall.

"No, Paddy. I need a decision."

"I propose Mr. Paul Thomas Gladstone." To everyone's utter bafflement, the nomination came from Nicole Cresson, whose high-decibel ire at the mere thought of an American as Secretary-General had filled the conference room only shortly before.

"I second." Though Borcht of Denmark was a confirmed Euro-Atlanticist, he grimaced as if he had bitten into bad cheese.

Had Gibson Appleyard been wearing a hat, he would have doffed it in admiration of Fanny's parliamentary performance this morning. "Tut-tut," the Englishman fussed. "A show of hands. For the record now, please." While all hands were still raised—before anyone could change his mind or make some legal objection; before anyone could even say *n'est-ce pas*—Fanny rushed to finalize the vote. "I now declare Mr. Gladstone's appointment has been unanimously approved." With another rap of his gavel, Featherstone-Haugh declared that the final meeting of this ad hoc Committee was adjourned.

From Fanny's point of view, the meeting had gone off well enough. The EC had shown again that it was a smoothly working part of a now widely established process that was patiently molding the minds and disposing the hearts—and the pockets—of millions of Europeans to think and therefore act as citizens of a unity greater than they had ever conceived. As the blue-blood Englishman he was, Featherstone-Haugh had some understandable reservations about that process. But for Fanny the EC Euro-Atlanticist, it was essential that all parts of that subtle, peaceful, constantly working process should function at various levels and from differing angles.

Those parts sometimes seemed to work at cross-purposes. But Fanny had the faith of a true believer. The EC, together with the EFTA nations, the CSCE, the WEU, NATO, the European Council—even the contentious Bruges Group—were slowly fitting into the process. All, that is, except that one sovereign ruler of a domain no bigger than a golf course down there on the banks of Rome's river Tiber. What a joke it was, Fanny thought contemptuously, for such a man to warn the EC that Europe was being "transmogrified" and "alienated."

Well, no matter. Rome's day was fast slipping away on the curve of history in the making. Bad Vatican jokes notwithstanding, then, the meeting had gone off well in the circumstances. True, the imposition of Paul Gladstone's candidacy from above had been awkward. Still . . .

For the last time that day, he gave Commander Appleyard a wordless glance and a rueful smile. Then he rushed to catch Nicole Cresson just as she was disappearing out the door. Their *"bonhomie professionelle"*—their "dear, dear fellowship" had prevailed. Europe had always been good to them. They would make sure that goodness continued.

Gib Appleyard had found his handgrips and toeholds, just as he had promised Admiral Vance he would. And he had used them well. His mission successfully completed, he lingered a while to shake hands with this and that Selector as they formed again into their easy groups and headed off. Like Featherstone-Haugh, Appleyard was subject to his own personality split. And the Slavic Pope's characterization of "poor, poor Europe" had brought that split to the fore.

Gib remembered his history. And because he did, those three words—"poor, poor Europe"—still played in his mind like a puzzle to which he had no answer. Or, perhaps, more like a dirge being piped from an unexpected quarter. As the mystic Rosicrucian he was in his heart, Gib Appleyard had no love for an imperial papacy, and certainly did not want to see its return. But as dispassionate executive officer for the Presidential

Committee of Ten, he did want answers to the questions those words had raised concerning the mind of the Slavic Pope. Nor was it a matter of mere curiosity. The Holy See had access to intelligence that any nation would give a third of its treasury to possess. And whether his house was divided or not, this Pope had shown himself well able to use that intelligence in geopolitical gambits of the highest order.

Those facts alone—those facts, and Thomas Jefferson's famous warning that anyone who dreams of being ignorant and free, dreams of something that never was and never will be—meant that it would be a long time before Appleyard would cease wondering what intelligence might lie behind the Pope's dirgelike lament for "poor, poor Europe."

XXIV

"DECKEL! . . . Deckel! . . . Deckel!"

Eyes half closed, Paul Thomas Gladstone turned his head toward the urgent cry, and then smiled in purest delight. His son was dancing about in happy excitement, shouting lustily as only a five-year-old can as he bounced his name off the ruined battlements of the O'Connor Castle standing some thirty yards offshore in the river Shannon.

As Paul lay on the riverbank, this third Monday of September, in this remote and private spot in southwestern Ireland's County Kerry, on this westernmost tip of Europe at the edge of the Atlantic Ocean, he was certain that life—the life he liked—was just beginning for him. Swathed in Declan's happy cries and in the warm embrace of the early-afternoon sun, and knowing that his wife, Yusai, was waiting in the Manor House eager for the faxed message that would tell them of their future, it seemed to Paul Gladstone that the cup of life's enjoyment was full to overflowing.

"Deckel! . . . Deckel!" Declan leaped about in the most amazing gyrations as the castle echoed his name in a voice that was faithfully, magically his own. He knew his proper name, of course; knew he had been named for Grandfather Declan. But Deckel had been so much easier for him to say as a toddler that it had become his nickname.

"Deckel! Deckel! Deckel!" The quicker he repeated the cry, the faster came the echoes, until his voice and his echo were one. Then he stopped just long enough to let every sound die away, so he could begin all over again. *"Deckel! . . . Deckel! . . . Deckel! . . ."*

Sequestered with the two people in the world he loved the most, Paul knew that the purity and exultation of his son's voice and its echo belonged here where all was untouched by stridency. On lazy days like today, the random cry of a lone curlew and the busy chirping of grasshoppers in the tall growth around him and the sound of Deckel's voice—above all, the sound of Deckel's voice—all seemed to belong in some satisfactory way to nature at its summer profusion. Here, all was in harmony, fresh, calming. Here, all was participant in some eternal now that bathed the sycamores and the copper beeches lining Carraig Road and that veiled land and water and skies with the contentment of permanence.

On his first visit here, Christian had been so struck by the similarities between Liselton Manor and Windswept House that he had teased his younger brother about it, wondering if Paul had chosen Liselton out of a secret desire to reproduce Windswept House without returning to it.

There was some truth in what Chris said. But for Paul, Liselton was far more than a mirror of Windswept House. There was nothing in Galveston or anywhere on earth to compare with the sweeping view of the entire Shannon estuary, of the rumbling and ever encroaching Atlantic Ocean, of County Clare to the north with its rocky coast, holiday beaches and central granite plateau. Surely enchantment had always been a condition of life here. For Paul, it was the Atlantic wind sweeping the river estuary and Liselton, particularly from late autumn to early spring, that sang to him of the special character of this place. Nothing would satisfy him but to belong here; to have this retreat here. And the call to do so—for he regarded it as nothing less than a mysterious call of some sort—was far stronger than his mental perception of its source.

In time to come, perhaps life with all its reckonings would sharpen Paul's perception. But for now, there was Yusai. There was Declan. There was Liselton. And there was the glowing promise of the near future.

"Declan!" Stirred from his reveries by a too long silence, Paul raised his head to see his son leaning too far over the riverbank. "Declan!" Gladstone was on his feet and beside his son in a few giant strides. "What is it, son? Didn't I tell you not to bend over the edge?" He scooped the boy into his arms. "Time to go back to the house, my boyo."

"There was a fish there, Daddy," Deckel protested. "A green fish. He was looking at me!"

"He wasn't looking at you, son." In spite of himself, Paul shivered as he recalled the local superstition—the "pishogue"—that said a fish looking at you meant you would join him soon. "Fishes sleep in the sun with their eyes open."

"But, Daddy!" With a touch of his father's stubbornness, Declan protested a second time. "When I moved, the fish moved his tail."

Paul ruffled the boy's black hair and settled him in his arms. "Little fishes do that to stay in one place. Otherwise the water flowing off to the sea would take them from where they want to sleep. See?" He turned so Declan could look into the Shannon from the safety of his embrace. "Those flat stones get warm in the sun, and the little fishes like a warm place to sleep."

So apparently did little boys. Paul could already feel Deckel relaxing, his face buried in his father's shoulder. Paul turned and headed up toward Liselton House. As he reached Carraig Road, he caught sight of Yusai running down the steep rise of the driveway waving a clutch of papers in one hand. Her face was as much a smiling picture of excitement as Declan's had been when he had called out to the echoing castle in the Shannon.

"Paul! Darling!" Yusai called in her picturesque English. "They're already screaming for you! The bonzes of Brussels! They want you there by the fourth week of this month!" Now that she was nearer, the odd look on Paul's face gave Yusai a sudden fear. What was wrong? Had something happened to little Deckel?

"It's nothing, darling." Paul glanced sideways at his son. "Just relaxed after all the sun and excitement, I guess. Worn out from calling Mr. Echo!"

"Here, then." In obvious relief, Yusai handed the fax to her husband and stretched her arms toward their son. "Give me my tired little boy."

Deckel opened his eyes in a sleepy sort of way. "I saw a fish, Mummy. . . ." With a child's unconscious gravity, he looked back toward the river.

Something of Paul's fear shivered through her own heart. "What happened down there, Paul?"

"It was nothing at all." Fully himself again, Paul was already scanning the fax that had filled his wife with such excitement. "So! We're to be the Gladstones of Brussels! And did you see? The message is signed by Cyrus Benthoek himself." Paul was exultant. "The bonze of all bonzes! Higher than that you can't go!"

"Do little fishes go to Heaven, Mummy? Does Holy God love them?"

Yusai drew the coverlet of his bed over her sleepy boy. "Of course, my pet. Of course He does."

"The very same Heaven where the Angels and Little Linnet are?" Deckel's pet canary, Little Linnet, had died the previous winter.

"Yes, sweet. The very same." Yusai spoke slowly and soothingly, but with no special conviction. She might have been singing a sleepy-time lullaby. "All God's Angels take care of the little fishes and birdies. . . ." Yusai's words trailed into silence. Exhausted by the day's adventures, Declan was already fast asleep. She brushed his cheek lightly in a blessing of love for this child who was so much like his father.

Outside on the landing, Yusai stood at the bay window giving out over Carraig Road and the estuary. Another few hours of sun, she thought, and then the slow tranquil decline of the evening. Entranced by the vista and the silence, she settled for a time into the love seat that nestled by the window. She loved Liselton. She loved it because she shared it with Paul and Declan. She felt at home here. Why, then, was there a mystery about this place for her? Some element or atmosphere she could not easily penetrate or ignore? Why was she disturbed? Why these bouts of uneasiness? And why had that strange look on Paul's face stirred all that in her again, shattering the order and tranquillity of her Confucianist mind?

Yusai had to smile. In her love for her husband, she had conformed to his decision that their child be reared in Catholic beliefs and devotions. That was why she knew at least the rudiments of the Catholic catechism; and that was why she could answer Deckel's questions about God and little fishes. But she herself remained the product of a type of Confucian culture and mind-set that had been stripped bare of those supposedly picturesque and invisible forces that still permeated the minds of uneducated Chinese.

Even when it came to her own Paul—or at any rate, when it came to the quasi-religious unease and disquiet she sometimes found in him—Yusai could only feel that unwelcome sense of mystery. Or maybe puzzlement was more like it. Having seen that look on Paul's face, how could she not be disturbed? He was always so sure of himself. So divinely sure. Never violently taken aback at events. Yet today she had seen—what? Surprise? Fear? Confusion? No, she decided. Like Liselton itself, Paul's expression this afternoon had been nothing so simple.

Yusai Kiang had first laid eyes on Paul Thomas Gladstone in the mid-eighties. As a twenty-five-year-old postgraduate student at the Sorbonne in Paris, she had been a guest of the Belgian government at a Brussels international conference on Europe-China relations. Paul, barely thirty years of age, had been the keynote speaker. She had fallen in love with him almost immediately. He had seemed to be some sort of god in human form. Or, as she told him at a later and tender moment between them, he had seemed like one of those "messengers from Heaven" commemorated in traditional Chinese mythology who were said to come down among mere mortals to share their toils and bestow happiness.

One of the things Yusai valued about her Confucianism was that she could indulge in such imagery and metaphor without any implication that they had any foundation in reality. They were meant to give a romantic elegance to life's marvelous happenings. In its centuries-old evolution, Confucianism had wisely dropped the theological underpinnings of ancient Chinese animism. But wisely, too, some of its fanciful language had been absorbed into a conventional humanism, the better to enhance the brute materialism of living. The Kiang family readily admitted the divinity of gods and goddesses and all the rest of religion's paraphernalia in a most practical and eclectic way: Use it if it fits your fancy; do not bother with it if it means nothing to you.

At any rate, time had not dulled even her romantic first impression of Paul. The Mandarin Chinese he had learned in Beijing was as smooth and effective and impeccable as his French. She was amused by the trace of

Texas twang that spiced his mid-Atlantic English. He had a truly global view of the society of nations, and she saw a dimension in Paul that exactly matched her whole family tradition. A dimension found in people who for generations have balanced the inherent miseries of human existence with continuous success and prosperity.

Yusai found herself unable to turn away from the window outside Declan's room. It was as if she was transfixed by the vulnerability Paul had displayed for just a moment today. And it was as if that vulnerability had something to do with the mystery of this isolated retreat. It was silly to sit here, she told herself, as if she would suddenly be able to put such things into a focus she could understand and cope with. With another look out over Carraig Road and the river estuary, Yusai resigned herself to living through this bout of uneasiness. It wasn't the first; and she supposed it wouldn't be the last.

Paul went to his study at the far end of the house. Cyrus Benthoek wanted confirmation that Gladstone would report directly to him in London before heading off to his new post—and his new life—as Secretary-General at the EC in Brussels.

As he composed his reply, it was easy to push Deckel's encounter with his "green fish" to a far corner of his mind. He thought instead, and with justifiable satisfaction, how far he had come in his chosen career in so short a time. And, as he anticipated his coming meeting with the indestructible Cyrus Benthoek, he thought, too, of how careful that old man had been from the start to direct him onto the politically correct and ideologically pure path of life in a transnational world. Not that Paul had minded such direction back then. Or now either, for that matter.

With his faxed message safely off to Cyrus Benthoek's office in London, Paul was more than ready for his shower, and then drinks with Yusai before dinner. The first rush of warm water over his body put him in mind again of Deckel leaning so precariously over that flat rock in the Shannon to investigate his "green fish." Nonsense, he decided, and soaped himself down as if that might wash the incident out through the drain. Yusai had the right idea about such things, he told himself. Her Confucian outlook—her idea of order and tranquillity; her mind-set that would have no truck with puzzlement and superstitions—those were things he treasured in her.

Of course, he treasured much more than that. She had always fascinated him. Yusai had challenged any stereotype that might have lingered in Paul's mind about Chinese women. She was more elegant and polished than any of the young women he had squired before he met her. She was well educated; fluent in three Western languages as well as in Japanese, Russian and of course her native Mandarin. She seemed to be without prejudice, and yet to feel and to be superior to most of her peers. And like Cessi and Tricia, Yusai recoiled from anything that was tawdry or trashy.

It had been her family history and culture as much as Yusai herself that had first made Paul a fascinated prisoner of this uncommon young woman. He had never come across any family like the Kiangs. He had never even heard of a Chinese mainland family that had survived the collapse of the Chinese empire in 1911; that still flourished in the period of Sun Yat-sen and the Kuomintang of Chiang Kai-shek; that escaped the Japanese onslaught of the thirties as well as the devastation of World War II and the subsequent Maoist purges in the forties and fifties and sixties. Yet Yusai herself was proof that the Kiang family had emerged from those eighty years of turbulence "beneath the Heavens" with their landed properties intact, their banking business in Hong Kong and Macao as solvent as ever and with an apparent acceptability for and access to the post-Mao clique of Chinese Communists in Beijing.

Paul had asked Yusai how her family had managed such a miracle. Every one of those regimes, she had said, needed families such as the Kiangs. Every one of those regimes needed money, and they needed access to foreign money markets. "And besides." Yusai had winked at him in a wonderfully provocative way. "My family never bought a house that hadn't got several back doors!"

Still, Paul had guessed quickly and correctly that the Kiangs' secret of success had less to do with back doors than with their perennial membership in a vaguely known international brotherhood of capital composed of individuals and groups whose interests spanned and outreached all nationalisms and all particular sovereignties. Thus it was that the Kiang family maintained a perpetual liquidity abroad, based on concrete assets at home and around the globe. And thus it was that they remained useful go-betweens for a Maoist regime facing the capitalist and anti-Marxist world outside China. The Kiangs practiced moderation in all their political affiliations, of course. Still, while that did result in a minimum of real enemies, it didn't eliminate the problem entirely. That was what Yusai had meant about houses with back doors.

By now Paul had learned that the Kiangs were not the only Chinese of that ilk. And yet, there was something special in them. For, while they remained quintessentially Chinese, it appeared that Yusai Kiang's family had been truly transnational in mind and policy long before it crossed the minds of Western European and North American CEOs that such a mind and policy were the keys to global success. For most people, such a realization would not have been the stuff of romance. But when Paul had first met Yusai, the transnational idea and way of life had taken hold in him as his supreme ideal. For Paul, then, Yusai was more than elegance and polish. More than beautiful and fun and wonderfully provocative. In a literal, flesh-and-blood way, his dream had walked right into his life. She was his ideal.

Yusai had not been everyone's ideal, however. She had not been Cessi's, for example; the awful scene at Windswept House when Paul had flown home to tell his mother of his intended marriage had made that painfully clear. Surprisingly, though, a few of Paul's in-house colleagues had had their own reservations about Yusai Kiang as the future Mrs. Paul Gladstone. One senior partner in particular, in fact, had come right out and said that the Kiangs were probably "international double-crossers." How else, he had asked, could old man Kiang have been on good terms with Mao Zedong *and* with Zhou En-lai *and* with Deng Xiaoping?

Cyrus Benthoek had remained above the fray over Paul's plans to marry Yusai. But Benthoek's CEO, Nicholas Clatterbuck, had given his support to Gladstone, and that was almost as good. Like everyone in the firm, Paul had always seen Clatterbuck as a kind of tweedy grandfather type. But no one at the firm ever doubted Clatterbuck's esteem in the eyes of Cyrus Benthoek. Nor did they question his authority, or his ability to manage any affair, large or small. It was at Clatterbuck's inspired suggestion, then, and with his able connivance, that Paul had invited all the firm's partners to a prenuptial dinner. And it was Yusai herself who had proceeded that night to charm and win them to the last man.

The couple married in Paris, and flew immediately to Yusai's birthplace in Mainling for their honeymoon. There, Yusai had put her stamp forever on those memory medals Paul still wore around his neck. Though his medals were religious in character, they were important to Paul because they represented layers of his life that stretched back to childhood—back to the day of his first Communion when Cessi had presented one of them to him as a gift.

That one, a small golden oval, bore the image of the Virgin Mary standing atop the globe of the world, and encircled with the petition "O Mary conceived without sin pray for us who have recourse to thee." Cessi had given Paul a companion to the Miraculous Medal on that now distant day—the crucified figure of Jesus on the traditional Roman Cross, an image meant to evoke penitence and repentance and sorrow for personal sins in the individual Catholic. But Paul had replaced Cessi's crucifix with a plain gold cross instead. It had seemed a suitable compromise.

Yusai understood all about Paul's gold cross. Her Confucianist mind had no problem with the accepted and universal symbol of Christianity. But as she and Paul had lazed in bed together, she had begun to finger the medal with the image of the woman. "Who is she?"

"Who is who?"

"This woman." Yusai lifted the Miraculous Medal on its chain. "Has she a place inside your heart?" The medal had been part of the furniture of his life for so long that he rarely gave it a thought. Even now, it wasn't the medal itself that was central in his mind, but his first experience of Yusai in a state of uncertainty.

"I really would like to know," Yusai persisted, "why you carry this woman so near to your heart. It's important to me, Paul."

"My sweet Yusai." Paul took the hand that held the medal and kissed it. "I'm married to you, not to her." Paul held the medal up in his turn. "It's a Catholic religious medal. I've worn it since I was a boy. It's a picture of Mary who was the mother of Jesus. Remember? She came up once in those instruction classes we went through before our wedding."

"Ah!" Yusai had beamed with the sudden delight of understanding. "That's her. The mother." The gremlins of uncertainty obviously banished from her mind, Yusai relaxed in her husband's arms.

Brief as that moment was, it had a remarkable and enduring effect on Paul. With her Confucianist desire to master uncertainty and doubt, Yusai had convinced him that their marriage had set them on a course that would bring them to an enticing land far distant from the Meiling of Yusai's parents and from the Galveston of Cessi Gladstone. A course that was irresistible. That night, Paul had tasted more than Yusai's sweetness and love. With a few gremlins of his own put away at last, he knew the giddiness of freedom from all that was old and outworn.

"Good show, Gladstone! Or should I say, Mr. Secretary-General!"

Paul had no sooner stepped into his corner office on the thirty-fourth floor of his firm's London headquarters than Nicholas Clatterbuck was hot on his heels.

"Thanks, Nicholas." Paul accepted the congratulations with a broad smile. "Is Benthoek here already?" It was barely eight o'clock.

"He's here all right. Asked me to bring you up myself as soon as you arrived." The two men headed for the private elevator that would take them to Cyrus Benthoek's penthouse office. "After you settle things with CB, we'll need a day or two of your time here in London. There's a lot going on. After that, your main liaison with us will be through Benthoek himself. He has an exclusive on you as long as you work with the European crowd."

The elevator doors slid open noiselessly on the penthouse floor, and at the sound of voices Cyrus Benthoek's private secretary popped her head into the corridor and pronounced herself ready to usher the pair into the inner sanctum.

Absolutely nothing had changed in Benthoek's office in the ten years since Paul's first interview. There was still that enormous desk with its curious inlaid design of the Great Seal of the United States. As always, there were a few piles of documents neatly squared on its vast surface. And of course that portrait of Elihu Root still surveyed the scene like an ageless monitor. Above all, Cyrus Benthoek had not changed. He was still straight and tall, and his blue eyes were as steady as his capable hands.

"I don't mind telling you, young man—" There were to be no congratulations from CB, it seemed. "I don't mind telling you that by some rather unexpected causalities over which none of your superiors have had any direct control, you have been thrust into a position of extraordinary relevance."

That was an odd way to start this meeting, Gladstone reflected. He knew better than to ask questions; there was no freewheeling in conversation with Benthoek. Were they to deal in cryptograms, then? Was Paul to spend his time here trying to figure out CB's hidden meanings? He knew the old fellow well enough to understand that "unexpected causalities" conveyed the idea of voices outside the firm. And, of course, the "position of extraordinary relevance" meant Paul's new career with the EC. He could only surmise, however, that lack of "direct control" must mean that the firm and its president had backed Paul for the post of Secretary-General because of some useful link between those outside voices and the interests of the firm itself.

"Mr. Clatterbuck's presence here today is as imperative as your own, Mr. Gladstone. He will be our go-between; yours and mine. It is therefore essential that he have a working knowledge of what we are about." Paul nodded.

"The first big date on your calendar will be December 10." CB fixed his eyes on Paul like an owl on a mouse. "You know about the Maestricht meeting, eh?"

"Just the essentials, sir." Like everyone else interested in transnational affairs, Paul knew that the EC Council Ministers would meet in Maestricht, Holland, on December 10 to finalize their plans for establishing the ultimate political and financial union of the European Community member states.

"Good!" Benthoek gave his young protégé a magisterial smile. "You know what you don't know. And that is the beginning of wisdom in my book. At this crucial stage—after getting acquainted with your official duties in Brussels, of course; and selecting your personal aides—your immediate task between now and December 10 will be to get a thorough knowledge of each of the twelve individual Ministers in the Council. And a thorough knowledge as well of the seventeen EC Commissioners."

Benthoek rose from his desk and planted himself beneath the portrait of Elihu Root. "I cannot stress the point too strongly, Mr. Gladstone. You must get to know each of those twenty-nine men individually. In detail. Personally. Politically. Financially. Get to know them; their associates; their aides; their friends; their enemies; their loves and hates; their weaknesses and their strengths. And in the case of the Ministers in particular, their day-to-day working relations with their home governments. Understood?"

"Yes, sir."

Satisfied that his most basic warning was clear, CB relaxed slightly and strolled the few steps back to his desk to lay out some of the particulars that concerned him. He went on to outline the most basic split within the EC—the fact that half its members favored close ties across the Atlantic, while the other half opposed them. "And of course"—CB sounded almost conspiratorial now—"there is also the rival organization to the EC. In our opinion, Mr. Gladstone, the Conference on Security and Cooperation in

Europe is the one unit functioning today that is most likely to become the chief organ of Greater Europe. We must not forget entirely the land of our birth, must we? The United States is a fully fledged member of the CSCE. And it is the principal moneybags behind the European Bank for Reconstruction and Development.

"The point I wish to make, Mr. Gladstone, is that we at this law firm are convinced Euro-Atlanticists. We are committed to the creation of a fully developed global economy, organized according to a globalized banking system. You must serve the EC Commissioners and the Council of Ministers, of course. But you must remember the position of your firm. We fully expect you to maintain close ties with us—*exclusively* through this office of mine. Of course—" Benthoek smiled like a professor pleased to instruct an apt pupil. "There is no doubt where your technical loyalties lie."

"Technical loyalties, sir?"

"Technical loyalties, yes, Mr. Gladstone. Once you leave the valley and walk upon the mountaintop, you will have a view of the valley dwellers that is very different from theirs. From the top, Mr. Gladstone, you will have the complete picture." The old man eyed Paul with a look that was at once prying and genuinely shy. "I'm sure you understand my meaning."

Gladstone hadn't the experience necessary to understand all of what CB meant to convey by those words. Not with his rational mind, at any rate. Yet it was a faculty of Cyrus Benthoek's peculiar character and temper that, with such simple phrasing and in a brief instant, he had succeeded in penetrating the privacy of Paul's sentimentality. With that look, he had succeeded in entering Paul's heart, that part of him that each of us must try to keep intact and inviolate from the necessary ravages that ordinary human intercourse wreaks on us all.

In that instant, and with those few words, it seemed to Paul that there was a sudden inner change in him that he was powerless to arrest right there and then. It was as if the solid ground—the well-known and well-beloved scenery of his familiar surroundings, his Yusai, his Declan, his Liselton, his Windswept House, his family—all dropped away and out of sight.

Paul's unexpected and involuntary reaction was part panic and part exhilaration. The sense of exhilaration said: Without any personal baggage, you can fly higher and higher. The sense of panic said: You will belong to no one; no one will care what happens to you. And a little voice of sad self-reproach whispered: This demon of loveless flight was always with you, always a part of you.

Cyrus Benthoek obviously noticed the look of puzzlement on the young man's face. "It takes time, Mr. Gladstone." He was almost paternal now, full of care and understanding. "It takes time to adjust. Take it in easy steps." He squared the already squared piles of documents on his desk. "Let me put it to you in a different way. By now you must have realized that things are never quite what they seem at first, eh? At least, not in this life. Would you not agree?"

Though he heard the words and met the cool look Benthoek leveled upon him, from Paul's point of view this was no longer a conversation between himself and the president of this prestigious and powerful transnational law firm. At this moment, Cyrus Benthoek seemed to be some hoary, human-faced repository of stark truth about the human condition. Someone who lived in a place where there was no condemnation for the blindness of that condition, and no compassion for its puny traits. Gladstone tried to clear his throat; tried to say something. But his mouth had gone completely dry.

Benthoek went on imperturbably. "You and I and Mr. Clatterbuck here—all of us moving at this level of affairs—are no longer merely ambitious and capable colleagues in an important transnational firm. Nor are we any longer merely responding as best we can to random events in the competitive life of international business.

"If that were so, Mr. Gladstone, you would not be sitting where you now sit. Nor, indeed, would I be where I now sit. Instinctively you know that. Do you not, Mr. Gladstone?" It was less a question than a command; and in any case, Paul understood it to be rhetorical.

"Now." Inevitably, the moment had come for Cyrus Benthoek to raise his hands in the *orans* gesture typical of him. "That brings us full circle. I am certain you will remember that I began this little interview with a mention of the extraordinary relevance of your new appointment. I am also certain that you will understand that you were not chosen as Secretary-General at the EC out of love for your beautiful eyes, as the saying goes. And not even for your talents, though they are admittedly formidable.

"But the simple fact is that your circumstances—the whole man that you have become through family, education, training, marriage—happen to make you suitable for a job of the highest importance within a vast and ongoing plan of human affairs. As *he* would say, Mr. Gladstone"—Benthoek stood up slowly and smiled, first at the portrait of Elihu Root behind him, and then at Paul—"all you need do is be faithful and follow the footprints of Mistress History in the sands of human time. If you will continue to do that, I have not the slightest doubt that my full meaning this morning will become clearer to you.

"Good luck, Mr. Gladstone. And God bless."

"Give me a couple of minutes, Nicholas." Back on terra firma of the thirty-fourth floor, Paul waved Clatterbuck off, headed alone for his own office and closed the door behind him. When his call to Liselton went through, it was Yusai who answered.

"Paul! Where are you? What's the news?"

"Everything's fine, darling. Just fine. Where's Declan?"

From the first syllable, Yusai heard the dead weight at the back of his voice. "School. He'll be back at three-thirty. But are you sure everything's all right? You sound peculiar, Paul."

"Couldn't be better," he lied. "Saw old CB just now and got my marching orders. Just wanted to hear your voice—say hello to Deckel—tell you both I love you and miss you. . . ."

"Paul darling, we know you love us. But . . ."

"What have you been doing since I left?"

Yusai recognized his need. Paul was reaching out from some rarefied and humorless plain far away from her. Despite a twinge of fear in her that had no name, she painted a sprightly picture of the morning's doings. They had got up extra early, she said. "You know Declan wakes up with the chickens anyway. But nothing would do for him today except to go and pick some fresh mushrooms. I wish you could have been there, darling. Declan was talking to the swallows, telling them not to eat too many morning flies.

"Oh and, Paul, there was one lone skylark up there, circling higher and higher into the bluest of skies—singing, singing, singing all the time in that lovely silence. It was like a sign from Heaven that all will be good for us. For the three of us. It was really a glamorous morning. Deckel shouted at the skylark to tell the Angels to bring you back soon. The sunshine was like a golden shower. The Virginia creeper was a cloak of yellow light. Liselton was all gilded glory. . . ."

At an odd sound on the line, Yusai thought they had been disconnected. "Paul? Are you there? Darling, have we been cut off . . . ?"

With his every sense, Paul absorbed the grace of the morning Yusai was describing for him. And with his every sense, he could feel a pain that was new to him. He could hear an inner voice; a nevermore bell of warning. Yes. That was it. A voice—a bell—that said, "Nevermore, as it has been for you. Never will you see with innocent eyes or with undivided mind, as before this moment. A part of you is consecrated now to all that excludes such simple joy and exultation. You were blessed to have it for a short time. . . ."

". . . Paul? Are you there? Darling, have we been cut off?"

"Of course, darling. I'm still here." Thankful that Yusai couldn't see his tears, Paul tried to master the huskiness in his voice.

Yusai accepted the lie and took up her description of the morning's adventures. She repeated Hannah Dowd's town gossip. She told Paul how many mushrooms she and Declan had found; how they had cooked them on a hot griddle; how many cuts of toast and mushrooms Deckel had put away. . . .

"What are you doing now, love?" Paul wanted to see that, too.

"I'm getting along with our packing and getting ready for the move to Belgium. And I'm missing you, Paul. It's not the same without you."

"Me, too. I'll call you again tonight."

Paul gave a hard look at the receiver as he rested it again in its cradle. Then, striding toward the door, he raised his eyes as though he could see through the ceiling of his office; through all the floors that connected him to the desk with the Great Seal and to the portrait of Elihu Root. "Damn your eyes, Mr. Cyrus Benthoek!"

XXV

BY THE FIRST MONDAY in October, comfortably installed in his new corner office on the third floor of the Apostolic Palace, His Eminence Cardinal Cosimo Maestroianni was set to launch the first stage of the three-step agenda he had outlined barely five months before to Cyrus Benthoek and Dr. Ralph Channing. Any nostalgia the little Cardinal might have suffered for his former status was all but banished by the intensity of his work to bring a new brand of unity to his churchly organization and to bring that organization into a new brand of unity with the society of nations.

It was fair to say, in fact, that his retirement from the all-consuming duties of guiding the Holy See's internal and external affairs as Vatican Secretary of State could not have come at a more opportune moment. Nor could his transition to what he considered a higher plane of activity have been more effortless or more promising. Paul Gladstone was in Brussels and already functioning as the newly installed Secretary-General of the EC. He had heard from Cardinal John Jay O'Cleary that Father Christian Gladstone had accepted the invitation to work full-time in Rome. And, most inspiring of all, he had received exactly the responses he had wanted to his last official letter as Secretary of State to the diplomatic representatives of the Holy See in eighty-two countries around the world.

That delicately worded letter had turned out to be one of the more skillful pieces of work His Eminence had ever done. Indeed, it could not have been more successful as an instrument to test the linchpin question of his entire agenda. The question: How united with the Slavic Pope did the 4,000 bishops of the Church Universal feel?

Just as Maestroianni had expected, the informal polls conducted by the diplomatic representatives at the Cardinal's request stressed the lack of unity between this Pope and his bishops. They also supplied Cardinal Maestroianni with a list of those bishops whose thinking on this issue still required some judicious revision. Equally clear was the lack of agreement among the bishops as to what kind of unity would be most desirable between themselves and the Holy See.

Responses that added up to such a total absence of cohesion might have told of chaos and nothing more. But for the little Cardinal, they provided a useful map upon which to chart the course agreed upon at Strasbourg. By early October, in fact, Cardinal Maestroianni had already plotted the two main lines of work that faced him.

The first and easier initiative would involve nothing more taxing than a little old-fashioned legwork in the field. With Father Christian Gladstone in Rome, and with his brother Paul installed as Secretary-General at the European Community, Maestroianni now had the means to assess both the needs and the weaknesses of every important bishop. And, through all kinds of political favors, he had the means to turn needs and weaknesses alike to his advantage.

Just as he had proposed to Channing and Benthoek, in other words, the Cardinal now had at his fingertips a process by which to guide even the most conservative bishops to an intimate appreciation of just how concretely the favors and considerations they required from secular authorities depended on a new kind of bridge to the wider world, and therefore on a new kind of Church governance.

The second of Cardinal Maestroianni's initiatives was more complex. This was the bureaucratic design he had spoken of with such candor to Channing and Benthoek. The design to use the multilayered Bishops Conferences around the world to form and to foment an open expression of the new Common Mind of the Bishops. Though the details of the process still required serious attention, His Eminence had a finely tuned instinct for the perfect bureaucratic machinery.

The last step—the use of the Common Mind of the Bishops to forge a canonically valid instrument to bring about the end of the present pontificate and, with it, the end of the papacy as it had heretofore been known—would itself be reduced to a matter of some additional bureaucratic engineering, once the process was in place. The operation Maestroianni had mapped out would be taxing. To achieve it in the relatively short span of time insisted upon by Dr. Channing would test even Cosimo Maestroianni's talents and experience. The Cardinal would have to keep a close personal rein on things. All must be done rapidly, but with method and great professional care.

That being so, His Eminence's calendar was already bristling with crucial meetings, planning sessions and private appointments. He would have to give the socially polished, politically naive Christian Gladstone his orders, of course. But Maestroianni anticipated no complications there. In the first instance, he would be sent off to canvass the needs of key European bishops, with American bishops to follow. And, with a little behind-the-scenes help from Cyrus Benthoek, he would entrain his brother's cooperation in satisfying those needs through the powerful EC contacts that came with the post of Secretary-General.

The revolutionary work to be done within the Bishops Conferences themselves, meanwhile—particularly the work of selecting and directing the first persuasive field commanders—would certainly require delicate judgments. The strategy must always be to build from strength. In this situation, that meant concentrating initially on Conferences headed by bishops whose names would carry weight well beyond their territory. Bishops like the remarkably powerful Cardinal of Centurycity in the United States, for example. Too bad there weren't more like him in the vineyards of the Church.

Adding to the complexity of Maestroianni's agenda was the fact that the nonclerical side of things had to be kept in mind and in balance. Cyrus Benthoek was as much a part of this brilliant scheme as Maestroianni himself, and there was the potentially powerful new alliance with Dr. Ralph Channing to nurture.

As important as all of that was, however, no one knew better than Cardinal Maestroianni how suicidal it would be to work in the worldwide vineyards of the Church without keeping the Cardinal Secretary of State reasonably well briefed. Not that there was any question of involving His Eminence Graziani in the intimate workings of the plan. That would be too much to expect of a man so politically coy as the new Secretary. Nevertheless, Graziani was now the second most powerful individual in the Vatican—nominally at least. Political reality therefore required that he be kept informed. Practical necessity required his cooperation in certain peripheral details. And expediency required a face-to-face meeting with the Secretary as a first priority.

"Most significant news, Your Eminence!" Early on that first Monday of October, Cardinal Maestroianni strode into his old office with proprietary confidence.

The new and unseasoned Secretary of State took such early-morning enthusiasm in stride. Even before his installation as Secretary, Giacomo Graziani had begun to behave with the gravity of the office. Now, with the Cardinal's red hat perched on his head and the Secretary's post secure as his own, he had become positively Buddha-like in his demeanor. Hands clasped on his ample middle, he responded to Maestroianni's elation with a pleasant smile, a slow but noncommittal blinking of the eyes and a welcoming nod toward the chair on the visitor's side of the desk that was now his.

His new manner notwithstanding, there were no questions about Giacomo Graziani in Cardinal Maestroianni's mind. To avoid a stalemate with the Slavic Pope, he had backed Graziani as Secretary, but did not regard him as one of his creatures. Graziani was nobody's creature, in fact. He was a calm and conservative man. A diplomat's diplomat. Not given to any excess in work or in thinking. Nobody's pushover, yet accessible and willing to learn. His greatest strength was that he had no ideology except to come up on the winning side.

"Most significant news," Maestroianni repeated, extracting his tabulations from the folder he carried. "I'm sure Your Eminence remembers my letter of last May to our diplomatic representatives around the world."

A single slow blink served as Graziani's acknowledgment. He remembered well Maestroianni's command of decorous language as a mask for brutal questions.

Maestroianni laid the typewritten sheets on the eighteenth-century Florentine desk with the touch of a poker player showing an ace-high straight.

Barely leaning forward, Graziani reached out with one hand to turn the pages as he scanned them. "The tabulations are most interesting, Eminence. Chaotic, but interesting, I'm sure. Significant was your word, I believe. To what significant use do you intend to put this data?"

"The purpose here, Eminence," the older Cardinal answered, "is to proceed toward an accurate sounding of what the bishops as a whole college actually think is necessary for the unity of the Church?"

Buddha blinked. That much had registered. "And the general lines along which that sounding will be conducted, Eminence?"

Maestroianni had thought it all through, and he wanted the Secretary to know that. "If Your Eminence is asking about the goal toward which we will be working, the answer is that we intend to facilitate the bishops. To ease their way. To aid them in overcoming any hesitations they may have, so that they can clarify their own thinking and beliefs in this all-important matter.

"But perhaps Your Eminence wishes to understand how we intend to conduct the sounding. Our principal instrument will be the vast global network of Regional and National Bishops Conferences that have grown to such maturity since Vatican II. I'm inclined to think of each Bishops Conference as a separate entity in itself. We will work at that level of compartmentation. Within each Conference, the matter will be managed as a normal internal-affairs issue. As always, we will construct ad hoc committees—Internal Affairs Committees. We aim for an IAC within each Conference."

Graziani glanced again through the data culled from eighty-two Vatican diplomats. "So." The Secretary raised an eyebrow. "We are looking at a series of Internal Affairs Committees? A worldwide network of IACs?"

Cardinal Graziani's appraisal of the immense complexities of such an operation was welcome, Maestroianni said. Most gratifying. In the same breath, and with the merest drop of acid in his tone, he assured Graziani that the dozen years and more he himself had put in as head of the State Department had proven his skills and had provided him with an intimate knowledge of personnel.

"Fortunately"—Maestroianni's smile softened the point—"we have a number of good men already in place who will surely want to aid their brother bishops in thinking through the matter of unity. Good men in key areas in Europe, of course. And in the United States I'm sure we can count on His Eminence of Centurycity. I only wish we had more like him."

"Ah, yes. His Eminence." A cloud of Buddha-like reflection passed over Graziani's brow. It seemed that the Cardinal Secretary now understood as much as he cared to concerning the machinery by which Maestroianni would dragoon the bishops into a single line of thought concerning the problem of episcopal unity with the Slavic Pope. There was another area of concern for him, however. An area that reached beyond the question of the tenure of the Slavic Pope, that touched on the office and jurisdiction of any Pope as the Vicar of Christ on earth. That touched on papal authority as a religious and social force.

"Several of Your Eminence's correspondents—not all of them in Anglo-Saxon countries—speak of the Pope as the Vicar of Peter." Graziani fingered the pages of Maestroianni's report. "Of course, I recall that at the Strasbourg meeting to which Your Eminence so generously invited me last May, Father-General Michael Coutinho of the Jesuits brushed that term lightly in his remarks. But to find it cropping up among so many of our bishops is disconcerting, is it not?"

Ah, Giacamo, Maestroianni thought, what a quick eye you have. "Disconcerting, Eminence? Not in the least. Probing and stimulating, yes. But not disconcerting. It is *the* issue."

There was no need to explain that if the Pope in Rome was merely the vicar of St. Peter the Apostle as the first Bishop of Rome, then logic dictated that every individual bishop was neither more nor less. Each bishop traced his roots back to the Apostles, after all; each was the vicar of an Apostolic predecessor. If such a view could be adopted as official teaching, it would be the bedrock foundation of a new governing structure of the Church. The centralizing role of the Pope—including his role as official, ultimate and infallible arbiter in questions of faith and morals—would give way. Power would shift from Rome to the whole body of bishops.

The look that passed between the two Cardinals now was a calculating one. Both realized what was at stake. As usual, Graziani was figuring the odds. And, as usual, Maestroianni was confident.

"Your Eminence." Cardinal Graziani was every inch the Vatican diplomat now. "The Church—the voice of the Church—must eventually speak clearly on this point."

Maestroianni was calm but watchful. For the moment, he did not require the Secretary to occupy anything more than a neutral position on this central issue. "That, Your Eminence, is precisely what this entire new operation is intended to achieve. The Church will decide! By the way," Cardinal Maestroianni added as if by way of coda, "the new Altar Missal now being put into use throughout the Church does speak of the Bishop of Rome as the Vicar of Peter."

"So I have noticed. But we all know that the new Missal has not yet received official Roman approval. As I recall, it was chosen by the International Commission on English in the Liturgy. Or at least by its extension, the English-Language Liturgy Consultants. But the status of the ICEL itself as a papal agency has still to be assessed."

"There's the crux," Maestroianni agreed readily. "The data I have put before Your Eminence this morning indicates that many bishops believe that the Bishop of Rome is not the sole Vicar of Christ on earth, but merely the Vicar of Peter. The new Altar Missal also reflects this belief. Now, if the Bishop of Rome claims to decide the question because he believes he alone is the Vicar of Christ, are we not facing the old logical fallacy of begging the question? Is this not the *petitio principii* of Aquinas and Aristotle?"

"Perhaps." Graziani had to hand it to the Cardinal. He barely blushed to invoke St. Thomas Aquinas in his argument. "Nevertheless, Eminence, to decide it all, we must still find the voice of the Church."

"Of course we must, Eminence!" Maestroianni decided it was time to bring the discussion full circle. "And where else can we hear that voice if not from the bishops of the Church? From the successors of the Apostles?"

The hint of a smile touched Graziani's eyes. "And that is the purpose of Your Eminence's present operation?"

"That, Eminence, and only that! Along the way, of course, we will be in a position to assess and improve the presently tattered condition of Church unity."

Once more Graziani took shelter behind a moment's silence. "Tell me, Eminence. What is the clearance on this document you have shared with me this morning?"

"Let us say, momentarily, 'celestial.' Compartmentation is an absolute priority."

Items classified as "celestial" were accessible only at the Cardinalitial level, only on a need-to-know basis, and at the ultimate discretion of Pope and Secretary of State. Compartmentation, meanwhile, though not peculiar to the Vatican, had certainly been developed to its highest form by this, the oldest political chancery in the world.

"So, follow-up action will be strictly 'celestial,' and strictly along compartmentation lines?" Graziani wanted unequivocal verbal assurance.

"Yes. Strictly." As if to underscore his confirmation, Maestroianni retrieved the report that had been the basis of discussion. "And for obvious reasons. We're talking here about the papacy, and ultimately about papal candidacy. According to Canon Law, this is the business solely and specifically of the College of Cardinals."

"At what stage does Your Eminence reckon things will encroach on the papal level?" That, as Maestroianni understood full well, was the language of *romanità* for "When will you fling this whole seditious mess in the face of the Pontiff?"

"When we have an accurate sounding of what the bishops as a whole college do think is necessary for the unity of the Church." That, as Graziani understood, was Maestroianni's *romanità* for "When we have the old man boxed in and there is no escape for him but total capitulation in his policies or resignation from the papal office."

Cardinal Secretary Graziani kept cool. "I suppose," he said almost as if musing to himself, "that Your Eminence will be working with Cardinal Aureatini as usual?"

Maestroianni filled his lungs with a deep breath. Graziani had left no doubt that he understood what was happening. His abrupt questions about personnel was as good as a tacit agreement to stand aside at least until the odds were clearer. "Aureatini is available, and he knows how I work. But I will also be relying very much on Cardinal Pensabene. In fact, I expect to meet with them both in my office within the hour."

Oddsmaker that he was by nature and experience, Maestroianni's use of Pensabene's name was deliberate. For, like everyone else, Graziani knew that the cadaverous-faced, bony-fingered Cardinal Pensabene had truly climbed to the top of the heap. By this time in his life, not much could budge in the Vatican Chancery without his blessing. More than that, his voice would be dominant in any discussion and choice of a future Pontiff.

With his point nicely made, and with everything accomplished that he considered needful, Maestroianni was impatient to be about his business.

It seemed, however, that the fledgling Secretary of State was not quite satisfied. "One last point, Eminence. I received a passport application yesterday from Your Eminence's office on behalf of a young American. Father Christian Thomas Gladstone."

"Sì, sì. Infatti." That expression on Maestroianni's tongue meant he was coating a pill. And it meant he expected no trouble on this question. No man knew better than he that the privilege of carrying a Vatican passport was granted to very few individuals who were not State Department professionals. But he felt detailed discussion to be unnecessary.

"I was just curious," Graziani probed cautiously, "as to why this young man should need a Vatican passport straightaway. . . ."

"Father will be our liaison with many bishops in the European Community and with certain governmental sectors. He will need the status of an official passport. And there may be good reason for him to take out a European Community passport. We must envisage the possible course of things. With a Vatican passport in his pocket, an EC passport will be easy to obtain."

"Bene! Bene!" For now, Graziani would have to be satisfied with the Cardinal's matter-of-fact explanation. Perhaps it was better not to know too many details in this dark affair. Still, the fact that this Gladstone was important enough to receive Maestroianni's patronage made him interesting.

The Secretary of State rose from his chair at last. "Let Father Gladstone drop in to pick up his papers. I would like to meet this new addition to

Your Eminence's staff. As to the rest, Your Eminence will keep me au courant, of course."

"Of course." Barely able to restrain his impatience to be gone, Cardinal Maestroianni all but sprang to his feet. "Your Eminence has been too generous with your time."

Graziani rewound the tape of his conversation with Maestroianni. As he played it back pensively, he ran his eye again over the archival dossier on the Gladstone family and the curriculum vitae of Father Christian Gladstone.

Was it merely coincidence, he wondered, that the Slavic Pope had sent the Gladstone material to him that very morning? There was no hint of an answer in the papal note attached to the material; it said merely, "For your information."

That was always the puzzle in working with this Pope. There could be no doubt that the Holy Father was au courant with world and Vatican affairs. And when he had his eyes on a new man, he was aboveboard about it. Yet he spent no effort in explanations.

That had been exactly the situation when Graziani had shown the Pontiff a copy of Maestroianni's letter to Vatican diplomats scattered over some fourscore countries of the world. Of course, there was no need for Cardinal Maestroianni to know the Pope had seen that letter; not soon anyway. But in the Vatican—in this world where finally there were no secrets—the Secretary did have to cover his own back.

At any rate, when the Pontiff had read that letter, he had given a short little laugh, as if to himself. But, as in so many situations, he had said nothing. Truth to tell, Graziani had not been altogether surprised by His Holiness' wordless reaction. New though he was to the job, there seemed already to be tacit agreement between himself and the Pontiff that the Secretary of State was the Pope's man for as long as the Pope remained at the top of the heap.

Still, while he was not privy to the deeper intentions of the Slavic Pope, Graziani had his own theories. As nearly as he could tell, the Pontiff's order of the day for the governance of his Church remained what it had been from the beginning. Undeclared though it was, to Graziani that policy seemed simple, clear and frank. By his actions—or more by his inaction on so many vital fronts—the Holy Father was saying: Let the bureaucratic machine rip ahead as it will, for nobody can stop it now. It appeared to Graziani, then, that the Pope was a gambling man. And the papal gamble appeared to be that he could outplay his adversaries by outwaiting them.

Listening to Maestroianni's voice on the tape, it was almost mechanical for Graziani to factor the odds. As far as he could see, bringing an obscure young professor like Father Christian Gladstone into the equation would make no appreciable difference. On the other hand, a man of such power as Cardinal Leo Pensabene could be decisive.

As he considered his own position in the explosive situation that was developing, Graziani remained unequivocally on the fence. It had been one thing—a judicious thing, in those circumstances—to raise a hand of agreement at that meeting of Roman and non-Roman huskies at Strasbourg. But any fool could see that it was still too soon to jump definitively into anyone's camp.

It was not too soon to wonder, though, just how close to the brink His Holiness would be willing to shave.

Maestroianni blessed his good fortune in having at his disposal Cardinal Silvio Aureatini's capacity for long hours of work and Cardinal Leo Pensabene's knowledge of ecclesiastical machinery and personages. Both of these colleagues shared Maestroianni's enthusiasm and interests. But it was Pensabene who had the most resources. And in the intricate scheme to establish special ad hoc Internal Affairs Agencies within the various National and Regional Bishops Conferences, it was Pensabene who came up with the key factor.

" 'Change agents!' " Cardinal Pensabene cocked a bony forefinger at Maestroianni and Aureatini at the outset of their very first working session. "If we can install 'change agents' and 'upper-level facilitators' within every ad hoc IAC in every Bishops Conference, we can meet our early timetable. Without them, we haven't a prayer—if you'll pardon the expression."

Pensabene realized that he had a lot of explaining to do to bring his two colleagues up to his level of understanding. On the historical side of the ledger, he told how the concept and implementation of "change agents" and "upper-level facilitators" had appeared first as prime factors in the rise of European dictatorships in the 1920s and 1930s. "Notably," he observed without apology, "in Joseph Stalin's Soviet empire, in Adolf Hitler's National Socialism regime and in Benito Mussolini's Fascist regime.

"To be accurate, the first page of this methodology was written by the Soviets. Hitler copied them. And, as Hitler's lackey, Mussolini tried to reproduce the Führer's version. The premier educational philosopher of the United States, John Dewey, studied the same methods and came up with his own version. A version tailored for use within two areas that concern us now.

"First." As he had at the Strasbourg meeting—as he was always doing, much to the annoyance of Silvio Aureatini—Pensabene raised his bony fingers as if to keep score. "First, Dewey tailored his methods for use within the educational realm. And second, he tailored them for use within the framework of Western democratic society. What is now called 'social engineering' took on a respectable air."

His nerves already grating at the sight of those fingers popping into the air like skeletal exclamation points, Cardinal Aureatini gritted his teeth and settled into silent attention.

"Now, as I see it," Pensabene continued, "the problem we face—the task of bringing the thinking of our bishops into alignment with our own views on the question of unity with the Pope—is exactly the problem faced by all those earlier theoreticians and practitioners of social engineering. And that problem is simple: How to persuade millions of people to change their outlook so as to fit ideologically into the mold the social engineers have in mind. For ultimately, it is not our four thousand bishops alone who must be persuaded."

Pensabene observed that the roots of the solution had been sought in the various forms of the abstract philosophy called phenomenology. "As a devoted student of history, Your Eminence will recall that phenomenology entered its great vogue among the intellectuals of Central and Eastern Europe during the twenties and thirties."

"Indeed, Eminence." Maestroianni was truly pleased to think that the solution to his bureaucratic problem might emerge from the very process of history. "Do go on."

Pensabene obliged. "It's quite simple really. Their solution was to create those 'agents of change' and 'facilitators' I spoke of earlier. An 'agent of change' might be any number of things. An institution. An organization. A lone individual. It might originate from either the public or the private sector—or sometimes from both. Indeed"—Pensabene could not resist a rare smile—"it might even be our own network of ad hoc Internal Affairs Committees set up within the Bishops Conferences. The purpose of an 'agent of change' is to replace 'old' values and behaviors with 'new' ones. And to do so by using psychologically based techniques developed specifically for the wearing away of attitudinal resistance.

"At some point, the practice of these techniques became known as 'facilitating,' or as 'facilitation.' But the object is always to change a previously held mind-set into a totally new and different mind-set. Even to a mind-set that previously would have been unacceptable and abhorrent." Another pointed look at Cardinal Maestroianni. "The process is fascinating. In this case, the process is a pyramidal affair. And the 'agent of change' is the capstone of the pyramid.

"The 'change agent' sets out to recruit a group of individuals or organizations who appear most susceptible to the desired and always attractively packaged new mind-set. Assuming the 'change agent' is capable, those who regard the new mind-set as a perversion of thought will be few in number. Any such dissenters are left by the wayside. The successful graduates, meanwhile, having emerged from the tutelage of the 'change agent' armed with a total acceptance of the new thinking—having been 'facilitated,' in other words—are themselves now rightly regarded as 'facilitators.' In his role as 'upper-level facilitator,' the 'agent of change' charges the newly converted to repeat the process. To go out into the world and spread their newfound beliefs. To coerce as many others as possible into accepting the 'new' and jettisoning the 'old.' As ever widening layers are formed in the pyramid of change, so too is the desired 'new' thinking formed about values, beliefs, attitudes and behavior."

At this point, Maestroianni felt it imperative to raise a practical concern. "Our present enterprise is delicate and dangerous. And we haven't the luxury of time. We cannot afford merely to assume such simple success as your 'facilitation' theory implies."

Pensabene's answer was as practical as the question. In the first place, he pointed out, there was no other model to follow. "And in the second place, Eminence, the process I have outlined is accomplished with relative ease. The basic thing to understand is John Dewey's own explanation of the techniques involved as—and I believe my quote is exact—'a control of the mind and emotions by experimental, not rational means.' The aim is to arouse emotions rather than to stimulate thought or intellectual perception. Assuming that the 'change agent' has chosen his initiates with cunning, he institutes a process in which his target audience participates actively. It is sometimes called a 'freezing and unfreezing' process—a relatively straightforward program of four steps."

Aureatini almost groaned audibly as Cardinal Pensabene held up the first of four bony fingers. "Having gathered a captive and complaisant audience, the 'change agent' begins by 'freezing' the attention and the experience of the group on its own isolation and vulnerability. The second step is to disaggregate, or 'unfreeze.' In this context, that means a distancing from the 'old' values on which the members of the audience once relied. It means, in sum, that those former values are made to seem no longer desirable or suitable. Stage three—reaggregation—follows with acceptance of the new structure of thought proposed by the 'facilitator.' The final step is routinization. The new structures of thinking are incorporated into the flow of normal, everyday life.

"That basic procedure can be repeated as often as necessary—and through as many converted 'facilitators' as possible—to perpetuate and spread the 'new' thinking. Equally important for our own present endeavor with the bishops, it can also be used to bring the participants in the ever growing pyramid to a still higher level of ideological persuasion intended by the 'upper-level facilitators.' "

Having suffered with remarkable patience through a rash of upraised fingers, perhaps Silvio Aureatini was merely on edge. Whatever the reason, he remained a holdout. Citing the importance of what was at stake, the junior Cardinal observed that this was not 1920. Nor would they be dealing with populations beaten down by a recent world war and a deep worldwide economic depression. On the contrary. In bringing the bishops into line on the unity question—or even in dealing with the clergy and layfolk who would have to be brought along at some level—they were dealing with people who felt themselves to be in the mainstream of life. It did not seem feasible that they could be made to feel "isolated and vulnerable," as Cardinal Pensabene's plan required.

Had Pensabene not known better, he would have thought the sharp-featured Cardinal to be one of the dullest colleagues with whom he had ever been obliged to work.

"My dear young friend." He cocked his sunken eyes toward Aureatini. "In my happy experience, it is one of the wonders of the human condition that, with a little care and attention, almost anyone can be made to feel isolated and vulnerable. When we planned the huge changeover in the daily Mass-going habits of fifty-five million Catholics in the United States, for example, we were not working in the 1920s, but in the 1970s. And when we undertook to transform parish life and the importance of piety, we were not working in the 1930s, but in the 1980s. And in both cases, we would have got nowhere without 'change agents' and 'facilitators.' Just think, Eminence. Think!" Pensabene tapped his bony temple with a bony finger. "Ask yourself, how did it happen in the United States that in the short space of two decades we practically obliterated any effective traces of a liturgy and parish life that had been ingrained—institutionally ingrained!—for nearly two centuries?"

"Well, I suppose if Your Eminence puts it in those terms . . ."

"And have we not all admired the work of our venerable brother Cardinal Noah Palombo? We have!" Pensabene answered his own question with unaccustomed vigor. "And rightly so! For under his leadership as a 'change agent' par excellence—as an 'upper-level facilitator' without peer—the Vatican's International Council for Christian Liturgy has restructured the very nature of priestly thinking in matters of approved prayer and devotion. I could cite other examples. . . ."

Such was Cardinal Maestroianni's command over even so powerful a figure as Leo Pensabene that a mere raising of his hand was enough to end the discussion. He had emphasized that time was a factor; and it was true that there was no working model to follow other than Pensabene's. But what really made him itchy to stop the debate and get on with practical planning and implementation was that he could see how neatly his recent data on the bishops dovetailed with the whole structure and process of "facilitation."

"You have both studied the informal poll taken by the Holy See representatives." Maestroianni spread the typewritten pages in front of him. "Correct me if I'm wrong, Eminence. But it would appear that our first task in this 'facilitation' process—the task of defining our ideological goals—is already accomplished."

A satisfied Pensabene agreed. "The goal is that the Slavic Pope resign voluntarily, in order to allow the Church to have a Pope who will enhance—not endanger—the precious unity of the bishops with the papacy."

"Precisely." Fired with energy, Maestroianni led the way quickly forward now. "We have a slight difference in terminology. For what Your Eminence refers to as 'the new mind-set' is what I've referred to in the past as 'the desirable conformity' among our bishops. Thanks to the data of this informal poll, we can already classify the various levels of conviction at which our bishops stand on the unity question. Without exception, all maintain that unity between themselves as bishops and the papacy is vitally important. That is the lowest level of conviction; the lowest level of conformity. But the data show that we can already capitalize on four higher levels of conviction in some quarters.

"At the second level of conviction there is a perception among many bishops that the desired unity does not presently exist and that something has to be done to reinstate such unity.

"At the next level, a smaller but still appreciable number of bishops feel that the desired unity should not be seen as the relationship between the Pope and individual bishops, but between the Pope and the Regional and National Bishops Conferences. This is capital for us; for among this group, any failure in the relationship can be reduced to a question of bureaucratic gridlock.

"Equally promising is a smaller group of bishops who see the failure of unity as due to a personality clash. Simply put, these bishops consider that the Slavic Pope's personality impedes the desired unity from flourishing.

"And that brings us to the highest level of perception, shared for the moment by the fewest number of bishops. A rarefied level of conviction that, for the sake of unity and in good papal conscience, the Slavic Pope should resign and allow the Holy Spirit to choose a Pope who can promote and enhance that unity."

Cardinal Pensabene raised his eyes from the tabulated data. "Neatly done, Eminence! You brought order into what seems on the surface to be a chaotic situation among the bishops. And you have rightly pointed to that fairly large number among the bishops who see the failure of episcopal unity with the papacy as a matter of bureaucratic gridlock. Clearly, your original IAC plan is doable. We know where to start in establishing our ad hoc Internal Affairs Committees within the bureaucratic machinery of the Conferences of Bishops."

"My thinking exactly, Eminence." Maestroianni smiled. "Nor need we be limited for long to those bishops who already see the unity problem in bureaucratic terms. For nowadays, the Governing Committees in each of these Regional and National Conferences, together with the Central Committees, can make life miserable for any bishop who steps out of line. Nowadays, in other words, individual bishops are far less free than they used to be to act autonomously."

Maestroianni was obviously pleased with himself. He placed the setting up of the first and most influential IACs as his team's priority work. But so, too, did he congratulate himself aloud on his forethought in having

Paul and Christian Gladstone—"the twin American arrows," as he described them—fitted into the bow of episcopal persuasion. With Father Gladstone canvassing the needs and the weaknesses of the bishops, and with his brother Paul in a position to help capitalize on that information in a concrete manner through EC patronage, any number of otherwise reluctant bishops would be moved to cooperate.

For the next couple of weeks, Cardinal Maestroianni inspired his little team of central collaborators to work without letup.

With "compartmentation" as the rule, with Pensabene's intimate knowledge of the various Bishops Conferences and with his own long experience as Secretary of State, Maestroianni's first task was to compile a list of potential "change agents." The need was for prelates—clergymen with the rank of bishop and upward—who could be easily "facilitated" and then relied upon as "facilitators" themselves and as the secretaries of the initial ad hoc Internal Affairs Committees in key areas.

Even as that list was being formed, a schedule was established according to which each of those chosen—some fifteen bishops, archbishops and Cardinals to begin with—would be contacted and invited to Rome for what would be billed as "a theological consultation." Late October or early November was agreed on as the target date for that meeting. After a week of intensive "facilitation," it was safe to assume that this core cadre would depart for their respective dioceses ready to form the first grid of IACs and to use them to broaden the pyramid of new thinking.

Inevitably, heated discussions arose concerning several names suggested for this premier roster. About one name, however, there was immediate and enthusiastic agreement. Cardinals Maestroianni, Pensabene and Aureatini knew beyond question that the most excellent "change agent" would be His Eminence the Cardinal of Centurycity.

Few American ecclesiastical personages had ever matched the position of power into which the Cardinal of Centurycity had "facilitated" himself over a period of less than thirty years. Indeed, many of his contemporaries remarked on how effortless His Eminence's rise had been. That was especially noteworthy considering that he had no silver spoon in his mouth, and certainly no sacred stole around his shoulders. There was no special backing from his family or any antecedent financial sinews. There had been nothing astounding in his intellectual performance as a theologian; no recognized orthodoxy as a Catholic. Nor had he enjoyed a special Roman connection in his early days. In the words of one of his colleagues in the American hierarchy, His Eminence of Centurycity was an "ecclesiastical phenomenon on the order of a flamingo born from ordinary, run-of-the-coop barnyard fowl."

Maestroianni, Pensabene and Aureatini knew their star American candidate. He had started his meteoric career in earnest as chancellor of a minor southern diocese. After a transfer to an upper East Coast see, His

Eminence had landed on his feet as Cardinal Archbishop of Centurycity—an archdiocese once famed for its financial solidity, its papist fidelity and its overwhelming if sometimes rambunctious Roman Catholicism. Within a short time, he had eclipsed his American fellow Cardinals, and at this critical moment occupied the catbird seat in the strangest of all ecclesiastical creations: the National Conference of Catholic Bishops—the NCCB; and in its no-bones-about-it left-wing political arm, the United States Catholic Conference—the USCC. Never mind the quip of one commentator that between those two arms of the American episcopate, the right hand did not always know what the left was doing. The Cardinal knew what both hands were doing at all times. His Eminence of Centurycity had the entire Machine at his disposal. His Eminence was the Machine.

While the personality of this man seemed ordinary and even banal to many who didn't know him well, three traits stood out as exceptional. His Eminence had always seemed to be acceptable to ecclesiastical leaders one rung above his own place on the ladder of preferment. Surely, he must have friends who had friends. Nevertheless, the basis of his singular acceptability was severely unclear to the naked eye. Second was his authority within the American episcopal Establishment. An authority that was unchallenged and that seemed unchallengeable. Cardinal O'Cleary of New Orleans was known to admire his tactics, but could not match them. The East Coast Cardinals feared his connections in Church and State. The West Coast Cardinals found it convenient to ride his coattails. Whether inside or outside Centurycity, with all the sanctions and inner discipline of the Machine at his velvet fingertips, His Eminence could isolate a recalcitrant cleric and strip him of all real power in the Establishment.

The American Cardinal's third trait was a turnabout of the second. For, as lethal as he could be to the careers of other clerics, he himself enjoyed an ironclad immunity from any attempt to short-circuit his own standing with Vatican authorities and with his American ecclesiastical colleagues. No matter how many complaints went to Rome from the Catholic Church in the United States—and no matter whether those complaints came from a fellow Cardinal or from parish priests or from layfolk—somehow they all ended up at the bottom of an unattended pile of correspondence or in one of a thousand "inactive" Vatican files. Apparently the Cardinal's chain of friends of friends extended up through all levels right to the papal throne.

Understandably, then, the American Cardinal became the standard by which Maestroianni measured everyone on his crucial list.

It was eight o'clock on a cold morning in early October when Father Sebastian Scalabrini's housekeeper, Kitty Monaghan, let herself into the apartment in the Royal Munroe Building in the Hillsvale suburb of Centurycity and found Father's body lying full-length on the living-room carpet in front of the television. The priest was mother naked, and there was blood all over his neck, upper torso, belly and groin.

As a former policewoman herself and the widow of a police sergeant, Kitty had seen her share of messed-up dead bodies. But as a Catholic and a grandmother, she was shaking with sobs as she dialed the police. Within minutes of her telephone call, Police Inspector Sylvester Wodgila arrived with three detectives, a battery of crime-lab technicians and a half dozen uniformed officers. The city medical examiner arrived soon after.

Immediately, Wodgila cordoned the building off. No one left or entered before being questioned by him or one of his men. The distraught Kitty Monaghan was asked to wait in the kitchen; she wasn't to leave until the initial stages of the investigation were completed. In any criminal case involving the clergy, the cast-iron rule laid down by the Mayor of Centurycity and the state Governor was clear: The Commissioner of Police was automatically in charge. No information about the case was to be given out. Especially not to the media. By noon, with all his data assembled, Wodgila lit his pipe, sat down at the phone and dialed. As usual, Wodgila's report was clear and orderly. The Commissioner listened to it without interrupting.

"We have a male Caucasian, sir. A priest of the archdiocese by the name of Sebastian Scalabrini. Assistant pastor at nearby Holy Angels parish. Forty-seven years of age. Death occurred about midnight. Found by his housekeeper at about eight this morning. Multiple stab wounds inflicted with a very sharp instrument. Forefinger and thumb severed from each hand, but so far not found on the premises. Castration. Genitals stuffed in the mouth. No signs of a struggle. Personal papers seem to be as Father left them. Nothing of note in them. Reputation as a quiet man. Little contact with his neighbors. Visited frequently by fellow clergymen. No one saw or heard anything unusual yesterday—evening or night. The doorman who was on duty says Father had a guest who left shortly after midnight. Didn't get a name. A priest by the look of him, he says. Youngish. The precinct has a file on Scalabrini. I have it here now."

The Commissioner had only a few questions. "How old did you say Scalabrini was?"

"Forty-seven, sir."

"And how many stab wounds in all?"

"Forty-seven, sir."

"Are the housekeeper and the doorman under wraps?"

"Yessir."

"Okay. The usual drill. I'll make the phone calls to BOSI and the Chancery. You wait for them, and then tidy up the details."

"Yessir." When Inspector Wodgila hung up, he knew his own part in the Scalabrini case was almost done. The usual drill meant that the Bureau of Special Investigations would take over. The usual drill meant that the city coroner would classify Father Scalabrini's murder as "death by misadventure." The usual drill meant that the body would be cremated; and it meant that Wodgila's own report and the autopsy findings would be sealed in BOSI's files along with those of similar cases over the past eleven years.

While he waited for the BOSI boys to arrive, Wodgila made one last check of the apartment—he wouldn't have another chance. And he leafed again through the precinct file on Father: Member of the Saturn Group 7 for twenty years. Pedophiliac activities confined to group rituals. Two and a half years as a police informant. Advised one week ago by his BOSI contact that his cover might have been blown.

"Someone's damn screwup!" Wodgila snapped the file closed and watched angrily as Father Scalabrini's mangled remains were zipped into the black body bag. It was always the same in these cases. The number of stab wounds always corresponded to the victim's age. Always the same mutilations, down to the last gruesome detail.

Inspector Wodgila was not fooled by the simple clerical clothes of the cleric who accompanied the BOSI boys. Like any of his professional colleagues, Wodgila was paid to recognize celebrities on sight. In this case, though, it was easy. This was also part of the usual drill. The cleric didn't act as if he was in charge, of course. But there was no mistaking the narrow, balding head, the round cheekbones in an otherwise gaunt face, the awkward gait, the imperious gestures of the black-gloved hands. All of that belonged to His Eminence the Cardinal of Centurycity.

The priestly blessing was a grim affair quickly done. His Eminence didn't ask for the body bag to be opened, and there was no anointing with holy oils and water. Within five minutes of his arrival, and without a word to anyone, including Wodgila, the cleric was gone. Scalabrini's body was removed. With her official statement taken and sealed, Kitty Monaghan would be released with a warning that she could endanger her own life and jeopardize the investigation if she were even to whisper anything of what she had seen. Wodgila would assemble his own men, remind them of the dangers attendant on the investigation of this particular crime, and order them to keep hands off. It was BOSI's case to handle.

Before he followed all the others out the door of this sad place, Wodgila took a last, long look at the carpet where the priest had been found. Once the blood that had been spilled there was gone, his own long memory would be the only accessible testimony to those mutilated hands, to that ugly black-and-crimson stain of castration, to the disgust and supreme agony etched around the victim's stuffed mouth.

Wodgila knew from experience it would be a long time before the images of ritual death ceased to haunt his dreams. For weeks, when his own parish priest held the Sacred Host aloft at daily Mass, the Inspector knew he would see Father Scalabrini's pathetic stumps. Wodgila looked for a long time at Scalabrini's blood, and offered what was in all likelihood the only heartfelt prayer for the immortal soul of that unhappy priest. "You poor bastard, Father. May God take your final pain and terror into account when He judges you. . . ."

Inspector Wodgila sent a copy of his preliminary report and all the documentation in the Scalabrini case to the Commissioner, the Mayor of Centurycity and the Governor. Because nothing could be done without an explicit go-ahead, he indicated the lines of investigation he wished to pursue. Within days, Wodgila received official notification that the Attorney General's office had decided to leave the matter alone and that the Inspector was not to pursue the investigation he had outlined. On professional grounds, Wodgila felt he had to protest. The case was still wide open, he insisted in a responding document; and if the past was any indication, they could expect still more cases of a similar nature unless strong measures were taken.

The final chapter of Inspector Wodgila's official involvement with the Scalabrini ritual murder was written within the month. The Mayor himself called to express his profound regret that the Inspector's name was on the current roster of men who would be given early retirement. Wodgila would receive his full pension, of course; and, in recognition of his years of superior service, he would be rewarded with subsequent civil appointments as well. At the same time, His Honor made it clear that there was no redress from the decision; and that silence—Wodgila's included—would remain the order of the day in all such cases as that of "poor Father Scalabrini."

The crowning touch to Inspector Wodgila's abrupt retirement came in the form of a letter awarding him the Catholic Hero Medal for that year. The letter, which cited "Inspector Sylvester Wodgila's unstinting loyalty to Holy Mother Church in the performance of his civic duties," was signed by His Eminence the Cardinal of Centurycity.

XXVI

CHRISTIAN GLADSTONE felt like a parvenu in Rome. Like a football suddenly tossed into a turbulent river, bobbing helplessly along with no sure way to keep his head above water. He had hoped to get some early advice from Father Damien Slattery. But the *portiere* at the Angelicum switchboard scotched that hope. "Father-General won't be back until this evening, *Reverendo.*" There was no getting around it, then. The imperious summons at the top of the small pile of messages and mail awaiting him on his arrival meant that his first meeting would be with His Eminence Cardinal Maestroianni.

If such an early encounter with Maestroianni wasn't a pleasurable prospect for Christian, neither was it a surprise. "You have come to the attention of no less a figure than His Eminence Cosimo Maestroianni himself," O'Cleary had said. Nevertheless, his early-afternoon meeting with Cardinal Maestroianni didn't help him to find his bearings.

Rather, from the moment he stepped from the elevator onto the third floor of the Apostolic Palace and was directed to His Eminence's new suite of offices, the whole mood of the place seemed oddly changed. Even the little Cardinal himself seemed different. As he had at their first meeting in May, His Eminence showed himself to be a master of condescending sociability and arrogant assumption. But there was something new. Chris would have expected that, removed now from the office of Secretary of State, Maestroianni would have less an aura of power about him. What he found, however, was just the opposite. Not exactly the sense of greater power, but the sense of power without the fetters of office to impede it.

After suffering his ring to be kissed by the American, Maestroianni's greeting was surely intended to be warm; but it cut Gladstone like a barb. "How pleasant it is to see you back in Rome so soon, Father."

Then, as he sat down behind his desk and waved his new protégé into the nearest chair, the Cardinal complimented Gladstone on his mother's strong sense of the Church. "We are all extremely gratified for that worthy lady's recent cooperation in the rather sad affair of the BNL." Completely at a loss, Chris could only return the Cardinal's smile and thank him for the intended compliment. He knew nothing more than he had read in the papers about the breaking scandal surrounding Italy's Banca Nazionale di Lavoro. But it was unthinkable that his mother could be involved in such dealings.

"Now, *caro Reverendo*"—Maestroianni was clearly done with pleasantries—"you too are being asked to do a man's job for the good of the Church." Briefly, but with a patience he would not have shown in other circumstances, His Eminence gave Gladstone a general outline of the job he had in mind. Christian would begin his full-time Roman service as a sort of roving Vatican emissary to a selected list of bishops. Maestroianni shoved a briefcase across his desk, but kept a hand on it. "Here you will find your first roster of bishops. You needn't take time to look through the material now, of course. There will be plenty of time for that, I'm sure. Let me simply say that you will begin your work for us in France, Belgium, the Netherlands and Germany. We have provided a dossier on each bishop—personal and professional. And there is also an analysis of each bishop's diocese. All the usual things are detailed—finances; demographics; media; educational establishments from kindergarten through universities and seminaries. As I say, all the usual things.

"Before you leave Rome"—Maestroianni raised his hand from the briefcase now—"you will study this material and make it your own. You are to know each diocese assigned to you, and each bishop you will meet, as well as you know your own name. During each visit, you will update our basic demographic data. We are always interested in such questions as the number of Catholic families still residing in an area. The number of conversions and baptisms. The use and frequency of confessions, communions, marriage annulments. The number of births and the number of children attending diocesan schools. Vocations to the priesthood. Books used in religious instruction. It's all set out for you. And without doubt, all such data as this will be made readily available to you en bloc from the officials in each diocesan chancery.

"There are other data, however, that can only be obtained by a trusted Vatican emissary in confidential, face-to-face conversation with each bishop. Data that will help us to overcome problems some of our bishops appear to be encountering. Do I make myself clear, *Reverendo?*"

Not by half, Chris thought to himself. "Up to a point, Your Eminence. I don't yet know what sort of confidential data is involved, of course. But it is unclear to me why any bishop would reveal anything of confidence to an outsider."

"My dear Father!" His Eminence appeared shocked at such a basic misapprehension. "You are not an outsider. Not any longer. You are one of us now. Your visit to each bishop will be announced in advance by this Chancery. By my own staff, in fact. And I assure you, the fact that you will carry the mantle of a Vatican emissary will do wonders to smooth your way. That mantle will assure your right of entry even into areas of information that are guarded from others."

The more he listened to Maestroianni, the more at sea did Gladstone find himself. So foreign was that idea to every sense he had of himself that Christian let his guard down. He asked a direct question. It was his only mistake. "If you will permit, Eminence, what is the main purpose of my full-time assignment to Rome? The work Your Eminence has outlined seems such a temporary thing—there are only so many bishops, after all. And Cardinal O'Cleary did speak of full-time teaching duties at the Angelicum."

Under the fire of a straight-out question, Maestroianni returned fire in the form of a withering look, a disapproving click of his tongue and a velvet rebuke delivered in a harsh tone. "Father dear! Of course we value your scholarly achievements. In that area, you have already garnered the highest approval of Roman authorities. Now, however, new undertakings will carry you into fields where *your* approval will be valued. As to the future . . ." His Eminence gave Gladstone a full-eyed stare for an instant, and then softened his expression. "As to the future, who knows? We must find God's will daily anew. Isn't that right?"

Christian found the Cardinal's appeal to God's will to be vaguely repulsive. The rest of his message, however, was straightforward and clear. Obviously the Cardinal had assessed him as a simple, scholarly priest given to fideistic attitudes and a childlike trust in the authority of superiors. The only thing that kept Gladstone from chucking the whole idea of a "Roman career" then and there was a sudden recollection of Father Aldo Carnesecca. Specifically, he recalled Father Aldo's passive, nonreactionary conduct and his unprotesting obedience in dealing with men like Maestroianni. Yet Christian knew Carnesecca to be as independent-minded as any man alive; and he had probably done more good in his long service to the Church than an army of firebrands.

"Now, Father Gladstone." Maestroianni took the young priest's silence for obedient assent. "You will obviously be traveling a great deal of the time in the near future. Your way across—er—many borders will be eased if you carry a Vatican passport. Yes!" Maestroianni responded to the utter surprise in Gladstone's eyes. "A rare privilege! But I myself have had a word with our new Secretary of State. Cardinal Graziani has been alerted of your visit here, and would deem it a pleasure to put that valued document personally into your hands this very afternoon."

There it was again, Chris thought. That sense of superiority, even over the Secretary of State. There was no time for further reflection on the point, for the meeting was all but over. Gladstone would be called for a final briefing within the week, Maestroianni told him. Meanwhile, he would master the information that had been prepared for him. Briefcase in hand, then, His Eminence's obedient new creature was packed off with a run-along-now touch to his second high-level meeting of the day. To another take-it-or-leave-it interview, this time with the new Secretary of State.

Christian had to admit that Cardinal Graziani seemed a pretty decent fellow, even personable. The Secretary did have a funny way of blinking his eyes. But his handshake was firm and sincere.

As though he, too, was aware of the power Maestroianni had taken with him when he had left this office, the Cardinal Secretary seemed more interested in establishing a bond of his own with the newcomer. "We share a milestone, Father." The Secretary passed the newly cut Vatican passport across his desk to Gladstone. "This is one of the first I have issued." Then, with a smile: "I've had occasion to read the Gladstone family file. Very impressive. Given such close ties to the Holy See, it is not to be wondered that your esteemed mother has once again come to the aid of the Church in the sorry matter of the BNL."

It was Gladstone's turn to blink now, and not with the wisdom of Buddha. This was the second time in less than an hour that Cessi's name had come up in connection with the international scandal swirling around the Banca Nazionale di Lavoro. Equally unsettling for Christian was the realization that his family's dossier was floating about in the upper reaches of the Holy See. Perhaps that was just part and parcel of being associated even in a minor way with the powerful Cardinal Maestroianni. But he sorely missed the protective cloak of anonymity that had been his as a part-time professor at the Angelicum.

"Before you go, Father." Graziani spoke with compelling sincerity now. "Let me assure you that if you ever need any special help, then please do ask. In this office, you will have complete confidence, no matter what or who is involved." The Cardinal couldn't come right out and say that any intended henchman in Maestroianni's power game should know where to find the exit; or that Maestroianni might be getting too big for his britches. But he could point out that it was not Maestroianni's patronage that counted now, but his own as Secretary of State. And he could emphasize his point by repeating his offer.

"Any help at all, Father Gladstone. You have only to ask." Graziani stood up then and walked Christian to the door in a most amiable fashion. "You will, of course, pray for us all. Especially for the Holy Father, that he be guided in his grave decisions."

Gladstone didn't have to wait until evening to find Damien Slattery after all. He ran into the Master-General in the upstairs corridor as he returned to his room at the Angelicum. Typically, the first word was Slattery's. "Just the man I was looking for. Let's have a word in your quarters, Father."

Better late than never, Christian thought as Father Damien seated himself in a chair not built for his massive bulk.

"Your first day back and already busy in the vineyards, eh?" Slattery watched Chris deposit his briefcase on the writing table and take his own seat across the room. "The message I have for you is a simple one, Father Gladstone. Some days ago His Holiness expressed a desire to have a few minutes with you. This is your first day back, and you must be exhausted. Still, are you free this evening? Say, at about eight-fifteen?" When there was no answer from the young American, Slattery's antennae finally went up. "Let's back up a step or two, Father. You've got something on your mind."

Christian's laugh was not pleasant. It was one thing to be treated as a mindless shuttlecock by the likes of Maestroianni and Graziani. But he didn't much relish the same tactics from Father Damien. Yet here the Dominican was, just issuing orders and instructions with no explanations. In fact, he was faring worse with Slattery. At least Maestroianni had given him a word of welcome, however disingenuous it might have been. And Graziani had at least offered his help, however backhanded his intent.

"The only thing I have on my mind, Father-General," Chris replied truthfully, "is a long list of questions and no answers."

Slattery crossed one timberlike leg over the other amid a sea of flowing robes. "Let's hear some of those questions, then."

In his discomfort, Christian began to pace the floor. For the first time he tried to put into words his feeling of having been tossed into a river with no terra firma for miles around. "The real question is whether I belong here at all. For the long haul, I mean. Maybe I'm too far out of my depth.

The more I'm told how much a part of things I am, the more I feel like I've landed among the little green men on Mars."

"Holy Mutherogawd, Gladstone!" In what seemed a mixture of anger and impatience, the giant Dominican lapsed into his Irish brogue. "Where d'yeh think yeh are? In some clerical kindergarten? What yeh need is a good dose o' growin' up! And while yer at it, yeh better learn there is no terra firma. Not in Rome! Not now! And yeh better learn that in the turbulent river yeh talk of, yer not bobbin' about with little green men! Yer swimmin' with a pack o' barracudas!"

Though stunned by Slattery's vehemence and stung by what he recognized as the truth, Christian was at least relieved that Father Damien wasn't talking like some Vatican robot skilled to the nines in *romanità*. He stopped his pacing and sat down. "I reckon I'm as willing and able to learn as the next fellow. But it didn't seem outlandish to hope that at least some of what Cardinal O'Cleary told me in New Orleans was true. When he said I'd be teaching at the Angelicum, I wasn't dumb enough to think that was the whole of it. But academia does have a way of putting order into a man's life. Even in Rome."

"Listen, Father." Slattery had a better rein on himself now. His brogue disappeared. "The long and the short of it is nothing your genius can't encompass. I don't know what O'Cleary was told about your teaching at the Angelicum. But the fact is, you're on special assignment. In Vatican jargon, you're 'detached for special duties at the request of the Secretariat of State.' What you need, then, isn't a schedule of entrance exams and lectures and seminars. What you need is a rundown on the barracudas.

"Let's settle for the moment on the two you mentioned. I gather you spent time today with Cardinal Graziani. As a diplomat, he'll do well enough. But like the old saw says, deep down he's shallow. He's everybody's friend, and nobody's ally. Not Cardinal Maestroianni, though. He's plausible and cunning. He has no ethics, but he plays by the rules—even if he has to make up his own. I'm not surprised you'll be working with him. In fact, I half expected it. And the best advice I can give you is to say your prayers, listen to every word and don't ask any questions. Not even obvious ones."

Despite the darkness of what Slattery was telling him, Chris had to chuckle. "I found that much out for myself."

"Asked one too many questions, did you?"

"I asked one question, period. Nearly got my face scorched off. But I'll ask you one. You know this BNL thing that's been breaking in the media? Well, twice today my mother's name was hauled into that mess. I can't figure it. I mean, do you know anything about it?"

"It's complicated, *Padre*." Slattery wasn't putting Christian off. The query was legitimate in his eyes. But he could only guess at the answer to the young priest's concern for his mother. "Here it is in the kind of language we financial pedestrians can understand. The Vatican Bank works with the BNL. The BNL worked with Saddam Hussein, facilitating the extension of up to five billion dollars in illegal loans and credits to help him pay for his Condor II missile project. And with the BNL's connivance, Saddam laundered money for the illegal purchase of strategic items. The BNL wasn't a lone operator, of course. Several other Western European banks were involved in the joint Iraqi-Argentine-Egyptian missile project. Some of your own U.S. banks were involved, too. And some high officials in the U.S. administration. The Bush crowd. Big illegalities on all sides.

"When the thing began to unravel in the media, a salvage operation was necessary to get the Vatican Bank out of any direct implication. Exactly what your mother had to do with all that I can only guess. But you Gladstones are hardly paupers, after all. And you are *privilegiati di Stato.* So my conjecture is that she was called on to help financially in that salvage effort."

Gladstone shook his head. When did a fellow ever get to know his mother? he wondered. Cessi abhorred Rome's stand on the religious side of things these days. But if Slattery was right, she had stood by the Pope's bank. All at once, though, another thought struck Chris. A thought that was too cynical, too much of a kind with the insider view of Rome that was piecing itself together in his mind. A thought that the Holy Father's wish to see him had something to do with the Vatican Bank and his family's financial usefulness.

No sooner had Christian shared that idea with Slattery than the Master-General surged out of his chair. His face irate and beet red, he bent nose to nose over Gladstone, making him a prisoner in his chair. "Can you *really* think that, Father? We're in a war with Satan himself! Maybe that war has already been won for us. But right now, we have lost, are losing and will continue to lose battle after battle! And you think the Holy Father has nothing better to do than buttonhole you about money like some ha'penny politician running for dog catcher? Well, think again! Perhaps you're too young to know what's going on. But you're not too young to learn that what's going on is far more complicated than you have any idea. Far more hellish, far more divine, far more hazardous than you can begin to imagine!"

Slattery straightened to his full, towering height and glared down at Chris with blue-eyed ferocity. "If you stop looking for adolescent assurances long enough, maybe you can join in this war. But I warn you, you learn from battle to battle. If all you want is a little order in your little life, and a little corner of academia is where you think you can find it, then I tell you, you'll be a lump of garbage just taking up space. There are hundreds of academics of that ilk in Rome. And do you know what they're really heading for? I'll tell you in one word. Death. You could take that road, too. And by the same token, you'd be damned. . . ."

Slattery stopped in mid-sentence, his face twisted by the ugly and repulsive thought he had begun to express. By his knowledge as an exorcist, and by his firsthand experience of the damned. He stepped away from Gladstone and moved toward the window. When he spoke again his voice was softer, but all the more riveting for that. "In the warfare that's going on, there are quite a few of us on the side of the angels. But we are not that many compared to the mass of camp followers trotting merrily along on the coattails of those out to destroy what we are trying to salvage.

"I don't know what choices Cardinal O'Cleary put to you, *Padre*. But I'll put you a choice, and I'll make it very simple. Are you one of us or not? If the answer is yes, start marching from battle to battle like the rest of us. If the answer is no, then get out from under our feet."

Chris held Slattery's stare for a long minute. The Dominican had not only made the choice clear; he had put it in terms that were eerily familiar. "Tell me, Father-General. Is Father Carnesecca one of—er, one of us?"

"Why do you ask?"

"I was just remembering. Your talk about warfare and about Satan reminded me of something he said a long time ago about our being in the middle of a global warfare of spirit. And about spirit being where true victory or defeat will lie. He said that the center of the battle is in Rome, but that a siege has been raised against the Pontiff from within the Vatican structure itself."

"Then in the name of Heaven, Gladstone!" Slattery let his full weight down into his chair so heavily that something in its frame cracked from the sudden strain. "If you can understand that much, why can't you understand the whole picture?"

"Is Carnesecca one of us?" Christian would have his answer.

"In the sense you mean, the answer is yes. In the larger sense, the answer is that Father Aldo is special. He already belongs wholly to God. But the question on the table isn't about Father Carnesecca." Slattery was determined to have the issue decided one way or the other. "The question, *Padre,* is whether you are one of us!"

"Yes!" He shot his decision back as if he were discharging an explosive device. "I am!"

"So! You will meet with His Holiness this evening!"

"Yes! I will!"

"Well! Why didn't you say so at the beginning, lad?" The Master-General rose from the chair and headed out the door, leaving it ajar. "There'll be a car down at the door at eight-fifteen," he called from the corridor.

When Monsignore Daniel led Christian into the private papal study on the fourth floor of the Apostolic Palace that evening, any vestige of cynicism concerning the Slavic Pope that might have survived Damien Slattery's onslaught was dissipated like smoke.

Seated in a pool of light at his desk, the Pontiff lifted his head almost imperceptibly at the slight sound of entry. Pen still in hand, he met Christian's eyes with a direct glance that changed immediately from querying to welcoming. It was more as if, simply by appearing in the room, Christian had captured the focus of the Holy Father's mind, pushing whatever had engrossed him to the periphery of his attention. In simple movements, rapid but devoid of any haste, His Holiness laid down his pen and came around the desk, his hands outstretched, the smile in his eyes softening his features.

From the moment he knelt to kiss the papal ring, Gladstone was certain that even if he were never to see this man again, he would be held nonetheless in that smiling glance, and in the quality of majesty that clothed the papal persona. All of that was this Pontiff's personal expression of a basic connection that binds every Pope with every priest of good faith. Gossamerlike in its seeming insubstantiality, that connection would be more lasting for Christian than a cord of tempered steel. A thing as primal as the feeling that once prompted Paul the Apostle to cry out, "Abba! Father!" As refined as Cardinal Newman's childlike sigh as he was received into the Church: "Incredible—home at last!"

On the face of it, this white-robed individual who took Chris's hand in his and guided him to one of two armchairs in a corner of the study was no different from many other men he had encountered. The Holy Father was obviously ageing before his time. He was gaunt-faced rather than full-cheeked. Fragile rather than ebullient. Illumined in himself rather than intense in manner. His deep voice, his accented Italian, the Slavic rhythm of his enunciation might have belonged to any of a thousand others. Yet there was that wisp of a difference. As a distant light implies a lamp, as a spoken word implies a speaker, as a spent wave fanning out upon a shore implies the deep ocean beyond, so, too, everything about the Slavic Pope—speech, gaze, gesture of eye and hand—implied some greater unseen presence.

The first thing on the Holy Father's mind was to thank his young American visitor for his aid in securing the photos of Bernini's *Noli Me Tangere*. "It is a blessing we will always share, Father Gladstone."

"It was little enough to do, Holiness."

"Perhaps." The Pope pursed his lips. "Still, as a priest you are reckoned to be always about our Father's business, one way or another. That means His special grace is with you. Yet Father Slattery tells me you feel disoriented by our present Rome."

Without mentioning Cardinal Maestroianni's name, Christian answered the Holy Father's implied question with a mild complaint about the imperious "plucking and tugging" at his sleeves. The pressure, he confessed, was difficult to manage.

"Indeed." The Holy Father shifted in his chair as if the thought had caused him some physical pain. "I understand that, believe me. But it is well to remember, Father Gladstone, that God does wag the tail of the dog; and that by himself, the dog can't do even that much!"

Chris couldn't suppress a smile at the image of the mighty, red-sashed Maestroianni as a dog wagging its tail.

"Tell me this, Father." The Pope seemed at ease again. "Would your discomfort prevent your sincere help to us in building the New Jerusalem? In building anew the Body of Our Savior? We are few. But Christ is the Master Builder. And"—the Pontiff smiled just a little now—"His Mother is in charge of operations."

Chris never could recall exactly the words he used to assure His Holiness that nothing short of death would prevent him from rendering whatever service he might. Nor was he in any way clear about the Holy Father's meaning. What he did remember—what conveyed a confidence beyond his comprehension and remained a constant refrain in his mind ever after—were the exact words with which the Slavic Pope welcomed him into the war. "Then come, Father Gladstone! Come! Suffer a little while with us all, and bear the present anguish for the sake of a great, great hope!"

"Jerusalem!" Secretary-General Paul Thomas Gladstone held the telephone receiver away from his ear for a second and stared at it in disbelief.

"Jerusalem, Mr. Gladstone!" The exasperation in Cyrus Benthoek's voice was as thick as London fog. "Do we have a bad connection? I did say Jerusalem. A private plane will be waiting for you at the airport in Brussels Friday evening. We have booked a suite for you at the King David Hotel. You will be back home in plenty of time for your Monday schedule."

"We, Mr. Benthoek?" Paul knew better than to cavil. But his question seemed a fair one in the circumstances.

"Yes." Benthoek sounded his normal, imperious self again. "An important associate of mine will join us. Dr. Ralph Channing. You may have read some of his monographs. If you haven't, you should. In any case, you will find this little pilgrimage to be well worth your while. Well worth your professional while." Benthoek rang off, leaving Gladstone disgruntled at this interruption in his heavy schedule at the EC.

Paul had not experienced any of his brother's difficulties in learning the ropes of his new job. He was putting in fifteen-hour days in his offices at the Berlaymont Building. And, though it was still early October, he had already sat in at his first plenary session of the EC Council Ministers. He had yet to finish reading the back records; and so a few of the details that had come up for discussion among the Ministers were beyond him. But luck had favored him in that the main issue had concerned the General Agreement on Tariffs and Trade.

That meeting had made it plain that the blockage in the so-called Uruguay Round of GATT negotiations had far less to do with the price of farm commodities than with the contention between Euro-Atlanticists and

Eurocentrics. Paul couldn't see the much vaunted goal of a politically and monetarily unified Europe coming about by January 1, 1993.

Wisely, however, Gladstone had kept quiet on that point in the meeting itself, and had followed the same cautious policy during a small reception given immediately afterward by the Ministers to welcome the new Secretary-General formally into their midst. He had fit easily into the company of those ranking diplomats, chatting with each in his own language.

That reception had also provided Gladstone with the opportunity to meet the EC members of the ad hoc Selection Committee who had elected him. As parliamentary secretaries, they accompanied their Foreign Ministers to any plenary meeting; and they had appeared as eager—or as curious, perhaps—to have a look at this American interloper as he was to get to know each of them.

Paul had formed a fair idea of what to expect from these twelve men and women who had connived together to ease his way. He had shaken hands with each of them. He had discussed England's cross-Channel interests with Featherstone-Haugh. He had commiserated with Corrado Dello Iudice over Italy's problems with inflation and the Mafia. He had shared an opinion or two with Francisco dos Santos about Portugal's current problems. With Germany's committed Euro-Atlanticist Emil Schenker he had speculated about the future of Russia. With all of them, in fact, he had exchanged pleasantries and had made arrangements to see each of them again within the next several days. Even France's Nicole Cresson had welcomed Gladstone warmly, and had agreed to join him and her good friend Schenker for dinner in the near future. But it was with Belgium's Jan Borliuth that he had struck up an immediate and genuine friendship.

The only real difficulty for Paul Gladstone in the early going was to find a permanent place to live. The apartment he had taken for himself and his family was ample enough in size, and it was within walking distance of the Berlaymont. But it simply wouldn't do for any length of time. He and Yusai both abhorred apartment-house living. And, fresh from Liselton, Declan was like a lion cub in a cage. Even their normally irrepressible housekeeper and cook, Hannah Dowd, was miserable. And the all-purpose domestic Maggie Mulvahill, who had come along with them to Brussels, was becoming downright moody. In the circumstances, Paul had sought the services of a local realtor and carried on a weekend search for a proper house. That, in fact, was the true cause of his dismay at Benthoek's imperious summons. He would do a lot better, he grumbled to himself, to have another go at the available real estate in the area than to make a pilgrimage to Jerusalem.

It was fortunate that Paul's lunch that day was with Jan Borliuth. A grandfather five times over, Borliuth seemed naturally to assume a paternal interest for anyone he met who was in need. Already he had been of considerable help to Paul in his advice about such practical settling-in problems as banking facilities, work permits for his domestic help, identity cards, Declan's schooling and suchlike. And he had set aside the coming weekend to help in Paul's search for a house.

As they sat together in the Berlaymont's canopied rooftop restaurant, the Belgian was crestfallen to learn that Gladstone would lose the weekend on that score. And he became all the more adamant in his offer of help. "If your wife is willing, and if you will trust me with your family while you are away, she and I will carry on the search this weekend as planned."

Paul jumped at the idea. He made a phone call to Yusai to explain his predicament and Jan's offer. And, in her Confucian way, Yusai agreed to the plan with a mixture of quaint hope and tough practicality. "Heaven must smile on us, Paul. Otherwise this simply will not work out for us."

"It's settled, then!" Borliuth raised a glass when Paul returned to their table. "With any luck at all, you will return to Brussels on Sunday night to find your problem solved!"

When Paul Gladstone checked into Jerusalem's King David Hotel shortly after nine o'clock on Friday evening, he found a brief note in Benthoek's hand waiting for him at the registry desk. "If you are not too tired after your flight, do join Dr. Channing and myself for a light evening meal in the dining room." This was not a social invitation, but a summons. He folded the note, had his bag sent up to his suite and headed for the dining room.

"How good to see you in Jerusalem, Paul!" Benthoek was the picture of octogenarian wisdom and fitness as he welcomed Paul to his table. "Dr. Channing here has been looking forward to our little meeting for some time now."

"Indeed, Mr. Gladstone." Ralph Channing smiled through his splendid goatee and raised a glass of Israeli wine. "Welcome to the Queen of Cities."

Paul was barely able to disguise his astonishment at Channing's toast. He hadn't known what to expect of this so-called pilgrimage; but he had not thought it would begin with the words of a prayer that was already ancient in the day of David.

He found Channing sympathetic. The Professor obviously enjoyed the academic turn of phrase. But he also showed himself to be a man accustomed to think in terms of large horizons, and to be above any vulgar prejudice or crude partisanship. In the course of discussing Gladstone's work in Brussels, for example, Professor Channing referred to the EC as "this continental organization," to its goal as "Greater Europe" and to the society of nations as "our human family." Paul found all of that to be most appealing.

As with the young American's work, so with his religion. "Your own tradition, Mr. Gladstone," Channing offered, "has been the epitome of globalism for quite a while. Despite some remnants of past idiosyncrasies, the Roman Catholic tradition is surely our best ally in the final phase of globalizing our civilization. Would you not agree?"

Despite a slow and reassuring nod from Benthoek, Paul thought it best to be reserved. It was simple enough to be both truthful and vague in his answer. "Any lapse in my own practice of Catholicism, Professor, has been precisely because of certain idiosyncrasies. Especially in matters of personal morality."

Channing was not to be put off by such a cautious non-reply. "I must be frank with you. Time is rushing by us all. And there is so much fruitful collaboration possible to make this a better world. Many of our friends in Rome think it is past high time for a change. And they are hoping that a solution may be found." At the same time, Professor Channing had to confess that the situation was a little complicated. "When the Vatican is involved, the situation is always complicated. But as far as your limited role is concerned, the matter can be put simply."

Surprise number two for Paul was that he should have any role at all, limited or otherwise, in Vatican matters.

That was understandable, Dr. Channing allowed. But perhaps Gladstone was conversant with the career of the renowned Cardinal Cosimo Maestroianni, recently retired as Vatican Secretary of State. . . . No? Well, no matter. The point was that His Eminence was not only one of Cyrus Benthoek's most valued friends but a friend of Channing's as well. And the point was that, when it came to the Europe that must be, His Eminence was of the same mind as the three men gathered at this very table. His Eminence would be devoting his retirement years to the welfare and wider education of Roman Catholic bishops in the affairs of the Greater European Community.

"I don't mind saying that such education is badly needed," Benthoek added. "RC bishops are woefully lacking in a real spirit of cooperation with that grand ideal of a Europe greater than it ever was before. You should be very pleased that your brother will be working in the most intimate collaboration with Cardinal Maestroianni."

"Christian?" Paul didn't even try to disguise his consternation. So far as he knew, Chris was as anxious as ever to finish his doctoral thesis on the Isenheim altarpiece and quit Rome for good. In fact, this was the time of year for Christian to be teaching at the New Orleans Seminary.

"I see we have taken you off guard, Mr. Gladstone." Professor Channing was a smooth number. "But I assure you, your brother is Rome-based now. I believe you and Father Gladstone will now have many opportunities to get together."

Surprise number three produced total confusion in Gladstone. But Paul couldn't see how his older brother's association with Cardinal Maestroianni's educational projects had anything to do with himself. He was happy if Chris had landed on his feet somewhere near the top of the Vatican heap. But . . .

Channing was about to follow up on Gladstone's surprise when a cautionary frown from Cyrus Benthoek warned him off. For all his brilliance, the good Doctor was not cunning about timing and finesse. As a connoisseur of men, therefore, and as a master at leading them into his own plans, Benthoek turned a smiling and benign face to his perturbed young protégé. He aimed a frown at Channing, and a smile at Gladstone. "Let us *all* remember. We have two full days ahead of us. We will go into greater detail tomorrow, when we are a little more rested. Suffice it to say for the moment that in this intended pilgrimage of ours, we are following in the forward footprints of history."

Paul passed a fitful night during which he was assailed anew by those nevermore-demons that had beset him after his initiation interview with Benthoek in London. But Saturday morning found him rested and eager to take up the conversation that had been left dangling the night before. To his frustration, however, Benthoek and Dr. Channing had other ideas.

"We have booked a limousine, Mr. Gladstone." Channing cooed that bit of information over his coffee and eggs.

"Indeed!" Benthoek gave his enthusiastic benediction to the plan. "I promised you a pilgrimage. And today it will begin. We have planned a tour of the archaeological sights in the Holy City."

So began an excursion that had obviously been meticulously planned. Paul had seen it all before, of course, on his earlier travels about the world. Nevertheless, with Channing's professional commentary as constant backdrop, and with Benthoek as a one-man Greek chorus, Gladstone gradually began to look at everything in this ancient place with a more refined understanding.

In the company of these two uncommon men, he all but relived Abraham's visit to Mount Moriah, where God's Covenant had been given to the Patriarch two thousand years before Christ; and under their guidance he examined the remains of King David's City with a liberating freshness of mind. He stood beside them at the Wall of the ancient Temple; peered with them into King Hezekiah's famed water tunnel carved through the rock of Mount Ophel; pored with them over the Dead Sea Scrolls in the Shrine of the Book; wondered with them at the blocked and mysterious Golden Gate of the Old City, through which—as Channing emphasized—many believe the Messiah will enter Jerusalem at the End of Days.

"So you see, Mr. Gladstone," Dr. Channing said as the trio headed toward the waiting limousine, "in the end, perhaps we all look to the birth of a New Heaven and a New Earth."

"To a time," Benthoek supplied the chorus, "when nations will beat their swords into ploughshares."

Though such observations were plentiful, and though they seemed perfectly designed to reopen the door to the discussions of the night before, Paul found to his bafflement and disappointment that he could not turn the conversation to matters of present interest. Even when they sat down to a late luncheon at the hotel, Benthoek and Channing refused to be sidetracked from their pilgrimage. "I only regret," Channing confided to his two companions, "that our time together will not permit us to visit other places of deep interest that surround us."

The Professor made up for the lack of time by launching into a verbal excursion. As Paul listened, he began to let go of his disappointment. He allowed his mind to be engaged instead by a new reverence, a sense of awe and respect that was unlike the old piety of his days at Windswept House. This land was holy, he felt, because of something more than its sacred history. Because of something Benthoek and Channing were trying to show him.

Nor was Channing content to be merely a guide on this verbal tour. He wanted Paul's comments, his questions, his observations, his reflections, his memories. He wanted Paul Gladstone's mind.

"Even though I am no Christian believer, Mr. Gladstone"—Professor Channing laid his fork across his empty luncheon plate—"I have to admit that this Jesus of history was the greatest teacher this earth has ever held. He literally went around doing good to all people without distinction, as your Bible clearly relates. Surely he was sent by a divine providence. Any man of spirit must see that. With that in mind, Cyrus and I would like you to come with us to make one more visit on this first day of our private little pilgrimage. To a place each of us has seen before, but that all three of us should see together."

Paul was not astounded to find himself next, with his two companions, at the Church of the Holy Sepulcher. There, at the spot where the body of Christ had been placed in its tomb after the Crucifixion, Paul was moved by the sadness in Dr. Channing's voice as he remarked on the partisan animosity that so obviously held sway among the different Christian denominations charged with the care of the Holy Sepulcher. "Is it not an unworthy spectacle, Mr. Gladstone? Even here, Roman Catholic Franciscans, Eastern Orthodox priests, Coptic prelates and all the others vie to be the most important custodians."

"Shameful," Benthoek agreed ruefully. "It really is time we all got together."

On the drive back to the hotel, as Channing reflected on the force of tradition and on the need felt by all religious-minded people to relive what he called "the foundational happenings of their tradition," Gladstone felt a true sense of belonging. A sense of privilege. A sense of camaraderie, and of shared ideals and sympathies. All the surprise and consternation of the prior evening had been replaced by a welcome, thoughtful peace.

It was only after the three companions came together again at the dinner hour that things turned to the specific purpose of these two remarkable men in regard to Paul Gladstone. The Professor turned to Paul with an imperious lift of his head. "We had hoped," he began with a sympathetic air of concern, "that this Pope would expand the universalism of your Church onto a truly global plane. Tell us, Mr. Gladstone. How do you assess the present Pontiff?"

"I see him in a contradictory light. In some ways, he seems to be the last of the old-time Popes. But he has some traits of what we can expect of future Popes. On the whole, I suppose I see him as an interim figure."

"A most interesting view." Channing ran a hand over his shiny pate. "Not unlike our own thinking. But tell me, young man. What about yourself on that score? Do you, too, still have one foot in the past?"

"Sir?" Paul knew he was being led in this conversation every bit as much as he had been led around Jerusalem. He didn't mind that so much now. But he wanted some additional direction.

"Let me clarify the question," Channing obliged. "As far as Cyrus and I have ascertained, you have quickly mastered the essentials of the post of Secretary-General. Overall, the Foreign Ministers and the EC Commissioners hold you in high regard. The issue, therefore, is this. Are you prepared to transit to another plane of understanding? Do you feel ready to grapple with the real issues at stake in our efforts to move forward to the goal of a globalized civilization? Of course, you can discharge your duties in Brussels perfectly well without making such a transition. Many of your predecessors have done just that, and have passed on to greener pastures. Ordinary, but greener."

In point of fact, such pastures were precisely what Paul had in mind. But he knew better than to say so.

"Or," Channing continued, "you can enter into an area of privileged knowledge and cooperation with those who watch over the whole globalist movement. That would require a certain detachment on your part. A certain independence of judgment. Cyrus and I do not want to influence you unduly." Dr. Channing lied on that point with practiced ease. "But from all I have seen you have all those qualities and more."

"Quite right!" Benthoek smiled handsomely at this point. "Quite right! But is it not time to set things out a little more clearly for our young associate?" Cyrus turned to Gladstone as a conductor to an orchestra. "Just as your abilities are held in such esteem at the EC, so, too, your brother's abilities as a scholar and a churchman are highly appreciated by his Vatican superiors. Now, as fate would have it, my good friend Cardinal Maestroianni has conveyed a mission of delicacy and importance to Father Gladstone. A mission in which many powerful men have a vital interest."

There was no doubt that Benthoek included himself and Professor Channing among such powerful men. The wonder of it for Paul, however, was that he, too, seemed to be included; and his brother as well.

Aware of his advantage—indeed, having come all the way to Jerusalem to secure it—Cyrus leaned forward. In a most confidential tone, he explained that in the course of his work in Europe, Father Christian Gladstone would need to ask Paul's assistance for certain bishops. "Facilitation in bank loans and mortgages, consultation in questions about landed property, tax reductions and so on. Now, let me put a scenario to you. A vision I have in which your own intimate connections with the Council of European Ministers will enable Father Gladstone to accommodate the bishops in these matters. A vision in which, with those favors done, the bishops themselves will surely be favorably inclined toward the Ministers. More favorably inclined toward a true spirit of cooperation with our grand ideal of the Greater European Community. More favorably inclined to bring the Church itself through what you have rightly called the interim phase currently presided over by the present Pontiff."

Gladstone listened carefully. Though he noted a number of gaps and omissions in Benthoek's account of his vision, he was pleased that Christian was apparently so much more attuned than he had imagined to the globalizing trend of world affairs. Still, Paul had his doubts. That the Foreign Ministers of the EC nations had a high opinion of him as Secretary-General was one thing. But it didn't seem likely that such powerful men would lightly render such favors as Benthoek had outlined to a newcomer. At least, not on such a regular basis as this conversation implied; and above all, not for the benefit of Rome. Such doors did not open just like that, willy-nilly.

With his clear statement of those objections, Paul Gladstone opened the door, willy-nilly, to his own final seduction. The way was clear for the cultivation in him of a spirit well adapted to the exigencies of his active life as Secretary-General of the European Community.

Cyrus Benthoek started the ball rolling on a seemingly new theme that was as surprising for Gladstone as hearing himself addressed familiarly now by his first name.

"Dr. Channing and I have asked you to join us, Paul, precisely to open many doors to you. Doors of cooperation and trust and concern and shared interests. And we have asked you to join us at this particular time—and in this particular part of the world—because here at this moment is a gathering of a most prestigious Lodge. Are you aware, Paul, that many high-ranking prelates in the Vatican belong to the Lodge?"

Paul took a moment to reply. "Yes. But there is still some official disaffection as regards Freemasonry."

Dr. Channing was quick to supply a corrective. "The only important source of disaffection that remains is the present Holy Father. But—as you have observed so wisely—in some ways he is the last of the old-time Popes."

Benthoek pressed forward again with a paternal smile. "Professor Channing and I have decided to make you a part of our little enclave. For you are family, my boy. That is what we have become today, isn't it? Members of the same family."

With that, and with many a graceful flourish of phrasing, Benthoek congratulated Paul on his good fortune in having been invited to appear before the Grand Lodge of Israel. Cyrus would take care that Gladstone would learn more in the coming weeks. It was enough this evening, though, for the young man to know that, while this Lodge was young—it had begun only in 1953—it flourished nonetheless as a Grand Orient, and worked the York Rite under the Supreme Chapter of the Royal Arch with its allied degrees. Further, it had the Supreme Counsel of the AAA Scottish Rite Lodges of Perfection, Chapters, Areopags and Consistories.

The flood of names was new to Gladstone. Still, he was taken by Benthoek's subtext. For what dawned within the inner reaches of Paul's easily captivated soul was the realization that he had been summoned to this ancient city not for the purpose of looking to the dusty past, but to enter fully into a new way of living. To join the privileged company of men who were engaged in building the New Jerusalem. To join a restricted number of individuals who always could and always did open doors for one another, for that noble purpose. To enter into the heart of his own success.

Everything Benthoek said confirmed Gladstone's understanding. "Throughout this day, Paul, we have been reminded of the importance of fraternal love among all men of goodwill. That is Bethlehem's message, and Calvary's message. But at the very foot of the Cross—at the Church of the Holy Sepulcher—we have also been reminded how elusive that message is for the citizens of this workaday world.

"What makes me proud to be associated with you—and I know Dr. Channing joins me in this—is the universalist outlook you have displayed to us. For that is the essence of our outlook; the essence of our life's work. You have come very far, my young friend. It was only last month in London that we spoke together of what it means to leave the valley floor and to walk upon the mountaintop. Yet already you are being called to the heights where there is no clash of rival faiths. No petty claims to priority, or to special privileges, or to religious exclusivism. Tomorrow, Dr. Channing and I will bring you to the crowning event of this pilgrimage. We will take you to that mountain where all acknowledge the same divine power and authority among men. We will usher you into a world of perfect ecumenism." Cyrus paused for a brief instant, then leaned forward as though the world he had just described depended for all its hopes on Paul's response. "Will you come with us to the mountaintop?"

Paul felt no tug of nevermore-demons now. Nor was there a trace of the panic or self-reproach he had felt in London. Rather, he felt like shouting his assent. However, Paul Gladstone simply gave the answer that would bind him with his brother in unwitting but essential cooperation to elicit from the bishops of his Church a Common Mind against the Slavic Pope.

"I will come with you, Mr. Benthoek. Most willingly."

❑ ❑ ❑ ❑

The invitation to the mountaintop turned out to be more than a figure of speech.

"Aminadab," Ralph Channing explained to Paul as the three Americans left their hotel together the following morning, "is one of the highest points in the environs of Jerusalem."

"Too bad the weather is turning against us." Benthoek scanned the sky. "We won't have a view down to the Sinai, or over to the Jordan or the Mediterranean. But we will have an expert driver to bring us safely to our destination and home again."

The expert driver—an Israeli who spoke English with an Oxford accent and who introduced himself as Hal—welcomed his passengers into his four-wheel-drive Jeep with a word of advice. "Fasten your seat belts, gentlemen, we're going to be climbing at an acute angle most of the way."

An initial low-grade ascent brought the pilgrims to a steeply inclined dirt road. Given the condition of the road and the worsening weather, there was no question of attaining any great speed. As they climbed higher and ran into swatches of dense, swirling gray mist that hid the way ahead, it seemed to him that some primal force had molded rocks and boulders into the shapes of ruined temples and crouching mastodons and unnamed monsters petrified with age. Only now and again, when the mist broke for a time, did he catch glimpses of the valley receding in the distance below.

As they headed up the final approach to Aminadab, the full force of the storm broke around them. The heavy veils of mist, the sharp reports of thunder and the momentary brilliance of lightning slashing over the gray-black face of the landscape created an impression of some ancient resident god angered at their approach, and inimical to all that was human and pleasant and accommodating. Then, suddenly, just as the road flattened out to an almost level plane, the sun broke through, splaying its gold-red banners across the sky.

"See!" Cyrus laughed in exultant good humor. "The very heavens smile upon us at Aminadab! It will all be very good!"

At that magical moment, Hal rounded his Jeep past a corner of rock, ascended for another three hundred yards or so, and brought them all safely into the small hamlet of Aminadab perched in tranquillity on the mountaintop.

Paul looked about in some disappointment. After the wonders of Jerusalem, this was not an inspiring spot. There were some half dozen cinder-block houses grouped around a few more impressively constructed buildings. Except for some thirty or forty vehicles in the car park adjacent to the largest building, the place seemed deserted.

It was in front of that building that Hal drew to a halt. Gladstone clambered out of the Jeep and followed Channing and Benthoek to the door, where the Professor called his attention to a plaque above the entryway.

"As you see, the Star of David and the Christian Cross and the Crescent

Moon are all framed within the Square and Compass of Freemasonry. Now, come with Cyrus and me to see that very human miracle in the flesh."

Channing led the way up a staircase that gave onto an open, wide, sparsely furnished room occupying the full extent of the building. At the center of the room had been placed what appeared to be a miniature ark. Solidly built, about two feet high, two feet wide and perhaps three feet in length, it rested on a royal-blue cushion and was surrounded by pedestaled standards, each bearing a lighted taper. An enormous Bible lay open on the ark and covered its upper surface.

The two end walls of the chamber were covered almost from floor to ceiling by black velvet curtains, the one emblazoned in silver thread with the emblems of Judaism, Christianity and Islam; the other, with the Square and Compass of the Craft. Ranged along each of the long side walls were three rows of pews from which, as Paul stepped forward flanked by Channing and Benthoek, silent men turned to inspect the new arrivals. A gentle-faced man with a great shock of white hair came forward, his hands outstretched.

"Welcome, Brothers." He addressed Channing first, and then Benthoek.

"Please welcome Paul Thomas Gladstone." Dr. Channing turned solemn eyes upon Paul. "Mr. Gladstone, I have the honor to present Shlomo Goshen-Gottstein, Sovereign Grand Commander."

"You are most welcome here, Mr. Gladstone," the Grand Commander responded generously. "Please come, all of you, and take your seats with us."

From his place at the center of the room beside the miniature ark, the Grand Commander began with a little address to Paul. "As you may know, our Lodge was founded in 1953, just five years after the founding of the State of Israel itself. We presently have seventy-five Craft Lodges working in three different rituals and in eight languages—Hebrew, Arabic, English, French, German, Romanian, Spanish and Turkish. These men you see sitting here are united in their efforts to spread the message of Freemasonry. The message of Brotherly Love, Relief and Truth. Thus do they build bridges of understanding among themselves and their peoples."

In unhurried succession, a half dozen men representing as many traditions rose, each in his own place, to extend a most solemn invitation to Paul to become a duly inducted Brother.

"I am Lev Natanyahu," the first man announced. "The God of Israel is One God. Accept our fraternal embrace, Paul Thomas Gladstone."

"I am Hassan El-Obeidi." The second man rose to his feet. "There is but One God and Muhammad is His Prophet. Accept our fraternal embrace, Paul Thomas Gladstone."

"I am Father Michael Lannaux, priest and monk of the Benedictine Fathers." A third man stood to face the neophyte. "God so loved the world as to send His Son to found His Church among men. Accept our fraternal embrace, Paul Thomas Gladstone."

The scales fell away from the eyes of Paul Gladstone's inner mind. He felt almost light-headed as, in that calm and calming moment, he came to understand the oneness of all religions. He came to understand their reasons for diversity. And, yes, even for their traditional opposition to each other. At that ultimate moment of his seduction, Paul had no words or mental images with which to clothe his new understanding. But for now he had been lifted as high above all the particularisms of Catholic, Protestant, Jew and Muslim as Aminadab was raised above the Holy City of Jerusalem. Never had he felt so acceptable to God and his fellow man. Never had he known such a safe haven for his mind and being.

When the last solemn formula of invitation had been extended, Paul responded firmly and with gladness. "Yes!" He rose in his place beside his two mentors. "Yes! I do accept your fraternal embrace!"

The bargain, offered and accepted, was sealed with a final brief ritual. The Grand Commander called upon the congregation to answer a single question. "Is there any reason why Paul Thomas Gladstone should not be admitted as one of our number?"

"No." The congregation answered as one. "There is no reason against him."

"Mr. Gladstone." The Commander gestured for Paul to step forward. "In appropriate ritual and at a suitable time, a more formal induction will be accomplished. But come forward now. Kneel, lay your hands on the Book of the Word and repeat our simple oath."

Paul saw that one side of the arklike structure was embossed with the seal of the Grand Lodge of Israel. The Bible lay open so that its left-hand page showed Scripture, while the right hand page displayed the letter G framed within the Masonic Square and Compass. With one hand resting on each of those pages, Paul repeated the words of the oath administered by the Grand Commander.

"I, Paul Thomas Gladstone, remembering always to maintain affinity to the sons of light, do solemnly attest my acceptance of this invitation. So help me God, the Father of all men."

"And Wisdom is His name!" The Commander bowed his head.

"So mote it be!" The chorus came again.

It remained only for the Grand Commander to confirm the young Secretary-General in the role he had taken upon himself in Jerusalem, and to confirm that those hard-to-open doors he had spoken of not twenty-four hours earlier would be no barrier. "On this day, Brother Gladstone, when the dust seems to fall so heavily upon the hearts of men, you shall walk in peace. For you have entered into the building of the Temple of Understanding among all men."

❑ ❑ ❑ ❑

Alone in his suite at the King David Hotel, his bag already packed and waiting for him in the lobby, Cyrus Benthoek took a few moments to dial through to Cardinal Maestroianni's private number at the Collegio Mindinao in Rome.

His Eminence was delighted to learn what a splendid weekend his old friend had passed in Jerusalem. Delighted to learn that the second of his American arrows was in place.

Alone in his suite at the King David Hotel, his bag already packed and waiting for him in the lobby, Paul Gladstone took a few minutes to dial through to his wife in Brussels.

"Paul, darling. Wonderful news!" Yusai was not in any mood for understatement. "Jan has turned out to be our own private angel!"

"Jan?" Paul laughed at the thought of that big Belgian sprouting cherub wings.

"You'll see for yourself!" Yusai was laughing, too. "We can hardly wait to show you the house he has found for us! Oh, Paul, it's a marvelous place. It's called Guidohuis after an early-nineteenth-century member of Jan's family. The finest lyric poet Flanders ever produced, he says. Anyway, Guidohuis is out in Ghent. Well, really, it's in a little township called Deurle. We arrived there in no time on the *autostrade,* so you needn't worry about the commute."

Yusai made the place sound irresistible. She described a 150-year-old farmhouse with endless rooms and a gaily tiled roof and almost as many nooks and crannies as they had at Liselton. Guidohuis sat on two acres of land encircled by the most beautifully slender birch trees. And there was an ample orchard beyond, and five acres of farmland besides. She was almost in tears with happiness. "You should have seen Declan! He ran like a deer in the orchard, climbing trees and picking apples. Hannah Dowd can hardly wait to start baking pies and puddings and dumplings and strudels!"

"You mean we have our own private angel, and an apple orchard, too?"

"Isn't it exciting? And there's an international elementary school. All the grades are taught in English, French and German. And it's practically in our backyard . . ."

A glance at his watch told Gladstone he would have to ring off if he were to get to the Tel Aviv airport in time.

"But, Paul," Yusai complained, "I have so much to tell you! Where are you rushing off to now?"

"I'm rushing home to you, my sweetest! I'm coming home from the mountaintop."

Alone in his room at the Angelicum, his bag already packed, Christian Gladstone read again the note that had come in the nick of time from Father Angelo Gutmacher.

Chris reckoned he was ready to embark on the maiden voyage of his work for Cardinal Cosimo Maestroianni. He had memorized all the data, and had been briefed by Cardinal Aureatini on the finer points of interrogating bishops in a way that would secure their confidence and buoy their hopes. The memory of his audience with the Slavic Pope had remained with Christian and had calmed the worst of his Roman jitters. Chris knew now that Rome was where he belonged.

Yet in another sense he was as perplexed as he had ever been. He knew in his bones that there was a subplot going on under his nose, but he had no clue as to what he had got himself into. He had managed to find time for a chat with Aldo Carnesecca. But since he, too, was about to leave on a two-week mission for His Holiness in Spain, there hadn't been nearly enough time to explore such puzzles as what the Pope might have meant when he had talked about building the New Jerusalem and building anew the Body of Our Savior.

Such questions apart, though, Christian had hoped to spend some time with his old friend and confessor, Father Angelo, before he plunged into the thick of things. Fresh from Galveston himself, Gutmacher was as new to the Roman insider game as Chris. Nevertheless, there was no man who understood better how to find one's way along uncharted terrain. And there was no man in Christian's life whose judgment he trusted so completely. Try as he might, however, Chris hadn't been able to raise Father Angelo in Rome. He had left a succession of messages for him at the Collegium Teutonicum, where he knew Gutmacher was billeted; but to no avail.

Finally, though, this short note had come in the post. Brief as Father Angelo's words were, and however quickly they had been scribbled, they provided the best direction Christian could have asked. They brimmed with priestly purpose. They supplied the compass he had wanted for his soul.

"Forgive me." Chris read Father Angelo's note aloud to himself one last time before his departure for France. "I had hoped to see you upon your return to the Eternal City. At the Holy Father's request, however, and on shortest notice, I find myself in the land of my birth. Beginning at Königsberg, and then in other cities, I am to establish Chapels dedicated to Our Lady of Fatima. Do give that news to your mother, for I will not have time to write her. Perhaps it will ease her anguish for the Church, and for you as her son, to know how serious the Pontiff is about such work. Pray for me, as I do for you. Serve Peter, Christian. In all you do, serve him faithfully. Serve Peter in Christ, and Christ in Peter. For that is why you have returned to Rome."

XXVII

IN SPITE OF Cessi Gladstone's fame for having faced down Cardinals, bishops, priests and errant politicians, she had never seen herself as another Hildegard, say, who scolded Popes and emperors in the twelfth century; or as a late-twentieth-century version of Catherine of Siena, who threw herself with such passion into the affairs of papal governance in the Great Schism of the 1300s. For all of her own complaints about the present condition of the Roman Catholic Church, in other words, Cessi had never thought seriously of taking on the Pope.

Not long after Christian's departure for Rome, however, seemingly unrelated events during one harried week in early October focused her attention on Vatican affairs in a new way.

The visit of Traxi Le Voisin to Windswept House marked the beginning of the change. Just as he had spearheaded the formation of the Chapel of St. Michael the Archangel in Danbury over twenty years before, and just as he had secured Father Angelo Gutmacher as its pastor, so Traxi had again thrown himself into the frustrating work of finding a new priest for St. Michael's after Father Angelo's abrupt summons into Vatican service.

Traxi's difficulty wasn't in finding applicants. A single advertisement placed in a militantly traditionalist Catholic publication had attracted more responses than he could handle. The difficulty was that, despite the surprising number of priests out there who hankered after traditional Roman Sacraments and observances, and despite the fact that many of them had been shunted out of their parishes by bishops unwilling to put up with their traditionalist leanings, to date Traxi hadn't found a single man who came near the practiced priestliness, the solid theology, the pastoral experience and the zeal of Gutmacher.

"I tell you, Cessi"—Traxi paced the study at Windswept House—"if this Slavic pretender of a Pope lets things go much further, it won't be long before we'll be left with no priests at all!" Traxi remained a *sede vacantist,* as convinced as ever that the Church had not had a true Pope since 1958.

Cessi allowed herself to think he was just being his usual overdramatic, overemotional self.

Once she went over some of the applicants' dossiers he had brought with him, however, she began to see another dimension of the ecclesiastical tragedy against which she had battled for so long at Windswept House. She began to have some inkling of the numbers of good and willing priests who had been dismissed by their own bishops. Branded as troublesome clerics, and therefore unable to find a bishop willing to take them in, they had been left with no means of fulfilling their sacred vocations. Sadly Cessi had to admit that she had no solution to the problem.

Even the news that the Pontiff had sent Father Angelo off to establish Chapels dedicated to Our Lady of Fatima failed to ease the anguish Gutmacher knew she felt for the Church. For it made no sense to Cessi that any Pope who professed such fervent dedication to Fatima should also allow priests of obvious faith to be inadequately trained in the first place, and then hung out to dry by their own bishops, with no protest or protection from Rome.

As disturbed as Cessi was by these developments, a sudden crisis in Tricia's health forced her to put everything else aside for a few days. She was recommended to a specialist in Toronto who had had some success in treating at least the symptoms of keratoconjunctivitis sicca. Because his treatment involved drugs not licensed by the American Food and Drug Administration, Cessi and Tricia set off together for Canada.

Immediately on their return home, however, Cessi's thoughts were focused on the Vatican with a vengeance, by an urgent call from her New York financial advisor, Glenn Roche V. He had proved his worth many times over. Under his guidance, the Gladstone fortune of some $143 million that had been left by old Declan on his death in 1968 had multiplied handsomely. That, plus the fact that the Roches were one of New York's leading Catholic families, made Cessi's trust in him all but unshakable.

"I'm glad I found you at home."

"It sounds serious." Cessi responded more to the tension in Roche's voice than to his words.

"It's another crisis at the IRA, I'm afraid."

"Good Lord, Glenn!" When she heard the acronym for the Vatican's Institute of Religious Agencies, Cessi could hardly believe her ears. "The Vatican Bank again? The ink is hardly dry on my signature authorizing that loan to help bail them out of the stupid mess the BNL got us all into over Saddam Hussein's Condor Cannon, or whatever it was. They can't have gotten into another jumble so soon again!"

"Looks that way, Cessi."

"What's up with the IRA anyway? These crises have been going on for nearly twenty years. In 1974, they came to us for help in connection with the billion dollars Marco Santanni managed to siphon from their accounts. Then in 1982 they had to cover another billion or so that disappeared in connection with that other Italian financier—what was his name?"

"Rodolfo Salvi." Roche filled in the blank in Cessi's memory. "In fact, you could say we're dealing with the return of Salvi."

Though she hadn't remembered the man's name, there was no need to remind Cessi of the main points of the brouhaha he had created. An eminent international financier, Rodolfo Salvi had headed up the Banco Finanziario of Turin. Like the BNL, the Finanziario was an institution in which major equity was held by the Vatican Bank. And it seemed that Salvi had used IRA letters of credit to lend over a billion dollars of investors' money to persons or institutions unknown.

Suddenly, Salvi had fled Turin, taking with him a suitcase containing $400,000. Also in the suitcase, however—or so it was surmised—was documentation on the destination of the embezzled funds; and possibly some evidence to explain the reason for his own miserable ending. The embezzlement scandal that had been triggered when Salvi had turned up dead, suspended at the end of a rope from a bridge over the river Thames, had been a major calamity for Vatican banking. After bitter litigation, the IRA had agreed to reimburse some of the original investors with a token sum of $250,000—not as a tacit admission of guilt, but as a goodwill gesture. That was where Cessi had come in.

"Let me guess, Glenn." Cessi rested her head against the back of her chair. "Somebody has come up with Salvi's suitcase at last, and now there's the Devil to pay."

"You're only half right," Roche corrected her. "News of the suitcase has surfaced, but not the suitcase itself. It seems there was a conversation in which a bishop was involved. A junior member of the IRA and an expert on Eastern European finances by the name of Karol Novacy. Novacy hasn't revealed the names of the other men involved. But he felt under such pressure to get his hands on the Salvi suitcase that, after a hasty telephone call to Rome, he wrote his interlocutors a cashier's check. Financial circles got wind of it. Once that happened, the net result was that the check was cashed, and everyone ran to ground. A complete blanket of secrecy dropped around Novacy and the suitcase."

The story was intriguing. Still, what with her worry over Tricia, her concern for Chris's welfare and Traxi Le Voisin's incessant phone calls, she saw no reason why she should be involved.

"I think you've already guessed the reason, Cessi," Roche countered. "Novacy himself is safe and sound in the sovereign sanctuary of Vatican City. The whole world still wants to get hold of Salvi's suitcase. And they'd love to get their hands on Novacy, too. But the crisis for the Vatican Bank is that Novacy's check has placed a dangerous strain on the IRA's liquidity."

Roche was right. Cessi had guessed. Once again it was a question of succoring the IRA.

Even in ordinary circumstances Cessi had no qualms about approving the financial moves Glenn proposed. But the concrete circumstances within which the Vatican's calling for renewed Gladstone intervention began to lend a sudden new fascination to the moment. It dawned on her that if the Gladstone millions had been useful over the years to the IRA, she might reasonably think of speaking her piece in return. After all, she reasoned, she now had a son permanently stationed in the Rome of the Popes. And things had come to such a sorry pass at home that, for all of his *sede vacantist* fervor, Traxi Le Voisin was probably right. It wouldn't be long before the faithful would be left with no priests at all.

"I'll tell you what, Glenn." There was no mistaking the mischief in Cessi's response. "I'll sign the new documents. But this time, I want to do it in Rome. And this time I want to sit face to face with Dr. Giorgio Maldonado. And with Cardinal Amedeo Sanstefano." A lay banker, Maldonado was Director of the IRA. And, as head of the Vatican's Prefecture of Economic Affairs—the fabled PECA—Cardinal Sanstefano managed all the economic and financial holdings of the Holy See, and wielded extraordinary influence in and outside of Rome.

"Do you think they'll see me, Glenn?" Cessi thought it best to confront the question head-on.

"See you!" Roche laughed with surprise at the question. "In the mess they're in now, if you were to appear at their door at three in the morning they'd rush from their beds."

"It's settled, then. You'll have to give me some coaching, of course, if I'm to speak intelligently to the IRA officials. I'll go to New York on the way to the Vatican, if that's necessary."

Roche found the proposal worrisome. "Don't be bitten by the Roman bug," he warned. "Many have blue-skied about intervening in the hidden workings of the IRA. But there's something more over there. Something more than clever bankers."

"If they had clever bankers, Glenn," Cessi objected, "we wouldn't be having this conversation so soon after the BNL debacle. But we agree about one thing. There is something more over there. Or there should be. Maybe it's time they were reminded of that. Will you make the necessary arrangements with the IRA?"

Roche had no idea what plan Cessi might be hatching; but he knew he had little choice. He would make the necessary arrangements. He would even accompany her. But he had a condition of his own. "I've made scores of visits like this to our foreign associates, Cessi. I mean, highly confidential visits to deal with matters of grave international implications. And the Salvi suitcase affair ranks right up there with the most sensitive. For your own sake and for the Vatican's, our visit will have to be secret and short. In principle, no one must know what's going on. That means no visit with Christian while you're there, not even a phone call to say hello. We go in. We do the needful for the IRA. And we get out. All in one Roman hour. Agreed?"

"Agreed." Cessi purred into the phone. "We do the needful for the IRA. And maybe just a little bit for the Church."

Cessi Gladstone was not the only one impelled by urgent circumstances to focus with a lively interest on Vatican affairs. Nor was she anything like the most powerful. In the drama of the world's rush toward a new economic and political order among the nations, all the main protagonists understood that the coming two to four years would be seminal to the competing plans of the United States, Europe and the society of nations. By the fall of the year, one of those protagonists—the ad hoc Presidential Committee of Ten in Washington—had faced up to the need for a clarification of the policies of the Holy See, with specific and pointed reference to the Pontiff's near-term policies regarding the Soviet Union and its changing role in the wider world. The man appointed to carry that decision forward was the Committee's senior executive director, Admiral Bud Vance. And the man appointed to do the legwork—the man assigned to the required no-nonsense meeting with the Slavic Pope—was the junior executive director, Commander Gibson Appleyard.

In official Washington, where understanding concerning Vatican policies runs about as deep as a rain puddle, that procedure made sense. Appleyard, after all, not only had ample Soviet experience as a onetime Navy Intelligence officer. He had also been the one tapped by Cyrus Benthoek to sit in on that strange antipapal meeting in Strasbourg. And, after he had heard the Pope's "poor, poor Europe" letter read at the EC meeting in Brussels, Gib had been the first one to raise serious questions about the Pontiff's policies concerning Europe. That was enough to qualify Gib Appleyard as a ranking expert.

The meeting at which Admiral Vance gave Appleyard his orders was specific in its main purpose and fairly wide-ranging in its scope. "We both know the situation in the Soviet Union, Gib." Bud Vance settled himself behind his desk in his D.C. office, and took a swallow of black coffee. He wasn't much for sunrise briefings. "Still, I've been instructed to lay it all out for you; so here it is in a nutshell.

"We know the shaky position of Mikhail Gorbachev following that bogus coup attempt in August. We know the ambitions of Boris Yeltsin. We know the persistent strength of what the Western press calls 'the right,' or 'the conservative party'—and we know those are euphemisms for the leftover elements of the Communist Party, complete with the still surviving armed civilian apparatus of the Leninist Party-State. We know the economic dishevelment of the U.S.S.R. We know how ambitious, volatile and unreliable the officials of the Russian Orthodox Church are in the political mix. And we know that the population at large—nearly 150 million people—have no idea what the West means by 'democratic liberty'; and that they don't even know what they themselves want, much less how to go about getting it.

"In the face of all that, the Committee of Ten knows it can only be a matter of time before the personal dislike and political rivalry between Gorbachev and Yeltsin flares up. In other words, they've known that a policy decision would have to be made about the leadership over there."

Appleyard smiled at his senior officer. As a man who liked rising early, he was in a sprightlier mood than his boss. "You'll pardon my saying so, Bud. But it doesn't take a Committee of Ten genius to figure that Yeltsin won't forget he was bounced by Gorbachev as Moscow Party chief, and then deprived of his membership in the Moscow Politburo."

"Be that as it may," Vance conceded the point. "Since the failure of that pseudo coup d'état, the relations between those two men has deteriorated visibly. As long as Gorbachev remains in power, Yeltsin can't feel safe. As long as Yeltsin continues to amass popularity and power, Gorbachev will be foiled. Until now, the administration has been able to dance around the problem. On the one hand, we backed Gorbachev in an obvious way. As leader among the Europeans, Helmut Kohl of Germany dutifully followed suit. At the same time, we also courted Yeltsin. It was all very discreet, of course. For example, there were those among the inner circle of power brokers who entertained Yeltsin handsomely enough through the auspices of the Esalen Institute in California's Big Sur area."

Gib Appleyard knew the waffling American policy as well as Vance did. Well enough so that hearing some of the details this morning made him impatient. "Let's be frank. The fact is that our people can't agree on what sort of a post-Cold War world they really want, or on what role they want the United States to play in that world.

"First they came up with a position paper placing us as the world's so-called globo-cop. Then they came up with a new position for the United States as a diplomatic super-maven, insisting on a policy of collective action by the nations, and leaving little room for us to take unilateral action. If we follow that course, we'll become one with the community of nations all right; but only one.

"In a word, Bud, our people are at sixes and sevens. Some are in the Gorbachev camp, and some favor Yeltsin. But what we do about those two men matters in the wider scheme of things. It matters for the EC, for instance. Yet even there, we don't seem to have a clear policy. Within the Administration—and in the State Department, too, for that matter—there's something close to a shooting war between those who love the EC, those who hate it, and those who laugh at it."

"Okay, Gib." Bud Vance sighed. "We're in a mess over here. But now that you've brought it up, let's make the link between the Soviet Union and the EC. Specifically, let's talk about the Committee's decision to put our muscle behind Paul Gladstone.

"Despite Gladstone's influence or maybe because of it, that's one of the questions we need answered—the EC's new spirit of conquest and expansion that threatened us before has redoubled. When their planners speak nowadays of a Greater Europe, there's no doubt that they mean to include not only the original EC states but all the European states not yet a part of the EC, plus the newly liberated Soviet satellites, and eventually some if not most of the Soviet states.

"In other words, we're still faced with the possibility of a competitor too big for the United States to handle at this stage. We're still faced with the EC's race to form a Greater Europe that will include the entire Eastern bloc."

Appleyard could only agree. "We're right where we were last spring. We want the EC, but not quite yet."

"Not quite yet." Vance latched on to Gib's thought. "Not until Gorbachev is ready for his new position. Our only way of controlling this new Europe of the EC is through the Conference on Security and Cooperation in Europe. That is, through the CSCE with Gorbachev as its head."

Appleyard was taken aback at Vance's casual announcement that the United States intended to concentrate its geopolitical eggs, and Gorbachev, too, in the CSCE basket. At the same time, though, he was relieved that the high-muck-a-mucks had come up with a Soviet policy at last. "So if it's Gorbachev for the long run in Europe, then it has to be Yeltsin inside Russia. At least for the moment. What I don't see, though, is where a face-to-face meeting with the Slavic Pope comes into the plans of the Committee of Ten. They think the Pontiff is an idiot. What's more, they just plain don't like him."

"They don't exactly love Yeltsin either." Vance frowned. "But that's not the point. The Slavic Pope—and I underline the word Slavic—has shown that he is a geopolitical gambler of the first order. And in Eastern Europe and Russia, his personal experience is so deep, so extensive and so detailed, that he can probably run rings around the best of us. In our strategy to back Yeltsin inside Russia, then, we can't just bypass the Pope. Like it or not, he's a player. So we need two things.

"We need to know where the Pontiff will stand—where he's likely to throw his weight—when it comes to the impending changes in the Soviet Union. And we need to let him know that the United States will not brook any real interference by the Holy See in the disposition of Gorbachev."

Appleyard groaned. "All to be done in clear but diplomatic fashion, no doubt."

"No doubt. But there's a little more to the mission."

That figured, Gib thought. It made little sense to send an intelligence officer on what amounted to nothing more than a diplomat's mission.

Vance swiveled his chair around and pulled a file out of the cabinet behind his desk. "Our people have come up with a number of intercepts lately that suggest the Holy See has an active finger in a lot of pies. Take our friend Paul Gladstone, for instance. Do you recall the data we included in his dossier about that brother of his?"

Gib remembered. "A priest by the apt name of Christian, if I'm not mistaken. Does a part-time stint as a professor in Rome."

Admiral Vance thumbed through the file until he came to the pages he wanted. "It seems he's not a professor anymore. He's suddenly been tapped as a full-timer attached to the Vatican's Secretariat of State. He's begun traveling around Europe at a fast pace. And he's taken to seeing a lot of his brother on some sort of official Vatican business.

"We'd like to know more about what's going on there. Aside from that, though, another name has popped up in our intelligence intercepts. A priest by the name of Angelo Gutmacher. It seems he's a close personal friend of the Gladstones. And it seems that, like Christian Gladstone, he, too, has recently been inhaled for full-time service to the Holy See.

"I don't believe in coincidence. His link with the Slavic Pope on the one hand and with the Gladstones on the other is too curious to overlook. We don't know what to make of him exactly. Like this Father Christian, he travels a lot. Sets up Fatima chapels. But we don't think that's the whole thing. Gutmacher goes from Germany to Lithuania to Russia to the Ukraine. He stays a short while in each place. Preaches. Blesses statues. That sort of thing. Then he moves on and starts all over again."

Appleyard followed Vance's logic without difficulty. "So you think these two are papal couriers of some sort? Or perhaps they're into humint—influencing minds, turning spies, laying down networks."

"Maybe a bit of both." Vance nodded. "We do know from intercepts that the Pope is in communication with Gorbachev, though. And that's obviously capital for us just now. We know they talk by letters; but they don't use the diplomatic pouch or any ordinary means. How, then? If the answer to that question is Angelo Gutmacher, then we're not dealing with some small-fry itinerant priest." Vance turned the pages of the intelligence folder with a sudden show of impatience. "To tell you the truth, Gib, I'm nervous about this whole idea of approaching the Pope. We just don't know enough about him, or the people around him. I keep coming back to that Strasbourg meeting you attended last spring. If that group is serious about an in-house insurrection against this Pope, then a lot of things will be up for grabs. But we can't get a line on any of it. It doesn't seem to be going anywhere. We've tracked the Vatican huskies who were there—Cardinal Pensabene and Cardinal Aureatini and the Jesuit Father-General and the rest of them. But it looks to me like they're all just going about their normal business. Cardinal Maestroianni has been retired as Secretary of State, so he may be out of that loop altogether. And the Pope himself has made this fellow called Graziani a Cardinal and bumped him up to be the new Secretary of State.

"As for Maestroianni's pal Cyrus Benthoek, he's got more connections in high places over here than you can shake a stick at. And they all vouch for him a hundred percent. Everyone seems to be straight, in other words. The only real mystery man at that Strasbourg gathering is Otto Sekuler. We're still on it, but so far we can't make head or tail of him. You'll see what we've got when you study the data for yourself."

Appleyard listened to Vance's troubled musings with a sympathetic ear. He didn't like unexplainable situations dangling over his head any more than the Admiral did. Surely he had been invited to that Strasbourg meeting to receive an off-the-record message. Still, if Bud was right—if nothing more had come of the Strasbourg plot in the several months since May—

then the message simply was that daggers were drawn inside the Vatican administration. That was interesting; but it applied to just about any administration in the world these days.

"Listen, Bud." Gib finally intervened in his partner's speculations. "The fact that we know trouble may be brewing around the Pope puts us that much ahead of where we were before. We know enough to be on the lookout. But this Pontiff's in the driver's seat for the moment. So the Committee is right. He's the man we have to deal with. Let's just have our man in Rome set the meeting with the Pope. I'll go to Rome a few days early and try to get a line on those two wandering priests, Gladstone and Gutmacher. Who knows? If we keep digging long enough, one thing may lead to another."

"Let's hope so." Slim pickings though it was, Vance shoved his intelligence file across his desk to his colleague. "So, Commander." The mischievous glint in Bud's eye broke the tension. "That leaves just one more question to answer this morning. Are you up to a face-to-face meeting on Soviet policy with the man who brought the Berlin Wall tumbling down?"

"Up to it!" Gib grinned. "I can hardly wait!"

Appleyard couldn't believe his luck. It wasn't only the Strasbourg meeting that had piqued serious interest in the Slavic Pope. Ever since that day in Brussels when England's fussy Herbert Featherstone-Haugh had read the Pope's enigmatic personal letter to the EC's ad hoc Selection Committee—ever since he had heard the Pontiff's words that had echoed his own thoughts about "poor, poor Europe"—Gib had longed for a chance to probe the papal mind. To find out if he was in fact an independent geopolitical thinker. To find out if he, too, was unconvinced by Europe's current fervor to remake itself into the guiding force in building the New World Order.

Appleyard hadn't expected an opportunity like this, of course. So he had decided to get at the papal mind through a study of the Pontiff's major speeches and published writings. And the more he had read, the more intrigued he had become.

Given his own bent of mind, colored as it was by the mystical elements of his Rosicrucian Masonry, Appleyard couldn't help but be encouraged by some of what he discovered. Nor did he feel he was being in any way unprofessional in such an approach. Any fool could see that some coordination between the Pope's policies and those of the United States would be enhanced if the same goals—at least, the same near-term goals—were shared by the Holy See and the Lodge. There was only so much to be gleaned from the public statements of any world-class official. But Appleyard had managed to form a fairly specific picture in his mind of the Slavic Pope. There was no denying that the Pontiff was a highly educated man; an intellectual of unusual caliber. He was a modern leader, and as widely experienced as any secular head of state. There were even signs that he might secretly have taken a step across the void from irrational attachment to primitive beliefs and onto the terrain of human reason.

The trouble was that there were also contradictions involved with this Pope that baffled Gib. He found documented evidence, for example, that the Slavic Pope saw all religions as true avenues to spiritual salvation. Even such things as African voodoo, Papuan animism and the millenarianism of Jehovah's Witnesses were included in this Pope's ministry. But the practical point for the American was that the Pontiff showed none of the usual insistence that all men and women become Roman Catholics.

On the secular side, there was evidence that the Slavic Pope was way ahead of all the One-Worlders, all the Bilderburgers, all the New Agers. Signs that he was way ahead of the Global 2000 stuff of Jimmy Carter and the Club of Rome.

Nevertheless, Appleyard found plenty of evidence within the Pope's published writings of the stark and radical differences that had set the Church at loggerheads with the Lodge in modern times. And at loggerheads with U.S. policy as well. Like the Lodge—and like the Church itself for all its history—the Slavic Pope refused to observe any boundaries of territory or peoples or cultures. Inherently universalist, the Pontiff included all lands, all nations and all individuals in his ambitions. He maintained the claim of his Church to be of transcendental character. To be able to nourish and develop the spiritual and moral nature of humankind. To be best and prime at teaching mankind how to live together, to develop spiritual and ethical values and thus to establish peace on earth and to prosper. All of that the Slavic Pope shared with the Lodge. But as he combed the Pope's writings and speeches, Appleyard ran up against one profound difference that overshadowed all the similarities.

Time and again the Pontiff harped on the Roman Catholic purpose to help all men and women achieve a goal above and distinct from human nature and natural capacities. He harped on that goal as the supernatural life of the soul, which is finally achieved only when physical death sets in and the individual is translated into another dimension by a gratuitous act of God. It was that super-nature aimed at by Roman Catholics, and apparently by this Pope, that simply did not square with the modern Masonic ideal of perfecting man's nature within the observable and attainable boundaries of the cosmos.

One of the many reasons Appleyard valued Masonry and the Masonic way of life was its humanly beautiful thought and language. Masonry was not a metaphysical system. Not a dogma. Not a definitive mystical revelation of a unique, unchangeable truth. It was a way of life by which the individual was initiated into the indispensable symbolic instruments for his becoming constantly more perfect in tracking and identifying the Supreme Intelligence present behind the facade of the cosmos.

By contrast, and for all of the beauty and marvelous humanism of its tradition, Roman Catholicism retained and even depended upon discordant strains not to be found in Masonry. There was a baby shivering in a manger with his homeless and indigent parents. There was a Crucifix with the twisted body of a man dying in his own blood. There was a resurrected Christ disappearing beneath a golden halo into the clouds. And there was that absolutist dogma about what some of Appleyard's more vulgar friends called "pie in the sky when we die."

Appleyard himself neither spoke nor thought in such lampooning terms. His empathy allowed him no such contempt. But he knew that the Masonic way simply made more sense. It was this rational, unheated, clear-minded confidence in man's creation of a peaceful, just and fraternal society of nations that gave Masonry its beauty and humanistic charm. Even when he was dealing with the starkest necessities and demands of U.S. policy, Gib had always looked toward the ideal of the Temple. And he had always kept the solemn oath that had marked his own induction into the 30th Degree of Scottish Masonry, the Knights Kadosh, some twenty years before. The oath to "strictly obey the Statutes and Directives of this Dreaded Tribunal . . . which I hereby acknowledge as my Supreme Judge."

It was supremely important for Appleyard, as a man and as a Mason, to find what appeared to be a kindred attitude in the writings of the Slavic Pope. There was a dimension to this man that clicked in Appleyard's mind like tumblers in a lock. A purity of outlook and a dedication of purpose he had found in no other world leader.

What was as surprising as it was appealing for a man as idealistic as Appleyard was this Pope's constant professional care not only for geopolitical strategy but for the strategic necessities of life. This Pontiff concerned himself with everything. With wantonness of agricultural policies. With the responsibilities and values of democratic society. With scientific irresponsibility, water rights, labor unions, housing, medical care, genetics, astrophysics, athletics, opera. The sheer impact with which his words were tailored to suit the cultures of over eighty nations was something to admire.

So impressed was Appleyard as the day approached for his departure for Rome that he had to remind himself that, without good and sufficient reasons of state, it would be out of the question in his conversation with the Holy Father to raise the question of the antipapal meeting at Strasbourg. Still, he couldn't help but wonder how the prelates he had met there could fail to realize what a giant of a leader they had in the Slavic Pope. And he couldn't help but anticipate his own meeting with the Pontiff in the most sanguine terms.

Unlike the main protagonists in the global push to a New World Order, the Cardinal of Centurycity did not look to Rome for anything. Beyond a certain level of mutual protection, in fact, the only thing His Eminence wanted from the Vatican was to be left to run his well-oiled Machine without interference.

Naturally, exceptions had to be made from time to time. At that special theological consultation to which he had been invited in Rome, for example. His Eminence's good friends Cardinal Maestroianni and Cardinal Pensabene had made a persuasive case for his close cooperation with them in the formation of a new ad hoc Internal Affairs Committee within the National Conference of Catholic Bishops.

The idea of the plan was appealing for the Cardinal of Centurycity. In the very heart of the NCCB, His Eminence's new IAC would be fundamental to the formulation of the Common Mind of U.S. bishops, and of bishops throughout the Church, about the all-important issue of Apostolic unity between themselves and the Slavic Pope.

His first order of business upon his return to Centurycity had been to form the foundational elements of his new IAC. That is, to induct those bishops who would serve as the Cardinal's principal "upper-level facilitators." Each of the five residential bishops chosen knew why he had been tapped by His Eminence. The first consideration in each case was moral character. His Eminence knew the weakness of each bishop, and felt no compunction about using that information. The second consideration was the mind-set of each man regarding Church matters.

The prime example of the desired type was the bishop from Connecticut, Kevin Rahilly. His Celtic frankness, animated by his unmitigated gall, had qualified him early as a leader in the effort to de-Romanize, and to Americanize, the churches in his diocese. A capital fellow, then. Equally desirable was New York State's Bishop Manley Motherhubbe, who had long been recognized for his dedication to rid the Church of what he called "its deplorable, outdated Romanism and superstitions."

A second man from New York State, Primas Rochefort, was intense in his glad handedness. The major quality that recommended him was a joie de vivre nourished at the fleshpots of the sweet life.

Michigan's influential Bishop Bruce Longbottham seemed a more substantial figure. He kept up a constant refrain of public apologies for "the sexist and patriarchal sins" of his Church, and was given to sporting designer slacks and pigeon-blue turtleneck sweaters. The Cardinal's core group was rounded out by the most eye-catching of his "upper-level change agents." Archbishop Cuthbert Delish of Lackland City, Wisconsin, who appeared to be nothing less than a walking advertisement for justice and probity.

The rapidity with which His Eminence of Centurycity was able to educate these five foundational members of his fledgling Internal Affairs Committee was wonderful. Admittedly, the Cardinal was at his best when presiding with a steel hand sheathed in a velvet glove over miscreant clerics of subordinate grade. The frost was barely on the pumpkin, then, before the Cardinal traveled to St. Olaf's parish in the diocese of Rosedale,

Minnesota, for a final operations briefing with his handpicked episcopal "facilitators." Immediately following the briefing, he would lead his collaborators into the first full meeting of his newly formed Internal Affairs Committee, set to take place in St. Olaf's basement hall.

Though the choice of this out-of-the-way site for their gathering was unusual, it was also wise. Certainly it could not have been held at the Washington headquarters of the NCCB, where media attention would have been attracted as a matter of course. Indeed, for all of its life span, the IAC would guard its inner proceedings as strictly confidential.

The Cardinal was adamant that his core collaborators be clear on the methods of operation to be used in order to affect the mental attitude of every United States bishop. Clarity was essential to success. The first point to be reviewed, then, was the need for strict compartmentation. Maestroianni and Pensabene had been emphatic about that; and so, too, was the Cardinal of Centurycity.

"This IAC will operate at the episcopal level." His Eminence looked at each of the five bishops in turn. "Although you will have to keep higher ranks informed, no one above the grade of bishop is to be meaningfully involved—present company excepted. The bishops themselves must be taught—inured, rather—to think as Kevin Rahilly does. They must learn to think in an American way. In essence, all of our IAC operations will be designed to this end. And always, crucial ecclesiastical and doctrinal issues will be involved. For instance, one of your auxiliary bishops will write an article declaring in good, egalitarian American style that it's high time women were ordained to the priesthood. Immediately, he must be backed up by a flood of supporting statements in diocesan newspapers, public conferences and the general media. The bishop originating the article will have to withdraw his statement—temporarily, of course—due to pressure that is sure to come from the papal office. We do not mind that. It does not count for much.

"What will count will be the effect on the NCCB. Because that proposal will have come from a bishop, and because of a flood of support from the grass-roots level, this Internal Affairs Committee will be forced to adduce the weighty considerations that have been raised. As an official Committee of the National Conference of Catholic Bishops, we could not be expected to do otherwise.

"Now, some of our bishops do still have a tendency to be unduly swayed by instructions from the papal office. And I want to remind you that we can expect a steady drizzle of such Roman interference as we proceed with our operations over the coming year. Therefore, I emphasize that the priority of this Internal Affairs Committee is precisely what its name declares it to be: *Internal* Affairs. Within the boundary limits of the United States, we are the Church. Rome is not based within our borders and has no place here. The general membership of the National Conference of Catholic Bishops will rely on this new IAC of ours to determine the official attitude of agreement or disagreement with the Holy See."

All heads turned as His Eminence's personal secretary, the attractive Father Oswald Avonodor, poked his face into the room and announced that all who had been invited to the general IAC meeting were assembled and waiting. The call was a timely one. His Eminence knew he had said all that was needed.

The bishops were happy enough to troop downstairs behind the Cardinal into the basement hall, where the bite of the cold weather was offset less by St. Olaf's meager heating plant than by the intensity of the thirty-odd individuals who greeted them. For, one and all, they were animated by the fervor of crusaders, of trailblazers, of an elite vanguard. Indeed, by the fervor of insiders at private plannings for great events. At least on the central proposition of this meeting—on the proposition that the Slavic Pope had to go for the good of the Church—all hearts beat as one.

Technically speaking, all present—including His Eminence of Centurycity—were guests of Rosedale's Bishop Raymond A. Luckenbill. And it was only to be expected that the easygoing Bishop would be surrounded by some half dozen of his easygoing parish priests and the easygoing Chancellor of his diocese. Still, no one had any illusions as to who was running this show. Still, as if to underscore the point, His Eminence of Centurycity was accompanied not only by Father Oswald Avonodor but by the Cardinal's well known hatchet man, Auxiliary Bishop Ralph E. Goodenough, a husky, balding, double-chinned bulk of a man with the small, calculating eyes of a barroom bouncer.

The procedure was orderly. As His Eminence called out their names, the three most prominent leaders of the U.S. feminist movement among women religious stood, each in her own place, to be recognized for her notable contributions to the American Church. Sister Fran Fedora from the West Coast was resplendent in her black-and-purple liturgical vestments. Sister Helen Hammentick of New Orleans paled by comparison in her severely cut business suit. Sister Cherisa Blaine of Kansas City, already famous for mixing Wicca practices in church worship.

Introduced next were a representative from America's largest group of men who styled themselves as "ex-priests," and a prominent member of Dignity, the Roman Catholic organization for homosexually active clerics and layfolk. Once the special guests had been recognized and welcomed, Sister Fran Fedora was invited to open the proceedings with a prayer. She invoked matriarchal blessings from Mother Earth and from Sophia, the goddess of wisdom.

With a perfunctory Amen to Sister's invocation, His Eminence turned his attention to the full gathering of residential and auxiliary bishops from twenty or so dioceses around the nation. Each had been handpicked for charter membership in this IAC by the Cardinal himself or, with his ultimate approval, by one or another of his core group of five. "Welcome!"

His Eminence greeted them all with a businesslike smile. "Welcome," he began again, "members and guests of the IAC of the U.S.A." Applause.

"At my request"—the Cardinal waved an imperious hand toward his distinguished associate from Lackland City—"Archbishop Delish has prepared a background report that you will all find useful." Archbishop Cuthbert Delish rose from his chair like justice itself, ready to separate the goats from the sheep. "We can safely assume two things," he announced. "First, there is currently a small majority of bishops in this country who have doubts about the possibility of any truly effective unity between themselves and the present Pope. Second, those who disagree openly with this majority are few. That is the strong basic foundation upon which we begin our work." It was true, of course, as Delish pointed out, that "a certain quota of dissidents is a healthy sign." Nevertheless, it only made sense to read out a short list of the most troublesome of those dissidents, and a considerably longer list of those whom he described as "fence-sitters."

That brought the Archbishop to the second portion of his background report. "Up until now, each of us has had some success at the skillful nourishment and development of new customs and attitudes among clergy and laity. Now, however, they must all be habituated as never before to hearing us disagree with instructions coming from the papal office. It must become a normal trait of Catholic life that our local churches disagree with Roman directives, and opt tranquilly instead to go their own way."

Archbishop Delish expanded on this principle with examples of sermons that might be preached, articles that might be published, interviews that might be given, public encounter groups that might be formed, media outlets to which they might make themselves readily available. "The point to keep in mind is this," Delish summed up neatly. "Once faced with customs already established and with attitudes already ingrained, there is not much Rome can do, is there?"

The response was a restrained but confident ripple of laughter. Only Bishop Rahilly of Connecticut felt the need to amplify Delish's remarks. "The point I make is this: We don't announce anything as new or innovative. We just go ahead and do what we will. That's how I arranged things in my own diocese with the modernization of the Mass. We didn't tell the people we were going to change, but we just went ahead and did it. The people fell into line like obedient dominoes. As simple as that."

Archbishop Delish gave a nod of approval to Rahilly for his contribution. Addressing the IAC's special guests, he gave his recommendation for "quiet persistence in action" and his assurance of support from this new Internal Affairs Committee of the NCCB. To the permanent members and "change agents" of the IAC, he gave a copy of his list of dissident bishops.

Never a man to gild the lily, His Eminence of Centurycity stood up abruptly, clapped his hands once as the seal of common resolution and, with Father Oswald Avonodor at his heels, carried himself out the door.

The Cardinal's auxiliary bishop, Ralph Goodenough, remained behind just long enough to run his little hatchet-man eyes speculatively over each attendee. The three visiting nuns stared him down as best they could. Bishop Luckenbill gave him an easygoing smile. The claque of bishops put up with the implied threat as an unnecessary bit of icing on the cake. It was only a minute or two before Bishop Goodenough traced His Eminence's footsteps out of St. Olaf's and into the waiting limousine. Everything was under control.

"Did you not assure us that everything was under control, Eminence?"

Angry but helpless at the obvious displeasure in the Guardian's voice, the Cardinal of Centurycity tightened his grip on the red telephone receiver until his knuckles showed white. Once back in his residence, he had relaxed from the strain of his trip to Rosedale over a quiet dinner and then had settled down in his study for a little catch-up paperwork. The last thing he needed was to have his peace of mind shattered by the red security phone jangling in its special case on his desk. In the dark about what might have raised the Guardian's dander, and unwilling to cop a plea in any case, His Eminence made no reply to what was obviously meant as an accusation and a reproach.

"You assured us," the Guardian supplied the missing clue, "that your handling of the Scalabrini case was secure. As I recall, your exact words were 'All's well that ends well.' "

His Eminence felt the blood drain from his face.

"Unfortunately," the Guardian continued, "the matter is not at all tidy. Our information is that the man who took care of Scalabrini may be ready to 'turn,' just as Scalabrini did. You must clean up this affair, Your Eminence. Definitively this time. Otherwise, it could be troublesome. Troublesome for us all."

The Guardian's voice was replaced by a click and the sound of the dial tone.

His Eminence frowned. Then, as the tumblers dropped into place in his mind, he buzzed for Father Michael Avonodor. By the time the young priest roused himself from bed and appeared in pajamas and robe at the study door, the Cardinal knew exactly what had to be done.

"Call Bishop Ralph Goodenough," he ordered. "I want to see him here first thing tomorrow morning."

"Right away, Eminence."

"And one more thing. Tell Goodenough to pack an overnight bag. I want him on an early flight to Detroit."

PART TWO
Papal Twilight

XXVIII

THAT GIBSON APPLEYARD had managed to glean even a meager sense of a consistent papal policy should have given him an advantage over every other geopolitical strategist in Washington and around the world, not to mention every expert in the Vatican as well. And yet, perhaps his main advantage was that he understood that it was evening time for the Roman papacy, just as surely as it was evening for the NATO alliance, for the European Community, for the Anglo-American Establishment, for U.S.A. world hegemony and for the Marxist-Socialist utopian dreamers of this almost spent twentieth century. A long and tedious and agonizing day was drawing to a close over the heads of the nations now. The clear reliable perspective of daytime was yielding to twilight. Accurate perception even of the most familiar objects was becoming difficult. Fears of dissolution, awareness of mortal enemies as yet unidentified, ignorance of the near future, growing discomfort with present conditions—now began to rustle and rise free from the darkening byways of the nations.

Thus an Appleyard would categorize the volatility in the wills of nations faced with a Bosnia and a Rwanda: the ethical clarity achieved in the glare of World War II had faded. Thus also he would classify the on-again, off-again papacy of the Slavic Pope: utter and obstinate firmity on sexual morality varying with an apparent looseness of former dogmatic tenets about who could be saved for Heaven and who had the last word on earth. Twilight over his papacy hastened to enshroud him, playing games with everyone's perception and making progress more dangerous by the minute. Thus the papal twilight enveloped all those—friends, collaborators, enemies—involved in his papacy. At the heel of the hunt, when the darkness of night fell upon this papacy, it would be difficult to decide who cut the most pathetic figure: The masses of faithful Roman Catholics? Those who had served the Slavic Pope at great personal cost? Or the Slavic Pope himself?

Of course, there were those in the Vatican and the world at large who welcomed twilight as a happy companion on their own journey of extremes. Indeed, as far as Cardinal Cosimo Maestroianni and his growing cadre of collaborators could see, the sun seemed already to be rising on their plans. After all, the Pope was unable to govern the Church Universal in any effective way.

Further, the machinery designed to pressure the Pope to resign for the sake of Church unity and for his own peace of mind was all but taking on a life of its own. The new ad hoc Internal Affairs Committees being established within the National and Regional Conferences of Bishops around the world were shaping up as the biggest and most perfect flywheel in the antipapal machinery.

No one understood better than Maestroianni that Europe had to be the linchpin in the antipapal mechanism. Catholicism in this ancient heartland of Christianity carried a special prestige that went far beyond theology and devotion, and reached deep into social life, culture and politics. Indeed, there never had been a time when the European hierarchies were not hip deep in politics—national, European and universal.

In principle, therefore, it should be easy to bring the National and Regional Bishops Conferences of Europe into line in the matter of the Common Mind Vote. Play into their divisions, and at the same time lever them into a politicking situation, and the European bishops would react predictably. Once Europe had been won, the Common Mind Vote elsewhere would be one of the few certainties in an uncertain world. His Eminence of Centurycity would oversee things in the United States because the National and Regional Conferences of Bishops in the U.S.A. all but belonged to him. As for the Canadians, it was the general Vatican opinion that they could be counted on to trot along about six months behind the Americans. In Latin America, the ravages of liberation theology had combined with post-Vatican II spirituality and liturgies to dig a deep fissure between the Slavic Pope and the National and Regional Conferences of Bishops. As for Asia and Africa, the Bishops Conferences on those continents would fall into step readily enough. For, like the Americans, the Africans and Asians had a follow-my-leader history with regard to Europe.

If it was true that the European bishops were the key to a successful Common Mind Vote around the world, it was doubly true that Cyrus Benthoek's inspired idea to deliver the European Economic Community as a major fulcrum of episcopal persuasion was the key to the European bishops. Not many even among the most retrograde bishops would long resist the political and practical advantages that could be brought to bear. Not many who would wish to be left behind by the new Greater Europe being fashioned by the EC. Not many who would long doubt the wisdom of being one with the Common Mind of their fellow bishops. With Father Christian Gladstone working the European bishops under Maestroianni's direction, and with Secretary-General Paul Gladstone's easy access to the EC's Commissioners and its Council of European Foreign Ministers, the table was set for the feast.

Wisely, His Eminence Maestroianni began to think about bolstering the roster of suitable candidates to replace the Slavic Pope. Surely it was time for Maestroianni to have a word with Cardinal Secretary Giacomo Graziani about securing the red hat for Father-General Coutinho. And for a few others besides. Nor was it too soon to see the last of a man like the Master-General of the Dominican Order, for one. Father Damien Slattery was more than a personal annoyance for Cardinal Maestroianni. He was one of the few stalwarts of any rank at the side of the Slavic Pope.

How fortunate, then, that the next General Chapter of the Dominicans was due to take place in March of the coming year. One such Chapter had voted Slattery in as Master-General of the Order. If Maestroianni's clout counted for anything, the coming Chapter would vote him into perpetual exile from Rome. After that, Slattery would be fair game.

Maestroianni wasn't the only Cardinal who had ideas about Vatican personnel. His Eminence Silvio Aureatini was becoming deeply edgy about Father Aldo Carnesecca. Ever since that October day in 1978 when he and Carnesecca had sat with the then Cardinal Secretary of State, Jean-Claude de Vincennes, at the triage of documents for two dead Popes, he had realized that evidence touching on the ceremony of the Prince's Enthronement within the Citadel might have been discovered and shown to the September Pope. Aureatini's suspicions had fallen squarely on Aldo Carnesecca.

Aureatini had never progressed from suspicion to certainty. The offending evidence had remained buried in the Vatican Archives, and no whiff of it had surfaced. Nevertheless, he felt it wouldn't do any longer to wait for Carnesecca to die a natural death. A more prudent way was needed to tidy the matter, a task His Eminence carried out with silken ease one afternoon in his office at the Secretariat.

The sharp-nosed Cardinal explained to Carnesecca that the Archbishop of Palermo and the other bishops of Sicily had decided to cooperate with the Italian police and the intelligence services of the Italian armed forces in an all-out assault on the Sicilian Mafia. The Vatican would serve as the clearinghouse for all communications between the bishops, the police and the intelligence operatives. One person in the Vatican would be designated as overall coordinator of communications and operations. The most sensitive link in the setup, as the Cardinal was sure Father Aldo would see, concerned communications. Everyone knew that telephones and the mails were unreliable. A courier was needed, therefore. Someone who had been engaged in clandestine work before and who could travel back and forth unnoticed for as long as necessary to secure all coordination points between the collaborating agencies and the bishops.

The timetable was still loose, of course. Until the courier system was running well, it would not be possible to pinpoint the exact strike date; the day when a general roundup of all active mafiosi would be carried out by units of Italy's Special Forces. But on the morning of that near-future day, the bishops themselves would issue the go signal in the form of a pastoral letter condemning and excommunicating all mafiosi. And television and radio would be coordinated to make this double blow of open condemnation and mass arrest devastating for the criminal organization.

Aureatini decided to whet the good Father's appetite with a detailed overview of the projected move against the Mafia. He took out a sheaf of briefing papers, and the two men went over everything. Maps, names, dates, contact points, passwords, statistics, personnel outlines, recognition signals, telephone numbers. Carnesecca made some recommendations based on past experience, and His Eminence adopted them without hesitation. "I'm young at this stuff, Father." He smiled in self-deprecation. "It's another case of the old dog for the long road, but the pup for the puddle."

Carnesecca laughed. But he knew Aureatini was already a trained bloodhound. And he knew in his bones that something was wrong. Instinct told him that buried somewhere was a lethal gap, a dangerous proviso, an innocuous detail that would leave his back exposed. Yet nothing seemed awry in Aureatini's explanations, or in the details of the plans they reviewed together. He could discover no plausible reason to back up his worry, and no reasonable excuse to extract himself from the situation.

"Now," Cardinal Aureatini wrapped up his sales pitch. "If you consent to the mission, you will have no cause for concern about the Vatican end of things. I shall be the overall coordinator at this end. So, what do you say, Father? Is it a go?"

Father Carnesecca cringed almost visibly at the news that Aureatini would be the Vatican coordinator; and he didn't like the narrow timing that had been left to him. He remained silent about the first point, but not about the second. "If everything is poised to begin, Eminence, my preparations will be rushed. Haste and hurry are the parents of fatal mistakes . . ."

Unwilling to hear any such thought, Aureatini cut in with a hasty disclaimer. "There's no worry about that, Father. You've seen all the plans. Your backup is professional. Strictly state-of-the-art."

". . . But," Carnesecca continued as if the Cardinal hadn't spoken, "given the pressure of events, Your Eminence, I shall undertake this mission for the Holy See."

The Cardinal slapped the desk with the palm of one hand. What a pity, he thought, that Cardinal Secretary Vincennes hadn't lived to savor this day.

During his first few months spent at the heart of fundamental confusion in this twilight Rome of the Slavic Pope, it was difficult for Christian Gladstone to sort out the different sectors of the Vatican that reached out to engulf him. Each one seemed to have an agenda for him. Despite his instinctive antipathy for Cardinal Maestroianni, the very simplicity of His Eminence's instructions fascinated the young scholar-priest. And it was a downright blessing for him that the M Project—for so Chris had dubbed his mission for Maestroianni—was grueling in its demands.

In the early going, the Cardinal assigned a new roster of European bishops for Gladstone to visit every few weeks, and each schedule came with a mountain of background data to be digested beforehand. The purpose of every visit was to enable Christian to complete a simply worded questionnaire. None of the bishops saw that document, of course; nor did they even know of its existence. But in the questions he asked all across the Continent, Gladstone was guided by the items on that questionnaire.

Chris found that most bishops he visited opened up to him with a candor he found disturbing. Perhaps it was that mantle of Vatican authority Maestroianni had spoken of. Whatever it was, Gladstone got an ecclesiastical earful wherever he traveled. He found among the bishops of Europe a universal feeling of a great lack in the Church. A general feeling that the unity of the Church itself was at risk. Still such sentiments came across to Christian as no more than that; as no more than sentiments. He found no real clarity of thought, no crispness of vision. Even the desire for closer papal unity itself was vague. Everything was expressed in terms of "perhaps." Perhaps the bishops would find again the solidity they had once enjoyed. Perhaps the Holy Spirit would inspire the papal mind to a new understanding of their difficulties in dealing with a new world that was defining itself in terms of finance and commerce. Perhaps . . . Perhaps . . .

At the same time—and despite their own laments over their bygone unity with the Holy Father—what also came across to Gladstone was the strength of the National and Regional Bishops Conferences that had been formed everywhere following the Second Vatican Council. Every bishop he met appeared to give more practical weight to those Conferences than to the Holy See. Rome was no longer the hub of authority; it figured now as only one of many hubs.

Among all of his discoveries, however, Christian never found any trace of love or any sense of deep respect for the Slavic Pope.

Disturbing though it was for him, the portrait of the Church that formed in Christian's mind caused him to hope that this assignment had been designed to do exactly what His Eminence had said at the outset—"to help us overcome problems some of our bishops appear to be encountering." With that thought as his spur, Chris was able to manage as many as three or four episcopal visits at a single regional swing. After each exhausting foray, he would hurry back to Rome, where he would complete the required questionnaires and prepare himself for thorough personal debriefings by Cardinal Maestroianni and other members of the upper echelons of the Vatican administration.

Those debriefing sessions gave him his first direct glimpse into the power structure of the Holy See. There were even isolated moments when he was tempted to a gentle hope that he was on his way into the heart of Rome. Moments when he almost thought that Rome as the Eternal City might open up to him as the best in beauty, the most ancient in wisdom, the most fatherly in sentiment. Moments when he felt he might glimpse its high gates accessing the universe, God's immortality and the lambent glory clothing the Rock of Ages. Yet each such moment gave way soon enough to reality. There was always something to remind Christian that he was a pygmy outsider, an impersonal cog in an unheeding machine, a gofer who would never penetrate beyond those gates of privilege or bathe in that glory.

After a month and more of intensive work, one debriefing session opened a day that was to provide Gladstone with a perfect paradigm of those two extremes that defined his early tenure in Roman service. Summoned without warning to an early-morning conference in the Vatican Secretariat, he was presented by His Eminence Maestroianni to no fewer than seven ranking Cardinals as "our valued new associate." Cardinal Silvio Aureatini and Cardinal Secretary Giacomo Graziani were present, and Graziani smiled his welcome to Gladstone, blinked often, said little and listened well. Two visiting prelates—England's Cardinal Lionel Boff and His Eminence Schuytteneer of Belgium—confined themselves to minor roles in the debriefing session, so Chris couldn't tell what to make of them. By contrast, Cardinal Azande of Africa's Gold Coast had many wide-ranging questions to put to Gladstone. Cardinal Noah Palombo was dour to the point of acidity, but his mind was incisive and his interest encompassed everything. His Eminence Leo Pensabene had a curious habit of emphasizing each of his questions by popping a bony finger into the air—an idiosyncrasy that seemed to annoy the sharp-featured Aureatini no end. As inquisitors, however, Pensabene and Aureatini were every bit as penetrating and all-inclusive in their probing as Palombo or Azande or Maestroianni himself.

Without exception, those Cardinals showed a lively interest in Christian's assessment of the bishops he had seen so far in France, Belgium, Holland, Austria and Germany. All appeared worried that the Holy Father was not understood by some of his bishops. So satisfied did they seem, in fact, with Christian's answers that when the moment came for him to leave them to their private deliberations, Cardinal Azande rose to shake the American's hand and give him a generous word of appreciation.

" 'Well done, thou good and faithful servant.' The Shona people in my Africa say, 'The sugar is over.' But you, Father Gladstone, have sweetened life for us. Thank you!"

It wouldn't have been half enough true to say that Christian was elated as he left the Apostolic Palace that morning. With Azande's sentiments fresh in his ears, Chris was halfway across St. Peter's Square when he heard his name called in the unmistakable Irish baritone that belonged to Father Damien Slattery.

"Have you had lunch yet, lad?" The Master-General forced a smile as he fell into stride beside Christian.

All during the cab ride to Springy's eatery and through most of lunch Slattery was regaled with a rundown of the heavyweight Cardinals who had so earnestly sought Chris's advice that morning. Damien was alarmed that Chris had been swept off his feet by the Cardinals who had shown such an interest in his work for Maestroianni. It was clear that the young American was becoming disillusioned all over again with what he saw as the Holy Father's disregard for the declining state of the institutional Church.

"Look, *Padre.*" The Master-General took advantage of the first significant pause in Gladstone's excited monologue. "I don't want to prick your balloon. But those huskies you met with this morning could have set a lot of things right in the Church before now, if that was what they were after."

Gladstone shook his head. "That's just it, Father Damien. No one is more surprised than I. I'd give my life in service to the papacy if it came to that. But fair is fair; and as far as I can see, Maestroianni and the others are at least trying to get a handle on things. It's the Holy Father who should answer for the way he lets things slide out of control."

Slattery had no answer for what was essentially a complaint about a papal policy he himself didn't understand. The best he could do was to air his own complaints about the brace of Cardinals who had turned Christian's head with their civilized pursuit of rough games. "Now, let me get this straight, Gladstone." Damien weighed in full bore. "The way you have it figured, Maestroianni and his cronies are looking to restore equilibrium to the Church. Have I got that much right?"

Christian cocked his head to one side in grudging admission.

"All right, then. Just for the sake of argument, let's say this is Cardinal Maestroianni." Slattery plunked his untouched water glass down in the middle of the table. "And let's pretend this is Cardinal Palombo." Damien drank the wine remaining in the second glass before putting it into the breach. "His face may not be pretty to look at, but a lot of Vatican heads turn when he passes by. Pensabene here—" The Dominican commandeered Christian's water glass for his symbolic circle of Vatican power. "Pensabene is unchallenged as the leader of the major faction of Curial Cardinals. And then there's Aureatini." Christian's wine glass served the purpose this time. "He may not measure up to the others yet. But Maestroianni has marked him out as a rising star; and his work for CARR in de-Catholicizing Catholic ritual has set the pattern, and given him a good deal of clout in the upstart Conferences of Bishops in every part of the world. Unless he trips over his own red sash, he could be a papal contender somewhere down the line.

"That brings us to our old friend Cardinal Giacomo Graziani." The Master-General chose a wine cork to stand in for the fifth man. "As Secretary of State, he's about as useful to the Pope as this bit of flotsam. He doesn't care which way the tide flows, as long as he pops up with the winner." Slattery had run out of glasses and corks; but it didn't matter. As far as he was concerned, they could forget men like Boff and Schuytteneer. "And forget Azande, too," he added. "I'll grant you, he started off differently; and he's a likable man if ever there was one. But he's become a toady. Like so many others, those three will eat whatever Maestroianni dishes up.

"Now." Father Damien reached for the salt shaker and set it down with a thump in the circle he had formed. "Here's the Holy Father, flanked on every side by the men you fell in love with this morning."

Christian tried to protest, but the Master-General tapped each of the tumblers sharply with a fork in a striking, off-key little concert. "If these five Vatican powerhouses truly wanted harmony and equilibrium in the Church, then I promise you that Boff and Azande and Schuytteneer would join the chorus in a minute. In fact, there isn't a soul you've met on all your travels over the past couple of months who would dare to sing a sour note."

"Now, let me get this straight, Slattery." Chris flung the Dominican's challenge back at him. "The way you have it figured, the Holy Father is ringed around by some sort of cabal. Have I got that much right? The man we have as Pope—the man who's traveled a million miles around the world; the man who knows every political and religious leader there is, and who is probably recognized on sight by more people in more places than all the famous headliners you can name rolled into one—that man is as hemmed in and as helpless as this salt shaker."

The Dominican sat back in his chair. For all the good it might do, he had got his mind across.

"I don't buy it, Father Damien. For openers, I don't see what would be in it for Maestroianni and the others to tie the Pope's hands while the Church falls into such a sorry state. I don't pretend to have the answer to the papal riddle. But your theory doesn't wash." The trouble for Chris at that moment was that he couldn't ask the ultimate questions about his own mission for the Secretariat of State without breaching the compartmentation edict he'd been given. The trouble for Slattery was that he wouldn't have known the answers in any case. Maestroianni was a master at holding his cards close to his chest. Damien had no idea what was in it for the wily little prelate.

In the end, therefore, he figured the most useful thing would be to give Gladstone the kind of advice he would be likely to remember when the going called for it. "Listen, lad." The white-robed cleric sighed. "I've told you what I think about the people you're working with these days in the Secretariat. Now let me tell you just two things about working with the Holy Father. The first thing is this—and remember it well: His Holiness trusts you. And second, there's no introduction to papal work.

"You complain about the piddling assignments that have come your way since your meeting with the Pope, and I can understand your impatience to get your teeth into things. You're not alone in that, believe me. But the fact is that he'll call on you when he thinks you can help. When he does—if he does—the answer is up to you. Purely voluntary. And once you're called on, it may be the first of many times—in which case you learn as you go. Or it may be the last and only time."

Christian looked across at his companion in stunned silence. It wasn't that Slattery's advice was so unexpected; or even that it had brought him up short in what he suddenly saw as pride in his hankering to be given a papal assignment. Rather, it was that Damien's words came across like a dose of parting wisdom; as something in the nature of a bequest. Gladstone wasn't much for gossip; but not even an alien from outer space could have avoided the incessant rumors that the head honcho of the Dominican Order was on his way out. Was it true, then?

Father Damien wasn't a man to coat the pill, even when he was the one who had to swallow it. "The rumor mill has it right, *Padre*. The General Chapter meets next March in Mexico City. When it's over, there'll be a new Master-General of the Order."

"And then?" Christian knew the answer, but he had to ask.

"And then I expect I'll be transferred out of here. A few months from now, I'll be as far away as my enemies can fling me. Probably in some hellhole that only corrupt sons of St. Dominic can concoct."

"You could be wrong, Father." Chris was aghast. Gone from him was every sense of gentle hope, every thought of Rome as the most ancient in wisdom or the most fatherly in sentiment.

"Dream on." Slattery's pain was obvious in his eyes as he surveyed the mute circle of water and wine glasses that still stood where he had arranged them. "You know the way Father Carnesecca always says that the enemy is within the gates? Well, he's seen it all; and he's called it just the way it is. They hold the levers of power. And if they have their way for much longer, we're all going to be eliminated. We never amounted to much in this place anyway. You know that, surely."

Christian found himself shaking with indignation. "But you must have some say, Father. There must be something you can do. What about appealing directly to the Holy Father . . ." Gladstone almost choked on his words as, in his turn, he looked again at the tableau of papal impotence Slattery had arrayed on the table.

Father Damien watched Christian's initial disbelief turn to indignation and then to anger. He watched until he felt he couldn't bear much more. Abruptly, then, he signaled to Springy to initial his tab for him. "Come on, lad." The Master-General clapped a ham hand on Gladstone's shoulder as they wound their way among the crowded tables and out the door into the thin sunlight of winter. "I've got a bit of time left, don't forget. Rome hasn't seen the last of me yet."

□ □ □ □

There was to be no balm for Christian in labor that day, however. For once, the scholarly discipline of his mind failed him. Time and again, his concentration was broken by the memory of the pain he had seen in the Master-General's face. Time and again he found himself trying to imagine what it must be like for a man to know he was going to be stripped of everything—of the most intimate fabric of his life. That was what it came down to. Everything that was important for Father Damien could be defined in terms of his life as a Dominican priest and his work for the Holy Father. Now, Rome had reached out to brutalize him in a way Christian had never imagined possible. Nor was Slattery the only one to be brutalized. In the space of a few hours, Rome had yanked Gladstone from the heights of his silly exhilaration. One of the beacons of his own life was about to be extinguished. One of his few anchors to stability would be gone.

Chris flung his pen down and shoved the neat stacks of papers on his desk into a jumble of disarray. Damien was right. No one amounted to much in this place in the end. If a man of Slattery's stature was expendable, then a man like Christian Gladstone was about as valuable as the shift key on a typewriter.

With a dozen Cardinals expecting a sustained input from him, and with bishops all over Europe primed to welcome him into their private enclaves, he had begun to fancy himself as somebody. But now he had ample reason to berate himself both for his pride and for his puniness. He was somebody, all right! An obedient, unquestioning mule among thousands of other equally obscure mules occupying thousands of obscure niches in the giant bureaucratic machinery of the Vatican. Somebody who had been fooled like some starry-eyed tourist by Rome's architectural grandeur and dazzled by its antiquities.

Chris was startled out of his bleak thoughts by the sound of the telephone from somewhere under the mounds of papers scattered across his desk. It wasn't until the third ring that he laid his hand on the receiver and heard the welcome voice of Father Carnesecca. Gladstone's pleasure was short-lived, however. His friend was calling from a phone booth, he said, to take a rain check on the walk the two had arranged for the following Saturday. "I'm on my way out of Rome right now, Chris. I've been trying to reach you since this morning to let you know."

Despite his own foul mood—or perhaps because of it—Chris picked up at once on the undertone of strain in the other man's voice. "Is everything all right, Father?"

"Nothing all that unusual." In the circumstances, Father Aldo could only reveal that he was already on a mission. The rules of security meant he would be incommunicado until he had completed the first leg of his mission.

"I see. I understand all about compartmentation and the rules of security."

It was Carnesecca's turn to wonder if things were all right. "Is something up, *Padre?* You don't sound like yourself."

"Don't listen to me, Aldo," Chris apologized. "I'll survive, old friend. And do you also survive, please."

"I'll do what I can to oblige."

No sooner had Chris put the receiver on its hook than Cardinal Maestroianni rang through. By contrast to Christian's frame of mind, His Eminence sounded full of beans. "If you can spare the time, *Reverendo*"—Maestroianni purred his best rendition of humility—"perhaps you will drop by my office tomorrow morning. But let me not keep you entirely on tenterhooks. I have taken the liberty of asking one of my associates to contact the Secretary-General of the European Community . . ."

"*Paul?*" The surprised exclamation was out of Chris's mouth before he could think.

"I knew you would be pleased." For once, His Eminence didn't seem to mind being interrupted. "It is rare that our arduous labors for the Holy See bring us into the embrace of our loved ones. You are indeed fortunate, Father Gladstone. Shall we say eight o'clock tomorrow morning? You're booked on a midday flight to Brussels. That should leave us plenty of time to go over the details."

Christian stared at the phone for a long time after Maestroianni had rung off. It seemed that His Eminence had his hands in Paul's new career as Secretary-General of the EC. Well, Chris sighed to himself, he might worry about the state of Paul's religious life, but never about his independence of mind. For better or worse, Paul had even managed to distance himself from Cessi. Now that he had obviously landed squarely on his own two feet, he wasn't likely to become anybody's unquestioning mule. Paul was a man who could take care of himself.

Cessi Gladstone knew as much as Christian about indignation and unexplainable forebodings. Indeed, her own lightning visit to Rome with Glenn Roche was motivated by her anger at the deplorable state of the priesthood that had left St. Michael's Chapel in Danbury without a pastor, and by her constant foreboding for the future of the Church at large.

Still, Cessi enjoyed a number of advantages over her son. Her first advantage was that she would be in and out of the Apostolic Palace within a few hours, just as she had promised Roche when he had phoned her at Windswept House. Second, the Institute of Religious Agencies—the Vatican Bank—needed a whopping loan from her in the aftermath of the Salvi suitcase affair. Third, she was clear-minded about the limited objective she wanted to achieve in return for her cooperation. And fourth, she had spent a day in Manhattan so that Glenn could coach her in advance about the terrain she would be treading.

"All I want," Cessi had reminded her financial advisor, "is enough coaching so that I won't sound too stupid when we walk into the Vatican Bank."

Roche made sure Cessi understood that the Vatican Bank was a real bank. The portfolio of the Institute for Religious Agencies, he told her, was right up there with the major financial institutions the world over. There was hardly any sector of human life in which the IRA hadn't invested Vatican funds.

Of course, Roche hastened to add, the fact that his bank was a real bank did not mean that the Pontiff was a real banker who micromanaged the financial affairs of the Vatican and the Holy See. Glenn had provided a fair rundown of key IRA personnel and the impressive scope of their operations, with detailed emphasis on the two men Cessi would be visiting, Dr. Pier Giorgio Maldonado and canny old Cardinal Amedeo Sanstefano, who, as head of the Prefecture of Economic Affairs, answered directly to the Holy Father for all economic and financial dealings of the Vatican, including those of the IRA.

Nonetheless, Glenn observed, the Pontiff had more control over the Institute of Religious Agencies than over most of the other Vatican ministries. The IRA, it seemed, had a special charter that couldn't be tampered with by anybody except the Pope. And that fact was basic to his independence of action, was the essential underpinning of his freedom from in-house constraints and external pressures.

All of that was simple enough for Cessi to grasp. But Glenn had insisted she see just what a major financial portfolio looked like these days. And that had required an excursion to a bleak building in midtown Manhattan where they had been escorted by a trio of guards through a warren of locked rooms monitored at every turn by television scanners.

Finally, they had found themselves standing amid the components of a massive computer. "This is the brain that organizes and makes possible the globalized financial dealings of our brave new world." Roche bowed in mock politeness.

"This electronic doodad?" Glenn explained that something approaching a trillion dollars passed through this unthinking brain each day; a sum that was more than the entire money supply of the United States.

"Remember your shares in the Racol-Guardata Corporation, Cessi? Well, that's the outfit that makes this electronic doodad. These black boxes you see here and a pair of Unisys A-15J mainframe computers manage coded orders that come in through one hundred and thirty-four dedicated telephone lines from everybody who is anybody in the financial world, including the Gladstones."

"Including the Church of God?"

"Including the Pope's bank," Roche confirmed as he signaled the guards they were ready to leave.

Glenn's little crash course in world finance wasn't finished yet. Once back in his office at Glenn Roche Securities, he pulled a thin volume from the bookshelves behind his desk and flicked its pages until he came to the passage he wanted to read aloud to Cessi. " 'Since I entered politics' "—Glenn settled into his chair as he read—" 'I have chiefly had men's views confided to me privately. Some of the biggest men in the U.S., in the field of commerce and manufacturing, are afraid of somebody, are afraid of something. They know that there is a power somewhere so organized, so subtle, so watchful, so interlocked, so complete, so pervasive that they had better not speak above their breath when they speak in condemnation of it.' "

Roche snapped the little book shut. "Woodrow Wilson wrote those words in 1913."

Cessi got the point. Those black boxes and the Unisys A-15J were exactly what she had said. Electronic doodads. Somebody engineered them, programmed them, manipulated them. "So." She spoke softly as if to herself, or perhaps to her guardian angel. "The Devil is wired to the world at last."

As arranged, Cessi and Glenn Roche arrived at Rome's Fiumicino airport on an early-morning flight. A taciturn Vatican guard met them at the gate and rushed them to a waiting limousine. An equally taciturn chauffeur sped them to the Apostolic Palace. And there, a smile was bestowed on them at last by a young priest-banker who waited for them just outside the entrance to the Secretariat. The IRA man was full of apologies. Ordinarily, no matter what the business at hand, any visiting *privilegiato di Stato* such as Francesca Gladstone would be expected to pay a brief courtesy call on the Secretary of State. However, His Eminence Giacomo Graziani was away on business for the day.

"How unfortunate!" Cessi tried not to look too relieved as she and Roche followed their guide through corridors that connected the Apostolic Palace to the sixteenth-century tower that housed the central offices of the IRA. And she tried not to sigh as they were ushered past banks of computer screens and clicking keyboards. Surely, she thought with a glance at Roche, these Roman electronic doodads were in constant contact with the Racol-Guardata doodads she had seen in Manhattan.

There was no time for reflection on the point; for their escort opened the door to a spacious office overlooking the Vatican gardens, where they found themselves in the presence of the two men Cessi had traveled nearly 5,000 miles to meet. So exact had Roche been in his descriptions that Cessi would have recognized those men anywhere. There was nothing to distinguish Pier Giorgio Maldonado as Director-General of the IRA. He was dressed like any other banker she had ever met, and appeared every bit as personable when the occasion called for it. But His Eminence Amedeo Sanstefano was another kind of man. As he turned his head to study her advance into the room, Cessi thought he looked the way Cardinals should. Redoubtable was the word that came to mind.

The American woman was barely through the door before Dr. Maldonado fairly leaped from his chair and rushed forward to greet her. "You are most welcome, Signora. All of us are extremely grateful for your cooperation in this too sad affair of the unfortunate Mr. Salvi. Extremely grateful, are we not, Your Eminence?" Maldonado guided Cessi across his office and presented her to the Cardinal.

His Eminence remained seated and silent for a moment. But his face was wreathed in smiles as Cessi knelt to kiss his ring. "We are grateful, indeed, Signora Gladstone." The Cardinal's English was hard to grasp at first. But his eyes were radiant with expression as he hobbled to his arthritic feet and escorted Cessi to a chair beside Maldonado's desk. "It is truly gratifying in these troubled times to find a daughter of the Church who is so devoted, and so well endowed by God with material wealth. We know you are motivated by the deepest concern for the Church and for the salvation of souls.

"And you, Signor Roche." His Eminence turned his attention to Cessi's companion. "It is always good to welcome you here."

"I am Your Eminence's servant." Glenn responded in kind to the sincerity of the greeting.

Cessi was surprised at the ease she felt in this very strange place. Perhaps it was the confidence she had gained from Glenn's expert coaching. Or, after so many battles with so many drooping prelates for so many years back home, perhaps it was her delight at finding herself face to face with a Cardinal who truly was a Prince of the Church. Whatever the reason, she held her own quite nicely throughout the small talk that is a prelude to any civilized meeting. Of course, the moment came for Dr. Maldonado to mention the document he had prepared for the Signora's signature. Perhaps she would care to take a few moments to read it over.

"I'm sure it is quite in order, Professor." Cessi took the two sheets of paper Maldonado held out to her and passed them over for Glenn to peruse.

"Indeed." Glenn read the agreement quickly through and then placed it on the desk in front of Cessi. "Everything is in order as usual, Dr. Maldonado."

"Well, then . . ." The Director-General offered his pen across the desk. To his surprise, however, Cessi made no move to sign. Instead, she placed the pen atop the papers that were the focus of everyone else's attention, and turned with that consummate grace of hers to the Cardinal.

"Your Eminence." She smiled. "I would make a small request of you."

Maldonado turned a desperate eye to Roche. Was this to be a bargaining session, then? Roche could only shrug his shoulders and listen; he knew the technicalities of such dealings as this, but Cessi was operating out of his range now.

Of the three men in the room, the Cardinal was the only one not perturbed by Cessi's unexpected detour. Sanstefano had spent half his life bartering deals for the Holy See. He and Cessi were two hard-nosed people who had bargained often with life, and who had liked each other on sight. "I am at your service, Signora."

"It is a small request, Eminence. I would be so pleased if the Holy Father would give me some moments of his time in a private audience in the near future."

His Eminence smiled at Cessi with great good humor. He knew a good bargain when he saw one. "A small request, indeed, Signora Gladstone. And a most fitting one. Of course, these things do not happen overnight. His Holiness' schedule is a very full one. The more so as he is so often away on his papal travels. At this very moment, in fact, the Holy Father is in Africa."

Cessi felt a tremor flow through her spine. Was this Sanstefano's Vatican double-talk for: Go fly a kite, signora?

The Cardinal decided not to prolong the situation for long. He had good reason to know the Gladstone file. And unless his eye had failed him, this woman was a Gladstone to the core. "Nevertheless." His Eminence broke the tension. "I have no doubt that an audience can be arranged for you. It will only be a question of time."

It wasn't Cessi but Dr. Maldonado who sighed with relief as, at last, he saw the Gladstone name etched on yet another document that would save the Vatican Bank another embarrassing episode. If just a few men on his staff could match this woman's mixture of guile and gumption, Maldonado mused to himself, the IRA might not have gotten itself into this Salvi suitcase mess in the first place. What wouldn't he give, then, to know what the charming Signora Gladstone had in mind for the Holy Father!

XXIX

"CARDINAL REINVERNUNFT has come over from the Congregation for the Defense of the Faith, Holiness. He asked me to be sure Your Holiness knows he's here." Monsignore Daniel Sadowski eyed the Pontiff with ill-disguised concern as he recapped the day's heavy schedule. "Cardinal Secretary Graziani knows his usual briefing session will be a bit delayed. He will come by at nine-thirty. That will leave an hour before the consistory of Cardinals at ten-thirty . . ."

"Reinvernunft is ahead of his time." The Slavic Pope glanced at his watch as he turned from the window of his third-floor study. "He was to come at eight o'clock as I recall. It's barely seven-thirty."

"Yes, Holiness. . . ." Monsignore Daniel caught his breath at the sight of sudden pallor on the Pontiff's face. If he had his way, the day's schedule would be scrubbed in favor of a thorough and long-overdue checkup with the Pope's internist, Dr. Giorgio Fanarote. The Holy Father, and many who had traveled with him, had all come down with the same symptoms following the recent papal visit to the Ivory Coast: severe fatigue, abdominal pains, breathing problems and a soreness of eyes and throat. Medical opinion was that they had doubtless fallen victim to the effects of the clogging red dust of the region and that the symptoms would pass. But Sadowski didn't accept that diagnosis, however. He was convinced that His Holiness had never fully recovered from the effects of the assassination attempt of 1981. At the very least, interior scar tissue had surely built up after the operation. And there was that still unidentified megalovirus he had contracted from the contaminated blood transfusion he had received. Had the doctors really got rid of that virus, or had it flared up all over again now that the Pontiff's physical defenses were at a low ebb?

"It's just a twinge." Intent on getting down to business, the Pontiff brushed aside all thought of doctors and checkups.

As usual, the Slavic Pope's schedule was chockablock. He never made any secret of the "issues weighing on my mind and heart," as he often put it, and took every opportunity to reach out for solutions to the specific problems pressing in on the world with increasing urgency. And when he was in Rome, so, too, did he use every turn of the papal day to confront virtually every problem of the day with candor, persistence and in the clearest possible terms.

The Pope moved a little too slowly from the window to his desk and scribbled a few notes to himself. "That should keep us all busy, Monsignore." He laid his pen aside.

"Yes, Holy Father. But about Dr. Fanarote . . ."

"Soon, Monsignore. For the moment, however, we mustn't keep Cardinal Reinvernunft waiting too long."

Though he had suffered a minor stroke three months before, Cardinal Johann Reinvernunft had lost none of his deadly logic or his acuity of expression. As Prefect of the CDF, the subject that most concerned His Eminence this morning was the need to issue a directive to the bishops concerning the civil rights of declared homosexual men and women. Predictably, he said, the matter had come to a head in the United States, Canada and several countries in Europe where legislation had been proposed on the issue, and in some cases already made into law. "Not so long ago," Reinvernunft observed, "there would have been little need to discuss the Church's response to such governmental legislation, much less to issue a CDF directive to the bishops concerning homosexual behavior. But these days . . ." The Cardinal managed a sad little smile.

The Slavic Pope glanced up sharply at His Eminence's reference to times gone by. But he picked up on another of the Cardinal's phrases instead.

"Your Eminence knows and I know that, if left to themselves, a minority of bishops will do nothing at all to counter the effects of such legislation. A still smaller minority will oppose it. And the great majority will endorse it."

That was as fair an assessment as the Cardinal himself could have given. But the Slavic Pope wasn't prepared to leave it at that. "In fact, Eminence"—the Pontiff rested his hand on a thick folder resting on his desk—"I have been particularly concerned with a number of reports sent to me privately about the spread of active homosexuality in North American seminaries and among the clergy at large. Have we any reliable idea of how bad the problem is in that region? Do we have any figures?"

The Cardinal shook his head. "Short of sending a special investigator to America, I see no way of coming up with hard data."

The Holy Father had thought more than once about sending an investigator on just such a fact-finding mission. For now, he wished Reinvernunft to send a papal directive to the bishops. There was to be no change, he said, in episcopal insistence that homosexual activity is an intrinsic evil that must not be endorsed by the Church.

His Eminence had a question: "Holiness, supposing the bishops treat this directive as they do your other papal directives. Then what?"

"You are quite right to ask the question, Eminence." The Pontiff rose from his chair and began to pace the study. "I have been puzzled by a sudden surge in the already abysmal unwillingness among the bishops to cooperate with the Holy See. Lately, and no matter how great our efforts, the gap seems to widen between Pope and bishops; between papal Rome and the provinces of the Church. But the problem doesn't end there. There seems no end to the decline in priesthood and religious life. The decline in Catholic practice of the faith seems only to accelerate. And the failure in evangelization is nothing less than dismal.

"In a word, Eminence." The Slavic Pope stopped his pacing abruptly. "In a word—and whatever measure you apply—we are recording such failures in evangelization throughout the Church Universal that I have slowly become convinced that there must be some specific reason to account for it. Some new element has entered among us. It is laying waste in the priesthood, among my bishops, among my Cardinals, in monasteries and out among the Catholic population.

"Just think a minute. Even the picture of decline I've just summarized doesn't encompass the enormity. We've barely touched on the vogue of a newly active homosexual way of life among layfolk and clergy. And we haven't even mentioned the extraordinary surge in Satanism of a ritualistic kind."

The Cardinal looked somberly at the Pontiff. Up along the ladder of his career, he had heard vague rumors, unreliable reports, whisperings that his belly told him were the outward mask of important things. Things that you did not retail to a reigning Pope, however, unless you were willing to put everything on the line.

The Pontiff returned Reinvernunft's somber gaze. This was not the first time he had reached out to the Cardinal Prefect with what amounted to an invitation for his decisive cooperation. In the past, when it had come to a choice between furthering his ecclesiastical ambitions and the need for trenchant action, His Eminence had plunked himself squarely on the fence. Like so many who might have made a difference in the Vatican, he had made a career of compromise instead. When the Cardinal chose not to respond, therefore, the Pope decided to widen his invitation.

"What new factor has entered the equation, Eminence? For some time now, I have been asking myself that question. Personally, I am convinced that something extraordinary has happened that has given the ancient Enemy of our nature a terrible freedom. I can be certain of nothing, Eminence," the Pope conceded. "But if I am correct, then it is something that must be undone. . . ."

The buzz of the intercom on his desk interrupted the Pontiff's speculation and, to Cardinal Reinvernunft's relief, ended the conversation.

"Yes, Monsignore Daniel?" The Holy Father betrayed no sign of his disappointment as he walked back to his chair and lifted the receiver.

"The Cardinal Secretary is on his way, Holiness."

"Good." The Pope's open glance at his visitor underscored his words. "His Eminence and I were just wrapping things up. Anything else?"

"One thing of note, Holiness. The U.S. Ambassador to the Holy See called to alert Your Holiness confidentially that his government is sending a special emissary to discuss the question of papal policy vis-à-vis the Soviet Union. One of the President's men, I gather, by the name of Gibson Appleyard. I've penciled him in for mid-December, subject to confirmation."

Sadowski had barely rung off when, with a tap at the study door to announce himself, Secretary of State Graziani came into the papal study and, armed with folders and smiles, held the door open for Cardinal Reinvernunft to make his exit.

Once urgent Secretariat matters had been dealt with, the Pontiff cut short any lengthy discussions with Cardinal Secretary Graziani. He discussed briefly his wish and intent to make a papal pilgrimage to the Soviet Union. Pope and Secretary knew that His Holiness' friend Mikhail Gorbachev would be out of power—and probably out of Russia—by year's end. Boris Yeltsin would be the predominant figure; and Yeltsin was no friend of this Pope.

"We must seek the right time for my Russia pilgrimage. Meanwhile"—he shuffled through the papers and documents on his desk—"has Your Eminence seen this?"

A suddenly tense Graziani took the document the Pope held out to him.

Though he had not been privy to its planning, he had read it. All the Cardinals had read it. It bore no signature, but there was no mistaking the hand of His Eminence Cardinal Silvio Aureatini.

The brief text began with a question: What mechanism of governance would take over if the Pope were totally incapacitated for a foreseeably long period? What if His Holiness were incapacitated in his vital powers of mind? The document proposed no solution to the fabricated problem.

"What do you make of it, Eminence?"

"I have never had the impression that Your Holiness envisaged the possibility of papal resignation." Graziani waved a hand as if to brush such an absurd thought out of the air. He suggested that His Holiness consult the Cardinals in this morning's consistory about the matter.

"A timely thought, Your Eminence." The Pontiff tapped a finger on his watch. "The Cardinals must be waiting for us."

As the pair set out for the conference room on a lower floor, the Holy Father opted to take the stairs instead of the elevator. By the time he reached the landing below, he stopped for a moment to lean one shoulder against the wall.

"Are you all right, Holiness?" Graziani was taken aback by the Pope's bloodless pallor and by his need to catch his breath. "Do you want to postpone the consistory?"

"No, no!" His Holiness forced himself to stand erect. "The years have taught me, Eminence, that going downstairs can be just as strenuous as climbing up them." He tried to smile. "The poor old body is protesting."

Secret consistories—or, plainly put, private meetings between Pope and members of the College of Cardinals present in Rome—have been a much used instrument of papal government for over a thousand years. While the Pope is endowed by law with absolute authority and is empowered to take decisive actions by himself, the Cardinals have always had a consultative role.

Today, many of those advisors had grouped themselves around the conference table in predictable little cliques.

Cardinals Pensabene, Aureatini, Palombo and Azande were seated with two or three minor Cardinals, including Onorio Fizzi-Monti, whose red hat had more to do with old money than with personal abilities or muscular faith. Cardinal Reinvernunft of the CDF formed the center of another group that included old Cardinal Ghislani, Prefect of the Congregation for the Divine Liturgy. They and a few more were supportive of the papacy after their fashion. Which was to say that, while they belonged to the large Vatican contingent that was nominally propapist, they spent much of their time hiding their loyal heads complaisantly in the sand.

As usual, there were a few strays in attendance. The powerful Cardinal Sanstefano of PECA chatted easily with His Eminence Odile Cappucci. Cappucci, a veteran of five papacies, had allied himself with no political group. As a bred-in-the-bone traditionalist, he was out of step with many of that stripe who had isolated themselves from the Holy See and the Curia. As a papist, he yearned for the kind of overt leadership that was not forthcoming from the Slavic Pope. And as a survivor, he hung on the hope that he might yet get a chance to do some good. At the far end of the table, Cardinal Alphonse Sabongo had taken a seat apart from all the groups. Prefect of the Congregation for Saintly Causes, and the only black African present besides Azande, Sabongo was a tough-minded man and a solid papist who seemed to be biding his time while he tried to figure out what this Pope was doing.

The Pontiff made his way slowly to the head of the conference table, exchanging greetings with each of the prelates as he moved past them. His movements seemed still to require a certain effort; to lack the accustomed ease. In the main, however, the Holy Father was in command of himself again. With all greetings duly exchanged, His Holiness recited a prayer to the Holy Spirit, took his chair and lost no time in introducing the first of the topics that weighed most heavily on his mind and heart this day: the now urgent question of an early papal visit to the East that would take him beyond Poland and into Russia and three more key states of the CIS.

A number of Cardinals expressed their worry that the Pontiff's physical strength was precarious and that such a pastoral trip would endanger it to an unacceptable degree; but Cardinal Leo Pensabene spoke up on the political dimension of the proposed trip. "In the current charged atmosphere between Gorbachev and Yeltsin"—His Eminence poked a couple of his bony fingers in the air to represent the two rivals as he named them—"a visit by Your Holiness would be taken as an endorsement of Gorbachev. And then, if Gorbachev is ousted—and that's the betting these days—where does that leave the Holy See?"

Cardinal Ghislani seemed impatient with the whole discussion. Since His Holiness had always envisaged such a papal visit within the framework of what the three Fatima children had said about the Blessed Virgin's intentions, why was the Holy Father consulting his Cardinals at all?

The Pontiff responded to Ghislani's frank question with an answer that struck many as enigmatic, and that raised eyebrows up and down the table. "I consult you on the issue, Eminence, because that framework is not so simple as Your Eminence assumes. According to those instructions, I am to collaborate with the Virgin's intentions through the advice of my Cardinals. At this time, apparently she is saying no to me. Ultimately, however, she will let us know in her own way about the Russian visit."

With that matter settled for the moment, and with an unobtrusive little nod to Cardinal Graziani, the Holy Father moved on to the trial balloon that had been floated anonymously concerning, as he put it, "some legal disposition to be put into place to deal with an incapacitating papal illness."

"What is this!" Indignant at the mere thought of such a move, Cardinal

Odile Cappucci rose in his place beside Cardinal Sanstefano. "Are we looking at a blatant effort to force a resignation? Does anyone here think such situations haven't arisen in the past when the Holy Father was incapacitated? This is disgusting!"

If anyone was up to returning Cappucci's icy stare, it was Cardinal Palombo. "Not at all, Your Eminence. It is no more than realistic. Life for world leaders has become dubious, and plunging into crowds all around the globe compounds the danger. It seems high time that some legal disposition was taken."

Aureatini was quick to second the thought. "At any event, should the Holy Father ever undertake the proposed visit to Russia and the other CIS states, simple prudence would suggest that some prior legal arrangements must be made."

Cardinal Cappucci was not mollified. "If simple prudence were at work here," he shot back, "such a question would never have arisen." It was perhaps out of simple prudence that everyone else at the table chose to keep his silence. With only Cappucci willing to speak out against it, for all practical purposes the matter of a possible papal resignation was left to simmer.

Next, the Pontiff again tackled the idea of a possible investigation into homosexual activity among the clergy.

This time, it was the normally laconic Cardinal Fizzi-Monti who rose to the boiling point. He began by warning against witch-hunts and latter-day inquisitions; those buzzwords always worked. And he pointed out that at least some residential Cardinals were already taking their own active steps in the matter. "His Eminence of Centurycity is one good example. His Eminence is considering the need of a special diocesan reviewing committee to handle all cases of pedophiliac clergy." Fizzi-Monti was not the cleverest fellow; but when his enthusiasm for the Cardinal of Centurycity fell flat among most of his colleagues, he retreated to his cry against unjust and divisive witch-hunts. "The day we in Rome must investigate each local bishop, that will be the day of real crisis."

Frustrated beyond telling with the Vatican's paralysis, Cardinal Sabongo countered Fizzi-Monti to his face. "In case you haven't noticed, Eminence, such a day of crisis is already upon us. And diocesan reviewing committees are not the answer!" Apart from that single heated exchange, reactions to the topic of homosexuality among the clergy were predictably guarded.

The Pontiff brought the consistory to a close. "Would you all, Venerable Brothers, please pray for the light of the Holy Spirit?" With that and no more to sum up his mind, His Holiness blessed all present and left the conference room.

"A word, Holiness?"

Cardinal Sanstefano of PECA followed the Pope out the door as quickly as his arthritic feet would allow. At any consistory, the agenda belongs strictly to the Holy Father. As the Pontiff hadn't opened the discussion to financial matters, Sanstefano hoped to snatch a few minutes of unscheduled time.

The Pontiff turned back with a smile. "Have you ever heard such sterile bickering in a consistory, Eminence? I don't know about you, but as I listened to the Cardinals this morning, I couldn't help but remember a little rhyme Margaret Thatcher used from time to time. 'Give me six good men and true,' she used to say, 'and I will get the policy through.' My problem seems to be that too many good men in the Vatican are no longer true; and that too many true men are afraid to act on the good they know they should do. But forgive me, Eminence. You have PECA matters to discuss, I take it?"

"A few decisions to be finalized, Holiness. And a problem or two for Your Holiness' consideration."

Once seated at his desk, the Pope approved a few IRA staff appointments in accordance with His Eminence's advice; and, finally, His Eminence addressed the Pope's concern over the homosexual question.

"As the discussion this morning wasn't a financial one, I didn't raise the problem in this morning's consistory. But I am alarmed at the number of appeals coming in for Holy See approval to make out-of-court settlements. The number and variety of transgressions is unprecedented. The money paid out is approaching one billion dollars. I have to agree with Cardinal Sabongo that we are facing a crisis."

"I take it, then, that Your Eminence favors an investigation?"

"The sooner the better, Holiness. But"—His Eminence brightened—"speaking of good men and true, Holy Father, I've been asked by a great supporter of the Church to request a private audience with Your Holiness. Signora Francesca Gladstone paid a visit to the Vatican Bank a few weeks ago . . ."

"Ah!" The Pope had every reason to recall the name, and to respond to it with a smile. Father Christian Gladstone was showing early signs of promise as a churchman of substance. And, like earlier members of her family, Signora Gladstone had come to the financial aid of the Holy See more than once.

"And she has done so again, most handsomely." Sanstefano encouraged the thought.

"I take it then, Eminence, that your advice is positive."

"As the lady said to me, Holy Father, the request is a small one. With Your Holiness' permission, perhaps Monsignore Sadowski can squeeze some time from the papal calendar early in the coming year."

With the Pope's consent willingly given, Cardinal Sanstefano set off to have a word with Sadowski before heading back to his own offices and his own busy schedule. All the while, and even as the day wore on, the simplistic little Thatcher rhyme the Holy Father had quoted to him pricked at his mind like a thorn. The more he thought about it—the more he considered the Pontiff's constant accessibility and frankness, say, or his geopolitical acumen; and the more he stacked those and other qualities against the talents of a Margaret Thatcher or of any other world leader—the more the Cardinal was convinced that the Pope had put his finger on the right button, but for the wrong reason.

Even if it was true that His Holiness couldn't find six good men and true to get his policy through, the underlying cause of that problem was what counted. And that cause was that there probably weren't six men in all the world, true or otherwise, who had yet been able to make out what the Slavic Pope's policy might be.

For all of his own experience, Sanstefano admitted to himself with a sad and troubled sigh, that was a problem for which he could find no parallel and no justification in papal history. And for all of his own goodwill, it was a problem for which he could see no solution.

XXX

EARLY ON THE EVENING of December 17, Father Angelo Gutmacher entered the Holy Father's private study on the fourth floor of the Apostolic Palace. Bone tired after one of his constant trips as papal courier to the East, he carried with him as usual a cluster of highly confidential written communications for the Slavic Pope. As usual, too, he sat in silence while the Pontiff read each letter. In the hour of uninterrupted conversation that ensued, Gutmacher answered the questions His Holiness put to him and, when called upon to do so, gave his own opinions frankly. Then, with new instructions in hand that would have him depart early the next morning—this time for Poland—he set off to get a few hours of much needed sleep.

For some time, the Pope remained at his desk. As he read again the correspondence Gutmacher had delivered—particularly the two letters written to him on different dates by Mikhail Gorbachev—his thoughts were primarily on change. In the first, the Soviet President confided that he would have to resign on the coming December 25. "I have lost the patronage of the West," he had written. "They want to put me on hold. Boris Yeltsin will succeed me. The Soviet Union will be legally dissolved, will cease to exist, within some weeks. Only this will satisfy my patrons in the West. The Soviet Union as such does not figure in their alignment of states in the New World Order. And this holding situation will be sustained until sometime after January 1, 1996."

The second of Gorbachev's letters was an amplification of his thoughts on the coming alignment of states in the New World Order, with emphasis on his expectation that his so-called patrons in the West would foster a working relationship between the Soviet Republics and the United States that would be closer by far than Gorbachev himself had envisioned.

Was that the explanation, then? Was that why Gorbachev had been passed over, at least for now, as a leading figure in the new machinery? "Part of the explanation," the Holy Father dialogued with himself in his mind. "Only part of the explanation."

Gorbachev's mention of the United States led him to a review of his own current and specific concerns in that region. He would be meeting with the American President's special emissary tomorrow. That hefty folder of reports concerning homosexual activity among the American clergy was never far from his mind. The data was anecdotal and far from complete. But it looked as though the clergy in North America was in a far worse moral condition than anyone had realized. Far worse than Europe. And that was to say a great deal by way of change.

As long as he was thinking of the tenor and tempo of change these days, it was well to remember the anonymous letter that had been circulated among the in-house Cardinals. At the very least, such a naked move to stump for new and specific legal machinery covering a possible papal resignation signaled a change in mood among the antipapal contingents within the Vatican. In the same vein, it was not inconsequential that Father Damien Slattery, one of the Pontiff's closest personal advisors for more than a decade, would soon be out as Master-General of the Dominican Order.

Come to think of it, perhaps a good session with Slattery and his other advisors would bring some crucial light to bear on things. A conference with those advisors was likely to yield more fruit by far than a dozen consistories with his Cardinals.

Monsignore Daniel Sadowski's telephone summons caught Father Damien Duncan Slattery just as he emerged from the Angelicum Chapel after Vespers. The Holy Father wished to see the Master-General straightaway, and he was to bring Father Christian Gladstone along.

Since there was no discernible reason for his sudden inclusion in a confidential papal meeting, Gladstone could only reason that once again Father Damien's advice to him had been on target. There is no introduction to papal work, Slattery had told him. The Pontiff will call you when he thinks you can help, and when he does, your response is purely voluntary.

By the time he followed Slattery into the Pope's fourth-floor study, four of the six high-backed chairs drawn into a semicircle facing the Pope were already occupied. Monsignore Sadowski was there, of course. And, to Chris's surprise, so was Aldo Carnesecca. The two men who flanked Carnesecca were strangers to Christian. He knew Giustino Lucadamo by name and by reputation as chief of Vatican security. The fourth member of the group, however, was not a Vatican man. His brogue pegged him as an Irishman. And, to judge by his clothes, he belonged to the teaching order of Christian Brothers. Augustine, as everyone called him, looked to be in his late thirties or early forties.

"I have a few decisions to make, my brothers." The Pontiff brought the pair of latecomers quickly into the discussion by repeating the essentials of the first of Gorbachev's letters. He made it clear that he was not startled by any of the news Gorbachev had communicated. Not by his coming resignation, or by the impending dissolution of the Soviet Union, or by the involvement of those Gorbachev called his "patrons in the West" in that coming dislocation.

"I expect no one here needs to be reminded that Boris Yeltsin is not a friend of the papacy or the Church. Or that Yeltsin's mind has been strongly colored by all that strange spirituality he drank in as a guest of the Esalen center in California. Or that one of Yeltsin's strongest allies is the new Russian Orthodox Patriarch of Moscow, Kiril, who has been a mole for the KGB all these years and no more a friend of ours than Yeltsin himself. Given that situation, my pastoral visit to the East comes into question. Not the fact of the visit, mind you; but only the timing. If we have any indication from Heaven, it is that the real conversion of Russia, as the Blessed Mother called it, will originate from the Ukraine, and that it will take place on the occasion of my pilgrimage to the East.

"The question I put to you now is whether to force the timing of my visit, despite Mr. Gorbachev's resignation in favor of Boris Yeltsin."

In the twenty minutes or so of give-and-take that followed, Gladstone was the only one who remained silent. He barely followed the deeper threads of the conversation, and he recognized only a few of the names that cropped up. Still, as the analysis gathered steam and everyone had his say, Chris realized that when these men talked about Gorbachev's patrons in the Western world, political figures didn't hold a candle to industrialists and financial leaders of a global kind. It was enough to give new meaning to the old saying that money talks.

When comment turned to the situation Gorbachev expected to see after the dissolution of the Soviet Union, and that he expected to stretch until after January 1, 1996, it was Brother Augustine who had the first word. "We can throw that date out the window, my friends." He flashed a toothy grin. "If the European Community achieves monetary and political unity by January of 1996, I'll eat Mr. Gorbachev's fedora!"

"Gorbachev doesn't wear a fedora, you Irish oaf!" Slattery laughed. "But you raise an interesting point. The Holy Father's visit to the East isn't going to take place in a sealed chamber. If things are going to be kept up in the air pending EC unity, there are real logistics to consider in the papal visit. Shouldn't we ask ourselves what's going to happen to the fifteen Republics of the U.S.S.R.?"

Giustino Lucadamo jumped in quickly. "Let's confine ourselves to the

Republics that will be included in the papal pilgrimage. To Ukraine, Belarus and Kazakhstan. A considerable portion of the Soviet nuclear arsenal is based in those states. Until the problem of how to secure that arsenal is solved, there isn't a country in the world that won't be watching those Republics."

It was interesting for Chris that Father Carnesecca was the first to see Lucadamo's point. He had thought of Carnesecca as one who never took a public initiative.

"If I understand you, Giustino, you're reminding us that Heaven has a long memory. So is it not providential that the Virgin pointed to the Ukraine as the epicenter for the conversion of Russia? And I mean to use the word 'providential' in our classic Christian sense. In the sense of God's all-wise plan for the universe and His all-loving fulfillment of that plan. I grant that the world's power brokers are too taken up with other considerations these days to pay much attention to Heaven's predictions. But you can bet they'll get the point that the papal mission to the East isn't to some out-of-the-way sheep station on the Russian steppes. They might even get the point that more than seventy years ago the Fatima mandate targeted an area that has since become one of the most important geopolitical hot spots in the world.

"That being so"—Carnesecca sat back in his chair again—"I expect that the Holy Father's Eastern pilgrimage will take place before Father Damien has an answer to his question. Before the status of the fifteen Soviet Republics is settled."

"That still leaves a wide berth of time, Father Aldo." The Pope pressed for more precision. "Gorbachev's assessment is realistic. And so is Brother Augustine's. The holding pattern will stretch for a period of years once the U.S.S.R. is dissolved. So my question remains. Should I press Yeltsin for an early date? Or should I wait for some sign, some indication in world events?"

Carnesecca's reply this time was not an answer, but a question. "What did Angelo Gutmacher counsel, Holiness?"

Gladstone gaped in astonishment. To be at sea in geopolitics was one thing; but to be at sea about such a lifelong intimate friend as Angelo Gutmacher was something else. As far as he knew, Father Angelo was doing the pious work of an itinerant priest, just as he had said in the scribbled note he had sent over to the Angelicum back in October. Was nothing in Rome what it appeared to be, then?

With an interested eye on the young American cleric, the Pontiff answered Carnesecca's question. "Father Angelo thinks we should sit tight for now. In his view, indications are that Gorbachev is the chosen instrument of real change, and that we should wait Yeltsin out." Then, while Gladstone's consternation was still plain on his face—catch a man at such an instant and you will likely catch the true mettle of his mind—the Slavic

Pope turned the question over to him. "And you, Father. What do you think?"

"I am no geopolitician, Your Holiness," Chris admitted. "In fact, I am learning things I never guessed at before. So I can only comment on the basis of my reading of contemporary history. On the basis of public knowledge. As far as Boris Yeltsin is concerned, that reading tells me he may be the man of the moment for a lot of Russians who live in pigsty apartments and get seventy percent of their daily calories from potatoes, sugar, bread and vast quantities of vodka. For those Russians, Yeltsin is a national hero.

"But he doesn't strike me as another Mikhail Gorbachev. In fact, based on what I've heard tonight about Gorbachev's treatment at the hands of those Western patrons of his, my judgment has to be that Yeltsin will fare no better. Once he's served their purpose, whatever that may be, he'll doubtless pass into obscurity at best. As to the timing of Your Holiness' visit to the East, I would take Father Aldo's observation as the touchstone for my own judgment. We're not dealing with coincidence, but with providence. By any human reckoning, Gorbachev should have perished in that August coup against him . . ."

"He's right, Holiness." Brother Augustine broke in. "One side in that coup was after Gorbachev's life, and no mistake about it."

"True. But go on, Father Gladstone. Your reasoning, I take it, is that it was not coincidence but providence that came to Gorbachev's aid."

"And, Holiness, it was providence that Gorbachev got back to Moscow on August 22—the feast day of the Queenship of Mary. It seems to me that the Blessed Mother watches over Gorbachev in some special way, and for some special reason. In the logic of faith, Holiness, I can make the argument that if the Russians have a national hero for the moment in Yeltsin, the Holy Virgin has some sort of international puppet in Gorbachev. And I can make the argument that, when the right moment is at hand, he is the agent who will be used to facilitate Your Holiness' Eastern pilgrimage."

There was an obvious stirring among his companions as Chris fell into silence.

"It is decided then." The Slavic Pope had heard all he needed. "We won't force the timing of my Eastern pilgrimage." Then, with a twinkle in his eye for Carnesecca, and a nod to Gladstone, "If God in His providence sees fit to protect Mr. Gorbachev, surely He will see fit to give a little nod to His Vicar when the time is right.

"In fact—" His Holiness rose from his chair and walked the few paces to his desk. "Speaking of providence in our classic Christian sense, we have great need of providential guidance in another matter I want to discuss this evening."

The Pontiff placed the Gorbachev letter in a folder and, fingering the much thicker file of reports that had come to him concerning homosexual activity among the clergy in North America, launched into a somber, no-holds-barred summary of those reports. A full-blown portrait of clerical homosexuality and pedophilia seemingly run amok. A portrait of deep moral crisis.

"I do not think that the majority of my Cardinals—especially my in-house Cardinals here in Rome—realize the extent of what is happening. Indeed, part of the tragedy is that they live behind office doors in their own world. That doesn't excuse them. And it certainly does nothing to mitigate the catastrophe for the Roman Catholics who are being battered and drowned by the tides of homosexuality and pedophilia among their clergy.

"But even that isn't the total of the disaster. All over the Church—but again, the epicenter appears to be in North America—ritual Satanism is more and more rife, among both clergy and laity. I think it is Brother Augustine who can make it clear just how deadly serious that situation, too, has become in the United States. The organized Satanist activity going on in America seems to bring us into a further dimension of unbridled evil."

At a nod from the Pope, Augustine supplied a brief rundown of the detailed written report he had given to the Holy Father. "Mine-joo—" The prelate's emotion brought his brogue to the fore. "Mine-joo, I was only doin' a bit o' spot reportin'. But it's a bad business. There's the case of a certain Father Sebastian Scalabrini, a member o' the Archdiocese of Centurycity, who was murdered in his apartment some months ago. The police treated the case with sensitivity, and the whole matter was kept quiet. Then, a short time ago, another priest member o' the same Archdiocese was murdered. And in the same brutal fashion." Augustine ran through a shorthand version of the details of both homicides.

"The clincher to all this was that both o' these priests had been talkin' to officers in Centurycity's Bureau of Special Investigations. Seems there's a whole nest o' filth and corruption in that Archdiocese, but there's a lid been put on the entire mess."

Damien Slattery was astounded that Augustine had been able to get a line on that kind of activity and still come out alive.

Augustine gave Damien a mirthless little smile. "The truth is that I stumbled onto the whole thing. One o' my couriers is a fire chief in Centurycity. He's married to the sister of a recently retired police inspector. One o' those funny American names. I have it down somewhere in my report . . ."

"Wodgila!" The Pope groaned in mock exasperation. "Inspector Sylvester Wodgila! It's a Polish-American name." The little wave of laughter at Augustine's expense took the worst edge from the tension, but the respite was over in a few seconds.

"I've made it plain that this problem is critical." The Holy Father got to the specific matter on his mind. "The fact remains that spontaneous reports are not always reliable. They are not systematic. Brother Augustine's discovery shows that they don't begin to cover the whole problem. And I am not certain in every case of the trustworthiness of the informants."

Everyone understood by now where the Pontiff was headed. But Giustino Lucadamo put the problem plainly. "The only way to satisfy those deficiencies, Holiness, and to avoid a witch-hunt, is to send an investigator you can rely on to canvass the situation in the United States."

"Correction, Giustino." Damien Slattery spoke as an exorcist. "What's needed is two investigations. Every ritual Satanist may be engaged in pedophilia. But not every pedophiliac belongs to a Satanist cult. There are probably any number of men who could run a systematic check on homosexual behavior of a general kind. All you would need is a good man with a strong stomach who knows how to follow leads. But when you talk about ritual worship of Satan, you're into an area where you need some expertise. Brother Augustine has made it plain that investigating organized Satanic worship means taking your life in your hands."

His Holiness knew Slattery was right. "Do I take it, then, Father Damien, that you would limit early investigations to what you call homosexual behavior of a general kind among the American clergy?"

Damien nearly popped out of his white robes at such a thought. "What I'm saying, Holy Father, is that I'm your man for the Satanist end of things. I know a bona fide case of possession when I see it. I've had enough experience with cults to know that when you deal with Satan worship, you're into demonic possession with both feet. And, once my Dominican brothers hold their General Chapter next March, I'll be looking for work."

Slattery's reasoning made sense. But it left two practical questions. First, how to persuade the Dominicans to post him to the States once he had been replaced as Master-General. And, second, given the mortal danger of the mission, how to arrange the posting without tipping anyone to the fact that a papal investigation was in the offing.

"I think I can manage that part of things," Lucadamo offered. "As head of Vatican security, I can tell you that not all of Father Damien's Dominican brothers are lily white." Though he chose not to say so in the Pope's presence, he was sure that a bit of judiciously applied blackmail in a good cause would do the trick. Giustino turned to Slattery. "I may not be able to find a friendly base of operations for you in the United States. But I can get you there. And I can promise we'll come up with a good cover for your work."

It was the less dangerous side of the papal mission to the United States that posed the bigger problem. His work elsewhere for the Holy See put Augustine out of the running. Carnesecca would have been ideal, but no one yet knew for sure when he would come free from his present mission. And the security chief was dead set against Gladstone on the grounds that he was too green. "And anyway, Padre Christian, Cardinal Maestroianni is keeping you busy hopping around Europe. I doubt he'd take kindly to the idea of sending you Stateside."

"Don't be too sure of that." Gladstone wasn't willing to be counted out so easily. "There's been talk of my heading in that direction at some point. No dates or anything like that. Nothing definite at all, in fact. But it's not necessarily out of the question. Maybe I could even push it a little."

Brother Augustine came down in Gladstone's favor. "Maybe we should settle for maybe, Giustino. If it worked out that way, it wouldn't be half bad to have an American digging out the truth. Father Christian's work for Cardinal Maestroianni would be the perfect cover. Green he may be. But he knows the territory, and we know him."

"I suppose you're right." Lucadamo took the suggestion without enthusiasm. "For the time being, let's settle for maybe."

"The hour is late, my brothers." The Pontiff knew his security chief well enough to sense his unease. Apparently Lucadamo wasn't ready to take the American as a known quantity without running a more thorough check on him. "We have made a good start. As Father Damien will not be available until March, I suggest we make that our target date for both missions. That will leave us some time for final decisions and for needful preparations. Agreed?"

After a session like that, there was no heading straight for home. There was too much talking out to do. Too much left up in the air about the Pontiff and his concerns. About Yeltsin and U.S. policy. About Gorbachev and Fatima. About the morass in America. And besides, what better moment would there be for a little politicking on Christian's behalf? The five papal advisors chatted for a time in the chill December air of St. Peter's Square before they decided to carry on their conversation in the warmth of a café on the Via Mazzini. As they set off, Slattery and Brother Augustine had a private word or two with Lucadamo. Walking a few paces behind, Chris took the opportunity to invite Father Aldo to an old-fashioned Christmas gathering.

"I'll be visiting my brother and his family in Belgium. They have a most ample house in a little suburb of Ghent called Deurle. If you're of a mind, Father, you'd be most welcome."

It was a tempting offer, Carnesecca said; and he meant it. But he expected to be spending this Christmas season attending to business as Cardinal Aureatini's gofer in Sicily. So he could only say that his time wouldn't be his own until sometime early in the new year. "If all goes well, perhaps we can meet for dinner in January."

Carnesecca's conditional "if all goes well" wasn't lost on Christian. Yet he couldn't help but brighten at the prospect of a wide-ranging talk with his good friend again. "After Deurle, I'll be doing some work in Belgium. Then off to Holland and Liechtenstein. But I figure to return by January 5 or 6."

"Well, then." Carnesecca looked back toward the still lighted windows of the papal study. "Let's see if providence will give the nod to a couple of itinerant priests to celebrate the Epiphany together in Rome."

The abdominal pains the Pontiff still suffered had lessened over the past week, but fatigue showed in his movements as he worked with Monsignore Daniel to clear his desk.

"Tell me, Monsignore." The Slavic Pope handed over the folder containing Gorbachev's correspondence first, and then the file of worrisome reports from America. "Tell me. Do you think our five visitors this evening understand what I am about?"

"All the goodwill Your Holiness needs is in those five men." Daniel gave an honest answer. "But real understanding of papal policy, let alone the reasons behind it? No, Holiness. I don't think so."

"I expect you're right." The Pontiff strolled to the window and caught sight of those five visitors heading off together across the square. "And yet, lack of understanding didn't prevent them from giving their full measure of cooperation tonight. More, they responded to each question I raised in the light of its moral dimensions. Everything had that deeper dimension to it. And each of them had solid Catholic reasons for the advice he gave.

"Obviously, those five haven't followed the trend to substitute dialogue for their sacred vows of obedience. And they haven't abandoned their allegiance to the basic, binding moral precepts of the Church in favor of carnal convenience."

"Far from it!" Sadowski was adamant in his agreement. "Father Damien has even volunteered to risk his life."

"And not Father Damien alone." The Holy Father watched as, side by side with Gladstone, Aldo Carnesecca turned his steps toward the Via Mazzini. "How different such men are from my venerable colleagues in the Sacred College of Cardinals. Surely I am not wrong to place my hope—the hope of the Church—in the fidelity of those men. And in the fidelity of other men and women like them, wherever they are to be found.

"I want you to promise me one thing, Monsignore Daniel." The Pope let the curtains fall back against the window and turned full face to his secretary.

"Anything, Holiness."

"So many men change so much once they get the purple. If ever I am tempted to make any of those five a Cardinal, stop me. Do I have your word on it?"

"You have my word, Holy Father." Daniel grinned. "Count on it."

XXXI

BY THE TIME the Slavic Pope met with his confidential advisors on the evening of December 17, Gibson Appleyard had been in Rome for some days, had settled himself into the Raffaele and had set about preparing for his audience with the Holy Father.

Tucked away discreetly on the Piazza della Pilotta on the periphery of Old Rome, the Raffaele could not have been more convenient, more expensive or better suited to the needs of its exclusively foreign clientele of government emissaries and diplomats. Aside from its excellent cuisine, it offered such unique fare as scrambler telephones and a full range of electronic facilities, secretarial help of the most confidential kind, special couriers, well-trained bodyguards and bulletproof limousines driven by chauffeurs with unusual qualifications.

The real draw at the Raffaele, however, was its proprietor, Giovanni Battista Lucadamo. Possessed of an extraordinary wealth of classified information derived from his former Army comrades who now occupied key positions in government offices, this Lucadamo—uncle of Giustino Lucadamo, and the idol on whom the head of Vatican security services had modeled himself—was a glorified version of the traditional "fixer." He could solve most difficulties for his guests, provided his own sympathies went along. When those sympathies were crossed, however, he would reject any request for help with a peremptory lack of interest. "*Non c'entra*" he would say. "The matter is not relevant." And that would be an end to it.

Appleyard and the elder Lucadamo had been friends since the early seventies, when Gib had cut his teeth on the anti-Americanism rampant in a Europe menaced by an increasingly desperate Soviet Union. Fortunately for the rangy Yankee operative, Lucadamo wasn't a man to go along with doctrinaire fads. In the twenty or so years of their friendship, he had never rebuffed Gib with so much as a single *Non c'entra*.

Given the multilayered nature of preparations for his present mission, the Raffaele was the ideal base of operations for Appleyard this December. As chief on-the-spot problem solver for the President's ad hoc Committee of Ten, he never lost sight of the fact that his main objective this time around was to pin down—and, if possible, to influence—the Slavic Pope's policy intentions toward the U.S.S.R. But that didn't mean he would be content to get himself a slot on the papal calendar and then walk into the Apostolic Palace just like that.

Appleyard had long since learned to value, and had adapted to his own craft, what French farmers call *goût de terre,* an indefinable but indispensable taste of the land that makes the difference between success and failure. For Appleyard, that meant a familiarity with people. And that was why Bud Vance had been right to point out how little was known about the men who worked closely with the Pontiff. Whatever the details of the Holy Father's Soviet policy might be, it stood to reason that some general knowledge of that policy, and perhaps some means of influencing it, would come with a better understanding of the individuals who served in the papal entourage.

And yet, all the names that had come up in Gib's Washington briefing with Vance were little more than ciphers. They didn't know if Cardinal Cosimo Maestroianni was really out of the loop, as Vance had surmised. They didn't have any idea what Vatican business the seemingly innocent priest-professor Christian Gladstone might be discussing with his brother at the EC. The newcomer to the scene, Father Angelo Gutmacher, was so totally unknown that he was all but faceless. And they knew next to nothing about the ubiquitous Herr Otto Sekuler—about why he should have turned up for the antipapal doings at Strasbourg and then at the EC Selectors meeting at Brussels in September.

While they were excellent for taking care of visiting firemen, Appleyard had learned to distrust any claim the two U.S. Embassies in Rome might make to accuracy. They relied on secondary sources even for information on the Pope and his ranking Vatican officials. Not surprisingly, they had nothing to offer on such seemingly minor players as Gladstone or Gutmacher.

Well before he set off for Rome, therefore, and even as he did what legwork he could in Washington, Gib had taken advantage of the Raffaele's secure facilities to provide Giovanni Battista Lucadamo with an advance request for data on those figures and on others who might have a bearing on U.S. interests. Because the request was difficult even for Giovanni Lucadamo, Appleyard prepared himself for disappointment as the two men settled down in the high-tech clutter of his old friend's office on the second floor of the Raffaele.

Inevitably, the session began with a little catch-up chatter. To Gib's delight, the Italian had aged little since their last meeting. Like the wonderful old Church of the Twelve Apostles that stood nearby, Giovanni seemed a permanent part of Rome. His aquiline nose was as sharp as ever. And his big ears still caught every nuance of rumor and gossip.

Once the personal talk was over, Lucadamo pulled a couple of piles of folders from a drawer and began a methodical run-through of the information Appleyard had asked for. "Let's start with His Eminence Cardinal Maestroianni." Giovanni handed the first and fattest folder to Gib. "A lot of things in Rome start with him, as you'll see when you read this dossier. He may be retired as Secretary of State, but you can be sure he's not on the shelf.

"Among other things, in fact, he's the key to your young American priest." Lucadamo thumbed the next in his piles of folders. "Father Christian Gladstone has been attached to Maestroianni's office. As you said, he does a lot of traveling. And he's good at what he does. But it's all on the square. Even routine, you might say. He visits bishops with a view to assembling a profile on the condition of the Church in Europe. When he has a spare moment, he likes to study local church paintings. You'll find a complete rundown of his activities."

"Anything on Father Gladstone's visits to his brother at the EC?"

"Nothing you wouldn't expect. As Secretary-General of the EC, Paul Gladstone is in a position to fix a few minor problems some bishops get themselves into. It's just one of those common little conveniences of Vatican life that, as Paul's brother, Christian is nicely placed to ease that process along."

"As innocent as that?" Gib cocked an eyebrow.

"No one said anything about innocence, old friend." Lucadamo laughed. "Not in this city. Still, both Gladstones come up as clean. No women—leaving aside Paul Gladstone's wife, that is. No boys. No gold. And the same thing goes for the next man you asked about. I grant you, it's odd that such a longtime and intimate friend of the Gladstones as Father Angelo Gutmacher turned up in the Holy See at the same moment Father Christian opted for a Roman career. He's a friend of the Gladstones, but there's no professional connection between those two. No contact at all, in fact, since they arrived here last fall."

Appleyard couldn't argue with the facts. He was less interested in Gutmacher's connection with Gladstone than with Bud Vance's theory that the East German refugee might be a major courier for the Holy Father.

This time, it was Lucadamo who cocked an eyebrow. The question was interesting enough to tuck away for future use. "Maybe so," he conceded. "But there's no trace of any activity like that in the data I have. Gutmacher shapes up as a pathetic figure, really. Lives out of a suitcase. A regular traveling salesman of a priest. Take his most recent trip, for example." The Italian glanced at the final pages in the third of his folders. "After a brief stopover in Kraków, Poland, he set off to Moscow carrying prayer books and fifty thousand plastic Rosaries. Recited the Rosary in Red Square. Prayed in all the cathedrals of the Kremlin. Spoke over the Russian Orthodox Radio Sophia and the Roman Catholic Radio Blagovest. Ate at the Pizza Hut on Tverskaya . . ." Lucadamo wrinkled his nose.

"Next stop: Lvov in Ukraine. Prayed there with the Roman Catholic Primate in Lvov's Cathedral of St. George. Then it was on to the island monastery of Valdai, halfway between Moscow and St. Petersburg, where he was accompanied by Eparch Lev of Novgorod. That's the story of Angelo Gutmacher's life for the moment. He's due back in Rome anytime.

But he'll be off again before anyone even knows he's been here. I can even tell you where he's going next, if you want to know, and with whom he'll be talking."

"Not Gorbachev, by any chance?"

Lucadamo tucked a second interesting question into his newly formed mental file on Gutmacher. "No. Not Gorbachev. He'll head for Poland again. Then to St. Petersburg to see the Metropolitan Russian Orthodox Primate, Joan. After that, it's back to Moscow and another chat with Patriarch Kiril. They'll talk some more about the Virgin, and about shrines and saints and Rosaries. That sort of thing. For what it's worth, he doesn't even visit the Pope's man in Moscow, Monsignore Colasuono. Nor the Roman Catholic Bishop of Moscow, Tadeusz Kondrusiewicz."

Appleyard shook his head. Although Gutmacher spent a lot of time in the U.S.S.R., his activities there pointed to nothing useful. Nothing more than the Holy Father's interest in the Fatima predictions, in all likelihood; and that was no rational policy base for a man as intelligent and as deeply engaged in world affairs as this Pope.

"It's a puzzle, isn't it?" Lucadamo was sincerely apologetic. "I've compiled dossiers for you on others who are close to the Holy Father. But for your purposes, it's more of the same."

"For instance." Appleyard stretched his long legs in front of him.

"For instance, you may have heard of the Master-General of the Dominican Order. Father Damien Duncan Slattery. He's been one of the Pontiff's close confidants for years. A confessor to His Holiness, in fact. Heads up a team of exorcists for the Holy See, and has quite a reputation in that field. He has lots of friends and lots of enemies. But the word is that his enemies have got the better of him. Anyway, he's on his way out as Master-General."

Appleyard saw a ray of hope. "That's too bad for Father Slattery. But if he's angry enough to do a bit of talking, it may be a break for me. Any chance I can meet with him?"

"Every chance in the world. He's a most affable fellow. Very approachable. The only trouble is that he'll talk to you about everything—except what you really want to know. And I wouldn't be too sure of his grasp on papal policy. He may be a pro when it comes to exorcism, but geopolitics isn't his field."

Appleyard waved his hands in frustration. "Tell me, Giovanni. Isn't there one man in Rome who can shed some light on things? One man who can make some sense when it comes to Vatican policies in the East?"

"Well." Lucadamo smiled. "There is one man who could probably answer all your questions. A priest—a gofer, really—by the name of Aldo Carnesecca. He's been here forever. Works in the Secretariat and around the place in general. He knows all there is to know about Rome. But he's mostly away these days in Sicily. And—I hate to tell you this, Gibson—I don't think he'd talk to you in a million years."

Appleyard would spend time before his papal meeting going over all the information Lucadamo had compiled for him. But, convinced by now that nothing in this mounting pile of dossiers would lead to anything useful as far as the Pontiff's Russia policy was concerned, he turned to the riddle posed by the Schuman Day meeting he had attended at Strasbourg.

Here again, Lucadamo had assembled a number of files for his friend. In the main, however, they added little to what Gib already knew. The only exception was the material on Otto Sekuler. But even there the data was sparse.

An ethnic German born in Kiev, Sekuler had escaped the Nazi German sweep into the Ukraine and had lived with the partisans until war's end. Educated at the Free University in West Berlin, he had joined the cultural section of the East German government and had eventually secured a place with UNESCO. His UNESCO career appeared ordinary and undistinguished, but it had led to his current posting with the Conference on Security and Cooperation in Europe. One way and another, he had traveled extensively in Europe and North America. Specifically, as Lucadamo pointed out, he had had some dealings with the Grand Orients of France and Italy; and, more particularly, his dealings with the GO in Italy often involved the Grand Master himself, Bruno Itamar Maselli.

Neither the data on Sekuler nor the intelligence concerning any of the others in the Strasbourg cabal served to answer Appleyard's main concern. Specifically, he wanted to know if the plans at that meeting to oust the Slavic Pope and change the governing structure of the Church were serious. "If they are, that would change the whole complexion of things."

"They're serious, all right," Lucadamo confirmed. "At the level where it counts, the game is so private you could say it's hermetically sealed. But they want him out."

"Who?"

"Who what?"

"Don't turn cute on me, Giovanni. 'At the level where it counts,' you said. Should I assume, then, that it doesn't stop with the men who were at the Strasbourg meeting?" Lucadamo shifted his eyes toward the windows and the piazza beyond.

"Names, Giovanni," Appleyard persisted. "If my guess is right, I need names."

"You need more than names, Gibson." Lucadamo turned back to the American. "But I can't give you even that much."

"Can't? Or won't?"

"It comes to the same thing. That Strasbourg list you sent me has clues enough. You'll be more apt to get a line on things in London or New York than in circles close to the Pope here in Rome." It wasn't exactly *Non c'entra,* but Lucadamo was clearly done with any further discussion of a plot to force a papal resignation. In fact, he was already moving on. "Now, Gibson, about that meeting you asked me to set up for you with

Grand Master Bruno Maselli. I thought about arranging for you to meet him at the Grand Orient offices on the Via Giustiniani. But it's too close to the Vatican. You might be observed. A meeting there might prejudice the outcome of your audience with His Holiness. It's never wise to be too blatant.

"Anyway, I've arranged for you to see Maselli at his private residence." Lucadamo scribbled an address in the Parioli district of Rome and handed it across the desk.

Gibson Appleyard's decision to pay a visit to Grand Master Bruno Itamar Maselli had been prompted by Gib's extensive study of the Slavic Pope's speeches and published writings. He had a sense that the near-term, practical policies of this obviously open-minded, intellectual Pontiff might not be so different from those of Rosicrucian Masonry; and he hoped to test that possibility in a meeting with no less an authority on the subject than the head of the Scottish Rite Supreme Council and Grand Orient of Italy.

Appleyard did have to admit that the exercise might prove pointless. If the plot to force the Pope from office was serious enough to make even Giovanni Lucadamo flinch to talk about it, maybe the Pontiff's policies toward the Soviet Union would be mooted, and the whole geopolitical game was about to change. On the other hand, his words to Bud Vance still held. Whatever about the future, the Slavic Pope was the man to deal with now.

By the time he settled himself into the rear seat of one of Lucadamo's bulletproof limousines and set out for the Parioli district, Appleyard had decided his theory was still worth testing. And, besides, he had looked forward to his meeting with Grand Master Maselli as more than a professional duty. As a spiritual pleasure, in fact. As onetime Commander-in-Chief of the Ancient Accepted Scottish Rite, Northwest New York State, Gib relished the chance to discuss Craft matters with the man at the top of the Scottish Rite Supreme Council and Grand Orient founded by Giuseppe Garibaldi himself. Despite the fact that Italian Masonry was the most secretive in the Masonic world, Maselli himself was a known personality. As far back as 1966 and 1967, as a still youthful member of the Grand Central Council, he had helped to pull Italy's GO out of a slump when some American GOs had withdrawn recognition following a series of political scandals. Then, as Grand Master, he had done the same thing again in 1980 after a bogus Masonic Lodge, the infamous P-2, was implicated in a national scandal involving billions of lire and such dark doings as assassinations and "suicides."

Apparently, anticipation of tonight's meeting was mutual. When his driver pulled up at Maselli's residence, Appleyard found his smiling host waiting at the door to welcome him as a distinguished guest and honored Frater. A pharmacist in civic life, Bruno Itamar Maselli was a well-fed man whose intelligence was obvious in his wide-set eyes. As the Grand

Master led Appleyard through his hillside home to an enclosed veranda overlooking the river Tiber, Gib was struck by the contrast between Maselli's open smile and the lugubrious, almost funereal tone of his voice.

The Italian invited his visitor to take a comfortable chair, splashed excellent brandy into a couple of snifters and turned his plump face to the American Frater as if to ask what he might have on his mind. Evidently Maselli wasn't much for small talk.

Gib was not coy. He had one main question for his host, and he put it straight out. "In dealing with this Pope, am I dealing with an enemy of Masons and Masonic ideals? Or is all that Catholic anti-Masonry stuff over and done with?"

Maselli lifted his glass to savor the aroma before he took a first sip. "Truthfully, this Pope is an enemy of no man."

This was more like it, Gib thought. Not only did this man know about the Slavic Pope but his assessment seemed to fit with the picture Appleyard had formed in his own mind.

"However," Maselli went on, "Masonic ideals are something else again. You must take this Pope's background into account. And above all, you must take into account the radical difference in ideals between his Church and the Lodge."

Gib's satisfaction faded. Of course he knew about the bad blood between Church and Lodge dating from the early-eighteenth-century beginnings of the Masonic Order in its modern form. But surely all that was *acqua passata*. Water long gone under the bridge by now.

"*Acqua turbolente* would be more like it," Maselli offered a polite correction. "In the Slavic Pope's homeland in particular, friction and enmity have always marked the relationship between Masons and the Catholic Church. The Pontiff's great friend and mentor, the late Cardinal Primate of his country, always treated Masons as the architects of an anti-Christian force. So it's only to be expected that churchmen there are not pleased that, just since the collapse of the Stalinist government, no fewer than thirty-eight new Lodges have opened in their country. They see in that a new effort by Masonry to undermine religious faith."

Appleyard thought about that for a moment. He wasn't about to challenge such an authority as Grand Master Maselli. But he decided nonetheless to set out his own more optimistic view of the Slavic Pope's attitudes.

Maselli listened patiently. Perhaps tolerantly was more like it. Either way, he was not impressed. "Surely you know, my dear Appleyard, how we have fared with this Pope. All our efforts to establish a working relationship have failed. We even went public with our invitation to comity between Church and Lodge. But"—he swept the air with one hand as if to brush away a gnat—"all to no avail."

"What happened precisely? Was the invitation rebuffed?"

"Precisely?" Maselli smiled as he echoed the word, but there was no change in his funereal voice. "Precision is not always easy to come by in these matters. But let me refresh your memory.

"There has been a convergence of views between the Fratres and many Church officials. You will recall, for instance, the *Bible of Concord* published in 1968 by the Italian Grand Master at the time, Giordano Gamberini, with the imprimatur of the Church itself! Yes! There was a great convergence!"

The Grand Master went on to put things into a wider context. "It has always been known that there have been a steady number of clerics of all three main ranks—priests, bishops and Cardinals—who have become active Lodge members. The venerable Grand Orient of France that dates from 1773, by the way, and now boasts over five hundred Craft Lodges, published an exhaustive list of Roman Catholic clerical members that included priests, bishops and members of such major Religious Orders as the Benedictines, the Dominicans and the Jesuits.

"At least once in the history of papal conclaves—specifically, in the Conclave of 1903—a Masonic Cardinal received a sufficient number of votes to become Pope. His election to the papacy was quietly nullified, of course. The official Roman reaction of fear was explicated in Canon Law 2335: Any Catholic whose name was included in the roster of any Masonic Lodge would incur immediate and automatic excommunication, even if he had never attended a meeting of the Fratres. The new Code of Canon Law promulgated in 1983 wiped out the ban of excommunication contained in the old Code.

"Then—" The Grand Master's disappointment became more evident as he drew matters up to the present moment. "Then there was another sudden and unexpected development. The name Bugnini—Annibale Bugnini—may not mean much to you, Signor Appleyard." Maselli leaned forward to replenish Appleyard's glass.

"Never heard the name," Gib replied.

"Just as well, my friend." Maselli gave a short laugh. "Actually, this Monsignore Bugnini was a member of the Lodge. And actually he did persuade the then Pope to try and eliminate the Roman Catholic Mass. When this present Pontiff heard about Bugnini's Masonic identity, he hardened in his attitude to the Lodge, and thus he turned his back on our approaches. This is the only possible answer to your question why this Pontiff rebuffed our invitation. After all, he has welcomed everybody else—atheists, animists, agnostics, fanatics, schismatics. But not the Fratres!"

"So you put the rebuff down to fear?" Appleyard was not convinced by the Grand Master's reading of the Slavic Pope. He was prepared to agree that the Pontiff was no man's enemy. But it seemed unlikely that a man with his record would be shocked by any confrontation with Masonry. After all, this Pope had survived the Nazis. As priest and prelate, he had faced down the Stalinists for years in his homeland. And within his first year as head man in the Vatican, he had risked his person and his pontificate, and won, in his astonishing face-off with the Soviet Union.

"Your doubt is understandable, I suppose." Maselli eyed his visitor with impatience. "Especially as you have had to rely on books and speeches to form your idea of this Pope."

"It's not doubt, exactly," Appleyard offered. "It's just that we heard rumors that some Fratres or some Craft Lodges had indulged in Satanist rituals. We thought that might have motivated the papal rebuff."

Maselli stared in utter disbelief. "You can scour the official records in all our Craft Lodges in this jurisdiction, Appleyard! You won't find a trace of such goings-on. Such wicked rumors begin in the Vatican, surely. This Pope is obsessed with Satan or Lucifer or whatever he calls this mythical being. Wicked, vicious rumors, Mr. Appleyard!"

Gibson was astonished. His own remarks might have been clumsy, but they hadn't been intended as a personal accusation. It was a moment worth remembering; but for now, it would be better simply to change the subject.

"I wonder . . ." As smoothly as the situation allowed, Appleyard set off in a new and more benign direction. "In my recent travels about Europe, I've come across a character called Otto Sekuler. I believe he belongs to some Lodge in Germany. He appears to have some international mission that brings him into your jurisdiction. Perhaps you know him."

"You have an interest in this—what was his name?"

"Sekuler." Gib hadn't expected a game of cat and mouse over such a simple query. "Herr Otto Sekuler."

The Grand Master stood up abruptly and led the way into his study, where he took a thick volume from a bookshelf. "Let me see now if I can be of some help. Sekuler . . . Sekuler, Otto . . . Ah! Yes, here it is." When Maselli raised his eyes again, his face was a perfect mask of composure. "He appears here as a prominent member of the Leipzig Lodge. Nothing unusual about him. He works for some of UNESCO's nongovernmental committees. Nothing at all outstanding."

The Devil you say! Gib spat the words silently in his mind. When Maselli made no move to head back toward the veranda, Gibson was ready enough to take the hint. "I fear I've overstayed my welcome, Frater."

"Not at all!" In a contrast of mood that struck Appleyard as chilling, the Grand Master was back to his smiling self. "Not at all! Always feel welcome to come or call. Anytime. Anytime you like."

The more Appleyard reviewed things during his ride back to the Piazza della Pilotta, the more somber his thoughts became. He remained convinced that there was nothing hidden or Machiavellian about the Pontiff. Yet he was equally convinced that no one he had spoken to understood either the Holy Father or his policies. Despite the advance work Lucadamo had done for him, Appleyard had learned only two things. No one who could be described as a papal intimate seemed to be accessible in any way that mattered. And no one who was accessible could offer anything more than the most routine knowledge of this Pontiff.

Then, to top it all, his meeting with Maselli had been worse than a dead end. Gib had hoped to establish a relationship of amity with the Italian Grand Master. Indeed, he had expected tonight's encounter to be rational, unheated and clear-minded; for such was the humanly beautiful advantage of Masonry and the Masonic way of life. Instead, he had come away with a sour taste in his mouth. He didn't like the contradiction between Maselli's sunny-day smile and his dead-of-night voice. He wondered at the raw nerve he had touched at the mention of Satanism. And he was just plain baffled over Maselli's charade concerning Otto Sekuler.

According to Lucadamo, Maselli and Sekuler had met face to face. And if it came to a choice between the proven reliability of Lucadamo's sources and Maselli's professed ignorance of even so much as the German's name, Lucadamo would win. Why the reticence, then? Why deny even the slightest personal knowledge of Sekuler? It was enough to throw doubt over the entire conversation, including Maselli's judgments concerning the Holy Father.

By the time his driver deposited him at the Raffaele, Gib had more questions than when he had arrived in Rome, and his mood was positively foul. This was not the best way to end the evening before his papal audience. Gib glanced at his watch. Memories of good times gone by told him that Giovanni probably had his feet up by now, with his collar open, something by Mozart on his tape deck and a glass of the best Marsala wine in his hand.

That was the ticket, he told himself as he headed for the second door. If anyone could help take the ragged edge off his mood, the levelheaded, worldly-wise proprietor of the Raffaele was the man.

On the chill but sunny morning of December 18, the Vatican protocol welcomed Gibson Appleyard as a distinguished emissary of the President of the United States. A young freshly scrubbed monsignore greeted him with formal cordiality at the door of his limousine and escorted him to the third-floor office of Cardinal Secretary of State Giacomo Graziani. His Eminence blinked his way through a pro forma conversation, during which a score of nice things were said by both men and nothing of consequence was addressed by either. Then the Cardinal himself led Appleyard to the papal study, presented him with smiles to the Holy Father and retired.

As the Slavic Pope took his visitor's outstretched hand in both of his own in welcome, Appleyard was impressed with the resident strength of the Pontiff's broad chest and solid shoulders. But what struck him—held him, in fact—were the Pope's eyes. Nothing could have prepared him for those eyes. Clearest blue—not hostile or anxious or indifferent, but smiling—they were the eyes of a man who has no fear. Eyes that carried a message that was not unpleasant but was too subtle to read at first sight.

The Holy Father made a few welcoming remarks as he walked his visitor to a pair of facing armchairs near one of the study windows. Appleyard responded in kind to the Pontiff's generous welcome. He extended the good wishes of his government. He complimented His Holiness on his journeys earlier in the year to France, Poland, Hungary and Brazil. And he commented with unfeigned sincerity that he knew of no other world leader, religious or political, who could have attracted 1.3 million young people to Fatima, as the Pontiff had done in May, and another 1.5 million to Czestochowa in Poland. "It was truly impressive leadership, Your Holiness. Most inspiring."

The Slavic Pope responded with a modest smile of his own, and then inquired by name about a few people he knew in the State Department. Though their exchanges were leisurely, there came a moment when, by some indefinable gesture, the Pope invited Appleyard to speak his mind.

"I have some specific subjects to discuss with Your Holiness on behalf of my government." Appleyard felt a sense of ease as he responded to the invitation. "But, as just one ordinary human being, I must confess that I have so much more weighing on my mind and heart, as I'm sure Your Holiness has. There is so much misery among our fellow human beings. Your Holiness' heartfelt interventions about the tragic condition of the Sudanese Christians, the East Timor people, the Somali people and the horror unfolding presently in Yugoslavia have given a voice to the universal feelings of all men and women of goodwill."

For an instant, the Pope focused on the middle distance as though he could see there what he had seen in those death-infested lands. "Evidently, Mr. Appleyard, you and I—and the bodies we represent—are fearful of what our Supreme Judge and Lord Arbiter of our fate will say about man's inhumanity to man."

A sudden, annoying memory plucked at Appleyard's mind. A fleeting recollection of his Masonic induction so long ago, and of those Knight Kadosh ceremonial words about "this dreaded tribunal . . . my Supreme Judge." But the moment passed quickly in the unspoken commonality of sentiment he had discovered in himself for this man in the white robe.

"And"—the Holy Father's eyes were on his visitor again—"we are concerned about impending matters in Europe and in the U.S.S.R. of Mr. Gorbachev." As easily as that, the Pontiff brought Appleyard to the focus of his visit.

The principal subject of his Roman mission having been opened for him, Appleyard inquired whether the Pope was aware of the imminent change in the top echelons of Soviet leadership that would see Boris Yeltsin take over from Mikhail Gorbachev. Yes, His Holiness indicated by a nod of his head. He was aware. Things had to come to a head, given the dynamics of the situation.

That was too interesting—too inviting—for Appleyard to let pass without exploration. "Those dynamics being what, in Your Holiness' appraisal?"

The answer was unhesitating and remarkably direct; but somehow its stark realism did nothing to lessen the total empathy that might have been shattered by a lesser man. "Once the top-level decision was taken that the Cold War would end, and that the Soviet bloc would move actively into the economic and financial sphere of the Western nations, the leadership change we both know will come within a few days was inevitable."

His Holiness paused briefly at the mild but open surprise written on the emissary's face. He had shifted the focus of conversation only slightly. In effect, he was saying that it was something other than mere blind and irrational forces of nature that was at work in the U.S.S.R. But he wondered if the American had taken the point fully.

"We both know, Mr. Appleyard, that there was no spontaneous 1989 revolution among the peoples of the former Soviet satellites or among the peoples of the U.S.S.R. The Soviet system did not implode, as it were, and fall into its own ruins. There was no sudden failure of Soviet nerve. Something unpredictable and unpremeditated by men did not suddenly break over our heads. Any such analysis as that is a hoax. It's at least a myth, if not a fabrication, foisted on the print-reading and television-viewing audiences of the world.

"Something far more significant in the making of history took place. The will of man—of men—went into action. There was an 'arrangement,' wasn't there? Let's forget for the moment by whom and for what motives. Agreed?"

The Pontiff's questions were obviously rhetorical, for he went on to speak of things other men only whispered. "What there was, concretely speaking, was a series of telephone calls from Kremlin offices telling Communist dictators and strongmen in the satellite countries to make themselves scarce, to get out. It was under President Gorbachev's direction all that was done. But we all realize, don't we, Mr. Appleyard, that he was not acting on his own personal initiative, but in obedient concert with the real men of power who decide life and death in the society of nations; and, if it comes to that point of macromanagement, in the cosmos."

Appleyard drew a long breath. He was stunned that this Pope, who seemed so enigmatic to the world, had opened his mind so readily. "We had hoped," he offered gingerly, "that President Gorbachev's desperate attempt to hold the states of the U.S.S.R. together would succeed."

"But it couldn't have succeeded." His Holiness held both hands out as if to present the gift of his long experience in the matters under discussion. "I believe our planners realized early on that if, by some wild fluke, it had succeeded, we would all have ended up with a mere change of name in the U.S.S.R. The old ideological status of things would emerge in a new garb.

"No, Mr. Appleyard. Gorbachev's Federation of Socialist Soviet States was a mushroom growth. Born at midnight, it was dead at sunrise. Midnight came for Mr. Gorbachev, I think, with the somber realism that reigned at the meeting of the G-7 in London last July, where he met with the heads of the seven most industrialized nations. The seven Wise Men had heard the message conveyed by the June election of Boris Yeltsin as President of the Gorbachev Federation in a universal vote by the Soviet peoples. And midnight passed for Gorbachev during the bogus coup staged the following August. From then until now, it was a matter of time until he would step aside and let Yeltsin try his luck."

Appleyard's astonishment had given way to something else by now. He no longer had to wonder what sort of intelligence lay behind the "poor, poor Europe" letter the Pontiff had sent to the EC Selectors meeting in Brussels. Instead, as he looked into those steady blue eyes, he read the subtle message that had escaped him earlier. Not only do I have the benefit of Holy Water and Agnus Deis and beautiful Latin hymns, that message said; I also have state-of-the-art information and communication at my fingertips, as you do. I am a Slav, that message said. And as a Slav, the Slavic community from the Oder to the Sea of Japan is my heritage. I am Pope, that message said. And as Pope, all nations are my bailiwick.

Appleyard was a quick learner. "I see, Your Holiness," he said. And with those words, he accepted not only the premises of the Pontiff's statements but all that passed unspoken between them. He now felt free to move on to the Committee of Ten policy concerns that had brought him here. "What actually preoccupies my government, Your Holiness, is the fate of the component states of the U.S.S.R. once the red flag is lowered from the Kremlin at midnight on this coming Christmas."

Again the Pope responded with the basic fact of the situation. "The old official Kremlin policy of *sliyanie,* melding all ethnic groups into the glorious homogeneity of the Leninist Party-State, that was always a mirage. In spite of Moscow's economic and military pressures, the Baltic States have already declared their intention to secede. So, too, Ukraine. And so, too, Belarus' Popular Front, the Adradzenie. I needn't mention Muslim states such as Tajikistan, Uzbekistan and Kyrgyzstan; in the next five years or so they may drop off the edge of significance. But the same spirit of secession flows among the Tartars, the Bashkirs, the Chuvash, and among Chechens in the North Caucasus."

By now, Appleyard wondered if the State Department experts assigned to monitor the East knew as much as this Pope. "Doubtless the remaining Soviet states will go the same route. But they are not viable by themselves. Not those Your Holiness has mentioned. And not Estonia or Latvia or Lithuania or any of the rest of them. We are heading into a period of fragmentation, contention and experimentation. And during that time—

the dangerous period of transition—Boris Yeltsin seems to us to be the safest short-term man to back. He will be dogged by hyperinflation and by huge drops in production and income. But he should survive for a couple of years. Perhaps even longer.

"We are aware of Your Holiness' warm relationship with President Gorbachev . . ." The Pope's raised eyebrow told Appleyard he had misstepped. "We are aware," he began again, "of the unusual exchange that has taken place between Your Holiness and President Gorbachev." A little shrug of the papal shoulder indicated acceptance of the modified remark. "Still, Holy Father, we would like to feel that we have Your Holiness' support—and, if the need arises, Your Holiness' collaborative efforts—in making the Yeltsin regime as successful as possible."

"But of course. I have collaborated with U.S. policy during the Gorbachev period. I reestablished the Roman Rite hierarchy in Belarus. I have incurred the displeasure of Premier Stanislav Suskievic to such a degree that he vented it publicly in the Parliament and on television. But I acted in accord with Moscow's wishes, not the wishes of the very patriotic Belarus populace. As in the past, so in the future. We intend to fulfill our obligations as co-signatory to the Helsinki Accords.

"Yet, Mr. Appleyard, I must remind you of the Holy See's disillusioning experience in this century vis-à-vis the Western powers. In World War II and during the trying years of the Cold War that followed, this Holy See made more than what you have called collaborative efforts to achieve the military outcome and the peace sought by Western-based forces." The Slavic Pope told of the unusual lengths to which the Pope of World War II had collaborated secretly with the Western Allies. "That Pope and his services were used by all the Allies, Mr. Appleyard. Yet the Holy See was allowed no effective say in postwar agreements."

In the Cold War, the Slavic Pope had only to recall how Solidarnosc—organized with the blessing of the Holy See—had been used by the Western powers in the seventies and eighties to create a first breach in what some had called the "evil empire" of the Soviets. "Again there was full collaboration by the Holy See. Now that the 'evil empire' is no more, however, the Holy See, which I now embody as Pope, has been and is excluded from the planning of Western leaders about the post-Cold War world. You may not know that, toward the end of World War I, Britain, France, Italy and your United States made the secret Treaty of London, explicitly to exclude the Holy See from any and all peace negotiations.

"In other words, Mr. Appleyard, there is a fixed principle observed by those who make major geopolitical decisions: to exclude this Holy See, no matter how cooperative it may prove to be. That is a brute fact of our time, Mr. Appleyard. You will understand that as Pope I have no intention of being used yet another time while that principle is still operative."

Appleyard did understand. He couldn't have asked for greater candor, in fact. But the Slavic Pope had blocked any further progress toward identifying papal aims in Eastern Europe, much less influencing those aims.

Having cut the diplomatic ground from under his visitor's feet, the Pontiff began to construct a little bridge of hope. "Mind you, sir"—it seemed no more than an afterthought—"my statements do not mean we will not continue to extend the usual diplomatic courtesies. It was a Church-owned Moscow radio station that alone made it possible for Yeltsin to broadcast to the Soviet peoples during the August coup. I myself gave permission for that. And doubtless you also know of our collaboration in financial and diplomatic matters during your invasion of Panama. And also before and during the Gulf War. The list could be extended."

Appleyard had to wonder if it had been such a good idea after all for the Committee of Ten to send a spy on a diplomat's mission. So far, the Slavic Pope was running rings around him. Still, he decided to make a feint across the Pontiff's bridge of hope.

"We have no doubt about the friendly and courteous attitude of the Holy See," Appleyard began speculatively. "That being so, there are naturally a few aspects of the present situation on which we would appreciate Your Holiness' estimation. Your Holiness alluded a few moments ago to the reestablishment of the Roman Rite hierarchy in Belarus. Your Holiness also reestablished the Roman Catholic Latin Rite hierarchy of bishops in Russia and Kazakhstan. And we have also heard that Your Holiness will shortly nominate five new bishops for Albania.

"Of course, we realize that these moves are apostolic. Yet Your Holiness must be aware that they do not sit well with the Patriarchate of Moscow. May I ask Your Holiness, then, the general policy of the Holy See toward the Russian Orthodox Church?"

Appleyard's effort to use a query concerning ROC and the Moscow Patriarchate as his entrée into the Pontiff's Eastern policy evoked an unequivocal reply. No one understood better than the Slavic Pope that Moscow's Patriarch Kiril was one of Yeltsin's allies, and that the interest of the Western governments in ROC had to do with helping to stabilize Yeltsin's regime. "Your government knows the long-standing commitment of the Moscow Patriarchate to the cause of the old Leninist Party-State. As with the upper-echelon membership of that now officially dead system, so with the Russian Orthodox authorities. They may change their commitment, or they may not. It may be that both the Orthodox authorities and the upper-echelon Leninists may yet mellow. But that is not the issue. The issue is camouflage! For, despite their new nomenclature, the same crowd is still at the center of power. And, in very truth, isn't this the crux of the difficulty with the present fracturing of the U.S.S.R.? That eventually the truth may out? You have only to ask yourself: What has changed really?

"Have we seen any settling of accounts for genocide? For deception? For perpetuating the Great Lie? For untold millions who lived lives of agony and died slow, excruciating deaths? Are we to believe that the

Leninist system with its spymasters and spies, its propagandists, its concentration-camp commandants, its jailers and wardens and torturers—the entire apparatus of the malevolent, lying Big Brother State—has all ceased to exist?

"We have all been watching a sleight-of-hand operation, Mr. Appleyard. Presto! Now you see the U.S.S.R. led by Mikhail Gorbachev. Presto! Now you see the Gorbachev Federation. Presto! Now you see the Yeltsin-governed Russia. Should this Holy See collaborate in preserving that sleight of hand?"

Appleyard sat a little straighter in his chair as a show of his diplomatic resolve. "In view of all this, Holiness, should my government take it that this Holy See will find it difficult to be in unison with the other signatories of the Helsinki Accords? At least on certain points?"

The Slavic Pope's rejoinder was immediate, smooth and unsmiling. He had been at this crossroads of diplomatic negotiation too many times to accept the choice that had been put to him. "Mr. Appleyard, those Accords provide escape clauses of which any signatory can avail itself when its own national interest is involved. You have already had my answer, therefore. This Holy See will not find it difficult to fulfill its obligations." In absolute terms, there was no need to say more. Silence itself was an implicit question. If it pleased the American to do so, he could end all discussion right here.

Gibson Appleyard turned aside from that alternative. Perhaps it was the mood of commonality that had been created at the outset of this meeting; or the picture he had formed in his mind of this Slavic Pope as a man of some enlightenment bade him prolong the discussion.

"Holiness, ultimately we are all aiming to make our world as peaceful and prosperous a habitat as possible. On this, surely we agree."

The Holy Father had no difficulty in following the shift in thought. He had such men as Appleyard within his own Vatican. Prelates whom he described privately as "good Masons." Men of good faith who were true innocents. Unaware or unconvinced of deeper workings and a deeper intent within the elements of Masonry, they saw no difficulty in combining their Catholicism with Masonic ideals. "Yes, Mr. Appleyard. In view of our eternal home with God, yes. Agreed. But not in view of making this world the exclusive, ultimate temple of man's existence."

A glance was enough for Appleyard to know he had not been entirely mistaken in his reading of this Pope. The Holy Father understood and accepted him for what he was. He was encouraged, therefore, to a further exploration of parallel interests between his government and the Holy See. "Our pluralistic system, Holiness, has standards that can be accepted by all. By those who aim at the eternal home of which Your Holiness speaks; and by those who aim at the ideal earthly temple of mankind."

Again, the Pontiff took the common ground offered as the entry to his answer. "In abstract principle, such standards are fine. Separation of

Church and State is a cornerstone of your American social contract to pursue life, liberty and happiness as the ultimate ideal. That conception is utopian, of course. Always aimed at, never achieved. You yourself obviously share that utopian ideal; you have faith in that ideal. However, there are others who place the achievement of that ideal under a banner in this cosmos that does not and will not tolerate those who, like this Holy See, aim at the eternal habitat."

The look on the American's face was more like perplexity than surprise. But it was enough to tell the Pope that he had gone as far as he could with this man of good faith.

Appleyard had obviously reached the same conclusion, for he used a personal request to break off from the conversation. He asked for access to some archival material for his own reference; and he mentioned a colleague of his at Stanford University who needed an introduction to the Pontifical Academy of Sciences of the Vatican.

"Happily, Mr. Appleyard." The Slavic Pope crossed the study to his desk and wrote out a memo directing immediate facilitation of the American's requests. Then the Holy Father put a request of his own. He was concerned with the investigations that were mushrooming into alleged U.S. government illegalities connected with the Vatican Bank and the Banca Nazionale di Lavoro. "I may be overstepping the given boundaries of our discussion," His Holiness acknowledged. "But on the Vatican side in this BNL affair, it would be a help to the Prefecture of Economic Affairs if these financial matters could be cleared up."

"No difficulty, Holiness. Your PECA was of service to the United States. The moment I return, I shall attend to it."

The Holy Father rose and retrieved a small package from a nearby side table. Carefully, he removed the wrapping to reveal an icon depicting the Monastery of Czestochowa under siege by Swedish armies in the seventeenth century. "It's an early-eighteenth-century piece, Mr. Appleyard." There was no mistaking the pride in the papal voice. "A private and personal gift from me to you and your family."

Appleyard accepted the gift from the Pope's hands with genuine pleasure. "Truly a beautiful work of art, Holiness." Appleyard understood fully the emotion that lay behind the treasure he held so gently in his hands. An emotion based on an abiding love of homeland. "Your Holiness has been most generous with . . ."

The Slavic Pope raised a hand as if to object to such finality in their parting. "Perhaps providence will bring us together again, Mr. Appleyard." The Pontiff walked slowly beside his visitor as far as the elevator. "Perhaps we will have another opportunity to discuss these grave matters."

"For my part, Holiness," Appleyard responded with sincerity, "I relish the hope that this will not be the last time we will meet."

❑ ❑ ❑ ❑

Gib Appleyard changed into slacks and a sweatshirt and ambled into the living room of his suite at the Raffaele. He had a lot of sorting out to do before he would be ready to make his preliminary telephone report to Bud Vance. He had learned a lot of lessons this morning. But he still knew next to nothing about the Holy See's policy with respect to the East.

Gib spent a solid hour critiquing his papal audience. At the most objective level, he reflected, he had been dealing with a world leader of a different kind from any other he had met. In a world where democratic capitalism had become the first and indispensable ticket of entry into the new society of nations, the Pope still reigned politically, diplomatically and religiously as an absolute monarch.

Nevertheless, the Pontiff was a man of these times. He headed a global organization unique in the depth of its contact with other leaders, and in the depth of its influence among hundreds of millions of people of the world. And he had made it plain that he had at his fingertips—and knew how to use—all the advantages of the oldest and most experienced political chancery on earth. Moreover, the Slavic Pope had shown that he was not an enemy of democratic capitalism. True, he clearly doubted capitalism's tolerance of a religious base for its moral judgments. He had demonstrated reservations about capitalist morality itself, in fact. But at least he favored the Western system over any Marxist or socialist stance.

At a more subjective level, meanwhile, there was no need for Appleyard to temporize his first face-to-face impression. Those eyes had said it all for him, because they had been able to see beyond all the deep differences that might have been a barrier this morning, and to establish instead a peculiar depth of communication. The eyes of a man who wanted nothing less than peace and the betterment of life for all mankind.

Come to think of it, Gib mused a little wryly, the Holy Father appeared to be one up on him when it came to the behind-the-scenes factors that had caused the abrupt transformation of the U.S.S.R. from Cold War superpower opponent to petitioner for inclusion in the economic and financial life of Western Europe and the U.S.A. The Pope had talked about Gorbachev acting in obedient concert with the real men of power in the society of nations. Gibson knew that orders and decisions came down from above. He had spent his professional life in that atmosphere. But he wasn't foolish enough to think the Slavic Pope had been talking about statecraft in the ordinary sense.

Appleyard tussled again with the problem of the Strasbourg plot to force this Slavic Pope to resign. The men at that gathering had spoken of a radical change in the topmost level of leadership in the Church and of the need for a papacy that would conform to today's reality. But the more he had come to know about the Slavic Pope, the less sense any of that made. He couldn't imagine a more radical change in papal leadership than had already been effected by the present Pontiff. And having met the Holy Father now, he was at a loss to fathom the reasoning behind such a cabal.

Surely the man he had met this morning could not be more attuned to present reality. He could not be accused of oppression or heresy or of any crime. Nevertheless, Gibson had to credit Giovanni Lucadamo's judgment. "They're serious," his old friend had said. "At the level where it counts . . . they want him out."

"Well," Appleyard told himself, "whatever the who and the why of that plot, according to Lucadamo I won't find the answers in Rome." That being so, and the hour having come around, he reached for the scrambler phone and dialed through to Bud Vance in D.C. "What have you got for me, Gib?" The Admiral sounded sprightly, but clearly he was all business. "How did it go at the Palace?"

"I think I've got what I came for." Appleyard was ready to boil things down to a few words. "The Holy Father didn't spell out his policies. But if any man knows the score, he does. As far as I can make out, he has an accurate picture of what plans have been made and of what our U.S. planners expect to happen. In fact, he gives the impression of strength in his convictions and surety of foresight. In the long term—say, over four or five years—I can't predict a definitive papal stance. But he will avoid embarrassing the United States."

"So he'll back our pro-Yeltsin policy?"

"He can't be quoted as backing Yeltsin. He's benign. Salutary, even. But he hasn't put his eggs in one basket the way we have. Still, that's not to say he won't cooperate if necessary, at least on a temporary basis."

"You're beginning to sound like a Vatican ambassador yourself, Gib. Speak English. What does that mean?"

Appleyard could almost see the Slavic Pope's eyes again as he laid it out for Vance. "It means, Admiral, that if it comes to a matter of security interests, 'this Holy See will not find it difficult to fulfill its obligations.' "

"We can settle for that." Vance sounded pleased. "But it leads to another question. I'm still concerned about Strasbourg. Did your sources in Rome give you anything more on that?"

"Not a lot, Bud. It's serious enough to be a worry, though. The institution is useful to us as it stands. If somebody manages to change the way it's governed—and that's what Strasbourg was about, after all—you can bet it would jigger our normal mode of access to a lot of things."

"My thinking exactly. Let's keep on it."

"I plan to." Appleyard's assurance to his boss seemed almost glib, but it came from his heart. "I practically promised the Holy Father I'd come back to see him. I'd like to think he'll be here when I do."

Unthinkable Realities and Policies of Extremes

XXXII

WHEN CHRISTIAN ARRIVED at his brother's home at Deurle fully a week before Christmas, Flanders was blanketed in snow. The song of the northwest wind swept deep blue skies clear of clouds and piped a melody of cozy contentment around the eaves of the house. It was a wordless chant composed by angels to increase the quiet of the placid land and to sequester Chris for a time from the moil and toil of the world.

He had slept over at Guidohuis several times during his various visits to different dioceses in Belgium and Holland. But he had spent most of his time with Paul at his EC offices in Brussels, attending to what Cardinal Maestroianni called "easements" for various bishops. By contrast, these would be family days for Christian. "Days of blessing beneath the broad palms of Heaven's hand," Yusai said as she hugged him in welcome.

This was his first real chance to savor the wonders of housekeeping Yusai had accomplished. Like Cessi, she had an instinct for the tradition of wonderful old houses. Most of the rooms had already been restored to their original homeyness. She had scoured Ghent for furnishings that were as attractive as they were fitting and serviceable. And the quarters she had set aside for her brother-in-law—a bedroom and an adjoining room where he could say Mass each day of his first true visit here—were already known in the family as Christian's Retreat.

On Chris's first evening among them, as the family sat down before a blazing fire to steaming bowls of black-bean soup served with *tartine flamande,* Paul announced that he had managed a few days off from his schedule at the EC. Then he proceeded to lay out the plans he and Yusai had devised for his brother's stay. The adventures would begin the next day, and would include a visit to Ghent's Gothic Cathedral of St. Bavon. "That place is right up your alley." Paul beamed at his older brother. "St. Bavon took over two hundred years to build, and it was finished back in the early 1500s. The Dean of the Cathedral is looking forward to meeting you. And my friend, Canon Jadot—Monsieur le Chanoine, le Directeur, as he's called officially—has a surprise for you. A special treat!"

"But that's just the beginning," Yusai chimed in. "We have sights to see and Christmas shopping to do and presents to wrap and a tree to decorate with all the trimmings."

"Lights, too?" Declan urgently wanted to know about that. "Will our tree have lights?"

"Lights, too, Deckel!" Yusai scooped her son into her arms and took him off to get ready for bed.

Paul and Chris moved into the large family room, where they settled in before another of the many fireplaces of Guidohuis. Hannah Dowd brought some brandy she had warmed for them and, almost before they knew it, the brothers were deep in reminiscences of holiday seasons gone by. They talked of boyhood days at Windswept House and the heritage that had begun there with Old Glad. They remembered outings with Grandfather Declan and marveled at the patience of dear old Aunt Dotsie. They thought together of a younger Cessi, and of Tricia in the days before she had become so painfully and dangerously ill.

So vivid and so full of joy were such memories for Chris that he decided to put a call through to Windswept. He wanted to hear Cessi's voice and Tricia's, and to share with them the happiness of this moment. But it was Beulah who answered the phone in Galveston. Cessi had taken Tricia off on still another medical pilgrimage in the hope of finding some relief, if not a cure, for her daughter's worsening condition.

Though Paul was as saddened as Chris at Tricia's plight, he felt a selfish relief that he hadn't had to chat with Cessi. Memories were fine; but the rift between them was still wide, and the wounds each had inflicted on the other were still raw. Yusai rejoined the men and enlivened the conversation again. Curled up in a chair and happy in their company, she listened to their memories, shared wonderful stories of her own childhood in her native Meiling and told of the colorful year-end celebrations there.

It was nearly midnight when Chris remembered a special gift he had brought with him. It was a housewarming gift really, he said; a reminder of the Catholic roots that were so much a part of the Gladstone heritage at Windswept House. With that, he retrieved a package he'd left in the entry hall, and displayed a handsomely framed photo-portrait of the Slavic Pope bearing a personal inscription. "To the Gladstone family," the Holy Father had written, "faithful sons and daughters of the Church."

Not wanting to disturb the warm ambience that embraced them, Paul took the portrait, joked about the high company his brother was keeping these days and reminded everyone, including himself, that they had better get to bed if they were to make an early start of it the next morning.

The days leading up to Christmas were everything Paul had promised, and Chris entered into it all with gusto. Each morning the foursome set off together, little Deckel clutching his uncle's hand like a new prize and adding to his pleasure. They visited every street and lane and square in the proud medieval and Renaissance city of Ghent, all of them filled with reminders of its ancient faith, its exploits and fame, its past heroes and heroines. They explored churches that dated from medieval and High Renaissance times—places like St. Nicholas and St. Jacques, St. Michel and St. Pierre—whose stained-glass windows glowed with magnificent colors.

They took Declan to see the gaily decorated shopwindows. They stood in the cold to listen to carol singers and warmed themselves with bowls of hot soup in pleasant little restaurants. They even spent some time going through the deserted ruins of the Béguinage of ter Hoyen, where, with Yusai listening in rapt fascination, Chris told Declan all about places like this—enclosed *béguinages* where lay sisters once had lived lives of prayer and charitable works, and had earned their keep by their needles and crafts, until corruption and Napoleon's revolution laid waste to it all.

At the Cathedral of St. Bavon the Dean was waiting to greet them with all the considerable charm at his command. But it was Paul's friend Canon Jadot who took the Gladstones into his special care. Dressed elegantly in regulation clericals, Jadot invited the foursome to join him for a tour of the place, including the three-hundred-foot-high belfry that stood apart in the center of the city. "On Christmas night, Father Gladstone," Jadot was pleased to tell his Vatican-connected visitor, "our fifty-two-bell carillon will peal out music to delight the soul. The air of Ghent will be filled with themes and variations of our joyful celebration."

The special treat Paul had promised was saved for last: that was a private viewing of St. Bavon's polyptych altarpiece, *the Adoration of the Mystic Lamb* by Hubert and Jan van Eyck. But as Jadot showed off every detail of the great masterwork to him, Chris began to feel uncomfortable. It dawned on him that Jadot felt in this great work less reverence for what was depicted than pride that his cathedral possessed such a priceless treasure.

Thinking back on it later, Christian wondered if the change that came over him as he listened to Jadot's erudite irreverence hadn't begun much sooner. Perhaps the trigger had been all the questions Declan asked on their tour of sacred places. Questions that made it clear how little the boy knew of his religion. More than likely, though, the real trigger had been the emptiness of all those old churches and chapels he and his family had visited. All those places that should have evoked the unforgettable awe of the miracle they would celebrate at Christmas. Instead everything he saw—the empty churches; the deserted chapels dedicated to Our Lady of Flanders; the votive offerings of past generations left to lie in the dust; the desolation of the *béguinage* buildings—evoked a poignant remembrance.

Not long ago Ghent had been ardently Catholic. Its holy places had overflowed with worshippers, and were filled with the smell of incense, the cadence of chants at Mass and benediction and the murmur of prayers in the confessionals. Now, however, in Ghent as everywhere else, parents no longer took their children to manger scenes erected in churches and chapels, or marveled with them at the wonder that the Christ Child had been born for them. They went to shops and malls, and marveled at the wonder of the computers and high-tech toys and electronic gadgets that had been manufactured for them.

To Chris's relief, little Declan wasn't entirely taken with the craze of the season. He loved the excitement and the lights and the carols, and he could hardly wait to help decorate the family tree and open all the presents. But, when Paul and Yusai wanted to do a bit of shopping without him, Deckel was happy as could be to take his uncle's hand and chatter about the new friends he had made at the International School near Deurle and about the excitement that life in general holds for a bright and adventuresome five-year-old. One of Deckel's new friends—the one who had truly captivated the boy—was a young professor by the name of De Bleuven. "He isn't stuffy like some of the others, Uncle Chris," Deckel said proudly. "He shows us caves and things, and tells us all about them."

It wasn't long before Chris gathered that this De Bleuven had organized a Junior Spelunkers Society, and every week, weather permitting, he plunged with his pint-sized enthusiasts into the local maze of caverns for which Deurle was famous. Concerned that Declan was too young for the dangers of spelunking, Christian thought he might have a cautionary word about it with Paul and Yusai.

The weekend before Christmas marked a change of pace in the life of Christian and Paul Gladstone.

Saturday afternoon was the opening bell; the time for everyone to pitch in and prepare in earnest for the holiday. With Maggie Mulvahill to help her, Hannah Dowd set about baking for the coming feast, and the house was filled with the aroma of the breads and cakes and cookies rising fresh in her oven. Chris, Yusai and Declan began to decorate the tree, while Paul, who was all thumbs about these things, pointed out the bare spots that needed attention.

Holiday preparations came to a temporary halt when Jan Borliuth stopped by to deliver a few gifts for Deckel. Proud grandfather that he was, Jan had three of his grandsons in tow, and in no time at all they were romping outside with Declan, building snow castles and defending them against imaginary invaders with stout cries and squeals of delight.

His grandchildren weren't the only visitors Borliuth had brought along. "Say hello to Gibson Appleyard. He's in Brussels for a few days after a bit of business in Rome. We're off to the airport after we leave here, so he can get back to hearth and home in time for Christmas."

"Any friend of Jan's will always find a welcome here, Mr. Appleyard." Paul's words were not mere form. Jan was practically a member of the family by now. The conversation was easy and familiar as they sipped piping-hot mugs of coffee and devoured an early batch of Hannah Dowd's chocolate-chip cookies, and even Gib Appleyard seemed like an old friend. He had an advantage in the conversation, of course. He made no mention of the behind-the-scenes role he had played in Paul's election as Secretary-General; or of his knowledge about Christian. But neither did he disguise a lively interest in both brothers. He liked Paul at once and admired his quickness of mind. He was charmed by Yusai and pleasantly surprised at her urbanity. It was the priest, though, who impressed him most. He recognized in Christian a genuine and uncomplicated sincerity. Here, he felt, was a Vatican man he could talk to, if only he could devise the occasion. As he had a plane to catch, however, it would have to be enough for the moment that an initial bond had been established.

The holiday preparations were completed by the time Chris celebrated Mass for the entire household on Sunday morning. Accustomed to the *Novus Ordo* Mass—"the newfangled, heretical Mass," as Cessi always insisted—Paul listened for the first time in years to the sounds of the Latin Mass that had been so much a part of his youth. Guidohuis wasn't Windswept House, of course; and Christian's Retreat was a far cry from Old Glad's Tower Chapel. Still, he was filled with a rush of bittersweet memory as he watched Chris in his Roman vestments. The moment came for Christian to hold the sacred Host in his left hand and strike his breast as he repeated the words of unworthiness and faith once spoken to Jesus by a pagan centurion. *"Domine, non sum dignus . . ."* Three times Paul heard those words repeated over the consecrated Chalice containing the Precious Blood of the Savior. "Lord, I am not worthy . . ."

Once not so long ago, Paul had desired to hold that Host as a priest and to say those words of repentance and faith. But now he couldn't bring himself to take Communion from his brother's hand or say even so much as a silent prayer. Head bowed, his hands covering his face, he had all he could do to deal with the unexplainable sting of tears at the back of his eyes. When Paul looked up again, Chris was kneeling at the altar. After listening to a few prayers of thanksgiving, only Paul stayed behind in his place, thoughtful and silent as he watched his brother clear the altar and fold his vestments away.

"Everything is still the same for you, isn't it, Chris?" Christian could only look at his brother in puzzlement. "I mean, the whole idea of the Cradle and the Cross," Paul clarified his thought. "The idea of humility and holy poverty and sacrifice and all that. It's all still the same for you, isn't it?"

"The Church doesn't change in its essentials, Paul." Chris closed the doors of the wardrobe where he had put the vestments. "And I am a priest, after all."

"But the Church does change. It has changed, in fact. It's not us-and-them anymore. Everywhere you look, the Church is reaching out as never before. Even the Pope sees that. He embraces Jews and Muslims and Hindus and . . ."

Chris straddled one of the wooden prie-dieu chairs. "What's really on your mind, Paul?"

The younger Gladstone had to smile. Christian always had been able to see through his little deceptions. Though he supposed there would be a confrontation over it, what he really wanted was to get the matter of his recent induction into the Lodge off his chest. "It's not just any Lodge, mind you," Paul defended himself in advance. "Cyrus Benthoek and one of his associates—an impressive character by the name of Dr. Ralph Channing—arranged for my acceptance into nothing less than the Grand Lodge of Israel itself." And with that, he launched into an enthusiastic description of his excursion to Jerusalem, of his voyage to the mountaintop of Aminadab, of how he had been made to feel so close to God and to his fellow man in that place. "Don't you see, Chris? We're all after the same thing, really. It's not membership in the Roman Catholic Church that's the important thing, but membership in the human family."

Christian listened quietly. When his brother had finished, he had only one question to ask him. "What about salvation, Paul?"

The younger Gladstone could only stare at him. Surely no one—and especially not Paul's own brother—could be so medieval in these modern times. Surely he must understand that even his own special privilege as a priest was different now; that everyone had a share in priesthood. And surely Chris must realize by now, after all their work together over the past few months, that the aims of the Lodge were anything but incompatible with the aims of the Church. "The important thing—the Christ-like thing—is to build bridges of understanding. You don't have to be a priest, or even a Catholic, to do that. And that's not just me talking, Chris. I mean, all you have to do is look at the major documents of the Second Vatican Council to know I'm right.

"Oh, I know—" Paul held up a hand to fend off his brother's objections. "I know. I left the Seminary, and I'm not the theologian you are. But even I know about the document they call *Gaudium et Spes.* And I know it couldn't have a better name. Joy and Hope. Joy at the new spirit of reaching out to non-Catholics and non-Christians. Hope that all the old barriers of distrust can be wiped out and replaced by a new unity. In fact, *Gaudium et Spes* has a thing or two to say about salvation, since you brought the matter up. It says that Christ achieved salvation for everybody. It says God wants everyone to be saved, and that nobody is excluded. Isn't that so, big brother?"

"Yes, but . . ."

"No buts about it. You know I'm right. And you know that *Gaudium et Spes* also insists that there's great value in all religions. We're told we should respect them all, especially as that's what God has allowed develop.

"That document emphasizes exactly what I agreed to do at Aminadab. It speaks not of the Catholic Church, but of the people of God. As Christians, we're all supposed to join in building mankind's habitat; in building prosperity for all people. In other words, Chris, we're not to be separate any longer. At long last, all the old prejudices are to be dropped. Including our differences with the Jews. We're finally to accept the importance of the Jewish people in Salvation. It wasn't the Jews who were responsible for the Crucifixion of Christ. Our sins did that.

"The overriding idea behind the Council—the spirit of Vatican II—is to join with the whole human race for a better world. And whether you like it or not, Chris, my membership in the Lodge has opened up doors that allow me to be more a part of that than I could ever be on my own."

Christian studied his brother's face for a moment, flushed with excitement of the utopian vision he had just shared with such passion. It was all so alluring, Chris thought. What he had to offer in return was not attractive—and, without the grace of God, never would be—to those whose lives were suffused by the credo Paul had just set out. Still, there was nothing for it except to face into the issue. "Look, Paul! We both know that there is not one exhortation in Christianity to build a material paradise. Humanly speaking, that's a bleak statement. But it's a fact. And even worse from your point of view is that there will never be peace between Christianity and the world. We have God's word on that. The world is the domain of the Prince, Jesus told us. He told us that our reason for being on this earth isn't to build a paradise here, but to earn salvation in Heaven. He told us that the only way to do that is to cooperate with Him. With the merits He won for us, and that He convinced us of by His specific words and His specific works, and that He communicates to us by His Sacraments.

"So the contrast is clear. Dedication to the attractive things of this earth. Or dedication to God who has seen fit to give us His laws to live by. It's a difficult doctrine because it runs against the tide of our passions. To take a page from the Gospel, it contradicts the desires of our flesh and the concupiscence of our eyes and the pride of life. It demands sacrifice and pain and loss.

"The beauty of Christianity is that it does ensure eternal life for all who believe in it. It ensures that we will live in the company of God for all eternity, and that we will have full share in His beauty, His truth and His infinite happiness. So you're right about me, Paul. The Cradle and the Cross and the idea—the goal—that lie behind humility and holy poverty and sacrifice are all still the same for me.

"And I'm bound to tell you that the strong prohibition against membership in the Lodge still stands. No matter how high-minded your intention, you are in mortal sin."

Paul had to tear his eyes from Christian's or risk his resolve. He had to recall to his mind the new sense of purpose he had discovered in Jerusalem. The sense of privilege, of camaraderie and of shared ideals. The sense that he was working now for something more than greener pastures for himself and Yusai and Declan. Above all, he had to reassert within himself that independence of judgment he had felt in the company of Benthoek and Channing.

Come to think of it, he had every reason to remember CB's words now, and he repeated them almost verbatim. "Are you aware, Chris, that many high-ranking prelates in the Vatican are Lodge members?"

Christian's eyes turned to stone, but he made no reply. He had a fair idea of the transgressions of some churchmen in the Vatican; he had complained about them often enough in his conversations with Aldo Carnesecca. But this wasn't a numbers game. He wasn't concerned about the Vatican but about his brother.

Left to fill the silence, Paul went on. "If I'm in mortal sin, I can only say that I'm in pretty good company. And I have it on good authority that my membership in the Lodge doesn't make me an outcast from the Church. The day after I got back from Jerusalem, I dropped in at the Cathedral Rectory to see Canon Jadot. I hadn't entirely forgotten the old stricture against joining the Lodge, so it was a confessional visit."

"Let me guess," Chris interrupted. He could almost imagine the scene. Instead of the old Catholic confessional box, the urbane and worldly-wise Jadot had probably invited Paul into some snug little Confessional Room, as such places were called these days, complete with the latest in banner art and track lighting and furnished with comfortable chairs. "No doubt your friend was in complete agreement with your friends in Jerusalem. With Benthoek and Channing and whoever else you met there. No doubt he told you our Catholic mind has evolved in this matter of Lodge membership. And if he gave you any penance at all, no doubt it was to care for your fellow man."

Paul laughed. "As far as it goes, Chris, your guess is perfect. If I didn't know better, I'd take you for a Conciliar Catholic. But there was a little more to it than that. Based on his own years of experience as a Lodge member, Canon Jadot did advise me to be discreet. And after this little tête-à-tête with you, I can see why.

"As long as we're at it, though, it was Canon Jadot who reminded me about *Gaudium et Spes.* In fact, he reminded me of something I had almost forgotten. Back when he was a lowly bishop attending the Second Vatican Council, the Slavic Pope himself was one of the chief architects of that document. And since the guiding aim of the Grand Lodge of Israel is to do exactly what that document tells us to do, you might say that I have the imprimatur of the Holy Father himself for my Lodge affiliation!"

"I wouldn't say that in a million years," Chris objected. "But since that's the way you look at it, let me respond point by point to what you've just told me. In the first place, if you decide to go to confession again, avoid Jadot as a man who's lost his faith. That's unfortunate. But he's not the first cleric that's happened to; and given the times we live in, he won't be the last. Second, Jadot has some of his facts right, but his judgment about them is badly off. He's right that our present Pontiff was one of the architects of *Gaudium et Spes.* That's the way it was. But many a man has had heterodox views and then has had to correct those views once he became Pope. Peter the Fisherman even went so far as to disown Jesus. Remember?

"And that brings me to point number three. Now that our Pope is

Christ's earthly Vicar—he'll have to correct his earlier errors that have led to such problems of confusion in the Church."

Paul threw his hands up in a gesture of impatience. "One of those errors being *Gaudium et Spes,* I suppose."

"Don't give me that, Paul." Chris wasn't buying his brother's show of exasperation. And he wasn't about to be turned away now. "It may be a long time since you read *Gaudium et Spes.* But you know as well as I do that it was sloppily conceived and badly written in the most ambiguous language imaginable. The thing that still has to be done is to reconcile that hodgepodge with the traditional belief and teaching of the Church. His Holiness will have to do that some day soon or pay for his mistakes in Purgatory.

"Traditionally, we ask God to help us detach ourselves from the world and to love the things of our true home in Heaven. How reconcile that with a call to join the world in fashioning some sort of material paradise? We believe that salvation comes through cooperation with God's grace in order to be delivered from the consequences of sin. From death, in other words. And we believe God gives us that grace through the Church He founded for that specific purpose. How reconcile that with the idea that nobody is excluded from salvation? All that and a lot more has still to be brought into line with traditional Catholic belief. And it's the Pope's responsibility to do that, especially since he was the architect of this very ambiguous document."

Paul knew better than to challenge his brother's theology. But his practicality was open to question. "If you ask me, the Slavic Pope seems a lot more interested in trotting around the globe, showing us how to cooperate with voodoo sorcerers. Maybe he'll get around to squaring the documents of Vatican II with your precious tradition. But what are the rest of us supposed to do in the meantime? Just ignore Vatican II and its documents like *Gaudium et Spes*?"

"In the meantime, Paul, and just for starters, you might try reminding yourself that Vatican II was not convened as a dogmatic Council. Neither *Gaudium et Spes* nor any other document that came out of that Council is dogma."

"In the meantime, my beloved brother-in-law—" Yusai's emphatic voice from across the room made Chris and Paul jump like startled cats. "In the meantime, you can both come and eat your breakfast!"

Paul had no idea when his wife had slipped quietly into Christian's Retreat, but the expression in her eyes told him she had been standing by the open door for some time. She had been giving serious thought lately to becoming a Catholic—to becoming a more intimate part of the world in which she lived at Liselton and Guidohuis—so these were matters that concerned her. Finally, though, it seemed better to intervene before confrontation reached a point from which there might be no return.

Their remaining days together at Guidohuis were as busy and almost as happy as ever. But at a certain level, a little pool of sorrow and loss gathered inside of Christian. It seemed to him that the sincerity of his brother's ambition to repair the world of its misery and poverty was beyond doubt. But how had Paul lost sight of the meaning of the Incarnation they were about to celebrate? What had they gathered here to celebrate at all, in fact, if not God's birth in time, and the eternal generation of that same God, and the involvement of the whole of humanity in those fundamental events?

Only by degrees did Christian find the courage to admit the obvious. Only by degrees was he able to tell himself in so many words that, like Canon Jadot, Paul Gladstone had lost his faith.

In Rome, the Slavic Pope prepared to leave the papal apartments to celebrate the first Mass of Christmas at midnight in St. Peter's Basilica. On his way out, he stopped in one of the private rooms at a small table standing alone beside an ornate fireplace. Upon that table, covered with a cloth-of-gold veil inscribed in silver thread with a large letter M, lay a humidor-sized box. And in that box lay a single sheet of notepaper; a carefully worded document that had been sent to Rome in the 1950s by Sister Lucia as the sole surviving seer of the 1917 Fatima vision. Highly confidential, that document had been entrusted to the Vatican office charged with guarding the faith of Roman Catholics, and had been placed here in the box that bore three Latin words: *"SECRETUM SANCTI OFFICII."*

To date, the Pontiff had read that document only twice. But neither its contents nor the current plight of the aged Sister Lucia as a virtual prisoner in her convent was ever far from his mind.

At this moment, as events were coming to a new pass in Russia, he ran his hand lightly over the veiled box. Before he joined his entourage and his mind would become wholly absorbed in the coming Mass and ritual protocols, he wanted to trace a finger along the lines of the silver-threaded M. He wanted to pray, as he so often did, for constancy and strength and light; and for the fruitfulness of his pontificate in an age of wholesale apostasy.

One of the misfortunes Giustino Lucadamo suffered as chief security officer for His Holiness was that he could participate only peripherally in papal ceremonies. Whenever the Pontiff moved away from the Apostolic Palace, Lucadamo directed a minute and multifaceted surveillance of every stage in the schedule until the Holy Father was back within the safety net perpetually flung around the papal apartments.

Lucadamo orchestrated the process tonight from one of his control centers. Together with two of his best men, he was surrounded by rows of electronic gear that kept him in total contact with his personnel, and by banks of monitors that flashed live pictures permitting him to scrutinize every step of the Pontiff's progression from apartments to Basilica.

It was smoothly done. As the Pope left each succeeding area, teams of guards took up their positions, sealing off all access to the rear as surely as steel doors closing behind the Holy Father. Once His Holiness was inside the Basilica, Giustino relaxed a little. A cat couldn't appear anywhere in that whole complex without being noticed. Every quarter and section of the congregation was swept continuously by monitors and human eyes. In the worst of scenarios—a gun raised suddenly against the Slavic Pope again, for example—none of the six strategically located sharpshooters would hesitate to fire.

When the Christmas ceremonies proper were under way, Lucadamo checked briefly with his chief lieutenant, Machali Bobbio, on duty in a second command complex. He sharpened the transmissions from the papal apartments and the approaches to it. Then, just when it seemed that there was nothing more to do but lean back in his swivel chair, Lucadamo sat bolt upright as if his spine had been stiffened by lightning. He punched the in-house extension code linking him directly to Bobbio. "How many are detached for the apartments?"

"Five men, sir."

"Right! Now, look at your consoles. There's Maschera and Fontanella. Okay? And there's Silvano and Crescenza. Torrente makes five. But who in the blazes is *that* one? He's heading for the room with the box, damn his hide! Get your tail up there, Bobbio! I'll be right behind you. And it's code of silence. Got it?"

Before he streaked out of his control center, Lucadamo had to alert Maschera and the others to the breach of security. He directed his men to the trouble spot, and ended the transmission with a curt "Code 500." In rapid-fire succession, the acknowledgments came back to him over the portable devices carried by each guard. "Code 500. Over and out," came Maschera's curt response. Likewise for Silvano and the other three. "Code 500. Over and out." There was no sixth response.

Whoever the intruder was, either he was too smart to speak on the encrypted channel or he didn't have access to that channel. Lucadamo tore off his earphones and was out of the command post at full speed. By the time he reached the fourth-floor corridor outside the private room of the papal chambers, the place was alive with agents, each with his Austrian-made Glock out of its holster and at the ready.

Giustino Lucadamo approached the door from one side, Machali Bobbio from the other. In one rapid movement, Lucadamo threw the door open, and both men took dead aim at a figure bending over the table with a pillbox camera in his hand.

Resplendent in white and gold vestments, the Slavic Pope stood at the altar in the great nave of St. Peter's Basilica. Beneath the ornate baldachin, and surrounded by the four black spiral columns holding the bones of 30,000 martyrs, he took in his two hands the Christ of Cradle and Cross.

"Behold!" The Holy Father held the Host aloft for all the world to see. "Behold the Lamb of God . . ."

XXXIII

BY EARLY MORNING of Christmas Day, Giustino Lucadamo knew the essentials behind the break-in of the papal apartments and reported what he had discovered to the Slavic Pope.

By the evening of the twenty-seventh, having been recalled on a red-alert basis from Russia, Father Angelo Gutmacher slipped into the fourth-floor papal study for a meeting of the Holy Father and members of his confidential circle. Already present with the Pontiff and Lucadamo were Monsignore Daniel Sadowski, Father Damien Slattery and Brother Augustine. But neither Aldo Carnesecca nor Christian Gladstone was in attendance.

After a nod of welcome to Gutmacher, the somber-faced Pope turned to Lucadamo, who proceeded to sketch the situation out for the group.

The security chief began by confirming the rumors already buzzing around at a certain level in the Vatican. It was true, he said, that a break-in had occurred. The intruder, a Sard by the name of Kourice, was a part-time soldier in the Palermo mob who freelanced his talents on the side. The plan had included the duplication of a guard's uniform by a local tailor and the top-notch forgery of an identity card. Kourice's job was to photograph the Fatima document reserved in the papal apartments. Kourice himself was of minor significance, of course. But Lucadamo had learned from the Sard the name of the insider who had made the intrusion possible, and his reason for doing so.

"The Vatican man involved"—Giustino turned a knowing eye on Damien Slattery—"was Archbishop Canizio Buttafuoco."

"That figures," Slattery growled. His face-off with Buttafuoco after the Pontiff's urgent call from Fatima the prior May had only been one in a number of confrontations between those two. "Buttafuoco is just stupid enough to get tied up in a scheme like that. But the question is, who put him up to it? And why?"

Lucadamo had already come up with answers to both questions. "We set Buttafuoco up. He was to meet with Kourice a few hours after the break-in to retrieve the film. Naturally, we let the meeting take place. And, once we had him, the Archbishop was willing to cooperate. Turns out he's a link in the Moscow line. And this time, the line terminates at Mikhail Gorbachev's desk."

Gutmacher and Brother Augustine traded a look of some surprise.

With the essentials on the table, His Holiness was quick to supply the missing background. "I think the lines of this foolish attempt trace back to my first meeting with Mr. Gorbachev. He showed a lively interest in the Third Fatima Secret. In fact, he wanted a private reading of the text. Of course, I refused. But I can say it was clear to me that he had studied the transcript of my remarks at Fulda back in 1981. Offhand remarks in which I had alluded to the fact that the reason the Secret had not been published by the Pope in 1960 was that the text could provide the Soviets with a strategic advantage over the Western allies.

"Gorbachev was in desperate circumstances. He needed a miracle. He thought he would have it with this letter of the Third Secret. Never mind that his idea of a new federation of Soviet States run by political consensus was really a noxious dream. And never mind that Russia itself is nothing more than a decomposing corpse. Suffice it to say that his desperation obviously drove him to that underhand way to achieve his miracle.

"There are some obvious ways to deal with the matter, but I'm not comfortable with any of them. I could confront Gorbachev directly. Or I could say nothing. Presumably our newly cooperative Archbishop Buttafuoco can be persuaded to keep his mouth zipped, and I can let Gorbachev stew for a while over the matter. Or I can order the preparation of a bogus text and let that make its way through Buttafuoco to Gorbachev's desk."

It was clear that no one in the room was any more comfortable with the obvious choices than the Holy Father himself. Brother Augustine—an expert in the Soviet mind if ever there was one—summed things up for the group.

"By reproaching Gorbachev, Holiness, you lose him. Leave him in the dark, and you can be sure he'll find out eventually what happened. So you'll end up with the same result. And if you use a bogus text, you stoop to his level."

The Pontiff agreed. "The alternative, then?"

"Let me talk to Buttafuoco, Holiness." The eager suggestion came from Damien Slattery. "Let me turn him around. Let me offer him amnesty on two conditions. First, that he identify his handler and any other links he may know about in this particular Moscow-Vatican chain. And, second, that he tell his handler the truth—that Kourice botched the job and that security has been so beefed up that another attempt would be suicidal." Slattery's suggestion satisfied the Pope. But it left the question of how to deal with Gorbachev himself.

"Why not tell him the truth as well, Your Holiness?" The suggestion this time came from Angelo Gutmacher. "Why not write an innocuous letter for me to take to him? Without pointing a finger or giving any details, mention the attempt to photograph the letter. Assure him that the text remains safe. And assure him that if and when the time comes to publish the text of the Third Secret, he will be the first to have a copy of it."

The Slavic Pope turned to his security chief. Lucadamo nodded. "Provided Father Damien can secure Buttafuoco . . ."

Slattery's laughter cut the question short. "Count on it, Giustino! After I paint a picture of the alternative—the prospect of living out his remaining years of Vatican service in the picturesque desolation of the Soviet Republic of Tajikistan, for example, or in the romantic seclusion of the isle of Penang in the Federation of Malaysia—Buttafuoco will turn out to be one of the best double agents we ever had."

Lucadamo was sold. "I agree, then, Holiness. It's a good solution."

The first person in Rome to know of Father Aldo Carnesecca's near-fatal accident in Sicily was Christian Gladstone.

When Chris returned to the Angelicum on the Sunday before Epiphany, the news wasn't about the break-in at the Apostolic Palace, or about Gorbachev's recent departure from power. The airwaves and newspapers screamed throughout the day with the headline story that a combined task force of civil and federal police and special units from the armed forces had launched the biggest and most thorough cleaning operation ever attempted against the Sicilian Cosa Nostra. For once, government preparations for the operation hadn't been betrayed. The surprise had been total. Over two thousand mafiosi had been netted in a predawn raid. Throughout Sicily and southern Italy, every bishop and most parish priests had gone on the attack from their pulpits, declaring the Cosa Nostra "a national cancer" and hitting at Sicily as its tumorous womb.

With late-breaking radio bulletins as background, Chris unpacked, and then began the review of his notes in preparation for the debriefing by Maestroianni and Aureatini. He broke off from his work several times to try to reach Carnesecca by phone, but without success. Still, it wasn't until the surprise call came through that Christian began to put two and two together. Gladstone couldn't hear anything on the line at first except static. Then, when the faraway voice of his friend crackled through, the news was dreadful. Carnesecca's car had been totaled in a hit-and-run accident on the main coastal road in northwestern Sicily. He was safe for the moment at the house of a priest in a town called Caltagirone, but he had been badly injured and had lost a lot of blood.

"Write the name down, Chris. Caltagirone. It's in the interior, southwest of Catania." Carnesecca's voice was fading beneath the static. "Get hold of Giustino Lucadamo as fast as you can, but say nothing to anyone else. It's a matter of my survival. Tell Lucadamo I have a couple of hours at best before they find me . . ."

There was a long burst of static. The line went totally dead. But Christian had heard enough to send him on a feverish telephone chase after Giustino Lucadamo. He had no doubt that the security chief was up to his hips somewhere in the middle of the anti-Mafia operation; but after an hour of frantic effort, he managed to run him down at the Naples airport. After he heard everything Carnesecca had managed to get across to Gladstone, and vented a string of earthy curses for "the Roman supervisor," Lucadamo was ready to take charge. He paused only long enough to give Christian a secure number for emergency use and to reinforce the warning that he speak to no one else. "You know nothing, Father." Giustino barked the order. "Make no more calls. Ask no questions, and answer none."

Chris was left to stew with no further news of Carnesecca's fate. Then, late in the evening, Cardinal Aureatini rang through. "It's about Father Carnesecca," His Eminence spoke up without waiting for so much as the sound of Gladstone's voice. "We expected word of Father Carnesecca this morning. Have you heard anything from him, Father Christian?"

Though he came within an ace of blurting out his own questions, Chris caught himself. "Of course, Eminence." He slurred his words as though he'd been awakened from a sound sleep. "I'll be there first thing in the morning."

"Father Gladstone!" The Cardinal carved each word out sharply. "Are you awake? Have you heard from Father Carnesecca?"

"But, Your Eminence," the sleepy-possum answer came back to Aureatini. "I did not hear anything about fasting from flesh meat."

"Reverend Father! I am not asking about flesh meat! I am asking about Father Carnesecca! Do you hear me, Father Christian?" Chris snored lightly into the phone, and could just make out Aureatini's frustrated comment to himself as His Eminence hung up the phone in disgust. "These *anglosassoni!* They sleep like their own oxen!"

A few minutes of troubled reflection was enough for Gladstone to understand that if Aureatini had expected to hear from Father Aldo this morning, Aureatini was part of the Sicilian operation. Maybe he was even "the Roman supervisor" Giustino had cursed. In any case, the Cardinal was clearly out of the loop now, and that was curious. It wasn't exactly an emergency, but Chris dialed the number Lucadamo had given him. He was patched through within seconds this time, and passed along word of Aureatini's call. By the sound of things, the security chief was airborne in a helicopter. "I'll bet the Cardinal would like to know where Carnesecca is!" Lucadamo shouted above the racket of the engine. "The worst is over, though. Just sit tight and play dumb."

It was Monday afternoon when Chris got word from Lucadamo that Father Carnesecca had been returned to Rome and taken to Gemelli Hospital, where a team of doctors had set to work on him in earnest and a team of armed guards was set up for a round-the-clock watch outside his room.

Gladstone was visibly taken aback at his first sight of Father Aldo when he was allowed visitors on Tuesday.

"What did you expect, Chris? My accident was no accident. I wasn't meant to survive."

Father Aldo explained nothing about his work during the months of preparation for the predawn Sicilian raid, except to say that he had functioned as a courier. But he seemed unusually interested in telling Chris about the details of his "accident." It had been his good fortune that when he had been forced off the road, his car had plunged into an overgrown ravine that was hard to reach. By the time the goons had got down there, Carnesecca had managed to crawl out of the wreck and drag himself to cover. His pursuers had beaten the bushes for a while, and then had gone off to get help.

Father Aldo barely remembered how he had managed to get himself up to the road, or who it was that had carried him to the priest's house in Caltagirone. But from that point on, it had been a race against time. "They knew I was still alive, and they still wanted me dead."

Carnesecca's problem had been how to keep his own security intact and still get to the Vatican security chief in time to do any good. His call to the Angelicum had been a gamble; but it was about the best one he had. "I remembered your saying you would be back in time for Epiphany. I knew there was no reason for you to be under surveillance. And I figured that if I could get to you, you would get help to me or die in the attempt. I owe you my life, Chris." The injured priest shifted uncomfortably in his hospital bed. "But I don't expect this is an end of it."

"But the Sicilian operation was a success, Aldo. Unless you think the Mafia will be after you for revenge, surely the danger is over."

Carnesecca made it clear that both he and Lucadamo were sure his accident had nothing to do with Mafia vengeance. "Giustino has his own theory. I'm sworn to secrecy about it for now. Maybe he'll tell you about it in time. He has evidence to back his main line of thinking. But I want you to understand, Chris, that this is one time when Lucadamo may be right for the wrong reasons."

Gladstone knew better than to pry into anything Father Aldo was bound to hold as a confidence. But if both Carnesecca and Lucadamo were convinced that the Mafia was in the clear in this bloody affair, what was behind it?

"It's a story—a Vatican story—that dates from long years ago, Chris. Back to the early sixties, in fact. I can't be sure, of course. But I'd say that my 'accident' means someone thinks I know too much for their comfort these days."

"Are they right?"

"I hope you'll never have a reason to find the answer." Father Aldo's strength was beginning to fade. "But if it comes to that—if ever I have an accident that's successful—get hold of my diary and give it to Lucadamo."

Though he sickened at the idea, Gladstone's logical mind drove him to the obvious question. "Where do I find this diary?"

"Always with me, Christian." Carnesecca was slipping over the edge of sleep now. "Always with me. Find me, you find my diary . . ."

After a consultation with Giustino Lucadamo in the relative quiet that always descends on the Apostolic Palace of a Saturday morning, the Slavic Pope laid aside the notebook in his hand, buzzed his secretary on the intercom and asked for Master-General Damien Slattery to be summoned at once. Monsignore Daniel rang Springy's eatery. Within a quarter of an hour, Father Damien joined the twosome in the Pontiff's study, where the pallor on the Holy Father's face told him that whatever was up spelled deep trouble.

"Trouble comes in bunches, they say, Father." The first words out of Lucadamo's mouth confirmed Slattery's assumption. "We had the break-in at Christmas. Then Carnesecca nearly had his chips cashed this week in Sicily. And now something else has come back to haunt us."

"Let's have it, then." Damien chose a chair near the desk where the Holy Father sat in silent agitation.

"Remember back last May when we found out about that private meeting Cardinal Maestroianni arranged at Strasbourg? 'A gathering of wolves and jackals,' you called it."

Slattery remembered. "Are they at it again?"

"They've been at it all along, Father." Lucadamo picked up the notebook from His Holiness' desk and glanced over some of the pages. "We haven't got all the pieces yet. But the long and the short of what we do have is this. It turns out that Strasbourg was the starting gate for a systematic, in-house initiative to force the issue of episcopal unity with the Holy See. Some mechanism has apparently been devised to organize a series of votes by the various National and Regional Conferences of Bishops. So far, we haven't found out what that mechanism is. But we know the goal; and we have an idea of the time frame. The upshot of the votes is to be a petition for the Holy Father to resign for the sake of Church unity. And the timing seems geared to His Holiness' seventy-fifth birthday."

Frozen in his chair, his face beet red with anger, Slattery shot one question at Lucadamo. "How many of the Strasbourg crowd are in it?"

"For openers, the whole list of Vatican men we came up with in May. As nearly as we've been able to find out, to one degree or another every man jack who went to Maestroianni's private Schuman Day gathering."

"The same old cabal, in other words, Father Damien." The Slavic Pope spoke for the first time since Slattery's arrival. "But, if I'm to believe this report, it goes well beyond the Vatican now. The indications are that Cardinal Maestroianni has established close links with some powerful non-Catholic and even non-Christian sources. How those centers cooperate, exactly who all of them are or where all the lines lead, what their various contributions may be, what they expect to get in return for their cooperation—all of that remains vague. But the basic fact that such outside centers are participating in the plan against my pontificate is solid information."

The more Slattery heard, the more his rage boiled up. He had never really penetrated the mind of the Slavic Pope, nor had he ever uncovered the fundamental strategy behind some of the Pontiff's puzzling words and actions; he had himself been taken severely aback by some of the Slavic Pope's actions. Nevertheless, the greater truth for Slattery was that the Slavic Pope was Peter's successor and the Vicar of Christ. He had never allowed anything this Pope said or did to dilute the strength and constancy of his own loyalty. This morning, though, even Slattery was at a loss for words. If Lucadamo's intelligence was accurate, the issue had gone far beyond criticism. Even beyond the private little war some of his in-house prelates had carried on for so many years against the Holy Father.

"Are you sure of the main facts?" Damien was grasping at straws as he turned to Lucadamo.

"Absolutely. Everything's been checked and rechecked. And it explains a lot of things. It puts a different perspective on the sudden surge in the open disobedience to the Pope among a growing number of bishops. It gives us a rational explanation for the rash of media stories and books that have been coming from so many quarters all at once and that speak as if a papal resignation were imminent and assured. And it puts a more ominous face on that anonymous letter circulated among the in-house Cardinals a few weeks back to test the waters about papal resignation in the event of incapacitation. In fact, we only have to look at poor Father Carnesecca to know just how ominous that face may be."

"Carnesecca!" Slattery was drowning in surprises. "Is that how you read his 'accident'?"

"We can't prove anything. But I can tell you in the first place that Father Aldo has been the source for some bits of our information about the antipapal plot. He picks up conversations, reads memos, is the recipient of grumbles and complaints. You know how he is. And, in the second place, the incident in Sicily didn't bear the marks of a Mafia job. Besides, I doubt they even noticed him. He's a clever man in the field, and he was all but invisible."

The Holy Father intervened again. "Aldo Carnesecca isn't the only one who concerns us, Father Damien. I'm afraid there may be another dimension to our problem. There seems to be a possibility that Father Christian Gladstone may be a part of Maestroianni's cabal."

"No!" Slattery's consternation was complete now, and painful to see. "I know Father Chris! I don't care what evidence we have, Holiness! I can't believe . . ."

"Easy does it." Lucadamo tried to calm the situation. "I don't think for a minute he was connected with the attempt on Carnesecca's life. But the fact is that all his politicking for Maestroianni among the bishops begins to look mighty like collusion. Maybe Gladstone is just a pawn. Maybe he's more than that. The point is, we don't know; and until we do, he remains suspect.

"And, since this whole antipapal affair is such a tangled, intertwined morass, my suspicions force me to bring up another matter. Father Christian may be a little too eager to be part of the papal investigation into homosexual and Satanist activity among the U.S. clergy. I don't have to remind you, Father Damien, that your end of that inquiry is dangerous. There have already been two priests murdered in connection with Satanist cults. Two we know about, that is.

"So, let's say Gladstone gets the okay from Maestroianni to go Stateside; he's already put in his bid, by the way. And let's say we use his work for the Cardinal as a cover for his end of our investigation. Innocent or not, don't we have to ask ourselves who would be using whom? I mean, look at what we're facing, man! Keep in mind what almost happened to Carnesecca. And what did happen to the now very dead Father Sebastian Scalabrini in Centurycity. And keep in mind how much Maestroianni loves you! Now, if Father Christian really is part of the antipapal pact, or even if he reports back to Maestroianni as nothing more than an unwitting stooge, how long do you think you'd last in the States?"

Slattery heaved his bulk out of the chair and strode to the windows. "It's insane, Giustino, and that's all there is to say!" Slattery's robes whirled like a white cloud around him as he turned back toward the room. "It wouldn't take much for me to believe anything about Maestroianni. But I'd stake my life on Christian Gladstone."

"Would you stake the whole U.S. investigation on him, Father Slattery?"

"Without a minute's hesitation!"

It was a standoff, then. The fundamental question regarding Christian Gladstone would be decided by the Slavic Pope.

The silence that settled on the room was almost unnerving. The Holy Father plunged for a few moments into a deep and private reflection. It was almost an automatic reflex for him to put the dilemma into a wider context. The papal investigation in the United States shaped up as crucial. The question to be decided was no different in its essence than the question that always presented itself in the Slavic Pope's policy of extremes. Always, it was a matter of where the greater gamble might lie.

Assuming that Slattery could take care of himself—the choice this time was clear. A possible compromise of the American investigation would mean delay, but that could be repaired. The injustice of jettisoning Gladstone without giving him a fair chance to prove himself would be irreparable.

In the end, the Pontiff decided his policy regarding Christian Gladstone exactly as he had decided the entire policy of his pontificate: he would play the hand that had been dealt him.

"Forewarned is forearmed, is it not, Giustino?" The Pope broke his silence at last. "We will have that advantage at the very least—assuming Maestroianni will agree to send Father Gladstone to the United States at all. Whether Father Damien's estimation of Christian Gladstone is correct or not—and I have to say, I share his judgment—our young American will show his colors soon enough by what he does with the investigation.

"If Father Damien and I are right about our young American, I will have secured one more good priest for lasting service to the Church and one more strong supporter for intimate service to this Holy See.

"Meanwhile, I will defend the integrity of the papal office as I have done until now. I will intensify my policy, in fact. I will devise every opportunity I can to double around behind His Eminence Maestroianni and the others. I will use every situation that presents itself to take the ground they stand on out from under their feet."

Trouble was not entirely confined to paradise in the early months of the new year. It reared its head for Dr. Ralph S. Channing when, on an otherwise tranquil winter morning at Cliffview House, he found himself on the receiving end of a painful telephone communication from Capstone.

"Among ourselves, my dear Dr. Channing, we must recognize the facts." There was no heat in Capstone's words; nothing that smacked of anger. Yet there was no mistaking the threat behind the clipped words and imperious tone.

"But, sir . . ."

"Your devotion to the Prince is beyond doubt. Nor do we question your dedication to the Chosen Alternative as the means to secure the Ascent of the Prince in the Citadel of the Enemy within the Availing Time. I need not remind you, therefore, of the importance of our timing. Or that, as master engineers of the Process, you and the other members of Concilium 13 have been charged with the gravest responsibility: to render the papal office useless to the Nameless Other, and to deliver it into our hands as servitors of the Prince."

"But, sir." Channing tried again. "Have you not read my reports? Things are proceeding according to plan. The link of interests we have established between the bishops of Europe and the European Community is already firm. We are driving it home as a wedge between bishops and the present holder of the papal office. Gynneth Blashford's newspaper chains and Brad Gerstein-Snell's multimedia communications networks have all been effective in broadcasting repeated and convincing materials to build pressure on the side of papal resignation. And Cardinal Maestroianni has devised an ingenious mechanism by which bishops around the world will make it virtually impossible for the present holder of the papal office to govern . . ."

"Dr. Channing." Capstone's quiet voice commanded silence. "You need not continue your litany. Your reports have been read. But satisfaction with your progress is not justified. Specifically, it is that ingenious mechanism, as you call it, that is the object of our concern. These so-called Internal Affairs Committees that have been set up in the various Regional and National Bishops Conferences are supposedly to deliver a timely and universal vote for papal resignation. The Episcopal Common Mind Vote is the parlance in use, I believe."

"Yes, sir," Channing confirmed. "ECOMMIV for short."

"Thank you." There was no trace of gratitude in the acknowledgment. "Let me direct your attention to two words I have just used: Timely. Universal. Those two words are the key to our concern. But again, let me be specific. We are satisfied for the moment with the progress in Europe. We have every reason to agree with you that the IACs are becoming increasingly effective there.

"But the European IACs won't deliver your Common Mind Vote on the required scale unless the United States leads the way. The financial and political power that U.S. bishops command—and the fact that they speak for a population of over sixty million Roman Catholics—will be a decisive leadership factor. So our question is clear. What is holding things up in your own backyard?"

Ordinarily, Ralph Channing dealt with all questions magisterially. But the fact was that he had no answer for Capstone. He knew, he admitted as he swiped at the sweat beading on his forehead, that there was some blockage to progress in the American IACs; but he had no ready explanation for it.

"We are not looking for explanations. Let me make it plain to you. The Availing Time for the Ascent of the Prince is gridded in part on an overall timetable of world events. On developments in the financial and economic structure of the society of nations. In the main, those events continue to go well for us. The post-Soviet condition of Eastern European states and the various republics of the now defunct U.S.S.R.; the thrust of EC and CSCE policies; the formation of the East Asian Pact countries; a similar formation for Middle East countries—all of that and more is proceeding nicely from our point of view.

"But we must not allow ourselves to be blindsided by partial victories. The one solid and tangible threat to the New Order is the continued existence of the papal office as the stronghold of the Enemy. We have accepted your plan to secure that target. We do not accept the blockage to that plan that has arisen in the United States.

"We expect the problem to be solved."

Because panic is contagious, in a matter of days Channing carried it with him like a virus from New York to London to Rome.

He flew first to England, where he closeted himself with Nicholas Clatterbuck in his office. As a member of Concilium 13, that gentleman understood the gravity of Capstone's complaint. As the efficient CEO of Cyrus Benthoek's London operations, he understood how to present the matter to the head man himself.

Channing and Clatterbuck flew down the corridor and closeted themselves with Benthoek in his penthouse office. There was no mention of such matters as the Availing Time, or the Ascent of the Prince, or the Citadel of the Enemy. But other terms were available for use with equal effect. Such terms as the accelerated pace of history's footsteps; and the dictates of intelligence in the universe; and the imperative to keep faith with destiny in the cosmos; and their common loyalty as servitors—as master engineers—of the Process.

Channing and Benthoek flew to Rome, and bearded that great Apostle of the Process, Cardinal Cosimo Maestroianni, in his penthouse study. Things were going well in Europe and elsewhere, they cooed. But what could possibly account for the peculiar situation in the United States? Why did the mechanism of the IACs in that region appear to be faltering so badly in its progress toward ECOMMIV? "Are your people purposely dragging their feet?" Channing put a sharp edge to his questioning. "Or has some problem arisen that might have escaped Your Eminence's attention?"

The little Cardinal flew to his office and called His Eminence Silvio Aureatini on the carpet. "We're in a real mess. You were supposed to be monitoring the IACs in the United States. Must I see to everything myself?"

Forthwith, His Eminence Aureatini flew to his own defense by laying the blame elsewhere. "The Internal Affairs Committees of the National Council of Catholic Bishops in America are under the care of our Venerable Brother of Centurycity," he reminded Maestroianni.

"And?"

"The Cardinal of Centurycity has not been in the best of health lately, Your Eminence." Aureatini tried to appear sympathetic as he lowered the boom on the Yankee Cardinal. "And he has been—er—distracted. He has a number of civil lawsuits on his hands involving some of his priests who have been accused of sexual abuse of minors. In fact, considering that something like a billion dollars has been paid in out-of-court settlements over the past eleven years or so in the United States, and considering the rash of lawsuits in Centurycity alone, I wonder whether the Cardinal himself is approaching the status of a problem."

Maestroianni eyed the junior Cardinal in silence while he sorted out his priorities. If His Eminence of Centurycity was becoming distracted, that was enough to account for the laggardly performance of the IACs in his territory. But without the Cardinal's leadership, nothing was likely to move forward in a timely way. In that regard, the Cardinal of Centurycity was indispensable. Who else could open the clerical and episcopal closets where all the skeletons lay? Who but he understood the specific trade-offs that would be most telling to secure the cooperation of this or that bishop?

"If I might make a suggestion, Eminence." Silvio Aureatini understood the problem. "In dealing with the European bishops, we have got on extremely well by sending our personal emissary to canvass their needs and difficulties, and to help solve concrete problems for them. Just as a stopgap measure, of course, until His Eminence of Centurycity is out from under his troublesome legalities, why not use the same technique there? We have the perfect candidate for the task."

"And who might that be?"

"Father Christian Gladstone. Your Eminence will recall Father Gladstone's own interest in extending his work for us to the States. He has proved himself an able worker in the field. As a simple priest, he presents no threat in his episcopal interrogations. Yet at the same time, he's learned to carry the Vatican aura like a true Roman in his dealings with men who outrank him. And as an *anglosassone* himself, he should have no difficulty in reading the mind of the American bishops for us on the question of Church unity.

"If Gladstone were to travel as Your Eminence's personal emissary—if he were to mention your name discreetly in such a manner as to indicate Your Eminence's interest and concern—I'm sure we could manage to improve their ecclesiastical welfare in ways that would prove persuasive. I doubt there are many bishops in America who would fail to appreciate the special facilities that might be opened to them at the Vatican Bank, for instance. Nor would they be ungrateful that difficult cases involving Canon Law might be solved. Or that elusive appointments to Rome might be secured. The examples are endless, Eminence."

"Endless, indeed." Maestroianni smiled at last. "Tell me, where is our talented young Father Gladstone now?"

Cardinal Maestroianni held out his hand to accommodate Christian Gladstone's usual ritual of kissing his ring. It was a small price to pay to keep such a promising young protégé happy. "How good of you to interrupt your itinerary on such short notice, *Reverendo*."

Christian brushed his lips to the ring and then took his usual chair beside Maestroianni's desk. "No difficulty, Eminence. Your secretary made it sound urgent."

The Cardinal seemed amused. "Monsignore Manuguerra tends to be excitable, I'm afraid. Your sister's health hasn't improved, I take it?"

"I'm afraid not, Eminence." That part of Gladstone's bid to be sent to America was not a ruse. The word from Windswept was that Tricia was in constant agony, and Chris did want to spend some time with her, if he could.

A click of his tongue expressed His Eminence's sorrow. A few nicely chosen words expressed his appreciation that Father Gladstone was so dedicated as to have suggested combining his work for Church unity with a little visit to his family. "Of course"—the Cardinal was back to the main point within seconds—"timing is a consideration. I fear we have been neglecting the needs of our bishops in America. But neither can we afford to dislocate your current schedule of episcopal visits. The itinerary we've already set out for you in Europe must be accommodated before you set out for your homeland. Still, we will need a bit of time to prepare a list of the bishops we would like you to canvass for us in the States."

"Of course." Maestroianni had given Chris the opening to suggest the timing he wanted—the timing that would mesh with Damien Slattery's departure from the Angelicum—and he took it. "For my part, Eminence, I expect to be on the road in Europe through most of February. Taking into account the time required to write up my reports and prepare for our usual debriefings, I think early March would be realistic."

Maestroianni nodded agreeably. This Gladstone was such a clear-minded fellow. All things considered, he was shaping up as excellent timber. A prime candidate for the Process. There wasn't time to go into that now, of course. But a preliminary little pep talk was surely in order. "Tell me, Father." Cardinal Maestroianni took on a more confidential air. "Have you given much thought to the importance of your part in our work as it relates to the felicitous achievements of the Second Vatican Council?"

Loath to pick his way through the minefield he had been invited to enter, Chris questioned His Eminence with uncomprehending eyes.

"Perhaps you're too young to know this matter in the round"—the Cardinal smiled—"but at my age, I have come to realize that the Council gave us a new ecclesiology. A new beginning. A new constitutional structure for the Church. One in which the power of Christ as head of the Church is suitably and harmoniously exercised by all its bishops, including the venerable Bishop of Rome. And you, Father Gladstone—even you, by your collaboration with this office—are helping mightily to enforce that new structure.

"We are both pressed for time just now. I expect the moment will come, however, when we will explore such matters at greater length. Meanwhile, think carefully on what I have said. Think on the work you have been doing for this office in Europe and the work you are about to take up for us in America. Think about that one word, unity. About the benefits unity will bring to our bishops, and to the Bishop of Rome—our Holy Father—as together they guide the Church toward the new millennium."

As he made his way through the corridors of the Apostolic Palace, Chris balanced things up. He had to admit to himself that in all the months of his work for the Cardinal, he still hadn't penetrated the thick layer of *romanità* that made it so difficult to get at the mind of that enigmatic

Vatican administrator. But if he had read the signals right today, he could be on the way to finding answers to some of the puzzles that had troubled him for so long and that he had explored so often with Aldo Carnesecca. Meanwhile, he felt he had managed things well. He had secured his work for the Cardinal as a cover for his efforts for the Holy See in America. He had even managed to set March as the target date. The rest should be easy. If he wasn't too green to handle even the likes of Cardinal Cosimo Maestroianni, surely he wasn't too green to handle his end of the papal investigation into the clerical scandals that were piling up like dung heaps in the United States.

His only problem now was to track Giustino Lucadamo down and make his case.

XXXIV

INSOFAR as he could foresee the near-term sufferings that would be caused for many in his Church by an intensification of his policies, the Slavic Pope felt the utmost anguish and regret. Indeed, he realized that even among his faithful supporters there were some who already felt that his papal policies implied an abandonment of his role as teacher, guide and governor of the mores of Roman Catholics, and of his role as witness and exemplar to the world as Christ's Vicar. But the Pontiff's reasoning was guided by an iron logic and analysis of his concrete situation.

The Holy Spirit had seen fit to place him as Christ's Vicar at a moment in history when the world's populations were moving holus-bolus into irrational modes of thought, and when whole continents were becoming resecularized and repaganized in accordance with a new kind of belief structure. As Pope his endeavor from the outset had been to occupy a high profile in that irrational and increasingly antireligious global context, to minimize the differences of religious opinion between Roman Catholics and non-Catholics and at the same time to maintain the revealed doctrines and essential practices of his Church. In practical terms, that endeavor had led him to visit with ordinary people on their own level. To frequent the circles of movers and shakers in political and cultural spheres. To establish easeful bonds with whatever powerful groupings existed or came into existence.

That endeavor was being made more urgent than ever by the two recent discoveries that had been presented to him. There existed a sophisticated, detailed and global plot among Catholic prelates against his pontificate. More ominously, there was an organizational connection of that plot to non-Catholic, non-Christian and even anti-Christian centers.

Nor could the Pontiff neglect the question he had raised so recently with Cardinal Reinvernunft: that some new factor had surely entered the equation, and seemed to be hastening the corrosion of basic Catholic faith. The possibility was that they were living in the aftermath of some action or event of such significance that it had caused a severe loss of divine grace and had increased the ability of God's ancient Enemy to wreak havoc. Given Brother Augustine's persuasive evidence of ritualistic Satanism and murder among the clergy, it didn't take a genius to figure that a sinister and vicious force had penetrated at least one important sector of the hierarchy and had linked that hierarchy in a most baleful way to the secularization and paganization under way among the nations.

The Pope had no choice for the moment but to press his policies to a new level. He would sanctify the activities of mankind by his active presence among them. He would raise his public profile still further. In circumstances that would have eliminated other Popes, he would remain active in the affairs of mankind. He would emphasize those things that unite all peoples, Catholic and non-Catholic; for all religion was facing the same threat of liquidation. He would redouble his efforts to carry the grace of God with him as Pope while talking in the language of the world.

The Pontiff was accurate about the effects of his stepped-up activities. Among supporters and adversaries alike, bafflement and confusion caused by his policies until now were child's play compared to the fallout as he applied his latest initiatives with surprising twists.

Among the first of his adversaries to feel the direct effects of his resolve was His Eminence Cardinal Cosimo Maestroianni. Invited to join the Pontiff in the papal study one morning, he found himself on the receiving end of a special mission the Holy Father had in mind.

"I am sure Your Eminence has noticed"—the Pope began the novel interview on familiar ground—"that I have made sure every important piece of news has continued to reach you since your departure from State."

"Sì, Santità." Still flustered at having been summoned for this meeting, Maestroianni kept up his guard as best he could.

"And," the Holy Father continued at his own confident pace, "I'm sure we have come to similar conclusions about the intergovernmental memos of January 5 and the ancillary intelligence reports we have received concerning those memos."

Whatever about conclusions, His Eminence acknowledged his familiarity with the data. Two major powers had secretly decided to foment age-old ethnic hatreds in Yugoslavia into a local war. The apparent idea was to reduce the area involved to a greater dependence on help from international organizations; that is, to advance the status of supranational bodies to act in the affairs of individual states. The data made it clear, as well, that five Yugoslav leaders had bought into the idea; that they had readily and deliberately planned, plotted and promoted a civil war. One result of that "managed" war, however, was that Western powers had come to the brink of a military intervention of their own to meet the unforeseen tide of public outcry against blood and destruction.

Satisfied that the Cardinal knew the essentials, the Pontiff outlined the conclusion he had in mind. "It is the duty of this Holy See, Eminence, to remind the society of nations that negotiation is a far more human solution to problems than internecine wars bubbling from ancient ethnic feuds and fed by lethal armaments from the usual unscrupulous merchants of death."

"Yes, Holiness." If that was the conclusion, Maestroianni saw no harm in assenting to it. "The danger is great that 'managed' conflicts like that may become generalized over a whole region."

"Besides the cost in human life and suffering."

"Of course, Holiness." Still at a loss as to the point of this discussion, the Cardinal was not at ease.

"What I propose, Eminence, is that you address a plenary session of the United Nations on behalf of the Holy See, and as my special legate. And I propose that Your Eminence draft the text of the address for my revision. We must help the society of nations to build our structures of global peace by delivering a letter on the subject of negotiations. That is to be the title, by the way. *Negotiations.* And its message—the message of this Holy See—will be exactly that. Negotiations, not war."

The Cardinal steeled himself; waited for some duplicitous catch to this curious assignment. But as far as he could see, there was none. Arrangements had already been set with the UN, the Pontiff told him, and the Secretary-General had assigned an early date for the special plenary session.

"I am relying on your expert guidance in this matter, Eminence." The Pope rose from his chair in courteous dismissal. "If you have the preliminary text of *Negotiations* ready for my revision in a week or so, that should do nicely. Give it your best, Eminence. The Church expects it of you."

Maestroianni did give it his best. Still on his guard, and aware that the speech would be read and received at the UN as coming from His Holiness, the Cardinal took special care to papalize the text, while still inserting his own idea of negotiations into the draft text of the future address. Faithful to his word, His Eminence completed what he considered a splendid draft of *Negotiations* within a week and sent it over to the papal office for revision.

When it came back to him a day or so later, the Cardinal was more perplexed than ever. Not only had the Pontiff maintained all the themes of the speech exactly as Maestroianni had set them out. He had all but depapalized the text by the changes and insertions he had introduced in his own hand. Puzzled and wary, Maestroianni went over the revisions, trying to understand, for instance, why the Pope had deleted the Cardinal's description of the United Nations as "the central forum for settling our human quarrels" and substituted a statement lauding the UN's "precious and irreplaceable role." He wanted to understand why the Pope had cut the reference to the papal voice as "a voice whose words come to you with the moral authority of God and the revelation of God's love for his children" and had substituted "a voice whose words are meant to be the echo of the moral conscience of humanity in the pure sense."

The text was pockmarked throughout with such adaptations and changes. Where he, Maestroianni, had described the aims of the Church as "the fruits of the Holy Spirit and that peace which Jesus Christ alone has been able to promise mankind," the Pope had substituted the aims of "cooperation, mutual trust, fraternity and peace." Where His Eminence had reaffirmed "this Holy See's dedication to spreading Christ's message of love tempered by justice," the Pope had written instead, "I reaffirm my confidence in the power of true negotiations to arrive at just and equitable solutions." Even the end of the speech had been changed to a plea that mankind "not lose the hope of being able to master its own future" and an exhortation that "men can and must make the force of reason prevail over the reasons of force."

The puzzle was too much to fathom. In every case, the Holy Father's changes had replaced the Cardinal's typically Catholic phraseology with typically this-worldly statements. The Pontiff had transformed it into a non-Catholic and non-Christian document, into a speech that might have been delivered by a Hindu member of the UN delegation from India, or by a Muslim delegate from Syria, or an animist delegate from the Congo, or a freewheeling atheist delegate from France. With a few minor changes, it might even serve as the annual address of the Grand Master of the Scottish Grand Orient.

When a dozen readings of the revised text did nothing to explain such a gross anomaly, Maestroianni decided to seek counsel among friends. In short order he was on the scrambler phone to Belgium's Cardinal Piet Svensen. What was the catch in this curious papal assignment?

"You worry over nothing, Eminence!" Cardinal Svensen was categoric in his advice and unremitting in his contempt for the Pontiff. "You are a seasoned diplomat, and you have been given a plum assignment. Perhaps the Pontiff has some trick in mind. But he's put you in a position to hoist him by his own petard. My advice to Your Eminence is to hoist away!"

Encouraged by Svensen's spleen, Maestroianni decided to consult Cyrus Benthoek, who asked for a copy of the revised *Negotiations* text to be faxed to him in London, with another to be transmitted to Dr. Ralph Channing in New York. The three-way conference call that ensued within the hour was more speculative at first than the Svensen conversation had been. In the beginning, in fact, Channing was downright incredulous.

"Do you really mean to say that the Pontiff authored these impressive elements of the message, Eminence?"

"Emphatically, I cannot explain it. But you have seen it with your own eyes. The words of the message are deliberate. But what is the intent?"

"It's not going to halt the plan in Bosnia-Herzegovina." That was Cyrus Benthoek's analysis.

"No," Channing agreed. "We know that must proceed as long as the CIS issue is unresolved. And yet, I must presume that the Pope knows of the Five-Man Plan."

"Emphatically," Maestroianni confirmed. "In fact, he brought it up specifically in our discussion as the springboard for this UN initiative."

"He knows, therefore"—Channing drew one conclusion—"that, for the moment, the Bosnia plan excludes negotiations. So it's safe to assume that the real purpose of this *Negotiations* message has little and nothing to do with its title."

Annoyed that they were still at square one, His Eminence cut in on Channing. "That brings me back to my original question. I seek the real purpose of this message. I don't know the answer, but I don't like the smell of it."

"Maybe he's just getting desperate, Eminence." Benthoek sounded hopeful. "Maybe he's beginning to see how far out of step he is with the new order of things and wants to get back into line."

"Desperate, Cyrus? He may be confusing the issues, but he's too confident to be desperate."

"Confusing identities would be more like it," Cyrus countered. "He sounds like one of us. He's invading our turf."

Dr. Channing listened with half an ear. As a dedicated servitor of the Prince, he had some private thinking to do. Channing was a man of Spirit. He was led by Spirit; had an unerring instinct for the movement of Spirit. And, unlike the other two, he knew of the Enthronement ceremony that had been celebrated decades before in the Citadel of the Enemy. Now, if the whole significance of the Enthronement had been to advance the power and the agenda of the Prince in the age-old warfare of Spirit, to embrace the Citadel of religion itself into the folds of the Process, it was only logical to think that the Slavic Pope had finally been affected in some primary way.

Not that the Pontiff had been co-opted. His dedication to the basics of Catholic morality was convincing testimony on that score. But it would appear on the evidence of the *Negotiations* text that he had been cornered; that willy-nilly he was being secularized.

A moment or two of such clear-headed analysis was enough to make the fundamental situation plain to Channing. He was ready to weigh into the conversation again at a persuasive and practical level. "Your Pope may not be desperate, Eminence." There was a buoyant edge to his voice as he broke into the dialogue. "Nevertheless, I think Cyrus may be right. The

Pontiff is making a bid to be included in the affairs of mankind. It beats me why he thinks talking like us in this *Negotiations* message will strengthen his position. But I have no doubt, Eminence, that it will strengthen ours. When you deliver that paper, it will help to mitigate the tension that still exists in some quarters against the new order of things. Language molds thought, after all.

"So, let's help him in this worthy effort. Let's hope he continues to confuse the issues, and his identity as well. Let's hope he confuses the conservatives and traditionalists who still hang on to the fringes of his Church. If we manage our plans well and keep things on a timely schedule, all of that will make it easier to deal with him definitively when the time comes.

"Now." The supremely confident Professor Channing turned the focus of the conversation on a dime. "Speaking of our own plans, your Eminence. I presume your new tactic to bring the Common Mind Vote program back into line among the bishops in America is firm?"

"Firm and ready to go." Maestroianni sounded like his old self again. "Limited as he is, I have high hopes for Father Christian Gladstone."

"Well, then." Channing was satisfied for now. "Unless we intend to let such an advantageous moment pass us by, I would say your man Svensen has given splendid advice. Let's welcome the Slavic Pope onto our terrain!"

While the Slavic Pope set about his latest gamble by redoubling his already troublesome policies, Giustino Lucadamo prepared Damien Slattery and Christian Gladstone for the papal investigations into Satanism and homosexuality among the American clergy.

Lucadamo still held Christian's loyalty to be an open question. For the moment, though, he was satisfied that Father Christian had put the basic elements of his mission neatly into place. The arrangement he had made to include the American bishops in his work for Maestroianni took care of his posting to the United States. The travel it required would provide him with the perfect cover for a wide-ranging investigation into homosexual activity among clergy and religious. And his family concerns justified his use of Windswept House as his base of operations.

Slattery's posting fell out perfectly, too, and almost of its own accord. As the date drew near for the General Chapter of the Dominican Order to take place, it became clear that another Irish friar, one Donal McGinty, was a shoo-in to succeed Slattery as Master-General of the Dominicans. McGinty, an astonishingly permissive man with a single-minded passion for golf, seemed overjoyed at the prospect of shipping his Dominican brother off to the Order's faraway priory in Centurycity, U.S.A.

Damien wasn't half so pleased as McGinty at the prospect of taking up residence at the Centurycity priory. Rumor had it that the House of the Holy Angels, as the monastery was known, had become a haven for several homosexually oriented members of the Order. And then there was the matter of Father George Haneberry, the man who would be Damien's superior in Centurycity.

"He hates my guts, Giustino." Slattery put the case frankly to the security chief. "Ever since I got at him about a scandalous monograph he published—"Homosexuality and Humanness," he called it; a blatant plea for homosexual rights—he'll do everything he can to smear me. Given half a chance, Haneberry will have me in a vise."

Lucadamo was sympathetic but insistent. "He won't have half a chance, Father. Officially, you'll be in the States on behalf of the Holy Father. As far as Haneberry knows, your job will be to lecture to pro-life groups and give retreats to priests and religious. That work will be real. It will give you as much latitude as Father Christian has to travel around the country. And the fact that you'll be working as the Pontiff's official representative should be warning enough to Haneberry—and to anyone else with an ounce of brains in his head—to keep hands off."

With the basic setup for the two neophyte spy-priests in place, Lucadamo crammed several briefing sessions with Slattery and Gladstone into a short span of time. "His Holiness needs more than lists of names and dates and places," Giustino began his review of the papal mandate. "His thinking is that the practice of Satanist rituals may have achieved some networking vogue among the American clergy. We need an overall picture. And the same goes for homosexual activity. We need to know the extent to which homosexuality as a way of life has been adopted—or at least accepted and tolerated—by that same clerical body. In other words, is there anything resembling a homosexual network among the clergy over there?"

Because both priests would be on unexplored territory, and because they were rank beginners in the business of covert operations, the security chief was rougher than usual in instilling the caution he was sure would be needed. "Never lose sight of the fact"—he drove the point home over and over again—"that sexuality and Satanism are the nitroglycerin of human relations. In practical terms, that means you'll both be fair game for the volatility of the liar and the irrational impulses of blind passions.

"You'll be dealing with informants. In the early going, you'll be dealing with people we know; people we've been able to check out. But that's just the starting point. When it comes to recruiting new informants as you go, deal with single individuals only. It's always one-on-one. Always proceed from individual to individual. Never recruit from groups—even from groups of two.

"In case you trust the wrong person, be sure you've taken every precaution in advance to limit the damage. Your reputation can be mangled. Your efficiency for this mission—and your whole career, besides—can be compromised. So don't leave yourselves open to false accusations. Whenever possible, meetings with people you have any reason to doubt should take place in public. Wherever you go, even alone, try to distinguish yourselves in some way, without being blatant. If you take a cab, for example, ask the driver about his family, the weather, the time. Anything that will make it likely he'll remember you. In restaurants, overtip. Or don't leave a tip at all. Or spill a glass of water. Complain about the service, or give effusive compliments. The idea is to be remembered. To be able to prove where you were, in case false accusations are raised against you.

"Establish safe phones at home base. That won't be a problem for Father Chris at Windswept House. But you might have a problem, Father Damien, given the situation you describe at the Centurycity priory. Insofar as you can, let one another know in advance where you expect to be, along with your times of departure and expected return—in case you don't return. And devise some simple code so you can avoid using names of people and places.

"As far as this papal investigation is concerned, you will seek no help from ecclesiastical authorities. Never consult them. And no matter what you may discover, never confront them or threaten their official capacity. Never antagonize them unnecessarily. Never step onto their bailiwick. Remember, they have Canon Law on their side. And, given the basic stuff of this mission, always—I repeat, always—remember that any ecclesiastical officeholder has two nightmares: financial failure and public scandal. They fear those two things more than Heaven's judgment or the pains of Hell."

When Gladstone and Damien were as ready as he could make them, Lucadamo gave them a set of briefing documents to be memorized and then destroyed. He then gave each man his initial contact.

Slattery would start with the retired Centurycity police inspector Sylvester Wodgila, the officer in charge of the Scalabrini murder case, who had put together the plan for the official investigation he had intended to follow. Included in Slattery's materials was one document he would keep intact. Courtesy of the Slavic Pope, a certain Father Danitski—a monk in the Monastery of Czestochowa, and a first cousin to Wodgila—had provided such an innocuous letter of introduction to the prematurely retired police inspector that it made Slattery laugh. "Give the bearer of this letter any assistance you can," Danitski had written. "He wants to see the sights of your famous Centurycity."

Christian Gladstone's point of departure was dicier and gave no cause for laughter. Father Michael O'Reilly had been recently ordained for service in the New Orleans Archdiocese by none other than Gladstone's former superior, Cardinal John Jay O'Cleary. At the end of his first year as an assistant pastor, however, he had discovered that three fourth-year students in the Archdiocesan seminary were active homosexuals. Boldly, he had taken the information to Jay Jay O'Cleary. Even more boldly, he had told His Eminence that the three men should be expelled from the seminary.

After a short inquiry during which the three seminarians in question had confirmed the truth of the allegations, Jay Jay had approved their ordination as priests of his diocese.

For O'Reilly, the whole affair had escalated into wholesale disaster. He was removed from his parish, placed on six months' probation and ordered to undergo a psychosexual evaluation. When he refused, he was sent to cool his heels in the seminary and was given no diocesan assignment. O'Reilly had decided to make the matter known to the Vatican's Congregation for the Clergy. The idea was to write a letter detailing the case and to use the diplomatic pouch of the Holy See's Apostolic Delegate in Washington, D.C., to transmit it to Rome.

Father O'Reilly's mistake had been to send that letter in strict accord with seminary rules: he handed it in to the Rector's office in the normal manner for transmittal to Washington through the mails. Not surprisingly, it made its way rapidly to the Archdiocesan Chancery, where it was intercepted by the Cardinal's red-haired junior secretary, Father Eddie McPherson, who had charge of whatever seminary mail might be sent through for His Eminence's attention. Jay Jay himself found that O'Reilly in his letter named names and gave dates and locations, and that he had complained that Cardinal O'Cleary had deliberately ordained three certifiably homosexual men, thus swelling the already growing ranks of pedophiliac priests.

O'Reilly had been called on the Cardinal's carpet, had been told he was a very sick young man and had been again ordered to submit to a psychosexual evaluation at the Raphael Institute in New Orleans. When O'Reilly had refused to obey, Jay Jay had declared him "insubordinate and psychologically undependable," and had told him he would be defrocked and expelled from the Archdiocese. Reduced by every circumstance to total frustration, O'Reilly answered by cursing Jay Jay to his face, flattening Father Eddie McPherson with a left hook to the jaw and storming out of the Chancery.

After that brouhaha, O'Reilly had dropped out of sight altogether for a couple of months. Finally, though, he had turned up on the long-abandoned Western Bordeaux Plantation in Louisiana, where, supported by a monthly stipend from his family, he now lived a hermit's life.

"What do you make of all that, Father Christian? As an old protégé of Cardinal O'Cleary, does it stack up as credible to you? And do you think O'Reilly would be reliable enough to serve as a first lead for your inquiry?"

Chris began with Father Eddie McPherson's alleged role in the outrage against Michael O'Reilly. "That part of the story is certainly credible," Christian confirmed. "McPherson is jealous enough of his own standing to see an advantage in heading off any scandal that would reflect directly on the Chancery. He's always ready to curry favor with His Eminence. And his duties for the Cardinal put opportunity in his way in the form of O'Reilly's letter."

As far as Jay Jay O'Cleary's alleged role was concerned, the report not only fit with Gladstone's perception of the Cardinal's character. His Eminence was known to be a man who wanted to be loved by everybody. In this instance, he would certainly be loved by the three grateful seminarians who had made it to priestly ordination. And he would be loved by any member of the academic faculty who might be homosexually active, or who just plain wanted to avoid trouble.

"And what about O'Reilly?" Lucadamo pressed the remaining point. "After what he's been through, do you think he'd be a reliable starting point for your investigation?"

Gladstone smiled a sad smile. "For my money, the question is whether O'Reilly has any objective backup proof like the material he showed to Cardinal O'Cleary."

"Maybe so." Damien had his own two cents to offer. "But if I'd been manhandled by my superior the way that young fellow has, I'd be gun-shy of any Roman Catholic clergyman who came within a country mile of me. So, for my money, the first question is whether you can get at him at all."

"I think I can manage that." Chris's smile was almost mischievous this time. "It just so happens that the plantation where O'Reilly is holed up belongs to the New Orleans Bank of Southern Credit. And it just so happens that some of the Gladstone millions you like to rag me about have bought us a major interest in that bank. And it just so happens that Thomas Barr Rollins, the president of that bank, is a regular visitor at Windswept House."

"And"—Slattery came back with a bit of mischief of his own—"I suppose it just so happens Rollins bounced you on his knee when you were still in short britches, so he'll do anything you want, no questions asked."

"I never wore short britches." Gladstone laughed. "But you've got the picture. I baptized one of his grandsons not long ago."

With the O'Reilly matter essentially settled, Lucadamo tackled what he called his Mayday provision. "The idea, reverend gentlemen"—he displayed a wolfish grin—"is not to be able to get yourselves out of trouble. The idea is to see that you don't get into trouble in the first place. But, just in case that nitroglycerin mixture of sexuality and Satanism explodes in your hands, and you do get into trouble, don't try to rescue yourselves without help." The security chief supplied them with one final piece of paper. "Memorize this name and the addresses and phone numbers that go with it. Then destroy the information along with the rest of the briefing data."

"Len Connell," Slattery read the name aloud. "A friend of yours, Giustino?"

"A friend, a colleague and a foursquare Roman Catholic." Lucadamo was emphatic. "But from your point of view, the main thing is that he's FBI. He knows how to get greenhorns like you out of hot water."

Finally, the only matter to take up was the question of communication with the Holy Father. Slattery and Gladstone would return to Rome to deliver their preliminary findings to the Pontiff sometime around the end of spring, before His Holiness left for the papal residence at Castel Gandolfo; or, if circumstances warranted a delay, they would hand in a final report by summer's end. Should communication become imperative before that, their contact was to be through Father Aldo Carnesecca.

"He'll be stationed in Barcelona for a while," Lucadamo told them. "Out of the direct line of fire, you might say. You'll be given secure mail drops, when the time comes."

At the mention of Carnesecca's name, the expression on Chris's face changed abruptly. "Now that we've been through this briefing with you, Giustino—now that I've had a glimpse of the life Carnesecca has lived during all the years of his service to the Holy See—I think I'm just beginning to see how tough a man he really is."

That remark went into the plus side of Lucadamo's continuing evaluation of Gladstone. He could only hope that this innocent-looking American would turn out to be half the man Father Aldo was.

XXXV

CESSI GLADSTONE opened her eyes at first light, peered about in confusion and, only after some seconds, remembered where she was. The Excelsior Hotel on the Via Veneto in Rome. "Ridiculous woman," she chided herself. Her mind still not focused, she reached for the bedside phone with the foggy notion of calling Chris at the Angelicum before he began his day. "Ridiculous woman," she scolded again as she gathered her robe around her and headed for the shower. "Get your wits about you, old girl. Chris is the one at Windswept House now. You're the one in Rome. And you'd better make the most of it."

The bargain she had sealed with Cardinal Amedeo Sanstefano during her lightning visit to the Vatican Bank had paid off. The Gladstone bailout in the Salvi suitcase affair last fall had been her ticket to a private audience with the Slavic Pope. Just as Sanstefano had said, it had taken a long time to arrange—from the previous autumn to this early spring. Not the least benefit from the delay, however, had been Cessi's discovery of a new friend in Sanstefano. He had become a potentially invaluable ally for the accomplishment of her mission with the Pope.

❑ ❑ ❑ ❑

As imposing as His Eminence had been at that first meeting in Rome, Cessi had not found him too formidable for her. Nor had she been content to ask the Cardinal to arrange a papal audience for her and leave the matter at that. When she had received the letter of invitation from the Pontiff's secretary confirming the details of her papal audience, she called him in order to register her dissatisfaction at the arrangements.

"It will not do, Your Eminence," Cessi had complained. "The details set out by this Monsignore Daniel Sadowski are exactly what I expected, and it will not do. His Holiness has set aside an hour for me. He will receive me in one of the upstairs reception areas of the Apostolic Palace. He will share some refreshments with me and listen to what I have to say.

"I am one of the Roman Catholic laity, such as we are these days. And in that role, I can tell Your Eminence that I don't need a Pope to shake my hand and ask me how I am. I don't need a Pope to pass the sugar for my tea while we relax together in a pair of easy chairs to discuss this or that or the other bagatelle. In other words, Eminence, I deplore the idea of having tea with the Vicar of Christ as though the Barque of Peter were the Good Ship Lollipop on a holiday cruise.

"I need a Pope whose instep I kiss because he walks in the awesome presence of God, and because he lives in the preserve of Christ Whose Vicar he is. I need a Pope to approach in awe because of the wisdom beyond all human calculation with which God has seen fit to endow him. I need a Pope to venerate because his fatal mortality and his puny human mind are absorbed by the power God has invested in him."

"It is true, Signora Cessi." His Eminence was candid, too: "We who live in Rome have been despoiled of something precious and irreplaceable. It is true that Rome itself has been despoiled of its ancient cloak of religious reverence. This Eternal City has been invaded by the mystery of iniquity, and everyone is infected to some degree with its banality and its indifference."

"Everyone," Cessi had intervened boldly, "including this most extraordinary and enigmatic of Popes?"

It had been a measure of Sanstefano's professional integrity that, rather than fall into the trap of open papal criticism, he had channeled Cessi's obvious anger and dislike for this Pope into a more positive course. His Eminence allowed as how he, too, would love to see a return to the old pomp and regalia of a formal papal audience conducted in the richly ornamented but now little used Sala della Sede Apostolica. "And yet, Signora, you will excuse an old man for suggesting that if your hope is to use your papal audience to evoke that religious reverence again, you will do well to recognize reality and to deal with it intelligently."

Grateful for Sanstefano's corrective, Cessi had decided to share with him her own dismal assessment of the Slavic Pope on the chance that he might collaborate in some meaningful way in the twofold petition she intended to make to the Holy Father.

"The real basis of my request for a papal audience," she confided, "lies in my view of how matters stand in the Church: we are facing into an eclipse of our traditional Roman Catholic life as any kind of visibly effective force. Further, it is my view, Eminence, that the Pope must consider the traditional structure of his Church to be passé and useless. For he seems deliberately to allow it to decay. If that is not his idea, there is no way of understanding him other than as totally aberrant and as neglectful of his Petrine office as Pope."

Sanstefano had finally made it plain that he wanted to hear more. And Cessi had a good deal more to say. "The decay of which I speak, Eminence, has already gone very far. Neither bishops nor priests nor the ordinary parish-and-diocese structure of the Church any longer guarantees the basics of that Roman Catholic life. Now, I won't detail what I consider to be this Holy Father's errors of judgment. Simon Peter made such errors. We all do. It is human. We do not share with the Pope either the authority or the responsibility of the papal throne. But we do most emphatically share with one another the responsibility to make up for his deficiencies.

"Unless we can agree on that much, Eminence, further collaboration between us will be impossible."

There was a silence while Sanstefano digested what he had heard so far. Clearly this woman made more sense of the Slavic Pope's policies and motives than men who had spent their lives tucked snugly in their Vatican careers. Clearly, without some expression of a common mind with her, His Eminence would learn nothing of her plans to tackle the Pope. "Those deficiencies you speak of, Signora Cessi. Would you not agree that they are most probably caused by the tight net of control and restriction drawn around the present papacy by internal enemies? By Roman Catholic enemies of that sacred papacy?" Then, on the assumption that his meaning had been clear enough, Sanstefano decided to take the exchange to the payoff. "May I assume, Signora, that you have a specific proposal to lay before the Holy Father during your audience with him?"

The Cardinal had not only met Cessi's challenge. On the condition that what passed between them now would be as confidential as anything said in the confessional, Cessi told Sanstefano the twofold purpose of her papal meeting.

His response had been more than Cessi had dared to hope. "It seems to me that the proposals you wish to present to the Holy Father do reflect the exceedingly dangerous condition of the Church. I will assist actively in the success of your venture. I will prepare the way for you to be received by the Holy Father in a format that is fitting and worthy of the occasion. There will be no grand processions, mind you. But neither will it be a tea party on the Good Ship Lollipop. And, with your consent, I will assist at the audience myself. Provided His Holiness agrees to your proposals, it will be clear to him by my presence that I stand ready to fill the role of Cardinal Protector for your venture."

□ □ □ □

At three-thirty sharp, dressed and coiffed in conservative elegance, Cessi stepped out of the elevator into the Excelsior's ornate lobby. As eyes turned on every side to watch, this graceful woman strode toward the entrance where the limousine with its unmistakable Vatican plates was waiting for her.

During the ride to the Apostolic Palace, Cessi exchanged pleasantries with her friendly young driver, but her mind was elsewhere. On the heavy congestion of traffic that slowed their progress. On her meeting with the Pontiff. On her worry about Tricia. On her questions about Chris and where his career as a Roman priest was taking him. On the advice and coaching Cardinal Sanstefano had given her.

At last, her driver was heading across the Victor Emmanuel Bridge. At the familiar sight of Castel Sant'Angelo topped by the famed figure of St. Michael, sword in hand, Cessi said a silent and equally familiar prayer for the Archangel's help and protection. Apparently, Michael was paying attention, for the traffic on the Via della Conciliazione began to move at such a clip that her driver pulled into St. Peter's Square and drew to a halt inside the Court of St. Damasus on the dot of three forty-five.

To be on schedule in Rome, she reflected with a little smile of thanks to the chauffeur, was a small miracle in itself.

The chamberlain waiting at curbside handed her out of the limousine. Through the Secretariat doors they went. Into the creaky old elevator. Up to the third floor and into a spacious reception room overlooking the square, where her escort left her with a bow and the barest touch of a smile. Cessi took a quick but critical look at her surroundings. She ran a hand over the dark wood of the conference table; frowned at the group of easy chairs assembled hard by the window; noted the delicacy of the cornice work above her.

The door opened. With Cardinal Sanstefano and another man, a monsignore, following, His Holiness walked into the room.

Cessi was astonished at the sense of happy solemnity that ran through her as His Eminence made the formal introductions. She knelt to kiss the Fisherman's ring, and then allowed the Holy Father to take her hand in both of his and draw her to her feet.

"Signora Gladstone." The Pontiff's blue eyes met hers squarely. "I am glad to have this opportunity to speak with such a faithful daughter of the Church and with the mother of such a fine priest as Father Christian."

The warmth of the Pope's greeting fell around Cessi like a cloak as Cardinal Sanstefano led the way skillfully but unobtrusively to the conference table. She waited for the Pope to be seated before she took the chair held out for her by the man who had been introduced as Monsignore Daniel Sadowski. Then there were a few minutes of ceremonial small talk—a reminder from Cardinal Sanstefano of the good signora's most recent act of generosity toward the Vatican Bank; a word from His Holiness about the selfless Father Angelo Gutmacher who was so close to the Gladstones; a word again about Father Christian's valued service. Cessi began to feel that Heaven itself was smiling upon what she was about to propose.

At a certain point, with no more than a slight gesture of his hands, His Holiness invited his honored guest to take center stage. Cessi did so with a formality that was rarely heard within the Vatican these days. "Your Holiness be blessed by Christ Our Lord for giving me this privilege. And if it please Your Holiness, allow me to present a twofold petition."

The Slavic Pope nodded his consent.

"I know we differ in our perspectives. By necessity, Your Holiness must take a world view. By necessity, as a woman, a mother and a private individual, I must view matters on a one-to-one basis. Nonetheless, I believe we can agree on one important fact. Every month fresh evidence pours in to show that the decadence of the external structure of the Church is proceeding at a geometric rate. For twenty-five years and more this has gone on with no sign of a turning." Cessi raised one eyebrow ever so slightly in query.

The Slavic Pope nodded somberly.

"In imitation of Your Holiness, I have no difficulty facing this desolation of Catholicism—this decadence and obsolescence—on one condition. Namely, that we who are so often referred to now as the People of God have access to the Sacraments. To valid Sacraments, Holiness." Stiffening suddenly as though some pain had assailed him, the Pope raised an eye to Cardinal Sanstefano, and then to Sadowski. Each man read those gestures differently, and each was correct. Sadowski was sure the Pontiff was truly in physical pain again. Sanstefano was sure the Pope had not expected this turn in Cessi Gladstone's argument.

"Unfortunately, Holy Father, the supply of validly ordained priests and therefore of validly administered Sacraments are both diminishing at the same rate as the Church structure is imploding on itself and disintegrating into dust."

The Pontiff was obviously fascinated by the self-possession of this Signora Gladstone. Her head slightly inclined, she never took her eyes from his while she spoke. She rarely paused except in silent query. She seemed to be pouring out her inmost concerns without haste or hesitation, but with an edge of passion that deepened the character of her language. Being of steel himself, the Pope recognized the steel in her.

"As I have said, my perspective is different from Your Holiness'. And in that, I have the advantage. For, despite Your Holiness' many personal pilgrimages, Your Holiness must deal with a sea of people; and with emotionless graphs and charts that tell little of the people's discontent and moral confusion. With faceless, voiceless letters of pain and incomprehension. From my vantage point, I have only to listen to hear the mourning of my fellow Roman Catholics. I have felt the suffering of Father James

Horan, a genuinely good, orthodox, papist priest in my own diocese. At forty-five, he has been defrocked and banished by our bishop. Why? Because he insists on preaching Roman Catholic morality in marriage. Because he refuses to accept the many strands of the modernist heresy that have been embraced and fostered by the Conciliar Church. Because he denounces the homosexuality bubbling to the surface among some of his fellow priests. Because he is chaste and celibate.

"Father Horan has now been abandoned, with no friend in our local Chancery and no advocate or defender in Your Holiness' Chancery. He and others like him twist slowly in the winds of corruption, while our bishops cry crocodile tears that there are not enough priests.

"And from my vantage point, Holiness, I know the danger of those who present themselves for their first Communion. Two of my own godchildren were both forbidden to go to first Confession before their first Communion. The Rosary beads I had given them were taken away from them as superstitious objects. The priest gave each of them a red, white and blue balloon to carry in one hand instead, and a square of soda bread to carry in the other. Each was told, 'Eat with Jesus.' The whole congregation clapped and chanted, 'Eat with Jesus.'

"Those two children, Holy Father, did not receive the Body, Blood, Soul and Divinity of Our Lord and Savior. Instead of being led into a state of grace, they were probably led into mortal sin. For, if they worshipped anything at all that day, it was nothing more than bread. And that is material idolatry."

His face drained of color, the Pontiff raised his hands in something between prayer and protest. "But, Signora! You must catechize those little ones. You must teach them . . ."

"Of course, Holy Father." Cessi was merciless. "But teaching them is not enough. For where are they to go now—where are any of us to go now—to receive valid Sacraments? These examples are not exceptions. They are not even the rule, for there are far worse cases. Your Holiness must surely know there are entire regions where the validity of all the Sacraments, beginning with priestly ordination itself, are in serious doubt; where the Body and Blood of Christ no longer resides in the tabernacles. Where the bread on the Altar is just bread. Where the wine is just wine—unless something else like grapefruit juice is substituted instead.

"Your Holiness must know all of this. But if you do not, then I cannot say whether the greater sin lies with those who hide the truth from Your Holiness or with Your Holiness for not taking the pains to find out the facts about the Church and its abandonment of the faithful."

Cessi raised no eyebrow in query now. She neither wanted nor expected a response to her implied questions. Though she had not used the word, Cessi had accused her Pope to his face of what amounted to malfeasance. She had not enjoyed the exercise, but it was the bedrock reason for the two related petitions she was now ready to present to the Holy Father.

"My two requests to Your Holiness will not solve the bitter grief into which the Church is descending. But in a time when the world has been all but denuded of grace, they will supply at least something of the abundant treasury of our faith. I have in my possession a list of fifty-four priests in the same quandary as good Father Horan. There are hundreds more. Perhaps thousands. But these are men I have interviewed and investigated. I can vouch for each of them. My first petition, therefore, is to work with a person of Your Holiness' trust to organize these men on a private and confidential basis, and without any juridical structure that would involve local bishops."

To his credit in Cessi's eyes, the Holy Father responded with a straightforward question. "To what end do you make such a request, Signora?"

"To a very simple end, Holiness. To provide in at least some localities a pool of validly ordained, apostolically authorized priests with full faculties to recite the Roman Mass, to hear Confessions, to anoint the dying. And, when the local bishop is in heresy or de facto schism, to confer the Sacrament of Confirmation."

"Signora," the Pontiff objected, "such a step would require the Canonical cooperation of several Roman Congregations. And there are other problems as well. Problems of a serious nature."

Cessi had done her homework. "With respect, Holy Father. Your Holiness disposes of immediate, direct and absolute jurisdiction over every single diocese and every single parish. The need in the present circumstances is for a one-on-one commission—Your Holiness to each priest individually and under solemn oath."

Intrigued that this petitioner could hold her own when it came to Canon Law, the Slavic Pope probed with professional interest. "Tell me, Signora. Have you considered the sustained control required to guarantee that such priests would not fall into their own abuses?"

"Yes, Holy Father." Cessi knew that pious fervor was no guarantee of priestly integrity. "One trusted priest should be appointed to be in charge of all these priests, and to report directly and regularly to Your Holiness. And two ironclad rules are essential. First, no use of diocesan churches or halls or other facilities and no appeal for diocesan aid of any kind. In short, no involvement by these priests with the local bishops in the external forum of episcopal authority. And, second, an obligatory system of confessions and open reporting. Each priest would have a fixed Confessor whom he would be obliged to see regularly for the Sacrament of Penance. Each would consent that his Confessor be free to report directly and only to Your Holiness if certain mortal sins are manifested. Sexual activity, for example. Or political activism, which would be a sin against obedience to papal directives. Or financial motivation and gain beyond the sufficiency required."

Such measures, Cessi admitted, would not be an infallible guarantee of integrity. But they would reduce potential abuses to a minimum; and they would provide sustained control of valid priestly activity in sensitive circumstances.

The Slavic Pope wasted no more words on petty objections. "And the second part of your twofold petition, Signora?"

Cessi was as cool now as she might have been in discussing a business proposition. "In those areas where such a pool of priests would be active, Holy Father, the Sacrament could not be reserved in diocesan churches. Moreover, there are so many locales where the Blessed Sacrament almost certainly no longer exists that they can't all be covered by a handful of priests. The second element of my petition, therefore, is that tried and trusted laymen be allowed to reserve the Blessed Sacrament in their homes. Again under strict rules."

The Holy Father was taken aback. He gave voice to his concern about what he called feasibility.

"The practice is already under way, Holiness." Cessi met the objection head-on. "Therefore it is feasible."

The Pontiff lapsed into a long and thoughtful silence. For the second time, he raised his eyes to the solemn face of Cardinal Sanstefano. His Eminence must have realized what had been afoot. Was His Eminence in accord with the assessments of Signora Gladstone? And if these assessments of the Church and of his own policies as Pope reflected Sanstefano's mind, how many more might there be like him in Rome and elsewhere? Men who were not aligned with the likes of Cardinals Maestroianni and Pensabene and Aureatini and Palombo. Men who remained loyal to the Holy See, and therefore to himself as Pope, even while they held his policies to be inimical to the interests of the Church. Men not unlike those priests Francesca Gladstone was talking about. They had not been defrocked or put aside, of course; but neither could they find scope any longer for a cohesive voice of their own.

No sooner had that stream of thought formed itself in his mind than the Slavic Pope banished it as a slithering worm of self-doubt. To entertain the validity of Signora Gladstone's concern—to consider it and to deal with it appropriately—was a matter of simple justice. But to allow himself to be tempted to the thought that he had miscalculated in papal strategy would be irrational to the point of ruin.

"Very well, Signora." His Holiness took a deep breath, as people do when preparing to make a great concession. "Let's take a preliminary step. Monsignore Sadowski will give you a special post office box number so that you can in confidence send me that list of priests as candidates for the undertaking you propose. Send only the names. Put nothing else in writing.

"As to the second element of your petition, again send me the names of laymen whom you know to be worthy to reserve the Blessed Sacrament in their homes. But in this case, please provide everything relevant about them. Full biographies, including Baptismal and Confirmation certificates;

marriage certificates when appropriate; testimonials. All that is needed to justify such a grave responsibility. Now, is there anything else, Signora?"

The Pope wasn't just being enigmatic now. He was completely opaque. Like any man brought up short and confronted with his mistakes, he was sensibly withdrawing from his visitor.

Eyes flashing green anger, Cessi gritted her teeth to keep from screaming: It won't do! Send a list, you say! Wait ten years for an answer is what you mean! I'll send you all the lists in the world, Holy Father! But give me an answer. An indication. Don't wait until there are no more Baptisms. Until, aborted or born, our babies are conceived without a thought for their immortal souls. Don't wait until there are no more Confessions, no more valid Masses. Don't wait until there is no one left to anoint the dying. Don't wait until poor Father James Horan—until all the Horans of the Church, and all the rest of us to boot—are sucked down and buried in the shambles of your Church!

"Signora Gladstone?" It was Cardinal Sanstefano come to rescue Cessi from the sudden assault of her anger. He answered the green fire of her eyes with a look of warning. A look that told her she had already gone the limit. As it was, her petitions would be given serious consideration.

Recalled to her senses by His Eminence's gentle mention of her name, Cessi turned to the Pope's question. "Yes, Holiness. There is something else." As virulent as her sudden flash of anger had been, it had not touched her sense of God's power vested in him as the Vicar of Christ. "My children, Holiness. I would ask for a special blessing for each of them, each for a different reason."

"Willingly, Signora Gladstone." The Pontiff rose from his chair. Cessi knelt to receive the blessing she had asked of him. Then, in a voice that was barely more than a whisper above her bowed head, the Slavic Pope added something more. "Father Christian has mentioned your daughter, and has asked for prayers for her health. I shall remember your son Paul in my Mass intentions. As to Father Christian himself, both he and his important work for the Holy See are in my prayers. Be assured of that, Signora."

Chris Gladstone would have been happy for the Pontiff's promise of special prayers.

This was the morning he had fixed with Tom Rollins to meet with Michael O'Reilly. If all went well, he expected to know by ten o'clock, whether O'Reilly could produce hard proof of an ecclesiastical cover-up of verifiable homosexual activity in the ranks of the local clergy.

In general, Christian had a very positive attitude toward his two missions in the United States. For all of his respect for Damien Slattery, he still couldn't buy the idea that his work for Maestroianni in the United States was somehow designed to make trouble for the Slavic Pope. After all, Chris told himself, he could see how the data he had amassed from among the European bishops had already helped overcome some ecclesiastical difficulties—thanks in part to Paul's help at the EC. And it hadn't been Maestroianni but Christian himself who had suggested extending his work to the States.

And besides, now that the Pontiff seemed determined to take the measure of some extremely serious problems, Christian felt justified in his expectation that his work and Slattery's would provide the long-overdue wake-up call that had been lacking to the Holy See. If he and Slattery came up with the goods as expected, surely the Holy Father himself would take a firm and corrective stand against the abuses laying waste to the Church. Surely he would lay down the law for seminaries, for example. Surely he would bring his backsliding bishops to their senses, and his priests to the fullness of their vows.

As he organized himself during his first few days at Windswept House, the only thing clouding that hopeful tenor of mind for Chris had been his first sight of his sister. Cessi had kept him more or less abreast on the medical side of things, but that hadn't prepared him for the physical change wreaked in Tricia by the pain that was now her constant companion. Not that Tricia ever complained. But she was unable to paint any longer. She insisted on getting out and about, but the pollution in the air even on the clearest days was enough to amplify her agony. Late one night, though, as they had sat alone together, Tricia had made a request to him. "Promise me one thing, Chris. Before you leave again for Rome, I want some time with you. Not now. I need to think how to explain things so that you'll understand. As a priest, I mean. So that you'll understand as a priest."

"You have my word, Tricia. Before I leave again for Rome."

Father Michael O'Reilly was a big-boned, big-headed, athletic man with dark hair and steady, almost unblinking brown eyes. According to Tom Rollins, the young priest was of German-Irish descent; the Irish in his heart could burst into anger, while the German in his brain could take fire with an idea and turn into a conflagration.

Sure enough, once they were alone, O'Reilly looked as if he might explode from his chair and out the door any second. Gladstone was careful not to spook the younger man, therefore.

He might have saved himself the trouble, though. When O'Reilly realized what Chris had come for and whose side he was on, everything about him changed. He was still angry. Still resentful at having been mauled so unjustly by his Cardinal. But not once did Christian hear any abusive language about His Eminence or Father McPherson or the Archdiocese.

Yes, O'Reilly said in answer to Chris's most important question. He had kept copies of all the photographs and documents he had given to Cardinal O'Cleary. But there was more. And that, he explained, was why he hadn't tried to contact Rome again. "Everyone takes it for granted that

I've been holed up like some hermit on that old plantation. And that's what I wanted them to think. But I haven't just been wandering around in the swamps and backwaters of Louisiana. There are lots of snakes and alligators in other places, and I've been up to my keister in them."

What O'Reilly proceeded to lay out for Christian was sickening; but it was also an unexpected bonanza for his investigation. O'Reilly's information about those first three seminarians had been the entrée to still more leads about other clerics. He had developed a roster of names of informants mostly, but also men he styled as "sympathizers and hothouse flowers in the stinking cause of active clerical homosexuality." And, to hear him tell it, the list ranged up and down the clerical ranks from simple priests to archbishops, and it stretched from America to Rome.

"Why else do you think they were able to scupper me, Father? And why else do you think Jay Jay caved in and shirked his sacred duty? It's a system, Father Gladstone. A mutually protective system that reaches all the way from O'Cleary's Chancery right up to the College of Cardinals. And many of the guys who'd like to get out haven't the guts."

O'Reilly didn't want to imply that Jay Jay was necessarily one of his so-called hothouse flowers. "But the truth—or what I take to be the truth—isn't a whole lot better. His Eminence wants to be promoted to a Roman post. So, rather than face into a major scandal, he's willing to jettison the moral standards of his Church and abandon his priests and his flock to the wolves. Yours truly included."

Incensed as much by O'Reilly's defrocked status as a priest as by the picture of abuse he had painted, Chris suggested he might be able to remedy the young cleric's personal situation through the Holy Father.

"No!" Father Michael's Irish temper exploded. "I'm just another member of the faithful who've been cut off by the man who's supposed to 'feed My lambs, feed My sheep.' When the Holy Father does his duty in this diocese—which he hasn't—then he can put my affairs in order. But until that day comes, thanks but no thanks!"

His bitter personal disappointment and his anger at the Slavic Pope off his chest for the moment, O'Reilly calmed down. "There is one thing you can do for me, Father Gladstone. If you have the stomach to dredge up the filth and the will to expose it unvarnished to His Holiness, then I'd like to help."

Because Chris was serious, the two priests shook hands on it.

O'Reilly agreed to give Chris all the data he had in hand.

Mindful of one of Lucadamo's rules—the one that said the simplest means are often the safest—Gladstone told his new recruit to use the mails. "Here's my address and phone number. If you call and I'm not there, leave nothing but your name. I'll be traveling a lot, but I'll call in for my messages. If I need you, I'll leave word with Tom Rollins, so check in with him. And one more thing, O'Reilly." Looking into those unblinking, angry eyes, Chris could easily imagine the scene at the Chancery when

Michael had flattened Father McPherson. "We both know there's still a lot of sludge to be waded through."

"So?" O'Reilly was wary again.

"So"—Gladstone laid down the law—"if you work with me, your job is to tag those snakes and alligators you talked about. Tag as many of them as you can. But keep your own counsel, and keep your temper down. You're not alone anymore, Father. So don't go off half cocked again. And don't try to drain the swamp."

"His Holiness can't get away with this much longer, Monsignore!" Despite the urgency with which he had been called, Dr. Fanarote had been unable to get the Slavic Pope to submit to the physical examinations that were called for. Livid with frustration and worry, Fanarote took his temper out on the papal secretary. "That pain in his side is becoming too frequent. I've given him a stronger painkiller. But there are bouts of nausea, and he admits to a decrease in vitality. I worry about that megalovirus we discovered in '81. I don't like it, Monsignore Daniel!"

Sadowski bore Fanarote's tirade with resignation and deep concern. He had given up trying to explain this Pope to anybody. How would it sound, after all, to answer Fanarote's warning with the fact that this Pontiff, who was leading his Church along the cutting edge of the New World Order, was still drawing lessons for himself from medieval spiritual writers? Or that he thought of his body as Frater Asinus? As Brother Donkey? It would be no balm for Fanarote to know that the Pope had lived by that epithet ever since his seminary days. His idea was to drive his body. To ride it. To keep it well nourished. To give it some respite when it was hurt, but to take no nonsense from it.

"The first sign of any change in the Holy Father's condition," Fanarote growled as he headed for the door, "and I want to know about it at once! His Holiness can't get away with this much longer!"

Though the day was drawing late, the Pontiff gave a good deal of thought to this afternoon's meeting with Signora Francesca Gladstone. Her blunt assessments had taken their toll on him, no doubt about that. Still, there was no doubt about the justice of everything she had laid out. His perspective as Pope was different from hers, just as she had said. He did get reports. And letters. Endless streams of letters. But that was not the same as being in the teeth of the daily struggles going on in the parishes. He knew about priests like Father James Horan; knew about too many such priests, in fact. But he was shielded from their agony, just as he was shielded from so many thousands of scenes like the blasphemous First Communion of Signora Gladstone's two godchildren.

The trouble was that he could do nothing of a thoroughgoing nature to correct all those abuses. He could not interfere with his bishops in their dioceses. This was his principle: he and they were equal in power and jurisdiction. And, though he couldn't say as much to his visitor, the trouble was that there was worse still to come. In a matter of days, Cardinal Maestroianni would deliver His Holiness' *Negotiations* message to the United Nations. In a matter of months, it would be clear to the world that he would be unable to keep the promise he had made many times, and publicly, not to allow girls to serve in the Sanctuary. Then there would be the question of female deacons and their ordination. And there would be more. Much more.

How would Signora Gladstone take all of that? Reflecting on the impression his visitor had made on him, he knew the answer. Until she drew her dying breath, that woman would take it all in fighting spirit. A great natural talent with formidable economic assets, she had shown him a selfless, practical, reasonable faith housed in a clear mind and girded by a will of steel. More, she had faced foursquare into the fact that the old structural organization of the Church was without force. She obviously knew it couldn't be patched together again; that it couldn't be put back into working order.

Apart from a few uncommon men like Father Aldo Carnesecca, there weren't many in the Vatican itself who had faced that reality. There were so many groups and individuals who came to him so regularly with the idea of forming cadres of zealots to man the ramparts of their Church and put everything to rights again.

He had refused to have anything to do with such proposals. In his perspective, this would be tantamount to interfering with the action of the Holy Spirit in Bishops Conferences, and priests' senates, and national and international organizations of prelates and clerics. The new evangelization was opening the Church to the wide world. Any of the former exclusivity of Roman Catholics would be a disaster.

But he studied her two petitions with a great interest: her idea of forming what amounted to an underground Church in order to maintain traditional Roman Catholic belief, practice and devotion; and her idea of manning that underground Church with solid priests who had been unjustly rejected by the hierarchy. The two proposals had one merit for the Slavic Pope: together they could provide a means of defusing the growing enmity between the traditionalists and the progressives among his Catholic people. It would be one way of establishing a certain peace. For, the Pope had no doubt, the traditionalist groups could not last for long. This way, their immediate needs would be satisfied. In time, the situation would right itself.

The Pontiff was startled by the sound of the buzzer on his desk. "Yes, Monsignore Daniel?"

"Cardinal Sanstefano would like to come over from PECA, Holy Father. He wants to follow up this afternoon's audience with Signora Gladstone. And the delegation of Ukrainian Catholics will be here to see Your Holiness within the hour."

"Tell me, Monsignore. Before Signora Gladstone left, did you make the necessary arrangements to receive those lists we talked about?"

"Yes, Holiness. It's all taken care of."

"Good. Ask Cardinal Sanstefano to come around at once. But be sure to let me know when the Ukrainians arrive. I don't want to keep them waiting."

"Right away, Holy Father."

The Pontiff stood up and stretched as if to test his energy and his strength. "So, Monsignore Daniel." He smiled as though Sadowski were standing there and he could see the look of worry on the face of his old friend and confidant. "Let's get another ride out of old Brother Donkey!"

XXXVI

THERE WERE NO SURPRISES for Father Damien Slattery on his arrival at Centurycity, and no friendly hand to smooth his way at the Dominican priory. The House of the Holy Angels received the once supreme Master-General of the Order "like a ruddy skivvy," as he grumbled to Christian in one of their early phone conversations. He had once made life miserable for men who were now his American superiors, and they were more than happy to even the score.

The squalid little dungeon assigned as his quarters was the first sign that Slattery had been marked out by the community as a pariah. A single room in the basement, it was barely large enough to accommodate an antique washbasin, a small desk, a two-shelf bookcase and an iron bedstead made for a midget. The uncarpeted floor was of the same tile as the bathroom down the hall and the ten-stall shower room at the far end of the corridor. Apart from a lamp on the desk and one by the bed, the only light came from a tiny, grated window with a bleak back-alley view.

The first man to make Slattery's new status plain to him in so many words was the Dominican Provincial for the United States—the same Father George Haneberry who, as Slattery had complained to Giustino Lucadamo, cordially hated his guts. Obliged to check in with Haneberry, Damien prepared his soul as well as he could before he knocked at the door of the Rector's office.

Though the advantage was Haneberry's that day, he did find it hard to be patronizing to a man who towered over him like an outsized Old Testament Prophet. Standing with his back to the window, he invited the giant Irishman to be seated. There, that was better.

"We understand, Father Damien, that you have a few pet projects for the Pope that will keep you busy." Aside from his habit of sucking saliva through his gapped front teeth, the Provincial's manner was smooth as silk. "Now, we have received instructions from our new Master-General in Rome that you are to be free to pursue those projects in accordance with the Holy Father's wishes. However, I must stress that the Archdiocesan rules set out by the Cardinal are not to be violated. As Archbishop of this diocese, the Cardinal is the successor to the Apostle. Our Order is in good standing with His Eminence. We are happy to collaborate with the Holy Father. But always within His Eminence's guidelines."

Haneberry proceeded to deal with this alien personality who had barged like an unwelcome bull among delicate and fragile arrangements. Given the travels required by Slattery's papal assignment, he dispensed Damien from the ordinary duties of the community. Nevertheless, Damien would be required to appear at the monthly Chapter meetings. And, insofar as his work for the Holy Father allowed, he would be on twenty-four-hour call as Chaplain for St. Anne's, a local hospital not far from the priory that had earned a curious reputation in the area.

Those and a few more basics taken care of, Haneberry salivated his way through a little contest of wills regarding Damien's work for the Holy See. "You'll be giving pro-life lectures, will you, Father?"

The how-the-mighty-have-fallen contempt in all of Haneberry's remarks was bearable for Slattery. But the attempt at control implied by the Provincial's question was something else.

"Lectures, Father," Damien countered. "And retreats for priests and religious. But not to worry. All the funds for my work will come from Rome." Slattery assumed the substance of his message—his private declaration of independence, financial and otherwise—was clear.

"Of course, Father." Haneberry was anything but unmindful of the hands-off subtext of Slattery's reply. He was so incensed by it, in fact, that he almost spilled the beans. Almost reached into his desk drawer for the dismissorial papers already made out in the name of Father High-and-Mighty Damien Duncan Slattery. Almost told him that the mind of the General Chapter of the Order in early March hadn't been merely to oust him as Master-General but to expel him from the Order and be done with him.

Unfortunately, Slattery's signature was required on those papers. Haneberry's assignment as Provincial was to make life so miserable in so many ways that Father Damien himself would demand to be released from the Order. Haneberry swallowed hard. The moment would come. Time was on his side. Time, and His Eminence of Centurycity.

Given the records he would have to keep once his investigation into Satanist activity was under way, Slattery had the toughest lock he could find put on the door of his basement hovel. Given his need for secure communication, he had a telephone and message system installed, and acquired a handy little cellular phone to carry with him. Given the misery of his situation, meanwhile, it was only natural in the early stages as he set up his cover for the coming investigation that his conversations with Gladstone amounted mostly to a running account of his daily trials.

What hurt him the most, he told Christian, wasn't his living quarters or the disdain of George Haneberry. What pained him to his soul was the malice of Dominican for Dominican. In a disturbing sense, his religious brothers in the House of the Holy Angels comprised a group of men who chose to be together and who excluded any alien spirit. "That means me," Slattery growled to Chris. "They all watch me like lynxes."

Christian grimaced for the plight of his friend. Soon, though, the reports from Centurycity became more hopeful. True to his character, Slattery lost as little time as possible in launching the pro-life lectures and the occasional religious retreat that were to provide cover for his coming investigations. He stayed close to home base at the start, but he could see that the plan was a good one.

"It's not just that Haneberry hates the idea," he laughed over the phone one day to Chris, "or that it gets me out of this den that passes for a priory. Would you believe I'm actually getting something of a reputation as a speaker? I think I could make a living at this if I had to."

"Not so fast, Slattery." Chris laughed to hear Damien's laughter again. "Don't forget what brought you to Centurycity!"

"Never fear, me boyo!" The Dominican took the warning in good part. "I've set a schedule for myself. Things will start to pop around here before you know it."

On his own while his wife was off visiting her cousins in New York, the retired police inspector Sylvester Wodgila put his coffee on, took the makings of a splendid breakfast from the refrigerator and had just begun clanging about among the pots and pans in the kitchen of his two-story wooden frame house in the Holland section of Centurycity when the door chimes rang. "What kind of uncivilized oaf," Wodgila wondered, "would disturb a peace-loving man at the crack of dawn!"

"Good morning to yeh, Inspector Wodgila! I am Father Damien Duncan Slattery, fresh in from Rome. I've come to nose out the trail of clerical Satanists."

With that Irish brogue washing over him like morning sunlight, Wodgila—by no means a pygmy himself—blinked up at a mountain of a priest with the most extraordinary mane of white hair and the most winning smile. In one enormous hand, the giant offered him an envelope—a letter, as it turned out, sent all the way from the Monastery of Czestochowa by the Inspector's sainted cousin on the Danitski side of the family.

"What took you so long, Father!" Wodgila opened the door wide. "The bastards are getting away with murder!"

The fit between these two men was perfect. For, if Damien Slattery was an emissary of God for Sylvester Wodgila, the Inspector was a gold mine for the Dominican. And it wasn't just the good Christian breakfast he served up either. As he dished steaming platters of eggs and Polish sausage and inquired whether his visitor used cream or sugar—"both, if y' please"; Slattery smacked his lips—Wodgila made it plain that he had a good bit of information to share.

He began with a detailed recap of the Scalabrini murder case. The Inspector had been nothing daunted by his early removal from the force or by the Attorney General's warning that it was to be hands off everything to do with that bloody affair.

"You kept up the investigation, then?" Slattery finished off his third cut of toast.

"Retirement has its advantages, Father. It leaves a man with a lot of free time. And it doesn't take away any of the professional contacts—local and otherwise—that come with a lifetime spent on the force." The Inspector put his empty plate to one side, lit up a comfortable-looking, well-used pipe and, coffeepot in hand, led the way into the den, where he opened a nicely hidden safe packed to the gunwales with file folders.

"The fruit of my labors, Father." Inspector Wodgila piled the material like a tower on the table beside Slattery's chair. "Here's the Scalabrini file if you'd like to examine it. But there's another I'd like you to see. Meet Father George Connolly." Wodgila opened the folder. "Not a local boy. Served at the Church of the Miraculous Medal up Careysville way. As these photos show, he came to the same end as Scalabrini. All the same earmarks. Mutilated and killed. Ritual murder of a kind."

Damien winced. He hadn't forgotten the meeting in the Pope's study, or Brother Augustine's description that night of a second priest murder in Centurycity. But no words could have prepared him for the police shots of Father Connolly lying all maimed and bloody on his living-room floor.

In the police-procedure tones that were second nature to him, Wodgila sketched out what was known about the two murders. "We had turned Scalabrini. He'd been working with us as an informant. We don't know who ordered either of these homicides. But we do know both killings were meant to send a message. And we know it was Connolly who killed Scalabrini."

Slattery looked up from the grisly photos. "You were able to follow the trail, then?"

"Up to a point. We knew Scalabrini had only one visitor on the night he was killed. When I finally tracked Connolly down, he was scared and ready to spill his guts. He wanted out of the whole mess, he said. Wanted to make it public. All of it. But I had a better idea. I persuaded him to fill Scalabrini's shoes. To turn informant. I wanted more than names, I told him. More than his uncorroborated word. I wanted the kind of data that can't be weaseled out of with lies and denials. There's an interesting thing about these Satanists, Father Damien. They keep photographic records of their most important gatherings, if you can call them that. I wanted Connolly to get that kind of evidence."

"And?"

"And I came within an ace of it, Father. Connolly called for a meeting. But it never happened. He was killed first. Just like Scalabrini, he died in the stink of his filthy sins. And I'm to blame for that."

"Listen to me." Slattery leaned forward in his intensity. "As men and as clerics, Scalabrini and Connolly were slime! They lived their lives in a bucket of sludge. That was their choice. When they tried to climb out of that bucket, they were killed. That was someone else's choice. As a good Catholic and good law enforcement man, you tried to do the only decent thing that could be done. That was your choice. And now you're the one marinating in self-recrimination. So Old Scrat has the last laugh!"

"Maybe so." Wodgila rubbed his forehead roughly. "That would be Old Scrat's way, I suppose. Everything upside down and backwards. They say that's one of his trademarks."

"It is. And as an exorcist from way back, I can tell you it's a deadly trap!"

"You're an exorcist, Father Damien?" Wodgila's mouth all but dropped open. "Well, why didn't you say so!" Buoyed by that astonishing news, and in part by his own reading of Slattery as a priest who loved God, the truth and food in that order, the Inspector was primed for battle. "We've got a mountain of work to do. So let's get at it."

For the next hour, coffee cup in hand and smoke curling from his pipe, Wodgila gave Slattery an overview of everything he had discovered so far. He had names. And he had dates and places and background. But it was all anecdotal. Without his two priest-informants, he had no witnesses.

"There is a link, though, Father. A priest by the name of Oswald Avonodor. He works for His Eminence in the Chancery of Centurycity. His private secretary, in fact. So he's privy to just about everything that goes on in the Archdiocese." The Inspector reached for another folder. "We have a lot of data on Avonodor. His pedophiliac history goes all the way back to his early days and comes right up to the present. Grew up as an Army brat. At nineteen, he joined up himself and breezed through Officer Candidate School. At twenty-six, he was accepted in the Special Forces and entered a highly secret training in deep psychological conditioning in North Carolina. Participated in several confidential missions abroad. Then, in '79, he was unceremoniously discharged, no reasons supplied.

"At age thirty-one—twelve years ago—he entered Centurycity's Major Seminary. He was ordained a priest by His Eminence in '86 and was immediately snapped up by the Cardinal for his private staff at the Chancery. He's been there ever since, and the post has been a good one for him."

"A little too good, the way it sounds to me." Slattery frowned.

"True. But my idea was never to expose Avonodor. My idea is to bag him. All the names in these files are just that. Names. But I wasn't kidding when I said I smelled the makings of an intricate network, and . . ."

"And you think Avonodor is the key."

"I think he's the weakest link in a long chain." The correction was important for Wodgila's mind. "I think he can be used to get to other links until, somewhere down the line, we can reach the anchor post."

"Any ideas yet, Sylvester, about where that chain might lead?"

"Vancouver is one good bet." Wodgila eyed his tower of dossiers. "Most of the clerics in these files seem to spend a lot of time there."

"Avonodor among them, I presume?"

"Funny you should ask." Wodgila smiled and lit a match to his pipe again. "The Cardinal's secretary will be off for a few days' vacation come this weekend. And guess where he's headed."

Happy to leave all the jangling telephones and diocesan emergencies behind him, Father Oswald Avonodor streaked northward along Highway 93 toward the state line until he came to a favorite stopping place, a pleasant motel perched on a wooded bluff some miles from downtown Centurycity. A quick meal, a hot bath and a good night's sleep would put him in shape for tomorrow's long drive to Vancouver. He had the tub half filled and was stripped to his shorts when there was a sharp knock at the door. Who the blazes . . . ? Avonodor had no sooner opened the door than he was riveted by the stare of a gargantuan specter—a white ghost, all eyes and wild hair.

"How nice to find you in, Father Avonodor."

Transfixed, Avonodor hadn't even noticed his second visitor—the one who held up the badge. Alarm bells screaming in his head, he tried to slam the door shut. But it was too late. The ghost and the badge were already inside.

"Perhaps you remember me, Father." Wodgila put his ID back in his pocket. "It was the case of poor Father Scalabrini, I believe. You telephoned me from the Chancery with messages from His Eminence. Allow me to introduce Father Damien Duncan Slattery, emissary of His Holiness."

"Hadn't you better get some clothes on, Father?" Slattery eyed the scrawny cleric standing there in his boxer shorts and his unnatural butter-blond hair. "You don't want to catch a chill."

Avonodor fumbled into a pair of trousers and pulled a T-shirt over the gold phallic symbol hanging on a chain around his neck. Slattery shut off the gushing tap in the bathroom. Wodgila motioned the trapped priest into the seat between himself and the giant ghost who had turned out to be all too real.

"Now, Father Oswald—you don't mind if I call you Father Oswald?" Wodgila was the picture of patient tranquillity. "We needn't even get to the point of warrants. We just want you to look at some photographs. And we want you to pay attention, because there'll be a quiz."

One by one, Inspector Wodgila slid a series of glossy photos under Avonodor's unwilling gaze. Death photos. Photos of Father Scalabrini. Scalabrini's naked body stretched askew on his living-room carpet. Scalabrini's chest riddled with razor-thin slashes, each with its little rivulet of dried, blackened blood. Scalabrini's severed fingers. Scalabrini's mangled groin streaked with blotches and stains. Scalabrini's face, his mouth stuffed with his genitals, his eyes frozen in the misery of his horrid death.

Sweat tingling over his scalp, Father Avonodor kept his eyes on Wodgila's hands. He watched as a second series of photos was shoved under his nose. Horrified, he looked at his own face smiling back at him. A wedding, he remembered. Yes. There he was, himself and a couple of other priests, seated with His Eminence in a church pew, all in mufti. There was the happy couple—two young men, each in lavender-colored robes with a wreath of flowers on his head. The celebrating priest, vested in lavender, too, solemnizing the marriage with bell, book and candle. The exchange of rings. The nuptial kiss.

"The Church of St. John the Beloved Disciple, if I'm not mistaken." Wodgila's quiet voice was the only sound in the room. "We know all the faces, of course. We know yours. We know His Eminence's. And we know the man seated beside you. Father George Connolly. Remember? Now, what ever happened to Connolly, Father Oswald?"

His mouth dry, Avonodor stared at a third series of photos. Connolly's naked body all askew on his living-room floor. Connolly's chest. The razor-thin slashes. The black rivulets of blood. The severed fingers. The mutilated groin. The mouth stuffed with his genitals. The eyes. Oh, God! Connolly's eyes. . . . Damn these bastards! What did they want from him, anyway? Avonodor's stomach lurched. He turned a sickly yellow. Vomit—a stream of dinner and panic and defeat and the blood-red filth of his rage—boiled from his mouth.

When his retching stopped, the priest felt something wet slapped onto his face. "Clean yourself up, Father. We're not through yet." Avonodor looked up to see Slattery throwing a handful of towels over the mess, and then heard Wodgila's voice again, calm and clinical as if nothing had happened.

"It's time for that quiz I mentioned, Father Oswald. We know a lot about Scalabrini and Connolly. We know Scalabrini's coven cooperated in his death. We know it was Connolly who killed him. We know all about the ritual number of stab wounds. We know His Eminence is guilty of complicity—at least that—in blocking the investigations into both murders. What we want from you is information. If you work with us, we can help you. If you don't cooperate—but still if we make it appear that you've turned informant like Scalabrini and Connolly—how long do you think it will be before someone finds you in the same condition?"

Avonodor threw a glance of frustration and hate at the Inspector, and then at the photos. "I'm dead either way. They'll know. They'll come. When I return to the city . . ."

"You won't return. We have an ambulance waiting not far from here, ready to transport you to an Army hospital for special duties and cases. It's run by a man who knows his stuff. Dr. Joseph Paly. Believe me, it's very private. Even the President can't reach into it. So let's get down to business. The first thing we want you to do is have a little chat with your man in Vancouver. That was where you were headed?" Silence from Avonodor. "Tell him you became so extremely ill with food poisoning that you've had to call for help. Tell him exactly that, and no more. If you add or omit anything, our deal is off. Understood?"

When Father Avonodor swayed unsteadily in his chair for a second, Slattery thought the fellow might pass out. But Wodgila reached for the telephone and put it between him and Avonodor. "You don't even have to dial. We'll do that for you. You just write the number down, along with the name and address that go with it."

"He'll want my location." Avonodor's voice was raw. "I'll have to give him the number here. It's his insurance." His hand trembling, he took the pen Wodgila held out to him and scrawled a name, a number and an address—a residence in a Vancouver suburb, just as Wodgila had expected.

The drill went like clockwork. The Inspector dialed through to a special Centurycity police operator who made the connection to Vancouver and patched the call to Avonodor's room. When he heard a man's quiet voice come on the line, he handed the receiver over to his glassy-eyed prey. Avonodor gave his location and phone number. He was helpless with food poisoning, he said. Needed treatment. Had called for an ambulance. Then he hung up. A few seconds passed. The phone rang.

"Father Avonodor here."

"Just checking," the same voice responded. "Be careful."

Again the line went dead. The Inspector punched the number for the special operator. Satisfied that the call had been recorded, he turned matters over to Damien Slattery.

"That was a very good beginning, Father." Slattery got to his feet and saw the hard look that swept across Avonodor's face. "Now I wonder if you can tell us how many clerical covens you know of in this area, besides your own."

Father Oswald said nothing.

"You've no choice, my man." The Dominican kicked lightly at the photos beside Wodgila's chair.

"Three." Avonodor's whisper had an unnatural edge to it. "I know of three. But I don't know the names of all the members. I swear."

"But you do know the organizer in each case. And you do know the meeting places. Give, Avonodor! And I want real names, not coven codes."

His voice still a tortured whisper, Father Oswald obeyed. Willowship, Harding and Roantree were the places. In each case, the Pastor was the organizer. "Lotzinger, Keraly and Tomkins," he rasped the name of each man.

"All three are pedophiles?" There was only a slight change in his demeanor; but it was Slattery the exorcist who was questioning the younger priest now.

A grotesque smile deformed Avonodor's mouth. "Little boys are always the guests of honor, Father Slattery. I'd have thought you knew that."

"Are any of these covens the Mother Chapel?"

"No."

"Have you been in the Mother Chapel?"

"Yes."

"Do you know the founder?"

"Yes."

"Where is the Mother Chapel, Father Oswald?"

"North. South. East. West." Avonodor's voice took on a silky, singsong quality. His misshapen smile turned to a toothy grimace.

Slattery bent forward. He knew the signs, and he didn't want to lose Avonodor. "I command you in the name of Jesus Christ. Tell me where to find the Mother Chapel."

Too late! Avonodor's eyes were glazed and bulging. His lips were drawn back. He raised his face, opened his mouth to its widest. "A virgin lives in the highways of virginity. A virgin virgins in the byways of virginity . . ."

At his first scream of mad, raucous laughter, Wodgila was on top of him, stuffing a towel into his mouth. Then, just as suddenly, his body went limp. He was like a silent spectator now. He felt the towel taken from his mouth. Flaccid, he watched as if from a great distance while these two strangers who had plundered his life went about their business.

Slattery packed Avonodor's belongings and retrieved the photographs. Wodgila made one last call—for the ambulance this time—and then went to the manager's office to explain poor Father Avonodor's sudden illness.

"Food poisoning." The Inspector clucked his tongue, flashed his badge and paid the bill. "Of course, we don't want to get you mixed up in anything that might cost you your license. But I'd be careful of any inquiries. Keep your distance, if you get my meaning." The ashen-faced manager stamped the bill paid and gave Wodgila a copy. He had no idea what was going on, but he knew a serious warning when he heard it.

Within minutes an unresisting Father Avonodor was trundled into the back of the ambulance and was speeding off into a night that had turned dark. So exceedingly dark.

XXXVII

AT THE OUTSET of his papal investigation, Chris Gladstone's best informants were men like Father Mike O'Reilly. Idealistic young priests who hated living side by side with homosexually active clergy, but who found themselves helpless in their outrage as bishops shuffled their boy lovers back and forth from parish to parish, and church after working church was closed and sold off to pay the mounting costs of out-of-court settlements.

Over time, each good lead he got from O'Reilly tracked inevitably to two or three more until he had a cadre of homosexual priest-informants supplying him with evidence of broken vows, failed vocations and abysmal betrayal of the trust of their congregations.

In city after city, Gladstone heard from this man or that how, two or three or seven or ten years before, he had fallen into the trap of easy passion with a brother cleric. How he had been introduced into the wider circle, where everybody knew the worst about everybody else. How he had been trapped still further by the position he came to occupy in the Church hierarchy; by the economics of life; by friendships and sociality. How he couldn't find the social or moral or physical courage to break away.

Gladstone began to understand the workings of what O'Reilly had called "a mutually protective system reaching all the way from O'Cleary's Chancery right up to the College of Cardinals." Only, system wasn't exactly the word for it, Chris decided. No. It was more like a shared understanding. A dirty little secret whispered just loud enough to draw those with similar interests into the circle. Just threatening enough to keep the secret safe. In a way, though, and whatever you called it, the whole setup functioned like a clerical protection racket. And in that sense, O'Reilly's description was accurate. Innocent or not, anybody who spilled the beans was almost certain to end up like Michael O'Reilly, isolated and buried under an avalanche of ruinous counteraccusations.

Those who played the game to the hilt, on the other hand, protected and promoted one another up through the ranks of the hierarchy. Nor did such preferment end with professorships at seminaries and the like. What hit Gladstone like a blow to his belly, in fact, was the credible evidence that built up in his files concerning high-ranking clergy—including auxiliary and residential bishops—who were participants in this ecclesiastical club of homosexual and pedophiliac activity.

If his growing understanding of the workings of clerical miscreance was an eye-opener for Gladstone, the interviews he had to conduct for Cardinal Maestroianni among the American bishops became a trial for him. An expert by now at the business of interrogating bishops, Chris found at least a partial answer to his dilemma by devising a few queries—seemingly statistical, demographic and financial in nature—to investigate active clerical homosexuality as what he called "a possible drain of diocesan resources."

The ploy was almost too effective; it told Christian almost more than he wanted to know. There wasn't a blush or a stutter in the answers the bishops gave. But neither was there much by way of traditional Roman Catholic morality. The hot headlines, bitter controversy and radical policy agenda fostered by such militant groups as Dignity and Lambda and Act Up and Queer Nation carried more weight among the American bishops than anything said two thousand years ago by St. James or St. Paul, much less anything written two minutes ago by the Slavic Pope or by Cardinal Reinvernunft of Rome's Congregation for the Defense of the Faith.

"It isn't really a question of a drain on our diocesan resources," one West Coast prelate lectured Chris patiently. "The problem is delicate. It requires special care. As bishops, after all, we must be pastorally sensitive to the needs of everyone."

In one form or another, that argument—the psychosexual argument, as Christian came to think of it—seemed to carry weight with a number of the bishops he interviewed. "What are we to do," ran the line, "if some of our priests are different by nature? Are we not to recognize that fact? Are we not pastors for all our priests?"

There were a few bishops who made a run at the Gospels in an attempt to excuse homosexual activity among some of the clergy under their pastoral care and guidance.

Christ, they argued, talked about visiting prisoners and about caring for the sick and aiding widows and orphans. Homosexual priests did all of that and were a caring group of clergymen. And Christ never mentioned homosexuality. It was the rare bishop who worried any longer that the actively homosexual priests under his pastoral care were in a state of serious sin. That the act of sodomizing men and little boys rendered impossible the exercise of priesthood. That daily they added sin after sin of sacrilege to their lives and the lives of others.

When a few bishops did try to take corrective measures, they found themselves cut off from effective dealings with the Regional and National Conferences of Bishops; excluded from important committees; unable to get urgent petitions attended to in Rome.

Given all of that, Chris almost expected the broader pattern that emerged from his systematic interrogation of American bishops. But he had never imagined that the magisterium—the ordinary teaching matrix of the Church in union with the Pope—could have been so thoroughly shredded. Fully two-thirds of the bishops he visited maintained an active opposition against the Slavic Pope. His Holiness was "backward," they complained. His Holiness was "medieval." His Holiness was "a bum leader." His Holiness was "the wrong man to head the Church." He was "weak-willed." He was "at a loss to deal with his hierarchy." He was "incapable of papal governance."

Christian found the American bishops united on one more issue: an intense dislike for Rome. They disliked any outsider telling them what to do. "Catholicism must be of a different kind on this side of the Atlantic," insisted some. "We're developing a vibrant new Catholicism for America," boasted others. "Let's have no more papal visits," was a common demand. "It's not Rome or the Pope that's setting the pace for the twenty-first century, but our American Church."

The message they had for Christian boiled down to a dissolution of the administrative structure of the Church as previous generations had known it. It was a revolt against centralized authority. Fragmentation was the new order of the day. Each diocese operated now more or less as an independent region. And each region thumbed its ecclesiastical nose at Rome. "Tell Rome to leave us alone"; that was the chief idea the American bishops wanted Gladstone to take back to the Vatican. The more he saw, the more Chris was beset with queries: What had happened to the magisterium, then? What had made it possible for so much error and ambiguity and confusion to replace the wisdom of the Holy Spirit in so many pastors? What was it that had clouded the ability of the clergy to sort what was true from what was false? Because those questions were vital and urgent for him—because he was slowly coming to the Slavic Pope's puzzlement over the failure of the hierarchic system—Chris scoured his list of bishops for one man who might give him some handle on what amounted to a massive weakening of faith among the higher reaches of the American hierarchy. That man turned out to be Bishop James McGregor of Hardcastle, Kansas. The forthright manner of this small, wiry man with red cheeks and smiling eyes had made him one of Cessi's favorites among the guests at Windswept House during its social heyday. But behind that bluff manner of his resided the deep piety of a first-rate theologian.

On the day Chris arrived at McGregor's Chancery and the Bishop began to get an inkling of the kind of information his young friend was after, he led the way into a spacious garden. It would be better, he said, to chat about these matters where they wouldn't be disturbed. In the sunny isolation of that place, Chris laid out as much as he could about what so many bishops thought of now as "the American Church." He spoke candidly of the growing number of actively homosexual clergy, about the complicity of some bishops and the connivance of those who weren't directly implicated. Above all, he set out the broad profile of the Church in America—a portrait of diluted faith and altered minds among a once muscular Roman Catholic hierarchy.

"Look, Christian." McGregor poked at the soil here and there as the pair strolled toward the farther end of the garden. "If it's corruption of the faith you're trying to understand, the first lesson to master is the corrosive effect of self-protection. A majority of the bishops are good in the ordinary sense of the word. Like a lot of other decent men, all they want is to keep their jobs and get ahead. Their corruption lies in the fact that they don't raise their voices against the corruption around them. They're corrupt in the sense that they let the Church decay while their parishioners bleat like lambs being led to slaughter by the dogs."

"But why? What's happened to our bishops? You haven't caved in, Excellency; and they don't have to either."

"Haven't I?" McGregor stuffed his hands in his pockets. "Oh, I still manage to say the Roman Mass on the quiet in my private chapel. I manage to consecrate enough hosts validly so that I can feed my parishioners with the true Body of Christ. I play golf a lot with my priests and give them eighteen holes of good theology to keep them in line. I try as best I can, in other words, to do what St. Paul did; to hand on the faith as it has come to me from the Apostles.

"But that's about it. In every other sense, I've bowed to the prescriptions of the Conciliar Church. Your pals in Rome have seen to that. Your pals who run CARR have changed the skin and bones of Catholic ritual. And your pals who run the ICCL have rammed a whole new liturgy down our throats. Between them, they've altered my Church for me, and there isn't a lot I can do about that out here on the prairies."

Still, Chris reasoned, McGregor had found some sort of solution. True, he had been forced to devise a series of dodges to keep things reasonably sane. At least he made sure his parishioners received valid Sacraments and that the priests and laity in his care heard the truths of their Roman Catholic faith. Why, then, Christian wanted to know, couldn't other bishops do at least that much?

"I'll show you why." McGregor headed back toward his Chancery office. "You've already discovered that most bishops live and work now as though there were something called 'the American Church.' But there's more behind that idea than independence from Rome.

"The plain fact is that a different creed is taking hold in that Church. It's a logic stripped of the Logos. It's not the creed of John's Gospel, the Word Who was God and with God. Not the creed of the Word made flesh. In this bowdlerized creed of the so-called 'American Church,' the flesh has been made word. And the word is 'digital.' "

McGregor threw open the door to his study and made for a row of file cabinets. "Here, Father Chris. Look at the new gospel we bishops live by these days. Take a gander at what pastoral care looks like." With every word he spoke, McGregor piled up papers; stacked up printouts filled with electronic type and images. "We live by polls and graphs and charts and statistical reports and bean-counter assessments. We get psychosexual profiles and pie charts of drug and alcohol abuse. We get analytical tables and bar graphs of all the social ills you can name. We get this stuff every day from liturgical committees. From sacramental committees. From committees for women, and committees for children, and environmental committees, and population committees, and economic policy committees. It comes at us from committees at the parish level, from diocesan and archdiocesan levels, and from the Regional and National Conferences of Bishops. In fact, we get so much of this garbage, and our minds are so stuffed with it, that it actually changes the way we think.

"You've come here for the truth, Chris." McGregor turned from the files at last. "And for my money, the truth is that life and thought and faith itself are becoming digitalized. We're all barreling down the same Infobahn the way gold grubbers thronged to Sutter's Mill. But gold isn't the big attraction now. Even the best bishops I know are being enticed down that highway by one word that sparkles and gleams at every turn. Digital. More and more, the information we rely on to run our dioceses and our parishes comes from a computer network that fuses everything into one mode. Religion—and the morality based on that religion—are being reduced to endless streams of zeros and ones. And something in that process—or maybe something about the way it's being used—is stripping supernatural meaning away from facts the way our good Kansas corn is stripped from cobs.

"That single word—digital—is like one of those computer viruses we hear about that travel around the world like lightning, wiping out whole storehouses of information. Only this virus is wiping out the whole vocabulary of faith. It's transforming Roman Catholicism from a religion that must adhere to the truth or die into a culture that must change with the world or be left behind."

Trusted family friend or not, it seemed to Chris that McGregor was going too far. It was one thing to say that professional episcopal thinking had changed; he could see that much for himself. But surely it was too much to say that computer language was the culprit.

"Maybe you're right." McGregor reached out for some of the material he had stacked in front of Chris. "But the same watchwords keep cropping up in every conversation I have these days with my brother bishops. And they all come out of this new creed."

"Like what, for instance?"

McGregor reeled off a miniature lexicon that left Christian glassy-eyed. "Ecumenical resurgence. Social renewal. Gender equality. Biblical computeracy. Social facilitators. Catechetical facilitators. Liturgical facilitators. Programmatic pastoral development. Task forces. Ministry teams. Problem solving. Communal healing. Inculturation. Horizontal prayer.

Outcome-Based Education. Virtual reality. Collaborative ministry. Concept of giftedness. Strategic planning. That's the digital vocabulary of faith in America now, my young friend." McGregor ignored the intercom that buzzed behind him on his desk. "It's a vocabulary that looks sophisticated, but in reality it's primitive beyond belief. It's a vocabulary that deals only in material images. And there are no material images that can express the nonmaterial dimension of life. The more you think in those terms, the less able you are to think in terms of the supernatural as the fundamental basis of everything. Indeed, it becomes impossible to think in terms of supernatural reality at all. If words are reduced to nothing more than images, and if everything is made material, how is it possible to think in terms of the love of a God Whom no man has seen? How is it possible to think about the Incarnation, Sacrifice, Resurrection and Ascension of the Son of that God?

"No, Chris. In this new vocabulary of faith, the whole thing begins to slip away from us and drift off into cyberspace.

"It becomes impossible to deal with Christ's revelations about the Trinity. Impossible to think in terms of a supernatural gift called grace. In terms of humility and purity. In terms of obedience and chastity and piety and holiness. In terms of Christ's suffering and self-denial on the Cross as the divine model for trust in God. In terms of charity as the human face of divine and therefore perfect love. In the end, it becomes impossible to think in terms of good and bad; in terms of sin and repentance. All of that comes from the old dictionary of our faith.

"And that, Father Chris, brings us face to face with the answers you came here to get. Face to face with corruption. After all is said and done, once the endless layers of toughness and richness and subtlety encompassed in God's revelations are stripped to the bone by the zeros and ones of the new digital mind-set, the bishops are faced with a problem about the Church's constant teachings and moral attitudes that have always been based on that revelation.

"You know yourself that even the Real Presence of Christ in the Sacrament is fast falling out of the day-to-day creed. An Immaculately Conceived Virgin is a problem. Angels and saints are a downright embarrassment. The infallible authority of the Pope is intolerable. Heaven itself—the idea that we can participate in the life of a God no man has seen—is treated as a cultural myth. It's okay to study Hell and Purgatory in comparative culture courses. But it's not practical to live your life—including your sexual life—as though they mattered. As though sin were as real as, say, virtual reality."

Christian was quiet for a long time. Perhaps to wrench his own mind from such high-tech razzle-dazzle, he began to think in terms of the old dictionary of faith. Began to muse aloud about Luke's account of the two disciples who had hightailed it to Emmaus on the very day of Christ's Resurrection. Of how, engrossed in their own hasty view of events, they had failed to recognize the risen Lord even when he fell into step right beside them. "Maybe the bishops today are a little like that," he suggested. "Maybe they're blindsided by their own idea that there ought to be some glorious, this-worldly manifestation of their faith. Maybe . . ."

"I don't think so." McGregor cut in abruptly. "The bishops are not worried or disappointed. If God's only role is to be patient and forgiving—if there's no Heaven and no Hell; if the only sin is to deplete the ozone layer, say, or contribute to overpopulation—then things are moving in the right direction. The trouble is that if you think that way, you've ceased to be Catholic. If you think that way, you've already been affected by a darkening of the intellect. And because that's the cleverest work of Satan—because darkening of the intellect is always demonic—it's the darkest darkness of all.

"If you think that way, you're ready to dump the teaching of all the great theologians—Peter and Paul and John and Augustine and Aquinas and all the rest. From Jerusalem to Vatican I, none of the great Church Councils means twaddle. It becomes perfectly acceptable to substitute the theories of social mechanics for the knowledge of faith. Life becomes horizontal. Everything that matters is right here, right now. And the upshot of all of that is that you cease to hope in what once was hoped for. Any day now, I expect some committee or another to send us a replacement for Aquinas' *Summa Theologica.* They'll probably call it *The Sensitive Pastor's Essential Guide to Politically Correct Theology.* And it will probably come with a handbook telling us how to search the Internet for the specific data we need.

"And I remind you, Chris. We're not talking about the momentary lapse of a couple of disciples running for cover to Emmaus. We're talking about the defection of whole nations barreling at the speed of light along the Infobahn. And we may be talking about the Slavic Pope himself. About the Vicar of Christ."

"Not you, too, Excellency!" Gladstone threw up his hands.

"Hold your fire, my friend." McGregor reached behind him into his desk for one document he hadn't filed away. "I know you're busy with your investigations. But take the time to read this. It's a copy of a papal message delivered at the United Nations last March by Cardinal Maestroianni. The text is secular to the core. *Negotiations,* His Holiness calls it. And he couldn't have chosen a better title, or a better place to deliver it. It's as if he's telling the world that the Church has no grace or wisdom or principles of its own to offer. It's as though he's run out of anything truly Catholic to say."

The sound of the intercom again, more insistent this time, forced McGregor to look at his watch. The hour he'd set aside for this interview was stretching into two. Yet as both men walked together through the Chancery, neither seemed ready to end their conversation.

"I've given the best answers I can to your questions about corruption,

Father Chris. Now, I wonder if I can turn the tables and put a puzzle to you?"

"Ask anything you like, Excellency."

"Maybe this investigation of yours is a good thing. But why has the Pope let the fraud get so far in the first place? Why has he let it go on for so long? Why hasn't he just laid an ax to the root of it? And in the midst of all the confusion, why does he go out of his way to deliver this *Negotiations* speech of his—and hundreds more like it—to the nations of the world?

"As far as I can see—as far as a lot of us can see who are trying to hold on out here—those are the central questions to ask. And you're not going to find the answers in Hardcastle, Kansas."

"He's asking too many questions, Silvio!" Annoyed by the static on the phone connection, His Eminence of Centurycity shouted. "When I agreed to take Damien Slattery into this Archdiocese until he could be cashiered, you and Maestroianni told me he was already a beached whale. But if you ask me, he's a dangerous meddler."

Cardinal Aureatini controlled his anger. He didn't like being addressed with such intimacy by his first name. And he didn't like being tracked down and called from the bedside of his ailing mother by a Cardinal to whom he owed nothing. Still, he and Centurycity did have a certain commonality of aims; and he had heard about Father Avonodor's sudden disappearance soon after Slattery's arrival in the States. If other things had begun to go wrong as well, it might be wise to hear the worst of it.

"You remember Lotzinger, I'm sure? Pastor over at Willowship?"

What Aureatini remembered about Lotzinger was the number of times His Eminence of Centurycity had had to move him into new parishes to save his hide, and the public rumors about sexual abuse of children that always followed him. What he remembered was that ex-nun of his, the former Sister Angela, who always popped up as principal of Lotzinger's parish schools. The Cardinal's lawyers had always been effective in protecting Lotzinger. So what was the problem?

"The problem, Silvio, is that Father Keraly of Harding has come to me with the same complaint. And so has Father Tomkins of Roantree. Slattery has been nosing around all three parishes."

"That is curious." Aureatini began to see the difficulty in a more serious light.

"My thinking exactly, Eminence. But there's more. It looks like Slattery has been seeing a retired police inspector here by the name of Sylvester Wodgila. He was in on the investigation of the Scalabrini affair."

"I see." Cardinal Aureatini drew a deep breath. "Any more coincidences?"

"Maybe. As far as I can make out, Slattery goes out of his way now and again to meet another Vatican man who's all over the landscape these days. Ever heard of a Father Christian Gladstone?"

"Beh!" The Italian Cardinal gave the verbal equivalent of a shrug. "Gladstone is a puppy dog, and Maestroianni has him on a leash. He's over there doing some work for us on the Common Mind Vote."

"So." Centurycity insisted on his own point. "What's Gladstone's connection with Slattery?"

"They know each other from the Angelicum, and Slattery probably needs a drinking buddy." Aureatini was guessing. "It's been my experience that Americans of Gladstone's wealth and social class are always polite, even to oafs like Slattery."

Damned Wop snob, Centurycity breathed to himself under cover of the static. "I'll take your word for it, Silvio. But that still leaves the problem of the Irishman. These pro-life lectures of his take him everywhere. My people can't take a step without tripping over him. It would simplify life over here if we could get him to sign those exclaustration papers. Or, better still, why can't Father Haneberry just be empowered to dismiss him from the Order?"

Thickheaded Yankee clod, Aureatini thought. "I wish it were as easy as that, Venerable Brother. But you're dealing with Rome in this matter. As former Master-General, Slattery has status. We still have to be careful with the Pontiff. It would be far better if you could precipitate matters locally. It will make Haneberry's job easier if you put your own position as Archbishop to good use. Call Slattery on the mat. Read him the riot act. Anger him. As you say over there, get his Irish up."

Aureatini chuckled at his little joke, but the American was not amused. He was dealing with Rome, all right; and as usual, Rome would be no help. As with everything else, it would be up to Centurycity to see an end to Damien Duncan Slattery as a priest. "I thank Your Eminence for your suggestion."

"Not at all, Eminence. What are friends for?"

On the surface of things, there was no inherent difficulty for Damien Slattery and Sylvester Wodgila in capitalizing on the leads they had been able to get from Father Oswald Avonodor. It was mostly a matter of surveillance, patience, travel and the willing cooperation of the endless web of contacts Wodgila had built up during his active career on the force in Centurycity.

While the Inspector set off to discover what he could about Avonodor's friend in Vancouver, Slattery concentrated first on the three covens in Willowship, Harding and Roantree. Before long, with the framework of his speaking engagements as cover, and with his credentials as a friend of Inspector Wodgila to gain him the confidence of interested law enforcement officers far beyond the confines of Centurycity, a flood of anecdotal evidence began to fall into Damien's hands like a deluge of acid rain.

He was made privy to "can blotters"—massive ledgers kept as a matter of routine in precinct after precinct, records of insidious doings protected from prosecution because no one's rights had been violated and no actionable crime had been uncovered. Called in more than once by authorities frustrated that the pedophiliac priests they apprehended wouldn't be charged, he heard firsthand accounts of Satanist child abuse and ritual sacrifice. He learned of abortionists who did a thriving side business in supplying babies, still alive but with no legal status, for use in local covens. He listened to tales of torture and despair; to accounts of bodies mutilated on Altars and bones disposed of in portable crematoria; to the cries of souls aching in their own remorse.

As his own records grew, Damien was struck by one name that came up over and again. "Mr. F——," it seemed, was in such common use among pedophiliac priests as a pseudonym for Satan that it followed Slattery all across the country.

There was that awful night in Iowa, for example, and the confession of a middle-aged parish priest fatally injured in a head-on collision with a truck during a driving rainstorm. "For all the little ones we hurt. Please, Father . . . for all the little ones we hurt . . . forgive me . . . please, Father . . . the little ones we hurt . . ."

The signs were clear, but time was short. Slattery needed to extract some precision from the man. "Did you serve Satan?"

"As a slave, Father . . . as a slave . . . Mr. F—— . . . as a slave . . . forgive me, Father . . ."

Kneeling in the rain, illumined in the lights of a police car, Slattery absolved the priest from his sins, comforted him and sent him to God's eternity with contrition on his lips and hope in his heart.

Despite all the dramatic testimony that fell into his hands, by mid-June Slattery still had no way to fit all the pieces together.

Everything pointed to a network of Satanist clergy right enough. From the moment Avonodor had confirmed the existence of no fewer than three covens in the environs of Centurycity, logic and his experience as an exorcist told him there had to be a wider network of covens. That, in fact, was why he had homed in on Avonodor with his questions about a Mother Chapel. There had to be a Chapel with which all continental covens were ramified. But where was it? If he was to fit the puzzle together—if he was to clinch the case for systematic clerical involvement in ritual Satanist activity in America—he needed to find that Chapel.

No matter how far he traveled, however, no matter how many can blotters he studied, or how many anguished confessions he heard—the only clue to the existence of a Mother Chapel was the delirium of Father Avonodor's singsong reply that night in the motel. "A virgin in the highways of virginity. A virgin virgins in the byways of virginity." Slattery had dealt with that kind of programmed reaction before. It bore all the marks of a mechanism by which a possessed person could evade a specific answer to an exorcist's question. But somewhere in that mechanism there was a clue; some inkling of the answer to the question asked. In this case, Slattery was convinced the key was Avonodor's repetitive use of the word "virgin." Yet the crucial meaning remained concealed.

Though he was as frustrated as Slattery was, the Inspector's advice was of a piece with his policeman's mentality. "Let's wait and work at the clear leads we have," Wodgila urged. "If we keep slogging along the trails of evidence we uncover, we'll get a break." Finally, though, time was getting too short for Slattery's comfort. In another six weeks at the outside, he would have to put all his energies into producing a detailed, airtight report convincing enough to impel the Slavic Pope to take early and decisive action.

Because Father Avonodor hadn't come out of his crisis, there was no possibility of questioning him any further. But there was always Dr. Joseph Paly. Maybe he could get to Avonodor in a way Slattery and Wodgila couldn't.

"I can't go with you, Father Damien," Sylvester begged off when Slattery broached the idea to him on the phone. "I've finally got some hot lines going here in Vancouver, and I don't want to let them slip away. But I'll give Paly a call at the hospital and ask him to see you on a priority basis."

The trouble with Slattery's plan turned out to be that Dr. Paly wasn't entirely sure what he was dealing with in the Avonodor case. He engrossed himself fully in the riddle of "the virgin in the byways." He agreed that Avonodor had been programmed so that certain words—in this case, "Mother Chapel"—acted like a trigger to produce the mad delirium that had overtaken him so suddenly. But, Paly said, the nature of the programming was the problem. Until he understood more about that, he could do nothing.

That was interesting, Slattery thought. "Perhaps you're thinking of Avonodor's training in the Special Forces, Doctor. But I've seen the same reaction in possessed people; and in this case we're talking about a man who's been deeply involved in organized Satanist activity. In either case, mind control is involved. And in either case, Father Avonodor could be deprogrammed. Deep analysis is the term used over here, I believe."

Paly was reluctant to talk much about psychological programming willingly undergone for the military; but he had to confess that was the nub of his problem. "Filthy stuff, that. The Army is tight as an oyster about it. We'll get Avonodor's records in the end. But even when we know the details, we may have a problem putting him into deep analysis. Any effort to get past military programming could trigger something far worse than the delirium you saw. We could lose him altogether."

"I'm not a medical man, Dr. Paly. But I know a fair amount about possession and exorcism. I know that psychological programming of whatever kind—even if it's willingly undergone—can be the unwitting means of opening oneself up to demonic possession. Given the possibility that Avonodor's service in the Special Forces involved such programming, and given the certainty of his Satanist activity, it's a fair bet that you're dealing with both problems at once."

"You could be right." Paly nodded. "Either way, though, it doesn't help you. I mean, I don't think Father Avonodor will give us the key to your riddle of 'the virgin in the byways' anytime soon."

"You'll be keeping Avonodor here, I take it? Life could be dangerous for him otherwise."

"So Sylvester told me." A sympathetic Dr. Paly accompanied Slattery as far as the hospital elevator. "In a case as complex as this, I think it may be a long time before we get everything sorted out." Then, not entirely as a joke: "We might even need an exorcist before we're through. Let me know if you ever need a job, Father Damien."

Late that week, Slattery returned to his dungeon in Centurycity and listened to the messages stored up on his answering machine. There was a check-in call from Gladstone, which he returned in kind. Several requests for lecture dates would have to be attended to. The curt, do-as-you're-told voice of Father Provincial George Haneberry commanded him to show up at the Chancery for a meeting with His Eminence of Centurycity the next afternoon at four o'clock sharp. And the excited voice of Sylvester Wodgila, back sooner than expected from his own travels, suggested that Damien drop by for dinner at the first opportunity.

Though Martha Wodgila was delighted with Slattery's huge appetite, she had been a policeman's wife long enough to know this wasn't to be an evening of small talk.

"So." Slattery followed Wodgila to the den after dinner. "What brought you back home in such a rush? What've you got, me boy?"

"Everything! I hit the jackpot!"

"In Vancouver! The Mother Chapel is in Vancouver?"

"No." Wodgila chose a pipe from his collection. "Vancouver is in a different league. Security up there is tighter than anything I've run across, but my sources peg it as an organizational hub for international Satanist activity. But the trail we did manage to find up there led to a closed-door group in South Carolina. Like Vancouver, the whole setup is tight as a drum, but it's the Mother Chapel we've been looking for all right, and you wouldn't believe the names that figure in their files."

"You got into their files, Sylvester?"

"Not exactly." Wodgila was savoring the moment. "But I did find the answer to our riddle of the 'virgin in the byways.' And you were right, Father. It was the key we needed."

When his efforts to get access to the man currently in charge at the South Carolina Chapel bore no fruit, Wodgila had decided to search for Church officials who had retired or been transferred out of the area, in the hope of finding someone willing to talk. "The logical man to approach seemed to be Archbishop James Russeton. Bishop Leo, everyone called him. He served in South Carolina for decades before he went into retirement in the fair state of Virginia." Wodgila watched in silence as that bit of information took hold in Damien's mind.

"Of course!" Slattery was stunned by the sudden clarity of the riddle. "Avonodor couldn't reveal the location of the Mother Chapel in South Carolina, but neither could he avoid giving some clue. 'A virgin in the byways of virginity.' So, if you're saying this Bishop Leo was part and parcel of the Mother Chapel, and Avonodor knew that, then the riddle fits like a glove. Substitute 'Virginia' for 'virginity,' and it fits." In his excitement, Slattery almost missed the past tense that had cropped up in Wodgila's remarks. Was Russeton dead, then?

"Talk about crucial timing." The Inspector nodded. "His body was being packed into the meat wagon when I drove up. I got a look at him, though."

"Natural causes?"

Wodgila nodded. "My friends in Virginia will fax the coroner's report when it's ready, but that's the way it looks. Lived out his days in a splendid house. Part of a development called Fantasia Foundation. Can you beat that?

"Anyway, his nickname suited him. Had a lion's mane of gray hair. Made me think of that passage from St. Peter's letters comparing Satan to a lion prowling after prey. Taller than average. Handsome, except for the look frozen on his face. Something between anger and confusion, as though he'd been overtaken at the last minute by some hateful visitor he hadn't expected to see.

"When I made a quick call to one of my contacts down there and explained what I was after, I was welcomed as part of a special team detailed to search the Bishop's house. And it turns out that Leo was an orderly man. The kind who keeps thorough records of his proudest accomplishments." Thorough was hardly the word to describe the boxes of materials Wodgila retrieved from a locked closet. The files Wodgila had brought back in copy from Virginia revealed everything, including the structure of the Mother Chapel and its frequent involvement with correspondent Chapels all across the country.

Hardened as both men were, it was cold and discouraging for them to see the degree to which the most banal, frightening, demanding elements of evil had penetrated the Roman Catholic Church in America. They pored together over meticulously detailed papers of induction and membership ledgers, records that went back for decades and that coupled true names with the coven names adopted by adherents of the Mother Chapel.

Russeton had made a special point of following an upside-down mimicry of religious life. In the same way the Church keeps official records of the many priests, brothers and nuns who take names of saints or angels, so had Bishop Leo kept his own records of the star-studded membership he had attracted to his Chapel.

As important as it was to have such a roster, Wodgila had more to lay out for Damien's inspection. He followed the membership ledgers with piles of dated records of Black Masses, and with photographic materials of human and animal sacrifice so demoralizing as to traumatize the mind and unseat reason.

And yet, Wodgila confided to Damien, the worst was yet to come. One by one, he passed a set of photographs to Slattery. "At first I thought I must be out of my mind when I saw these. But when I checked the official records, I knew there was no mistake. Earlier in his career, way back when he was a monsignor, His Eminence of Centurycity was stationed as Chancellor to Bishop Leo."

"No . . ." Slattery spoke with acid in his voice and a deep melancholy in his soul. "There's no mistake." The face was younger, but there was no mistaking the bespectacled features of the Cardinal. There he was, decked out in nothing more than open robes. Some shots showed him preceding Bishop Leo in solemn mockery of Church processions, a single black candle in his hands. In others he was reaching toward the Pentagram on the Altar, or standing at the lectern between the Black and Red Pillars. In still others he was immersed in elements of the ceremony so vile, so bestial, so sacrilegious that Damien had to force himself to look at them.

But even that wasn't the end of it. Wodgila took Slattery through clusters of memos and letters he had found locked away in a floor safe in Russeton's basement. It was this collection of documents, the Inspector said, that completely vindicated Slattery's insistence that clerical Satanist activity in America must be a highly organized affair. Most of this material consisted more of cryptic, stenographic messages than normal communications. Still, while hard to decipher, there could be no doubt that these were Bishop Leo's records of the many celebrations his Mother Chapel had undertaken with correspondent chapels. With the help of some of his cryptologist friends, Wodgila hoped to come up with the names and locations of those chapels.

As Slattery pored over the gruesome treasure of information, he came across one series of memos that were far more cryptic than any of the other materials. They dated from June of 1963, as far as Damien could make out. But they were of particular importance in that they did appear to involve a direct link to Rome.

"What do you make of this, Sylvester?" Damien held the sheaf of papers up.

"It's a funny thing about those memos." Wodgila recognized them at a glance. "We found them tucked away in an ornate box apart from all the other records, as if they were especially important for Russeton. But I couldn't make head or tail of them."

"That makes two of us." Slattery squinted through the pages, and read aloud the few words he was able to decipher, as though that would supply meaning. Two notations—"Call Pol. 10 o'clock Rome time" and "Call Sek." appeared on a single sheet of paper. "S. Paulus . . . Open line . . ." he read from a following page. "Synchronicity of beginnings" and "Ascent" figured several times in the jottings, usually underlined. And so, too, was the notation "Sure fitting."

When both men were too exhausted to go on with their examinations, they began to pack the materials back in their boxes. In that matter-of-fact way of his, Wodgila began to talk of his new understanding of what had happened to him. "Given the evidence," he mused, "it's no wonder I was removed from the Scalabrini case, or that His Eminence gave his blessing to my early retirement."

"Given what happened to Scalabrini," Slattery offered by way of dubious consolation, "you're lucky His Eminence settled for your retirement."

Sylvester piled the last of the boxes back into the closet and poured a couple of short brandies. "I've been thinking a lot since I came back from Virginia about that photo we showed to Father Avonodor. The one of His Eminence and the others at that homosexual wedding."

"What about it?"

"The link is what's about it," the Inspector answered. "His Eminence seems to be a link. A functionary in a wider network than either of us expected to find."

At exactly four o'clock in the afternoon, as he followed a close-lipped young priest through a corridor in the Centurycity Chancery and sat down in the small anteroom beside the Cardinal's study, Damien Slattery set foot into the opening stages of a nightmare beyond the scope of any mere dream.

Slattery rose to his feet as His Eminence emerged with a companion. A German by the sound of his accent, the visitor was still engrossed in conversation with the Cardinal when he turned to examine Slattery for a second through the glint of his steel-rimmed spectacles. The Cardinal seemed not to notice Slattery at all. He walked his visitor through the anteroom, then returned to his study without so much as a nod.

It was well past four-thirty before a doorman appeared and gestured in Slattery's direction. His Eminence would see him now. But even inside the study, the dreamlike silence was prolonged as, without the barest acknowledgment of Damien's presence, the Cardinal worked through a stack of papers. It was only when a third man joined them that His Eminence finally looked up.

"Bishop Goodenough here tells me, Father Slattery, that you have been making it your business to visit parishes in this Archdiocese . . ."

The Cardinal's words reached Damien as if from a great distance. He was staring His Eminence in the eye, but what he saw in his memory of those horrible photographs was the younger monsignor carrying a black candle in procession; the younger monsignor fingering the Pentagram; the younger monsignor flanked at the lectern by those infernal Black and Red Pillars; the younger monsignor engaged in unspeakable sacrilege at the Altar . . .

"By what authority do you take such liberties, Father Slattery . . . ?"

Every nerve and muscle in Damien's huge body was strained with his effort at self-control. He repeated Giustino Lucadamo's instructions silently to himself like a mantra. "No matter what you discover, never confront ecclesiastical officeholders . . ."

"Have you nothing to say?" His Eminence threw a frustrated glance at Bishop Goodenough. Aureatini's advice wasn't working. It wasn't so easy to get this man's Irish up after all.

"Never confront ecclesiastical officeholders . . ." Damien repeated the mantra and gritted his teeth in silence. "Never threaten their official capacity . . . They have Canon Law on their side . . ."

"His Eminence is speaking to you, Slattery!" At the challenge from Bishop Goodenough, Damien turned toward that double-chinned bulk of a man. Maybe the Cardinal's rank put him off limits. But Goodenough was temptation incarnate! Bishop or not, he was nothing more than a two-bit goon; a troubleshooter. And he was nearly as big as Slattery himself. Big enough to take a couple of roundhouse punches to those calculating little eyes of his and survive . . .

"Father Slattery!" Unsettled himself now by the silence that enveloped the Dominican friar, His Eminence was close to the edge of his patience. "I haven't time for these games. You are to make no more visits to any installations or properties of this Archdiocese without my explicit permission. Do I make myself clear?" The Cardinal's puzzlement gave way to a sudden, unexplainable panic. Was there some mystery about this Irishman? Or was he about to attack them physically? Apparently Goodenough had the same thought, for he cast a nervous eye toward the door as though to make a break for it.

"No!" Slattery held up one hand. "Don't leave, Your Excellency!"

After his long silence, Damien's voice seemed to startle both men; made them cringe as if a whip had cracked over their heads. Slattery looked down from his enormous height at the Cardinal trapped in his chair.

"Your Eminence." His words might have come from some giant avenging angel delivering a personal promise of justice. "You have but a short time in which to repent."

"The man's a menace!" Seized with a fear he had never felt before—fear at some nameless threat embodied in Damien Duncan Slattery—the Cardinal screamed into the telephone at Father Provincial George Haneberry.

"Just ask Bishop Goodenough. He's standing right here. He'll swear Slattery threatened us both!"

"But, Your Eminence, Cardinal Aureatini's instructions were clear. We're to wait . . ."

"Aureatini be damned! This clown nearly massacred us. I'll send you an affidavit to that effect within the hour. We must be rid of him. Not next week or next year. Now!"

Within the hour the Cardinal had an affidavit on its way to Haneberry, attesting to Slattery's physical attack on Bishop Goodenough and citing it as a technical violation of Canon Law that would not be tolerated within the Archdiocesan jurisdiction of Centurycity.

Damien Slattery felt like anything but an avenging angel.

Trapped in a sense of isolation so baleful that his soul was entombed in its darkness, Damien walked the streets of Centurycity for hours, trying to find his balance again amid the normal things of life. Instead, however, relentless signs of demonic cruelty dogged him everywhere. He saw fear in the faces of men and women scurrying to reach home before dark; saw hopelessness in the faces of beggars left to bed down for the night in doorways of banks and investment houses; saw lovelessness in the faces of whores preening on street corners, and lust in the eyes of men who cruised them; saw addicts in search of a high, and ready to kill for a dime or a dollar to get it. In his frame of mind, the whole of Centurycity seemed to him like a river raging toward the bottomlands of damnation, swallowing everything in its tide.

The passing scream of a siren propelled him into a torrent of too vivid memories. Living images of the darkest things he had discovered in America assailed his senses. He heard that terrified priest, that dying slave of Mr. F——, pleading for his soul on a rain-soaked highway in Iowa. He heard all the tales he had been told of covens run by priests and nuns. He saw all the unspeakable photographs Wodgila had brought home from Virginia. All of it flashed in his mind as if projected by some demonic kaleidoscope; rolled out in front of him like a carpet of madness and violence leading his steps straight into Hell.

It was past midnight when, still in the throes of his demonic attack and exhausted by it, Slattery let himself into the priory of the House of the Holy Angels. He was just heading for the stairs to his basement hovel in the hope of finding an hour or two of much needed rest when the sound of several voices raised in laughter drew him to a kitchenette at the back of the house. Astonished into silence at the sight of the huge figure in black clericals staring down at them from the doorway, four men dressed in terry-cloth robes nearly choked on their snack of toasted muffins and milk. Two of the group—men in their late teens—were strangers. But Slattery recognized the other two as members of the Community. "Fer

Chrissake, fellas . . . ," one of the visitors cursed and scrambled to his feet. Everyone knew there was no mistaking the situation.

Damien stared at each man in silence. There were no words to express his shock. Each face etched itself into his mind, intensified the demonic nightmare he was living. With whispers and giggles following in his wake, he backed out of the doorway and half stumbled down the stairs to the basement. The usual rank odor from the showers made his stomach lurch, but he managed to reach his room and close the door against the world.

He sat as still as a statue on the edge of his bed for a long time before he noticed the envelope that had been slipped under his door during his absence. Eventually, the familiar coat of arms of the Master-General in Rome registered in his mind. He reached down with a dreamlike effort, retrieved the envelope and read the documents inside. Documents that drove his mind reeling to the edge of collapse.

The first of those documents—signed in Rome in March by the new Master-General of the Order, and countersigned that very day in Centurycity by Father Provincial George Haneberry—made a mockery of Dominican life. "For the harmony of the Order, and for the good of your own soul," Master-General McGinty had written, "we think it advisable that you spend some time outside the religious cloister. After a trial period of no less than six months and no longer than one year, we will again consider the circumstances of your life. We join you in praying to the Holy Spirit that together we will find God's will in your regard."

Because such a letter of exclaustration could not be presented without cause, a second document had been attached as justification. This one, signed by His Eminence of Centurycity and witnessed by Bishop Ralph Goodenough, made a mockery of Canon Law. Obviously prepared after his meeting with the Cardinal, it accused Slattery of behavior more fitting in a barroom than in a Chancery.

Damien looked at the dates on both documents again, and then dropped them onto the table. Every excruciating detail of the future that had been planned for him by his "brothers in Christ" played itself out in his mind's eye. He was not only an alien in America but an alien in the Dominican Order. He was to be left adrift outside any welcoming wall. He could search for a bishop benign enough to accept him as a priest in his diocese. He could try to explain inexplicable letters like the one attached to the exclaustration order; letters smearing his character and warning everyone to beware of this disturbing man, this stormy petrel. For the good of the Church, he would be met with bland refusals until, failing any acceptance by a bishop, there would come the inevitable decree of laicization. He would be defrocked, stripped of the most basic fabric of his life and told to live as a layman, to fend for himself.

In a very real sense Damien had only been able to drive himself forward through one horrible discovery after another on the assumption that no matter how much evil he encountered, he knew he was secure in his base of operations. Secure in his dedication to papal service. Secure above all in his priestly vocation as a Dominican. Now, however, His Eminence of Centurycity had turned that solid ground into a sinkhole.

All at once, Damien groaned aloud in his misery and, with the sheerest effort of his will, forced himself to his knees beneath the Crucifix he had hung above his bed. His face covered in his hands, he prayed to the Crucified Lord whose priest he was. Prayed for strength. For light. For help. Prayed that Love had seen his weakness, was ready to give him courage. He emptied the violence of his suffering into the sacred passion God had endured at Calvary, and endured still upon the Altar, for the salvation of all who would call upon Him.

Still motionless beneath the figure of his bloodied Savior, Damien was flooded at a certain moment with a first answer to his petitions. With a little straight talk from God. With a sense of shame and anguish bitter to the taste but essential to the soul. After the foul misery he had seen on these shores, had he forgotten that such pain could exist as the pain he now felt? Or that tears could sting with such intensity as the tears he now wept? How had he waited even a moment to join his own puny sufferings, and all the sufferings he had encountered, to the sacred passion Christ had suffered for his salvation?

Little by little, as he tore at the demon-shroud of anger that clung to his every sense, as his soul strengthened itself in contrition and trust, Damien's prayers seemed to rise more easily to Heaven. Insensible to the passing hours, impervious to his fatigue, he knew at last what to ask for. "Dear Jesus . . ." He spoke to his Lord with a different sort of passion now. "Crucify my self-pity and my self-seeking . . . Strengthen me for the trials to come . . . In the tide of violence and cruelty and Christlessness rising in this land—in this place where there are so many victims, yet where suffering has become so sterile—make a cleansing crucible of my sufferings . . ."

At the sweet sound of distant bells, Slattery stirred. Was it morning already . . . ? It wouldn't do for the Rector of Rome's Angelicum to be late for Mass, or to keep His Holiness waiting . . . Still on his knees and fully clothed, Damien opened his eyes. This wasn't Rome's Angelicum. The Pope wasn't waiting for him. There was no sweet sound of bells. This was the House of the Holy Angels in Centurycity, and his telephone was jangling raucously in his ear.

"Damien! Damien! Are you there? Wake up, man. It's past six o'clock. There are souls to be saved and graces to be won."

Slattery had never been so happy to hear the sound of Christian Gladstone's voice. "There's only one thing worse than a talkative Irishman at six in the morning, Gladstone. And that's a talkative Roman theologian!"

"Blame yourself." Chris laughed. "Your message was waiting for me when I got in late last night. It set me to thinking, in fact. What about coming down here to Windswept for a while? My mother and my sister are heading off to Ireland, so we'll have Beulah Thompson's cooking all to ourselves. And we have a lot of catching up to do."

"You don't know the half of it, me boyo!" Slattery winced at the cramps in his legs as he got up from his knees, and then again at the sight of the exclaustration document awaiting the inevitable finality of his own signature. "There are a few loose ends to tie up here, but I should be able to shake the dust of this place in a day or so."

His most urgent news, Chris decided, couldn't wait that long. "One thing, Damien. Father Aldo rang a few minutes ago from Barcelona. The public announcement won't come for a little while yet. But Dr. Fanarote has scheduled His Holiness for surgery."

Damien stiffened. "How serious is it?"

"They won't know for sure till they have him on the table. But the message to us, Carnesecca says, is that the Holy Father expects us to pray the best prayers and do the best work we've done in all our lives, and that he'll be waiting for us in October."

"Amen to that, Christian." All Slattery wanted now was to stay in one piece long enough to finish the work he had come to do for Christ's Vicar and get back to Rome. "Amen to all of that!"

XXXVIII

WELL BEFORE the official public announcement that the Holy Father would enter Gemelli Poly for surgery, a fever of whisperings and speculations ran through the Vatican Chancery like a summer cold, infecting all the main protagonists in the Slavic Pope's pontificate.

Cardinal Cosimo Maestroianni was among the first to know of it. His first thought was to call Cyrus Benthoek. "We may not need the Common Mind Vote after all, Cyrus! Word is that the Holy Father may be riddled with cancer and that the operation is merely to find out how long he has to live."

"Don't be mesmerized by possibilities." Benthoek took a more level-headed view of things. "We cannot afford to assume anything. We must always remember that our agenda is attuned to the Process. We must not allow ourselves to be sidetracked by rumors. We must work on the basis of the larger reality."

Reality in this case focused Benthoek's mind more urgently than ever on the need to accomplish the public spectacle of the Common Mind Vote. Even if the Pope's health should decide the question of his removal, Cyrus argued, the CMV would make it clear what kind of Pope the bishops felt necessary for unity; what kind of Pope the bishops would accept as leader. It would stand as a powerful persuader in the next papal Conclave. "In truth, Your Eminence, I would be happier to receive this news if I knew you were ready with the CMV right now. With that, plus the creation of a legal instrument of papal resignation, we would have all eventualities covered."

Such a cold dose of *Realpolitik* from anyone else would have provoked a storm of contempt from the seasoned Cosimo Maestroianni.

But coming from his close friend and most trusted advisor and colleague, and couched as it was in terms of the Process, the little Cardinal took it as a timely corrective. Within an hour, His Eminence had a letter on its way by courier to Christian Gladstone in Galveston. "Your preliminary reports have been excellent. Your work in America ranks with the contribution you and your dear brother have made to the well-being of the Church in Europe. Therefore, I send a double expression of thanks for your cooperation in the past and in the future. Please God, all will end well."

In a hastily called session with Cardinals Aureatini, Palombo and Pensabene, Maestroianni's aim was to come up finally with a workable document of papal resignation. Nor had he any need to be so circumspect with those three colleagues. "The Pope's illness is a natural springboard," he stressed. "It is our duty to raise again the question of the Pontiff's possible incapacitation."

"The Pope's illness puts the whip in our hands," the acid-faced Cardinal Palombo stated the case more bluntly. "And Your Eminence is suggesting we crack it over his head before he goes into the hospital."

"For the good of the Church, Eminence." Maestroianni saw no need for such language, but the issue was to get the job done. "Always for the good of the Church."

It was for the good of the Church as well that Maestroianni took pains to jockey his own man into position among the most desirable candidates to succeed the present Pontiff. His Eminence congratulated Cardinal Graziani on the expert manner in which he had guided the Holy Father's choice of the Father-General of the Jesuits, Michael Coutinho, as the next Archbishop of Genoa, and he mused on the fact that the Genoa post always carried with it the red hat of a Cardinal. "You must agree, Eminence, Father-General Coutinho's qualifications are impeccable. Unblemished record as a religious. Advanced degrees in theology. Acknowledged expertise in Holy Scripture. Au courant with public affairs. Though barely sixty-three, he has years of experience in clerical government. His physical presence makes him a graceful and dignified celebrant of public liturgies."

Yes, Graziani blinked, that was impressive. But what was the hurry? Both Genoa and Coutinho would still be there after the Holy Father's surgery and recuperation.

Without the slightest hint of friction, Maestroianni raised the Secretary's enthusiasm quotient with the mention of support that had already come to the surface regarding Coutinho's advancement. Surely he needn't mention all the names.

Surely not, Graziani blinked again. But he made his own mental tally anyway. His Eminence Cardinal Palombo was certain to be appreciative. And so, too, His Eminence Cardinal Pensabene, who in turn had the support of the dominant faction in the College of Cardinals. And, of course, there was the prestige of Maestroianni himself. In the event of a deadlock in Conclave, such powerful men might find it in their hearts, or at least in their interest, to support Graziani himself as successor to the Throne of Peter.

Having fanned the fires of the Secretary's cooperation in Father-General Coutinho's speedy advancement into the College of Cardinals, Maestroianni arranged a quiet dinner with one among the many newsmen whom His Eminence could always interest in a bit of insider intelligence. In the course of a most civilized evening, the Cardinal mentioned Jesuit General Michael Coutinho as an interesting man to watch. A man willing to envisage changes and adaptations of Church disciplinary law regarding contraception, for example, as well as abortion and fetal research. As a man not unfriendly, either, to changes in the Church's position on homosexuality, married priests and the ordination of women. In sum, as a man of the future.

Though aware he was being handed the makings of a major scoop, the reporter needed a wider context to make sense of it. When pressed, however, His Eminence counseled patience. Everything would fall into place soon enough, he said. In Rome, everything finally fell into place.

After a call from Cyrus Benthoek, Dr. Ralph S. Channing passed the news up the ladder in the most urgent fashion.

"I agree with Benthoek's thinking, Professor." Capstone spoke quietly. "Nothing as banal as a carcinoma is going to be our ally. Ours is a war among titans, my friend. And the Prince does not fight such a crucial battle for control of the Enemy's stronghold with a flubbed surgical intervention or a messy termination by hired hands. Tell me, then. Do we know how close Maestroianni is to achieving the Episcopal Common Mind Vote?"

"Almost there, sir." Channing didn't want to run afoul of Capstone again on that score. "The Cardinal assures me that the U.S. bishops are lining up as expected."

"And the instrument of papal resignation?"

"Our own associates are deeply involved in that effort."

Capstone cut the conversation short with a clipped message meant for all the members of Concilium 13. As servitors of the Prince and engineers of the Process, their supreme responsibility was to see that all would soon be ready for decisive action. "After all," he reminded the Professor, "the Availing Time will not last forever."

Cardinal Silvio Aureatini was the logical choice to prepare a legal instrument to be signed by the Pope himself, as a guarantee of his resignation of the papacy under certain specific circumstances. Taking Maestroianni's general instructions and his own sense of *romanità* as his guides, the junior Cardinal produced such a worthy instrument that even Maestroianni agreed that it suited the purpose.

The importance of the resignation document notwithstanding, Aureatini had other things on his mind. It fell to him to keep up a steady contact with the European bishops in order to clinch the CMV work Christian Gladstone had done among them before his departure for America. In addition, he was part of the standing committee charged by the Pope with the important work of drafting another document—a new *Universal Profession of Faith*.

Some seven hundred pages long in its present form, and already run off on the press in draft for its first full review by the Pontiff and his advisors, the *Profession* was a delicate piece of work. It had to encompass all the dogmas of the Faith. Yet, as had been the case with the documents of the Second Vatican Council and the new Code of Canon Law of 1983, the trick was to satisfy the general standard of Catholic belief, but to do so in such general terms as would allow the greatest latitude of interpretation.

It was a wonder Cardinal Aureatini had time to give any thought to Father Aldo Carnesecca. Nevertheless, there was still that crucial uncertainty about Carnesecca; that seed of doubt stemming from the 1978 triage of papal documents; the possibility that the innocent-seeming Father Aldo knew of matters touching on the Prince's Enthronement. And the Cardinal did still suffer a barrage of criticism from certain associates for having botched the job in Sicily.

With the same dedication that went into all of his work, therefore, Aureatini set about a meticulous study of Carnesecca's latest mission for the Holy Father. He set a watch on his movements. And, taking advantage of the fact that the Cardinal's office paid his living expenses and received at least pro forma reports from him, he tracked Carnesecca's dossier closely. The old boy was slick; no doubt about that. His reports concerning his work for the Holy Father in Spain told Aureatini nothing significant. Aureatini kept at it, though. Even to the point of searching line by line, receipt by receipt, through Carnesecca's monthly expense vouchers for clues to his needs and habits; for any little sign of vulnerability that might be useful.

With everything else coming so rapidly to a head, it really was time to throw a halter around Carnesecca's neck.

❑ ❑ ❑ ❑

Gibson Appleyard at home in the United States felt betrayed. He knew it wasn't a rational reaction; but when Giovanni Lucadamo called from his listening post at the Raffaele in Rome with news of the Slavic Pope's health crisis, Gib took it as something more personal than a glitch in his own near-future plans.

In his struggle to put his thoughts in order, fragments of a prayer popped into Appleyard's head. Prophetic words written more than a century before for men like himself by the great Frater Joachim Blumenhagen: "*When the Masonic Temple shall shine over the whole universe, when its roof shall be the blue heavens, the two poles its walls, the Throne of Peter and the Church of Rome its pillars, then will the powers of the earth . . . bequeath that freedom to the people which we have laid up in store for them. . . . May the Master of this world give us yet another hundred years and then shall we attain that end. . . . Grade to Grade, progressing from Entered Apprentice through the Holy Royal Arch, through the Golden Veil, past the Altar of Incense and the Rose-Croix, by the Order of the Temple, in the light of the Reconciled Countenance; all the way to the Heart Divine in the Sovereign Reason of the Center . . . and then the ne plus ultra, the Spiritual Temple, the New Jerusalem. . . .*"

That must be it, Appleyard told himself. The Spiritual Temple. The New Jerusalem. That must be why he cared so much what happened to this Pope.

"In light of your efforts to firm up another interview with the Pontiff"—Lucadamo's voice from across the Atlantic recalled Gib to the moment—"I thought I'd better get on to you about this surgery business as soon as possible."

Confident that Giovanni was in on every rumor, Appleyard pumped his old friend for information about those pillars; about "the Throne of Peter and the Church of Rome." Then he dialed through to Bud Vance. An urgent meeting over the Presidential Committee's idea was essential, he told Vance. For the matter in question this time was an element of U.S. policy so crucial that it was regarded as fundamental for national security, and so fundamental that it not only transcended American party lines but was paramount in planning the prosperity and progress of the G-7 Group of industrialized nations.

Officially entitled *National Security Study Memorandum 200: Implications of Worldwide Population Growth for U.S. Security and Overseas Interests,* but known to all concerned with it simply as *NSSM 200*, the 1974 NSC memo had fixed U.S. policy for the next thirty years.

As a basic document, *NSSM 200* pinpointed thirteen countries with strategic roles to play as sources of raw materials vital to U.S. security and as important markets for Western goods and services. The nations involved were India, Pakistan, Bangladesh, Nigeria, Mexico, Indonesia, Brazil, the Philippines, Thailand, Egypt, Turkey, Ethiopia and Colombia. The concern cited in the memorandum was that the birth rates of those countries were considered to be too high for stability.

NSSM 200 was simple and straightforward in its recommendations: across-the-board financial assistance by the U.S. government to these countries and to others, in order to increase their use of contraceptives, abortion and sterilization of both sexes; and to further fetal research. The basic premise of *NSSM 200,* in other words, was that population control abroad was strategically as necessary for the United States as the integrity of its own territory, or as its right to ensure its fundamental freedom and viability as a sovereign nation.

NSSM 200 was rapidly woven into the fabric of U.S. foreign policy. On November 26, 1976, by means of another memorandum—*National Security Decision Memorandum 314,* or *NSDM 314* for short—President Ford enshrined *NSSM 200* as an obligatory guideline for all U.S. government agencies, including everything from the Departments of State, Treasury, Defense and Agriculture to Health and Human Services, the Agency for International Development and the President's Economic Council. As a result, the United States spent more than all other countries combined during the succeeding years to implement this policy of population control. But other countries, too, saw the wisdom of joining in to some degree. Together with the United States, they funneled financial grants through the United Nations Population Fund (UNPF), the International Monetary Fund (IMF), the World Bank (WB), the Planned Parenthood Federation (PPF) and a host of private organizations.

By the nineties, however, despite undeniable progress, the time had come to launch a full-scale population control policy. The next President, whoever he might turn out to be, would have to assure the steady availability of resource materials from the still unindustrialized nations, and the viability of those nations as markets for the G-7 industrial giants. In order to make that coming thrust viable, however, U.S. planners had to overcome political reluctance on the part of some of its G-7 partners for whom population control remained a political taboo. Simply put, and whatever about their official disdain for papal Rome, local politics made the Pontiff's acquiescence a must if America's G-7 partners were to back the policy of population control on the scale deemed essential by U.S. planners.

In view of this by now sacrosanct policy that tied America's national security to systematic population control, and in view of the timetable for the next presidential election, there had to be fresh, substantive talks between the U.S. government and the Slavic Pope. The choice of Gibson Appleyard as the man to conduct those talks—as point man in the official U.S. effort to induce a change in the mentality of the Slavic Pope—had been a matter of some debate.

The main factor on the negative side had been Appleyard's personal philosophy. If this Pope was to be persuaded to mitigate his Church's traditional opposition to the methods of population control fostered by official U.S. government policy, it might not be wise to rely on a man whose Rosicrucian principles put him at odds with those methods.

Vance had been adamant, however. Appleyard was as American as Old Glory, and he understood as well as anyone that U.S. planners could have no more powerful backer than the Slavic Pope in their quest to limit human births. Further, he understood that no other organization was as universal as the Roman Catholic Church. And he understood that no other organization, including the Lodge, was as opposed as a matter of official policy to U.S. population control methods.

And besides, Vance had reminded his colleagues, when it came to the Slavic Pope, Gib Appleyard had winnowed and sieved every available word this Pontiff had spoken or written since he had come into prominence. If he hadn't gotten the Holy Father's total backing for U.S. policy regarding the former Soviet Union, at least he had come away with the assurance that the Pope wouldn't stand in the way of that policy.

Vance had won this argument. It was agreed that if the government was to have any hope of coming away with even that much on the issue of population control, Commander Appleyard was the man to send.

For the better part of three months, therefore, Gibson had been working on the details of his new foray into papal Rome. He had even got so far as to instruct the Embassy to set things up for him on the papal calendar again. Now he was confronted with the possibility that the urgent timetable Vance had given him would be badly jiggered. In fact, if Lucadamo was right—if the Slavic Pope's coming surgery had to do with cancer—his preparations might be out the window altogether.

"It can't end like that, Bud." Appleyard was visibly upset. "I can't believe things will end for him with the awful whine of the heart monitor, or with his slipping into a coma under the ravages of disease."

Though sympathetic, Vance had no time for private speculations. What this Pope thought and the direction he was moving his Church had become questions of paramount consideration in higher policy planning. The Admiral was forced to turn his mind to another level of Vatican politics: What did Appleyard know about possible successors to the Slavic Pope?

"Little and nothing." Gib was frank about his ignorance. "According to my Roman contact, this whole thing came as such a surprise that no one was ready for it."

"What about private speculations inside the Vatican itself? Has your man in Rome heard any names at that level?"

"He came up with a couple of names. He'd heard Cardinal Noah Palombo mentioned. And Cardinal Leo Pensabene. But he doesn't put much stock in the rumors. Quoted an old Vatican adage to the effect that any man who enters Conclave as Pope comes out as Cardinal. It could be interesting for us, though, in a more general sense. Have our people been keeping an eye on the Strasbourg players?"

"For all the good it's done us." Vance shoved the Strasbourg surveillance dossiers across the desk. "We've kept a select team on it, but everybody still seems to be minding his business."

"Maybe." Appleyard ran quickly through the folders. "But what do you suppose Herr Otto Sekuler's business is? In Brussels last year, he billed himself as the CSCE's special Liaison-Delegate to the European Community. People I spoke to in Rome connect him with UNESCO and with the Leipzig Lodge. He's also the chairman of WOSET, which is a minor member of the UN's nongovernmental section. Something to do with world ethics. But according to this tracking data, he shapes up as a stranger duck than that."

"He's mainly a lecturer, I'd say," Vance put in. "In any case, he's no threat to national security."

"Maybe." Appleyard scanned the file through all the same. Sekuler spent a fair amount of time in the States and drew liberally on two foreign-source accounts in major banks of five U.S. cities. He lived mainly in private hotels, and was on intimate terms with such eminent public personalities as the Cardinal of Centurycity and the celebrated scholar Dr. Ralph S. Channing, among many others. In fact, Herr Sekuler was a bit of a celebrity himself, a man called upon as a frequent speaker for several dozen philanthropic and cultural organizations patronized by architects, physicians, engineers, university professors and prelates of both the Catholic and the Protestant persuasion. A number of those organizations had been investigated by public authorities for cultist behavior, but that was about all that could be reliably documented about Sekuler's activities in America.

The anecdotal side of the record, on the other hand, included a darker dimension. There was nothing remarkable in the fact that Sekuler held private meetings with top-level officials of the principal pro-choice organizations and that witnesses to those meetings pegged him as pro-choice. But Gib drew in his breath as he scanned the report of one singular meeting where, for the benefit of some twenty-five abortuary professionals gathered in the operating room of a private clinic, the German had demonstrated the latest method of dealing with the carcasses of aborted babies. "In a brief preamble to his demonstration"—Appleyard read the text aloud—"the subject of this surveillance assured his audience that there need be no more trouble with blocked drains, or with unpleasant discoveries in public trash containers, or with nuisance demonstrations by extremists.

"The subject said nothing. He had brought with him a valise, and several metal cases about the size of double filing boxes. From the valise he extracted and assembled the parts of what amounted to a newly designed and technically advanced grinder. From the metal cases he removed fresh fetal body parts in various states of development, which he used to demonstrate the most efficient and sanitary means by which to reduce that material to a semi-liquid that could be caught in a basin and washed into the sewer system as safely and inoffensively as pink toothpaste.

"The subject assured his audience that he was advocating no radical change in the normal running of abortuaries. There was no question of depriving themselves of income from researchers who required live fetuses for the study of pain tolerance or for work on such afflictions as Parkinson's and Alzheimer's diseases and diabetes. Nor was there any thought of leaving cosmetic companies short of material for skin collagen or of neglecting the cult market interested in using fatty tissue for candles. The new system was neither more nor less than an improved method of dealing with troublesome leftovers."

Gibson closed the Sekuler dossier and tossed it onto Vance's desk. "Nice company I've been keeping."

"You're not alone. If you noticed, there are plenty of endorsements here, including one from Cyrus Benthoek, attesting to Sekuler's standing as an international servant and humanitarian."

That was cold comfort for Appleyard. Endorsements or not, there was too little information of substance. Nothing really tangible about the source of Sekuler's funds. Nothing about his superiors; or even if he had any superiors. "We're looking at a ghost, Bud. There's no ID track on the individual. But, speaking of Benthoek, let's get back to that Strasbourg gathering. Given what we do know about Sekuler, it's disturbing that he was invited to discuss the future of the papacy. And it makes me think about the fact that Palombo and Pensabene are being mentioned as papal candidates."

"Hold it, Gib!" Appleyard was going beyond the evidence, and Vance didn't like it. "It seems to me that the interest at Strasbourg was to bring the Church into line with aims we all share. With the aim of building a human society of nations on a rational principle of regulating economic growth and development.

"Provided Palombo and Pensabene were really serious about the need to join the real world, maybe it wouldn't be so bad if we had to deal with one of them as Pope."

"Or," Appleyard countered testily, "maybe we'd be dealing with an ecclesiastical thug wearing a tiara. The Strasbourg meeting was a nasty piece of sedition. Besides, at least we know what we're dealing with in the Slavic Pope. I grant you that in some ways he comes across as conservative to the bone. But side by side with that, you have to take other things into account.

"Take that *Negotiations* speech Cardinal Maestroianni delivered for him at the UN recently. Maybe you read about it, Bud. He plumped foursquare on the side of joining the society of nations in the real world. Or take this new Catechism he's been working on. My Roman contact sent me an early draft of it, and it bears all the marks of every major document that's come out of Rome since the Second Vatican Council, including the new Code of Canon Law he promulgated back in '83. Lots of room for new doctrinal interpretations of all the old dogmas.

"In some ways, he's downright permissive, in fact. A true macromanager. Refuses to interfere at the lower echelons of governance, no matter what. Refuses to interfere with bishops. Refuses to enforce laws banning clerical membership in the Lodge, or the use of Altar girls. Refuses to expel heretical theologians. Refuses to put a stop to phony marriage annulments issued by the Church, even when they amount to some fifty thousand or more annually. Retains thousands of actively homosexual clergy, even while he exhorts the faithful to observe the Church's teaching on sexual morality."

Gibson wound up his litany: "And he refuses to insist on his unique claim to be infallible in teaching, or to take advantage of the absolute monarchic power he enjoys as Pope. Clearly, he regards himself as nothing more than a very important bishop among four thousand other important bishops."

Vance got the point. Appleyard was saying it's better to deal with the devil you know than the devil you don't?

"I wouldn't put it like that," Gib objected in all seriousness. "This Pope is way ahead of all the propaganda about the need for religions to wade into the work of building a new world. In fact, he takes it as a God-given assignment for the Church he heads. And on top of that, he claims to include all religions in his ministry, but without any of the usual old insistence that everybody become Roman Catholic."

"I'll take your word for it, Gib. I stand corrected. This is no 'grin and bear it in this life, pie in the sky when you die' Pope. But the crucial issue for U.S. policy isn't the Pontiff's religious ministry. The issue is his Church's public stance regarding population control."

"Give a fellow a chance." Gibson lightened up a little. "I was just coming to that. The Slavic Pope is on record as favoring the limitation of human births in view—I'm not kidding now—in view of possible environmental disaster stemming from overpopulation."

"Well, I'll be . . ."

There was one catch, Appleyard admitted. "I doubt he'd go along with overt governmental pushing of abortion facilities with public funds, or with the use of a drug like RU-486, or with obviously repugnant fetal research. We're not dealing with the likes of Herr Otto Sekuler, in other words. There must be some care about *how* births are limited if this Pope is to go along with us."

"You're forgetting one thing." The Admiral cast a somber glance at Appleyard. "We're not dealing with Otto Sekuler, and thank God for that! But we don't know if we'll be dealing with the Slavic Pope either. We don't know if he'll live or die."

Gib lowered his head. "I hadn't forgotten. But I still say it can't end for him like that. This Pope and his Rome are moving into position as the pillars of the Temple."

"Come again?"

"Forget it." Gibson smiled. The Admiral wasn't the man to talk with about Joachim Blumenhagen and his prophecies, about Masonry and the Church and the New Jerusalem. On the other hand, though, there wasn't a better man than Vance to lay a bet with. "I'll give you odds, Bud. Five to one on the Slavic Pope to come through this operation as strong as a bear. In fact, ten to one that I'll be sitting down with him again in plenty of time to pull your precious G-7 population policy out of the fire."

"You're on, old man!" Vance eyed the dossiers on Sekuler and his high-ranking friends in the Vatican. "And I don't mind telling you this is one bet I'd love to lose!"

It was true that Father Aldo Carnesecca's quarters in the sad and largely deserted old Monastery of St. John of the Cross on the outskirts of Barcelona were some five hundred miles and more removed from Rome. It was not true that Carnesecca was as distant from papal activity, or such a minor player, as Cardinal Aureatini assumed. Along with such papal confidants as the Vatican security chief, Giustino Lucadamo, and the Pope's secretary, Daniel Sadowski, Aldo was one of a handful of men who were briefed by the Pontiff himself.

The call had come through just as Carnesecca was settling down after his latest visit to the Papal Nuncio's office in Madrid to catch the diplomatic pouch reserved for special dispatches to the Holy Father. The Pope's principal concern had been to pass news of his operation along quickly, to Father Damien and Christian Gladstone and a few other men of confidence around the world.

But also on His Holiness' mind at this critical time was the much ballyhooed new Catechism. The *Universal Profession of Faith* was ready now in draft for review and revision, the Holy Father said. Monsignore Daniel had already dispatched copies to Father Aldo. He was to keep one for his own reading and critique during the Pope's absence from the Apostolic Palace; and he was to enlist Gladstone and Slattery for the same purpose.

Carnesecca had briefed the Pontiff on his work in Spain, about his quiet soundings in preparation for a papal Consistory with the Spanish bishops, about one or two men who might be candidates for the College of Cardinals, about the dismal condition of the Church in that once vibrantly Catholic land.

One thing Carnesecca had not mentioned to the Holy Father was his sure sense that he was under surveillance. It wasn't a new happening in his life, after all, and he had been at this sort of clandestine work long enough to know how to take precautions. But he was getting a little weary of it all. Weary of exile. Weary of being constantly on the watch. Weary of being so totally alone.

The reading of this *Universal Profession of Faith* only increased Carnesecca's weariness of soul. Like the documents of Vatican II, and like the tremendously important new Code of Canon Law promulgated in 1983, the *Profession* reflected the changed mentality of the Roman Curia. Like those documents, the new Catechism included all the basics of dogmatic faith. But, again like its predecessors, it was replete with cajoling and deceptive ambiguities. It was, in other words, another major document that would open the Church to still more invented spirituality, invented liturgies, invented doctrine.

How, Carnesecca wondered, was he to discuss a document like this with Christian Gladstone? Carnesecca remembered the anger Gladstone had shown at the Slavic Pope's penchant for strategies that had left his Church in shambles, and how unwilling he had been to let the Holy Father off the hook on the grounds that his enemies in the Vatican had ringed him around and laid siege to the papacy itself. "If the Pope is a prisoner in the palace as you claim, Father Aldo," Christian had complained, "maybe it's because he's acquiesced all along. Maybe it's because he allows all the abuses of power and all the deviations from apostolic duty to go on in the Church."

With such memories as background, Carnesecca had every reason to worry that Chris might see this Catechism as the last straw of papal acquiescence; that he might revert to his idea of leaving Rome to its scheming chamberlains. Because it was as unacceptable to him now as it had ever been that Rome should lose such a good priest as Gladstone, and because he was convinced that the *Profession* itself was nothing less than a major campaign in the long war for control of the papacy and the Church, Carnesecca ignored his own weariness and put his mind to a thorough analysis of the Slavic Pope himself.

Carnesecca knew this Pontiff was no clown pretending to be Pope. In worldly matters, he was as brilliant as any of his expert advisors. Somewhere along the line, then—somewhere after they had made him Pope, or perhaps even before that—a man with such qualifications must have made a grave decision about the papacy and the Church. For fully a week, therefore, as Carnesecca traveled to Grenada or Seville or Saragossa, as he walked about in Barcelona, as he worked in his rooms in the Monastery of St. John of the Cross, even over the meals he took with the Monastery's fussy little caretaker, Jorge Corrano, and his wife, María, Carnesecca's mind remained fully engaged in his analysis of a papal leadership that appeared to so many to have been fatally compromised.

For Father Aldo, only three ideas were open to serious consideration as possible explanations for this Pope's actions.

First, and no matter what his qualities as priest, prelate and scholar, there was the possibility that His Holiness was simply an incompetent governor of his Church. The second possibility was that the Holy Father had decided to go along with the so-called progressivists in his Church, and with the power centers outside his Church, in the hope of turning the situation around somewhere down the road. Go along to get along, in other words. The only remaining possibility was that the Slavic Pope had come to papal power with his own ideas already formed about the coming world of the third millennium. That he considered the whole present structure of his Church to be expendable, and expected it to be replaced by an as yet unknown structure.

None of those explanations was attractive. But the third theory had always made the most sense to Carnesecca. It was reasonable to think, then, that His Holiness had operated from the start on the principle that what was happening to the Church was all for the best. He regretted nothing. He didn't want to bring the old structure back. That much said, it followed that his basic idea was to insist on the essentials of morality while he waited upon events.

And if that was the Slavic Pope's policy, then His Holiness was making an enormous mistake, in Carnesecca's opinion; he was consigning the Church to flames instead of fighting for it as other Popes had done. Aldo Carnesecca was too holy a man to be dour. But a week of tussling with such thoughts did leave him in a sober state of mind.

"You work too hard, Padre Aldo," Jorge Corrano told him more than once. As one of the few people who saw him regularly, the caretaker had noticed a change in Carnesecca and was concerned by it. "You're in and out of this Monastery like a fiddler's elbow. Slow down, *Padrecito*. Learn to take a siesta now and then."

The caretaker's wife had her own remedy. "I'll fix a nice paella the way we used to do in Málaga," María offered one afternoon as she delivered the eyedrops she had picked up at the pharmacy for Father Aldo. "You need to put some flesh on those bones." Carnesecca wasn't much for siestas. But that day he did enjoy Señora Corrano's paella; and the kitchen conversation with this most *simpático* Spanish couple provided him with an hour of relaxation. So relaxed was Father Aldo, in fact, that he decided to put his work aside and make an early night of it.

Abandoned by the Carmelite Sisters since 1975, the sad old Monastery of St. John of the Cross embraced him in the cool silence of its Catalonian marble walls like a lonely friend; it seemed in some sense to attend him in his evening prayers. No traffic echoed any longer on the main staircase that wound past the landing outside his door and down to the bronze gates of the Chapel on the floor below. Even the few pilgrims to whom the Monastery was open these days as a hostel, and who came here to venerate this shrine to the great Spanish saint, seemed quieter than usual. Was this not a fitting place, then, for prayers like Aldo Carnesecca's prayers? Prayers for faithful men like Christian Gladstone and Damien Slattery and Angelo Gutmacher and Brother Augustine. Prayers for himself. That come what may, and until it was time for him to be called to his eternal home, he would remain a faithful, fruitful servant to Christ and to His Vicar.

As he rose at last from his knees and set about the routine of preparing for bed, Carnesecca chatted for a while longer with his guardian angel about that last point. He didn't know when he would be called home, he told his angel. And he wasn't exactly asking about that. Yet he was beginning to tire. Not physically or mentally. It was more like nostalgia. A desire to see the home of his childhood; to see the Rome of his youth; to see such rare friends of his later years as Christian Gladstone. He felt he had almost drained the chalice of his life's sufferings.

Without disrupting the intimacy of prayer, Father Aldo reached for the little plastic vial of eyedrops María Corrano had fetched for him. This, too, had become a part of his routine ever since he had consulted Dr. José Palacio y Vaca about the tiny, sporadic flashes of light he had begun to notice on the periphery of his vision. The good doctor had given him a long technical explanation; but the long and the short of it had been that Father Aldo suffered from angle-closure glaucoma. He could be operated on if the condition grew critical; but for the moment it would be sufficient to water his eyes twice daily, morning and evening, with a 0.5 percent formula of Isopto Carpine, and to continue with regular examinations.

Obediently, therefore, Carnesecca was just squeezing the drops into his eyes—reminding himself as he did so to add the pharmacist's latest receipt along with the bill from Dr. Palacio y Vaca to his expense folder before he sent it off to Cardinal Aureatini's office in Rome—when the sharp sound of his telephone shattered the silence of the Monastery like an alarm, and the sharp sound of Chris Gladstone's voice, as troubled as Carnesecca had known it would be, shattered any thought of an early night.

"Father Aldo, about this so-called *Universal Profession of Faith* the Holy Father asked you to send me . . ."

XXXIX

LIKE THE OFFICIAL Vatican announcement put out by the papal spokesman, Miguel Lázaro-Falla, the cables sent out to papal representatives around the world by Secretary of State Graziani were bland and low-key: On the advice of his doctors, the Holy Father would enter Agostino Gemelli Polyclinic on the evening of June 29 to undergo exploratory surgery.

By the following morning, the papal health crisis was international news. To a degree that was not merely curious, however, but unprecedented, all sides played the situation down. The Vatican, the Catholic hierarchy around the world, diplomatic missions in Rome and elsewhere, Catholic newspapers and news services, the international media—each for its own deliberate motives—minimized the event as of no great significance. There was no sudden influx of news correspondents to Rome, nor did Roman Catholic bishops pass resolutions or statements of sympathy in their various Conferences. Three bishops—only three—organized public prayers in their dioceses for the successful outcome of the operation. In consequence, no popular mood of apprehension or speculation set in among the general body of Roman Catholics. There was no noticeable outpouring of sorrow; no deluge of sympathetic cables and letters to the Holy See promising prayers for the Holy Father.

Perhaps the bishops were feeling their oats, Sadowski complained privately to Cardinal Sanstefano. But such terrible silence seemed to him as uncaring as it was peculiar.

"Uncaring?" The busy Sanstefano lingered just long enough to give his own opinion. "No, Monsignore Daniel. I'd say too many bishops just care about the wrong thing. They're caught up in their own ambitions. What we're witnessing, I think, is an unexpressed hope that this might be the end of a papacy most of them find unsatisfactory."

It was a wonder to all, and a puzzlement to many, that the Slavic Pope himself seemed impervious to the strange unresponse that followed the official announcement. He seemed to be far more preoccupied with the pressure being exerted on him to follow up his appointment of the urbane Father-General Michael Coutinho as Archbishop of Genoa with the red hat. Like many before him in the long line of Pontiffs, the Slavic Pope's long and lasting service to the Church would be the composition of the College of Cardinals, the destined electors of his own successor. Yet this looked like another battle lost in a long war. Supported as he was by Leo Pensabene, and reinforced by the considerable prestige of Cosimo Maestroianni's backing, it would have been surprising had Pensabene's dominant faction in the College of Cardinals not voiced support for the Jesuit; and more surprising still had men like Aureatini, Graziani and Palombo not lined up behind Coutinho's candidacy.

"People think the Pope can do what he likes," His Holiness grumbled to Monsignore Daniel. "If they only knew! The Pope has to listen to his bishops and his people."

It was during those eerie days, too, that the matter of Father Damien Slattery's fate came suddenly to the fore. The word from the Vatican security chief, Giustino Lucadamo, was that Father Damien had retreated to the momentary safety of Christian Gladstone's family home. From a security point of view, that would do until his current mission was completed. But temporary security for Slattery wasn't enough. The prospect of abandoning such an open supporter of the papacy to the doubtful mercy of the bishops—the thought of Father Damien begging fruitlessly for some hovel in which to hang his priestly hat, while men like Coutinho moved so easily, so steadily up the power ladder—was unacceptable.

There was no question of railing about the injustice that had been wreaked on the Dominican. There was no justice in the system at present; only power. And in that system, the Cardinal of Centurycity had too many important allies in the unruly Vatican Chancery to allow direct papal intervention in such a matter as exclaustration. The Pope moved another plan into high gear instead. He set about the speedy canonical formation of the new network of underground priests first suggested by Signora Francesca Gladstone and championed since then by Cardinal Amedeo Sanstefano. The Holy Father placed the new order under that Cardinal's patronage. In the Vatican power game, few men could or would challenge the head of the Prefecture of Economic Affairs. Sanstefano was only too happy to draw up the simple rule by which the new network was to be governed, and submit it for approval to Cardinal Reinvernunft at the Congregation for the Defense of the Faith. The strictest secrecy was to apply all around, Sanstefano told his Venerable Brother. Even Damien Slattery wasn't to be apprised of the plans until he returned to Rome in the fall and could be told face to face in the secure setting of the papal study. But everything was to be in readiness before the Pontiff entered Gemelli Polyclinic.

The Pope didn't view this solution to Slattery's predicament as ideal. Through no fault of his own, Father Damien would remain forever under suspicion in some quarters. Yet the Pontiff couldn't have found a better director anywhere for his new network of underground priests. And what more could he hope for in the circumstances?

Side by side with such feverish efforts on Damien Slattery's behalf, His Holiness was given a foretaste of the critique he knew would come from such men as Carnesecca and Father Christian Gladstone—and from Slattery, too, if he knew his man—concerning the vague and permissive language that had blossomed again in the new *Universal Profession of Faith*. Cardinal Reinvernunft himself came to the Pontiff with a challenge to the doctrinal integrity of the Catechism. As Prefect of the Congregation for the Defense of the Faith, His Eminence was particularly troubled by a section of the *Profession* that echoed the language of *Lumen Gentium* in its description of the hierarchical structure of Pope and bishops and their working relationship in governing the Church Universal. The Holy Father was dedicated to vindicating the teaching of the Second Vatican Council. More, His Eminence knew the Pontiff himself had had a good deal to do with *Lumen Gentium*, way back during the Council sessions. But as head of CDF—as the one official in the whole Church whose principal charge was to maintain the purity of the Faith—he felt strongly that statements of Vatican II which had not yet been reviewed by the Holy See in the light of the Church's long tradition should not be included in the new Catechism.

And he felt just as strongly that he had no choice but to press his case, apologetically but firmly.

"At some point, Holiness"—the Cardinal Prefect came to the issue head-on—"the obscurity of certain capital questions will have to be cleared up. For example, the question of whether the bishops, ex officio, share the same universal power and authority over the Church as does the Pope, ex officio."

Though the tone of His Holiness' response was measured, there was no mistaking the harshness of its substance. Sooner or later, perhaps such statements as the Cardinal Prefect found too obscure might have to be modified. "But at this moment, Your Eminence, my pontificate and the unity of my Church depend on adherence to the will of Vatican II. All who wish to serve this papacy must remember that."

The Pontiff did not think Cardinal Reinvernunft was right. But Reinvernunft represented only one faction among the theologians of the Church. Given the disheveled condition of his churchmen, most of whom were not capable of understanding the transformation of Catholicism being effected by the Holy Spirit, the Pontiff had concluded that he should continue to rally everybody to a broad, median band of principles distinct from those of the madcap progressivists who wanted everything to change and from those of the stubborn traditionalists who wanted everything to be restored. In time, the will of Christ would be manifest in His Church and in world events.

In such a context, the *Universal Profession* seemed no worse than other compromises, and better than some. For all of its ambiguities, it did state the basic dogmas of the Roman Catholic faith, after all. It was even reasonable to think its promulgation might do some good. And what more could be humanly effected in the circumstances?

Because the will of Christ upon which he waited had everything to do with all of the affairs unfolding in the world, His Holiness continued to concern himself with the aims of the new global order. And he kept fully abreast of the reports that came continually by pouch from his observers at the EC and the CSCE.

In those quarters, at least, there were few surprises. Their names and their stated aims notwithstanding, there wasn't much in either the EC or the CSCE that was European in any forward-looking sense. Both remained unrelentingly materialist in their outlook. Both had managed to strip themselves of their Christian heritage. Both were all dressed up in new, one-size-fits-all parliamentary clothes, but neither was making much headway. True, the CSCE was inching toward a getting-together of nations, and the Pope did expect Russia to come into that group before long. When it came down to the hard decisions, however, there was no wealth of cooperation in the Conference on Security and Cooperation in Europe. It was still every member state for itself.

Like a spurned lover, meanwhile, the EC still chased after its twin goals of early and extensive political and monetary union among its member states and abolition of all customs and tariffs between them. "Things on this side of the world are not yet ready for such advances." Cardinal Secretary Graziani agreed with the Pontiff's assessment when one of their early-morning briefings touched on EC affairs.

"Things in the United States are not yet ready," His Holiness countered. "U.S. policy doesn't envisage such an extensive union until later. Until then, the EC will have to balance all the items on its geopolitical tray the best way it can."

At least on the geopolitical level, this Pope's strategy and his expectations were vindicated by objective events. And what more could he hope for in the circumstances?

It was still some few very busy days before the Pope was scheduled to enter Gemelli Polyclinic when, with the exquisite timing of a torture master, His Eminence Noah Palombo asked to be received by the Holy Father along with a delegation of senior Cardinals. In view of His Holiness' coming absence from the Apostolic Palace, there were a number of administrative questions to discuss—not least among them the delicate question of the Pope's possible incapacitation.

The stony-faced Palombo did his best to imitate the legendary *romanità* of Cardinal Maestroianni as he cracked the whip of papal resignation over the Pontiff's head. "For the good of the Church, Holiness—and in light of this crisis in Your Holiness' health at such a critical time for the Church in various parts of the world—it has seemed to a majority of Your Holiness' Cardinals that some extraordinary disposition is required to ensure continuity of governance. Some guarantee against disruption. A legal instrument to take effect, should the need arise."

With that, the Slavic Pope got his first look at Cardinal Aureatini's latest bit of handiwork. Without any visible sign of dismay, he read every deft word of the legal instrument by which he would, if he signed it, agree in advance to resign the papacy should certain conditions come to pass.

If there was any consternation at that meeting, it did not appear to be in the Pontiff. As though he had anticipated just such a conversation, the Slavic Pope parried the attempt to force his hand with a few documents of his own. Indeed, he had the notarized opinions of the oncologists ready for the occasion.

"As you see, Your Eminences"—His Holiness passed the affidavits over for examination—"this operation will mean a few weeks of rest for me. But it will coincide nicely with the summer exodus. In fact, as I will recuperate at Castel Gandolfo, I will probably be more accessible, and therefore more able to deal with any emergency, than most of my vacationing prelates, including yourselves."

Palombo's first impulse was to point out that the resignation letter was not meant to deal with the Pope's recuperation, but with graver possibilities. With no way to counter the oncologists' prognosis, however, he decided not to overplay his hand. It would be enough to have the papal death warrant signed somewhere around the time of the Common Mind Vote of the bishops. The following spring would be time enough, therefore—at least according to Maestroianni's present estimates. Come this fall, other opportunities would simply have to be arranged to tighten the screws.

With such thoughts as comfort, it took no time at all for His Eminence to regain his composure. Considering the welter of problems mounting for His Holiness these days, the very fact that the resignation letter had been presented to him by a senior delegation of his Cardinals must have had some impact on him. A demoralizing impact. There was no reason at all to worry over the Pontiff's little victory.

Palombo was right.

The Pope wasn't demoralized exactly. But the slithering worm of self-doubt began to nibble away at him again. He was troubled anew by his failure to stir the consciences of his Cardinals; by his failure to get them to act in fealty to Christ, to Peter and to the faith handed down to them from the Apostles. He was beset by worry that, in keeping so many bad bishops and bad theologians and bad priests in place, he had himself abandoned those who remained loyal to the Holy See and to the faith. He was troubled by thoughts that he had allowed things to slacken to such a degree that men like Palombo felt they could pluck the very reins of governance from his hands.

Still mentally convinced of his papal policy, the Slavic Pope managed to steel his will against such depressing thoughts. This was not the only troubled period in the history of the papacy, he told himself. If he could just hold long enough—if he could just maintain those broad, bedrock principles of faith and morality; if he could just keep his eyes steadfastly on Christ and His Mother while he waited for the signs promised at Fatima—everything would come right for the suffering Church he served, and for the suffering world he loved so much. If he could just hold . . .

The June 29 date scheduled for His Holiness to enter Gemelli Polyclinic was the very date he was called upon to preside over Michael Coutinho's installation in the College of Cardinals at a ceremony in St. Peter's Basilica. Because that was the feast day of the great Apostles Peter and Paul, and because Roman gossip is always ready to spice its reading of papal goings-on with a dash of superstition, there were some who saw a certain fatefulness in that sequence of events. Some turned their thoughts to another June 29; to a ceremony of promise in St. Paul's Chapel; to the Prince enthroned in the Citadel.

By the time he laid aside his work at last and set off to keep his date with Dr. Fanarote and his team of medical specialists at Gemelli Polyclinic, His Holiness was in grievous pain. The only men with him were his secretary, Monsignore Sadowski, and his security chief, Giustino Lucadamo. From the next morning on—from the moment the Pope would enter the operating room, and for the early days of his recovery—Sadowski and Lucadamo would be part of the five-man team to whom the exclusive direction of papal household affairs would belong. The other three officials in charge—"my keepers," the Holy Father called them—were to be Cardinal Sanstefano of PECA; the papal spokesman, Miguel Lázaro-Falla; and, of course, Dr. Fanarote. The Secretary of State and the other in-house Cardinals could not intervene until the Holy Father returned to normalcy.

Lucadamo had already executed concise and concrete plans for the near term by means of a hard-nosed briefing for hospital personnel, including the surgeon and all attending physicians. For the duration of the papal stay, there would be total electronic surveillance of every part of the hospital and of everyone who entered or left it. Each person involved with the care of the Pope, no matter how menial the task, would be accountable for every detail of his or her duty.

To his own handpicked agents posted throughout the hospital, Lucadamo's orders were stark. They were to maintain total control. They were to answer only to him. And in this case, justice was to begin and end at the muzzles of the weapons they carried. "If you have good reason to suspect danger, don't wait to ask questions. Do your best not to end up with dead bodies. But we must not end up with a papal cadaver."

Of all the world leaders and public personalities who were so regularly in touch with the Holy Father, only one broke the strange silence that had lately fallen over them in his regard. As those eerie, turbulent days drew to a close, the Slavic Pope was alone and already in bed when, late on the eve of his operation, a brief note was delivered to him by hand. "I cannot believe," Mikhail Gorbachev had written, "that the providence of the Almighty will terminate Your Holiness' services just at this crucial moment in human history."

Windswept House turned out to be more than a retreat of safety for Damien Slattery. From the entry hall of Windswept House, where the chimes of Oakey Paul sounded the hours, to the Tower Chapel, where he offered Mass every morning, there was something here that burned away whatever instinct of self-pity had sprouted in his heart, and dissipated whatever littleness of spirit had constricted his mind. Some trait of heredity seemed to fill this great mansion. Some indelible mark of far-off times when Christian's ancestors had decided not to cling to their ancient moorings in Cornwall—not to rot in resentment; not to wait to be carried off into oblivion by the malice of the enemies of their faith—but to face the open sea instead, and to find their footing in a different world than they had ever known.

Not that Slattery could really get away mentally from Centurycity. He knew as well as the Pontiff did that the Cardinal's accusations against him would shred his reputation for a lot of people. And, because he didn't want that to be an issue between himself and Gladstone, he laid the whole sorry mess out for his friend frankly and in detail.

It said a great deal about the effect of his eye-opening labors on Chris that Damien's story didn't surprise him. On the contrary, most of it was familiar to him by now. From beginning to end—the contempt dished out to Slattery at the House of the Holy Angels; his final showdown with the Cardinal; even the brazen homosexual priests he had come upon with their imported lovers in the priory kitchenette—the situation Damien described was of a piece with the cases of so many other priests Christian had interviewed and whose stories he had checked.

It still seemed odd, though, Chris said, that not even the Dominican Father Provincial had offered some religious sentiment, however insincere it might have been. "Didn't he say anything about the sons of St. Dominic sticking together and supporting each other?"

"Haneberry?" Damien had a hearty laugh at that. "He was like a hen on a hot griddle. Couldn't get rid of me fast enough. That's what they set out to do, and they pulled it off like pros. They've fixed it so I'll have to live outside the Order until they finalize their decision in my regard. Meanwhile, I expect hotter complaints against me from Haneberry and the Cardinal. I'm out of control, they'll say; psychologically unbalanced. They'll make it impossible for me to find a bishop who will incardinate me. And if I can't find a bishop, I'll be out. Laicized. Released from all my religious and ecclesiastical vows. Canonically, I won't exist for them any longer."

"It's Mike O'Reilly's case all over again." Disgust was written all over Christian's face. He remembered Father Michael's charge that he was just another member of the faithful abandoned by the man who's supposed to 'feed My lambs, feed My sheep.' " That's what O'Reilly had said to Chris. And, in essence, that's what Chris charged, as he let loose with both barrels about his Pope.

"This Holy Father is the key." Gladstone's face was flushed with anger. "Perhaps Father Aldo is right. Perhaps this Pope is the obedient slave of Our Lady. Perhaps he will bend to her Son's will as she gave it to us at Fatima. Perhaps he is looking at the bigger geopolitical picture and knows the New World Order won't take hold; that it would change the family of man in such a way that religion would have no place any longer; that the Fatima message has to do with all that. But maybe the Pope is just plain mesmerized by geopolitical change. And in the meantime, he's causing more problems than any of us can solve!"

"Hold on there, Chris!" Slattery had seen Gladstone's temper before, but never an explosion like this. And he didn't understand how Aldo Carnesecca had suddenly come into the picture.

"I'll tell you how, Damien!" Christian retrieved the draft of the new Catechism Father Aldo had sent him and flung it across the room to his friend. "I've had a long talk with Father Aldo about this screed the Holy Father intends to pass off as a universal profession of our faith. I was just about ready to buy into Aldo's point of view. But now I think it just won't wash. Call it a Catechism if you want. But it's a perfect reproduction of all that stinks in the post-Conciliar churchly organization. All the fundamental dogma is there in black and white—it always is! But it's chockablock with the kind of go-with-the-flow garbage that leads to the crucifixion of good priests like Mike O'Reilly and you and a couple of hundred more I can tell you about.

"Suddenly, Hell isn't feasible for us anymore because it doesn't square with God's milquetoast mercy. All you have to do to be saved—whatever that may mean now—is to be a conforming member of this floundering society of nations. If a framework like that is Roman Catholic, I'll eat all seven hundred pages of this so-called Catechism for dinner!

"So, tell me, Father Damien. Was it all a prearranged plan right from the bosom of the Second Vatican Council? Was this Pontiff in on the whole thing, the whole miserable transformation of Catholicism? Or is it just a coincidence that Council documents like *Gaudium et Spes* and *Lumen Gentium* look exactly like the Canon Law of 1983? And that they all look like this new Catechism? Tell me if you can, Damien. What's the key to the puzzle? The Slavic Pope was at the Council. He composed those two documents. He's their champion. So whose side is he on? Once he became Pope, why did he allow the Church to get to this point of corruption? Tell me if you can, Father. Have the bishops over here got it right? The Pope and his papacy don't really matter anymore, eh? Isn't that what they think? Isn't that how he acts?"

Slattery was frozen into silence. Even that afternoon at the Angelicum when he and Chris had had another donnybrook over papal motives, he hadn't heard this kind of sentiment from the young cleric. Suddenly Damien's own crisis didn't seem to matter so much anymore. "There is another possibility, Christian." As deep as it was, Damien's voice sounded like a whisper after Gladstone's barrage of accusations. "It's just possible that from the very beginning of his pontificate, it was already all over. It's possible that the seeds of apostasy had already been sown and were already flourishing. It's possible that Christ had already given up on this version of the churchly organization. It's possible that, like Peter, this Pope was chosen by the Holy Spirit more for his weakness than for his strength. More for his lack of understanding than for his wisdom. More for his love for Jesus than for his understanding of what sort of kingdom Christ intends His creatures to build. Perhaps the Almighty has had enough of all the corruption, in other words. Enough of this generation. Perhaps we're all destined to be replaced by a new generation. Another race of Catholics. A better, truer, cleaner race. It's just possible that the Slavic Pope is in truth the last Pope of these Catholic times. And it's just possible that he knows it. That he has known it all along."

In a few seconds, Slattery had outstripped all the theories about the Slavic Pope; had wrapped them all into a possibility so terrible that it was almost impossible for the mind to encompass. Almost impossible to accept. Suddenly a stranger in these most familiar surroundings, Chris was searching for solid struts to hold on to.

"Suppose what you say is true, Damien." Slowly, Gladstone began to grope his way onto new terrain. "Would that give His Holiness the right to let so many good men like yourself go down to ruin? Does he see that as Christ's will? Or is he just taking a big gamble with other people's lives?"

Questions like that weren't new to Slattery; for him, the answers were as old as Christianity. "I expect he thinks what I think about Christ's will. If good men are going down, God must be allowing that to happen. Willing it to happen, in fact, just as He willed the Crucifixion. And for the same reason. There's always a serious discrepancy between God's priorities and the priorities of the world. It's out of just such suffering that He brings greater benefit than you or I or the Pope or anyone else can begin to imagine.

"I suppose you could say that the Pope is taking a big gamble. And it's always hard to make choices in a world so full of thunder and lightning and the sound of man's groanings and babies' cries. Human reality is all untidy."

"So that's it?" Christian wasn't ready to cave in. "The Pope's choice is to wait on a gamble, while the world gets too untidy to manage?"

"No, Chris. That's not it. I do not know the sum total of this Pope's policy. He is reaching out in a new way to all and every kind of human being. That's part of what he means when he talks about 'the New Jerusalem.' If that policy of his is painful to us as individuals, if we do not fit into the Conciliar Church this Pope is fashioning, if we find ourselves marginalized by his creation, we do what your ancestors did. We do what Roman Catholics have always done. We go on. We don't have all the answers. As far as I know, the only avenue of access to the answers on this earth is the Holy Father. So we stay always with that basic datum of our faith: The Pope is Peter. For as long as he's alive, the Slavic Pope is Christ's Vicar. That's his job. Christ will take care of us and of him.

"And for as long as we're alive, you and I are priests. That's our job. We can walk a few steps behind the Holy Spirit, always confident in the faith revealed to us through the Apostles and manifested by the teaching of the Church through the ages. Even in the hardest circumstances, we can bend our backs to accomplish our puny part in the work Christ always entrusts, knowingly and lovingly, to unworthy hands."

"In other words"—the hint of a wry smile played at the corners of Christian's mouth at last—"you're telling me to get back to work."

"In other words"—Slattery tossed the Catechism back to Gladstone—"I'm telling you to stop trying to be Pope. Let's both pray that His Holiness comes through surgery. And let's give the man the gift of a job well done."

While they waited for news from Gemelli Polyclinic, therefore—and while Chris, still unconvinced by Damien's stout defense of the Slavic Pope, continued to grapple with his suspicions—the two priests pored over the mounds of data each had assembled.

Day by day, they huddled in the library, reviewing their records of names and dates and places, analyzing documented activities each had collected and verified independently of the other. And day by day, Damien became more and more convinced that he was right. It wasn't just that the material showed that homosexual activity and ritual Satanism had both reached an organizational level among U.S. clergy. It was that the same names and the same places cropped up in both sets of data.

Chris, for example, had catalogued hundreds of cases of pedophiliac priests whose bishops moved them from parish to parish. Slattery's records showed that a few of those same bishops were themselves involved in established covens. Some, in fact, even turned up in the mysterious records of Satanist activity Bishop Russeton had kept during his days as head of the Mother Chapel. True to his word, Sylvester Wodgila had quickly found the help he needed to decipher the names and locations of affiliated chapels around the country; so there it was, all set out as clear as you please.

So compelling was the pattern that emerged, in fact, that Chris found he could literally map the coincidence between clerical pedophiliac activity and known Satanist covens. He was able to mark the location of all the dioceses—too many dioceses in too many parts of the country—where the names of known pedophiliac priests were identical with the names of priests Damien had linked to Satanist covens.

"That's quite a picture, wouldn't you say?" Slattery studied Christian's map with sickening disgust.

"It's the picture of a cover-up. But I can't figure how such a thing is possible. Given the total number of bishops and priests in the country, we're dealing with a relative handful. But we do have a big dirty bubble in the center of the Church over here. And yet no official is screaming. Are all the baddies in charge? And are all the good ones blind? Or are they all little tintypes of Cardinal O'Cleary? Are they frightened that if they burst the bubble, the sludge that comes out will cover their own faces with filth?

"Out with it, Damien!" Christian was getting too good at reading Slattery's eyes.

What Damien came out with wasn't the answer to Gladstone's questions, but a series of questions of his own. "Doesn't it all seem to tie up, Chris? If you put it all together, I mean. There's Cardinal O'Cleary's decision to ordain three priests who'd been shown to be homosexually active. There's the matter of all those pedophiliac priests who are moved about by their bishops, and a consistent refusal to laicize known offenders. There's the special fund the bishops have had to set up to pay hundreds of millions of dollars in out-of-court settlements. There's that evidence Wodgila found linking Centurycity to Bishop Russeton, and linking Russeton's Mother Chapel to other dioceses all over the landscape. And now this map points to a de facto connection between pedophiliac homosexuality and ritualistic Satanism among the clergy.

"It's bad enough that the faithful are paying for the maintenance of such awful games, and that the bishops are pitting the Church against Catholic families in lawsuits. But if we keep at it, we may find that there's something more than a cover-up here. At this point, mind you, it's only a private notion of my own. I have no proof. But I think the question to ask from here on out is whether there's an effort to transform the Church into a safe sanctuary for known pedophiles. And, in the process, to create a perfect field of harvest for Satanist cults.

"If we ever come up with evidence to answer that question, we may find that what we're witnessing is an effort to bankrupt the Church, both morally and monetarily. A deliberate, expertly orchestrated attempt to demolish the Church from within."

To the depths of his soul, Christian was sorry he had asked for Slattery's reading. He tried to argue that Damien was seeing everything through the eyes of an exorcist. That he was seeing Satan in every dark corner. That his "private notion" was too gruesome to be tenable. Yet hadn't Father O'Reilly come up with something like the same conclusion? Not that he had seen the Devil behind the deeds, except in the most general sense. But he was convinced that they were dealing with a network of protection reaching all the way to Rome.

In the end, Gladstone had to ask the questions that might make his own situation untenable. If such an effort was under way against the Church, how far did Slattery think it reached into the hierarchy? "Does it reach as high as Maestroianni and the other Cardinals I've been working with? Do you suppose it reaches into that level?"

Again Slattery fell silent. And again Christian probed. He'd come this far. Best to hear it all.

As dispassionately as possible when talking about such things, Damien recapped Giustino Lucadamo's suspicions stemming from a meeting that had taken place some time back at Strasbourg. Suspicions that encompassed Maestroianni and Aureatini and Palombo and Pensabene in a scheme to devise a series of votes by the various Regional and National Conferences of Bishops around the world. According to Lucadamo, that scheme was to be the trigger for some mechanism to secure the resignation of the Slavic Pope.

Gladstone winced. "If Lucadamo suspects that whole crowd, then he must suspect me, too!"

Slattery's response was silence. Eloquent silence.

Chris buried his head in his hands. He didn't know whether to laugh or cry. The world had gone berserk. He suspected the Pope. Lucadamo suspected him. Slattery suspected the whole hierarchy. Maybe they all belonged in an asylum, himself included. Otherwise . . . Otherwise, what? He couldn't force his mind that far. Not yet.

Fresh from his own severe misery, Damien tried to comfort his friend by backtracking as much as he could. "Don't bother about Lucadamo, Chris. He's paid to be suspicious. But he's a fair man; and he's devoted to the Holy See. He'll come to the truth about you. In fact, I think we'd do best to follow Lucadamo's example. Let's continue the work we've come here to do. Let's ask all the questions that have to be asked. But let's be fair; and let's keep an open mind.

"As to Maestroianni, he may be no friend of this Pope. And he's no friend of mine, that's for certain. He's part of the worldly crowd who think that wisdom resides entirely in history. But it would be a big leap to say that puts Maestroianni in the same league as a Bishop Russeton. There is arguably a break-off point between what Maestroianni would probably call a worldly-wise, commonsensical attitude toward the concrete conditions of the Church—toward the hard realities of finance and politics, for example—and the idea of a kingdom devoted explicitly to Luciferian principles.

"The professional Luciferian acts as if there is a wisdom behind the changing decor of mankind's everyday life. These days, a lot of people see that sort of wisdom—Luciferian wisdom, if you will—moving history along by the apparent accidents of human affairs. Nevertheless, just because a cleric identifies his professional ideas and ambitions for himself and his Church with those that fit the Luciferian mold, does that make him a Luciferian? Or, to come down to cases, just because Maestroianni hobnobbed in Strasbourg with a motley crowd of worldly globalists, I'm not prepared to argue that he falls on his knees at the thought of the Fallen Angel."

Gladstone stared wide-eyed at Slattery. At some other time, it might have even been interesting to debate such theological reasonings with his friend. At just this moment, however, his worry was strictly practical.

Chris had always known that in Rome he didn't amount to much. The Gladstone name was something else again; and that was reason enough for a man like Maestroianni to groom him for some future role. Until today, he hadn't been able to think of any other reason why the little Cardinal should have plucked him out of nowhere for an assignment that boosted his standing among bishops on two continents.

Now, though, Slattery had given him another reason. If Lucadamo was right about the nature of the Strasbourg meeting, then Gladstone wasn't being groomed for anything. He was being used right now. As a stupid pawn. As an unwitting gull in a filthy game of antipapal politics. The work he had been doing for Maestroianni—those touchy-feely questions he had been asking the bishops concerning their perceptions of the Pope; all of those exhaustive debriefings in Maestroianni's office; all the favors he'd been doing for bishops at Maestroianni's request—all of it was being used to further a plot against the Pope!

"You've no idea what's been going on!" Christian took his fury out on himself and on Maestroianni. "You don't know the extent of my career as a water carrier for those bastards! It's all supposed to be super-confidential, and now I can see why!

Slattery was at a loss to follow Gladstone.

"Let me tell you, Damien!" Unable to contain himself, or even to sit still, Chris began pacing the floor. "I've been obtaining favors and facilities for some thirty or forty bishops in Europe. Things like the relaxation of zoning laws in Antwerp so the bishop, or some friend of his, can build a villa in a certain place. Things like the filing away of a report on some priest's indiscretion with a woman. Things like the preferential treatment of some archbishop's nephew or sister in view of a government sinecure."

"But how, Chris?" Slattery was confused. "How were you able to maneuver such things?"

"My brother!" Gladstone glared down at his friend. "My brother, Paul. He's Secretary-General to the EC's Council of Ministers. Thanks to me, we've both been shat upon. Me, because I've been at Maestroianni's beck and call in Rome. And my brother, because he's in a position where he really can pull strings. And the worst of it is that Lucadamo is right about me! I was the one who made it all possible! I shrugged off all my doubts. I bought into the line that my major assignment was to help Maestroianni improve the unity and solidity of the Church. I told myself I was doing it all for 'the exaltation of Holy Mother Church and the welfare of the Holy See,' as the old prayer says. All the canvassing of bishops. All the statistical tallies. And, yes, the favors, too.

"But all along, I've been giving Maestroianni and the others a working model of the whole episcopal mess. I can tell you—and I have told Maestroianni—how the bishops stand on every major issue and what their local problems are. And as if that weren't enough, the favors I've been doing have put a lot of bishops on Maestroianni's side."

Gladstone shook his head and sank into his chair. He couldn't believe his own stubborn stupidity. "You tried to warn me, Damien. Remember that lunch we had at Springy's? You told me Maestroianni and Palombo and the others could have done a lot to set things right in the Church already, if that's what they were after." In his rage at himself, Chris almost envied Slattery. "At least your enemies found you so indigestible that they've had to vomit you out of their mouths. But me? I'm the perfect fall guy. But not anymore! Maestroianni has seen the last of this stooge!"

"So that's it. . . ." Slattery's face hardened as he took in the full scope of Gladstone's situation. But he brightened almost as quickly. Maybe, he suggested, they could turn Maestroianni's game against him. "What with you as errand boy for the Cardinal and his cronies, maybe we can play this thing for all it's worth."

"Hold on, Slattery!" Gladstone sprang out of his chair again. "You're not suggesting . . . I mean, you can't be serious . . ."

"No, no! You hold on. Until a minute ago, you had no idea what was going on. But now that you do, you're in a better position than Lucadamo or anyone else I know to get a handle on the whole Strasbourg setup."

Chris had barely begun a string of objections to Slattery's brainstorm—had barely asked, "What if Lucadamo won't go along?" and "What do I do when I get back to Rome and have to face Maestroianni again?"—when Beulah Thompson knocked on the library door.

Between Damien and Beulah, it had been love at first sight. As far as Beulah was concerned, Father Damien Duncan Slattery just naturally belonged in such a grand, big mansion as Windswept House. And as far as Damien was concerned, the New World had never seen a grander cook, nor ever would, than Beulah Thompson.

"You two been holed up for so long, a body'd think you was fixin' to rob Fort Knox!" Beulah put on her fiercest scowl. "First thing I know, you'll be wastin' away to skin an' bones. Why, Miss Cessi'll have my hide, an' Miss Tricia, too, if they comes home from Ireland to find a couple o' pale ol' scarecrows here!"

"Not much chance of that, Beulah!" Convinced that a break in the intensity of things would be all to the good, Slattery patted his frontage with both enormous hands. "But if dinner's ready, I'm your man!"

"You, too, Mister Chris!" A victorious Beulah trailed the words behind her as she headed off to dish up a proper feast.

Damien was already on his feet, but Chris still wanted some answer to his problem of how to handle Maestroianni and the others who had used him the way a pimp uses a whore.

"Well, I'll tell yeh, me darlin' lad." Damien unleashed his broadest brogue, and a grin to match; but his advice couldn't have been more serious. "It's the oldest formula in the book fer men who're sent like sheep among wolves. When we get back to Rome, yeh'll be as wise as a serpent. Yeh'll be as simple as a dove. In short, yeh'll be a priest."

Early on the morning of June 30, the Slavic Pope was anointed with the Holy Oils of Extreme Unction by Monsignore Daniel. Then he was wheeled through guarded corridors into the operating room, where, under the watchful eyes of Giustino Lucadamo, the anesthetic was administered.

Hazily, his thoughts coursed back to an earlier day in this same hospital. To an August day in 1981 when Ali Agča shot him in St. Peter's Square. The Blessed Virgin had appeared to him that day; had warned him about the errors of Russia; had shown him the Miracle of the Sun as Lucia and Jacinta and Francisco had seen it on October 13, 1917. But today was not a day of miracles. Today there was silence. Darkness.

But wait . . . . What was that sound? What was he doing here, on the sheerest edge of a cliff? He could feel the presence of a vast crowd pressing behind him. He tried to turn . . . something held him . . . yet he could hear the murmurings. Men. Women. Children. Murmurs of protest. Querulous murmurs. A babel of languages. Garbled questions. Why couldn't he understand? He had spoken so many languages to so many people in so many lands. Why couldn't he understand?

Suddenly, someone flung him from the cliff and into St. Peter's Basilica. It was the Feast of the Assumption. December 8, 1965. The end of the Second Vatican Council. The old Pope was at the High Altar . . . speaking . . . staring at the thousands of bishops seated in serried ranks in the nave. But why did nobody seem to be listening? Why was Sister Lucia running to and fro? Why couldn't he hear anything? Why were the bishops not listening? Where had they got those little white skullcaps they were wearing like so many Popes? What had they done with their miters?

And who were those bald men? Those scores of tall, black-robed men with eyeless sockets moving about among the bishops? Why were they screaming at the bishops like that? Like a clockwork chorus? "Man! Man! Man!" Filled with distress, the Slavic Pope covered his ears. Ran to the High Altar. Maybe he could remove that strange dark cloth draped around the bronze serpentine pillars under the baldachin. If he could tear those drapes away, the bishops would be able to hear the old Pope.

He ripped at the darksome veil and, to his horror, saw that all four pillars had been smashed at the base. The bones and dust of 30,000 ancient Roman martyrs cascaded out from them like a tide gorging from ugly mouths, engulfing everyone in the Basilica. Someone began clacking those bones together. He turned. Who was clacking the bones? But all he could see was that dark veil enclosing itself around the old Pope, hiding his face. All he could see were clouds of balloons floating upward to the lofty dome of the Basilica.

He wanted to see the face of the old Pope. He fought against the tide of bones. Again he tore at the veil. But still he could not see that face clearly. Why not! The whole Basilica was lit. But not with lamps. There were no lamps. It was a garish, fearsome light. A conflagration. Yes! That was it! A conflagration outside the Basilica, enveloping its venerable walls, licking at its high dome . . .

Why could no one hear his warning? He could hear his words inside his skull casing. But why could he not be heard? Why couldn't he make Slattery and Gladstone hear him? Why couldn't he make Angelo Gutmacher hear him? Why couldn't he make Maestroianni hear the words of the exorcist's blessing? Why couldn't he make Christ hear how much he loved Him? The words poured out of his mouth in a babble of Latin and Italian and Polish. "*Credo in unum Deum . . . Maryjo, Królowo Polski . . . Introibo ad altare Dei . . . Proszę Cię . . . Io, figlio dell'umanità e*

Vescovo di Roma . . . Blogoslaw dzieci Twe . . . Ubi Petrus, ibi Ecclesia . . . Io, figlio dell'umanità . . ."

Faces pressed in on him. Why could they not hear? Why could no one, anywhere, hear those words? White and black faces. Yellow and red and brown faces. Bloodstained faces. Starving faces. Smiling faces. Angry, scowling faces. Faces he recognized and faces he could give no name to. Faces that stifled his every effort.

These armored divisions surrounding him at the Shrine of Czestochowa in his beloved Poland . . . why could they not hear? These jeering crowds in Amsterdam, flinging excrement at his Pope-mobile and burning him in effigy . . . why could they not hear? These crowds threatening to pour gallons of AIDS-contaminated blood on the streets of Denver . . . why could they not hear? Why could Ali Agča sitting beside him in his jail cell not hear? "Michael!" Surely, the great Archangel would hear him. Time and again he called out for help. Called out in prayer. "Michael . . . Michael . . . Michael . . ."

"Prayers are answered, Father Damien!" The news from Dr. Fanarote was precise; and if it didn't solve all of Christian's problems, it did lift him from the torpor of one major worry. The tissue removed by the surgeon had been dangerously close to cancerous, and there was some concern that the Pontiff still carried that stubborn and mysterious megalovirus. But the prognosis was good. His Holiness was out of danger and resting.

"The Holy Father has come through with flying colors!" Chris was so elated, he nearly forgot to hang up the phone.

"Prayers are answered!" Slattery repeated Gladstone's words with a great sigh of relief. Fanarote's report told him all he needed to know for now about his Pope. And the emotion that suffused Christian's face told him all he could hope to know for now about the will of this good but troubled priest to stay the course.

It was time to get back to work.

XL

IT WAS NEARLY TEN in the evening before Father Aldo Carnesecca made his way back to the Monastery of St. John of the Cross on the outskirts of Barcelona. Late enough so that he had to ring the bell for the caretaker, Jorge Corrano, to open the double-locked outer door for him. At the sound of Carnesecca and her husband chatting, María Corrano popped her head out of the ground-floor apartment to say hello. There were comments all around about how short the summer had seemed. Now that September was here and the pilgrim visitors had gone, the Monastery would be very quiet. "Too quiet," Jorge lamented. "Not like the old days."

After their good-nights had been said, Carnesecca decided to spend some time in the Chapel before heading up to bed. He was more than usually tired, but he wanted to give thanks at the Altar for the labors of the day. As he climbed the marble stairs to his room at last, he made a mental note to tell Gladstone about Jorge and María and their kindness. By the time he had prepared for bed, he was so tired he almost forgot to treat his eyes with the Isopto Carpine drops Dr. Palacio y Vaca had prescribed for him. Wearily, he reached for the vial, tilted his head back and with a quick movement—he was an expert at this by now—pinched a drop of the solution into each eye.

No sooner had the liquid flooded in than pain—vicious needles of searing pain—stabbed through his eyes and deep into his brain. Pain so awful that he shrieked in agony, lurched to his feet, still shrieking, his hands clutched to his face. "Corrano! Corrano!" He staggered to the door. Had to get it open. Had to get down the stairs. Had to get help. "Corrano!" Again and again he screamed the caretaker's name. The needles of agony were paralyzing him, shutting his brain down, numbing his muscles, making it impossible to move. "Corrano!" He stumbled across the landing toward the top of the marble stairs, but the pain was too much. It was overpowering him. He was losing consciousness, losing all control. There was no way he could go any farther on his own. "Corrano!"

The caretaker tore full tilt out of his rooms just in time to see the worst. The momentum of Carnesecca's rush propelled his body down the dozen marble steps in a terrifying, ungainly, higgledy-piggledy mass of legs and arms, his head banging loosely on the sharp surfaces as he tumbled from step to step. "*¡Aaaeey!*" Corrano streaked forward, arms outstretched, his own screams filling the empty house now and echoing from the marble walls. "*¡Aaaeey! ¡Qué calamidad! ¡Padre! ¡Padre!*" But there was no answer from the mouth that gaped open. No pulse in the madly twisted neck. No sign of life.

And then he saw them. The eyes! *¡Ay, Dios mío!* The eyes! What had happened to this holy priest! What had happened to his eyes!

As summer drew to a close, and vacationers said farewell to the beaches and oleanders of Galveston Island, Windswept House came alive with activity. The mood of the place, however, was not one of gaiety and celebration. Not like the old days.

Christian wound up his work on the road and, with Father Michael O'Reilly as house guest and associate, set about writing his final report for the Slavic Pope. But it was that very chore that flooded his mind again with a sentiment of bitterness that had been a stranger in his life until this curious season he had spent at home.

He showed O'Reilly the map he had prepared, and shared Damien's idea that some upside-down version of religious sacrifice might be at the back of it. Maybe Slattery was right, he said. Maybe there was some theoretical cutoff point between Luciferian thinking and outright dedication to the Prince of this world. But surely the unbroken uniformity of behavior among some hundreds of individual pedophiliac clergymen, many of them unknown to one another—the terrible unity of single and separate acts of violation—surely that must imply obeisance of some kind to the will of one superior intelligence.

It was during these late-summer days, too, that, with his own papal report to prepare, Father Damien finally gave up his good-faith effort to find a bishop who would take him. "The Cardinal of Centurycity controls the National Conference of U.S. Bishops," Slattery grumbled to Chris on his return to Windswept. "And since that's the machine that regulates each bishop, it's no surprise that I've come up empty." Well, not entirely empty. Damien had spent some productive time with Sylvester Wodgila. The Inspector had tracked still more evidence for Slattery's report on clerical Satanists and, like a dog with a bone, he intended to stay at it.

In the midst of all this activity, Cessi and Tricia came home from Ireland to take charge of Windswept House again. Though she was brimming with stories to tell, Cessi's first concern was to restore order to the household schedule. Work was all very well and good, she said, but there would be no more haphazard skipping of meals. And at eveningtime they would all sit down together like a proper family. "That includes you, Father Damien! And you, too, Father Michael!"

Her second urgent concern was to attend to the welcome news contained in a letter from Cardinal Sanstefano. The Holy Father had not only given full approval to her plan to form an underground network of priests, His Eminence wrote, but intended to have it operational as quickly as possible. As Cardinal Protector of the project, Sanstefano would be pleased if Signora Cessi would arrange the necessary independent financing for the Order, begin to address the problem of suitable housing for its members and continue to suggest additional candidates.

That news was almost enough to leaven Cessi's disappointment at the results of her and Tricia's summer in Ireland. She had had such high hopes that the specialists she had been referred to in Dublin would come up with the answer to her daughter's worsening eye ailment. "It all looked so promising at first," she told Chris and the others over one of their first dinners together at Windswept. "The relief Tricia experienced seemed like a miracle. She slept so well. She was able to sketch and paint again. Oh, Chris! I wish you could have seen her!" Cessi reached for her son's comforting hand as she had in years past. "I suppose it was only the Kerry air, though. Anyway—as you can see by her absence from the table tonight—it was a passing thing . . ."

"Don't you worry, Miss Cessi." Her ear cocked as always for talk of the family, Beulah weighed in on the side of hope. "I just been up to her room, an' she's in good spirits. Miss Tricia's a special lady, so don' you get down on things."

As usual, everybody took Beulah's advice to heart. While Chris and Damien and Father Michael spent their days working on their mysterious projects, Cessi spent hours making plans and phone calls. She tracked Cardinal Sanstefano down at his summer retreat to work out details with him. She was in contact with Glenn Roche in New York. As her chief financial advisor, she would rely on him to set up a self-perpetuating, independent fund to finance her network of priests.

Still, Cessi had never been one for solo occupations. Busy though they were, she enticed all three men into her confidence. It was the best way she knew to widen the roster of candidates as rapidly as Sanstefano had asked; and it had its special rewards.

Once Cessi learned the history of Michael O'Reilly at the hands of Jay Jay O'Cleary, she was more than outraged. She was determined that O'Reilly himself should be at the top of her list of candidates. "Nonsense, Father Michael!" Cessi demolished his objections. "How dare you demand that the Pope set everything else right before you let him put your situation in order! In case you didn't know it, this just happens to be the most troubled time for the Church, and the most disharmonious pontificate, since the sixteenth century! And you're being given the chance to be the priest you were meant to be. To be the kind of priest all of us need. All of us, including the Holy Father. So stay angry if you want to. But be smart about it! Be intelligently angry!"

Michael was sufficiently chastened to agree to Cessi's proposal. And Chris took Cessi's battle cry to heart for himself as well. His own anger and resentment at the cynical way he had been used were every bit as justified as O'Reilly's. But Slattery had been right. Provided Lucadamo would agree, the best thing Christian could do to help the Pope would be to double around Maestroianni and find out all he could about Strasbourg. As much as it went against the grain, the best thing he could do would be to deceive while pretending to be deceived.

All in all, then, there was a better balance to things now. With Tricia pitching in as much as she was able, Chris, Damien and Michael were as deeply involved in Cessi's project as in their own work during their remaining days at Windswept. And night after night, gathered in Cessi's sitting room after their family meal, they listened and laughed together at Father Damien's store of tales about the Ireland he had known; about the Land of Saints and Scholars that had nurtured him.

Chris laughed as heartily as all the rest. But he knew what his friend must be going through; and, when they were alone, he shared his thoughts with his mother. No man of Slattery's age, he told Cessi, and no man with his history as a member of a religious Order and an honored personage in the clerical way of life, could be torn from all that as suddenly and unjustly as Damien had, without suffering terribly. Such a violent upheaval had often unhinged the mind, if not the morality, of otherwise strong characters. Gladstone could only imagine, and was grateful, that this time at Windswept was part of Slattery's restoration. These lightsome evenings of storytelling and memories were part of a sorting-out process for Slattery, part of his preparations to deal with the future.

On one such evening, though—it was in early September—the general delight at Damien's tales gave way to Cessi's more recent memories of Ireland. "Ah, Father Damien." The tears of laughter still wet on her cheeks, Cessi cast her mind back over the summer just past. "I wish it were all still the way you remember it."

Not everything in Ireland had changed, Cessi admitted. Never before had she found herself in a land of such undisturbed tranquillity; such purity of air, such benign sunlight; such freshness in foliage and field. Paul's summer home at Liselton had overwhelmed her with its distinctive grace. As at Windswept, so at Liselton she had felt that sure sense of the supernal—an almost tangible surety that those Shannon waters and the ocean beyond opened out to the whole wide world of man, and to all the invisible shores of God's creation.

"The skies," Cessi said, "are never without clouds, yet never cease to be visibly blue. The sun showers borne in on southwesterly winds irrigate the land, but never leave it sodden. So the fields become almost golden with the ripening of wheat, barley and rye. Liselton's orchards and Yusai's kitchen garden were loaded this year with apples and pears, all readying themselves for Hannah Dowd's cooking pots."

As they listened, Cessi's descriptions seemed idyllic to Chris and Damien and Father Michael. Tricia, however, knew otherwise. She had been there, too. She, too, had been captivated by Ireland's wild beauty and the brooding testimony of its ruined monasteries, castles and chapels. With Yusai and little Declan as their guides and companions, the places they had visited—each named for Saints she had never known existed—had filled her imagination. And yet, the sketches that filled her notebook told of the inescapable melancholy that graced the Irish countryside. It was almost too easy to commune with the spirit of Ireland's famed Saints and Scholars who had lived with "No Quarter" as their unspoken motto, and who had died as often as not by the sword of foreign oppressors. But it was almost impossible to find any living embodiment of the faith of those Irish who slept beneath seas of grass, with Celtic crosses rising like stone hands held in prayer to mark their places of rest.

"Perhaps," Cessi mused, "all of that is meant as a divinely arranged memorial to the glory that once was." The abrupt change in Cessi's tone shattered the mood she herself had woven. "And perhaps the modern Irish will never completely neglect or forget or destroy it. But neither do they give a tinker's damn themselves about Heaven and Purgatory and Hell! Attendance at Mass is sparse, the churches have all been modernized beyond recognition. In most places, the Tabernacle is hidden out of sight. Confessionals, the Crucifix, the Stations of the Cross, the statues of Mary and the Saints are rarely seen. In Killarney's magnificent cathedral, the old marble Altar and Tabernacle have been broken into sections and stuffed away in cubbyholes and corners. All those solid objects that bind us to Revelation are being replaced by fakery. It's as if everybody expects life to turn into the fable of Snow White, and the bishops are the Seven Dwarfs whistling a happy tune of independence.

"And as to the clergy!" Cessi threw both hands into the air. "I have to tell you, Father Damien, they are either elderly men who are tired, confused and totally at a loss. Or they are young, theologically ignorant and brashly modernist in their ideas of religious belief and clerical behavior. The younger generation no longer holds any regard for the Church. They have no understanding of the Eucharist as Sacrifice and Sacrament; no idea that it not only gives grace but contains the Author of grace Himself. They are anticlerical and antipapal, and they dislike the Slavic Pope in particular. They no longer even want to be called Roman Catholic.

"The only faith they have is in the almighty American dollar; and in practical terms they have become as morally permissive as so-called Catholics in this country. Physical comfort is what they're after. Compromise has led to acceptance of formerly unacceptable things. And acceptance of compromise has replaced the universal truth of their Roman Catholicism. It's taken a long time, but the cruel ghost of Oliver Cromwell has found a friend in the ghost of Walt Disney. And for the moment, they appear to be winning the battle for Ireland."

His coffee cold and forgotten on the table beside him, Chris glanced at Father Damien. Everywhere, people's lives were being transformed just as Bishop McGregor had said that day in Hardcastle, Kansas. It really was becoming a borderless world. A new human community, independent of national borders, local cultures, local educational systems and local traditions. Independent of the blood ties of the family; independent of all social bonding such as sacramental marriage implies. A community with no geographical location. A community without propinquity, whose commonality resided only in their current, concrete experiences and their undisciplined intuitions. A community isolated from its original sources of knowing, and with no background silhouettes of a greater reality behind the visible, the audible. A global community of phenomenologists.

All of that was bad enough. The worst disillusionment for Cessi had to do with Paul and his family. Yusai, it seemed, had been serious about being received into the Catholic Church. But Paul had arranged for her to be instructed by his friend at Ghent Cathedral, Canon Jadot, who had schooled Yusai in prayers to "Mother Earth," taught her all about "holy meals" and organized "ecumenical dances" with groups of Buddhists and Hindus. "The whole process has left her no nearer to Roman Catholicism than she ever was," Cessi fumed. "Jadot has actually told Yusai that being a good Confucianist is the same as being a good Catholic.

"And as for little Declan, he's the victim of gross neglect on his father's part. He speaks English, French and Flemish as fluently as you please. He can recite all sorts of jingles about pet dinosaurs and baby seals—all of which he learned in religious education classes in Belgium, by the way. Yet he can't recite Catholic prayers in any language. He has a vague idea about Jesus as a man who lived a long time ago, but hasn't a clue about the Sacraments."

In his regret for the beauty lost to Yusai's brilliant soul and to Declan's youthful being, Chris asked what Paul had to say about Declan's ignorance of his faith.

Was it the hint of tears that made Cessi's eyes glisten so behind that little smile? No one was sure. Paul, she said, was more fired up about some ongoing crisis in the EC than about Declan's ignorance or Yusai's conversion.

"Oh, come on, you two!" The seriousness and sadness visible in Chris and Cessi impelled Tricia to turn the conversation to brighter things. "The last time Mother started talking like this, we nearly set out on a thirty-day walking pilgrimage to Rome!"

Cessi was as quick as everyone else to take the cue. Such a special bond of sympathy had grown up among them all during these few days that they vied with one another now in a competition of storytelling that drowned passing time and sorrowful thoughts in new tides of laughter.

It was late in the evening, and Father Damien was just coming to the best part of one of his best stories, when the phone jangled everyone into silence.

"Hold your thought . . ." Chris turned to Slattery as he covered the step or two to Cessi's writing table. "At this hour, it's probably a wrong number."

Within a moment, however, everyone knew it wasn't a wrong number. Chris listened for a long time. When he did speak, his voice was hoarse and his words few. Yes, he said; he would tell Slattery. And he would catch the next flight out. There seemed to be some disagreement about that, but Gladstone was adamant. "I must come," he insisted. "I'll charter a flight if I have to, Giustino, but I must come! Wait for me!"

At the mention of Giustino Lucadamo's name, and given the lateness of the hour, Damien knew the news had to be bad. But there was no way to imagine how bad until Christian turned again, the blood drained from his face, tears streaming down his cheeks.

"It's Father Aldo . . ."

After a few sleepless hours, Chris was up at 4 A.M. He offered Mass alone in the Tower Chapel for the eternal soul of Aldo Carnesecca, and then headed to his rooms to throw a few things into an overnight bag. To his surprise, he found his sister perched on a chair in his sitting room, wrapped in a summer robe and waiting for him.

Her timing might seem strange, Tricia said. But as there was still an hour before Chris had to leave for the airport, she had come to cash in on a promise. "Remember last spring," she asked as she took over the packing chore, "when I said I wanted time with you before you left again for Rome?"

Still half numb with grief, Chris nodded. He remembered.

"Well, what I wanted to explain to you—what I wanted you to understand as a priest—is about my eyes. I had almost decided to let the whole thing go. But the death of your friend in Barcelona—your reaction, I mean—changed my mind again.

"Remember Father Franz Willearts?" Tricia settled back into her chair, and Chris drew another close beside hers. But now he was more puzzled than ever. Father Willearts had been very special for a lot of folks in Galveston during Tricia's years at school. As teacher, confessor and friend, he had seemed the ideal priest. Then one day he had turned up missing. Ran off just like that with a woman, got married to her and ceased to live as a priest.

"I had long since graduated by then," Tricia recalled. "But he had been my confessor and my friend for so long. I was so devastated by what he had done that I made a deal with Christ about it. I was ready to receive the punishment due to Father Franz, I told Him. I asked Him to accept me as a victim, in other words, and to join my victimhood with His own. I told Him to take anything he wanted from me. My life, or any part of my being. But in return, I asked Him to give Father Franz the grace to repent and to come back to his priestly duties again.

"And that's exactly what happened. Shortly after that, I began to feel the first symptoms of what was soon diagnosed as keratoconjunctivitis sicca. Not much later, Father Franz came back to Galveston. Like a lot of other people in trouble, he made a beeline for St. Michael's Chapel, where he asked our beloved miracle worker, Angelo Gutmacher, to help him. It took some doing, but you know Father Angelo! First he managed to regularize Father Franz's priestly situation, and then helped him make good on his decision to devote his life to missions among the poorest of the poor in Africa. We still get word of Father Franz now and again, so I know Christ has kept His end of the bargain. And as you can see, I keep mine as well."

"But . . ." Christian fumbled for words without success. "I never guessed . . ."

"I know." Tricia smiled. "Except for Father Angelo, I never told anyone. Not even Mother, though in a way I think she'd be the first to understand. Anyway, Father Franz wasn't the only one who made a beeline for St. Michael's Chapel. Once I began to feel the real agony of this eye ailment, and once I realized what it might cost me—my sight, and possibly my life—I knew I needed more than medical help. So I went to Father Angelo and asked for his guidance.

"I showed him all the medical records. He checked with the doctors firsthand. He satisfied himself that there's no underlying condition to explain my case, as there usually is for this illness. So he knew. Of all the experts I've seen, only he could understand Christ's acceptance of my offer to make up for Father Franz's betrayal of his sacred vows. From that point on, Father Angelo was much more than my confessor. Until he left for Rome, he was my spiritual guide. Without him, I think I might have been as untrue to my vow as Father Franz had been to his. He trained me in the traditional asceticism of the Church. He showed me how to make my whole life—my person included—into a continuous act of adoration and expiation to the Divine Majesty in this time of wholesale apostasy.

"God's purpose in allowing evil, Father Angelo told me once, is to bring about greater good. He said that in the victory of Christ, each holy victim is victorious. And he said that in the victory of each victim, Christ is again victorious."

Tricia leaned forward and took her brother's hands in both of hers. "From what you and Father Damien told us last night after that phone call, I can only think Aldo Carnesecca knew all about the lessons Father taught me. I can only think Father Aldo's life was a continuous act of adoration. Even though his death was accidental—I mean, even though he didn't die as a victim in that narrow sense—surely he offered every day of his life as a priest to Christ. And surely every day of his life as a priest was another victory for Christ.

"That's all I wanted to say, Chris. That's all I wanted you to understand."

"That's all, is it?" Christian rose from his chair and drew this innocent, uncomplicated, uncomplaining victim soul of Windswept House into an embrace of gratitude and love. Tears—but not the tears of sadness any longer—welled in his eyes. "You put us all to shame, Trish. Faith and constancy like yours amid all the betrayals put us all to shame."

The heat in Barcelona was suffocating. Accompanied by Giustino Lucadamo, Chris stepped into the sparsely furnished room that had been home to Aldo Carnesecca during the last months of his life and opened the two large double windows that looked out on the monastery garden. A few letters lay unopened on Father Aldo's desk beside his wallet and some pages of scribbled notes. His Breviary was there, too, and his Rosary beads. A score or so of books stood on the shelves above the desk. His personal papers were tucked neatly in the drawers. His cassock hung in the wardrobe. His clean linen was folded in a chest. The bed was turned down. It was the room of a man called away suddenly at bedtime. It was hard to believe . . .

As Gladstone moved slowly about the room, Giustino Lucadamo gave him the information he had come to hear firsthand. "The caretaker was badly shaken. But once he was able to gather his wits, the first phone call he made wasn't to the local authorities, but to a number Father Aldo had given him for emergency use."

"Your number in Rome?"

"Just so. But the story he told me was so strange, so out of character for Carnesecca, that I got the Apostolic Delegate in Madrid to alert the locals; but to make it clear that, while I would need their help, this was an affair that was strictly under the jurisdiction of the Holy See. When I arrived a few hours later, the Guardia Civil was waiting outside, but nothing had been touched. Everything was as you see it, except that the caretaker, Jorge Corrano, was kneeling in vigil beside Father Aldo's body at the foot of the marble staircase."

As far as Chris could see, it was a tragic accident that could have happened to anyone.

"Accident my Aunt Fanny!" Lucadamo took a little plastic vial from one of his pockets and plunked it on the desk beside Carnesecca's personal papers. "The immediate cause of death was a severed spinal cord. Simply put, his neck was broken in the fall. But when Father Aldo rushed out of this room—that was the first thing Corrano told me; Carnesecca rushed out shrieking for help—his eyes were being destroyed by a powerful acid. He was in the extremest agony, and totally blind! In my book, that adds up to murder."

Gladstone picked up the innocent looking vial. "Dr. José Palacio y Vaca," the prescription label read. "Isopto Carpine 0.5%. One drop in each eye morning and evening." He unscrewed the cap.

"Don't bother." Lucadamo sat down on the bed. "It's odorless and colorless. But it's not Isopto Carpine. It's a solution of hydrochloric acid. Strong enough to burn its way right through to the brain in a matter of seconds. He hadn't a chance." It was almost too much for Gladstone to accept. Almost incredible. Who would want to kill Father Aldo? Why? And how could anyone have substituted acid for his Isopto Carpine?

The security chief had some of the answers. It wouldn't have been all that hard to switch one vial for another in this deserted place. Routine surveillance by a "pilgrim visitor" would have done the trick. And the substitution might have suggested itself in the first place to anyone with access to Carnesecca's expense vouchers and a little imagination—but that covered a lot of people in the Vatican. So the second question Christian had asked was key. If he could find out why, he would probably know who.

"No, Giustino! I take it back!" Chris was out of his chair now, rooting about in Carnesecca's papers like a madman. "It's not incredible. The diary . . ."

"What are you talking about? We've been through everything. There wasn't any diary."

Gladstone flung clothes from the wardrobe. He took all the linen from the drawers. He took the books from the shelves. He stripped the bed. He even checked Carnesecca's shoes. And all the while he tried to make Lucadamo understand. "After that so-called accident of his in Sicily, Father Aldo told me that wouldn't be the end of it! If he ever had an accident that was successful, he said—those were his exact words, Giustino; I don't know how I could have forgotten! If he ever had an accident that was successful, I was to find his diary and give it to you. He said you'd ferret out the truth. And he said the diary was always with him. 'Find me, find my diary.' That's what he said."

"Did he say anything about what was in the diary? About what made it so important?"

"Carnesecca said the accident in Sicily had nothing to do with the Mafia. He said you had some theory about it. He wouldn't tell me what it was, but he said he thought you might be right for the wrong reasons."

"And? Think, man! Did he tell you anything substantive?"

Gladstone shook his head in frustration. "He said something about a story that went back a long way."

"That doesn't help much!" Lucadamo was more than a little frustrated himself by now.

"Maybe not, Giustino, but . . ."

"*Con permiso.*" The timid voice from the open doorway belonged to the caretaker's wife. "The day is so hot, I made this pitcher of lemonade . . ." While the startled María Corrano surveyed the mess these two visitors had made, Lucadamo took the tray with a smile and set it on the desk.

"Poor Padre Aldo!" Señora Corrano turned to Christian. Clearly she had more than lemonade on her mind, but she cast sidelong glances at Lucadamo and seemed reluctant to speak in his presence.

"Señora Corrano . . ." Chris led María to the chair by the desk and did his best to gain her confidence. Hesitantly she stuttered her way into incoherent apology and explanation.

"Maybe I should have told Señor Lucadamo . . . He's a kind man, too . . . But it was addressed to you, *Padre* . . . He gave it to me just a few days before . . . Padre Aldo . . . He said I was to put it in the mail in case . . . But it's addressed to you, Padre Gladstone. So I thought . . . Jorge and I thought . . ." The good woman extracted a small package from the recesses of her apron. She held it for a few seconds, as tenderly as she might have held the relic of a Saint, and then placed it in Christian's hands.

Even before he opened it, he knew. It was Carnesecca's diary.

For the rest of that afternoon and far into the night, Gladstone forced himself to pore over the record of Father Aldo's long career as a man of confidence in the Vatican. The diary—a worn, leather-bound notebook about the size of any normal volume—was a journal in the strictest sense of the term. In script so tiny it made Christian's eyes swim, terse entries spanned four pontificates. It was line after line of bare-bones, factual happenings. One day was often compressed into a single sentence, and a single page often served to cover several weeks. But nowhere did Chris discover any sign of fear or horror or anticipated violence.

"It's no use." Chris surrendered the diary to Lucadamo over the light breakfast María Corrano prepared for them early the next morning. "I don't even know where to begin."

"Well." Lucadamo flipped through the leather volume. "Father Aldo said the story went back a long way, so I suggest we begin at the beginning. By rights, Father Chris, this diary belongs to you. But why don't I take it with me and make a photocopy? You'll be back in Rome in a couple of weeks. I can return the original to you then. Maybe together we'll come up with whatever it was Carnesecca intended us to find."

"He knew, Giustino." Christian's words were so quiet and unexpected that Lucadamo was caught off his guard. "He would never have let this diary out of his hands, or said what he did to Señora Corrano, unless he'd known. He was so good, so gentle. Yet he knew someone was so determined to get him that he couldn't account for his own safety any longer." Gladstone lapsed into the silence of recent memory. There could be no doubt that each day of Father Aldo's life as a priest had been a victory for Christ, just as Tricia had said. But now Christian knew something more. He knew the truth about his friend's death. He knew Aldo had died as a victim in the narrow sense.

The security chief was grateful for the brief silence, but his thoughts were of another kind. He had no answer for his failure. The horrid images—Father Aldo's agony, his panic, his screams, his bone-breaking fall down the stairs of this monastery—would make up the sludge of nightmares for Lucadamo. Images like that could evoke uncontrollable demons in a man. They could summon the red-eyed spirit of revenge for Carnesecca's murderers.

"He knew, Father Chris." Lucadamo said Gladstone's words back to him. But the rest was left unspoken between them.

PART THREE
Papal Night

XLI

IN A MANNER OF SPEAKING, geopolitics was all there was for the Slavic Pope. Unless you were attuned to him geopolitically, you could have no real understanding of his ecclesiastical behavior, his moral judgments, his public relations policy, his piety and devotions or his interpretation of contemporary history.

More to the point, unless you could see how intricately the twilight of his papacy had been bound up with the fifty-year twilight of the international system known as the Cold War, neither could you appraise the clarity of his understanding of how swiftly the old system had faded into night and of how deftly it was being replaced by another whose landscape he could see as clearly as if a blazing searchlight displayed every detail of its terrain.

During the weeks of his recuperation at Castel Gandolfo some twenty miles from the center of Rome, for once His Holiness obeyed Dr. Fanarote's orders to rest from the usual rigors of his schedule. In relative solitude and tranquillity, he had time and every motivation to review the change—the seeming evolution—that had begun in 1989 to set the world on a new and definitive course.

Never in world history had two such dire and thoroughgoing enemies as the former superpower adversaries of the Cold War become so reconciled and so trustful in such a short time, and with so little ceremony, as the capitalist West and the newly dismembered East. The Pontiff was too dutiful a pastor for the obvious religious significance of such a geopolitical shift to escape him. And he was too fine a geopolitician to doubt that the years since 1989 had been a seeding time for what was now about to wrap itself around the society of nations and the Roman Catholic Church as a universal institution.

Had tragedy not struck him down, Father Aldo Carnesecca would have been the confidant for many of the Holy Father's thoughts during those late-summer weeks. Carnesecca alone had seemed to possess something like a supernatural vision of the Church and the Vicariate of Christ. His loss at this critical moment of His Holiness' pontificate was more than deeply sorrowful. It was irreparable.

Monsignore Daniel Sadowski knew he was no Aldo Carnesecca. But in his fidelity, and in his love and concern for the Slavic Pope, it was he who shared the Pontiff's mind during sessions in the papal study, and it was he who came to know intimately the mounting urgency with which the Pontiff regarded the coming fallout from the definitive settlement between East and West that had been prepared by two dramatic events of the recent past.

The first of those events had been the *Joint Declaration of Twenty-two States* signed in Paris on November 19, 1990. That *Declaration* had told Mikhail Gorbachev's U.S.S.R. that East and West were no longer adversaries. Gorbachev's own top strategist, Georgy Arbatov, had put the case more bluntly—more usefully, in the Pope's opinion—when he had solemnly declared that "Communism is dead." The Cold War was over. The second and far more theatrical event had been the coup d'état in Moscow during August of the following year, when the U.S.S.R. regime of Mikhail Gorbachev was virtually terminated. Gorbachev's resignation had followed on Christmas Day, and the new regime of Boris Yeltsin had come into power.

It was a telling element of the new rapprochement of East and West that, like Tweedledum and Tweedledee, Gorbachev and Yeltsin both insisted that now there was a total break with the Soviet past; that there was no continuity between the former Soviet regime and the new regime. "Indeed," the Pope underscored the significant point to Monsignore Daniel, "the West had to be convinced that this was so."

It was essential as a basis for the economic and financial help expected from the West. Essential, too, for the inclusion of Russia as a member of the institutions to be built for the New World Order. Essential above all for unifying and stabilizing what Gorbachev had called "the European space from the Atlantic to the Urals and on to the shores of the Pacific"; and what Eduard Shevardnadze, dictator of Georgia, described as "the Great Europe, united Europe, from the Atlantic to Vladivostok, the European-Asian space . . ."

Well before the August coup, and like every other deeply informed world-class leader, the Slavic Pope had known that the terrain had been prepared for both Yeltsin and Gorbachev in their new roles. By 1991, Yeltsin had already publicly quit the Communist Party and had publicly challenged Mikhail Gorbachev. It was top-flight theater, and as such it had been witnessed by the Soviets and all the peoples of the West crowded around their television sets. It was during that time that Yeltsin had been treated to the first of several private tours of the United States, tours that had included the Esalen Institute, where he had imbibed the basic principle of the Esalen programming method—"breaking everything down and building it up again." On that and subsequent visits, he was also introduced to a number of American legislators, bankers, industrial CEOs and foundation heads.

Mikhail Gorbachev's future path was likewise smoothed. Even before the August coup, he knew his next location and destination. His was to be a global role on a transatlantic basis. Ultimately, he would be at the center of the Conference on Security and Cooperation in Europe. More immediately, however, his base of operations would be the Gorbachev Foundation—GF for short. Its motto, chosen by Gorbachev: "Moving toward a New Civilization."

As early as April of 1991, his American friends and sponsors had set up the nonprofit nucleus for that Foundation, calling it the Tamalpais Institute of San Francisco. They couldn't decently call it the Gorbachev Foundation while Gorbachev was still the master of all the Russias! But they could—and in May of that year, did—hold a fund-raising dinner at New York's Waldorf-Astoria. There, in the presence of Henry Kissinger, officials of the Rockefeller Brothers Fund, the Carnegie Endowment for International Peace, the Ford Foundation, and the Pew and Mellon Funds all pitched in with a guarantee to supply the Gorbachev Foundation with its start-up bankroll of $3.05 million.

Thus, well before Gorbachev ostensibly quit national Russian politics at the end of that year, plans for his future role were nicely on their way. And not for GF/USA only. A Moscow branch of the Gorbachev Foundation—GF/Russia—would be housed by Yeltsin in the long-established International Lenin School. The ILS offered such advantages as its location at the center of Moscow and its trained working staff of one hundred academics, all provided at government expense.

Within two years of Gorbachev's "ouster," GF/USA had moved into the disused military offices of the Presidio in San Francisco. There, with the fantastic view of the Bay to cheer him, Gorbachev set about his new role in earnest. He launched GF/Netherlands and GF/(Rajiv Gandhi)India. And he formulated plans for Green Cross International, his own version of ecumenical activity for the "spiritual alliance of all true believers in man's earthly habitat." As she had always done, Raisa Gorbachev entered into the spirit of her husband's latest endeavors, including his new ecumenism. Though a convinced atheist, she had even sported a cross around her neck during a recent visit to the United Kingdom.

All told, then, by the time the Pontiff had entered Gemelli Polyclinic, Gorbachev had been well outfitted and perfectly placed for his two main tasks: To promote the political, monetary and cultural unification of "the European space from the Atlantic to the Sea of Japan." And to promote his own new role within the CSCE.

What made the Slavic Pope's geopolitical antennae vibrate during his time of rest and recuperation at Castel Gandolfo were the results he anticipated from that seeding. "Is it not a wonder to behold?" With a wry smile, the Holy Father asked Monsignore Daniel the critical questions. "Is not the wholly new configuration of the once monolithically solid U.S.S.R. a wonder to behold? And are not the bonds being forged between the U.S.A. and the 'new' Russia under the title of 'Partnership for Peace' an even greater wonder? Once there was the Soviet Union. Now, in the blink of an eye, we behold Russia; and we see all of its former component parts, the so-called New Independent States, the NIS. Russia and the NIS, are now described in the West as the CIS. The Commonwealth of Independent States!"

The Slavic Pope and his secretary both knew that "confederation" was a poor translation of the hybrid Russian jawbreaker *"sodruzhetvo,"* which means something like "co-friendship" or "partnership." It was a word that struck the Pontiff as belonging squarely in the Soviet lexicon of benign terms signifying deadly serious intent. Like Nikita Khrushchev's description of an atomic explosion as "a bucketful of sunshine," its very whimsicality seemed sinister. And this seemingly sudden political realignment of sovereign states promised to be no less sinister.

Amnesia was one early component of that realignment. Amnesia about the Cold War had seized all the minds of Western politicians. Amnesia about the Gulag prison camps. Amnesia about the hundreds of thousands of KGB operations—camp commandants; wardens; jailers; torturers; spies; trained assassins; couriers; cryptographers; special assignment militia. Amnesia about the array of special aerodromes, Army divisions, Navy ships, ballistic missiles and logistical equipment under KGB control. Amnesia about the estimated 75,000 carefully placed KGB moles and double agents disseminated throughout the world, particularly in the Americas. Amnesia even about the approximately 35,000 American GIs captured by the Soviets, interrogated by the KGB, but never returned to the United States. In the "gentleman's agreement" between Russia and the U.S.A., a mere change in the name of the KGB had wiped everyone's memory clean.

For the Slavic Pope, minds that could find satisfaction in such an arrangement were thoroughly corrupt. Yet such minds were among the guiding lights of the new society of nations. And with the connivance of those minds, an even more special deal had been worked out. With a wink and a nod from the Western allies, Russia was now allowed to dominate the New Independent States; and to do so in ways that Western democracies had found inappropriate and inconsistent with international law in other members of the society of nations. So it was, then, that when the freely elected President of the Independent State of Georgia, Zviad Gamsakhurdia, tried to act independently of Moscow, his poisoned and bullet-riddled body had turned up in a shallow grave. And so it was that Eduard Shevardnadze, Gorbachev's ally, was now the claimant dictator of Georgia.

Far from decrying such behavior, America, the UN and all major powers had admitted Russia as a player in the global game of politics. Only one example was enough to make that plain. Russians, with their Western allies in London, Washington and Paris, had insisted that Russia's pro-Serbian views be paramount in dealing with the current civil war in Yugoslavia. Clearly, the West could have kept Russia out as defender of the Serbian cause; there would have been a certain advantage in doing so, in fact. Just as clearly, however, greater advantage had been perceived in strengthening Russia's hand.

Collective amnesia about an evil past and connivance in the uses of bloody warfare were not without precedent in history. What was more disturbing by far was that, de facto, the U.S.S.R. was still in its geographical extent and sociopolitical influence. Except for the Baltic States and the Ukraine—or so the Pontiff hoped—the same national security infrastructure of the U.S.S.R. remained throughout the NIS, with the same personnel, the same headquarters, the same privileges and the same methods.

Externally, since 1991 Russia had established a complex network of bilateral treaties and declarations. By the second quarter of 1994, that network had included sixteen European countries. With Yeltsin working the political side, and with Gorbachev working socially and philanthropically, Russia was well on the way to achieving a new Stability Pact between the CIS and all the members of the European Union, as the rapidly expanding EC was now frequently called. Unlike the more clubby European Community, and happily for the new Russia, the EU envisaged itself as encompassing all the states of Europe in the not distant future.

Against such a background, those macromanagement bonds being forged between the U.S.A. and Russia—bonds being promoted aggressively by the new U.S. administration of the nineties under the title of the "Partnership for Peace"—were significant portents of the gravest kind. When His Holiness had first heard the Partnership for Peace mentioned, he had experienced a momentary frisson, as if somebody had stepped on his grave. The parallel was not lost on him between the "partnership" that united Russia with all the New Independent States and the Partnership for Peace now supposedly uniting the United States with Russia.

More than a few times during the summer of his searching review of present realities and imminent threats, the Pontiff commented to Monsignore Daniel that he had to admire the skill of the architects—the "master engineers and facilitators," as Cardinal Maestroianni thought of them—who had managed all this.

Several elements and many familiar names came readily to His Holiness' mind. There was the International Foreign Policy Association, for instance. Based in San Francisco's Presidio, the IFPA had been co-founded by Eduard Shevardnadze and Dr. James Garrison, a bureaucrat with executive experience in the Esalen Institute. Among those working with Garrison were Senator Alan Cranston of California and former U.S. Secretary of State George Shultz.

Then there was the U.S. Committee to Support Democracy in Georgia, the former Soviet Republic. George Shultz was co-chair of this organization, an honor he shared with former President Jimmy Carter, former U.S. Secretary of State James A. Baker III and Carter's erstwhile National Security Advisor, Zbigniew Brzezinski. And now there was the Partnership for

Peace. The big umbrella beneath which the current U.S. administration herded both the U.S.A. and the CIS.

It was small wonder that Russia had now been admitted into the deliberations and decisions of the G-7 Group—the seven most powerful industrialized nations on earth. Small wonder, too, that there was now the obviously intended integration of the U.S. and Russian space programs; of their public educational systems; of the overall logistical structures of their armed forces.

Given the implications of the Holy Father's analysis of the new global realities, it came as no surprise to Monsignore Daniel when, toward summer's end, the Pope sent an urgent message to Father Augustin Kordecki, Abbot of the Hermits of St. Paul, at Jasna Gora Monastery in Czestochowa in Poland.

Father Kordecki's clandestine radio had been a key factor in the dangerous maneuvers between the underground Polish resistance and the Stalinist government of the sixties and seventies. He still maintained that radio and the courier information network established during the Cold War, and to this day, he and his community at Czestochowa functioned as the most accurate source of news about the East. The Hermits of St. Paul sent a perpetual barrage of holy prayer from Czestochowa to the Heavens; but they were also the perpetual recipients of hard facts of life in the "post-U.S.S.R." epoch.

If you wanted to know how many of the original 2,800 Soviet Gulag prison camps still functioned in the nineties, Kordecki could tell you. If the status of former KGB officers interested you, Kordecki had the details. And if you wanted to be in touch with a clandestine papal operative such as Father Angelo Gutmacher without drawing notice to him, Kordecki was your man.

Shortly before the Holy Father was due to return to the Apostolic Palace in Rome, Father Angelo Gutmacher arrived for a couple of days of quiet consultation at Castel Gandolfo. His latest travels had taken him through Russia, Kazakhstan, Georgia, Ukraine and Armenia. He brought information and documentation from such varied sources as Russian Orthodox prelates; the Russian Interior Ministry, or MVD, in Moscow; underground groups; important political offices such as the mayoralties of Moscow and St. Petersburg. He brought copious correspondence from Gorbachev and other personal friends and acquaintances of His Holiness. And he brought a trove of firsthand observations—among them, reports of a new initiative only now becoming evident among the former members of the U.S.S.R. and its European satellites.

In his first and briefest session with the Pope, Gutmacher confirmed the Pope's analysis. "Something new is starting over there, Holiness. It's happening almost in silence. But it's real. You can feel it. The people sense it.

Yet I doubt if even a third of them yet realize what's really happened to their territories and nations—or to themselves as human beings."

"But there are always the exceptions, Father Angelo." The Pontiff turned from the window and its shining blue vista of Lake Gandolfo. "In that part of the world, there are always the ones who know. You've talked to many of them, I'm sure."

"Holy Father, what they're saying over there is that something has been set in stone now. A new system is in place. Most of the people I spoke to don't like what's happened; but they stress to me their sense that East and West have reached a definitive settlement. They use that word all the time, Holiness. Definitive."

By the time the two churchmen sat down together for a more protracted conference, the Pontiff had gone through most of the documents Father Angelo had brought with him. And from the outset, the most important element in their discussion was conveyed by one name. Russia.

"You are aware, Father Angelo, that I must make a papal pilgrimage to Russia. I wanted to go on the eve of Yeltsin's rise to power. But I was not able to elicit the collaboration of my Cardinals. You must realize by now that I have an absolute rule: I must have the agreement and collaboration of my Cardinals in my policies. And this, too, even when it is a matter of the Blessed Virgin."

"And now, Your Holiness?" Gutmacher was beginning to understand why he had been called home so urgently.

"Now, Father Angelo, I must review the whole idea of my pilgrimage in the light of Russia's new international role. So my first question to you is this: is it your opinion that Russia will soon evolve to the point of blocking a pilgrimage by the Pope of Rome to its 'near abroad' territories, to use Yeltsin's expression?"

Gutmacher was frank. "As you imply, Holiness, it's a question of timing. Yeltsin has never been a friend. And Russia's allies in the CIS are inimical to the Holy See, mainly on account of the Patriarch of Moscow and the Patriarch of Constantinople. In spite of all that, though, Holy Father, I think you stand a chance of being invited to visit Russia and Ukraine. The window of time is narrow. And Yeltsin will resist. But if enough moral pressure can be brought to bear through third parties . . ."

"Considering what is at stake, Father Angelo, and however I am able to arrange it, I am resolved to undertake my pilgrimage to the East—my 'Russia trip,' as Cardinal Maestroianni calls it with some disdain."

Gutmacher wasn't in disagreement. Far from it. But, given the Pope's dependence on his Cardinals, it was difficult to see how he could manage to go to Russia.

"I expect there will be a price to pay," the Pope acknowledged. "But every sign convinces me that the time has come to test Heaven's will to the limit in this matter. And besides, Father Angelo"—a mischievous twinkle touched the Pontiff's eyes now—"when it comes to horse trading, I doubt that even Cardinal Maestroianni is a match for our Blessed Mother!"

The days were still lazy and Rome was still largely barren of its major figures when Cardinal Maestroianni welcomed a select group of colleagues to his penthouse apartment.

Seriously disgruntled at having been recalled from the beauties of Stresa, Cardinal Aureatini was the last of the distinguished group to arrive. Like an unwilling Gulliver, he followed the tiny valet past those photographs of Helsinki to His Eminence's perpetually book-strewn study, and considered the group already gathered there. He smiled at Maestroianni himself, and at Cardinal Secretary of State Giacomo Graziani. He greeted the three purported if still unofficial papal candidates—Cardinal Karmel of Paris first; then the newest Cardinal, the handsome Michael Coutinho of Genoa; and, finally, his acerbic Vatican colleague, Noah Palombo. The struggle among those three would eventually have to be settled amicably and behind closed doors. With that thought in mind, Aureatini exchanged a nod with Cardinal Leo Pensabene, the acknowledged Pope-maker in any forthcoming Conclave.

In the high-pressure atmosphere that was bound to hold Rome in a tight grip in the coming months, it had been agreed that nothing must be left to the caprice of partisan politics or the whim of personal ambition, papal or otherwise. Cardinal Secretary of State Graziani, therefore, had felt the need to appoint this small, select ad hoc committee "to assist His Eminence Maestroianni in processing the earliest tallies of the Common Mind Vote." This tally wasn't the real thing, of course. Not quite yet. But once Cardinal Maestroianni could assure Graziani and the others that they were morally assured of a quasi-unanimous Common Mind Vote (CMV) from the bishops of the Church Universal, then all the phases of their plan could be initiated.

The first phase—the pressure of the public and highly publicized CMV—would be used as the trigger for the second. And the second—securing the consent of the Pope to sign the resignation letter—would encompass the third. For that letter had been redrafted so that the Pontiff's signature would make it *De Successione Papali;* the Pontifical Constitution regulating the resignation, voluntary or involuntary, of this Pope.

Thanks in large part to the excellent surveys being done by Christian Gladstone, it was already possible to construct a working model of the CMV and to assess it as the trigger mechanism for the Slavic Pope's resignation. If the early signs were right, it wouldn't be long before the actual vote among the world's bishops would be coming in from the scores of Internal Affairs Committees in the Regional and National Conferences of Bishops.

From everyone's point of view, therefore, it was time for a serious reality check. From Cardinal Graziani's viewpoint in particular, it was time to arrange for a little personal insurance. He could accept the idea of arm twisting and the use of quid pro quos in securing the CMV. But this ad hoc committee would assure that, prima facie, all would be correct in form; all would be legitimate in that sense. And it would ensure that others could be named as responsible in the event of a fiasco. The Cardinal Secretary of State was going to be nobody's patsy.

Cardinal Palombo had a bolder reason for an early check on the status of the Common Mind Vote. If these early tallies turned out as Maestroianni expected, it would be Palombo's signal to unleash the pressure moves he had in store for the Slavic Pope.

As for Cardinal Maestroianni, it was reward enough that his labors to galvanize the bishops into a quasi-unanimous CMV were about to come to full fruition. He had no doubt that this preliminary head count would be a successful dry run of the actual CMV. The real thing would be a simple matter of directing his network of colleagues, friends, appointees, disciples, dissidents and acquaintances in the many provinces of the Church and in the many lands and nations that had been His Eminence's bailiwick for so long.

Within hours of Aureatini's tardy arrival, everyone present had his wish. "All we lack now"—Maestroianni gathered up the tally estimates with deep satisfaction—"are the final episcopal surveys Father Gladstone will bring with him from the United States."

"And when will that be, Eminence?" Cardinal Palombo was intent on timing.

"Within the week, Eminence. Barring the unforeseen, we should be ready for the public spectacle of the CMV by spring, as planned."

On the second day of Father Gutmacher's visit to Castel Gandolfo, the subject of population control took center stage in the Pope's general review of conditions in the East. Soon after his return to Rome, as he told Gutmacher by way of background, the Pontiff was scheduled for an important conversation with Bischara Francis, the head of the United Nations Fund for Population Administration. And not long after that, a U.S. envoy by the name of Gibson Appleyard would be paying a second visit to the papal study.

"The first time around, Mr. Appleyard and I had an interesting chat about Holy See policy with regard to Russia. This time around, like Signora Francis, his concern is Holy See policy with regard to global population."

"Your Holiness' policy is hardly a secret," Gutmacher offered.

"Exactly, Father. So it looks like I'll be in for some serious international arm twisting." A few more bouts of arm twisting were the least of the Pontiff's concerns. "Let me be plain about this matter, Father Angelo." The Pontiff stood up to stretch his legs. "The American administration is insistent on pushing population control universally with abortion, contraception and all the other means at its disposal. And into the bargain, the Chinese and Thai experiments in forced population control have shown that, by draconian means, population growth can be reduced to zero without raising the standard of living. Those who have the money and the power, in other words, have found out the technique to maintain large areas of our world in a state of economic backwardness as a source of raw materials and what amounts to slave labor.

"I have not looked for this imbroglio with the American administration." The Pontiff's face darkened. "But I have made it clear to all the agencies of the Holy See, and to all of its representatives, that I will not sanction or allow anyone to back the artificial limitation of births, or even to propagandize the idea of limiting families to one or two children. I will tell Bischara Francis and UNFPA that. I will tell Gibson Appleyard and his President that. This is a battle we must fight.

"I know the enemies I'm up against in the West," the Pontiff concluded the brief outline of his situation. Powerful organizations like the World Bank, the Draper Fund and the World-Wide Fund for Nature and others were all quite openly genocidal in their intent. What His Holiness wanted to know was whether Gutmacher had seen evidence of any change—any worsening was what he meant—in Russia's policy of population control.

"The change is more in degree than in substance, Holiness. But speaking of draconian means . . ." Gutmacher reached into one of his pockets and came up with a videocassette tape he had brought back with him. "It's a sales presentation, I suppose you could say. It was prepared by the Moscow International Institute of Biological Medicine in conjunction with the Russian Center of Perinatology and Obstetrics. And what they're selling is their new prowess as mass-market abortionists. Between them, these two institutes now attract big sums of needed foreign capital into Russia and produce big profits for their American investors."

Grim-faced, the Pontiff watched Father Angelo insert the tape into the VCR and then listened to the voice-over explain how these Moscow-based medical centers now acted together as "the largest bank of medical raw materials in the world . . ."

The sales patter continued as the camera panned over nothing less than an assembly line of well-formed babies being aborted alive; dismembered, sorted and packed, part by part, in neat plastic sacks; then frozen in categories—brains, hearts, lungs, livers, kidneys, glands. The final scene showed special containers being loaded for speedy transport to foreign markets, like Beluga caviar.

One early sequence so shocked the Pope that he cried like one of those crying babies as he watched a woman—"the midwife," said the voice on the tape—hold up a freshly delivered infant boy still attached to his umbilical cord. He watched the baby react with cries to the cold of the operating room. Watched tiny hands shiver toward yet blind eyes while the umbilical cord was cut. And he watched as the infant was handed over—"to a surgeon," said the voice on the tape—to be dissected, alive and screaming, into "useful parts."

The Pope was too horrified to speak for some time after the tape had ended. Too horrified; and too stunned by the parallel between the gross, organized, market-oriented atrocities he had watched and what he knew had been predicted in the Fatima message of 1917. Surely he had just seen the very hoof of Satan. If Fatima meant anything, therefore—if Christ's Mother was to keep her promise of 1917, and if his own pontificate was to have as large a part in the conversion of Russia and in establishing a new reign of peace in the world as the Blessed Virgin had indicated to him in 1981—then nothing could be allowed to stand in the way of his Russia trip this time. Not the American government. Not the UN or the EU or the CIS. Not his Cardinals. Not any power on earth.

XLII

SO CHANGED did Rome seem to Christian Gladstone when he and Damien Slattery returned in mid-September that he felt off balance, like a sailor who had been too long at sea.

He put it down to natural things at first. Carnesecca's death hit him all the harder here; Rome would be a harsh and coarser place without him. It became all the more coarse when he was welcomed back as a member of the Angelicum family, while Slattery—an outcast among his Dominican brothers now—had to be housed at the Holy Father's pleasure as a permanent resident in a Vatican guesthouse, the Casa del Clero off the Piazza Navona. Insult was only added to injury when Father Bartello, the new Rector of the Angelicum, assigned Slattery's old quarters to Gladstone—"Courtesy of His Eminence Maestroianni," the Rector told Chris.

Within hours of his arrival at the Angelicum, though, Christian began to realize that the change he sensed had little to do with personal distress, and everything to do with the queer ecclesiastical and political atmosphere that had settled like smog on the Eternal City. "I'm not an accomplished Roman." Chris practically accosted Slattery when the two met before dawn on their second day back. Reports in hand, and with Christian grumbling all the way, the two friends headed for their first brief meeting with the Holy Father. "I know I'm not capable of the perceptions that were second nature to Father Aldo. But there's nothing subtle about the scuttlebutt making the rounds at the Angelicum."

He told Damien how students and faculty members alike gossiped about His Holiness as a lame-duck Pope. It was painful to hear their pitying remarks about "*il vecchio Papa,* the old Pope." But it was downright infuriating to scan the magazines and journals with their speculation about the Holy Father's resignation, about where he would live and the cost of his keep, what his title would be, what sort of an apostolate he would have, what degree of authority he would enjoy, what changes his successor would introduce.

Published speculation of that sort wasn't entirely new to Gladstone, or to Slattery either. Even in the States, editorial commentary along that line had spilled over from Roman Catholic publications into the secular press. But here, it seemed, the coverage had escalated into an onslaught. It didn't take an accomplished Roman to figure out the meaning of such a relentless commentary. For Chris Gladstone's money, it meant that for an identifiable section of clerical Rome and the Vatican bureaucracy, the Slavic Pope no longer counted as a formidable factor. It meant that those who were desirous of change were actively fomenting and nourishing a consensus that death or resignation and retirement would soon remove the Slavic Pope from the papacy.

"It means," Slattery interrupted as the pair slipped into the still deserted Vatican Secretariat, "that those who desire a change are tinkering with the grid on which power in papal Rome is transmitted."

When Monsignore Daniel Sadowski welcomed them to the fourth floor of the Apostolic Palace and accompanied them into the Pontiff's private study, it was a joy for Gladstone and Slattery alike to see His Holiness well again after his operation. It was like balm for their souls to kneel and kiss his papal ring. To hear the genuine warmth of his greeting and sense his mental vigor and strength of purpose made them grateful he was still alive, still their Pontiff, still their visible source of hope.

The little group settled into a circle of chairs near the window where they could see the early light creep over the rooftops of Rome. The Pontiff chatted for a few minutes about the general status of his returning collaborators—about health and family and associates; about their impressions of Rome after their long absence. There was talk of Carnesecca as well, but Chris saw no reason to mention the riddle of Father Aldo's diary. And, like the elephant in the room that nobody sees, the current gossip about the Pope wasn't mentioned either.

When the catch-up conversation turned inevitably to general political developments, Slattery asked about the situation in Eastern Europe.

"It's promising if you are one of the architects of the New World Order," the Pope replied. "But it's a bleak outlook for Christianity. They intend to build a new Europe from the Atlantic to the Sea of Japan, but without the faith of old Europe. My recent correspondence with Mikhail Gorbachev has been enlightening. All has been readied."

"For what, Holiness?" Christian made no bones today or any day about his geopolitical ignorance. "Readied for what?"

The Pope guessed what was behind the question. "For a different Europe from the Europe your brother helps administer, Father Christian. For a different U.S.A. from the country you were born into. For a different world from the world redeemed by Christ." The Pope cut his analysis short. In all likelihood, he realized, Gladstone and Slattery would not be able to envisage the new landscape until they came face to face with it. "Let us talk of this another day. It is time for us to turn to the urgent matter of Father Damien's status. As long as I am here, Father"—the Pope reached for a folder lying on the table beside him—"you will not lack a home and work . . ."

Maybe the queer atmosphere of Rome had gone to Christian's head, but when it became clear that the Pontiff wasn't going to mention Slattery's failure to find a bishop willing to incardinate him, he fell victim to a sudden flood of impatience. A promise like that is not what Damien deserves from you, Holiness, Gladstone said in his head. He's been through hell for your sake, Holiness. Supposing all the gossip is right, Holiness. Suppose you die overnight, Holiness. What then? He's suffering this dreadful ostracism—he's been thrown to the dogs, in fact—because he's faithful to you, Holiness. How can you allow that, Holiness?

In the next instant, however, Christian's vehemence turned to chagrin. Damien, it seemed, was to take over supervision of the new underground network of priests whose formation had kept Cessi so busy lately at Windswept House. The new post would be nothing like heading up the great Dominican Order. But at least Chris felt there would be some protection for Damien in the fact that no less powerful a figure than Cardinal Sanstefano of PECA had signed on as Protector. And it didn't hurt that Cardinal Reinvernunft of CDF had approved the rule for the Order.

"A clear and simple rule, as you will see." The Pontiff handed the folder to Slattery. "Of course, you will be traveling to the United States on a fairly frequent schedule—perhaps one week out of four."

"Yes, Holy Father." The assignment was obviously grist for Slattery's mill. "But it also means I will be in Rome, and at Your Holiness' disposal, for the other three weeks."

His satisfaction at Damien's enthusiasm plain to see, the Pontiff reached out at last for the reports the two priests had prepared for him. "This may be a turning point." The Pope thumbed the pages of both volumes as he spoke. "Great changes may come about now . . ." With no more than a glance at his watch, Sadowski reminded the Holy Father that the day's schedule was pressing in on them. "I won't have a moment today to start reading, I'm afraid. Cardinal Palombo is coming this morning with representatives of the Jewish Ecumenical Community of Dijon. They will be followed by ten American bishops . . ."

Christian winced inwardly as the Pontiff rattled off the names of the prelates whose turn it was to give their Pope an accounting of their dioceses over the last five years. All ten were from the East Coast, and all figured in Christian's report. Ideally, the Pope should know beforehand the distressing information documented about them. Given the obvious press of time, however—or was that no more than a cover for his own weakness?—Gladstone let the moment pass.

". . . and then, before I welcome my bishops again for dinner, I must have a very important conversation with Bischara Francis, who has come to plead the cause of the United Nations Fund for Population Administration."

Slattery was beginning to wonder if there would ever be a bright spot in the papal schedule again, when the Pontiff told them of plans for a brief pilgrimage to the Holy House of Loreto in central Italy.

According to tradition, this was the actual house where Jesus had lived his hidden years with Mary and Joseph at Nazareth; according to legend, it had been transported to Loreto in the thirteenth century by angels. His Holiness confided that he had long wanted to add his name to the long list of Popes who had visited the Holy House. But it was less his words than the look of expectation in his eyes that told of the Pope's deep devotion to the Holy Family. "Before I leave for Loreto"—the Pontiff still held the reports in his hands—"I will study this material with great care. Give me some days. Then we will get together for a full discussion."

Gladstone and Slattery left the papal study with hearts high. His Holiness had spoken of their reports as "a turning point" and of his expectation that "great changes may come about now." That could only signal his intent to bring his Curial Cardinals and his disobedient, recalcitrant and erring bishops into line and to elicit more willing collaboration from his Vatican officials. A turning point, indeed!

Monsignore Daniel's thoughts were of a different sort as he watched the two priests head for the elevator. After their long absence, he knew there was no way they could gather the seemingly disparate strands of this morning's conversation into one cohesive fabric. Nevertheless, such conversation meant that the Fatima mandate was foremost in the Pontiff's mind now. According to Fatima, the fate of the world would depend on Russia. If great changes were to come about, then surely the Holy Father expected his pilgrimage to the East to be the turning point.

In all likelihood the Pope had wanted to share some of his thoughts on that subject, and had been disappointed that time hadn't permitted him to do so today. And yet, Daniel reflected as he closed the door to the hallway, there were compensations. Perhaps Gladstone and Slattery had attained no real vantage point within the geopolitical loop; no deep understanding of the subject most dear to the Pontiff's heart and most constantly on his mind. But they did share the one trait that made faithful service possible. They believed in this man's holy office, the papacy.

Cardinal Noah Palombo was his usual taciturn self as he led seven delegates of the Jewish Ecumenical Community of Dijon into one of the reception rooms of the Apostolic Palace for their meeting with the Slavic Pope and Monsignore Sadowski. Beyond the required introductions, His Eminence had nothing to say. At least not directly. Brother Jeremiah was the spokesman. Like the other six delegates, he was a bearded man clad in a white ankle-length robe. He explained to the Holy Father that they wished him to hold an ecumenical service in St. Peter's Basilica as an act of reparation for Christian responsibility and culpability in the Hitlerian Holocaust.

The Pontiff fixed his gaze on Palombo as he listened to Brother Jeremiah. Try as he might, he could not get the Cardinal to look him in the eye; but he knew Brother Jeremiah's proposition had come from His Eminence's mind; that this was another piece of mischief on Palombo's part; another turn of the screw; another way of saying to the Pontiff, "We also run the Church; Peter is not supreme."

Finally, His Holiness turned from the Cardinal and began to address Brother Jeremiah's specific proposals one by one. The Pontiff said he did not think such an ecumenical service should be held in St. Peter's. Brother Jeremiah himself had included among his proposals the removal of any Cross or Crucifix during the ceremony; both symbols, he said, evoked painful memories for Jews. But there were so many Crosses and Crucifixes in St. Peter's that such an idea was impractical. "And," His Holiness added with another unreturned look at Cardinal Palombo, "it is also impermissible."

In fact, the Pontiff thought a memorial concert would be a more fitting event. Ecumenical services implied that the participants desired and prayed for eventual union with each other, and His Holiness did not think this was the desire or the intent of the Jewish Community. As to the site for such a concert, His Holiness felt the huge reception hall built by a recent papal predecessor would be suitable. It stood right beside St. Peter's; and it contained only one Cross, which could be temporarily shifted to a closet.

Once such points were clarified, the delegates accepted His Holiness' suggestion of a memorial concert. "The Shoah Memorial Concert"—Brother Jeremiah came up with the name on the spot—a fitting name that encompassed images of ravage and destruction, of waste and terrible horror.

His Holiness rose and shook hands with each smiling member of the Dijon delegation. "My personal secretary, Monsignore Sadowski, will be at your disposal. But His Eminence will be in charge of the event. He will be working with the Governor of Vatican City and the Cardinal Vicar of Rome, of course."

That was the only time—a fleeting second—when Palombo lifted his head and gave one steady look into the Pontiff's eyes. What that look was meant to convey was anyone's guess. But what the Pontiff saw left him with a sense of shock greater than the Cardinal's malign contempt had ever sparked in him. Had he been a man disposed to fear, it would have been baleful. As it was, it brought to mind how Damien Slattery had described the look in the eyes of those completely possessed by the demon.

"That was what I saw in His Eminence's eyes, Monsignore," the Pope confided to Sadowski when the visiting party had left. "A completely alien look. It was as though I was facing a hollow man; a total stranger with whom I had never exchanged a single word."

Chris Gladstone's schedule that day was no more pleasant than the Holy Father's. The time had come for him to begin his double game as a mole and a deceiver.

No sooner had he set foot again in Cardinal Maestroianni's office than His Eminence enveloped him in a genial welcome and sat him down beside his desk. The preliminaries were brief—Maestroianni hoped that Gladstone wasn't overtired after his journey and that his new quarters at the Angelicum were to his liking. Brevity and the implied disdain for Damien Slattery aside, however, every word was obviously intended to make the younger man feel like a long-lost son. Like a favored intimate. Like a Sancho Panza. Then, it was down to business.

Ripples of satisfaction soon filled the atmosphere as Maestroianni went through the packed envelopes Christian had brought back with him from America. "Excellent! . . . Excellent, my dear Father Gladstone! . . . Just the material we need! . . ." When he had concluded his preliminary reading and folded everything away, the aging Cardinal rested his elbows on the arms of his chair, his hands clasped beneath his chin. It was a solemn moment for him. In all probability, this young priest—so surprisingly able for an Anglo-Saxon—would be the last disciple he would prepare for service in the Process. "It is about time, my dear Father," Maestroianni began quietly, "that I tell you what we have launched. First, let me ask you discreetly if you've seen the Holy Father since your return?"

"Yes, Eminence. Briefly."

"Your impression?"

"It's hard to say, Your Eminence . . ."

"Yes. It's always hard to tell about him." The Cardinal seemed satisfied but pensive as he cocked his head sideways at Gladstone like a wise old owl about to hatch an egg. That impression, it turned out, wasn't far wrong. For the better part of thirty minutes, Christian was treated to a stunning revelation of Maestroianni's soul. With absolute candor, His Eminence laid out the extravagant conceptions that had animated his mind for so many years and that had exacted from him the pitifully heavy price of his faith. The little Cardinal's eyes shone as he shared the dream of his belief in the Process as the true force behind the forces of history. He seemed electrified with energy as he spoke of the need to suppress divisiveness and to develop the machinery for a cooperative spirit in the world.

"Tell me, Father Gladstone. In your academic career, have you read much about the great French statesman Robert Schuman?"

Christian was still reeling inwardly at how completely Cardinal Maestroianni had been stripped not only of his Romanism but of any trace of Catholicism. Not once in his paean to the forces of history had he mentioned Christ, much less the Blessed Mother or the Apostles or the Fathers of the Church. He was at a loss to understand why His Eminence asked now about such an outstanding Catholic as Robert Schuman; but he allowed as how he knew as much as most.

"Then, my dear Father"—the Cardinal came down to cases—"you must know how dedicated Schuman was to a new ideal for Europe. And you know enough to appreciate the significance of an ecumenical gathering that took place on the occasion of the official Schuman Memorial celebrations in Strasbourg early last year . . ."

Chris felt his heart skip a beat. Was it to be so easy, then? Was the Cardinal going to spill the beans, just like that, about the Strasbourg meeting Slattery had told him about at Windswept? Was he going to hear about the plans that had made him, and his brother, too, into such simple-minded pawns in Maestroianni's antipapal schemes?

"Are you all right, Father Gladstone?" His Eminence offered his visitor some water from the carafe on his desk. "You look pale."

"I'm fine, Eminence. Just the excitement of the moment . . ."

"Perfectly understandable." No stranger to such excitement himself, the Cardinal relaxed again. "I see you are quick to comprehend important matters. Let me come to the point. As a man of experience, you will not be surprised to hear that we are actually engaged in the transition between two pontificates. The present one, which clings to outworn ideas, and a new one, which will be more attuned to the enlightened future awaiting us. As loyal sons of the Church, we must all do our best to facilitate that transition. When I say 'we,' of course I mean the Church of Christ in the persons of his bishops, the successors of the Apostles. Peter and his brethren, to use the old phrase." The Cardinal cocked his head as if to elicit a response.

Unwilling to trust his tongue, Chris stared at Maestroianni, hoping that neither the expression in his eyes nor the color that flooded his face—a flush of anger, a blush of disgust—would betray him. At last, he managed to nod his head.

Apparently that was enough. Patiently and methodically, Maestroianni explained the basic concept of the Common Mind Vote, the Resignation Protocol, the link between the two, and the urgent timing of the plans under way. He spoke of the magnificent contribution Gladstone's work had made to the CMV. He expressed his debt of gratitude to Paul Gladstone for his timely interventions at the EC on behalf of individual bishops. "Pivotal work, Father," the Cardinal cooed with a throaty chuckle. "Blood is thicker than water, eh?"

That was not to be the end of the matter, but only the beginning. So certain was His Eminence of Gladstone as a young man of perception and promise that he had nominated the good Father for the grade of domestic prelate. "That touch of violet in your clothes and robes works wonders in this city and elsewhere."

"Your Eminence is too kind." Christian all but choked on the words. The last thing he wanted was to deck himself out in the violet-colored buttons and robes of a monsignore.

"Not at all, *Padrecito.*" The warm familiarity of that form of address on the Cardinal's lips wasn't lost on Gladstone. "I am presuming you will continue to work with us. We do still have some important loose ends to tie up . . ." Maestroianni was about to go into those loose ends in some detail when Monsignore Taco Manuguerra knocked at the door.

"I know you want no interruptions, Eminence." Manuguerra was all afluster. "But Professor Channing . . ."

Annoyed at what he regarded as a necessary evil, the Cardinal reached for his phone and signaled for Christian to remain where he was. "A pleasure to hear from you, Dr. Channing. . . . Yes, I was just speaking to a young colleague on the subject. . . . Yes, yes; you have understood correctly. The CMV is quite on schedule. . . . What's that, Professor? . . . Supplemental initiatives. . . . I see. . . . Yes, Dr. Channing. Why don't we leave it like that? The moment we're ready for definitive action, you will be the first to know. . . . Well, of course, if you feel the need to come to Rome. . . ."

For a moment, Maestroianni seemed to forget Gladstone was there. It was a fleeting thing, and almost unheard of in a man so adept at *romanità;* but, for the first time in his association with the little Cardinal, Chris thought he saw the flicker of open enmity.

"Do forgive the interruption, Father." His Eminence returned to form the moment he hung up. "Now, where were we? Ah, yes. The loose ends that must be tied up."

For the moment, those loose ends consisted of certain bishops in Spain and Portugal who needed a visit. Father Gladstone would find their names and the usual array of background information about them in the first of the folders the Cardinal handed him. In the second folder, he would find the tallies of the CMV to date, and a copy of the Resignation Protocol. "Study those, Father, and you will have a better understanding of the tactics we are using. Keep me abreast of your work on all fronts. My door is open for you day and night."

Assuming he had been dismissed, Chris tucked the two folders into his briefcase and rose from his chair.

"A moment." Maestroianni glanced at his watch. "I'm expecting two visitors right about now. Like you, *Padrecito,* they realize the need for radical change. I want you to meet them. Say a brief hello, and then be on your way."

The first man, dressed in the flowing white robes of a Dominican, was introduced to Christian as Father George Hotelet, an honorary member of the Pontifical Academy of Sciences and General Secretary of the International Theological Commission. "Father also functions as a theologian for the papal household," Maestroianni expanded on Hotelet's credentials. The second man, a layman, had the bearing and the name of a distinguished Italian aristocrat. "Dr. Carlo Fiesole-Marracci at your service, *Reverendo.*"

Again Maestroianni supplied the credentials. "Dr. Carlo is current President of the Pontifical Academy of Sciences and an outstanding demographer. And a very good friend."

Always adept at bringing trusted colleagues together, His Eminence explained that Father George and Dr. Carlo, along with six other experts at the Pontifical Academy, had just completed a superlative study of population control and demographic trends. "You will read it soon, Father, and with great satisfaction."

Equally adept at dismissing colleagues at the proper moment, Maestroianni made it clear that this was the cue for Gladstone to take his leave.

It was a hefty walk from the Apostolic Palace to Lucadamo's office in the Porta Sant'Anna. Just what he needed, Chris decided. He wanted time to himself after his meeting with Maestroianni.

Until today, it had been easy to dislike His Eminence and let it go at that. But it wasn't so simple now. The Cardinal's sermon on the bleak, inhuman, faceless thing called the Process forced him to wonder. It was disheartening to see a man so capable, so high up and so far gone. But when he began to ask himself what had happened to Maestroianni's faith, Chris wondered if the same might not happen to him. How could anyone working in present-day Rome manage to stay in God's grace?

In a mood somewhere between sadness and exasperation, and with no answers for his questions, Chris arrived at the Porta Sant'Anna, made his way through the Vatican's administrative complex to Lucadamo's office and found Slattery and the security chief already in deep discussion.

"I can't put my finger on it, Giustino . . ." Damien acknowledged Chris's entrance with a nod. "The Holy Father seems full of life, while burdened by life. He seems ready for combat, but retiring and mild. There was real fire in him when he told us about his meeting with Bischara Francis, but when he mentioned Cardinal Palombo and the Jewish Ecumenical Community of Dijon, there was a look in his eye . . ."

"You can't blame him for that," Lucadamo answered. "That Ecumenical Community is full of antipapal snakes. But you needn't worry about His Holiness' health. The doctors say his pontificate is good for another ten years."

"Not if Cardinal Maestroianni has anything to say about it." Chris settled into the empty chair beside Slattery and explained the details of the

Common Mind Vote of the bishops exactly as Maestroianni had explained it to him.

Lucadamo took in every detail. He knew that Strasbourg had been the launch for some sort of organized vote by the National and Regional Conferences of Bishops. He knew relations between the Pope and his Curial enemies had reached an all-time low, with both sides hardened in their attitudes. He had watched disintegration take its toll on the Holy Father's control of the levers of power in the Vatican bureaucracy. Like Slattery and Gladstone, he had read all the commentary that removed any element of surprise or shock from the idea of a papal resignation. And of course he knew about the resignation letter itself that had been drafted and redrafted.

But until now, he hadn't understood the mechanics of the CMV. He hadn't discovered how it was to function as the heart of the assault on the papal office; how the public spectacle of a vote of no confidence from his bishops, together with all the other pressures and humiliations Maestroianni and his colleagues continually piled up against him, would be engineered to convince the Slavic Pope that he could no longer effectively govern his Church. "And the culmination of all that," Lucadamo finished Gladstone's explanation for him, "will be the Pontiff's signature on the Resignation Protocol. Is that the way they have it figured?"

"Pretty much."

"Do you have a timetable yet, Father?"

"Spring is their target date. And, thanks to me, the Common Mind Vote is a sure thing." Gladstone popped his briefcase open as he spoke and handed the early CMV tallies to Lucadamo. "I'll need this material back. I have to have it down cold before I see the Cardinal again."

Lucadamo gave the CMV tallies to a secretary to copy. Then, turning to Gladstone and Slattery again, he allowed as how Maestroianni always seemed to have the Devil's own timing on his side. "If the Holy Father's present plan works out, he could be in Russia at about the time the CMV is supposed to take place."

"Russia be damned!" Slattery boomed his objection. "The Holy Father will have to scuttle this CMV plot right now!"

"We'll see, Father Damien. He's dead set on the Russia trip, but you'll have your chance to convince him. He's told me he has your reports. I'll be getting copies myself as soon as Monsignore Daniel gets them over to me. He plans to have a meeting with all of us as soon as he's read them through. In the meantime, you're to mention his Russia trip to no one. Either of you!"

Despite Slattery's outburst and Lucadamo's startling news that the Pontiff had put his plans for a pilgrimage to Russia into high gear, Chris was deep in his own thoughts. "There's a man called Channing. He's a doctor or a professor of some sort. That's all I know about him, except that he's somehow tied up in the CMV and that he has some supplemental initiative up his sleeve."

"Anything else?"

"Maybe." Chris asked Slattery about a Dominican by the name of George Hotelet. "He and the current head of the Pontifical Academy of Sciences turned up in Maestroianni's office just as I was on my way out. His Eminence is all excited about a study they're doing on population control."

"Father Georgie?" Damien scowled. "Yes. I know him. Butter wouldn't melt in his mouth, but he's definitely part of the antipapal cabal. If George is in on anything—say, this study by the Academy of Sciences—it's bad news for the Pope and for the Church."

That figured, Chris thought dejectedly. But he couldn't help wondering aloud what Father Aldo Carnesecca would think of him now. "Wouldn't he think," Christian answered his own question with another, "that it smacks of insanity that, for the sake of the Pope and the glory of God, I'm turning into a first-class deceiver? And wouldn't he think it smacks of moral cowardice that, for the foreseeable future, I'll be a brown noser to men like Hotelet?"

"You must be out of your mind!" Slattery rounded on Chris. "How the blazes do you think Father Aldo got through the fifty years of his Vatican career without a pratfall? He did everything he had to do in order to survive, and to do whatever good he could do within the system!"

Slattery's outburst hit Chris like a bucket of ice water. It brought him face to face again with the fact that his wise and gentle friend had finally run out of ways to survive. And it brought him back to the questions about Father Aldo's murder.

Lucadamo didn't need much prompting. The red-eyed demon of revenge was very much with him. "We've made copies of his diary." Giustino took the worn leather volume from a locked drawer and returned it to Gladstone. "I've gone through several years of entries myself, and I have a couple of my best men on it as well. But so far there's nothing that stacks up as a motive for murder."

"It has to be here, Giustino. Whatever Aldo wanted us to find has to be here."

Lucadamo was still prey to the grisly images of Carnesecca's agony. But he confessed that it wasn't only murder now that drove him to find the key. Above all, he said, it was the method. "Whatever he wanted us to find—whatever it was he saw—was so important that it wasn't enough just to kill him. It was as if some maniac wanted to burn his eyes out first for having seen it. As if someone wanted to burn every shred of memory from his brain."

Once dinner was over and the exhaustive personal interviews with his American bishops were behind him at last, the Slavic Pope took advantage of the first quiet moments of his long day to draft a handwritten reply to the latest letter from Mikhail Gorbachev. He had just settled down to that task when, pen in hand, he let himself be tempted by the two reports Monsignore Daniel had left on the corner of his desk. "I wonder . . ." He breathed the words half aloud to himself.

According to those ten East Coast bishops, their individual dioceses were vibrant with goodwill for the Holy Father and brimming with exhilarating examples of the religious renewal His Holiness encouraged and recommended. To hear those worthies talk, in fact, their dioceses were financially sound, internally cohesive, faithful to the directives of their bishops and pastors; and they were in the very forefront of zeal and religious observance. Of course, the Pontiff took such talk with a grain of salt. But what he didn't know was whether the bishops were pulling the wool over their own eyes or were consciously engaged in a facade of devotion to the papacy.

"I wonder . . ." He decided to dip into the thicker of the two reports. It was Gladstone's, as it happened, and its information was laid out with the care of a true academician. And sure enough, each of the visiting American bishops turned up in the inclusive index of names and subjects.

"We concentrate on the quality, not the quantity, of our priests, Holy Father . . ." So the Bishop from Albany had said. But according to Gladstone's report, that same bishop declared constantly that the old concept of priesthood was "obsolete"; that priests no longer needed "the medievalism of celibacy," that homosexuality was a "perfectly acceptable" way of life. The Pontiff shook his head like a dog emerging from a pool as he tried to shed the memory of the pious-sounding voices of the other bishops whose personal mores and moral teaching were outlined in Gladstone's report. He winced at the gullibility those men presumed in him. But inner hurt wasn't even the half of his suffering now. There was in him a cold, repulsive horror at his own guilt.

Was he not the one ultimately responsible to the Almighty? What right had he, then, to ask if the bishops were pulling the wool over his eyes? Did justice not demand that he ask another question? Instead of simply being deceived all this time, had he conveniently shut his eyes? Had he conveniently told himself, and all who asked, that such corruption of faith and morals in the hierarchy was ineradicable at this time? That the very splendor of the truth would dispel all the errors?

"Holiness . . . ?"

Though Monsignore Daniel barely breathed the word, the Pontiff was startled at the sound. Was it 5 A.M. already?

"How many people are coming this morning, Monsignore?"

Sadowski understood the question. One of the Slavic Pope's first innovations in the Vatican had been to admit guests to his morning Mass at six-thirty and then to breakfast with him afterward. But the sight of the

Pontiff left the papal secretary too shocked to answer. This was a man who never sought pity or commiseration for his inner pains. But Daniel saw the stain of tears; he saw the reports open on the desk amid a sea of handwritten notes; and he knew the deeper signs of turmoil in this churchman whom he had served for thirty-five years.

"Monsignore Daniel?"

"Twelve in all, Holiness." Still shaken, Sadowski answered the question. "The ten U.S. bishops you met with yesterday and those French Brothers from the Ecumenical Community of Dijon."

The Slavic Pope rubbed his eyes, as if that would clear away the weariness of his soul. "Please put them off, Monsignore. Today, let me say Mass and breakfast alone." The Pontiff stood up, stretched himself and was just heading off to bathe and shave and prepare for Mass when he turned back. "In fact, Monsignore, clear the week of all but the most important interviews and public appearances. It will be better that way. I will be tied to these reports for days."

"Of course, Holiness."

Daniel remained behind in the study for a time. He had begun to read his own copies of those reports and, like a lot of other things in the Vatican these days, he wished he could wish them away. But all he could do was ask himself the question he had asked a thousand times before. On whose shoulder could a Pope lean to shed his tears?

XLIII

ON THE POPE'S INSTRUCTIONS, Sadowski cleared the papal calendar as much as possible. As a convenient explanation, and with the connivance of Dr. Fanarote, he hinted at a great fatigue afflicting the Holy Father—a ploy that led to yet another spate of rumors about a papal resignation and, alternatively, the imminent death of the Holy Father. Rumors were the least of Monsignore Daniel's worries, however. It was the Slavic Pope's suffering that pained this faithful servant and loving collaborator.

Sadowski knew this man thoroughly. In the course of his career as bishop, Cardinal and Pope, merciless dilemmas and ugly choices had been thrown at him; but always he had devised acceptable alternatives. Always this Slavic Pope had walked a charmed life—never doubting, ever hoping; never resourceless, ever buoyant; never impatient, ever sure of his destiny.

Now, however, it became truly difficult to stand apart and watch the Pontiff wilt visibly. Most of his daylight hours were spent reading and analyzing the reports and taking notes. Once a day, on Dr. Fanarote's stern orders, he took a quick-paced swing through the Vatican gardens;

but then it was more reading, more analysis, more note taking. Nor were nights a time of rest. He took solitary nocturnal walks through the corridors of the Apostolic Palace. Once, he spent hours down in the Tombs of the Apostles beneath the High Altar of St. Peter's. And on three mornings, when Daniel entered the Pope's private Chapel at around 5 A.M. to prepare for Mass, he found the white-robed figure stretched prone on the floor before the Tabernacle, where he had obviously passed the night.

For once, Sadowski was truly helpless. He was reading the same materials as the Pope; knew the Pope had created many of the bishops and Cardinals who figured in the reports; knew how it must sicken the Pope to see the details of sodomy and Satanism in the clergy—to see all the names and dates and places.

But he also knew there was more to it for the Pontiff than that. His Holiness had become obsessed with finding an answer to some torturing question; a man engaged in a personal crisis that went beyond the unthinkable realities established in the reports as factual.

In his helplessness, Sadowski spoke to Dr. Fanarote about the strain on the Pope and on his vital powers. But he found precious little hope there either. "If strain could kill this man, he would already be dead. And anyway, Monsignore, he simply doesn't care one way or the other about that. I'm his doctor and I know. Whatever it costs him—including his life—he'll do what he thinks he should."

In and of themselves, the grim facts Gladstone and Slattery had documented in their reports did not surprise the Slavic Pope. Homosexuality and Satanism were among the oldest viruses lurking in the body politic of the Church. The difference now was that homosexual and Satanist activity had attained a new status within that body politic. In certain sectors of the Church, its members had come up from the underground and claimed the right to be represented in the public forum of Church life. Their apparent acceptability to their colleagues and associates was a signal that all involved had ceased to believe in Catholic teaching. Some had beliefs so alien that effectively they could no longer be reckoned as Catholics. And yet, none wanted to quit the Church, as Martin Luther had done. Nor did they intend to live somehow within the Church according to its laws and doctrine, as Erasmus had done.

Suddenly it became unarguable that now, during this papacy, the Roman Catholic organization carried a permanent presence of clerics who worshipped Satan and liked it; of bishops and priests who sodomized boys and each other; of nuns who performed the "Black Rites" of Wicca, and who lived in lesbian relationships within as well as outside of convent life. Suddenly it became clear that during this papacy the Roman Catholic Church organization had become a place where every day, including Sundays and Holy Days, acts of heresy and blasphemy and outrage and indifference were committed and permitted at holy Altars by men who had been called to be priests. Sacrilegious actions and rites were not only performed at Christ's Altars, but had the connivance or at least the tacit permission of certain Cardinals, archbishops and bishops. Suddenly shock set in at the actual lists of prelates and priests who were involved. In total number, they were a minority—anything from one to ten percent of Church personnel. But of that minority, many occupied astoundingly high positions of rank and authority in chanceries, seminaries and universities.

Appalling though it was, however, even this picture wasn't the whole cause of His Holiness' crisis. The facts that brought the Pope to a new condition of suffering were mainly two: The systematic organizational links—the network, in other words—that had been established between certain clerical homosexual groups and Satanist covens. And the inordinate power and influence of that network.

Of those two facts, the power of the network—so utterly disproportionate to its minority status in Church ranks—was the most devastating for the Slavic Pope. Both Gladstone and Slattery had accumulated evidence tending to show that this inordinate power and preponderant influence of the network was due to its alliances with secular groups outside the Roman Catholic field and to the overwhelming number of teachers in seminaries, universities and Catholic school systems who dissented openly and as a matter of course from Catholic dogma and moral teaching.

But there was a third fact: This Pontiff who had been called upon by Christ to be most directly responsible for His Church had made that influence possible. He had seen the corruption. He had even spoken of his suspicion that some now resident source of evil had entered the hierarchic structure of the Church and infected most of its parts. But his decision had been not to excommunicate heretics. Not to defrock errant priests. Not to dismiss apostate professors from their posts at pontifical universities. His decision had been to speak to them. To speak to everyone, everywhere.

Hadn't he, like Peter, been too headstrong? Hadn't he, like Peter, betrayed Christ?

Three times betrayed, Christ had asked Peter three times, "Simon, son of John, lovest thou Me . . . ?" Three times betrayed by Peter, Christ had told Peter three times to feed His lambs; to guide and guard and govern His Church. But hadn't the Slavic Pope many more than three betrayals to answer for? Hadn't he reason not only to doubt his own judgment but to question whether the entire enterprise of his pontificate had been a betrayal? A nasty joke giving rise to a rictus of contempt on the face of the ancient Adversary?

Many more than three times during those days and exceedingly dark nights, therefore, the Slavic Pope prostrated himself before Christ and, more anguished than Peter, gave his reply to the question he knew he must answer.

"Yes, Lord, I saw the corruption . . . But I presumed what my two predecessors in this sacred office presumed. I presumed that the spirit of the Second Vatican Council was Your spirit.

"Yes, Lord. I saw the corruption that had set in in the churchly organization during those two previous pontificates. And I decided that the traditional Church organization had been thoroughly dismantled; would never be restored; would never again be as it was.

"Yes, Lord. I saw the corruption. But I presumed the spirit of Vatican II was creating a new community of Christians—the New Jerusalem. As Pope for all peoples, I presumed it was my duty to give witness to that spirit among the nations of the earth. To assemble all the people of God in readiness for the appearance of the Queen of Heaven in human skies announcing a new era of peace and religious revival among the nations.

"Yes, Lord. I saw the corruption . . ."

"Yes, Monsignore Daniel, I've seen the reports. Finished reading them through last night, in fact. Thank you for bringing them over." Cardinal Sanstefano leaned forward to nurse an arthritic leg as he spoke quietly into his private phone at the Vatican Bank. He had no idea why his arthritis always flared when trouble was on the horizon, but years of experience had taught him how accurate a barometer it was. "Confession you say, Monsignore? Yes, of course. When would suit His Holiness?"

Sanstefano was somewhat surprised at the Pontiff's summons to come to the papal Chapel to confess him. Every Friday, a certain Father Jan Kowalski made the trip from St. Stanislaus Kostka Church in the Trastevere district of Rome to the Apostolic Palace, slipped into the small private Chapel of the Popes and there heard the Holy Father's confession. Father Jan was semi-retired now; but he'd become such a permanent part of this papacy that security personnel took notice only when he didn't turn up on schedule.

On the other hand, this wasn't the first time His Holiness had asked the head of PECA to confess him. He had done so twice before. And because each time had been a moment of crisis and of grave decision, Sanstefano prepared himself now by letting those two earlier occasions seep back into his memory.

The first occasion, he recalled, had been in late December, barely two months after the Slavic Pope had been elected. The newly elected Pontiff, so full of ebullience and sangfroid, had begun with the usual formula for declaring his intention to confess his sins. But instead of unburdening his soul of his personal faults, and mindful that his confidence was protected by the seal of the confessional, His Holiness had turned his attention to the Vatican Bank. Then as now, it was the IRA's independence that most interested the Slavic Pope. Its charter made the IRA totally untouchable by anybody in the Vatican except the Holy Father himself.

His queries were direct and pointed: How much had the Holy See lost in what popular reports described as international scandals and scams? Who was implicated in those losses? Had the failure been engineered? By whom? What great debts did the Holy See owe?

As number two man in the IRA back then, Sanstefano had called a spade a spade. In the first thirty years of the IRA's existence, there had been a solid hope that Vatican finance—including its financial arrangements with all the worldwide provinces of the Roman Catholic Church—could hold its own as an independent banking system, and present itself as a peer in association and competition with the other banking systems in the world marketplace.

But the IRA had been the focal point of financial troubles that had begun in the sixties and continued into the seventies. That series of scandals and scams the Pope had mentioned had led to a loss of professional standing and a grave loss of liquidity—"over a billion dollars at least," Sanstefano had said ruefully. The result had been a lessening of the IRA's autonomy and liberty of action in the money markets of the world. The former hope of becoming a player at the big board had been dissipated. The IRA's moves had to be tailored to those of the "real giants," as the Archbishop called them. All was decided in view of a financial hegemony wielded by powers outside the Roman Catholic Church. Sanstefano had wanted to put the best face on a difficult situation; but that wasn't easy. "We're up against a hegemonic strength greater by far than any we have at our disposal; greater than any other on earth. It's a situation that may severely modify Your Holiness' foreign policies."

The Pontiff took the news in the spirit of a fighter. As priest, bishop and Cardinal, he had already faced two alien regimes hankering after world hegemony. Not yet sixty, and Pope into the bargain, he intended to do nothing less in Rome than he had done in his homeland. "Let me think about all this," he had answered Sanstefano that day. "The strength of the papacy—its autonomy in the furtherance of faith propagation—was the whole aim of the Pope who set up the IRA. But it seems to my poor brain that someone set out to reduce us to the status of camp followers. Yet we have many friends abroad who share our dislike of such hegemonic control. Through them and with them, it may be possible to get back on track. We have to achieve autonomy."

The second occasion on which the Pontiff had called Sanstefano in as confessor had been a couple of years after Ali Agča had tried to kill the Slavic Pope in St. Peter's Square.

The Holy Father had made Sanstefano a Cardinal and promoted him to head the Prefecture of Economic Affairs, with full control over the IRA. And in those early years of his pontificate, the Slavic Pope had been as good as his word in matters affecting the Vatican Bank. One of his major undertakings had been to repair the losses in liquidity and in standing suffered by the Holy See in the seventies. In those years, and in the few recuperative years after the attempted assassination, the ebullience and sangfroid of the Slavic Pope were transformed. It was a time when one of the two superpowers was preparing to step into oblivion, and the other was likewise faced with a course of action none of its earlier leaders—the fathers of the American Revolution—had dreamed of. A time when the Pope acquired a clear perception of the machinery that administers the macromanagement of this world's complex structure—its matter, its energy, its physiology, its vitalism. During those years, the Holy Father deepened and expanded his contacts with many of this world's great figures whose decisions shaped the lives of billions of people. He nourished his contacts, too, with certain personages in the Soviet Union. With Russian churchmen, he formed an underground of priests. With Party members he found a commonality based on their mutual realization that a new order was dawning in the world. It was one of those Party members who wrote to the Slavic Pope so candidly and trenchantly about that world order—and in words so redolent of the Pontiff's discussion with Sanstefano in their first confessional encounter—that the Holy Father had shown that communication to the Vatican banker.

"At least," that official had written, "we are free of the illusion of superpower status; and Your Holiness, of any illusion that you are head of a super-church. In our world there is only one superpower; not our U.S.S.R., not the U.S.A. And now that the Church of Satan is established, your papal authority is no longer absolute."

Privately, Sanstefano had always been convinced that something about those wide-ranging contacts in the early eighties had prompted the Slavic Pope to insist on a private conversation with his would-be assassin, Ali Agča. In a Roman prison called Regina Coeli in honor of the Queen of Heaven, the two men had engaged in a conversation of such whispered intimacy that no other human being—no intelligence agency in Washington or Moscow—would ever know what had passed between them. The day after that meeting, the Slavic Pope had called upon Sanstefano to confess him for the second time.

"I have asked you to hear my confession, Eminence," the Pontiff had begun, "because I have some crises of conscience." Because his conversation with Ali Agča had taken place under the seal of confession, the Pope could reveal only those facts for which the penitent Turk had given explicit permission. The most important of those facts had sent chills through Sanstefano at the time.

"There need be no fear for an unnatural termination of my life," His Holiness had said with icy calm, "provided this Holy See does not seek a hegemonic position at the big board of the world market and in the new international order now emergent among the nations. We can survive—on that score."

To help the cause of human harmony, he would have to use the universally accepted prestige of the Holy See and its Catholic Church as a means of fostering a certain unity and commonality among all religions. Friction between Jewry and the papacy was singled out for particular attention because, as it was said by some, the Holy See had never really made amends for the role played by its members in the Holocaust; and because, it was said by some, the Holocaust was the brainchild of Christians and the final result of traditional Christian anti-Semitism.

Some papal action was called for—action plainly indicating that the Roman Church accepted the Synagogue as a peer within the scope of the world's great religions and honoring the Jewish people as bearers of a special historical mission.

With the arena of his concern set out in general terms, the Pope proceeded to details. "No Pope has ever visited the Jewish Community in this city of Rome. I must. No Pope has visited Auschwitz. I must. No Pope has established diplomatic relations with Israel. I must. No matter how long it takes, no matter what effect it has on others, I must do all of that, and all will be well with the Church on the material side of things. We must sue for peace, if peace is what we desire."

Sanstefano had the sense that the Pontiff was repeating actual recommendations that had been made to him. As head of PECA, he also knew full well that, in the marketplace of money and temporal power, the Holy See could no longer even plan to act autonomously. All efforts in that direction had been halted by the attempted assassination.

The Holy Father now had specific questions of conscience. Would diplomatic recognition of Israel imply any abandonment of Catholic tradition? Had the Church been wrong, theologically or morally, to abandon its previous teaching that the Jews' rejection of Jesus had incurred God's anger? Should the Jews be the object of Catholic proselytizing efforts?

"Follow the dictates of a well-formed conscience." Sanstefano kept invoking the old Catholic principle. "You must educate, not distort, your conscience."

"Do you think, Eminence, that I may distort, or already have distorted, my conscience?"

"Put it like this, Holiness. Many of the faithful—those most faithful to traditional teaching—do think so."

"Your advice, then?"

There had been a longish pause at that moment. The Cardinal had to make a choice: tell his papal penitent to pray for enlightenment or open the scope of this confession onto a wider plane. Sanstefano's blunt character predominated. "Holy Father"—Sanstefano spoke with quiet authority—"let me try to put these questions into the broader context of Your Holiness' pontificate.

"We both realize that you have a theology that is not orthodox and traditional; that your philosophy is not Thomist; that you are a phenomenologist. We also realize that you have given up on the present clerical organization of the Church; and that much of the clerical organization has given up on you. They want you out of their hair, definitively and soon.

"But for all of that, Holiness, we both know you are Pope of all Catholics and Christ's sole representative among men. My one strong precept to you is that you be morally sure of what you do *as Pope*. And because we mortals sin not only by commission but by omission, be just as sure morally of what you are deliberately *not* doing. For, in your case, Holy Father, it is what you are not doing—what you have not done—that distresses many of the faithful."

This was as far as Sanstefano had taken his advice at that second confession.

Arthritic flare-up and all, Cardinal Sanstefano was only a minute or two late. He put his head in the door of Monsignore Sadowski's fourth-floor office, and then went next door to the private Chapel while Sadowski informed the Holy Father that his confessor was waiting for him.

This confession was the shortest; but time was not its measure.

"Eminence." The Pontiff spoke in short sentences. Almost curtly. "You must answer my first question as chief of the IRA. Imagine for a moment that I accept the advice of my Cardinals. That I resign from the office of Peter. How would that affect our standing in the market?"

The Cardinal's Catholicism was bred in his bones. But under the icy blast of the Slavic Pope's realism, his inner grip on that Catholicism became bleak and joyless. "When would this resignation be expected to take place?"

"Any time between now and my seventy-fifth birthday."

"Provided you are replaced by someone with friends neither you nor I have cultivated, Holy Father, a resignation in that time span would probably boost our standing. We both know that those who exclude us now from certain investment sectors would open doors at the moment of Your Holiness' resignation. *Amici di amici*. Friends of friends . . ."

"You must answer my second question as one of my Cardinals and as my confessor. But first, a statement. Monsignore Daniel has told me you have read the two reports I sent over to you. Now, I have more than one reason for contemplating resignation. But my chief reason—the reason that concerns me uppermost at this moment—is the shocking condition into which I have allowed churchmen to lapse during my papacy. My chief reason, then, is that I am no longer effective as Pope. Now, Eminence, the question: What was my main mistake?"

Sanstefano leaned forward, his forehead resting on one hand. "Undoubtedly, Holy Father, your failure to interpret the doctrine of the Second Vatican Council authoritatively and—I repeat, Holiness: *and*—in agreement with tradition. Beyond any shadow of doubt, the documents of that Council, as they now stand, are not compatible with traditional Roman Catholicism. You thus allowed error to flourish without correction. That amounts to misfeasance—possibly even malfeasance—at the papal level."

"Given my motives, are we talking about mortal or venial guilt?"

"Given the damage, mortal."

"Is it your opinion, then, that I should resign?"

"Pontifex maximus a nemini judicatur." Sanstefano was quoting old Canon Law. "No one is entitled to pass judgment on the Pope. That judgment is yours to make. Yours alone and exclusively."

"But I am asking merely your opinion, Eminence. As my confessor."

Sanstefano's breath felt tight in his chest. "I cannot answer you as confessor, Holiness. I have no opinion. No one is competent to have an opinion in this matter. No sensible believer would hazard a guess. No one who knows his position would attempt a reply. I have only my faith in Peter's office. You are the Anointed of God. Who lays his hands on the Anointed will die the death. So Scripture tells us."

There was little more to say. With grave guilt at issue, both men knew the requirement to repair the damage done and to correct the fault. But both knew, too, that repair and correction added up to a tall order when policies of state and Church were involved. Like Dr. Fanarote, however, Cardinal Sanstefano was certain that whatever it might cost him—including his life—the Slavic Pope would do what had to be done. In that moral certainty, he imposed his penance and gave absolution to the Holy Father.

As he poked his head into Monsignore Daniel's office to say goodbye and then left the papal apartment, there was more than guilt for Sanstefano to think about. His hands shaking, his breath still tight in his chest as he retraced his steps through the Apostolic Palace, the Cardinal reflected that much had remained unsaid in this papal confession. Unspoken reasons—something beyond his own accountability for the systemic sins of his contemporary churchmen, beyond his own judgment of himself as useless—had brought His Holiness to the edge of the unthinkable. Sanstefano could only guess at what those reasons might be.

This Cardinal had seen five Popes come and go. Had known them personally before they were elected. Each of them, once he had accepted the papacy, had crossed an invisible line into a place of aloneness. For all the depth and breadth of his human sympathy, the Slavic Pope was no exception.

"No matter how much we care for him, or he for us," Sanstefano said in his heart, "on our terms and within our world, we cannot fathom his distress and discomfort. We can only give him the truth. Too often, the truth hurts. But it also heals."

XLIV

CHRIS GLADSTONE and the others saw right away that this private predawn meeting with the Slavic Pope to which Monsignore Sadowski had summoned them would be special. For one thing, instead of settling into comfortable chairs in the Pontiff's study, they gathered around a conference table in a small reception room in the papal apartments on the fourth floor of the Apostolic Palace. And for another, the Pope came in to this meeting, reports in hand, with a definitive agenda. Most of all, though, Christian was struck by the change that had taken place so quickly in the Holy Father's appearance. His very smile still warmed Gladstone's heart. But the pallor on his face, the lines of suffering around his eyes and mouth, the deep resonance of his voice, the noticeable curve in his shoulders—all these told of something far deeper than time's visible ravages.

Still, this was a gathering of loving and caring friends united by their common devotion to the Slavic Pope. Not one of them—not Christian Gladstone or Damien Slattery; not Angelo Gutmacher or Giustino Lucadamo; not even Daniel Sadowski—fully understood the Pontiff or his papal policies. More than one of them entertained severe doubts about his wisdom from time to time. Yet merely to be together with each other and in the Holy Father's presence was a joy for each one.

It was an added joy for Christian and Father Angelo to see one another again—the first time since that morning in the Tower Chapel at Windswept House when they had each answered very different calls to a life of service to Rome. There wasn't much time for catch-up talk today, however.

Immediately, His Holiness raised two items of particular interest. With a glance at Giustino Lucadamo, he made it clear that he had been fully briefed on Gladstone's detailed intelligence concerning the plans and antipapal motives for a public Common Mind Vote among his bishops. And, he informed Gladstone, he had signed the documents approving his advancement in clerical rank. Father Christian was now entitled to be addressed as Monsignore and to sport that distinctive violet touch on his clothing.

That opening was already too much for Christian. His new status as domestic prelate, he blurted out with some vehemence, was the direct result of his having been taken as an ally by churchmen who wished to encompass the near-future termination of His Holiness' pontificate. "In fact, ever since my permanent status in Rome was effected, I've been an unwitting ally of theirs. I've traipsed over Europe and the United States as a political shill for Your Holiness' enemies, and abused my family ties to boot, to further plans formed, I'm convinced, in the mind of Satan. And yet, here I am, totally accepted by Your Holiness and by your close associates."

Nobody stirred for a few seconds. Lucadamo broke the silence. "Don't kick yourself too hard for having been used by them. We also have used you. Your information on the proposed CMV has already filled some crucial gaps in our knowledge. But you're just beginning to understand what you've signed up for. In the mess we're all in, the task now is to take the initiative away from the other side. And that's why we're here this morning."

Having been yanked by Lucadamo out of his selfish personal anger and back to the plane of the papal agenda, Gladstone turned to the Pontiff again, an apology for his outburst forming on his lips. The Pope met his eyes with a humorous smile that spoke approval and confidence. All is understood, that smile said. Now, let's get on with the essentials.

The first of those essentials concerned the reports Chris and Slattery had given him a week or so before. But the conclusions the Slavic Pope had drawn from those reports turned out to be far different from the practical conclusions Chris had anticipated. "The total impact of these reports, together with the information Monsignore Christian has communicated to us on the Common Mind Vote of my bishops, makes one thing clear. The opposition has seized the opportune moment for all their plans to be implemented. They see what I now see so clearly; but they see it from a totally different point of view. From an adversarial point of view.

"They see the imminent schism between the papacy and the bishops of the Church. They not only see but have connived at a steady demise of Catholicism. It's fair to say, in fact, that a majority of Catholics are now alienated to one degree or another from the Catholic truth. Rome and the papacy are no longer objects of obedient devotion, but at best merely of a vague and romantic veneration. A vast number of Masses and confessions are invalid. An untold number of priests have not been validly ordained. And I have not yet attempted to assess how many bishops either are not validly consecrated or have become unbelievers.

"Christ is no longer honored in our Tabernacles, so He has left our churches, our convents, our religious orders, our seminaries and our dioceses. Indeed, why should Our Lord stay where He is neglected, insulted and denied? It is not He who needs us, after all. Now"—His Holiness looked at each man at the conference table in turn—"if I have any recourse at all, it is to the protection of the Queen of Heaven. As a special act of veneration, I must—if at all possible, I must—make my pilgrimage to Russia and Ukraine."

Everyone listening to the Slavic Pope at that moment knew the implications of what he was saying. Even Chris Gladstone understood that the rumors engulfing Rome might be true. That the Holy Father's outlook encompassed his own possible departure from the papal scene. That the end of his pontificate was at hand; and with it, the climax of his geopolitical endgame with the nations.

As if to confirm that collective thought, the Slavic Pope went on to give a further justification—a geopolitical justification—for his Russia trip. He listed such items as the serious and potentially vicious differences about population control coming to a head between the Holy See and the present U.S. administration; the equally serious differences on that and other bedrock issues between the Holy See and the UN, and between the Holy See and the European Union; the rising enmity of Russia and its allies in the CIS toward the Holy See.

"Will Your Holiness consecrate Russia to the Blessed Virgin during your time in Moscow?" Damien Slattery was still keen on the Holy Father staying in Rome to fight the CMV plot; but at this moment, though, he was thinking of the promise made by the Virgin at Fatima that, if the Pope of 1960 consecrated Russia to the protection of the Mother of God, the Church would be saved from terrible persecution, wars would cease and humanity would enjoy peace and prosperity.

"No." The Pontiff was blunt. "I am not the Pope of 1960. She did not tell me to do it. I have no mandate in that regard. What I want is to restore to the Russian people their beloved Icon of Our Lady of Kazan, which is presently in the possession of this Holy See. And I want to go to Kiev, because that is where Prince Vladimir baptized Russians a thousand years ago, en masse, in the waters of the Dnieper.

"But you are right, Father Damien. My Russia trip has everything to do with the Virgin's promises and revelations. And my determination to make this pilgrimage has been strengthened by these reports. I mentioned to Father Angelo recently that I have long suspected that my recent papal predecessor was right when he spoke about the smoke of Satan having entered the Church. Today, I am convinced of it. No one who has read these reports and digested the details of the CMV plot can doubt that we are in need of special help. In particular . . ." His Holiness' voice broke just this once, but he recovered himself quickly. "In particular, we need help for this Holy See of Peter, if it is not to collapse and be taken over by the Demon."

Gladstone shot a look at Slattery. When he had spoken a few moments before of the CMV plot as a scheme hatched in the mind of Satan, it had been a figure of speech. But it seemed to him that the Slavic Pope was dead serious.

"I am resolved, therefore," the Pontiff continued, "to make my papal pilgrimage to Moscow and to Kiev. My one purpose is to elicit the special help we need from the Blessed Mother. She must speak to her Son. She must tell Him of all the souls that are withering. She must tell Him again, as she did once during her time with Him on this earth: They have little or no wine of belief left."

The silence that followed was as deep as the Holy Father's voice had been. And again it was Lucadamo who broke the quiet of the room with a practical reminder. "Holiness, the news that Father—er, Monsignore Christian has brought us means that Your Holiness can expect renewed pressure to sign the Resignation Protocol. Unless we intend to be led by the nose to the place of execution, so to speak, we need to take the initiative."

"Agreed, Giustino." The Pontiff nodded; but his main focus was clear. "Father Angelo will fetch the Icon from Portugal to Rome. He will then pay another visit to Mr. Gorbachev to discuss what can be done to secure an early invitation for our visit to his land. As it would be unwise to put all our eggs in that basket, however, I will choose the opportune moment to . . ."

Gladstone didn't hear the rest of that statement. A while ago, he had been ready to apologize for having been duped by the Pope's adversaries. During much of his time in the States, and especially since his return, he had taken on the role of a double agent, dealing in half-truths and double entendre. The only positive fruit of all that double-dealing had been the report he had delivered to the Holy Father with all the documentary evidence needed—names, dates, places, affidavits, transcripts of audiotapes, photographs—to clean out the whole brood of corrupt clerics and false religionists. "Why"—in another sudden flare of emotion, Christian broke in on the Holy Father—"why, Holiness, do I get the impression that the reports are going to be put in cold storage?"

All eyes were on Gladstone, but only Father Gutmacher seemed prepared to tackle his young friend's argument straight on. "How long, Chris, do you think you and Father Slattery would last here in Rome or anywhere else once it was understood who drew up those reports? And besides, those reports will alert the Holy Father's opposition as to how much we really know about their mischief. Forewarned is forearmed. To put the reports in the hands of the Curial Cardinals would be to court greater difficulty for His Holiness than before. They would be ready for any initiative—any move at all—that the Holy Father makes against them."

Father Angelo's argument wasn't half good enough to satisfy Christian. "You can't just keep a lid on everything," he argued. "Your Holiness doesn't have to give the reports out to everyone. But you can follow the data of the reports. You can take action. You can expel any bishop shown to be leading an actively homosexual life; any bishop who has a mistress; any bishop allowing Wicca nuns in his diocese; any nun known to be an active lesbian. You can deal in some appropriate way with priests, nuns, bishops and Cardinals who are undeniably and identifiably un-Catholic.

"With all respect, Your Holiness, it might begin with the fact that already a number of American women have undergone a would-be ordination ceremony for the priesthood at the hands of a bishop still in charge of one American diocese. I have also submitted some evidence that the same has happened in one Canadian diocese. Canonically, those bishops are already auto-excommunicated. But I recommend that they be relieved of their positions by direct papal decree. The scandal is already vigorous among the people; they know something is wrong."

It was a grim-faced Slavic Pope who heard Gladstone out. The American was still rough in his approach to things; but, like the irreplaceable Father Aldo Carnesecca, he wasn't afraid to pursue painful problems. That being so, the Pontiff answered Christian with the candor he deserved. "What you proposed, Monsignore Christian, would be feasible only if it was in my power to make and unmake bishops in the Church, and to dismiss priests, and to expel nuns from convents."

"Hasn't Your Holiness that power? As Supreme Pastor?"

"Officially, yes. Actually, no." The Slavic Pope stared Gladstone in the eye, seeking his acknowledgment of reality. And finally, after an eternity of some few seconds, Chris nodded and lowered his gaze.

Angelo Gutmacher broke into that moment of bitter understanding with a new suggestion for a papal reaction to the data of the two reports. His Holiness should write an encyclical letter to the Church Universal—an ex cathedra letter—stating clearly the condemnation of homosexual activity and of all forms of Satanist rituals and organizations. According to the declarations of such a letter, anyone violating those mandates would be automatically excommunicated.

The idea appealed to the Pontiff. In fact, he began at once to expand on it. Even while Father Slattery took over supervision of Signora Gladstone's group of underground priests in the United States, he was to draw a first draft of an encyclical letter directed against the abuses—homosexual activity and Satanist ritual activity. But, especially in the light of the Pope's recent meeting with UNFPA's Bischara Francis—specifically, in the light of her information that the United Nations was about to embark on an intensive global campaign to formulate a consensus in favor of an accelerated and highly emphasized birth control policy—Slattery was also to include in the encyclical such basic issues of sexual morality as contraception and current methods of population control.

The enterprise was to be kept as quiet as possible, His Holiness cautioned; but he acknowledged that an ex cathedra encyclical letter couldn't be kept entirely secret for long. "Certainly not from the Secretary of State," he said by way of obvious example.

The Russia trip was a different matter. One that required a delicate balancing of logistics. "I must go public with it soon," the Pontiff said. "Unless I am to rely entirely on Mr. Gorbachev—and that would be unwise—a public announcement of my intentions must be added to my efforts to secure an invitation within the desired time frame. My Cardinals in Rome think so badly of that pilgrimage, however—they are so opposed to Marian devotion in general and to Fatima in particular—that I must choose the moment. To the degree I can catch the Cardinals off balance, to that degree I will have seized the initiative from them.

"Meanwhile, Monsignore Christian, I have heard your plea concerning the reports. When I first commissioned them, my intent was to use them to bring my Curial Cardinals back into some cooperation with the Holy See. But as Father Gutmacher has pointed out, that is not practical. There are some individual bishops to whom I can and should show the reports on an eyes-only basis. But I begin to think we can do more than that. Over the past several days I have been considering whether to call all my Cardinals in from around the world for an extraordinary Consistory. To use the reports to put them on notice that the Church is in crisis and that we can't go on as we are. Now, with so much on the table—the reports, the ex cathedra encyclical letter, my pilgrimage to the East—I see such a Consistory as imperative."

Father Damien had severe doubts about a secret Consistory as part of the Pope's plans. Given the politics of the Cardinals these days, he said, any sudden willingness on their part to cooperate with His Holiness would be nothing short of a miraculous conversion.

Gutmacher disagreed. "The Cardinals are important in the Regional and National Bishops Conferences," he reasoned. "It's those Conferences that will be the vehicles for the CMV. And it's the Cardinals, not the bishops, who elect Popes. If there's any chance to take the initiative from the Vatican cabal once and for all, a secret Consistory of Cardinals could be the best way to do it. The real question for me isn't whether the Consistory should be called, but when."

The Pontiff took charge again. He agreed with Gutmacher that timing would be crucial. But because the Consistory was linked in his mind to the Russia trip—or, more exactly, to his expectation of some sign from the Holy Virgin during that pilgrimage—the timing for a meeting with his Cardinals would have to remain open until the pilgrimage dates were set.

As far as His Holiness was concerned, everything was settled. He polled each of his collaborators with a look; and each nodded agreement—except Giustino Lucadamo.

"Frankly, Holy Father, I'm still concerned about the pressure I anticipate will be put on you to sign the Resignation Protocol." That was the best way Lucadamo knew to hint at what really worried him. Though he didn't have such an intimate view of the Pope as Monsignore Daniel did, Giustino had kept fairly close tabs on His Holiness during the week when he had been consumed in reading the reports. In his reckoning, it seemed possible that this Pope had been brought to such an extreme of choices that he might walk away from the papacy as being beyond his capacity. If the course of action he had outlined today failed to set things somewhat to rights in the hierarchy, he might actually sign the Protocol.

The Holy Father responded to Lucadamo's worry from a different perspective. Cardinal Sanstefano had reminded him of the moral necessity to correct the damage done to his Church and to correct his own grave fault. All the plans that had been laid out this morning had their justification within that context. "Frankly, Giustino, I also am concerned. But if my departure is what the Blessed Mother has in mind—if that is the price to achieve a true reform of the Church structure and to restore peace . . ." The rest—the unthinkable—he left unsaid.

Seizing the initiative from the opposition was everything now. And in his routine briefing with the Cardinal Secretary of State on the morning of his departure for his Loreto pilgrimage, the Pontiff had every reason to be pleased with the opening of his campaign.

"An encyclical letter, Holiness?" His Eminence blinked somewhat more than usual. "*Ebbene.* Good judgment is paramount in such matters."

"But do you not think, Your Eminence, that good judgment requires that the papacy pronounce an ex cathedra statement on such plagues as homosexual activities and Satanist cults? About contraception and the assault on the innocent in the name of population control? Is it not time for such a statement, in fact?"

"Holy Father, I have always thought the truth makes its way more thoroughly when there isn't too much strife and screaming. Such a categoric manner as an ex cathedra statement does usually evoke much strife and screaming nowadays."

"A point I have considered, Eminence." The Pontiff was smooth but insistent. "I plan a gentle-toned presentation. But we have to draw the line of definition, especially in view of governmental policies that are increasingly inimical to the Church's teaching."

"I suppose so, Holiness." It was uncomfortable for Graziani that the Pope was making it so hard to be noncommittal. "No doubt about it; at present we are in a cold war situation with the EC and the UN—not to speak of the United States and the vast majority of individual governments today. But my question is whether we want to escalate to a hot war status. After all, birth control is considered by the Americans to be a strategic necessity for their country." Satisfied that he had shifted the burden of the argument onto the Americans, the Cardinal blinked benignly in the Holy Father's direction.

"Haven't they got a phrase in America, Eminence, about letting the chips fall where they may?"

"Chips? Ah, yes. Indeed they have, Holiness." The Cardinal Secretary smiled a little and rose from his chair. The best thing he could do in the face of a warning like that would be to renew his good wishes for the Pope's safe journey to Loreto and make a graceful exit.

"A moment, Eminence." Graziani remained standing. "I'm sure Your

Eminence agrees we shouldn't let it be known that I am preparing this letter. Surprise may be a principal element in its success."

"I could not agree more, Holy Father. Surprise has saved Rome several times in the past. It shall remain an official secret until the date of its publication."

The Slavic Pope watched the Cardinal's receding figure, calculating how much time it would take for those interested in aborting his encyclical letter to hear the news. The time needed to walk the length of the corridor between the papal study and the Secretary's office? The time it would take to dial a telephone number?

According to Lucadamo's surveillance, at least some of those parties in Europe and North America were aware of the encyclical before the Pope reached Loreto that afternoon.

The enemies of the Slavic Pope, and most of his friends as well, were taken completely by surprise when the papal spokesman, Miguel Lázaro-Falla, called an unscheduled midday press conference on October 13. The date, chosen by His Holiness, was the anniversary of the celebrated miracle of the sun that had occurred at Fatima in 1917. In his most businesslike manner, he announced that the Holy Father would shortly summon all his Cardinals from around the world to meet with him in a special Consistory. The timing, Lázaro-Falla said, had not yet been decided; but it would not be later than one year hence. In the meantime, His Holiness was expecting an official invitation from the governments of Russia and Ukraine to visit their countries in a purely spiritual capacity. The Holy Father would travel as a pilgrim, not as the head of a sovereign state.

The hubbub of questions shouted by reporters left Lázaro-Falla unfazed. He declined to be more specific, referred all queries to the Secretariat of State and the two home governments and deftly disappeared from the podium.

All nerves at the best of times, Monsignore Taco Manuguerra appeared strained to the limit as he answered two phones at once, and nodded Gladstone into Cardinal Maestroianni's office.

". . . such unpredictable, Machiavellian moves on the part of this out-of-date Slavic mystic of a Pope . . ." Cardinal Silvio Aureatini stopped his protest in mid-sentence when the American stepped into the office.

"Ah, Monsignore Christian." For once, even Maestroianni was evidently caught off guard.

"If you would prefer to postpone our appointment, Eminence . . ." It was a sight to see the tables turned on these two men who specialized in behind-the-scenes moves, and Chris was enjoying every moment of it. "I can come back at a more convenient time."

"Our appointment . . . Of course . . ." Maestroianni was a picture of distress. "I'm always glad to see you, Monsignore. But . . . Yes . . . Could you remake the appointment with Monsignore Taco . . ."

The Cardinal was interrupted by Manuguerra's flustered announcement over the intercom that Secretary of State Graziani was on the phone. No rest for the wicked, Chris purred to himself as he caught the first words of Maestroianni's end of the conversation.

"But I knew nothing about it, Eminence. . . . Yes, yes, I was chatting with His Holiness yesterday. . . . Eh? . . . No, not a word. He told me the entire history of the Holy House of Loreto. . . . I'm not changing the subject, Eminence. . . . I don't know who arranged all this. I suggest you speak to the man in Moscow. . . . You did? . . . He knew nothing? . . ."

Chris closed the door behind him. The Pope had spoken about the tactical advantage of choosing the right moment for his announcements; and Lucadamo had emphasized the need to seize the initiative. To judge by the scene he had just witnessed, a fair beginning had been struck.

"Distressed, Your Eminence?" Dr. Ralph Channing settled into Cardinal Maestroianni's office as though it belonged to him. "Why should I be distressed? It's wonderful news that the Holy Father wants to visit Moscow and Kiev. Have the two governments issued a formal invitation?"

"We don't know." Maestroianni, distressed enough for both men, was extremely annoyed at the Professor's cavalier attitude. "Communication with either government is difficult and problematic. We will know in a couple of days."

"But we are not going to wait a couple of days, Eminence. One or the other government may demur; but it is in our interest that they issue the invitations, because it is in our interest that the Holy Father make the trip." Channing explained how difficult it had been for his colleagues to understand the way plans had been dragged out in Rome. Without mentioning the Availing Time, he explained the need those colleagues felt to devise supplemental initiatives to speed the final phase of their enterprise. And he explained how perfectly the Pontiff's Russia trip might play into those supplemental initiatives.

"You say you can evoke the Common Mind Vote overnight, Eminence. Well, why not do just that? Provided you secure His Holiness' signature on the Resignation Protocol, the Pontiff's Eastern trip will provide us with an excellent venue for our supplemental initiative, and with a happy ending to this protracted struggle!"

Maestroianni was enlightened, but still distressed on one major point. "But can you ensure that those invitations will be issued?"

"The least of our worries, Eminence, provided I can use your secure telephone facilities."

"You mean, right now?"

"Yes, Eminence. Right now."

"Please come with me." The Cardinal led the way to a private communications room where he had no choice but to leave the Professor to make his call in privacy.

In a mere ten minutes or so, Channing returned to Maestroianni's office to announce that all was in order. "By this time tomorrow"—he smiled through his goatee—"what we require will have been accomplished."

It was only after lunch at Massimo's, and a more thorough discussion of Channing's supplemental initiatives, that His Eminence was free to hurry back to his office to discover what he could about the Professor's call. Monsignore Taco was gone to siesta by then, so Maestroianni eased into the chair behind his desk and turned on the tape recordings of the morning's telephone calls. Eventually he found the one he wanted. Channing had dialed direct. The Cardinal listened to the ring of the distant phone, and then sat bolt upright at the familiar sound of the male voice that had answered.

"Hallo! Hallo! Sekuler."

"Hello! Herr Sekuler!"

"Jawohl!"

"Channing from New York. Speaking from Rome. I have a request."

"Very well." The answer came back in English. "One moment please, Dr. Channing. We are on an open channel."

His Eminence cursed at the sudden voice fade-out followed by a low-pitched buzz. He waited for about a minute. Then, with a sigh, he turned the machine off. The rest of the conversation was off-channel. Maestroianni had learned one thing, however. Herr Otto Sekuler apparently enjoyed a more exalted position in the hierarchy than had been evident at the Schuman Day meeting in Strasbourg. All in all, His Eminence figured, it hadn't been a bad day's work.

No one in the American government raised an eyebrow in surprise or curiosity at the media reports that the Slavic Pope would hold a Consistory of his Cardinals in Rome or that he intended to travel to Russia and Ukraine. At the State Department and the two U.S. Embassies in Rome, the news was barely worth a shrug. Another papal trip? Another meeting of Cardinals? Ho-hum. Gibson Appleyard did take notice of the announcements. But he already had received sufficient assurances from the Slavic Pope concerning his Russia policy. And the news came at a moment when Gib was preoccupied with what seemed a far more vital issue for U.S. interests—the decline of American leadership in Europe since the new administration had taken over, and the new belligerent role being assumed by Russia.

So it was that no subordinate official underlined these press items for the eyes of Admiral Bud Vance, or referred them to the acting secretary for the National Security Council, until the U.S. Ambassador in Moscow signaled Washington that the Russian government, conjointly with the Ukrainian government, had actually issued an invitation to the Slavic Pope that he come on pilgrimage to their lands within the next twelve months. The Ambassador's curiosity had been piqued by several details in connection with the invitation, and he proceeded to list them.

First, said the Ambassador, the two governments in question had been approached on behalf of the Slavic Pope by the presiding chairman of a remarkably insignificant member organization of the United Nations called the World Solidarity of Ethical Thought. Second, the name of the WOSET chairman was Otto Sekuler, and the Ambassador recalled seeing that name on a departmental questionnaire some time back. Third, it was normal practice for the Vatican to make its own requests of governments, or to solicit the intervention of the United States, Germany or France. In this instance, the Vatican had apparently bypassed the usual channels, and the Ambassador thought he should alert his superiors to that fact. Didn't it indicate a greater independence from Western powers and a greater influence by this Pope in other areas than the Department had ascribed to him?

Fourth, the invitation was backed by strong support from a very unusual source—namely, Russian Orthodox Patriarch Kiril of Moscow. As Kiril was a well-known former KGB agent and an acknowledged enemy of the Slavic Pope and his Church, what was behind this sudden favor for the Roman Pope?

It did not help Admiral Vance's bad humor one morning to find a copy of the Ambassador's signal on his desk, together with a sharply worded note from the Secretary of State: "How did this happen without my being warned about it?"

Almost by instinct, Vance dialed Gib Appleyard's number and asked more or less the same question. "What's your bloody Pope up to now?"

"He's not my Pope, Bud . . ."

"Yeah, I know. He's the Pope of all the Catholics. But thanks to him, I've got to face the Committee of Ten in a couple of minutes, and then I have a meeting with the NSC. Let's meet here about eleven-thirty. In fact, come in beforehand and brief yourself. I'll leave the stuff with my assistant."

"Sure, Bud. But can you give me a hint about what's going on?"

"Remember Otto Sekuler?"

"Yes."

"He's back to haunt us."

Gib Appleyard settled into Vance's office to study the materials the Admiral left for him. He found the Moscow Ambassador's memo interesting. But he spent a great deal more time on the backup documents concerning Otto Sekuler. The information was still thin; it was as if there were a wall of armor around him. Appleyard remembered how the head man of the Grand Orient of Italy, Grand Master Maselli, had been so evasive about

Sekuler. Still, what data there was made it clear that the German had become truly important within the past year. And that fit in with a number of other things that had been especially troubling for Appleyard.

One of those things was the appalling Lodge crisis of one year ago that had shaken the organization on both sides of the Atlantic and that had at least temporarily crippled the fraternal empathy between London and Washington. Variously referred to as the "split," or the "debacle," or "lightning over London," the crisis had affected Appleyard and Vance alike. Too, because the crisis seemed to be merely the staging for a deep change in U.S. foreign policy vis-à-vis Europe and the UN, it had affected both men professionally as well as Masonically.

Following the installation of the new U.S. administration, uncertainty and sudden changes had unsettled the equilibrium of the European bureau—the largest bureau in the State Department, responsible for thirty-eight countries and all international relationships. Vance was its Executive Secretary, next in authority to the Secretary of State; and Appleyard was number two to Vance.

Gib couldn't figure which came first, the "split" between London and Washington, and then the in-house changes at State. Or the in-house changes at State, and then the "split." But he knew the "split" had started with a division in Italian Masonry. A newly formed Grand Regular Lodge of Italy (GRLI) had broken away from the old GLI, the Grand Lodge of Italy. Then the Grand Master of the newly born GRLI had declared he was establishing a "European Grand Lodge" which was to be a confederation of all European Grand Lodges, East and West. The Masons of the United Lodge of England, led by their Grand Secretary, had opposed the idea of a "European" Grand Lodge. Masonry is universal, the ULE declared.

The United Lodge of England had convened a world conference of Grand Masters from sixty-seven Grand Lodges. They had met in Crystal City near Washington, D.C.—and they handed a defeat to the ULE. In reality, it was a defeat for "spiritualist" and "theist" Masonry, as opposed to the "relativist" and "atheist" version.

For Appleyard and Vance, and for those Fratres of a like mind, it was a defeat. Especially for their ecumenical attitude toward corporate religious bodies such as the Roman Catholic Church. They had always regarded such bodies as potential allies. "When the Masonic Temple shall shine over the whole universe," Frater Blumenhagen had written, "when its roof shall be the blue heavens, the two poles its walls, the Throne of Peter and the Church of Rome its pillars, then will the powers of the earth . . . bequeath that freedom to the people which we have laid up in store for them." The new attitude, however, was to regard all such bodies not only as expendable but as targets for elimination.

The practical consequences of all that were now beginning to be felt. Gone were the tightly coagulated transatlantic bonds of NATO and the

Anglo-American-European alliance. The U.S.A. was disengaging from European entanglements and aiming at global alliances. The New Covenant was being implemented in global decisions. By now, the new perspective had found its expression in the Brussels Declaration of 1994: The European Union was proclaimed, with broader and more inclusive aims than the EC; the new Eurocorps for defense was touted in place of NATO; Eastern European States—former satellites of the U.S.S.R.—were invited to become "Partners for Peace."

The latest expression of the new perspective was reflected in the intensified pressure for global implementation of the population control policies enshrined in U.S. National Security Memo 200, now the global policy of the UN.

It was in the context of that whole "debacle," Appleyard noted, that the mysterious Herr Otto Sekuler had come into his own. It was reasonable to conclude, then, that Sekuler belonged to the side that had come up winners in the "split." But that didn't explain Sekuler's influence in the ragtag remnants of the Soviet Union; or why Sekuler would come to the aid of the Pope. And, above all, it didn't explain why, of all the powerful parties Gib could think of, Sekuler had been the one to pop up at just the right moment to secure the papal invitation.

"A bad day at the NSC, Bud?" One look at his boss's face told Appleyard the whole story.

The Admiral sank into the chair behind his desk with a groan. "Not only do I ache in every bone from the pummeling I just got at NSC but I don't understand a damn thing any longer. What is it about this Pope that gets a whole NSC session so riled up over his attitude about condoms, and about the twaddle of that little nun from India—I declare to God, I've blotted out her name . . ."

"Mother Teresa?" Appleyard laughed. "The NSC had a meeting about Mother Teresa?"

"Part of a meeting, but that was plenty. She sure has made enemies in the White House!"

"So what about the rest of the meeting? And what about the Ten?" Gibson held up the Moscow Ambassador's communiqué. "Why are they suddenly so upset about the Pope's travels?"

"That was just the jumping-off point." Vance ambled across the room and poured himself some coffee. "Word is that this Pope is preparing an official letter about birth control. A real assault. Our people want something done about it. Otherwise . . ." The Admiral sat wearily down at his desk again.

"Otherwise what, Bud?"

"Otherwise, it's open war between this administration and the present Pope."

"I see." Gib felt a knot forming in his gut. "And our instructions?"

"Very simple. Go to him and get him off his high horse about population control. With the usual provisos."

Appleyard stirred in his chair. "They can't mean *all* the provisos. Surely they can't . . ."

"Of course they can, Gib. And they do. It's strategic, remember? Executive Order stuff. Has been all the time since Nixon. The last two administrations fudged it slightly. But nobody's fooling around now. You should have heard the Veep go after the encyclical letter at the NSC this morning. It was rough. And it was serious."

"Any deal to be offered?"

"That's for you to find out. ASAP. But if you're asking me do I think there's any possible deal, the answer is no. I don't think so."

Neither could Appleyard see a way to make any kind of deal with the Slavic Pope. They were faced with two irreconcilable absolutes. American insistence on birth control and the papal ban on birth control. Half afraid Vance might make his eyes and guess at the third absolute that was forming in his mind, Gib turned away. If anyone expected him to carry a threat of physical extinction to this Pope in Rome, or expected him to be the one whose report would set the macabre machinery in motion, they were crazy. He couldn't do that. Not on the issue of birth control. Not on any issue. Not to this man.

XLV

BY MID-NOVEMBER, the prospect of the forthcoming papal journey to Russia brought a fresh wave of current surging into the power grid of religion, politics, money and culture on which papal Rome has always functioned. Reasonable people began to entertain the electrifying near-future possibility of the triple event that periodically revivifies the whole of Rome—the end of one papacy, the Conclave election of a new Pope and the start of a fresh papacy.

No one who was anyone in Rome needed to ask why the mere announcement of yet another papal trip—the Slavic Pope's ninety-fourth—should draw such excitement and expectation. Everyone who was anyone saw this particular journey as the Pontiff's last major move in his papal endgame; as his only recourse in his straitened circumstances. It was a gamble that might pay off handsomely, routing and dispossessing his enemies, and leaving him supreme in the power grid. Or it might complete the failure of his pontificate.

Certainly, then, for such a consummate Roman as Cardinal Cosimo Maestroianni it was essential to move things along. Now that the end was in sight, it wouldn't do to leave the initiative to the Slavic Pope. It was time to take stock, regroup his colleagues and get on with the business of history's mandate.

Maestroianni gathered three of his chief collaborators in his office for a strategic planning session. Together with Their Eminences Palombo and Aureatini, the little Cardinal listened as Vatican Secretary of State Graziani grumbled about the recent visit of the Ambassadors of Russia and Ukraine on the same day, promptly at the opening hour for public business, to present the official request of their respective governments that the Holy Father make a state visit to their countries within one calendar year. "Notes of invitation," Graziani emphasized, "that were identical not only in their terms but in their phraseology. In each case, the same motive for the invitation was alleged: the Holy Father's already explicit wish to make the journey. What's going on around here?" Still angry and embarrassed that he had been blindsided by the Pope, he waved the two invitations in his hand. "They actually request the Pope's presence! Are we simply to swallow hard and accept the apparent fact that the ex-Soviet officials in both governments, together with the Pope-hating Russian Orthodox clergy, suddenly feel the need for the Holy Father's blessing?"

With the memory of Professor Channing's recent visit vividly in mind, Maestroianni chuckled. But what he really wanted from Graziani was the latest update on the Pontiff's Russia trip.

"It's a punishing itinerary." Graziani extracted the Holy Father's schedule from one of the folders he carried. "It's all still subject to change, of course. But as it stands now, the Pontiff plans to arrive in Kiev on May 8, and drive out to the Trinity Chapel at Hrushiv. On May 10, he's scheduled to visit Kiev proper. On May 11, he proceeds to St. Petersburg. On the twelfth, he arrives at the Troitse-Sergiyeva Lavra, a Monastery outside Moscow. There will be a semi-official welcome at the Monastery, followed by an ecumenical service conducted by His Holiness and Russian Orthodox Patriarch Kiril. The papal party will depart for Rome in the late afternoon of the twelfth."

"Haven't you left something out?" Maestroianni reached for the sheet of paper. "Ah, yes. Here we are. The immediate antecedents to the Holy Father's travel. I see that the Shoah Memorial Concert will complicate life for His Holiness at the brink of his departure. And I see he plans to convene the General Consistory of Cardinals a mere two days before he leaves Rome. Their Eminences arrive on the sixth and settle in. The Consistory starts on May 7."

"It's a funny thing about that, Eminence." Despite the indignity of having the schedule practically snatched from him, Graziani blinked pleasantly. "His Holiness hasn't said so exactly, but I have the impression that he intends for the Cardinals to remain in Rome until he returns from his Russia trip."

"Are you serious?" Cardinal Maestroianni seemed galvanized by that possibility. He could hardly believe the Slavic Pope would play so willingly into the hands of his adversaries.

"As I say, Eminence, it's only an impression I have. But, yes, I'd say it's a serious possibility."

"Well, then. Let's set the stage properly for such a great event. I've been discussing our enterprise with one of our secular colleagues, and we've worked out a series of what we might call supplemental initiatives. A little show-and-tell to demonstrate where the future authority of the Church truly lies." What Maestroianni envisioned was the type of operation that would demonstrate the ability of the new force at the organizational center of the Church to bring about changes independent of any papal strictures to the contrary.

The first such initiative Cardinal Maestroianni had in mind had to do with the issue of Altar girls—a ready-made field of contention if ever there was one. The Holy Father was not in favor of Altar girls. He had said so recently, both in private and in public. He had promised there would never be papal permission for Altar girls. There had been a time not so long ago when serving in the Sanctuary of the church had been reserved for boys, just as the priesthood was reserved exclusively for men. Indeed, this had been the immemorial practice of the Church during nearly two thousand years.

Nonetheless, for the past twenty years or so, bishops all over the Church had permitted young girls to function as servers at the Roman Catholic Mass. At first, bishops and the Roman administration had turned a blind eye. Then they had tolerated the use of Altar girls. Then they had allowed the usage. Finally, they encouraged it. In all that time, nobody had even pretended the practice was legal. But by now there were areas in the United States that had more girls than boys serving at the Altar. There was even an annual competition in some U.S. dioceses for the year's best Altar girls, affairs that bore all the marks of beauty contests, except that the local bishop gave out the prizes and there was no swimsuit parade.

The Slavic Pope knew this. The official guardians of the purity of Roman Catholic doctrine knew this. It was public knowledge. Yet the papal stricture remained. Maestroianni's first supplemental initiative, therefore, would be aimed at taking the whole issue of girls in the Sanctuary out of the hands of the Slavic Pope once and for all. A little added legwork among some few bishops would be required, but that was nothing the able Monsignore Gladstone couldn't handle once he was properly instructed.

The second supplemental initiative would target the Pontiff on the central issues where he had never given an inch: population control and the traditional moral teachings of the Church. Faced with the utterly unacceptable consensus being formulated by Bischara Francis' UN agency in favor of an accelerated global policy for birth control, the Slavic Pope had already begun a counterattack. He had been seizing every opportunity lately to go after the population control mentality and to plead against the use of abortion and contraceptives. And on top of all that, there was the forthcoming ex cathedra encyclical to consider.

What better time, then, to arrange for the unveiling of the population control study prepared by Dominican Father George Hotelet and Dr. Carlo Fiesole-Marracci under the auspices of the Pontifical Academy of Sciences?

"I think it's safe to say that both of these supplemental initiatives will be ready to be launched well before the Cardinals gather in Rome for the Consistory." Maestroianni all but smacked his lips. "Added to the other means we can devise, they will bring pressure on His Holiness to sign the Resignation Protocol—before he leaves for Kiev, of course."

Beyond that, Maestroianni said, they would play everything by ear. The closer they came to the climax, the more they could expect the field of battle to change. "But be confident, my friends. With the Common Mind Vote all but in our pocket, and with all the Cardinals in the world coming to town, the initiative remains with us. Despite the Pontiff's little surprises, the initiative remains with us."

"Gladstone here." Reluctantly, Chris answered the phone in his study at the Angelicum. He had managed to set aside most of this day to make some serious headway in deciphering the cramped entries in Aldo Carnesecca's diary before setting off on yet another round of chicanery among the bishops for Cardinal Maestroianni. He didn't relish the idea of needless interruptions.

"Gibson Appleyard speaking, Father. Forgive the intrusion. Perhaps you remember me. Jan Borliuth of the EC was kind enough to bring me along for a visit at your brother's house in Deurle at Christmas."

"Yes, Mr. Appleyard. Of course I remember."

"I know it's short notice, Father. But is there any chance we can have a talk?" The silence on the line told Gib he had some resistance to overcome. "It is important, Father. I'm to see His Holiness on Monday morning on behalf of my government. Our government. It would be to our mutual benefit to meet."

"How about tomorrow afternoon here at the Angelicum, Mr. Appleyard?"

Gladstone dialed Giustino Lucadamo to find out what the security chief might know about an American government man by the name of Gibson Appleyard.

Giustino recognized the name at once. And he knew of the Monday meeting with the Pope—something to do with the situation between the Holy See and the U.S. government on population control. "If he's reached out to you, see him." Lucadamo made it sound like an order. "Essentially, he's full of goodwill. But he's no mean personage. I'll send over a confidential dossier on him so you'll realize what you're up against. And I'll throw in a précis of the Pontiff's recent dealings with the American administration for good measure."

Within the hour, Gladstone had those materials in hand and began boning up for a meeting he really didn't want to have. Appleyard's personal dossier fixed certain salient points in Christian's mind. This American diplomat was a prominent and serious member of the Masonic Order in the United States. His history with the Order, as well as his academic background and his governmental career, marked him as one of those perpetual insiders who never cut a very visible public figure, but who are always at the forward edge of national affairs. Both Appleyard and his wife, a Catholic by birth, came from old and solid money. That part of the profile was one Gladstone recognized. All in all, Mr. Gibson Appleyard figured as a trusted American who enjoyed enormous credit at the upper levels of government.

Christian turned to the rest of the materials Lucadamo had sent over. Apparently, a complete impasse had developed between the Slavic Pope and the U.S. administration. The United States sided with the UN Fund for Population Administration in its push for universal population control, and the widespread use of abortion as a means to that end. Until recently, the UN had subscribed to the principle that abortion should not be actively promoted as a means of family planning. Now, however, that stance had changed. Ms. Francis and her colleagues were working their way toward a declaration that would promote abortion as a fundamental right and as a legitimate method of family planning throughout the world. If all went as planned, that declaration would be ratified in a formal document at a major international conference on population control scheduled to take place in Cairo.

As the situation stood even now, a number of nations represented in the UN Agency had already signed a consensus agreement recommending abortion and a wide gamut of contraceptives as their official weapons for birth control. That much was a fait accompli. Nothing could undo it. Only a handful of nations stood with the Slavic Pope's antiabortion and anticontraceptive position. Faced with this crux, the Holy Father had telephoned the American President to plead his case. But neither the President nor his wife had given him any satisfaction. Both were adamantly in favor of abortion and contraception. The President had promised to send an envoy who would explain the U.S. position to His Holiness. Gibson Appleyard was that envoy.

From the moment the two Americans sat down together in Gladstone's study there was a mutual feeling of respect and pleasure.

Assuming that Gladstone had checked him out, and relying on his own judgment of the priest as an open-minded man, Gibson plunged immediately into his subject with total candor. "In the matter of population control, there is a total breakdown of understanding between His Holiness and the President. Without some guidance, I feel I don't know how to create an understanding between them. Can you help me in that, Father Gladstone? My aim is solely to create understanding."

Christian detected no partisan note in the query. No defensiveness. No offensive undercurrent. "Is it your opinion, Mr. Appleyard, that neither man is really free to choose a position?"

Gib gave a straight answer to a fair question. "Correct, Father. His Holiness is in strict conformity with his duty as Pope and with the expectation of his sponsors—on earth and in Heaven! Likewise, the President is in strict conformity with his duty and with the expectation of his sponsors."

Gladstone rose from his chair and opened the window onto the piazza below. He needed a couple of seconds to find his way more deeply into the question his visitor had just raised. "Tell me, sir. Way back at the beginning of this year—before the UN-sponsored conferences made such headway for the cause of population control—many reports coming to the Holy Father were optimistic for the Pontiff's viewpoint. Reports, I should add, that came from His Holiness' own Mission to the UN. What happened since then?"

Appleyard showed no change of expression. "There has been a change in emphasis, Father Gladstone. It has been clear from the beginning of this administration that the Executive Order we know these days as NSM 200 would be strictly and categorically applied. However, the Catholic Liaison Group that works with the White House assured the President that the North American hierarchy would not judge the population question solely from a Roman Catholic point of view. It's fair to say that assurance cemented the President's policy."

Having learned so much about so many in the American hierarchy, Chris wasn't surprised at Appleyard's statement. But he was puzzled about particulars. "Refresh my memory, sir. The membership of that official Liaison Group escapes me."

"Well"—Gib ticked off the roster on his fingers—"there's Catholics for a Free Choice. And the Dignity people. The Call to Action people. The Cardinal of Centurycity. The Secretary of the American Bishops Committee for Democratic Affairs . . ."

Gladstone got the picture. "So those early and optimistic reports coming to Rome created the perfect climate in which the UN Agency could proceed toward a consensus, without a note of alarm being sounded beforehand in the Holy Father's ears."

Chris questioned Gibson with a look, and read assent in his eyes. "I see. Well, Mr. Appleyard, no wonder there's a crisis."

Not yet, Gib thought to himself. You don't see it all yet. It was one thing to understand the aims of those organizations who sent their delegates to the Catholic Liaison Group at the White House. For differing reasons, all were opposed to the Pontiff's stand on contraception, homosexual lifestyles, abortion and allied questions. But there was more to it than that. "We must remember, Father. The President's stand was bolstered in the American public arena by this Liaison Group. But the stand itself stems from a higher level"—Appleyard let a second or two pass; just a momentary pause to allow understanding to catch up with words—"which, of course, no wise President can afford to ignore." Gladstone thought for a minute, then drew a deep breath. In an absent sort of way he noted that daylight was fading. Already the streetlamps had been lit.

"Let me be frank with you, Father." Appleyard hoped Gladstone would see that he meant those words sincerely. "I for one do not share the demographic fears of our contemporaries. For one thing, human fecklessness always seems to come to the aid of nature to redress any excessive population imbalance. But I also believe the evidence concerning overpopulation has been inflated; that the claims of imminent danger to the planet are fueled more by ideology than by scientific knowledge. On that score, I consider such organizations as the Planned Parenthood International about on a par with the already discredited Club of Rome, whose professional reputation was ruined by all their scientifically false pother about a global winter in the eighties.

"And the entire world economic picture has changed since President Nixon's day, when that Executive Order was first issued. I see no solid scientific data indicating that imposing birth control and abortion on Third World countries measures up as a legitimate strategic necessity for the United States."

Appleyard leaned forward. "What I'm saying to you is that I'm glad someone as prominent as His Holiness raises his voice. That's my personal feeling. Nevertheless, I'm here to represent my government's brief. No one expects His Holiness not to protest this planned global population control. But a direct challenge to the United States in this area is something else again. It's war. Wars—even nonmilitary wars—kill people. Usually the innocent.

"I've come here to ask your help in avoiding the death of innocents."

The silence that fell between the two men was the silence of mutual understanding. Perhaps even the silence of trust. Still, Christian wasn't sure he would ever get used to shocks like this. He'd hardly had time to grapple with the possibility of a papal resignation; and now an even more unthinkable possibility had been shoved under his nose.

"I'm grateful to you, Mr. Appleyard." Gladstone stood up. "Please be assured of my cooperation. I'm certain the Holy Father will understand the President's position more deeply now."

The official public announcement of the formal invitations from Moscow and Kiev overshadowed the day's activities in Rome and in many another world capital. By the time Appleyard stepped into the papal study at midmorning, the Slavic Pope had already been deluged with communications that ran the predictable gamut from congratulations to complaint.

"We know a visit to those two lands has been a long-nourished desire of Your Holiness." Gib came down on the side of the well-wishers. "I do hope it satisfies all Your Holiness' desires."

The Pontiff recognized the personal sincerity of the envoy's sentiment, thanked him for it and then went straight to the point of the meeting. "Monsignore Gladstone has made it possible for me to understand and appraise the position of your President, Mr. Appleyard. And that is most important." The Holy Father took a chair near the window and gestured his visitor into another. "Equally important for me is to clarify the management levels of government in the United States. What I call the macromanagement level, as distinct from the micromanagement level. Of course, I know that both levels meld on the plane of practical administration. But they *are* separate levels."

Appleyard smiled. Gladstone had obviously understood everything he had said, and had been thorough in his report to the Holy Father. That eased the way for both men to deal now with harsh diplomatic realities. "Yes, Holiness. I would say that. And the ultimate answer is that the population control policy is strictly a product of the macromanagement level."

"And the forthcoming international conference—the one planned for Cairo? That, too, is macromanagement's bailiwick?"

"Of course, Holiness."

There was some conversation about the more obvious participants at that level and about the general principles animating them. But the Pontiff came quickly enough to his central theme, and stated it with the frankness and clarity that Gib so rarely found elsewhere and that he so valued in this man. "Mr. Appleyard, I want you and the President to understand our policy and our opinion on this side of the fence. In his last message, your President proposed to me that he and I agree to make a common statement in favor of a universal rule for Catholics and non-Catholics. A rule or norm of two children per couple at a maximum. Of course, I refused."

"Holiness, at that moment the President was speaking from the macromanagement point of view."

"And I am speaking from the point of view of Christ—the real governor and manager of this cosmos. From that perspective, it seems plain that the birth control policy of the United States as enshrined now in NSM 200 is the result of North American cultural imperialism imposed on Third World nations whose natural resources the U.S.A. covets for the strategy of its survival as a superpower. Moreover, the support given by the U.S.A. to the latest paper produced by the UN Fund on Population Control is a cause of shame to Christians and a serious setback for humanity. It would legitimize abortion on demand, sexual promiscuity and distorted notions of the family. In short, it proposes the imposition of libertine and individualistic lifestyles as the base and norm for the society of nations."

Appleyard flushed slightly. The Holy Father was being frank, all right. So frank that the American was pinned into a corner. He had said to Gladstone that he saw his government's policy in this area as driven not by facts, but by ideologues. But, like the Pope, he also saw it as antifamily and as inimical to the social order. Right now, though, there was the other side to the situation. He didn't believe in the efficacy of ultimatums in this negotiation—that was why he had sought Gladstone out. But if he was to head off a crisis, he needed an answer to one question. That being so, he decided to respond to the Pontiff's candor with an equal measure on his side.

"Holy Father, the official position of my government apart, I personally share Your Holiness' assessment of this situation. My difficulty—and Your Holiness', too—is that at the macromanagement level, the opposite view now reigns. And at that level, there is power enough to impose that view."

"And?" The Pope knew Appleyard hadn't come here merely to state the obvious.

"There are rumors, Holy Father. The urgent question is whether Your Holiness will directly challenge U.S. policy on population control by publishing an ex cathedra pronouncement condemning abortion and contraception."

Something more than rumors, the Pope thought with a glance in the direction of Cardinal Graziani's office. Then, returning his full attention to the American diplomat, he laid the situation out as plainly as he could. There was no need to enter into the consequences of such a papal challenge, he said. He had reckoned them all up, and they were insignificant in his eyes. "What does matter, Mr. Appleyard, is the timing of any such challenge. Now, this double invitation from Eastern Europe changes the timing for this Holy See. So the answer to your main query is that the President need no longer expect a near-future papal statement condemning his population control policies as irreconcilable with Catholic dogma."

Gib was relieved but mystified.

"You are wondering, Mr. Appleyard"—the Pontiff guessed the meaning of the quizzical look on the envoy's face—"what my trip to Moscow and Kiev has to do with the difficulty between the papacy and the presidency. The explanation is simple. That I am allowed to undertake this pilgrimage is a direct favor from the person we Catholics call the Queen of Heaven. She has been selected by God from all ages and in every age for a special role among us. She is in charge of all this. Of all of us. She has willed this papal trip—this pilgrimage, I should say—to take place. Therefore, I have good reason to believe that, in her own way, she will use the occasion of my so-called Russia trip to resolve the problem between my papacy and your American presidency."

Appleyard nodded benignly—an apt disguise, he hoped, for his bewilderment at the ease with which the Pope moved from the practical plane of life-and-death decisions to a level that seemed abstract and alien to concrete reality. The Slavic Pope's face was wreathed in such an expression of joyous confidence, and his eyes shone with such happiness, that Gibson had to turn his own gaze elsewhere. If I ever felt the way this man does now, Gib heard himself say in his mind, I would have to fall on my knees, crave his blessing and his forgiveness for my sins and weep tears I've never wept . . .

"In the meantime, however . . ." The Slavic Pope was back on what Gibson regarded as practical terrain. "In the meantime, and as I have written to all the heads of state—including your President and the Secretary-General of the UN—you cannot expect that those of us on this side of the fence will accept such an all-out attack on the values of nature, morality and religion without protest. But if you wish, Mr. Appleyard . . ." The Holy Father all but banished the tension of the moment with one of those open smiles of his. "If you wish, in good time I will send you an early copy of the letter I have planned on this subject. And you have my word that I will not publish it until after my trip next year to Russia and Ukraine."

The American's relief this time was clear and unclouded. A promise like that from this man was as good as gold. Perhaps the war hadn't been called off. But at least he could report to Vance that there was no immediate crisis. In the circumstances, Appleyard couldn't ask for more.

With Maestroianni's injunction to bring constant pressure on the Holy Father to sign the Resignation Protocol as his goad, Cardinal Secretary Graziani devised ingenious reasons to see the Pontiff more frequently than usual. Among the most legitimate of those reasons was the need to firm up as much as possible at this early date the main events of the Pope's Russia trip and the plans for the General Consistory of Cardinals.

"This is going to be a cruel pilgrimage, Holy Father. All of Their Eminences at home and abroad have expressed fear for Your Holiness' health and for the governance of the Church. At this perilous moment in the Church's life, we need Your Holiness' undivided attention."

With Graziani's intent clear to him, the Slavic Pope answered as casually as he could. "I will rely on my doctors' judgment, Eminence."

"Yes, of course, Holy Father. But medical wisdom extends so far, and no farther. The margin of error is wide. As Your Holiness' chief advisors and co-gerents of the Church's welfare, Their Eminences are convinced that their word should be the ultimate factor entering into Your Holiness' judgment."

The Cardinal Secretary had reminded His Holiness of a simple fact of papal life and Vatican administration. The Pope would not go on his Russia trip without the approval of his Cardinals as a college of Church advisors. That was how this Pope had acted from day one of his pontificate. That was how he would act now. And besides, according to the Pontiff himself, no less a personage than the Blessed Mother required the cooperation from the Cardinals for this particular pilgrimage.

His trump card on the table, Graziani rummaged among the folders on his lap, extracted one marked "Resignation Protocol" and laid it on the Pontiff's desk. "Have compassion on our worries, Holy Father. Let me leave the latest draft text of the Protocol Their Eminences hope Your Holiness will approve as a pontifical constitution governing papal succession. We *do* worry, you know, when Your Holiness is away on these strenuous trips. We need to take steps. We, too, bear the burden of the Church Universal."

A blink. A smile. And the Cardinal Secretary was gone.

"I have just been taught my lesson for today." The Pontiff was already scanning the Protocol as Monsignore Daniel entered from his adjoining office.

"What lesson is that, Holy Father?"

The Pope gave his old friend a sardonic smile. "Popes, too, must behave themselves. Otherwise, their Cardinals won't be nice to them!"

XLVI

NEARLY EVERYTHING about the closing weeks of that year and the opening weeks of the next left a bad taste in Gladstone's mouth. As general gofer in Cardinal Maestroianni's operation, he'd been detailed to make the rounds of key bishops in several European capitals and then go on to the United States again, where he would see some dozen or so ranking members of the American hierarchy, including the Cardinal of Centurycity. As Maestroianni explained it to Chris, and as Chris explained it to Giustino Lucadamo, his main function in all cases was to light a fire under the bishops in the matter of the Common Mind Vote.

"It looks like they're going to skip the public phase of the CMV," Gladstone told the Vatican security chief. "Maestroianni's idea seems to be to accelerate the timetable. He wants the formal results in hand from all the Internal Affairs Committees by April."

Lucadamo almost expected something like this, he said. If the Cardinal and his cronies could present at least a quasi-unanimous CMV to the full College of Cardinals in early May, that might be the final wedge in the effort to be rid of the Slavic Pope. "Anything else on your travel agenda, Monsignore?" Giustino seemed ready for more bad news.

"Some more polling and politicking." Chris shrugged. "His Eminence seems interested in stirring things up over the issue of Altar girls, but he hasn't told me what that's all about."

Chris had one question of his own before he left to pack for his travels. Aldo Carnesecca's murder was never far from his mind. But no. Lucadamo and his team had come up with nothing.

"Look at it this way, Monsignore," Giustino quipped. "With all the traveling you'll be doing, at least you'll have a lot of plane and train time to devote to the diary."

Gladstone began his weeks of travel in Europe with a couple of days at Guidohuis. Paul was away in London, but Yusai greeted him with open arms at the airport, and Declan seemed positively ecstatic to see him. Christian's arrival, it seemed, coincided with one of the happiest events in his nephew's young life. Still aflame with enthusiasm for cave exploration, Deckel was to be initiated the following day as a full-fledged Junior Member of the Royal Belgian Society of Speleologues. Nothing would do but that Uncle Chris should be his special guest on a tour he would lead through the famed cavern known as the Lesser Danielle. "Please come," Deckel pleaded as Yusai drove them home to Deurle. "Daddy has to be away for a special meeting, and I'd be so proud, Uncle Chris. Please say yes . . ."

Chris did say yes, and regretted it.

The next afternoon, it was a very proud Declan Gladstone who led his uncle and a small party of Society officials and guests into the Lesser Danielle. Through a complex of caves they went, around narrow hairpin bends, down sudden drops and up steep underground ascents. But by the time the group reached its destination—the vaulted chamber known as Sainte Chapelle—the excursion had taken its toll on Christian's mind. He listened to his nephew talk about "draperies" and "curtains"; but the echo of the boy's voice in the otherwise utter stillness of the earthen cavern assumed a macabre tone for Christian. The image of innocent childhood swallowed up in darkness would not leave his memory.

Chris tried to pass the experience off as part of his mood these days. But in all innocence Yusai made that impossible. She had her own worries, and she was grateful to be able to confide them to her brother-in-law before dinner that night at Guidohuis. "It's Paul." She looked at Chris with an embarrassed smile. "Sometimes I'm afraid I'm losing him. More than once in the past year he's had to be away for a few days . . ."

Infidelity? Paul? Not a chance! "He's been away before, Yusai. He's Secretary-General of the European Union, after all . . ."

Yusai shook her head. Not another woman; nothing like that. Something to do with Paul's Lodge association. Some sort of turmoil, some sort of split that had taken place, something that left him ill-humored and distracted for days at a time. "I've been so desperate that I've even begun to say the Rosary."

Christian promised to speak with Paul. He'd be busy the next day with the bishops of Ghent and Bruges, and then with the Cardinal Archbishop of Malines in Brussels. But he'd see his brother at the Berlaymont the next afternoon before going on to Paris.

Chris saw Paul all right. He even caught a whiff of that strange new element in his brother's character that Yusai had described. But whatever it was, there would be no time to get at it on this visit. Instead, there was a reception at the Berlaymont that evening for a dense crowd of luminaries from all the European institutions and the global organs of the UN. Paul's presence as Secretary-General of the European Union was mandatory; and he took care to introduce his distinguished brother from the Vatican to the Commissioners and to several important colleagues.

But Christian's adventures with Declan in the Lesser Danielle, his conversation with Yusai and his own day's work among the bishops of Belgium had left him in poor humor for crowd scenes. He saw Gibson Appleyard and was just making his way across the room to have a word with him when Jan Borliuth came up beside him, took him in tow and presented him to a little group whose central figure needed no introduction. "Mikhail Gorbachev, founder and head of the Green Cross International . . ." Chris heard the name and up-to-date credentials on Borliuth's lips; but all he could think of as he felt the firm handclasp was the Slavic Pope. Somewhere inside himself, he rebelled at the thought of this man as an intimate correspondent of the Holy Father.

"And," Borliuth continued the introductions, "this is Herr Otto Sekuler. He and Mr. Serozha Gafin here are board members of Mr. Gorbachev's GCI."

Sekuler—a spare, bald-headed bespectacled character given to clicking his heels—registered as an odd duck whom Chris would rather not get to know. The husky, slant-eyed Gafin, on the other hand, registered as someone he'd seen before. . . .

"You may know Mr. Gafin from the concert stage." Borliuth supplied the missing clue. "And Herr Sekuler is chairman of the World Solidarity of Ethical Thought."

Christian smiled his way through some minutes of small talk. He thanked Mr. Gorbachev for his invitation to visit him at San Francisco's Presidio or, better still, in Moscow's Red Square. "My thought and the Holy Father's thought coincide perfectly," Gorbachev offered with polished political grace. "The world environmental crisis is the real basis for our new ecumenism."

"*Ach, ja,*" Sekuler agreed.

"I hate to interrupt such a pleasant conversation . . ." Gladstone turned as Paul strode up behind him. "But if my brother is going to catch his train . . ."

Chris was grateful for the rescue. But he wished they could have had an hour alone. He wished he could have explained his fears for Deckel, and Yusai's fears for Paul.

There was a banal sameness about all of Christian's interviews this time around. Business was conducted on a rigidly impersonal note. The few personal comments that passed between him and the various Cardinals and bishops were nonspecific. He was offered neither a meal nor refreshments by any one of them. And though he knew the contents of the documents he carried, only indirect reference was made to the materials he conveyed to them. "A glorified mailman, that's what I am," he told himself as he rounded off the weeks of his European tour and headed for his flight to the United States. "And not very glorified at that!"

The story of his visits to the U.S. Cardinals was the same. Not even his visit to Jay Jay O'Cleary in New Orleans broke the pattern. From the moment His Eminence got a look at Maestroianni's accelerated timetable for the successful conduct of a unanimous Common Mind Vote, and then read the paragraph in which Maestroianni held each Cardinal personally accountable on this capital score, O'Cleary's reaction was marked more by fear for his Roman ambitions than by his well-known regard for his connection with the mighty Gladstones.

There was one exception. To Christian's mind, His Eminence of Centurycity didn't merely lack all sense of social propriety; he showed not a grain of ordinary civility. His eyes empty of feeling, he treated the Vatican messenger as he did any subordinate. What compelled him to deal with Gladstone at all—or Gladstone with him, for that matter—was their common relationship to Cardinal Maestroianni. Unlike O'Cleary, the Cardinal of Centurycity didn't blink at Maestroianni's accelerated schedule. The deadline was April? Well and good. It was all to be accomplished through the IACs now, with no public phase in advance of the General Consistory? Well and good. Maestroianni would hold Centurycity doubly accountable for a successful outcome in the U.S.A.? In a pig's eye!

"You will carry back one message to His Eminence, Monsignore." The American Cardinal folded away the last of the documents Maestroianni had sent him. "Tell him that now is the opportune time to publish the agreement already reached between the Holy See and the U.S. hierarchy concerning the use of Altar girls in the liturgy *and* concerning the appointment of deaconesses as parish pastors." The Cardinal's smile was mechanical. "I depend on you, Monsignore, to convey that message accurately."

Gladstone managed to show an impassive face to the Cardinal. He knew of no agreement between the Holy See and the hierarchy about Altar girls, but he had obviously been badly off the mark in reckoning the importance of the issue in Maestroianni's plans. What hit him hardest, however, was that this ecclesiastical turncoat should remain so powerful at the topmost level of the American hierarchy; and that he should make such a brazen push for catapulting illicit, invalid deaconesses into the role of parish administrators.

Gladstone's report to a delighted Cardinal Maestroianni and his debriefing by a grim Giustino Lucadamo added still more urgency to the high-pitched atmosphere surrounding the Pontiff's projected journey.

"No wonder His Eminence didn't care to commit his message to writing," Lucadamo growled when Chris got to that part of his story. "Of course there's been no papal agreement to allow the use of Altar girls, and certainly not to allow unordained deaconesses to serve as parish pastors. It's just more of their lies and their tactics. Clearly, the aim is to have women priests."

"That's not the whole aim." Gladstone was beginning to think like Maestroianni by now. "The goal is to misrepresent as meaningless any legislative statements of this Pope. And the real message they intend to drive home is that this Pope doesn't matter; doesn't count any longer. It's the bishops who count. It's the laity. It's the Roman Congregations. Ultimately, the message is that the Church has outgrown that medievalism called the papacy."

Still, Chris didn't see how the message could be implemented. "Surely they can't publish a bogus document just like that. It would have to carry someone's signature, and Maestroianni is too canny to come out in the open like that."

Lucadamo's response of tight-lipped silence set off an explosion in Gladstone's mind. Aldo Carnesecca had always said there was a plan behind all this, and maybe he'd been right. But Carnesecca was dead, and everything seemed to be spiraling out of hand. What kind of a plan was it that brooked such obvious contempt for the Pope? In the silent explosion of that moment, Chris knew Lucadamo had no answers for his questions. It was like a replay of the scene in the papal study when he had understood that the Pope would shove his report into limbo. But now he had to wonder if anything he did was going to make a difference. No matter how much evidence he uncovered or how damning it was, would any of it make a difference?

When Lucadamo filled the Holy Father in on Gladstone's report, the Pontiff agreed with their assessment of the goals of his adversaries. But the problem that vexed Gladstone almost beyond endurance was not enough to deflect the Slavic Pope from the larger offensive he was carrying forward.

Part of that offensive had to do with the burgeoning consensus of Bischara Francis' UN agency. It had become imperative that His Holiness step up his own counterattack on the battleground of population control and the traditional moral teaching of the Church. He used every opportunity to plead against the use of abortion and contraceptives. In his weekly public addresses, in his speeches to visiting groups of pilgrims and to the regular flow of VIPs who wanted to add a personal audience with the Holy Father to their public record, he carried his attack vigorously forward. Finally, he moved the action to the front where he knew he could make the most headway. To Embassy Row.

Rome was the official residence for most of the nations' ambassadors and consular representatives to the Italian state—to "the Quirinal," as diplomatic usage described them. Further, there were diplomatic representatives from at least 117 nations accredited to the Holy See itself. This double cluster of representation was, in fact, what gave the diplomatic corps of the Eternal City its peculiar luster. Its unique value as a source of information and an international whispering gallery was enhanced by the fact that Rome was considered the great global meeting ground; the capital where East and West mingled as a matter of daily necessity.

The Slavic Pope saw to it that his message countering the United Nations consensus ranged up and down this densely populated, international nerve center. By turns that message was pleading or protesting; prayerful or cajoling; suggesting or blaming; encouraging or annoying. But always it carried the same theme: "At present, there is an organized attack on the vital unity of the nation—each nation. Namely, the family. Ultimately, this is an attack on each nation, on the family of nations and on the human race."

Because the Pope's counterattack was open, because he mentioned names and because American participation in financing population control in Third World countries ran to the billions, the United States inevitably became the target of remarks and criticisms. Well-trained Vatican spokesmen repeated the same message as they made their way in the circuit of cocktail gatherings, buffets, receptions and dinners. Copies of the Executive Order mandating an imperative U.S. birth control policy popped up as if by magic and made the rounds.

The Slavic Pope had a single aim in this campaign. He had promised Gibson Appleyard that he wouldn't publish his ex cathedra encyclical letter without prior notice. But he had preserved his prerogative to use every other means at his disposal to force the U.S. government to open talks with the Holy See in this grave matter.

Perhaps it took longer than one might have expected. Bernard Pizzolato was not the brightest Ambassador the Americans had ever sent to the Quirinal. But the day finally came when even he got the message.

"Unless this campaign of papal rumormongering is halted, and soon"—Bernie Pizzolato aimed his rage at a confused Admiral Bud Vance—"the United States will have to come to the Pope's bargaining table; and that spells the effective elimination of the Executive Order!"

"What about it, Gib?" Bud turned to Appleyard. "We gotta get some clarity here. What's this Pope doing with all his rumormongering about the United States? Is it just a prelude? Is he secretly preparing a letter after all? Is he getting ready to condemn U.S. population control policy?"

"Come on, Bernie." Gibson glared at Pizzolato. "Let's cut out the hot air. If you spent less time cozying up to this Pope's enemies and more time cultivating the Pontiff, you might have a better feel for what he's doing."

"And just what might that be, Appleyard?"

"I'll tell you what it's not, Mr. Ambassador," Gib shot back. "There'll be no letter from the Holy Father for now. If he contemplates anything like that in the near future, we'll know it beforehand. And—I repeat, *and*—we'll have a preliminary look at anything by way of a letter or document he proposes to publish."

"Well, then." Pizzolato practically bared his teeth. "I guess you can say I don't trust the Pope in this matter. Or in much of anything else!" With that, he turned heel and stalked out of the office.

Left in the privacy of their own deliberations, Vance and Appleyard went to the heart of the matter.

"Look, Bud." Appleyard sat back in his chair and crossed his long legs. "We all know we're in a minefield. One false step and it will blow us to smithereens. We don't need the kind of secondhand information Bernie picks up." Gib was no Catholic, he reminded Vance, but he'd learned not to trust renegades. He wasn't about to stand by and let a mercenary go-getter like Pizzolato muddy waters for no good reason except that he hated the religion of his fathers. In fact, it seemed to him that a man who would welsh on his religion would welsh on anyone and everyone.

"You're sure of the Slavic Pope, then?"

"As sure as I am of anything. He's walking a tightrope, and he's very high up. I mean, it's a long fall down to where some of his own crowd want to push him. But he's given his word to us and . . ."

The look on Vance's face stopped Appleyard in mid-sentence. He'd seen that expression before. It said: I know more than you think, Gib! "Come on, Admiral. Cough it up. What is it?"

"Remember your old friend Cyrus Benthoek?"

"Sure."

"And Professor Ralph Channing?"

"I've never met him, but I know who he is. Everyone knows who he is. And if memory serves, he came up in Otto Sekuler's file."

"Well, they both breezed in here the other day. The NSC called over to announce them. That's why Pizzolato's reading of things has me so confused. Benthoek and Channing confirm what you've been telling us about the Slavic Pope. Not about keeping his word. But about the pressure to get him out."

"What exactly?"

"They say we'll have a new Pope in Rome by the end of May."

Appleyard stopped breathing for a minute. "Did you take that seriously?"

"Add it up yourself. The pressure by the Pope's own crowd for him to resign; the pressure from the White House telling him to shut up; the pressure on his central policies by the UN; the voices that secured his invitation to Russia and Ukraine; the papal doomsday balloon floated by the likes of Benthoek and Channing at the NSC itself; and now this pointed and personal attack on him by Ambassador Pizzolato.

"Yeah, I take it seriously. In fact, I don't know how your Pope has withstood that kind of pressure for as long as he has!"

Suddenly and unaccountably, Gib felt as sad as if Vance had just announced the death of an esteemed friend, a valued personality, an admired role model, a beautiful mind. In all his professional life, he asked himself, when had he ever regretted the passing of a high public official in any land? Even in the U.S.A.? When had he ever been as sad as this—as lonesome as this—over the disappearance of any of the greats he had known? Never, was the answer. Never. Then, why now? Why was this piece of news about the Slavic Pope so paralyzing?

"Are you okay, Gib?"

"Just a little taken aback. Guess you got me with that news forecast . . ."

"I know you like the old guy." The Admiral was truly sympathetic.

"No, Bud." Appleyard got hold of himself. "I don't think you can really like any of these public leaders. The really big ones, I mean. Their persona as public leaders sets them outside that category. But . . ." He fell silent again. He thought he understood why he would feel bereaved if the Slavic Pope disappeared so soon from his life. The trouble was that he had no words for it.

"Well . . ." Vance shuffled the papers lying on his desk. Sympathy or no, he had some contradictions to deal with, and he needed Gibson's help. "Channing and your pal Benthoek were probably mixed up in some way in those invitations for the Pope's Eastern trip. At the very least, they know that Sekuler and that pianist character named Gafin made the arrangements. They said as much. We've known since Strasbourg that Benthoek is wired into the Church scene in the U.S.A. and into the Vatican. And Channing is right up there in the same league. They were both very keen on the papal visit going through."

"Have I missed a beat, Bud?" Appleyard scratched his head. "I thought the administration's complaint about the Slavic Pope had to do with his stand on population control, not his Russia trip."

"The administration's complaint has to do with too many mixed signals coming out of Rome. But let's go back to population control for a minute.

"Everyone knows the Pope's stand on that score and on the traditional moral teachings of his Church. Even Bernie Pizzolato knows the Slavic Pope won't compromise with the U.S. government. And you yourself have kept telling us that this Pope is going to fight tooth and nail against all and every attempt by the UN General Assembly to impose a universal limitation on the number of children permitted in each family."

"Sure I have, Bud. He made that clear to me. And he made it clear to the head of UNFPA, Bischara Francis. I spoke to her myself, and I can tell you she was pretty steamed after her audience with the Holy Father."

"Right. But now we've heard rumblings that some blue-ribbon Vatican think tank—the Pontifical Academy of Sciences, I think it's called—is about to put out a paper contradicting everything you say this Pope says about population control and resources. Now, if that stands up as official—if a blue-ribbon pontifical panel headquartered in the Pope's own city-state of the Vatican actually issues a turnabout of papal policy—can you blame us for being confused? Or, to put it another way, can you blame us for thinking this Pope isn't a straight hitter after all?"

Appleyard was ready to weigh in on that, but the Admiral wasn't half finished with his problem yet. Apparently, analysts at State had told Vance's superiors, including the Committee of Ten, that it could be unwise to take at face value the Pope's statement that his Russia trip was simply a religious pilgrimage. They thought the Pope was up to something else, and that it could involve the security of the United States. Like Pizzolato, they didn't trust the Pope. The mixed signals coming out of the Vatican on the population question only added fuel to their argument.

"That's just garbage."

"Maybe, Gib. But listen to their reasons."

First of all, Vance said, there was the private relationship between the Pontiff and Mikhail Gorbachev. They had been closely in touch while Gorbachev was the Soviet strongman, and they remained so now. But their relationship hadn't started all of a sudden when Gorbachev became Boss of All the Russias.

During its rise in Stalinist Poland in the seventies and eighties, the Solidarity Movement was manipulated remotely by the KGB center in Moscow to serve its own long-range plans. Vance knew that. Gib knew that. Nobody in the intelligence game was ignorant of that.

"We're quite cozy with Gorbachev ourselves right now." Vance came to the point. "But we may be in bed with a family of cobras. Our new Partnership for Peace arrangement with Russia—Boris Yeltsin's Russia—is the biggest gamble since World War II. Yet we're always operating in the dark. We never see the bride—we're not even sure who she is! But we have to share the marriage bed with her. And we have to wonder if someone else is courting her on the sly."

"You figure the Slavic Pope as the wanna-be bridegroom?"

"I figure there's reason to question this Pope's statement of intent. A clear picture is beginning to emerge from intelligence intercepts in Russia, Ukraine, Belarus and Poland. The suspicions of those on the scene—the people carrying out this surveillance—center on two or three main facts. For one thing, most of the radios operating in Greater Russia are in areas whose local Russian Orthodox bishops have secretly acknowledged the Slavic Pope as their spiritual leader. And it also turns out that Belarus has been invaded by hundreds of Polish priests and Polish-trained Belarussians. So a case can be made that the Slavic Pope is slowly taking over the governing structure of the ROC. We can't afford to forget that this man used a bunch of clerics to beat the stuffing out of the Stalinists in Poland. We have to ask ourselves if he intends to scuttle the boat in which we've floated our still rickety Partnership for Peace."

There was still more, and Vance piled it on for Appleyard. Papal fingerprints were all over some of the data, he said. There were two papal emissaries or couriers—a German and an Irishman—who were continually traveling between Rome and Eastern Europe, including Greater Russia. Several letter drops that had been identified in Europe had been tied at least tentatively to the Holy See itself.

Appleyard leaned forward. "What you've got, Bud, is a clear picture of a Pope who's working to convert people. That's what he does. That's his job. Unless I miss my guess, your intercepts are probably filled with references to Fatima and the Third Secret . . ."

"How the blazes did you know that?"

Gibson ignored the question. What else, he wanted to know, had turned up in the intercepts?

Vance looked sheepish. He had to admit that the code being used in the radio transmissions and written communications hadn't been broken yet. The analysts pored over references like the ones Gib had mentioned. References to Fatima, the Immaculate Heart of Mary, the Third Secret, the Pilgrim Statue of the Queen, the Blue Army. But they couldn't put it all together. They couldn't make out precisely what was being communicated. "Nevertheless"—Bud went on the offensive—"there's no doubt about it. There is an ongoing plan. Some sort of D-day event is being organized. But there are too many crosscurrents for us to be able to make sense of it.

"I can't figure why Benthoek and Channing would come here to tell us they favor a papal trip to Russia. I can't figure the Pope getting help from Sekuler or Gafin or that humbug ROC Patriarch Kiril. On the face of it, none of them are friends or well-wishers of the Slavic Pope. Or are they? But most of all, I can't figure the Pope himself. Who's being suckered in this game? Who's managing whom? I grant you that if the Pontifical Academy of Sciences really does come down on the side of limiting the size of families—if that stands up as official Holy See policy—it could ease things between the Pope and the President. I mean, if it's okay according to the Pope to establish a lid of two children per family, it's only a hop and a skip to imposing a one-child limit. And it's a short jump from there to imposing childless marriages—to the President's goal of zero population growth.

"But it's not that simple. If this Pope is telling you one thing and doing the exact opposite in the critical area of population policy—or even if he's just waffling in indecision—what's to say he isn't doing the same thing in his Russia policy? I hate to say it, Gibson. But maybe we're being made fools of by a crowd of old men in skirts!"

Appleyard knew as well as anybody in State how delicate the arrangement was between the U.S. government and Russia. Vance had been right about the rickety state of the Partnership for Peace. And he had made a good case about the dangers inherent for America in the contradictions and confusions coming out of the Vatican over papal policies and intent. Gibson's money was still on the Slavic Pope as a straight hitter, and he said so. But he needed time, he told Vance. Time to sort out what was true and what was not. Time to find out what was truly in America's best interest. Time to get back to Rome.

"Do as you judge best." Vance barely managed a smile. "Things are heating up between the Pope and this administration, so I haven't got a lot of leeway to give you. But for now, it's your baby."

"With all respect, Eminence, I don't see where the confusion lies." Cardinal Maestroianni looked indulgently at Cardinal Karmel. The other members of Secretary Graziani's ad hoc committee who had gathered for an update on a few main items of business—only Pensabene and Coutinho were absent—decided to sit this contest out for the moment. France's Cardinal Joseph Karmel was not a man to be indulged.

"With all respect, Eminence," Karmel boomed back at Maestroianni in his redoubtable Old Testament style. "You can talk all you like about your so-called supplemental initiatives. The fact remains that the Pontiff has been consistent in his opposition to the use of girls in the Sanctuary. He has promised there will never be permission for Altar girls. Only a few months ago, he forbade Altar girls. And only a few weeks ago he told Mother Teresa he would never allow Altar girls. Therefore, I do not see how you expect to publish a counterstatement and get away with it."

"We've gotten away with much more than that over the years." Noah Palombo found it hard to believe that any man who hoped to be Pontiff himself in the near future, as Karmel did, could be so timid. "The formula is tried and true by now. Once we slip something past him and get it accepted as common usage, this Pope won't fight to undo it."

"Quite so, Eminence." Maestroianni smiled. "I've worked out the details. For the first time, a statement will come from this Roman Chancery permitting Altar girls. And close on the heels of that initiative, we have arranged for a crisis in papal proposals about population control and demographics. You must agree, Eminence. These will serve as two excellent examples of the bishops acting for the good of the Church, even if they must countermand known papal views to do it. As the Americans are so fond of saying, let us see who blinks first."

It was too mysterious for Karmel's taste; he would have liked to know the details. He was clearly outnumbered, however. And Maestroianni was keen to get on to the central matter of the Resignation Protocol itself.

At the slightest nod from the little Cardinal, Secretary of State Graziani launched into a detailed account of how he had managed to place the Resignation Protocol in the context of the papal trip to the East.

"Eminence!" Maestroianni interrupted. "Have we got a definitive text or not? If we have, please show it to us."

"We have indeed, Eminence. It's not perfect. But it will do." Graziani had no intention of putting copies of this dynamite text into four different pairs of hands. Not without taking certain precautions. Not today. "Chiefly," he continued with stately dignity, "what we have now, as a result of much labor on my part, is a text which clearly states that, in the event of a total physical disability on this Holy Father's part to govern during his Russia trip, he will be deemed to have resigned from the papacy legally, voluntarily and forever. Recovery, partial or complete, will make no difference. The Throne of Peter will be considered empty. We will have *sede vacante*. The normal machinery for the election of a new Pope will go into action."

Cardinals Palombo and Aureatini shifted in their chairs. They had been nervous about leaving such a tricky business in Graziani's hands, but apparently he had pulled it off.

"His Holiness did insist on two points, however." Graziani ignored the glance that passed between Palombo and Aureatini. "He insists that this new legislation have only one application, and only on a one-time basis. That it apply only to himself, and only during the time of his Russia trip. If no application of the Protocol takes place before his return from the East, then the legislation falls into abeyance. It cannot be invoked again in his case, or in the case of any other Sovereign Pontiff."

Maestroianni waved all possible objections aside. "We never envisaged more than one application."

That much accepted by all, Graziani continued with the next papal condition. "No matter what I said or did, I could not get the Holy Father's agreement to sign the document *before* his departure for the East. He will initial it. But he will sign it only if circumstances during the trip make it abundantly clear that he should do so."

It was Cardinal Karmel again who grumbled. How could a comatose Pope decide to sign anything? Unaccountably, however, he found himself steamrollered for the second time. No one else seemed to see his logic or to share his concern.

On the contrary, Graziani was ready to explain the whole question away in legal terms. "We all know, Eminence, that an initialing of a legal document can be probated into a full signature, under Canon Law."

"I, too, would prefer a full signature at the outset," Maestroianni chimed in. "But we can make do with a mere initialing. We've made do with less in other cases . . ."

"One final point." Graziani looked at each man in the room. "His Holiness wishes the document to be held secret until and unless it acquires the force of law by its implementation."

"We can live with all of those conditions, Eminence." For the final time, Maestroianni spoke for the group. "Now, may we have copies of the document?"

For the first time, Graziani bested Maestroianni at his own game. "Of course, Eminence. Just as soon as all the technical details are completed. The protocol classification and so forth."

The little Cardinal was tempted to insist. But what was the point? Thanks to Monsignore Gladstone, the CMV was assured; and the message he had brought back from Centurycity had been most timely. The Pontiff himself was tired; too tired, surely, to withstand the pressure of the double-barreled supplemental initiatives about to hit his pontificate. And, while Dr. Channing felt a shortcut might have to be arranged at some crucial stage, any way you looked at it, the Russia journey would be this Pope's final effort. It was a small matter, then, to let Graziani have his head for a while longer. "As you say, Eminence. All in good time, eh?"

If Cardinal Palombo had his way, history would soon be smiling upon him in particular. He stayed on after the others to share a glass of wine with Maestroianni and to work out a strategy to present his candidacy for Peter's Chair. Though his voice and his face were as blank as ever, he was plainly bent on having that strategy set before the General Consistory of Cardinals opened in early May.

"Absolutely, Eminence. I will turn my attention to it in the next few weeks!" Maestroianni knew how essential it was that he hold his own forces together. This was no more than a problem of success, he told himself. It wouldn't be long, in fact, before he would have all the other papal contenders like Coutinho and Karmel to bargain with—not to mention such obvious Pope-makers as Pensabene of Rome, Boff of Westminster and His Eminence of Centurycity. Still, no one with an ounce of experience and a desire to survive would tackle Cardinal Palombo frontally, especially on the subject of his own papal candidacy. It was with a great deal of skill that the little Cardinal managed to smile this most sullen of his colleagues to the door without the issue coming to a head.

"We will talk." Such was Palombo's skill with overtones that his three bland words of parting remained behind as a living presence in Maestroianni's life. As a request and a statement. As a suggestion and a command. As a prediction and a threat.

XLVII

BY MID-FEBRUARY, Damien Slattery was beginning to doubt his grip on things. With the Pontiff's Russia trip just ten weeks off, he could feel tension all around him as things heated up in Rome. But his precipitate fall from Dominican grace meant, among other things, that he was no longer at the center of action as he had been for so many years at the Angelicum. These days, in fact, when he wasn't holed up at the Casa del Clero working on the Pope's encyclical on contraception, abortion and homosexuality—*Current Errors and Abuses,* it was called—he was traipsing about the United States tending to his duties as spiritual director of Cessi Gladstone's growing corps of underground priests.

On the morning when he was due for a special catch-up conference with the Holy Father, therefore, Slattery called Chris Gladstone at first light and coaxed him to an early breakfast at Springy's eatery. He was looking for solace and a good, solid update on things. What he got was an earful of bad news.

"I declare to God and all His angels"—Christian tore into the platter Springy set before him—"if I hear one more bishop telling me of his plans to draft a new mission statement for his diocese, or appointing some new task force to identify intermediary objectives and ultimate goals for Church life, I might just throw the whole mess at Maestroianni and tell him what to do with it!"

"Which of them is it now?" Damien raised his coffee cup to Springy for a timely refill.

"That whited sepulcher and unworthy prelate, my Lord Bishop of Nashville, Connecticut. It's all just drivel, Damien. But he's a perfect man for Maestroianni. He's constantly stumping for female deacons and the ordination of women. Meanwhile, his diocese is the Devil's own joke. He has the highest rate of high school pregnancy and the lowest rate of Mass attendance on the eastern seaboard. No Sunday sermons ever. The two cases of priestly pedophilia he settled out of court last year alone cost him millions. And he's got Altar girls and female Eucharistic ministers coming out of his ears!"

Damien shook his head. "The Pontiff has been muzzy about a lot of issues, but he has been clear about that!"

"And so have all his predecessors. But prepare yourself, my friend. Maestroianni plans to publish some kind of bogus document to get around His Holiness on this score. I don't know how he expects to pull it off, but I do know why. If they're going to hijack the Holy Father into resigning, they'd better prepare people for the change."

"Have you told His Holiness?"

"Lucadamo has. But I'm afraid, Damien, this is going to be one more battle lost in a long and bitter war." Chris shoved his plate aside. "I've been rethinking our conversations when we were at Windswept. We were so eager to do a good job of work for His Holiness. But, like water poured out on cement, it's all come to nothing. So tell me. Do you still think this is the man Christ wants as Pope precisely at this critical juncture of events?"

"Yes!" Maybe Damien was losing his grip on some things, but about this he remained as certain as sunrise.

"Do you think this Holy Father is still a Roman Catholic believer?"

"Yes."

"On what grounds?"

"On the grounds of Roman Catholic faith. He refuses to abandon the basics. In morality, he maintains our Catholic opposition to abortion, contraception, homosexuality, divorce and bedrock rules of that kind. In dogma, he champions all the main beliefs—the divinity of Christ, the privileges of Mary, Heaven, Hell, the Last Judgment. He'll never change on any of that."

"Okay. So he keeps banging away about those four or five moral rules. But all the while, he lets the whole Church slide into chaos and ruin. Or are you prepared to argue that he's a competent governor of the Church?"

"No. Incompetent. But I am prepared to argue that he wouldn't be Pope—couldn't be Pope—if Christ didn't want him to be Pope. And I'm prepared to argue that anyone who expects a restoration of the old comfortable Church we knew when you were in knee britches can forget it. As much as we abhor it, we're paying the piper for the intent of all those bishops at Vatican II. It was as though they were saying, 'We don't know exactly what we're doing, but nobody—not God, not Christ, not the People of God, not the wide world of mankind—will tolerate the absolutist monarchy of the papacy any longer.' "

"Hold on, Damien," Chris flared. "I've been machine-gunned by too many bishops with all that pap about the intent of Vatican II. But you hit the nail on the head, my friend. Most of them didn't know what they were doing. They let themselves be suckered by a crowd of people who had lost their Catholic faith. They were taken over by the Rahners, the Maritains, the Reinvernunfts, the Küngs, the Courtney Murrays, the von Balthasars, the Congars, the de Lubacs. And they've been carrying the water ever since for all the others—for women who see Holy Orders as nothing more than another notch on their gun of equality; for homosexuals who think vindication lies in the Conciliar Church; for abortionists who beat a bloody path from their stirrup couches to their countinghouses."

"Wait a minute, laddie!" Damien held up a huge hand in mock defense. "I'm on your side, remember?"

"Sorry, Slattery," Chris relented. "I know you're right. The old Church isn't coming back. Not with this Pope. Not with any Pope. But neither do I think the bishops of Vatican II meant to shove us into this permanent state of war. So I just can't figure it. We both know the Slavic Pope isn't stupid. And we both know he's not an apostate. But I can't figure why he goes on allowing what he himself calls the fraudulence of our ecclesiastical life."

Damien had no sure answers. Maybe Christ had chosen this man to be His Pope more for his faults than for his other qualities. Maybe the Pontiff himself had let things go too far to get them in hand. Maybe he'd given up so much power because he knew the old system was dead. Still, come what may, Slattery was sure of two things.

"I'll bet you another breakfast at Springy's that His Holiness is not going to cave in and resign. He's more useful as Pope than any of the radical progressivists like Coutinho and Palombo and Karmel and my old pal from Centurycity who are panting for a chance to take his place. You and I both know that much. I reckon the Holy Father knows it, too."

"And?"

"Maybe this will turn out to be another battle lost, as you say. But always remember, Gladstone. The war won't be over till the Last Trumpet sounds. And no matter how many battles we lose, it ends with the victory of Christ."

The Slavic Pope seemed so confident that morning that Slattery was practically ready to collect his bet with Christian. This was not a man, Slattery thought, who was ready to cave in. The first thing His Holiness wanted was an update on the progress of Signora Gladstone's project in America, and this was one report Damien was happy to give.

"There are difficulties and some individual failures, Holy Father. But as a group, the underground network has met with immediate success in its main purpose. Our priests supply valid Mass, Confession and Baptism to small, dedicated groups of the faithful in their neighborhoods all across the United States. And as an organized group we have escaped detection by the American hierarchy. One of our priests—a youngster by the name of Father Michael O'Reilly—has a theory to explain that part of our success. He thinks the U.S. hierarchy is too arrogant to conceive of anyone flouting their authority."

The Pontiff pursed his lips. O'Reilly's name and something of his character had figured in Gladstone's report. "Overconfidence is the brother to arrogance, Father Damien. I hope you've made that point to Father O'Reilly."

"Cessi Gladstone made the point for me, Holiness." Slattery smiled. "I may be the juridical center for these priests. But that great lady is a lot more than the financial backbone of the new order. She's made it her business to stiffen the spine of anybody who needs it, including young O'Reilly."

"I can well believe it, Father Damien." His Holiness answered Slattery's smile with one of his own. He had his memories of Signora Gladstone, and he seemed delighted to hear how she had brought O'Reilly to heel. More, he was pretty sure she had warned O'Reilly about the ecclesiastical roughnecks and clerical thugs they were up against. In the Pontiff's mind, thoughts like that brought him naturally to the main purpose of this meeting with Slattery. "You're coming along well with the text of *Current Errors and Abuses,* Father Damien?"

"I have about two-thirds of the first draft ready, Holy Father."

"Well, then. I have another and related task for you. A second encyclical letter to be ready simultaneously with the first."

Slattery listened to the Slavic Pope with a special sense of satisfaction and privilege. What was wanted, the Holy Father explained, was a theological confirmation of the centuries-old and quasi-universal belief among Catholics that Mary, the Mother of God, had been chosen by the Most High from all eternity and for all time to exercise a special function in the mortal life of all who aspired to Heaven as their goal. To reach that goal, each one needed special help in the form of supernatural grace. By divine appointment, Mary was the mediatrix of that grace. Canonized saints had been guided by this belief. Martyrs had died for it. Popes had taught it. The Church at large had always presumed it. Now the Slavic Pope intended to promulgate it as a dogma of the faith. "Now all of us—and I in particular—need her special protection. It is my prayerful hope that she will be gratified by our action in celebrating her dignity as mediatrix of all supernatural grace. And it is my hope that she will therefore obtain from God the precise protection we need. For otherwise, Father, we are facing extinction. Pope, papacy, Church and the Roman Catholic people are facing obliteration. That is the essence of my thinking in this matter, Father Damien. I realize the time is short. We are talking about completing two encyclical letters before the General Consistory opens barely ten weeks from now. So the practical questions come down to two. Can you do it, Father? And will you do it?"

Could he do it! The only question in Damien's mind was what had taken the Holy Father so long! His very motto proclaimed the dedication of his pontificate to Mary. As Pope and as evangelist to the world, he had carried that motto like a second St. Luke to practically every nation of peoples. Now he was heading for the land Mary had specifically claimed at Fatima. For Russia, whose errors she had predicted. For Ukraine where she had appeared many times since then "in the Fatima mode."

"Do I gather, Holiness, that the second encyclical is to remain a secret until the right moment?"

"In this case, yes. The whole world knows about the first letter. Only you, Monsignore Daniel and I know about the second. It's better to keep it that way for the present."

As he left, Damien was tempted to ask at what moment the Slavic Pope intended to publish both letters. But he decided to hold back. It was enough to know not only that the Holy Father was preparing to make a stand against his enemies but that he would call on the Queen of Heaven as defender of the papacy.

Easter that year would fall in the second week of April. When he arrived in Rome in February, Gib Appleyard was certain there would be plenty of time to get back to the States before the usual influx of pilgrims and tourists into Rome took the place over. All Bud Vance was looking for was reliable corroboration that there was nothing in the offing on the papal scene that would upset the administration's plans or be embarrassing to the President. The Admiral couldn't afford to care about Vatican squabbles over power or about papal journeys to Russia or anywhere else. The Pope could travel to the dark side of the moon and back, Gib figured, just as long as U.S. interests weren't affected.

When he got down to it, the task turned out to be more formidable than he had anticipated. Papal Rome was caught in a peculiar spasm of excitement and confusion that made everything harder to decipher. And Gib found that Vatican politics were different from anything he'd unraveled in Beijing, say, or in Moscow or Paris or Bonn. No doubt about it; men like Maestroianni and Graziani and the others he'd met at Strasbourg were chasing after the same goal as any politician. Power. But the way they went about it was what made the difference. Their bastion, the Vatican Secretariat, was the oldest political chancery in the world, and they had learned its lessons well.

The first thing that hit Gib was a buzz saw of rumors about the Pontiff's health that plunged Rome into a new frenzy of speculation. Reporters and commentators gathered in like vultures come early for the feast. The atmosphere became a suffocating fabric of reports about "the Pope's physical frailty." Armies of "unnamed Vatican experts" were quoted as saying the Holy Father was deathly ill with something—with heart problems; with the aftermath of a series of small strokes; with cancer; with Parkinson's disease; with Alzheimer's disease. Denizens of Embassy Row like Bernie Pizzolato shaved close to the ghoulish in their enthusiasm for the Pontiff's demise.

"Good Lord, Giovanni," Appleyard complained to the proprietor of the Raffaele one evening over Mozart and wine. "What on earth is happening to your Church? If the Pope hears all the rumors I hear, he must be checking to see if he still has all his body parts!"

"I doubt it, Gibson." Lucadamo knew where to look for explanations. "It must be difficult for you to understand what is being done to our Holy Father. I know you have a great regard for him. But like most Popes, the present Pontiff has his enemies who are anxious for his demise, and who are certain that the next Pope will be *their* Pope."

Of course, when Giovanni talked about the Pope's enemies, he included Cardinal Maestroianni and the others who had been at Strasbourg. But that was the simple part. Even with the canniest instinct for upsetting the papal applecart, they couldn't have managed all this confusion in Rome without some serious help. But then, hadn't that been what the Strasbourg meeting was all about? Reaching out for some serious help?

Gibson was still tracking that line of reasoning through intercepts and intelligence reports and personal travels to key posts in Brussels and London when, as Holy Week approached, papal Rome was thrown into another spasm of excitement and confusion by one of the most peculiar documents ever to reach the National and Regional Conferences of Bishops all over the world. Though it purported to be official, it was unsigned. And it carried no protocol number.

These glaring deficiencies notwithstanding, the document declared in the name of the Holy Father that the usage of Altar girls had been found to be perfectly legitimate. That, in fact, permission for Altar girls in the liturgy had been implicit all along in Canon Law 230.

As it reached the far-flung Catholic world more or less simultaneously, the new interpretation of Canon Law evoked an immediate flood of reactions. Those in favor of it—including, apparently, a good majority of bishops and priests—were happy at "this step forward in liquidating the chauvinism of our Church." Those against the new measure declared it to be yet another challenge to the ancient faith of their fathers and "a sword of destruction aimed at the heart of the priesthood in the Roman Catholic Church."

It took another few days before it was claimed that the document came from the Vatican's Congregation for the Divine Liturgy. By that time, Cardinal Baffi's signature and a protocol number had been added. Baffi was a semi-retired Cardinal who filled various onerous but inconsequential jobs in the Vatican Chancery.

Appleyard had no sooner returned to the Raffaele from his latest fact-finding foray into Belgium than Giovanni Lucadamo took him to his private quarters and put the two versions of the document in his hands. "QED, my friend!" Giovanni was furious at the open deception. "Maestroianni has not only put the fat in the fire. He has set the whole Roman goose aflame!"

Gib had no idea why the issue of Altar girls was so important. Surely, then, it should be a simple matter for the Slavic Pope to rescind this bogus instruction and expose it for what it was. A piece of fraudulent mischief.

"Think again, Gibson." Giovanni shook his head. "You know that my nephew is security chief at the Vatican. We share information only now and again, when one of us has some overriding reason to do so."

"He called you about this?"

"The other way around. I called him. I told him this was a fraud plain and simple, and I asked him straight out what the Holy Father plans to do about it. Do you know what he told me? He told me the Pontiff declared that such fraudulence must stop. He told me that the Pontiff intends to mention the matter to Cardinal Secretary of State Graziani and the Cardinal of the relevant Congregation."

"And that's it?" Confused, Appleyard looked at both versions of the bogus papal instruction. "He's not going to rescind?"

"Of course not!" Pain was written all over Giovanni's face. "By now the news has been communicated worldwide. There's an 'official' copy, signed and numbered, in every one of over four thousand chanceries. It's probably in each of the nineteen thousand or so parishes in your own country, and in all the other dioceses and parishes throughout the world. It's a fait accompli. Too many Cardinals and bishops have already praised it as a wise move. The Holy Father couldn't rescind all that."

"Why not?" Gib didn't know if he was more incensed at the betrayal of the Slavic Pope or at the Pontiff's acquiescence.

"He hasn't got that power now."

"You mean, he has the power, but he won't use it."

"That, my friend," Giovanni said sadly, "is a distinction without any practical difference."

As if that telling point was the cause of a sudden collapse of his energy, Appleyard excused himself and retreated to the solitude of his own suite. There was a lot he needed to think about now.

For one thing, he was back to square one in his effort to make a realistic assessment of the intentions of the Slavic Pope. Vance had made it clear that the U.S. government's complaint about the Pontiff had to do with too many mixed signals. They wanted to know they were dealing with a predictable leader who could be relied on to keep his word. And who could blame them for that? The Pope's global reach was immense, and he had shown his ability to outflank and outwit the heaviest of geopolitical heavyweights.

Gib was understandably torn. There was his personal conviction of the Holy Father's good faith; his certainty that the Pope would keep the promises he had made concerning his current Russia policy, and concerning any near-future promulgation of an official stance against the U.S. position on population control. Now, however, Appleyard had every reason to question his own judgment. The Pope himself had tackled the issue of Altar girls as a major area in which he would not budge. He had made serious statements and given serious promises in the matter. But according to no less an authority than the Vatican security chief, those promises meant nothing. They could be tossed out the window, just like that.

Gibson realized that his deepening sadness over the Slavic Pope had to do with something more than questions of professional judgment. It had to do with age and its human analog, time. He had met the Holy Father at the midpoint in his life when he could look forward to his senior years and old age. He had met the Slavic Pope at the appropriate time for him to wonder about so many traits of his life; about the baggage of his psyche that poked up from the deepest recesses of his memory. About the questions he refused to answer and the doubts he refused to solve. The fears he failed to confront. The judgments he avoided making. The dusty corners of his life where dead mementos lay forgotten. The indifferent places in his mind he tolerated through laziness. His tacit decisions to cohabit with evil in others because it was convenient and conventional.

Of course, he had long since learned to deal with such baggage so that his judgment remained free and his self-confidence held firm. Yet every once in a while he felt some little pain of regret. Not disillusionment, exactly; more like a tendency to "if only." Even before he had experienced the Slavic Pope, he had begun to think how humanly valuable it would be if there were someone to whom he could describe himself without reserve. Somebody with the capacity to understand all, forgive all, placate and pacify all. Someone able to reconcile and unify all within him, assuring him of forgiveness for his mistakes. Of consolation for his losses. Of security from his fears. Of hope for the finale.

In the last few months, as he had drawn closer to the Slavic Pope—a surprising process that did not depend on frequent meetings—that "if only" tendency had begun to give way to something else. To a consoling wish. To a hope, perhaps, that one day he might find in this ageing prelate an ideal repository for that baggage of his psyche. More than once since his first papal audience he had studied a little gold medal the Holy Father had included among his parting gifts. There was nothing extraordinary about it. It was stamped with the Pope's likeness and his papal name followed by two letters. *Pp. Pater patrum.* Father of fathers.

"*Pater patrum.*" Appleyard repeated that title over and over again in his mind and asked himself sadly if those words should be invested with the lovely and consoling meaning he had begun to entertain. Perhaps they were no more significant than one more pleasant but empty honorific title. It was important for Gib to know the answer.

The high-tech screech of the scrambler phone on the nearby desk startled Appleyard out of his chair. "Gibson?"

Speak of the Devil. "I was just thinking about you, Bud. What's up?"

"That's what I called to ask you, pal." Vance did not sound pleased. "Remember those rumors that a blue-ribbon papal think tank was about to contradict everything your Pope has said about population control and the drain on natural resources?"

"The Pontifical Academy of Sciences Report?" Gib suddenly felt very old. "Yeah. I remember."

"Well, it's not a rumor anymore. It's not going to be published until May, but I have a copy in my hand. It's called *A Report on Demography, Economics and Natural Resources,* and it throws everything this Pope has said about population control into a cocked hat. Listen to some sentences. 'The need has emerged . . .'—remember, Gib; I'm quoting the Slavic Pope's own experts now. 'The need has emerged to contain the number of births . . . it is unthinkable that we can sustain a growth that goes much beyond two children per couple.' How do you like that for an about-face on basic papal policy?"

Appleyard thought he might be sick. "If that report really is put out by the Pontifical Academy of Sciences, then I guess you can score one for Bernie Pizzolato."

"It looks official to me. It's got footnotes and an afterword by Father George Hotelet, OP, who's billed as theologian of the papal household. And the introduction is signed by the President of the Academy himself. He's got one of those triple-tiered Italian names. Carlo Fiesole-Marracci."

Gibson picked up the fake Altar girl documents from his desk and crumpled them in his fist. "Let me do some sniffing around and get back to you, Admiral. There's a lot of weird stuff coming out of the Vatican complex that looks official these days."

"Okay." Vance sounded reluctant and very nervous. "But remember. The clock is ticking. Either we can trust this Pope to keep hands off our policies or we can't. This time it works out in our favor. But we can't afford to play Russian roulette."

Appleyard found Giovanni Lucadamo again, gave him all the details about the Pontifical Academy of Sciences Report and asked him to find out everything he could. Then, almost on impulse, he rang through to the Angelicum and asked to speak to Father George Hotelet. To his surprise, the Dominican came on the line almost immediately.

Yes, Father Hotelet said; Appleyard had heard correctly. The Report was a detailed argument for imposing a two-child limit on all families. But no, he said; Appleyard was mistaken to think there was any contradiction between what the Holy Father had said and what the Academy Report said. "You must understand, Mr. Appleyard. The Holy Father's concern is—as it should be—human ethics. He speaks on the basis of faith inspired by the Holy Spirit. We at the Academy, meanwhile, are speaking as demographers dealing with the hard facts of human life. Economic facts. Nutritional facts. Educational facts. Several times at the Vatican Council—that was before he was Pope, of course—the Holy Father himself recommended the limitation of families. Then he was dealing with facts. Now he's dealing with ethics."

And I'm dealing with a shyster theologian, Gib thought. He thanked Hotelet for his time, hung up the phone and poured himself a stiff brandy.

It was nearly nightfall by the time Giovanni Lucadamo came up with the information Appleyard wanted. "In fact," he told his friend, "I've come up with a copy of the actual Report. It's authentic. But there are some bad signs, I'm afraid."

"Like what?" Gibson took the slim volume from Lucadamo and turned a few pages.

"Well, for starters, the Report wasn't printed by the official Vatican Press, the Editrice Vaticana. It was printed by a company that belongs to well-known enemies of this papacy. An outfit called Vita e Pensiero of Milan. And a second bad sign is that His Eminence Cardinal Palombo had a hand in it all."

There it was again, then. The Strasbourg link.

When Appleyard put it all together in his mind, and when he aired it out for Giovanni Lucadamo over the dinner they shared, a few things seemed clear enough. It was evident, the two men agreed, that the antipapal cabal was ready to bring things to a head. And the timing of the mischief was linked to the coming papal trip to Russia. What was not evident was how far Maestroianni and his crowd were prepared to go in bringing off their palace coup. And for the life of him, Gib couldn't figure why the Slavic Pope appeared to be so acquiescent. "Why doesn't he defend against the plotters, Giovanni? I mean, if an outlander like me can see what's up, he must know what's going on. Doesn't he care?"

The discussion raised by questions like that went on for some time, but produced no answers that would satisfy Bud Vance and the Ten. It was late in the evening when Gib let himself into his room again. He wasn't ready yet to give up on the Slavic Pope. And he had plenty of reason not to buy into Vance's worry that the Pontiff was being duplicitous about his basic policies. But everything else—above all, the way the Pontiff was running things—was like a blank wall for him.

For the second time that day, he decided to make a phone call on impulse. His first meeting with Christian Gladstone had produced the results he wanted. Gladstone obviously had the ear of the Pope; and he still stacked up as the only straight-arrow cleric Appleyard knew in the Vatican. Maybe another conversation would provide at least some of the answers he needed so badly. Anyway, it was worth a try. As Vance had said, the clock in Washington was ticking.

It was confusing and unnerving for Chris Gladstone that his schedule during those early months of the new year was so out of synch with the excitement gripping Rome and that the fruits of his labors were so out of synch with his bedrock loyalties. Ever since he had come to Rome for good, his constant travels for Cardinal Maestroianni and his assignment for the Slavic Pope in America had barely left him time to breathe. But these days, while everyone else was caught up in the frenzy of preparations for the General Consistory, the Shoah Memorial Concert and the Pontiff's Russia trip, the rhythm of Gladstone's life geared down to a churning process.

Now and again he was sent off by Maestroianni to double-check on a few bishops in Europe just to be sure the Common Mind Vote was coming along as expected. The little Cardinal called him in frequently—sometimes to clarify this or that verbal message he had brought back from some of the Cardinals in the United States, but more often to chat with him about the Process, the forward footsteps of history and the architects and engineers of mankind's destiny.

Chris continued to keep Giustino Lucadamo up to date on what he learned of the plans of the opposition. The fact remained, though, that no matter how much intelligence he managed to ferret out, the opposition continued to make all the headway, and the Holy See continued to be hemmed in at every turn.

About the only good thing for Gladstone as Holy Week approached was that he finally had time to devote to Aldo Carnesecca's diary. Even though he never forgot he was searching for the clue that would explain murder, Carnesecca's journal turned out to be a consolation for Chris. Nothing would ever take the place of so great a friend, but reading those entries for hours at a time was a little like talking to Aldo again.

There wasn't much comment in the journal, of course. The entries were terse; there were gaps Chris couldn't fill in; some of the material was too elliptical to be deciphered. Still, everything Chris read put human flesh on the bones of half a century of Church history. This journal was Aldo Carnesecca's testament of love for his Church. Gladstone took it as that, and was grateful.

Once the weather began to taste of "high Roman spring," as Slattery liked to say—open skies and scudding clouds driven by a cooling breeze—Christian reverted to his custom of reading his Breviary up on the roof of the Angelicum. It was on just such a day when, in the midst of his prayers, he was seized by something like a brainstorm. "You idiot!" Gladstone smacked his forehead with an open palm as he scrambled down the stairs and back to his rooms. "It was right there in front of you, and you passed it over!"

He was still calling himself names as he sat down at his desk, Carnesecca's journal in hand, and riffled back through the pages searching for the entries he wanted. That was the thing that had thrown him off. It wasn't one entry Father Aldo had been talking about that day at Gemelli Hospital. It was a series of entries linked together by one common thread. Within twenty minutes Gladstone found what he was looking for. It took him another day to check a few things out and then have a chat with Monsignore Daniel. What he needed after that was to get to Giustino Lucadamo.

"I don't know what's in the envelope, Giustino!" Chris had finally managed to buttonhole Lucadamo in his office at the close of a hectic day. "But I'll tell you what I do know.

"I know that each of the two Popes who preceded the present Holy Father read its contents and left it to his immediate successor, so it's been opened and resealed. I know the envelope carries two papal inscriptions. The first, written by the old Pope, reserved the envelope 'For Our Successor on the Throne of Peter.' The second papal inscription written by the September Pope says its contents concern 'the condition of Holy Mother Church after June 29, 1963.' I know the envelope figured in the triage of papal documents at the beginning of the Slavic Pope's reign, and that both Father Aldo and Cardinal Aureatini—Archbishop Aureatini back then—assisted at that triage. I know that Secretary of State Vincennes conducted the triage shortly before he was killed in a car accident, and that he held that envelope aside. And I know from Monsignore Daniel that no such envelope was among the private papers of the two prior pontificates that were given to the Slavic Pope."

"Here, Giustino." Gladstone took a single sheet of paper from his pocket and laid it on Lucadamo's desk. "See for yourself. I've copied out the relevant passages date by date, word for word. If you think I've made a mistake or missed something, you can check it against your copy of the diary."

The security chief leaned forward to study the paper.

June 29, 1977. Confessional matter of the gravest kind.

July 3, 1977. Private audience with Pp. Confessional material. Pp too ill and too afflicted with domestic and foreign problems to undertake needful. Material sealed and inscribed, 'For Our Successor on the Throne of Peter.'

September 28, 1978. Long conversation with Pp about envelope left by immediate predecessor. Agrees no Pope will be able to govern Church through Vatican until enthronement undone. Pp will do what he can, but resealed envelope with second inscription, 'Concerning the condition of Holy Mother Church after June 29, 1963.' Insurance, he says.

Lucadamo raised a querulous eye to Gladstone for a second. He remembered the surprise that had attended the election of the September Pope, and the shock at his sudden death within barely a month of his enthronement. If memory served, September 28 was one day shy of his death date. Without comment, he returned his attention to the final entry. *Assisted Cardinal Vincennes at double triage of personal papal documents. AB Aureatini attending. All pro forma until both stunned by resealed envelope in first set of documents bearing two papal inscriptions. Vincennes took charge of envelope. Not certain if Pp's insurance may backfire.*

Lucadamo laid the sheet of paper down. "You're positive the Slavic Pope didn't receive any such envelope?"

"Monsignore Daniel is positive."

"And what about this enthronement business? Any idea what that means? Or what it has to do with papal governance in the Vatican?"

"None. I've assumed the relevant date is June 29, 1963. But the only enthronement I can find any reference for during that year was the investiture of the old Pope who sealed the envelope in the first place and left it for his successor."

"And what about . . ."

"Look, Giustino." Gladstone was at the end of his patience. "You said yourself that Carnesecca had seen something so threatening to someone that they wanted to burn it out of his brain and kill him for it. And you hinted to me that it was Aureatini who arranged that attempt on Carnesecca's life in Sicily. So at the very least, we have a possible connection between those two things. Now, I don't know what's in that envelope. And if that connection does hold up, I don't know why Aureatini would have waited so long to do something about it. I don't even know that he did wait. Maybe he tried even before Sicily and failed. But I'll tell you one thing. I'm going to find that envelope. With your help or without it, I'm going to find it and read it and go from there."

Once the basic decision was made, Gladstone and Lucadamo faced a simple logistical problem. After a triage of the papers of any deceased Pope—or two Popes, as in this case—documents considered to be of minor importance were consigned either to the special files of the Secretariat of State or to the Secret Archives of the Vatican Library. On the theory that the envelope was as damning as Christian's gut feeling told him it was, and on the further theory that Cardinal Vincennes hadn't destroyed it, it made sense to surmise that he would have wanted to put it as far out of reach as possible. That meant the Archives.

They decided that Gladstone had to be the one to do the search. The fewer who knew about the envelope, the better. Lucadamo and his staff were deeply engaged in the security arrangements for the Cardinals of the Church who would soon be assembling in Rome from the four quarters of the globe, for the thousands of distinguished guests who would attend the Shoah Memorial Concert and for the papal trip itself. And besides, the early searches Chris had done for the Slavic Pope in the Archives—the scout work that had made him so impatient during his first weeks of personal service to the Holy Father—had familiarized him with the terrain.

"Our difficulty"—Lucadamo frowned—"is to arrange matters so that no one knows we're in their bailiwick. Daytime searches would raise questions, and Aureatini has ears everywhere."

"There's another difficulty," Chris put in. "If I'm going to turn into a night burglar, there will be locks to open. I'll have to get in the main door. Then there are sectional gates all over the place. And some of the boxes that hold the documents are locked."

Giustino smiled and shook his head. That was the least of their problems as far as he was concerned. He would detach one man for Gladstone's exclusive use. Giancarlo Terragente, he said, could open any lock anywhere and close it again, with no one the wiser. And he was a wizard at deactivating and reactivating alarms.

The far greater difficulty would be timing. The Secret Archives were reckoned technically to form part of the Biblioteca Apostolica, the Vatican Library. The Archives were located within the complex of the Belvedere Galleries, which also included the inventories of the Gallery of Charts, the Hall of Parchments, the Room of Inventories and Indexes, the Records of the Consistory, the Picture Galleries and so on.

Supervision of the whole complex, and access to it, lay under the authority of Cardinal Alberto María Valdés, a crusty Spaniard legendary for his independence from Vatican politics and because of the extraordinary hours he kept at the Biblioteca.

"I happen to know," Lucadamo told Christian, "that His Eminence is consumed these days in the job of editing a series of correspondence between the nineteenth- and twentieth-century Popes and contemporary statesmen. He's up at six in the morning. By eight, he's said his Mass, had his breakfast and is hard at work in the Archives. He breaks for lunch, siesta and dinner; but the place isn't empty and records are kept of all visitors. Then he's back at work and stays until all hours." The only way Lucadamo could devise to get the young American priest into the Secret Archives was to find a near-at-hand place from where he could be spirited through the locked doors when the Cardinal finally retired for the night.

"Why not?" Chris agreed to the plan. "I'm already a double agent. I might as well add burglary to my priestly résumé!"

It was an irony of the gentlest sort that the most convenient place—near at hand and yet not under the jurisdiction of Cardinal Valdés—turned out to be that ancient Tower of the Winds that old Paul Gladstone had visited with Pope Pius IX over a hundred years before and on which he had patterned the Tower Chapel at Windswept House. Christian's first sight of that place was an eerie experience. It stood midway between two sections of the Biblioteca Apostolica, the Museo Sacro and the Museo Profano. Terragente led him up a steep stairway to the topmost floor of the Tower. "I'll be back for you the minute Valdés closes shop," the picklock promised as he disappeared down the stairs again.

Left to wait in the dim light of a single electric bulb, Chris knew immediately where he was. The Room of the Meridian. His memory of Old Glad's journal descriptions dovetailed with everything he saw. He surveyed the walls covered with frescoes depicting the Eight Winds as godlike figures and with scenes from ancient Roman bucolic life during the four seasons. He paced the zodiac diagram on the floor, designed to coordinate during daylight hours with the sun's rays slanting through a slit in one of the frescoed walls. He looked up to see the anemometer on the ceiling, and knew its indoor pointer was moved by an outside weathervane to indicate which of the Eight winds was blowing across the Eternal City.

That Room of the Meridian cast a spell, but it wasn't the spell Chris would have expected. He was lulled by the keening of the winds, by the movement of the ceiling pointer, by the peaceful scenes of a pastoral life that was no more. He was surrounded by the lonely emptiness of the room, by the gentle creaking of that ancient stairway, by the mausoleum effect of the surrounding galleries of the Archives. This place is all full of dead things, Gladstone's mind kept telling him. All dead things . . .

"Monsignore!" Terragente popped his head up the stairway. "It looks like the Cardinal is going to make a night of it."

Chris looked at his watch. Nearly one-thirty. "Let's pack it in, Giancarlo. We'll try again tomorrow."

In spite of Cardinal Valdés' erratic timetable, Terragente managed to get Gladstone into the Secret Archives with reasonable regularity. They had to pace themselves, of course, or run the risk of turning into zombies for lack of sleep. But before long they managed to develop a routine. On each foray, Chris waited patiently in the Tower for Terragente's all clear. Then Giancarlo sprang the locks and, flashlights in hand, the pair entered the sector Gladstone had blocked out for that night's methodical search. As adept at prowling in the shadows as he was at breaking and entering, Terragente was always on the alert for any interruption. Only once or twice, however, did the security man have to close himself and his companion into the search area, and then spring the lock again when things had settled down.

"You're a natural at this, Monsignore." Giancarlo smiled the compliment at Christian as he drove him back to the Angelicum after their fourth or fifth unsuccessful search for the mysterious papal envelope. "With a little practice, you could be the best cat burglar in Vatican service. Next to me, of course."

Chris laughed dryly at that. He was beginning to think the whole exercise was a waste of everybody's time. There were only so many places where old papers were stuffed away, and he had been through about half of them. Maybe Vincennes had destroyed the envelope after all.

"Not a chance!" Giancarlo considered himself an expert on human nature. "Remember your President Nixon? He could have saved himself a lot of trouble if he'd destroyed those tapes. I don't know why he didn't. And I don't know why Vincennes wouldn't have destroyed the envelope. But I'll wager anything you'd like to name that it's somewhere in the Archives. You'll find it, Monsignore."

Maybe in a hundred years from now, Chris thought as his companion in crime pulled the car to a stop in front of the Angelicum. But right now he was tired and discouraged, and all he wanted was to get a couple of hours' sleep before sunrise.

❑ ❑ ❑ ❑

"Who?" His eyes unwilling to open, Gladstone fumbled with the phone next to his bed. "Who did you say this is?"

"Gibson Appleyard, Monsignore, calling from the Raffaele. Sorry for ringing you so early, but you're a hard man to find. I have a little problem and I thought you might help me out again . . ."

XLVIII

THERE WERE seven Cardinals in the historic delegation of the Princes of the Church who, by formal appointment, came to a conference with the Slavic Pope as darkness fell over Rome on Monday of Holy Week.

The entire affair was stately. His Holiness, already seated at the head of the conference table, received a dutiful sign of reverential obeisance from each Cardinal. First came the two prime Pope-makers, cadaverous Leo Pensabene and tiny Cosimo Maestroianni. Close behind, the two individualists—the Frenchman Joseph Karmel and the agate-eyed Jesuit Cardinal Archbishop of Genoa, Michael Coutinho. Cardinal Secretary of State Giacomo Graziani came next. Then Noah Palombo, clothed in his usual mood of arctic darkness. Last of all, Silvio Aureatini bowed to His Holiness and took his place at the farthest end of the table.

The Slavic Pope's nod of recognition to each was a fraternal greeting; but just as much was it notice served that he knew each man for what he was. He had elevated some of them to the Cardinalitial purple. He had seen all of them flourish during his papacy. He knew their in-house allies and their external associations. When he had learned of their Masonic connections and their financial finaglings—when he knew enough to cashier them, in other words—he had not interfered with them. He had let them have their head even when they had encroached continually and substantially into papal matters and Petrine issues.

In front of each man lay a copy of the Resignation Protocol. For this was the subject of the evening's august deliberations. No one present would even pretend this was merely a personal matter between the Slavic Pope and the Cardinals, as if Their Eminences simply disliked the Pontiff personally and wanted to be rid of his annoying presence on the Throne of Peter. Rather, everyone here, including the Slavic Pope himself, knew that what they were about this evening was a threat to the spinal column of the Roman Catholic body: the papacy.

"You are Peter." So Jesus had said to Simon the Fisherman at Caesarea Philippi nearly 2,000 years before. "Yours are the Keys to the Kingdom of Heaven." The Slavic Pope's signature on the Resignation Protocol would be tantamount to his declaring: "I now use that unique power of the Keys to surrender them to you, my colleagues. Together now we will wield the power given to Simon Peter."

What they were handling, then, was explosive, revolutionary and ominous. Nothing less than explosive. For if the Slavic Pope acquiesced in this as he had done in so much else, Petrine power would be invested not in a papal persona, but in a self-appointed committee. Nothing less than revolutionary. For this unique power would now be shared by so many fallible men, without a divine guarantee. Until tonight, papacies had been limited by none but the hand of God. If these seven Cardinals were successful, the decision would henceforth be a collegial affair. Once that much power was surrendered, who would take it back? And who would set the farther limits? Nothing less than ominous. For, inevitably and sadly, all, including this Holy Father, would have forgotten the millenniar Roman caution: Whoever strikes at the Petrine papacy will die the death. Together, Pope and Cardinals would strike at the Petrine papacy.

The Pope had blocked out thirty minutes for the meeting. No preliminary maneuverings were expected. No palaver. No socializing. What was there to talk about? All the reasons for and against a papal signature had been thrashed out ad nauseam. The only thing lacking now was a definitive Yes or No.

By agreement among themselves, Their Eminences had neither an appointed leader nor a common spokesman. This would be a headless conference; for they had only one certain plank of consensus on which to stand together: This Pope should agree to dismiss himself from current papal history. With his signature on this Resignation Protocol—with his initials, if they could do no better—they would have an instrument to make his resignation legally effective because freely offered by him. "The rest," as Cardinal Maestroianni had assured them, "could be left to providence."

For once Cardinal Secretary of State Graziani felt he could make his position count as chief papal executive. He took it upon himself to state the case for Yes. "By signing the Resignation Protocol, Holy Father, you put into our hands—into the hands of Your Holiness' colleagues—the authority to determine when your papacy ends. You make the papacy collegial. Admittedly, this is a change. But I submit, Holiness, that you have already been following the example of two of your most recent predecessors in this matter." Graziani went on—a bit inventively perhaps—to recall for His Holiness how the good Pope of the Second Vatican Council had been inspired with the ideal of a collegial papacy. Somewhat less inventively he recalled how, by his actions over a reign of fifteen years, the good Pope's successor had approved the governance of the Church by a collegial papacy. Surely, therefore—especially as the Slavic Pope had in essence followed the same principle since his own election by the College of Cardinals in Conclave—it was time to formalize the de facto situation.

Graziani brought his argument to a tactless crescendo. The Pope did not appoint the bishops, he said. "We do—with Your Holiness." The Pope did not decide what teachings are heretical, he said. "We do—with Your Holiness." The Pope did not decide who would become a Cardinal, he said. "We do—with Your Holiness."

"If this is so—and it is so, Holiness—all that the majority of your Cardinals and bishops wish is that we formalize this present and actual collegial arrangement. Truth in our words! That is what the Church needs, Holy Father. Put an end to the misery of our self-doubts, of our quarreling, of our failure in faith. Confirm us in our collegial faith, we beg you."

The Slavic Pope listened in silence. None could tell if he cast his mind back over the two pontificates adduced by the Cardinal Secretary of State. None saw any sign that he questioned the agreement of those predecessors to a format of governance that had allowed abuses and extended freedom to progressivist extremists. None knew if he suffered a moment of regret at the confusion caused by those two prior Popes who had aided mightily in shredding the once seamless fabric of the Church's papacy. Nor would they ever know.

The Slavic Pope leaned forward ever so slightly and read the Resignation Protocol one more time. Seven pairs of eyes watched as he uncapped his fountain pen. Watched as he brought the tip down until it almost touched the signature line. . . . Then he paused. "As successor to the Holy Apostle Peter . . ."

At those words from the Slavic Pope, the blood froze in every heart but his.

"As successor to the Holy Apostle Peter, I take this most extreme measure in order to ensure the unity of my bishops with this Holy See. As Bishop of Rome, I initial this document. Each of Your Eminences is a cosignatory. This is truly a collegial act. So help us God, the Father of all."

None of the Cardinals knew exactly what distinction the Holy Father meant to draw, if any, between his role as the successor to the Apostle and his role as the Bishop of Rome. None knew; and none cared. With a quick flourish, His Holiness initialed the Protocol. Then, unwilling to wait for the attending power brokers and papal aspirants to affix their own signatures, he rose from his chair in unexpected haste. With Monsignore Daniel barely a stride behind him, the validly elected successor to Peter was gone.

Wearied by his failures and taxed by lack of sleep, Chris Gladstone faced into his dinner at the Raffaele that Monday evening with mixed feelings.

In their November meeting he had found Gibson Appleyard to be a decent man, and he retained that initial feeling of pleasure and respect the American envoy had sparked in him. Still, he didn't relish another discussion about his country's political problems with his Pope; and he didn't really feel up to a solo meeting with Appleyard. It was a relief, then, for Chris to find that Giovanni Lucadamo would act as host and make the party a threesome.

Though this was their first face-to-face encounter, the elder Lucadamo was so much a part of Vatican lore—so much a part of common knowledge and community talk—that Gladstone felt he was in the presence of a friend of long standing. More, because Giovanni Lucadamo's record of exploits had become the stuff of legend, he knew he was in the presence of a seasoned warrior; a man who had proven himself over the years to be invaluable as an ally and unyielding as an enemy.

Whether by design or not, everything about the early part of the evening put Christian at ease. The three men relaxed for a time over drinks in the living room of Giovanni's private quarters—a high-ceilinged, ornately decorated apartment that bore all the marks of a prosperous Italian with a fine taste for the classical and the means to indulge it. Gladstone was treated to a clinic in secular politics as Appleyard and Lucadamo dissected and analyzed various governments in Europe—including the new government of Italy, which now included both neo-Fascists and Communists. By the time they moved to the dining room and settled down to a meal prepared in the Raffaele's superb kitchen, Chris was on a first-name footing with his companions, and the conversation shifted easily to Vatican affairs.

Lucadamo had a good deal to relate about Cardinal Maestroianni—a subject Christian obviously found absorbing. And that created the opening for Appleyard to take up the "little problem" he had mentioned on the phone to Gladstone. "It's a problem of credibility, Monsignore." Gibson broached his subject in plain, unvarnished terms. "And again, strategic requirements for the United States are involved. There are two issues at stake."

"Whose credibility?"

"The credibility of the Holy Father." Appleyard shot a good-natured frown at Lucadamo.

"And the two issues?" Gladstone exchanged his own quick glance with the Raffaele's proprietor.

"Population control. And Russia."

Chris sat back to look at his countryman. "But you had it out with His Holiness already on population control."

"That's what I thought, too, Monsignore. But that Report from the Pontifical Academy of Sciences has put a monkey wrench in the works. It appears to some of my colleagues now that, despite what he's said, the Pope is not against *some* population control . . ."

"Provided it's not achieved by artificial means," Gladstone interrupted. Maestroianni had proudly shown him the Academy Report, and the thought of it still made his blood boil.

Gibson wasn't satisfied. He needed something more reassuring than a theological correction. "So, in principle, the Holy Father wouldn't be against a two-child limit imposed by law?"

"Yes, he would. That's fascism. You can't impose absolute limits without ending up with infanticide, like Mao's China. And over and above that, it's capital to remember that the preferred Catholic method does not countenance killing the child."

"But what about the Academy Report? Giovanni here thinks it's part of an effort to denigrate the Holy Father's authority."

"And to secularize Catholic morality." Lucadamo decided to speak up on that point, and to add another. "The Report is in the same category of Roman clerical politics as the scandal over Altar girls. Wouldn't you say so, Monsignore?"

Again Gladstone sat back in his chair. He wasn't willing to risk his delicate political balancing act in the Vatican by sharing his mind too freely. It wasn't Signor Giovanni who worried him; he was held in huge esteem by the Vatican security chief, and who would know him better than his own nephew? But what about Appleyard? Was it enough to rely on his personal sense of trust in that quarter?

"Monsignore?" Signor Giovanni's gentle prod was almost sufficient to tip the scales. But not quite. Before he would respond, Christian wanted to pursue the second strategic problem that bedeviled the American government.

"You mentioned the question of Russia, Gibson."

"Yes." Appleyard showed no sign of reticence. "Plainly stated, they're afraid back home that this Holy Father may interfere with the special relationship this U.S. administration is cultivating with Boris Yeltsin."

Plainly stated, indeed. Gladstone was mindful of Gibson's November warning about the death of innocents. As that warning had been coupled with the question of population control, it was sobering to know that Maestroianni's mischievous "supplemental initiatives" had muddied that situation for the Americans. But just as sobering was the idea that the Pontiff's forthcoming pilgrimage to Russia had been thrown into the same scales. If ever there was a moment for candor, Christian decided, this was it. "The best way I can reply to such insanity"—Chris turned a pair of blazing eyes on his companion—"is to answer the question Signor Giovanni asked a minute ago.

"The Academy Report apparently has the U.S. government up in arms again over their precious population policy. But that Report, as well as the counterfeit document on Altar girls, is part of a scheme to have the present Pope removed. Such tricks merely prepare the way. So you can go back to your colleagues in Washington, and you can tell them that they have not understood this Pope. And because they don't understand him, they're fair game for the crowd of theological thugs and geopolitical miscreants who feel compelled to remove him.

"As to Russia . . ." Christian relaxed a little in his posture, but not a whit in his intensity. "My advice to you is to go straight to the Holy Father, tell him straight out what you've told me. Tell him your government doesn't trust his word. Tell him how confused they are. Then carry on from there."

Both of Gladstone's companions were taken off guard by the honesty of his words and the force of his emotion. But it was his unequivocal statement about the plot to remove the Slavic Pope—the first in-house confirmation of the serious progress of that plot—that sparked a spontaneous and even violent response from Appleyard.

"You may find it hard to believe a word of what I say, Monsignore." His voice, normally so relaxed and measured, rose to an unusual pitch of intensity. "Even Giovanni may find it hard to believe. But I will do anything in my power to prevent the success of any such plot."

Gib was right. Chris did find those words hard to believe. Leaving aside the question of Masonry, he was talking to a senior envoy of the U.S. administration. It was one thing to be overcome by momentary emotions; but it would be something else for a man of Appleyard's rank and accomplishments to oppose the official stance of his home government.

"You would be making a mistake to take such a promise lightly, Monsignore." Lucadamo read the doubt on Gladstone's face and responded to it. "I have trusted my life to Gibson more than once over the years. And as you see, I am here to tell the story!"

For the remaining days of Holy Week, Appleyard shoved his nose as deeply as he could into papal politics. For all of his recently acquired expertise in Vatican affairs, the simple fact was that he didn't know half enough to make his argument in favor of the Slavic Pope. Not enough to make it count in Washington, at any rate. What he needed was as much data as he could find on the men lined up to replace the present Pontiff, should it come to that.

The two U.S. Embassies in Rome were all but useless; but that was only to be expected. With Giovanni Lucadamo to ease his way, Gib made the rounds of the best tipsters he could find. More often than not, they turned up among the city's resident newsmen who had been around for generations. And one of the first lessons they taught him was the difference between Pope-makers, papal wanna-bes and serious papal candidates. By Good Friday, he knew that among the antipapal prelates he had consorted with at Strasbourg, Cardinal Maestroianni and Cardinal Pensabene were Pope-makers of the first order. He knew that Cardinal Aureatini was a papal wanna-be. He knew that Graziani might be a long shot. He knew that most of others mentioned frequently in local gossip as *papabili* wouldn't even make it to a ballot in a papal Conclave. And he knew the struggle would be among three men.

Appleyard had learned much of what he needed to know about two of those three candidates in his face-to-face encounter with them at Strasbourg. Cardinal Noah Palombo and Cardinal Michael Coutinho were men attuned to the world. In their speeches that night, both had impressed

Appleyard as cynics. Palombo had seemed downright sinister. By the mere fact that they were involved in a clandestine plot against the reigning Pope, both had shown a dangerous and shifty side. And, not surprisingly, both had shown themselves in that meeting to be adept at striking a public pose of selfless idealism that was patently at odds with their words and actions.

The third *papabile*—a Frenchman by the name of Joseph Karmel—was an unknown quantity for Appleyard at first. But assiduous digging in that Cardinal's public record showed him to be cut from the same fundamental pattern as the other two. Karmel's authoritative, Old Testament demeanor and his charismatic behavior made him a little more entertaining, perhaps. Beneath the veneer, however, he was more unreliable—and therefore more dangerous in Gibson's view—than either Coutinho or Palombo. He appeared to use emotion rather than reason as his guide. And despite that Old Testament profile he cultivated, he made a meaningless blur of all distinctions between the religions of the world.

What it came to in the end, then, was exactly what Christian Gladstone had said at the Raffaele. If the plot against the Slavic Pope were successful, Washington would probably be left to deal with a crowd of theological thugs and geopolitical miscreants.

That was deeply important to Appleyard. As a Rosicrucian, as a universalist and as a career servant of his government, he believed there was and should always be room in God's cosmos for true diversity of belief, and that no one should be dragooned into a monolithic ideology. He had no doubt that the Strasbourg group—the individuals who hankered after the universal power of the Roman Catholic apparatus—were globalist in their ambitions. But that was so far from his own universalism as to make Gibson shudder. Globalism—at least as he thought of the term—meant the fashioning of a global village in which, come Hell or high water, no one would be different from anyone else. There would be one frame for everything, and everything in one frame. The element globalists did not insist on was the one element that made Roman Catholicism so valuable in a volatile world: the stability of a cohesive moral underpinning as the basis of personal and community life.

Palombo and Coutinho had made it clear at Strasbourg that they favored a looser, more worldly and morally permissive point of view. No doubt that was what Gladstone had meant by theological thuggery. And no doubt, either, that, without a stable moral base, such men would easily become geopolitical miscreants.

But the question was: Would Gibson's superiors in Washington care? Hadn't they been after a looser, more worldly, more permissive point of view on Vatican Hill? If the moral cohesion fostered by the Holy See could be fundamentally, formally and finally disrupted, wouldn't that make things easier when it came to such a basic U.S. strategy as population control and to such a precarious U.S. gamble as the Partnership for Peace?

The answers Appleyard gave to his own questions convinced him that Gladstone had been right on yet another point. As hectic as things were now, barely three weeks in advance of the General Consistory and the Holy Father's departure for Russia, Gib would have to ask for an urgent meeting with the Pontiff. To have any chance of making his case in Washington, he would have to tell the Slavic Pope what he had told Gladstone, and then carry on from there.

Appleyard would always remember his May 1 interview with His Holiness as the most painful and most insightful conversation of his life. A meeting whose value for him lay not in its details, but in the entire event.

In preparation for the hectic timetable that would rule his movements during the first two weeks of May, His Holiness had decided to rest up for a few days in the papal villa at Castel Gandolfo.

"The Holy Father is following an elastic schedule," Monsignore Daniel had told Appleyard when he had called so urgently for an audience. "We've eased up on deadline dates and fixed appointments. Come earlyish, but be prepared to wait."

Appleyard did come early. Giovanni Lucadamo's staffer guided the limousine along the drive that sloped gently upward through gardens still sparkling under the night's fall of dew. Immediately Gibson stepped out onto the cobbled courtyard, the double doors of the main entrance were opened and he was greeted by a pleasant-faced layman. His Holiness was at Mass and Benediction, the doorman said. Perhaps Mr. Appleyard would care to stroll on the grounds until Monsignore Daniel called him.

Gib was about to follow that suggestion when the sound of organ music changed his mind. The gentle cadence was his guide through a spacious, ornately decorated corridor and into a large ground-floor chapel. Except for the amber light of two chandeliers, the place was in semi-darkness. Mild incense evoked memories of the summer glories and autumn harvests of Appleyard's boyhood.

Gibson slipped into one of the rear pews and sat down to watch. A few priests and some half dozen nuns kneeling in the pews chanted a Latin prayer in harmony with the organ. The Slavic Pope knelt on the lowest of the three steps leading to the Altar, two acolytes knelt beside him. An enormous crucifix hung from the ceiling above the Altar. The gleam of candles played against the precious stones and richly embossed golden door of the Tabernacle. Atop the Tabernacle, a monstrance held the Sacred Host to view.

All at once, the music that had drawn Gibson here ceased. Amid the silence of sacred things, the Holy Father rose from his knees. His hands draped in cloth-of-gold, he raised the monstrance and slowly traced a cross of blessing upon all present.

It was a moment of grace that ended all too abruptly. A brief litany followed in praise of a bountiful Heaven. The Pontiff removed the Host from the monstrance, draped it with a cloth, placed it in the Tabernacle, genuflected and followed the acolytes from the Sanctuary. One of the priests stayed behind long enough to extinguish the candles and the chandeliers and remove the monstrance. And then Appleyard was alone. Only the small red lamp remained alight in the Sanctuary, flickering against the shadows.

"Mr. Appleyard?"

Gib turned to the chapel door. At a little gesture from Monsignore Daniel, he followed the papal secretary to one of the private reception rooms on the ground floor of the villa where a smiling Pope awaited him. Despite all the rumors of the many horrid afflictions about to claim his life, the Pontiff looked amazingly well. Gibson expressed his deep pleasure at seeing His Holiness so fit.

"I'm really not a city man, Mr. Appleyard." The Pope acknowledged the American's greeting with obvious pleasure and gestured toward the Alban Hills visible through the open windows. "As long as I can walk in the open air in the sight of woods and tall mountains, I'm fine. Now . . ." The Holy Father chose a pair of easy chairs beside those windows, and the pair settled down to their talk. "Tell me, Mr. Appleyard. Why is your government so afraid of my poor little Russian pilgrimage? I assure you, I'm not planning any interference in U.S.A.-Russia relations. But why this suspicion?"

"Holiness"—Appleyard responded in kind—"I think the key men in the present administration are less afraid of you than of their own memories. They recall the role played by you and the Catholic Church in defeating the Communists in your homeland. They remember how you beat them without guns or bullets, but just by organization and force of spirit."

"Ah!" The Pontiff brushed the air with one hand. "We're talking about apples and oranges. Your administration in the United States has special bonds with Russia now."

How like this Pope to give him the opening he needed, Gibson thought. "Would Your Holiness prefer that the present administration not forge those special bonds? Bonds, I admit, that are closer and tighter than my government has formed with any other power, East or West."

"Before I answer your pointed question, Mr. Appleyard, let me be explicit about those newly forged bonds as I understand them today. Take item number one. Recently, Russian warplanes manned by Russian pilots conducted bombing missions in Yemen. The Saudis financed that secret operation, and your present administration gave its blessing to it. Item number two. Your Washington people have given the Russian regime a green light to dominate not merely Georgia but any of the CIS states; and to do so militarily as well as economically. The massacre of Chechnya is still going on, even as we speak.

"Item number three. The United States voted in the UN to give the

Russia-dominated CIS equal 'observer status' with NATO, and regional status in the UN itself. That means UN sanction to throw Russia's weight around in the 'near abroad,' and eventually in the 'far abroad.' Item number four. Your present Washington administration is very much inclined to accept the new and secret U.S.A.-Russia alliance presented to them by Yeltsin's emissary, Vladimir Shumeiko. What the Russians now seek is joint rule with the U.S.A. over peacekeeping actions in the world. Condominium over global arms sales. Condominium over the export of military and civil technology to Third World countries.

"Now, Mr. Appleyard, you have asked me in effect if I like all this. Of course I don't like it! Nobody with a knowledge of the realities could like it. But does that mean I'm going to undermine it? Oh, no, Mr. Appleyard! It will come to grief all by itself. And in any case, I assure you that that is not the geopolitics which occupies me."

If Gibson had come to Rome seeking clarity, Gladstone and the Slavic Pope had each given him more than he or his government had any right to expect. He acknowledged as much to His Holiness and promised to make his position as clear as he could back home.

For the briefest moment, the Pontiff and the diplomat shared an easy silence. Together they savored the fresh morning air and the mingled sounds of daily life that reached them from the town beyond the gates. But Gibson savored something more—some remnant of his former wish that he could reach another, more personal plateau in his relationship with this Pope.

"Off the record, Holiness." Gib chose to break the silence. "Are you still in close correspondence with Mr. Gorbachev?"

"Off the record, Mr. Appleyard, you know better than I or the wide world will ever know that Mr. Gorbachev is financed now by U.S. dollars. He is totally dependent on his paymasters. He flies in their corporate jets. He travels in their bulletproof limousines. He gathers funds at their galas. He holidays in their spas and watering holes. He is the protégé, the creature, the marionette, the obedient servant of the macromanagers and the darling of the master engineers.

"I have always maintained a link with him. He has been a useful means of knowing what has really been happening to us all since 1989. But none of us has any illusions about him and his aims. On the personal level, he remains a convinced materialist and atheist. On the sociopolitical level, he remains a crass Marxist. And on the moral level, he is indistinguishable from a polar bear. Mikhail Gorbachev has mercy, compassion, sympathy for no one on this earth, myself included. Am I making myself clear, Mr. Appleyard?"

"Off the record, Holiness"—Gibson laughed the way he sometimes did with Giovanni Lucadamo—"that would be my summary also."

"Perhaps you remember a speech Mr. Gorbachev made in your country a while back, Mr. Appleyard, in May of 1992, at Westminster College in

Fulton, Missouri. He called that speech *The*
ative of Action. It is an obvious notion, but
on. You must take its tide, or miss the oppo
"I have told you what I do not plan to do o
I do not plan to disrupt your government's ar
tell you now is that I have accepted the dual in
Kiev because surely the tide in the river of my
open sea . . ." The Slavic Pope broke off gentl
did not need saying. "This morning, Mr. Apple
Lord that you should arrive just in time for Be
pleased God that you should be here for a special
give to Him for having sent you. You have mad much easier than many other diplomats would have done in similar circumstances. For that, our Father in Heaven will thank you with abundant blessings and grant your heart's desire."

There had been a time when the American would have responded to those words as an expression of gratitude for one more piece of diplomatic work well done. But he knew enough now to understand that the significance of the moment went deeper than the smooth surface of diplomacy.

"Will you be returning to your country at once, Mr. Appleyard?" The Pontiff rose from his chair. It was time for his morning walk with Monsignore Daniel.

"Not quite yet, Holiness." Gibson fell comfortably into step beside the Holy Father. "I have some business to get through up north in the Low Countries first."

"I see. Well, when you arrive home, please carry my blessing with you. For your family. And for your country—your people and your government. May the Holy Spirit give wisdom to all of you."

"I cannot tell you how reassuring I find that prayer, Holiness." Appleyard found himself responding with a sentiment no other human being had ever evoked in him. "I am impressed that you see the movement of the Holy Spirit as possible even in a political system such as ours, which sets such an alien face in our time to the essence of Catholicism and Christianity itself."

The Pontiff stopped just short of the door to the courtyard where Sadowski was already waiting for him. "Mr. Appleyard, if you see me traveling across the whole world to meet with people of all civilizations and religions, it is because I have faith in the seeds of wisdom which the Spirit has planted in the conscience of all those various peoples and tribes and clans. From those hidden grains will come the true resource for the future of mankind in this world of ours."

Appleyard and the Holy Father stepped into the sunlight. There was a handshake and a parting glance before the Pope turned and, leaning lightly on Sadowski's arm, entered the broad path leading into the private grounds behind the villa. As he watched them, Gibson considered his ne to do all he could to foster this man's permanence in considered, too, all the names that had figured in his s with the Slavic Pope. Yeltsin, Gorbachev, Shevardnadze, Bush, Thatcher, Kohl, Mitterrand, Clinton, Mandela. Those and more had come up explicitly or by implication.

Yet of all the greats, it seemed to Appleyard that only this one—only this Slavic Pope—was worth saving, worth protecting, worth perpetuating. So long as such a man cut a figure on the international stage, for so long would wisdom and salvation and progress be possible for the society of nations. "Poor, poor Europe." Not all that long ago, Gib recalled, the Slavic Pope had written those words to the EC Committee charged with filling the post of Secretary-General. "Poor, poor world," he might have said.

His mind deep in such thoughts, Appleyard watched the two figures recede into the gardens, one robed in somber black, the other in white. Before the path took them both from view, the figure in white turned back for an instant to wave farewell.

"Holy Father," Gibson said half aloud and raised his hand to return the gesture. *"Pater patrum."*

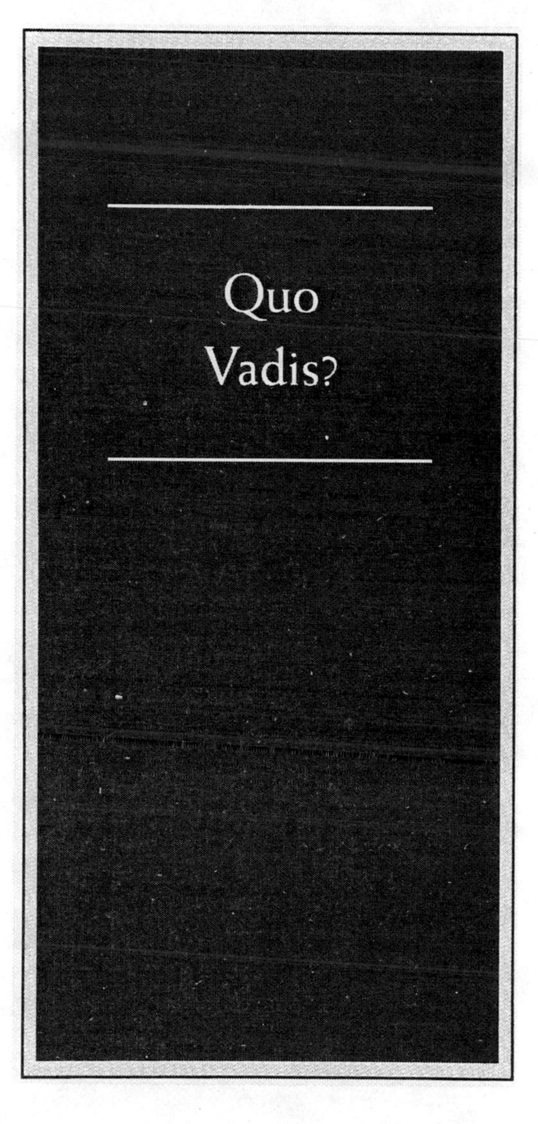
Quo
Vadis?

XLIX

HAMMER AND TONGS. That was the feel of everything in Rome during the first two weeks of May. So much so that even before he returned from Castel Gandolfo, the Slavic Pope was enmeshed as the centerpiece of events that everyone sought to control and that could only end in some shattering climax.

True, those who knew the details of the radical change being planned for the papacy weren't talking, and those who did most of the talking knew next to nothing. But because no real secrets are possible for any world leader whose decisions affect the lives and fortunes of millions, the general conviction that had been growing for so many months—the silent consensus that this Rome of the Popes was about to change and would never again be the same—strengthened in intensity, much as the size of the Roman press corps expanded from its normal complement of some hundreds to a little over three thousand. Given time, even news agencies caught the unmistakable scent of a big story and gathered in for the kill.

Contributing to the fever taking hold of Rome was the whirlpool of information and speculation flowing like contagion from diplomatic back channels, intelligence intercepts, specialized agencies' reports, inquisitive media, gossip columnists, spin doctors, vested interests and the gut instinct of ordinary people.

In that climate, Cardinal Maestroianni's "supplemental initiatives" wreaked their intended effect. The confusion caused by the illicit document on Altar girls and by the report on population control put out by His Eminence's allies in the Pontifical Academy of Sciences set media minds aflame like dry tinder. By the time the 157 Cardinals of the Universal Church began to arrive for the May 6 opening of the General Consistory—a mere trickle of them on May 1; some decades by May 4; the whole flood of them by May 5—a new pitch of uncertainty reigned everywhere. What was really going on at the Church's highest seat of government? Who was really in charge?

Instead of contributing answers to those questions, however, the Cardinals themselves were buffeted by the staged publicity and propaganda devised by the Slavic Pope's adversaries, and beset by the suddenly frenetic lobbying of contenders and pretenders in the papal race. Still, and despite the public confusion, none of these gathering Princes of the Church would be able to excuse themselves later by saying they weren't on the spot for the events about to take place, or that the issues were hidden from them. All had ample opportunity to consult together as colleagues in a closed society of their own, where no intruders could venture. They had the special status of brothers of Peter the Great Fisherman, who, they had been divinely assured, would strengthen their weaknesses and reinforce their faith. And the very fact of their physical presence underscored the truth that the universality of the Roman Church was at stake. Indeed, their lives during those two weeks would be lived according to one of two alternative scenarios, and guided according to each one's goals and alliances.

According to His Holiness' enemies, the last Roman Catholic Pope was about to be eased out of the papacy by a combination of his own deficient leadership, the firm will of those who listened to the lessons of history and knew their duty to humanity and, though few among them knew it, the covert tenacity of those Fratres intent on the sands filtering inexorably down through their hourglass of the Availing Time.

According to those who still believed in the Roman Catholic Church as the unique source of eternal salvation for all of humanity, the Slavic Pope stood on the brink of a near-apocalyptic change. For them, he was the last Catholic Pope not because his was the last papacy, but because an era was about to end. His pilgrimage to the East not only marked the climax in his personal drama as Pontiff and as a human being but signaled the close of these Catholic times that had begun two thousand years before.

With such considerations in the balance, it was unthinkable, but undeniable, that the greatest effect the assembled Cardinals managed to achieve was to heighten the public sense of spectacle. Their ethnic, linguistic, cultural, political and religious diversity made for great theater. And their stage presence was boosted by the fact that each was attended by a retinue of at least one bishop, two theological experts and any number of colorful and outspoken diocesan officials. Further spice was added when it was discovered that several bishops from the United States, Holland, Germany and Switzerland were accompanied by teams of Altar girls and female Eucharistic ministers. It was an exotic aspect of diversity tailor-made for tabloid rhapsodies.

The left-wing *Il Borghese* snickered that "*haute couture* now graces Church ceremonies," and that "the hierarchs have enlisted Chanel, Dior, Lauren and Klein in their search for divine beauty." The *Corriere di Roma* countered with heady headlines that trumpeted "Rome's feminization." Editorials elsewhere waxed poetic about "the Church Universal, replete with human inventiveness," and about the Cardinals—some of them, at least—as "worthy representatives of that prophetic humanism which is the crowning achievement of Roman Catholicism in this twentieth century." The appetite of the secular press was whetted all the more when it became known that several young American bishops were accompanied by women theologians in a private capacity. "Hopefully," winked the

Socialist weekly *Uomo Nuovo,* "these prelates, junior in age and standing, will outrank their seniors in virtue."

With the May 6 opening of the General Consistory coming up fast, newspapers in Europe and the Americas began to play the festivities to the hilt. Not all the media attention was lavished on such stories, however. During the opening days of May, the Eternal City was transformed into the ultimate showcase for the success of a patient and guileful strategy that, over a period of thirty years, had fragmented the sacramental unity and traditional piety of the Catholic Mass into a hodgepodge of invented rites that aped local cultures and that bore about as much resemblance to one another as water bears to oil.

Once upon a recent time, anyone attending any Catholic Mass anywhere in the world had been confident in his understanding and worship. Language and vestments, gestures and movements had all been redolent with the same identical motive and meaning. Now, however, Mass had to do with local tribal traditions, local political ideologies and, not infrequently, local sensual pathologies. The Mass said by the Slavic Pope in St. Peter's Basilica bore no resemblance at all to the so-called Dignity Mass celebrated at the same hour in Milwaukee, Wisconsin; or to the Liberation Mass taking place in the Base Communities at São Paulo, Brazil; or to the Goddess Gaia Mass chanted in the Archdiocese of Seattle.

Aware that revolution and diversity make for byline copy, representatives of the press swarmed over Rome to write about the spectacle. In a single day at the Church of Santa Maria Maggiore, an Indian stringer photographed Cardinal Komaraswami's colorful Hinduized Mass; an African reporter covered the amazing Congolese Mass of Cardinal Bonsanawi of Zaire; and a Brazilian television crew trained cameras and lavish commentary on the guitar-and-dance folk Mass of Cardinal Romarino of Belize.

In the midst of all this precedent-shattering activity, the Holy Father returned to the Apostolic Palace in a spirit of unshakable equanimity. Rested and vigorous, he received each of the visiting Cardinals for a personal audience—events well publicized in His Holiness' own newspaper with banner headlines and front-page photographs. He made himself liberally available to Cardinal Graziani when final details had to be worked out for the Consistory and the Shoah Concert. And he was the predictable target of a heightened level of diplomatic activity.

To some degree, such diplomatic attention had to do with the Pontiff's current contention with the U.S. President. To some degree, it was an admission that his forthcoming trip to Russia and Ukraine had already enhanced his unique status still further in the arena of world leaders. But it was also tacit recognition, at least among the Rome-resident diplomatic missions, that this Pope's availability was shortening; that now was the time to capitalize on their acquaintance with him for an unusual string of favors.

The face the Slavic Pope showed throughout all the hugger-mugger—his smiling performance in public; his acquiescence in all the arrangements made by the Secretariat of State for the General Consistory; his satisfaction at the vastly increased numbers of pilgrims and tourists thronging Roman streets and monuments—all this fed the festive and celebratory mood. But it seemed to papal intimates like Sadowski, Gladstone and Slattery as though, unmindful of the sharp cracks and lethal fissures in the wall of Catholicism being papered over by the bonhomie going on around him, the Pope had his eyes fixed on some North Star visible only to him.

For Christian, watching the situation was the easy part. As a bonus for work well and loyally done, and as a token of rewards yet to come, Cardinal Maestroianni made it a point to keep him at the center of things. He spent long hours each day in the Cardinal's office, where he helped to deal with the pressures of visiting consultants, diplomats, emissaries, couriers, conference members and the inevitable hangers-on.

Unavoidably, he spent more time than ever with Silvio Aureatini and Giacomo Graziani. He exchanged a word or two with his brother's great mentor, the fabled Mr. Cyrus Benthoek, and with the mysterious Dr. Ralph Channing, when the two "dropped in," as Channing was pleased to say, "to savor the exhilarating atmosphere." He was buttonholed by retired Cardinal Piet Svensen, who had come down from Belgium to install himself as a day resident in State's consulting rooms. On the lower end of the scale, he found it useful to strike up an acquaintance of sorts with Aureatini's gofer, the gossipy and not very bright Archbishop Buttafuoco.

Gladstone saw nothing of Damien Slattery during those first hectic days of the month. But in his capacity as double agent, he saw Lucadamo as a matter of necessity. For caution's sake and because of the demands each day put on them, they came to rely on late-night meetings well away from the Vatican.

One such meeting marked a new turning for Gladstone. On May 4 they met over a couple of sandwiches at a cappuccino café tucked away in the Trastevere district. As usual, Chris passed along a quick but detailed account of the information he had been able to pick up. But, also, he had a complaint to register. He was upset over the delay in the search operation for that mysterious double-sealed envelope still buried somewhere in the Secret Archives.

The security chief was sympathetic. He shared Gladstone's anxiety to find that envelope. But he reminded Chris that Cardinal Valdés' schedule had become more erratic than ever, and would doubtless remain so until the Consistory got under way. The search would have to wait until then. "By that time," Lucadamo cautioned his companion, "you and Giancarlo Terragente will have to work on your own. One way and another, I'll be with His Holiness every waking hour. From the time of the Holy Father's formal welcome to the Cardinals tomorrow night until we return from Russia on the thirteenth, I don't plan to let him out of my sight."

"Console yourself, Giustino. With the way Maestroianni and Palombo and Pensabene and Aureatini have been working Their Eminences over, it would be a downright relief to get out of Rome. I only wish I were going along."

"A relief for Maestroianni, maybe." Lucadamo picked up on Gladstone's thought with an ugly laugh. "He and Palombo and the others can't wait to get the Pope out of Rome so they can have full play with the College of Cardinals. They have the Common Mind Vote of the bishops in hand now to use as a whip. They have their precious Resignation Protocol initialed. What else do they need? After His Holiness departs, wouldn't it be providential in their eyes if something happened along the way that would allow them to invoke the Protocol into law? Hey presto! The College of Cardinals becomes a ready-made papal Conclave and proceeds to elect a successor to the Slavic Pope. *La commedia è finita!*"

"Assassination?" Gladstone had been alarmed enough to hear Gibson Appleyard touch on that possibility. But this wasn't Appleyard talking now. This was the dispassionate, realistic, coolheaded, professional security chief calculating the odds of papal disaster. "Are you talking about assassination?"

"That's my difficulty, Christian. I don't know what they're planning. I don't know when or how they intend to carry it out. But I start with the conviction that this will be the neatest chance they'll ever have to be rid of this Holy Father."

"But the whole idea of the CMV was to embolden the bishops and demoralize the Holy Father." More appalled than ever at his own involvement in the scheme, Chris was searching for solid ground. "The plan was to force his resignation, not to murder him. I've learned not to put anything past this crowd I'm working with. Not after Aldo Carnesecca. But we're talking about the Pope now, Giustino. And besides, your security on papal trips is always airtight."

"Maybe so. At least it's as tight as we can make it. All the same, I have this awful feeling at the pit of my stomach. I can practically hear Graziani's pious proclamation to Rome and the world that the Pope is dead or resigned or comatose, or whatever they've arranged."

"His Holiness must be aware of the possibilities, Giustino." Chris was grasping at straws now. "I mean, have you suggested postponing the Russia trip until the Consistory is over? I know it's late, but . . ."

Lucadamo waved the thought aside. "He's aware of the possibilities all right. That's one reason why he's insisted that Father Damien come along. If anything does happen, he doesn't want Slattery to be left here to be eaten alive."

Gladstone heaved a great sigh. It sounded to him as if the Pope was almost eager to be gone.

"No." Lucadamo turned suddenly pensive. "His attitude has to do with Fatima. He expects the Blessed Virgin to give him some sign of God's will on this pilgrimage. I'm not sure what that means. Some indication of Christ's will for his pontificate, I imagine. And for the Church. But whatever it is, His Holiness is confident. He's told me in so many words that no matter what motives anyone else may have—whatever motivated the governments involved to invite him, and whatever motivates Maestroianni and the others—they have all made this pilgrimage possible 'in God's providence.' Those were his words, Christian. 'In God's providence.' "

Absolutely speaking, Gladstone knew the Pontiff was right. Ultimately everything is part of God's providence. Given recent history, however, he was troubled beyond telling to think what His Holiness might do with what God had provided.

On the afternoon of Friday, May 5, one day shy of the opening of the Consistory, Cardinal Secretary Graziani provided each of Their Eminences with a dossier prepared by his staff. Among its contents were three items: A carefully tabulated report on the Common Mind Vote, bolstered by backup evidence and statements from the august members of Cardinal Graziani's ad hoc committee. A photocopy of the *De Successione Papali* document, together with affidavits from Cardinals Graziani, Maestroianni and Aureatini. And a summary of His Holiness' state of health that was worrisome. A separate letter signed by the Cardinal Secretary of State emphasized that there was to be neither public nor collegial discussion of this material. Their Eminences were to feel free, however, to discuss it privately with the "relevant authorities."

That same evening, from a control booth high above the second-floor amphitheater of the Nervi Hall of Audiences, Giustino Lucadamo and a couple of his top aides scanned the distinguished crowd gathering in for the Pontiff's address of formal welcome. The Cardinals had all assembled well before the time scheduled for His Holiness' arrival. So, too, the high-ranking officials of all the Vatican Congregations and the heads of all the Religious Orders. Emissaries from the Anglican and Eastern Orthodox Churches took their own places in the semicircular rows of seats. The expression on all the faces appeared to be a blend of satisfaction and expectation. Of particular interest to Lucadamo were the Roman officials who had gathered in Strasbourg for that historic meeting of the antipapal cabal. Patiently, he searched each of them out in the crowd. Not one was missing.

"Where the body is," Giustino muttered Christ's remark recorded in the Gospels, "there the vultures gather."

At nine-thirty on the morning of May 6, His Excellency Alberto Vacchi-Khouras arrived for an unannounced visit with Abbot Augustin Kordecki at Jasna Gora Monastery in Czestochowa in southern Poland. He was here on official business as the Apostolic Nuncio of Warsaw, His Excellency informed the Abbot, and he wished to address the entire community of monks on a matter of utmost importance. The Abbot summoned the Sacristan to his office. In turn, the Sacristan hastened to summon the full complement of Pauline monks. When all were gathered, His Excellency declared that the news he was about to share was to be sealed with the secrecy surrounding the Confessional.

Satisfied that all understood the severe penalties for violation of confidentiality, the Papal Nuncio was pleased to announce that, following the severe rigors of his journey to Ukraine and Russia, the Holy Father would be making a private visit to the Monastery. To ensure seclusion, His Holiness and a few companions would arrive incognito. The suite assigned to the Pontiff and six adjoining rooms would be off limits to all except the few monks required to attend the visitors' needs. The papal party would dine alone; and, while they would confine themselves for the most part to their quarters, the monks were to consider certain areas of the Monastery off limits to the community. Mentioned specifically were the Gothic Chapel of Our Lady, the Church of the Assumption, the library and the refectory.

For the few days in question, the monks would make do with the Chapel of the Last Supper for their devotions. Should there be any chance encounters between the community members and the papal party, the clandestine and recuperative nature of the visit was to be respected. Which was to say, no words or communication would be tolerated.

"In fact"—His Excellency covered the point smoothly—"I invite you all to enter into the reflective silence and solitude of a three-day retreat, beginning on May 12. Any television and radio sets on the premises will be put under lock and key. No monk will leave the Monastery, and no one will enter from the outside. All telephone lines will be disconnected for the duration of the papal visit. Let it be a time of prayer and penance, during which we will all ask God to endow our Pope and our bishops with a new wisdom for a new age."

It was shortly past ten-thirty when, having complied with his instructions to the letter, Vacchi-Khouras bid farewell to the Abbot and clambered into his limousine for the 125-mile journey back to Warsaw.

Kordecki watched as the sleek Mercedes-Benz, flags fluttering on its fenders, glided down the drive toward the superhighway. Come May 12, he and his monks would have no choice but to lock Jasna Gora down as required. From now until the papal party departed, he was bound to secrecy. Nevertheless, he knew as a Pole what no Palestinian like Vacchi-Khouras, and none of his masters at the Vatican Secretariat, would ever learn. Deep in his bones, Kordecki shared the bond that had always united the Slavic Pope to his people. They would know he was present among them. They would know he was in danger. Despite the precautions and the security, somehow they would know.

❑ ❑ ❑ ❑

At nine-thirty on the morning of May 6, Christian hunkered down in the anonymity of a small balcony atop the second-floor audience hall at the Nervi to watch the Princes of his Church file in for the opening of the Holy Father's General Consistory.

Though they were all decked out in their jeweled crosses and ermine cloaks, Gladstone was less impressed with their splendor than with their pathetic quiescence. Not many of them, he knew, were cut from the same cloth as His Eminence of Centurycity. Most were probably more like Jay Jay O'Cleary. But one and all, they were key to Maestroianni's plan to dismantle the Catholic tradition to which they belonged and to which they owed their only claim to ecclesial identity.

"Butter wouldn't melt in their mouths, would it, lad?" Father Damien slipped into the seat beside Gladstone.

"Slattery!" That deep voice was the happiest sound Chris had heard in weeks. "Where've you been! You've missed a lot that's been going on around here."

The truth was that Damien hadn't missed anything. He had seen the Pope at least once a day for the past month until he had finished composing and editing the two encyclical letters in accordance with His Holiness' specifications. Then he had supervised the printing of both encyclicals in time for the Consistory. As he was sworn to mention that work to no one, however, he kept his attention on the scene below.

"No wonder Christ is liquidating this Catholic organization, Chris." Slattery caught sight of Cardinal Pensabene chatting earnestly with a group of prelates from his old stomping grounds in Latin America. "Another ten years under the hand of men like that, and the destruction of the Church organization will be complete. But by now I guess we know enough not to be surprised. That was the plan, after all."

"I'm not surprised." Gladstone leaned forward to get a better view. "Just disgusted. Disappointed. Frustrated. And, to be frank, sometimes disillusioned with this Pope. Half the time I can't figure him at all. Mind you, I'm not ready to give up on him. He's Peter, warts and all. Wherever he resides, there is the Church of Christ. And he is Bishop of Rome. So here I stay, religiously and physically."

"I'm with you in all of that, Christian." Damien lowered his voice to a whisper as the amphitheater fell into silence. "And yet, we'd be fools not to know that we're looking down on the sclerotic backbone of an ecclesiastical organization that doesn't serve God faithfully, and doesn't serve man efficiently."

At exactly ten o'clock, the Slavic Pope arrived. He walked slowly but firmly to his place as presider over the assembly. In gestures that had become familiar to most of the world, he saluted all the Eminent Cardinals and all the eminent guests with a wave of his right hand and a smiling face. With his left hand, he lightly touched the pectoral cross suspended on its gold chain. Every movement showed the unmistakable picture of good health, of confidence and of welcome. His Holiness opened the Consistory by inviting all to rise and join with him in reciting the verses of a prayer to the Holy Spirit, the *Veni, Sancte Spiritus.* Then Monsignore Sadowski laid a manila folder on the lectern in front of the Pontiff.

"Venerable Brothers." The Holy Father turned the cover of the folder. "I have three documents to present to you for consideration. The first two are letters of instruction for the Church Universal. The third contains a canonical modification of existing Church legislation regulating the papacy . . ." With those words as preamble, His Holiness proceeded to turn his address to this first session of the General Consistory into a stunning blow to the egos of many Cardinals, and a surprise to all.

He began with the letter declaring the Church's bans on contraception, homosexual activity and all forms of Satanist observance to be infallible teachings; violation would entail the pain of automatic excommunication. Then he went on to the second letter, which declared it to be a dogma of Roman Catholic faith that all supernatural aid from God—in the traditional language of the Church, all divine grace—came through a special function granted to the Blessed Virgin Mary as the Mother of Christ. She was, therefore, to be revered as Mediatrix of All Graces.

The texts of these two ex cathedra letters were not yet definitive, His Holiness told their Eminences. He was confiding the documents to them now so that during his absence of five days in the Eastern lands of Europe, they could study them, discuss them, critique them and improve them. With their collaboration, he hoped to promulgate both encyclicals officially soon after his return to Rome on May 13.

The Holy Father spent a shorter time on the Resignation Protocol in its definitive form. He had initialed the *De Successione Papali* document, he explained, for one purpose only. To allay the filial fears of so many of his Venerable Brothers that the Church might be left suddenly without an elected head capable of governance. According to its terms, that agreement between himself and his Cardinals was limited to a one-time, one-case application. But that document, too, if rightly studied by Their Eminences, might give them solace from their worries and food for serious reflection during his absence.

"Now, my Venerable Brothers . . ."

Those were the last words Gladstone heard of the papal address. One of Giustino Lucadamo's aides had made his way up to the balcony and, at that precise moment, touched him on the shoulder. "There's a crisis, Monsignore. Come."

L

"WE DON'T KNOW, Chris. Declan may be dead. They all may be dead by now. We don't know!"

Paul's son dead? That vibrant, bright-eyed, inquisitive, beloved boy taken at the very threshold of his life? Within minutes of his brother's anguished call from Belgium, Gladstone was on the way to the airport in a helicopter mustered for him by Giustino Lucadamo. Thanks to Lucadamo, too, Alitalia held its flight to Brussels "for compassionate reasons involving a distinguished member of the Holy See"; and the mere mention of Paul Gladstone's name as Secretary-General of the EC was enough for NATO to hold a helicopter at the ready at the Brussels airport to rush Christian to the site of the accident. The whole of that wild dash from the Vatican helipad to the Danielle cave complex couldn't have taken more than four hours. But it was an eternity for Chris, torn by the threat of death to his nephew in Belgium and by equally dire threats to his Pope and to the papacy itself in Rome. Finally, though, he was able to control his emotions and force his mind to work.

It had taken a few seconds to calm his brother enough to get the essentials. In broken sentences Paul told how Deckel had been one of a group of young spelunkers chosen for a three-day foray into the Greater Danielle. "How could we say no?" Paul was on the verge of breaking down. Declan had been so excited, and everything had been so carefully planned. Their leader was an experienced guide. Radio contact would be maintained with an aboveground control center. The party would check in on an hourly schedule. The group had entered the Lesser Danielle on May 1. They passed into the Greater Danielle on May 2. Everything was fine. Then on May 3, when they were ready to start back through the caverns, a tremor had been felt aboveground and all contact with the spelunkers had been lost. A search party had gone down. Within a couple of hours they had radioed the worst possible message. A cave-in!

Paul and Yusai had spent the next two days at the surface entrance of the Danielle complex. The Royal Belgian Society of Speleologues had sent a series of teams to work in relays at the dangerous job of tunneling through the debris. But by the time Paul had made his call, hope was fading and there was whispered talk of death.

Once on the ground in Belgium, Chris had the feeling of moving through a lugubrious black-and-white dream sequence. The NATO helicopter that took him to the cave site sped over a countryside sodden with a steady drizzle of rain. Paul and Yusai were pale and numb with grief.

The experts who briefed Christian poured out a flood of dizzying technical information. But when they took him below to get a more precise idea of the situation, all the buzzwords came down to hard reality. The seismic disturbances were continuing. Conditions belowground were deteriorating. It was dangerous to venture even into the Lesser Danielle. No one could tell what things were like, or might happen next, in the badly destabilized portion of the Greater Danielle they were trying to reach. There was discussion of suspending the rescue operation lest lives be lost in the effort.

Toward midnight, the official in charge advised the Gladstones to go home to Deurle for a few hours of rest. "We'll keep at it for as long as we possibly can," he assured them. "It's a short ride by helicopter, and we'll call at the slightest hint of a breakthrough." Drenched by the misty rain, all three returned to Guidohuis, where Hannah Dowd and Maggie Mulvahill, half sick with worry themselves, waited up for any scrap of news. By the time they had changed into dry clothes, there was some hot soup on the stove and a log fire blazing in the living room. It would, they knew, be a sleepless night for everyone.

Yusai said very little. Chris felt there was a certain touch of fatalism in her reactions; but whatever her mind-set, her suffering was matched only by her self-control. She invented little tasks to busy herself for a while until, overcome with physical exhaustion, she curled up in a chair across the room in silent isolation.

Not so Paul. Once they were home, he wanted to talk. At first he rattled on to his brother about the odds that Declan and the others might still be alive. He knew they had taken plenty of water, he said a dozen times. By now, though, they were probably out of food. But what about air? And what if they hadn't merely been trapped by the cave-in? What if they had been buried by it? "Ah, God in Heaven!" Paul's nerves were wearing thin. "I hate thinking what if! Tell me, Chris. Why can't the good Lord just save my son without any ifs, ands or buts? What's my little Deckel done to deserve such an awful death in the dark and cold and muck of that place?"

What indeed, Christian thought. He knew Paul wasn't contending with God so much as he was trying to understand a very old mystery—the reason for human suffering. "I don't think it's a question of what Deckel deserves, Paul." Christian gave the only answer he could. "Christ is innocent, too. He *is* innocence, in fact. Innocence incarnate. But He suffered precisely to take your sins and my sins and all our sins on Himself as God's Son."

"Atonement?" Paul groaned and ran his hands through his hair. "I can't imagine the good God taking his anger or displeasure out on a little child because of the sins of his elders. I know I'm not a first-class Catholic, but I've done my best in difficult circumstances. . . . No, by God!" Sparks flew and flames danced high as Paul shot out of his chair and kicked the logs in the fireplace. "There isn't room for lies like that anymore.

"God knows I love my son. He's the pride and joy of my life. I'd do anything to save him. So would Yusai." He looked at his wife, who stared back at him, startled by his outburst. "And God knows I've given my boy every material advantage." Paul sat down beside his older brother again. "I've done my best to prepare him to live in a world that will be different than anything that's come before. I've even done my best to have a part in shaping that world. That's why my acceptance into the Grand Lodge of Israel was so important. Remember, Chris? I told you about that. About Jerusalem and Aminadab and feeling so close to God and my fellow man up there on that mountaintop. But my boy hasn't ended up on a mountaintop, has he? He's down in that freezing, rotten hole!"

Tears coursed down Paul's face. "I wonder if you can understand how right that moment seemed up there at Aminadab. So splendid with promise. Then, after that, the first two oaths were so easy—the Entered Apprentice Degree and the Fellowcraft Degree. So easy; so rewarding. The Third Oath was okay, too. It made me a Master Mason, after all; opened all the doors. But that one cost me something special. And it cost Declan and Yusai something special, too. And do you know why? For the simple reason that taking that oath was like cutting a ribbon with scissors. It was like killing something inside me; something that had always been a part of our family and our lives at Windswept House.

"That was okay, I thought. Just old-fashioned, outworn nonsense. Let it go. And that's exactly what I did. Even here, right now, I've reckoned the odds of life and death for my son in terms of air and water and food."

"Have you, Paul?" Christian's voice was as soft as the firelight. "Have you let it all go?"

How strange, Paul thought, that such a loving question from his brother should hit him like a sharp blow. "Yes." He had to answer truthfully; but he had to be clear about it. "It's not me I'm thinking about, Chris. It's Declan. It's what I never even thought to give him. All the things you and Tricia and I breathed in like the air at Windswept House. I've left him without that innocent, trusting sense of God's omnipotence. Of His love. Of His miracles. I never even taught him to pray. I've left him without any defenses down there in the Danielle. Can you believe that?

"So maybe you're right after all, Chris. Maybe God put this child of ours into our hands—Yusai's and mine—saying, 'This is your gift from Me; take good care of him.' And maybe now God is saying, 'If you can't do any better than that, I've decided to take him from you.' " Stripped of all his own defenses, Paul was reduced to naked agony. "Tell me! What am I to do? I'd willingly die to save little Deckel, if that's what God wants. Is that what it takes, Chris? Would that placate this God Who now seems to be taking His gift of a son? What does He want of me? Tell me!"

Christian had heard enough. Maybe he couldn't do anything to help

Declan. But he wouldn't stand by and let his brother cut himself to shreds with helpless grief or be seared to the bone by anger and self-pity. "Have you been listening to yourself, Paul? Have you been listening to the questions you've asked me? Why is God withdrawing His gift, you ask? Well, try turning that question around. Tell me, Paul. Why should God leave His gift with you? You took the gift, and forgot the Giver. What in Heaven's name have you done for God except spit in His face?

"You ask what God wants of you? I have no infallible answers; no special communiqués from on high; no premonitions of things to come, the way Mother has. But I can answer this one. You've been clever in bargaining with Mammon. Clever enough to deal your way right into mortal sin. So now, try doing what Christ said. You don't have to be half so clever in bargaining with God. You don't even have to go to Aminadab to strike a deal with Him. Tell Him what you want, and what you'll do to get it. Give back your soul to God, and He may well give back His gift to you!"

"Paul?" Yusai was always the first to admit that she'd become a Catholic without learning much about Christianity. But what Chris was saying now was simple to understand. "Paul?" she called a second time. But it was her eyes that drew her husband to kneel by her side and take her in his arms. Those eyes, glistening with tears of helpless dignity unmatched in the whole of God's universe. Those eyes, glistening with the tears of Rachel.

So they remained, those three, silent in sorrow and hope, until the gentle but insistent ringing of the telephone invaded that sacred moment.

"Say again?" Christian was nearest the phone, and answered it. "What was the name?"

"Régice Bernard, Monsignore. Giustino Lucadamo phoned me. I'm an old friend of his uncle. He told me about the boy trapped in the Danielle cave-in. Have they found him yet?"

It was like God, Chris decided, to send a huge ox of a Walloon like Régice Bernard thundering in on his company helicopter as a signal that He was ready to deal if Paul was.

Bernard was all business—crisp, orderly and raring to go. He could see that Paul and Yusai were in no condition to make clear decisions. So he drew Chris into the study and explained as briefly as possible what Giustino already knew, and why he had called. A hale and hearty seventy-something now, he ran his own heavy construction outfit in his native Liège. Back when the Germans had invaded Belgium in 1940, he had been a strapping lad in his teens. Naturally, he had taken to the woods and the Ardennes forest with the maquis. And because the network of underground tunnels and caverns honeycombing certain parts of his native country had been indispensable for him and his fellow partisans, he knew both the Lesser and Greater Sectors of the Danielle complex like the back of his hand. More importantly, he knew sections of the Greater Danielle that remained unmapped. And on top of that, he knew another way into the maze; a second entrance some three miles from the known entrance through the Lesser Danielle. "In fact," he told Chris, "I know ways in and out and around those caverns that would make those speleologues running the rescue operation sick with envy. That's why Giustino called me. I'm not saying we'll find the boy alive, Monsignore. There's no guarantee about that. But if there's any way at all to get to him, I know I can find it. So, if you're game . . ."

"I'm game, Mr. Bernard!" Chris knew the sound of hope when he heard it. "And I'm grateful. Let's put a call through to the rescue team. I guarantee they'll cooperate. Then give me a minute to explain the situation to my brother and his wife."

The next half hour was helter-skelter. Régice Bernard didn't so much plead his case with the Danielle crew chief as bark out a series of no-nonsense preparatory instructions. Yusai, alive with hope again, ran to tell Hannah and Maggie the news and then rushed to throw on some warm clothing. Paul, too nervous to stand still, asked his brother to wait outside with him. "I suppose it's not usual, Chris, to hear a confession strolling on the grass." Paul paced back and forth beside Bernard's helicopter, perched near the orchard. "I don't even know if you have the necessary Confessional faculties. I mean, I remember from my seminary days that there are certain sins that not every priest is authorized to forgive . . ."

"No." Christian put a stop to the waffling. "It's not usual. And it's not usual for brother to absolve brother. But I do have the necessary faculties, and all things are allowed in case of necessity."

In the time it took for silver-gray streaks of light to pierce the clouds along the eastern horizon on that Sunday morning of May 7, God chose to collect His end of the bargain with Paul Gladstone. Solemn-faced and still fearful for his son, the prodigal statesman made his first valid confession in fifteen years. He asked to be cleansed of sins that had culminated at Aminadab in his renunciation of Christ's Salvation in favor of prideful, ambitious dedication to the kingdom of this world. In view of his deep guilt, he asked for severe penance. And in view of Christ's personal promise of patience and endless mercy, he asked to be given pardon and peace in the absolution of his offenses.

Christian complied with the first request in terms both men knew might arrest Paul in the upward spiral of his career. He had just complied with the second when, with Yusai scurrying gamely by his side, Régice Bernard came striding toward the orchard. Chris exchanged a few quick words of explanation and a hasty bear hug with his brother. Then Paul turned to help Yusai into the helicopter and clambered in beside her.

"You won't be coming, Monsignore?" The strapping Belgian clasped the hand his new young friend held out to him in farewell and heartfelt thanks.

"Whatever happens in those caves, Mr. Bernard, I owe you a debt I can never repay. But there's more than one life-or-death situation being played out at this moment. I've done everything I can here. It's time for me to get back to Rome."

Had Cardinal Maestroianni been a believer, he would have thought it the hand of God that the Slavic Pope had caved in one more time and named him to the office of Camerlengo. As it was, he chalked it up to the tide of history, to his own prowess at bargaining and to the Pontiff's desire for peace at all costs. But any way you sliced it, as papal Chamberlain, His Eminence would hold all necessary authority to govern during the crucial days of the Holy Father's Russia trip.

Nevertheless, even with the smell of victory rising in the air, Maestroianni knew better than to rest content. He was up hours before dawn that Sunday to recap the risks and alternatives he and his colleagues would face over the next seven days. By seven o'clock he was ready to conduct a final run-through with the key members of the ad hoc committee at his penthouse apartment. With that same sense of victory to fire his soul, Maestroianni's perpetual associate, Cardinal Silvio Aureatini, was the first to arrive. But the others piled in close on his heels—Leo Pensabene, Cardinal Prefect of the Congregation of Bishops; Noah Palombo, director of the International Council for Christian Liturgy; Cardinal Secretary of State Giacomo Graziani.

The first order of business was to be sure all five men were clear on the plans and contingencies. Fully aware of every detail of the Slavic Pope's itinerary from the time of his departure the next day until his scheduled return on May 13, they had every reason to expect that His Holiness would fall prey to an occurrence of bad health. "Or at least," as Pensabene added gracefully, "to force majeure and the play of circumstance."

"Speaking of force majeure." Maestroianni turned to the Secretary of State. "May we take it that Monsignore Jan Michalik has been thoroughly briefed?"

"Thoroughly, Eminence. I met with him and Dr. Fanarote yesterday afternoon." Graziani was full of confident self-adulation as he reviewed that conversation for his companions.

Michalik himself was a known quantity to everyone listening to the Secretary. A minor but egotistical Secretariat of State bureaucrat, he was a tall, angular Italian of Polish extraction, fluent in Polish and blessed with the eyes of a lynx for details. The Monsignore had built his career on an almost fanatic attention to detail. As expected, he had taken it as his due that he should be assigned to travel with the Pope as a member of his personal entourage. Or, to be precise, as what amounted to Graziani's personal watchdog.

Dr. Fanarote had been less compliant, of course. Graziani recounted the papal physician's disbelief as he was told not only that he was to report even the slightest variation of His Holiness' physical condition to Monsignore Michalik but that all decisions in that area were to be made by the Monsignore. Fanarote had been wise enough to confine his objections to professional grounds. He could not discuss anything touching on His Holiness' health with any third party, he said, unless the Holy Father himself should give permission.

Unruffled by Fanarote's indignation, Graziani had made the sedate observation that such an extraordinary man as His Holiness would surely understand if the good doctor might not be up to the rigors of this most extraordinary of His Holiness' journeys. Faced with Hobson's choice—to obey Graziani or abandon his Pope—Fanarote had declared himself to be His Holiness' servant. Understanding on every detail had been quickly achieved after that.

"Well done, Eminence." Maestroianni was indeed satisfied.

There followed an equally satisfactory review of the report from His Excellency Alberto Vacchi-Khouras, Apostolic Nuncio of Warsaw, concerning the arrangements with Abbot Kordecki at Czestochowa. All was in readiness there. That left only two major if less troublesome items of business to review: the management of the Cardinals during the Pontiff's absence and the management of public opinion until a resolution of the uncertainty over the Pontiff's welfare was achieved.

As Camerlengo, Maestroianni himself would provide direction to the Cardinals in their discussions and deliberations. While the principal preoccupation of the Consistory would ostensibly center on the two encyclical letters proposed by the Slavic Pope, the reality of power play would dictate a different agenda devoted to an assessment of the Common Mind Vote, and the consequences to be drawn for the future of the Roman papacy. As to public opinion, Cardinal Aureatini had arranged for a press conference to be held at 5 P.M. each day of the papal pilgrimage. He had put Archbishop Buttafuoco in charge of that important chore. It would be his job to give out news bulletins about the Holy Father's journey and to dispense prepared statements about the pious proceedings of the Consistory.

Cardinal Camerlengo Cosimo Maestroianni adjourned the meeting in plenty of time to notify each of his counterparts abroad of the impending disposition of the Slavic Pope due to health. He placed a call first to retired Cardinal Svensen, who had returned to Belgium, then to Cyrus Benthoek, who had returned to his headquarters in London, and last to Dr. Ralph Channing in New York City. That, Maestroianni knew, was sufficient. By the time the Shoah Concert got under way this evening, the full network of friends and allies in this grave undertaking would be alerted.

Once back at the Angelicum, Christian found a message waiting for him from Damien Slattery. But his first call was to Windswept House.

"You mark my words, Chris Gladstone!" Cessi took the news about

Deckel in the grand manner that always irritated her enemies and made her friends smile. "My grandson is not destined to perish in the bowels of some dank underground cavern!"

"Not if Régice Bernard has any say," Christian agreed. "I'll let you know the minute I hear anything. We need a lot of miracles right now, Mother, so keep praying. And Tricia, too. She has a special pipeline to Heaven!"

Gladstone was about to return Slattery's call when his friend rang from the Casa del Clero and saved him the trouble. He asked for news about the search for Declan, but put off Chris's questions about developments in Rome. "First things first, lad. Lucadamo has been hoping you'd get back in time for a final briefing before the Russia trip. And I've got a mountain of work to get through before I leave with the Pontiff tomorrow. Maybe I'll catch up with you and Giustino tonight after the Shoah Concert."

Like the crisis call from his brother and his descent into the Danielle caverns, the Shoah Memorial Concert developed into a nightmare experience for Christian.

When the Slavic Pope stepped through the eastern entrance to Nervi Hall, all Gladstone could see was the ocean of faces that followed the Pontiff's advance along the red-carpeted aisle that sloped gently down to the stage. Five thousand men and women rose to their feet in solemn, unsmiling respect and greeting.

At a certain moment, His Holiness came into clear view, flanked by Chief Rabbi Elio Toaff of Rome and Italian President Oscar Luigi Scalfaro. That scene—the sloping floor and the undulating ceiling of the Hall that swallowed the Pontiff and his guests like a gigantic maw, just as it had swallowed Christian and the thousands around him as though they were few—was a sight Christian would never forget. He watched the three leaders approach the far end of the aisle, where the tapers of an outsized Menorah candelabrum had been lit by six Holocaust survivors in living memory of six million Jews who had perished so horribly in the Nazi Final Solution. He watched as Pope, Rabbi and President settled into a trio of thrones, symbols of the equal religious dignity of the three presiders and of the people they represented. He listened as the Royal London Philharmonic Orchestra launched gently into Max Bruch's variations on *Kol Nidre,* the most significant prayer said on the holiest day of the Jewish calendar, Yom Kippur.

Perhaps it was that wordless performance. Perhaps it was Lynn Harrell's throaty cello calling out in lament for those millions whose voices had been cut off in cruel death. Perhaps it was the thought of Declan trapped in the dark caverns of the Danielle. Perhaps it was only fatigue. But Christian found himself transfixed by Pericle Fezzini's enormous bronze sculpture—the largest in the world, he'd been told—splayed across the back of the Nervi's stage. He couldn't take his eyes off that sculpture.

Its naked figure leaned forward as if to snatch everything up in its zareba of branchlike arms and fingers and indiscriminate masses of bronze, irresistible in their flailing and rising, reaching and pointing. It seemed the perfect symbol of Shoah. The perfect symbol of human life, always on the edge of chaos and destruction.

Chris forced his eyes away from the giant bronze. Away from the stage. Away from the Pope and the lighted Menorah. But there was nothing to see. Aside from that Menorah, there was nothing that was Jewish or Catholic or Christian or human here. Certainly there was nothing that was traditionally Roman. No frescoes testifying to the faith of patrons. No statues of the Angels or the Saints. No cornice carvings of fleshly *putti* or cherubic *ignudi*. No oil canvases that spoke of Christ or the Virgin Mother, of life or death, of Heaven or Hell or the Last Judgment. Only two ovaloid stained-glass windows, one in each long wall, stared back at him like fish eyes.

Late that Sunday evening, after the crowds had dispersed and the Vatican's doors and gates were closed for the night, Chris made his solitary way toward yet another restaurant for yet another secret meeting with Giustino Lucadamo.

The Shoah Concert hadn't been so bad, he told himself. By and large, in fact, the evening had been filled with exquisite gestures and symbols and music. Surely it had been the right thing—the Christ-like thing—for the Pope to embrace everyone, the living and the dead, in words and a spirit that spoke of brotherhood and harmony. Still, the Nervi was such a protean place—so telluric, so of this earth—that Chris would have preferred a long and prayerful time in the chapel at the Angelicum instead of another late-night briefing with the Vatican security chief.

It was only when he reached the restaurant Lucadamo had chosen for their meeting that Chris realized he had been there before, back when he and Father Aldo had strolled the streets of Rome together. He had just settled in at a quiet corner table and ordered a beer when Giustino arrived, accompanied by a famished Damien Slattery. "Like you, Chris me boy," Damien said by way of greeting, "we're all learning to do without much sleep. But it feels like a hundred years since I had a decent meal."

While his two companions ate, Chris gave a full account of the Danielle situation, and thanked Lucadamo for having enlisted Régice Bernard in the rescue attempt. But he wanted to talk about Rome.

Slattery was quick to oblige with the essentials. "Once he laid those two encyclicals on Their Eminences," he recounted, "and once he turned the Resignation Protocol into a matter of conscience, His Holiness invited the Cardinals to two events. He asked them all to attend tonight's Shoah Concert, of course. And then he announced a farewell address to those Venerable Brothers and the general public tomorrow at St. Peter's. It's to be at nine A.M., immediately before his departure—our departure—to the East.

"You can imagine how well that much sat with the Cardinals," Slattery chortled. "Especially the two encyclicals. But the Holy Father wasn't done yet. In that cool, offhand manner of his, he went on to make a final statement that nearly knocked me senseless. I remember every word, and you will too, Chris.

" '*Upon my return to Rome on May 13,*' he said, '*and before Your Eminences leave for your home dioceses this month, we will as the College of Cardinals, plan the interpretation of all official documents of the Second Vatican Council in order to bring them into line with the traditional teaching of the Roman Catholic and Apostolic Church.*'

"The Cardinals were literally dumb with shock. And so was I. You could have heard a pin drop on a velvet cushion."

For a minute, Gladstone, too, was dumb with shock. Certainly an alignment of Vatican II documents was long overdue. But for the Slavic Pope to count himself as part of the College of Cardinals was yet another self-inflicted blow to his papal independence and supremacy. "It compounds the whole problem of his pontificate," Christian fumed.

Giustino Lucadamo lost patience with the pair of them. The security chief was worried about the Pope's independence and supremacy, too, he said. But not for the same reasons. He still had that awful certainty that somewhere along the way of the papal pilgrimage, the Resignation Protocol would be invoked; but he still didn't know how it would be done. That, in fact, was why he had wanted to see Christian. "Father Damien and I and the rest of the papal party will leave for Fiumicino Airport tomorrow, immediately following the Holy Father's address in St. Peter's. Once we're on that plane to Kiev, everything will be in the cauldron. And that's exactly the moment Maestroianni is bound to be feeling his oats.

"Now, since you're such a fair-haired boy for His Eminence these days, Monsignore, he might take you into his confidence, or at least drop some unguarded remark. In other words, he might yet tip his hand to you in time to do us some good."

Gladstone was doubtful, but he played the logic through anyway. "Suppose it falls out that way. Once you're gone, even your signals room will be under Maestroianni's direction. So how am I to contact you?"

Lucadamo wrote his answer on a small piece of paper. "Memorize this number and then tear it up. It's a secure line at the Raffaele. Camerlengo or not, that's one trick Maestroianni can't control. My uncle will know how to contact me, and his radio facilities are as good as anything we have at the Vatican."

Chris didn't doubt it. His own memories of dinner with Appleyard and Signor Giovanni fresh in his mind, he thought that scrappy gentleman would be up for any emergency. "In fact"—he smiled—"he'd probably be better than I am at rifling the Secret Archives."

"Don't worry." Giustino scowled at Gladstone's not so subtle reminder. "I haven't forgotten Father Aldo. And I haven't forgotten your search for that envelope. My instinct about its importance is the same as yours. Tomorrow night will be your next Archives night. I've alerted Terragente already. He'll meet you at the Tower of the Winds around the usual time. But there may not be many more nights after that, Monsignore, so you'd better find it pretty soon."

Chris raised an eyebrow in Slattery's direction at that. Piled on top of freshened memories of Aldo Carnesecca and the terrible uncertainty about Declan, all these dour precautions and warnings made a fellow wonder. Would they ever see one another again once the pilgrimage to Russia got under way?

"You should know Giustino by now, laddie." Damien clapped a strong hand on Gladstone's shoulder. "He's paid to be a pessimist! And anyway, it's not farewell for the three of us yet. We still have the Holy Father's departure from St. Peter's at nine tomorrow morning. After that, let's all just take it one step at a time."

It was well before nine o'clock on Monday morning, May 8, when Gladstone slipped into Lucadamo's control center perched high above the nave of St. Peter's Basilica.

"Better to see than be seen today." Chris nodded to Giustino and helped himself to an empty chair.

By eight o'clock the number inside St. Peter's had already swelled to about 15,000. By eight-thirty Lucadamo calculated the crowds within the Basilica and outside in the square at about 120,000. By eight forty-five necks began to crane and fingers pointed as the general public tried to get a glimpse of the important personages filling the two semicircles of seats—some hundreds of them—arranged on either side of the nave, facing the papal throne and the High Altar behind it.

To the right of the throne, the Cardinals assembled in scarlet-clad rows. To the left, more numerous rows of bishops presented their own spectacle in their ceremonial robes and miters. The seats placed almost directly in front of the Pontiff's chair were eagerly taken up by well over half the members of Rome's diplomatic corps. The comment circulating along Embassy Row had it that they would witness either a showdown between the Slavic Pope and his enemies or the unrepeatable overture to that event. Nobody wanted to miss it.

Secure in his refuge, Chris surveyed the entire scene as Lucadamo's various consoles panned across the Basilica. He caught sight of Gibson Appleyard down among the diplomats. And he saw all the members of the party who would be traveling on the papal plane as they filed into one of the tribunes some forty feet above the nave. Slattery was chatting with the papal spokesman, Miguel Lázaro-Falla. Father Angelo Gutmacher, who had retrieved the Icon of Our Lady of Kazan from Portugal and had disappeared again until this morning, sat beside a grim-looking Dr. Fanarote. The lynx-eyed Monsignore Jan Michalik looked very much the odd man out.

At exactly nine o'clock, the door to the Sacristy opened and the Slavic Pope entered the Basilica, accompanied by Monsignore Sadowski. Wearing his miter as Bishop of Rome and holding the slightly crooked crozier he had carried all over the world, he was greeted at once with tumultuous enthusiasm. Salutes echoed from every quarter and cascaded around him in a babel of languages. His Holiness welcomed the crowds as warmly as they welcomed him. He walked slowly past the security barriers, giving his blessing, smiling, touching children held up to him by their parents, pausing here and there for a word, reaching for hands that reached for his, acknowledging greetings with an intimacy that seemed somehow to embrace everyone.

That living image of the Slavic Pope and the sounds that engulfed him were carried everywhere. Individual monitors throughout the Basilica served those who could not see the Pontiff directly. For the people massed outside in St. Peter's Square, a huge TV screen conveyed everything taking place inside. Transmissions carried the events of the morning to some 500 million people abroad.

In time, the Holy Father made his way to the papal throne in front of the High Altar just above that part of the Basilica known as the Confession of St. Peter. Once seated, he handed his crozier to Monsignore Sadowski and beckoned to the Master of Ceremonies to bring the microphone closer to him. Then he looked around him, smiling quietly until the cries died away and silence reigned.

"It is not my intention here, my dear sisters and brothers, to say goodbye to you." Because the Pontiff held no prepared speech in his hands, and because his words were so conversational—so unlabored and natural—it took a moment for the crowds to realize they were listening to a formal address.

" 'Goodbye' and 'farewell' are not favorite words in the vocabulary of those who have a firm hope in the substance of things to come, of living together forever in the community of God's Angels and Saints.

"At most—and really as a pious human gesture—there is a cheerful arrivederci *at the back of my mouth. But if you don't hear that word pass my lips, you must hear it in the deep silence and tranquillity of your souls. For we shall see each other again."*

Spontaneous cries rose at that from the masses of people inside and outside the Basilica. "Do not leave us, Holy Father!" "Stay with us, Holiness!" "We are your lambs and your sheep, Holy Father!" "Go in strength, Holy Father, and return to us!"

The Pontiff acknowledged the cries with a gesture of his hand, and quieted them with the command of his words. *"Do not fear! Be not afraid! Either I shall return to see you and be seen by you again in this flesh of ours beside this Tomb of the Apostle. Or we shall see each other on the day of the Lord and in the heavenly mansions of the Eternal Father. Either way, we win, you and I! For our Crucified and Risen Savior has conquered death for us all."*

Except for a slight stirring among a few of the Cardinals, there was perfect stillness.

"As you might guess, parting is not the subject that occupies my inmost heart today. Nor do I think it is your preoccupation at this moment in human time when I am setting out on pilgrimage to the lands of the East.

"Our theme today is that victory of our all-powerful, all-loving Lord and Savior, Jesus Christ. That victory, brothers and sisters, is the truth Almighty God reveals to our minds. That is the feeling He now arouses in our hearts. His victory!

"Hear me, therefore, all of you! Children of the Father! In Europe, in Asia, in Africa, in the Americas, in Oceania. At all the points in our human cosmos. Hear me now! Hear me as Peter. As the personal representative of God among men. With the eyes of your faith, you can see this and know this. For I speak of Christ, a stumbling block for the Jews. Of Christ, a folly for the Gentiles. Of Christ, the Power of God for those who belong to the Father. Christ, the Wisdom of God. This is the dawning day of His long-expected victory. For Christ is alive! Christ has conquered! This is His victory speech!"

If there was a stirring again, a rustling among the crowds, it faded to profoundest quiet at the next words they heard.

"For anyone listening who finds the assertions of this Pope to be strange and unwanted here at the Tomb of the Apostle, know that there is no aggression in my intentions. I am not announcing dire sufferings. Nor am I declaring war. I am announcing that the bitter warfare we have been waging is almost at its end. Please open a window in your minds, therefore, and a door into your hearts. The authority of the office I occupy is the authority of Our Lord Jesus; but as I have walked among you all, I have tried to imitate His humility. Up to this moment in my tenure as Pope, I have chosen to speak with the authority vested in me; but I have not chosen to wield that authority.

"I have treated with my bishops as with brother bishops. With my priests, as with brother priests. With other Christians, as with separated brothers striving to be one in Christ's Holy Church. With my Jewish brothers and sisters, as with elders of my faith family. With my Muslim brothers and sisters, as with my co-believers in one God. With those of other religious persuasions, I have acted as one who sees in their religiosity and their piety the delicate hand of the Holy Spirit disposing them for Christ's Salvation. With those who profess godlessness, I have spoken nonetheless as one who knows they belong to God's human life as fellow human beings. Even with those who profess hatred for all I stand for and for the Church itself, I have extended the Blessing of Peter in the hope that

our mutually shared humanity can be a bridge for mutual acceptability and understanding as members of the human race.

"*Be my judges, then. Can anyone reproach your Pope for having repulsed any advance or proposal of genuine love and fraternal friendship? Can anyone accuse your Pope of refusing human solidarity? In my opinion, the answer must be No. Not even when the hard stones of obstinate hate and cruel calumny have been flung at my person, not even then have I stooped to pick up a stone and throw it back at those who first threw it at me. My answer has always been the answer of my Lord and Savior to the man who struck him across the face unjustly: 'If I have done wrong, state the wrong. If I have not done wrong, why do you strike me?'*

"*That, as the whole world knows, is the way your Pope has behaved at this level where divine Providence has placed him. That, my brothers and sisters, is the figure I have cut as I have walked among the nations and with the peoples of this world. And yet, if I have faltered now and then on these forlorn heights, forgive me. Remember that, like each of you, I am flesh and blood. And remembering, forgive my sins as Christ my Savior has forgiven you and me and all who truly repent.*"

His Holiness allowed so great a hush to engulf the Basilica that the sound technician working the acoustics scanned the dials in front of him. But everything was perfect. "It's as if angels were in charge," he muttered to himself as the Pope took up again.

"*I have said that I am going on pilgrimage today.*" His Holiness ran his eyes thoughtfully over the rows of bishops to his right. "*But I would not have you think that my pilgrimage begins only today. The first time I spoke to you from this Chair of St. Peter the Apostle, I announced myself as a pilgrim from a far-off country. And, like each one of you, as a person on his way to the far-off country of eternity. If these were ordinary times, I could leave it at that. But we live in extraordinary times.*" The Pope turned his gaze toward his Cardinals as his voice rose in volume and sharpness. "*Or I should say that we are living, you and I, at the end of extraordinary times. At the end of these Catholic times that began with the Sign of Emperor Constantine in the long-ago night skies above Rome. The Sign of the Cross. The Sign of Christ's victory over sin and hate and death.*

"*And so . . .*" The Pope raised his eyes to the general crowd again. "*We have come to a cardinal moment in the history of this Holy See of Peter, and of the Church's institutional organization represented by you. By all of you. My Venerable Brother Cardinals. My Venerable Brother Bishops. My Reverend Brother priests. My beloved sons and daughters, the sheep and the lambs confided to my care by our Sovereign Lord and Savior, Jesus Christ. On what you do, each one of you, and on what I do, hinges the near-future fate of Christ's visible Church.*"

What happened after that was so utterly unexpected that it would, within the hour, evoke a flood of cablegrams, E-mail, telephone calls and consultations between governments and diplomatic representatives around the world. And yet, the universal comment might have been: "We should have expected it; more fools we for being surprised." At that precise moment, the Slavic Pope got to his feet, took his pastoral crozier from Monsignore Sadowski, who was instantly by his side, and stepped forward from the Altar until he faced the members of the diplomatic corps.

"You have honored me and my Church today, distinguished ladies and gentlemen," he told those worthies, *"by assembling here and participating in this ceremony. Give me your indulgence, and out of your kindness toward this Holy See of Peter, convey to your home governments and peoples the salutation of this Pope in Rome. His blessing—the blessing of the living representative of Christ among men—is upon them."* With that, the Holy Father raised his right hand in the triple Sign of the Cross. Some among the diplomats knelt; some signed themselves; some wore smiles of embarrassment; some had no idea what to do. But upon each and all he pronounced the ancient invocation to the Triune God: *"May the blessing of the Father, of the Son and of the Holy Spirit descend from Heaven on you all and remain with you forever."*

The Pope turned to his left and faced the ranks of his bishops. *"My Brothers,"* he told those worthies, *"for more than fifteen years we have jointly governed the visible organization of Christ's Mystical Body. You became bishops and you remain bishops because I, the Bishop of Rome, decided so. But we have not nourished our unity. Most of you are not willing to implement what I have wished to implement for the betterment of our people.*

"The time has come for that state of things to end. The time has come for each of you—each one of you who will—to ensure our unity in exercising our functions as bishops."

Unsmiling, His Holiness moved to his right until he stood before his Cardinals. *"My Lords Cardinal, as I leave the city, I put you in charge of this Holy See until, under God, I return here.*

"You are called Cardinals because on you hinges the well-being of the Church. Your Eminences are the direct participants in the bureaucracy that aids me, the Pope of All the Catholics, to administer the Church Universal. The time has come for Your Eminences to ask yourselves whether your service to this Holy See has been and is now rendered according to the dictates of the Holy Spirit; or whether it is rendered according to the dictates of some who would subordinate this Holy See to the will of those who wish to destroy it."

The Pontiff drew in a long breath. *"We must, each and all of us, examine the alliances we have formed. We must ask ourselves if we will not be ashamed of those alliances when we are called to give an ultimate accounting of our ministry to God. We must remind ourselves that we are not in rehearsal for another and greater day. For this is the day. This is all the chance we have to make good, or suffer terrible shipwreck. I ask you, then, to wish me well on my journey. And I ask you to send me off with your blessing."*

Heads swiveled and whispers flew through the Basilica like rushing winds as the Holy Father knelt before his flustered Cardinals, bowed his head and waited.

It was old Cardinal Sanstefano who rose first. Not as the powerful head of PECA now, but as the venerable Dean of the Sacred College of Cardinals, he traced the Sign of the Cross over this Pope whose anguished confession he had so recently heard, and blessed him with a most solemn blessing.

"Amen," Sanstefano ended his benediction.

"Amen," came the abashed but compliant response from his brothers in scarlet.

"Viva il Papa!" came the thunderous public cry as the Holy Father rose to his feet. *"Viva il Papa!"* "Godspeed, Holy Father!" "Come back to us, Holiness. Come back to us soon!" *"Viva! Viva!"*

With joyous applause and shouts of farewell ringing in his ears, the Pontiff walked down the middle of the nave, blessing the people again. As he moved slowly toward the great bronze doors leading to the square, a contingent of six Swiss Guards and a dozen of Lucadamo's security men weren't enough to hold back the thousands who poured out of the Basilica in his wake until the white-robed figure was swallowed from view in their midst.

LI

GIUSTINO LUCADAMO stayed in his control booth monitoring the steady stream of voice reports from the escort guard. The instant he knew the Holy Father and the papal entourage had reached their limousines and were safely on the way to the helicopter pad behind the Apostolic Palace, he grabbed the black case that was his constant companion on papal trips and, with a hasty *addio* to Gladstone, hurried down through a private passage and sped to the waiting helicopters.

Within twenty minutes of liftoff from the Vatican Gardens, the papal party was boarding the white Alitalia DC-10 at Fiumicino. With the Vatican security chief by his side, the pilot—no stranger to this traveling Pope—greeted His Holiness, kissed his ring and escorted him to his seat in the forward cabin. As faithful keeper of the gate and all the secrets, Monsignore Daniel Sadowski followed a little distance behind and took a seat nearby. Directly across from him, the chatty and elegantly dressed papal press officer, Miguel Lázaro-Falla, settled in beside an unusually taciturn

Dr. Giorgio Fanarote. Damien Slattery, meanwhile, paired off with Gladstone's old mentor and the Pontiff's confidential international emissary, Father Angelo Gutmacher.

As at St. Peter's, that left the Secretariat's "liaison officer" as odd man out. Monsignore Jan Michalik took a seat toward the rear of the papal cabin.

Also aboard the plane, separated from the forward section by a bulkhead, some seventy passengers were already in their seats. Mostly layfolk, but with a few bishops among their number, they had all been invited personally by the Slavic Pope. They had stood by him through thick and thin in the losing battle he had been waging with his enemies for over a dozen years. It was only fitting that they should be associated with him in this last phase of his papal endgame.

Before he took his own seat beside Sadowski, Lucadamo accompanied the captain to the cockpit, where they and the rest of the crew ran through a checklist. Two other planes waiting nearby on the tarmac, already filled with journalists assigned to cover the Russia trip, would depart immediately after the papal plane, and would stay with it through the entire journey until the Pope's projected return six days from now, on May 13. The flight plans of the papal journey had been privately communicated to all governments whose airspace they would enter, as well as to the government of the United States and NATO authorities. The papal plane would be escorted by jet fighters throughout the entire trip. No nation wanted an accident to befall the Pope of Rome in its airspace.

By eleven-thirty the DC-10 was in the air. By early afternoon, the Slavic Pope's welcome in Kiev—a tumultuous scene of near delirium—was under way. Following a short rest and a meal at the Monastery that would serve as his Ukraine headquarters, His Holiness launched into a schedule that would, from that moment forward, tax him heavily both physically and emotionally.

In Kiev itself, a city of hills and churches, the Holy Father insisted on seeing everything and greeting everybody. For their part, the Ukrainian Catholics—long suppressed, imprisoned, persecuted and deprived of any public voice—welcomed the Pontiff as a champion and world-class leader who dwarfed every Russian Orthodox prelate within all the states of the former Soviet Union. Everywhere he went, ecstatic crowds pressed forward to see him, to touch his hand, to overwhelm him with their accolades and to receive his blessing. He held services at the Church of St. Sophia and St. Vladimir's Cathedral. He prayed at the building that had housed the eight-hundred-year-old Church of St. Michael until the Soviets had converted it into a political commissariat. He marveled at the walls of the Kiev subway, decorated with mosaic portraits of biblical saints. At all those places, the Pontiff spoke to the people, touched their hands, bent to their children, entered their hearts. At all those places, he blessed them.

Toward evening, and as the culmination of his visit to Kiev, the Holy

Father visited the ancient Pecherskaya Lavra, where, as still more crowds gathered outside, he prayed alone and undisturbed for two hours. A candlelight descent into the famous deep caves to pray at the tombs of earlier and long-dead monks was followed by a farewell gathering where the papal party was entertained by the Kozatski Sabovi Folk Group. Then it was on by hydrofoil to Kaniv, some way up the Dnieper River, to be with the eager crowds who awaited him at the tomb of Taras Shevchenko, their beloved poet, essayist, playwright, thinker and revolutionary, whom they still revered as nothing less than the founder of modern Ukrainian literature and restorer of the Ukrainian religious spirit.

When the papal party returned at last to overnight in Kiev, everyone, including the two planeloads of journalists, seemed done in already by the pace of this pilgrimage. Even Monsignore Jan Michalik headed straight for bed. Only His Holiness, Giustino Lucadamo and that inveterate traveler Father Angelo Gutmacher relaxed together for a time in the Pontiff's suite.

Lucadamo thought this might be the moment to review security for the next day's events. But the Pope's thoughts were elsewhere. He was disappointed, he said, that "as yet the Virgin has sent no sign of her intentions. Or even of her satisfaction with our pilgrimage so far." But no news was good news for Lucadamo. "Holiness," he spoke up in reply, "isn't it sufficient sign of her approval that her Son and she have brought us this far in safety?"

"Perhaps, Giustino." The Pontiff looked at this loyal man whose job it was to guard his life. "In any case, it will have to do us for now."

But it was not enough. In his constant resistance to his enemies' pressure that he resign, the Slavic Pope had run out of alternatives. In his estimation, everything depended now on the will of Heaven, and on the powerful intercession of the Mother of God.

"Stasera, Monsignore, pazienza!" Giancarlo Terragente wore such a mock-melodramatic expression on his face that Chris Gladstone nearly burst into laughter as he poked his head above the steep stairway to the Room of the Meridian. "Patience tonight, Monsignore! Consistory or no, His Eminence is working in the Biblioteca." With that, the genius picklock disappeared down the stairs to keep a close eye on the situation in the Archives, and Christian settled down to wait for the all clear.

Though frustrated at this further delay in his search for the mysterious double-sealed envelope, Chris was prepared for the wait. And, truth to tell, after the madness of the last couple of days, he welcomed the chance to go over things quietly in his mind; but most of what he had to think about wasn't pleasant.

Chris had called Deurle for news of the search for Declan, but there hadn't been much to report. Régice Bernard and a team of Army sappers and speleologues had entered the complex. Everyone figured contact with

Declan's party should be made sometime late tonight. Chris glanced at his watch. Eleven o'clock. "Soon," he whispered to the winds soughing around the Tower. "Soon we'll know if our Deckel is alive or dead."

Unwilling to allow himself to fall into a state of useless hand-wringing, Gladstone turned his mind to the situation in Rome. With the Pope gone now, and all the stalwarts like Slattery and Lucadamo and Sadowski and Gutmacher gone as well, he felt he had been marooned here at exactly the moment when Maestroianni was ready to bring things to a climax. If there was no miracle—if God's mother didn't somehow intervene—if Lucadamo was right and the Pontiff didn't return, Maestroianni as Camerlengo would turn the Consistory into an illicit Conclave and force the invalid election of a new Pope. What Gladstone was contemplating, therefore, was nothing less than the possible destruction of his entire world.

The winds keening around the Tower and the lonely emptiness of the Room of the Meridian sent such a sudden chill through Gladstone that he began pacing back and forth to get the blood flowing and restore warmth to his bones. He thought again of happy times long past when he and Paul and Tricia had huddled in the study at Windswept House reading descriptions of this place in Old Glad's journals. Back when he was a boy, those journals had seemed so heroic. A Gladstone had traveled halfway around the world with a million dollars in his pocket to come to the aid of the then-reigning Pope, Pius IX. And then he had founded a new dynasty of his own in Galveston, and had built his own Tower of the Winds as a visible pledge of enduring faith.

That memory was a small but significant happening in the life of Christian Gladstone. A reminder that, in the delicate pattern of God's all-seeing providence, his earliest beginnings at Windswept House were connected with his present life. A reminder that the Rome of Old Glad's time had been taken over by the Italian Nationalists; Pius IX had remained a virtual prisoner in the Vatican; and so had all the Popes after him until the Lateran Treaty had been signed in 1929. A reminder that the papacy had remained.

"Let's get to work, Monsignore!"

Startled at first by Terragente's stage whisper, Chris quickly packed up his thoughts and, flashlight in hand, followed his companion in crime down the creaky old staircase, through silent passageways and into the Secret Archives.

"If our luck holds," Terragente whispered as he sprang the lock on the first gate, "there will be no interruptions. But with Comandante Lucadamo out of Rome now, and with Maestroianni in charge, Cardinal Aureatini has special details all over the place. I don't know what that man is afraid of, Monsignore Gladstone, but word is that he's as nervous as a cat."

"If our luck holds," Christian whispered back, "we'll strike gold tonight. There's really only one place left to look."

With Chris leading the way, the pair carried on a careful, methodical drill. Terragente sprang the locks on one large damask-covered storage box after another. Then, while Gladstone picked through the contents of each, the Italian scouted the terrain around them, his ear attuned to catch the slightest sound.

Chris was examining the contents of what must have been the twentieth box, and was just about to admit defeat, when he lifted a pile of old ledgers, and there it was! Though he was too stunned at first to reach for it, Gladstone knew there was no mistake. Except for a series of letters and numbers printed in one corner—DN413F10; the Archival Destination Number, as Chris knew—every detail was just as Carnesecca had described it in his diary. He could see by the light of his torch that the envelope had been opened and then resealed with heavy filament tape. And he could see the two papal inscriptions.

"For Our Successor on the Throne of Peter."

"Concerning the condition of Holy Mother Church after June 29, 1963," he read the second inscription.

"L'ha trovata, Monsignore?" Terragente came up behind him with such stealth that Gladstone nearly jumped out of his shoes. The Italian eyed the treasure in Chris's hand, but he asked his question again anyway. "Have you found it?"

Christian's only reply was a thumbs-up. He stowed the envelope carefully in his jacket pocket. Together, priest and picklock placed everything else back in the box and locked it, and secured the Archives door again. Then it was up the stairs, through the ground-floor corridor to the postern door and out into the open air of the courtyard as fast as their legs would carry them.

On the morning of Tuesday, May 9, the papal party set off westward from Kiev by train for a twelve-hour journey to Lvov. His Holiness insisted on stopping at every town and village; and at each stop along the way, with Monsignore Michalik forever hovering in the background, he spoke of victory to the excited crowds of believers who thronged to greet him and to receive his blessing.

On that same morning, in the quiet of his rooms at the Angelicum, Christian recovered from the initial shock that had assailed him in the Archives. His nerves as cool as ice now, he sat down at his desk, fingered the double-sealed envelope for a minute and then, without any nod or say-so from Pope, bishop or priest, he slit the filament tape.

The first notice yielded by the envelope was a single sheet of paper. Narrowly cut to fit with the other documents, it bore a terse warning in Aldo Carnesecca's hand: "Whoever opens and reads here, know you are dealing with the fate of Christ's Church. Desist, unless you are authorized by the Apostle."

Chris could not have been more disturbed had he heard the voice of his dead friend among the morning shadows. As it had been for Carnesecca, so it was for Gladstone. To violate the papal office, separate and exalted as it was above any other office in human society, was to court lethal danger. Anything to do directly and intimately with the Apostle was sacrosanct. For Romans and papists such as Carnesecca and Gladstone, there was a deep truth encased in an old and crude Roman proverb. *"Chi mangia Papa . . . ,"* ran that warning: "Whoever eats Pope, dies of it."

Nevertheless, there was nothing for it but to enter the privileged reserve of the specially chosen; of those destined by God from before the foundation of the world to be the direct instruments of His divine will in the salvation of mankind. The rest of the contents of the envelope consisted of a second sheet of paper bearing a papal seal and coat of arms, and a series of fiches that were, by their nature, illegible without the aid of a microcopy reader. Of necessity, then, Gladstone focused on the sheet of paper, a letter penned in Latin and sealed by a dying Pope nearly twenty years before. He read the text through once, and then a second time. Finally, his body gone stone cold and motionless, he read the pathetic, courageous message yet again.

"Enclosed herewith," the old Pope had written, *"We have placed a list of those among Our Lords Cardinal and Our other personnel who have freely joined the Masonic Craft, together with a detailed* Rituale *enacted on June 29, 1963, in the Cappella Paolina, during which the Fallen Archangel was enthroned specifically as 'the Prince Ascending to Power,' and according to the plans and prophecies of 'the Enlightened Ones.'*

"It has not been given to Us to undo this enthronement. We have neither the bodily health nor the spiritual strength. Nor are We worthy to be chosen for such a task; for Our sins in this august office have been too great. We have been forgiven, We believe, and will be purified by God's hand in the passage of Our death. But We are no longer trusted as responsible. We therefore commit the enclosed to Our lawful successor in this holy Roman office of the Apostle. We do this believing firmly in the Resurrection of the body, in the Last Judgment and in Life Eternal. Amen."

It wasn't for lack of understanding that Chris read the old Pope's letter so many times over. From his own training, and above all from his conversations with Slattery, he knew something about the enthronement aspect of Satanist ritual. Enough to know that those who engaged in it lived with a view to reigning with the Archangel in his kingdom in this life, whatever about the afterlife. Enough to know that they dedicated themselves, and the buildings and homes they occupied, to the service of the Archangel on this earth. Indeed, enough to know that Satanist devotees expected a time to come—a time they called the Ascent of the Prince—when nations would hail the Fallen Archangel; would publicly acknowledge him as Prince Lucifer, and the Son of the Dawn, as their leader and divinity.

What Gladstone could not understand was how such a ceremony—a gruesome ritual, so far as he could remember, that required its own elaborate setup and involved a human sacrifice—could have been carried out anywhere near the Vatican, much less in St. Paul's Chapel. Nor could he understand what Aldo Carnesecca had to do with it.

Still, if such a ceremony had been enacted on June 29, 1963, the day had been significantly chosen. It was the feast day of the Holy Apostles, Peter and Paul; the quintessential Roman holy day. To carry out the so-called Ascent of the Prince on that day—and to do so not only in the Vatican as the household of the Apostles but in the chapel dedicated to St. Paul—would be a piece of Satanic insolence only the Fallen Angel and his devotees would think of perpetrating. What was more, if such a ceremony had taken place, it would explain a lot. For one thing, and at the very least, it would explain that enigmatic entry in Carnesecca's diary telling of his meeting with the September Pope. "*Long conversation with Pp . . .*" Chris knew the words by heart. "*Agrees no Pope will be able to govern Church through Vatican until enthronement undone.*"

More significantly, it would account for the astonishing speed of the deterioration of the Roman Catholic Church structure. Chris had always found it to be inexplicable that within the short span of fifteen years—a fairly definable time that had stretched from the close of the Second Vatican Council in 1965 to the end of the seventies—a solid, vibrant Church structure had been liquidated. It had been as if, say, the Panama Canal had suddenly been emptied of water. For in that brief period, the Roman structure—a vast organization built over the centuries at huge costs in blood and sacrifice—had suddenly been emptied of the spiritual and moral energy that had animated it and made it into the womb of a whole civilization and a formidable force among the nations.

No matter how impossible or outlandish it might be, the more Gladstone thought about it, the more he realized that a genuine enthronement of the Fallen Archangel in such a sanctified place would explain a great deal that had been so baffling and discouraging for him. Violation of the Vatican in the name of summary, incarnate evil would account for grace expelled, and for the buffeting of physical buildings and people alike by the influence of that dedicated Adversary of God and man. And it would account for what had happened to papal Rome, what had happened to four Popes and what had happened to the far-flung Church Universal.

It would explain the mystifying behavior of the old Pope whose reign, unbeknownst to him, had begun with that enthronement, and who had allowed and in certain ways even promoted the liquidation of the Church structure. It would explain the smiling resignation and the death of the September Pope, who had been tragically prescient when he had spoken to Carnesecca of "insurance." It would explain the manifest impotence of the

Slavic Pope—his prudential errors, his idiosyncratic ideas, his failure to align Council documents with Church doctrine and tradition, his tolerance of heretical teaching in seminaries and universities. It would explain the putrescence and corruption Chris and Slattery had detailed in their reports to His Holiness. . . .

In fact, Christian realized with a shudder, the microfiche material lying before him might even explain what was going on among the men who were, at this very moment, clawing after Peter's Throne at the General Consistory in Rome. Perhaps the data those fiches contained was the key to the inexplicable and corrosive hatred of a papal pretender like Cardinal Palombo, to the watered-down Christianity of a *papabile* like Cardinal Karmel, to the banality of an ambitious Cardinal Aureatini, to the secularism of a Pope-maker like Cardinal Maestroianni, to the darksome behavior of Centurycity's Cardinal, to the fecklessness of so many men like Cardinal O'Cleary.

Christian took one last look at the old Pope's letter before he folded it away. *"Enclosed herewith We have placed a list of those among Our Lords Cardinal and Our other personnel . . ."* His quiet time of reflection was over. The most urgent and pressing thing in his life now was to know what Carnesecca had discovered. He needed to know the names on that list. He needed to read everything that had been reserved for so long in the double-sealed envelope. For, if he was right, the solution to the Slavic Pope's difficulties did not lie in Russia. If he was right, the Slavic Pope had to get back to Rome as fast as his Alitalia DC-10 could bring him.

In the city of Lvov as in Kiev, the Slavic Pope wanted to see everything; and, again, he was all but overwhelmed by enthusiastic crowds every step of the way. He visited the ornate and beautiful churches adorning that major ecclesiastical center where once there had been a strong movement for the reunification of Orthodox and Roman Catholics. But the capstone of his visit came with the Mass he celebrated at St. George's Cathedral for what seemed to Slattery and the others like half the population of Ukraine.

As the day progressed and the energy of some in the papal party again began to flag, Monsignore Jan Michalik began to worry; for, like the Pope, he, too, was waiting for a sign. There was no doubt that the physical strain on the Pontiff was magnified a thousand times by the emotional tension he was undergoing. How was it, then, that he never seemed to tire? "Just give it time, Michalik," he told himself in an effort to calm his own mounting nerves. "Tomorrow it's on to Hrushiv. Then St. Petersburg and Moscow. The crowds and the excitement and the tension are bound to take their toll. No man can stand such punishment. He'll break. It's just a matter of time."

❑ ❑ ❑ ❑

Gladstone made two telephone calls before he left the Angelicum. The first was to his brother's home in Deurle.

"Praise be, Monsignor Chris!" Hannah Dowd was so aflutter with excitement when she answered that it took some doing for Chris to get things straight. Régice Bernard's rescue party, it seemed, had reached Declan's group in the small hours of the morning. There had been one death in the Danielle cave-in, and the others had been injured, some of them seriously.

"Declan," Chris pressed her. "What about Declan?"

"He had to be carried out on a stretcher, Father. They've all gone to the hospital. That's where Mr. Paul and Miss Yusai are right now. We're waiting for news. But he's alive! Our little Deckel is alive!"

Chris took in a deep breath, left messages of love and blessing for his family, said a fervent prayer of thanks and then dialed through to Cardinal Maestroianni's office, where Archbishop Buttafuoco was doing double duty for an absent Taco Manuguerra.

"I'll be sorry to miss your press conference this afternoon," Gladstone lied. "But I feel a virus coming on, and I'd like to nip it in the bud."

"Not to worry, Monsignore." Buttafuoco was all sympathy. "His Eminence will be tied up all day with the Consistory. And the press conference will be more of the same old pap for the media. Not to worry."

Twenty minutes later, at a call box some distance from the Angelicum, Chris dialed the secure number Giustino Lucadamo had given him for the Raffaele. "Of course I can help, Monsignore," Signor Giovanni said in answer to Gladstone's predicament. "I know just the place where you can study those microfiches without fear of interruption."

It was as simple as that. Within an hour, Christian was safely lodged in a quiet, well-staffed villa some ten miles south of Rome—an ideal place, as it turned out, for the baleful job of work that faced him. He had complete silence and a beautiful view of the Roman Campagna from the room where he installed himself. And because that villa belonged to the elder Lucadamo, it was fitted out with every imaginable device, including a secure telephone and a very efficient-looking microcopy reader.

For the rest of that day and far into the night, Christian immersed himself in facts and events that were worse, more unimaginable, than mere impious fantasy. Taking care not to disturb the order in which the material had been arranged in the double-sealed envelope, he inserted the first microfiche into the reader and began a descent into a world so dark and askew that he had to force his mind to reason, lest he drown in the mental and emotional reactions that washed over him.

The first fiche contained a single document—a testament written by Father Aldo at the request of the old Pope, and in his presence, summarizing the curious circumstances by which the horrid affair of the enthronement had come to light. For the second time that day, it was as if Carnesecca was speaking from beyond the grave; this time to tell how, on

June 29, 1977, he had been called to a private hospital in Rome to attend at the bedside of dying Archbishop D-G—a Frenchman Carnesecca had known in the Secretariat of State. Faced with imminent death and in gravest need of Absolution, the Archbishop had confessed to Father Aldo that he had been a member of a Satanist coven in Rome for many years, and had participated in a Satanist Rite in the Cappella Paolina on June 29, 1963.

Father Aldo had refused absolution unless three conditions were met. First, the Archbishop would have to indicate as much as possible about the Satanist Rite that had been used. Second, he would have to reveal as many names as he could remember; especially the names of Vatican officials and members of the hierarchy who had participated in that Rite. And third, he must allow Carnesecca to inform the old Pope of everything in this part of the Archbishop's confession.

Archbishop D-G gave his consent to all three conditions. More, he gave Father Aldo permission to retrieve two ledgers from his safe. One contained the full roster of names of all who had participated in the Rite. The second contained a detailed description of the Rite itself. Archbishop D-G died on June 30, 1977. On the night of July 3, Carnesecca was received in private audience by the old Pope, related everything the dying Archbishop had told him and watched while His Holiness examined both ledgers.

Already afflicted with extremely bad health—according to his doctors, he had only a few months left in this world—and beset by a host of worsening domestic and foreign problems in the Church Universal, the Pontiff had decided that, while he could not undo what had been done, he would make sure his successor on the Throne of Peter would be fully informed. The old Pope's plan, which Carnesecca had included in his short but comprehensive explanation, had been simple enough. Microcopies of the Archbishop's ledgers and Father Aldo's testament were made. The Pontiff prepared a brief letter of explanation and placed it in an envelope along with the microphotos and Carnesecca's trenchant hands-off warning. He inscribed the envelope: "For Our Successor on the Throne of Peter," dated it and sealed it with his papal seal. The ledgers themselves were sealed and consigned safely to the Secret Archives.

That was as much information as the first microfiche contained. Christian removed it from the reader and switched the machine off. Though his reaction was surprisingly unemotional, he needed some time to digest what he had learned so far. He could only surmise what had happened after July 3. He knew from Carnesecca's diary that Secretary of State Jean-Claude de Vincennes and Archbishop Silvio Aureatini had conducted a double triage of papal effects. As papal Chamberlain, Vincennes had doubtless put off the triage of the old Pope's papers until the brouhaha surrounding the election and installation of the new Pope should die down. Doubtless, too, Carnesecca had feared that Vincennes might not hand the envelope on to the new Pope. If Christian could assume that much was true, then it followed that Carnesecca would have found an opportunity to get that specially inscribed envelope into the hands of the September Pope.

In any case, Chris knew from the diary that on September 28, 1978, Father Aldo had indeed had a "long conversation with Pp about envelope left by immediate predecessor." He knew further that His Holiness had opened the envelope, had read its contents and had resealed it with that second inscription—"Concerning the condition of Holy Mother Church after June 29, 1963"—telling Carnesecca that it was "insurance."

Finally, Gladstone knew that, following the stunning death of the new Pope a mere thirty-three days after his election, the experienced Carnesecca had been called in by Vincennes to assist at the triage of personal documents left by two dead Popes. He knew that Aureatini had also been present. He knew that the double-sealed envelope had figured in that triage; that Vincennes and Aureatini had both been shocked to see it; that Vincennes had taken charge of it; and that Carnesecca had been worried that the "insurance might backfire."

A slight frisson ran through Chris as he leaned forward in his chair and switched the reader on again. There was no longer any doubt in his mind that an enthronement ceremony had taken place. He had the testimony of two dead Popes; and he had the testimony of his beloved friend, Aldo Carnesecca, to a deathbed confession of an eyewitness. It remained only to learn how it had been done, and by whom.

His mind totally concentrated on his work, Christian fitted the first of the remaining microcopies into the reader, focused the page and started reading. One after another he read them all. He paused now and then to check on this word or that phrase. But over the next several hours, he became privy to every horrid detail of the *rituale* that had enthroned the Prince as Ascendant in the Cappella Paolina on the significant date of June 29, 1963.

He learned of the stratagem of the double ceremony—a "Parallel Enthronement," it was called in the ledger—that had been devised to get around the impossibility of a full-blooded enthronement in the sacred and well-guarded "Target Chapel" within the precincts of the Vatican. He learned of the arrangements made with the "Authorized Sponsoring Chapel" in South Carolina, and the names of the central clerical participants in the ceremony there. The once renowned Bishop James Russeton had been principal Celebrant; and no less a figure than the present Cardinal of Centurycity had served as his Archpriest and co-Celebrant.

Gladstone had to force himself to read the account of the ceremony in the Sponsoring Chapel itself. An account which Archbishop D-G had done his best to set down faithfully as it had been reported from one "Ceremonial Messenger" to the other on an open telephone connection between the Sponsoring Chapel in America and the Target Chapel in Rome. An account of profanity and hate that was the more heinous for the laconic manner in which the Archbishop had recorded it. An account of the methodical profanation of everything that was sacred and the defilement of everything that was innocent.

Page after page was filled with the indescribably foul "Invocations" that had been chanted in both Chapels; the indescribably sadistic series of animal sacrifices that had been performed in America; the indescribably degenerate inversion of Holy Communion, coupled with the indescribably sadistic and repeated violation of the "Ritual Victim" on the Altar—a child whose name was given as Agnes—that had been perpetrated by priests and Participants alike in the Sponsoring Chapel.

Though enraged and sickened, there were still more horrors for Gladstone to face into before he had done with this blasphemous insanity. For, with the physical brutalities completed, the primary action of the Parallel Enthronement had switched to the Target Chapel in Rome. There, as Christian read, an "International Delegate"—a layman by the name of Otto Sekuler—had carried out the sacrilegious role of "Plenipotentiary Extraordinary." By the reading of a "Bill of Authorization," the text of which Archbishop D-G had recorded, the Chapel of St. Paul had been co-opted as the "Inner Chapel of the Prince within the Citadel of the Enemy." Then, by an act of his individual will, each of the Vatican Participants—"the Roman Phalanx," as they were called collectively—had completed the final two ritual requirements of the enthronement.

As a body, they had sworn "the Sacred Oath of Commitment" administered by the Delegate. Then each man had approached the Altar to give "Evidence" of his personal dedication. With blood drawn by the prick of a golden pin, each had pressed his fingerprint beside his name on the Bill of Authorization. Henceforth, the life and work of every member of the Phalanx in the Roman Citadel was to be focused on the transformation of the papacy itself. No longer was the Petrine Office to be an instrument of the "Nameless Weakling." It was to be fashioned into a willing instrument of the Prince, and a living model for "the New Age of Man."

Senseless of the hours that passed, or of the caring staff that kept an eye for his well-being, or of the concerned but discreet calls Giovanni Lucadamo made from the Raffaele, Gladstone turned at last to the final microcopies waiting to be read—the roster of Roman and American Participants in the enthronement ceremonies.

Gladstone was no longer surprised or shocked by the names he saw. Nor would he ever be puzzled again by the presence of so many unsuitable and unworthy clerics with their unholy ambitions and their neglect of Christ's faithful. Everything was now explicable. Of course such men found no difficulty in forming alliances with nonbelievers; with sworn enemies of Christ and of all religion. Of course they had no use for the revelations made by the Blessed Mother of Christ at Fatima. Of course they could not wait to rid the Church of the Slavic Pope.

If anything surprised Chris, in fact, it was the names that were not inscribed on the Archbishop's lists. Chief among the missing on the Roman roster was Cardinal Cosimo Maestroianni. And yet he, too, was in it up to his eyes. For, with the exception of Secretary of State Giacomo Graziani, the little Cardinal's closest associates in the Vatican turned up in the ledger. Maestroianni's unswerving obeisance to the forward steps of history and Graziani's dedication to self-aggrandizement had laid both men open as apt targets for such "advisors" and "collaborators" as Cardinal Noah Palombo and Cardinal Leo Pensabene, among others, who had sworn that blood oath against Peter at the enthronement.

Though the hour was late and Christian was very near exhaustion, he stared at the lists a while longer. Or rather, he stared at two names: Jean-Claude de Vincennes and Silvio Aureatini. He had speculated for so long about the contents of the envelope; about why men would kill other men in connection with it; about why Carnesecca had been murdered and by whom. Now he had his answers. Giustino Lucadamo had been right. What Father Aldo had seen was so important that it hadn't been enough to kill him. Some maniac had wanted to burn his eyes out for having seen it; had wanted to sear the very memory of it from his brain.

"It's the only possible answer," Chris reasoned with himself as he finally switched the reader off. Aside from the old Pope, the September Pope and Carnesecca himself, only two men had known of the existence of the envelope. But Cardinal Vincennes was dead and buried when Aldo was murdered. That left only one. Silvio Aureatini was the maniac.

Early on the morning of Wednesday, May 10, his last day in Ukraine, the Slavic Pope set out by car with his entourage for his visit to the village of Hrushiv. Its significance for the Holy Father was no secret. The focus of this leg of his pilgrimage was the little wooden Church of the Holy Trinity, where, as reliable reports testified, the Blessed Virgin had appeared recently, and more than once, to reinforce the Fatima message.

Inside the church, His Holiness conducted the Orthodox liturgy of Benediction, Moleben and Parastas. They proceeded outdoors to a temporary Altar that had been erected for this momentous occasion. There, his arms crossed upon his breast and his lips moving only now and again, he prayed silently and at length. Standing stock-still, he gazed so intently upward toward the dome of the church where the Virgin had been seen, and seemed so oblivious of the press and the vast public alike, that Father Slattery and Father Gutmacher wondered together if the Virgin might have chosen this moment to grant his desire for some vision; some guiding sign.

Apparently she did not. But if disappointment deepened the fatigue he must surely be feeling by now, the Pontiff gave no sign of it. On the contrary, he suggested a departure from his itinerary—a visit to the Carpathian Mountains in the Hutsul region. Dr. Fanarote dissuaded him, however. Deeply concerned for the pace His Holiness was keeping, and with an eye on the ever vigilant Monsignore Michalik, the papal physician insisted that the Pope return to home base in Kiev for a rest before going on to St. Petersburg.

"Is that a smile of triumph, Monsignore?" Giovanni Lucadamo welcomed Chris Gladstone to his study at the Raffaele after sundown on Wednesday.

"A smile of resolve, Signor Giovanni." Christian felt surprisingly fit after his ordeal at the villa. A few hours of sleep and many hours of thought had done wonders to clear his head. "Thanks to the service you rendered me so gracefully, I know what I must do. But I need to impose another urgent request on you."

"You owe me nothing, Monsignore Christian. And I will be happy to help further if I can." He had sized this young prelate up as a faithful servant of the Holy Father; as a man not entirely comfortable with Roman ways; as one who still relied on others for direction. Somehow, though, the last element of that description no longer seemed to fit, and he was interested to know what had caused such a radical change in him.

Before Chris got down to his urgent business, he asked for news of the papal party. To his relief, the older man didn't waste time by pretending ignorance. He had spoken to his nephew by radio early this morning, he said, and nothing untoward had occurred. "The Holy Father is showing signs of fatigue"—Lucadamo wound up his summary—"but there can be no wonder about that. Giustino is still on the lookout for trouble. But so far, so good."

"When will you speak to him again, Signor Giovanni?" With the Vatican under Maestroianni's control now, Chris assumed Giustino had set up a communications schedule with his uncle.

"You have a message for him?"

"I have a message for the Holy Father. He must get back to Rome without delay."

"Well." The older man stood up. "A request like that is likely to be refused. But at least your timing is good. Come with me."

Gladstone was still gawking at the amazing array of electronic gear installed in Lucadamo's private office when the security chief's recognition signal came over the airwaves from Kiev, followed by the familiar sound of his voice.

"Giustino." It was Gladstone who spoke up first. "We found the envelope. The information is as bad as it can be. If His Holiness doesn't return—if you're right; if there is a trap and he is induced to give up now—Lucifer wins and occupies the center. We can't allow that to happen."

More acutely aware than Chris that radio signals are easily intercepted, Giustino knew better than to ask for details. But he also knew the present mind of the Slavic Pope. "He's determined to go through with this to the bitter end. There's no way to get him to turn back now. We leave for St. Petersburg in a few hours. Then it's on to Moscow and the ceremonial return of the Kazan Icon. He's convinced that between now and then, he'll have the sign he's been praying for. He won't turn back."

There were a couple of brief exchanges after that. No, Chris replied to the most urgent question on the security chief's mind; he had learned nothing new from Maestroianni; had barely seen him, in fact. Yes, Giustino said, the Holy Father was standing up to the rigors of the journey well; but their projected return to Rome on Saturday, the thirteenth, was still three grueling days off.

Very quickly then, it was "over and out."

Gladstone's troubled silence was a clear enough sign that he had been left with a problem he couldn't solve.

"There's nothing like a little brandy to clear a man's mind." Giovanni Lucadamo's invitation as he led the way back to his study was his civilized way of offering to help if he could.

With vintage brandy warming in their hands, the two men sat by an open window looking out at the night traffic while Christian worked out in his mind how much he could share with this patient man of experience. The matter in hand was both Apostolic and confessional. But, he decided, the moral circumstances were such that practical judgment must prevail. "At our first meeting," Gladstone began at last, "you and Gibson Appleyard spoke of having entrusted your lives to one another more than once. It is in such trust that I would like to speak to you now."

"Whose life do we speak of, Monsignore?"

"Like your nephew," Chris responded evenly, "I believe the Pope is at serious risk. But, more than that, the life of the Church is at stake as well." In grim, staccato phrases, Chris went on to tell of Aldo Carnesecca's discovery, of his attempt to get two Popes to deal with it and of the martyr's price he had paid for his concern. He told of the *rituale* that had been carried out simultaneously in Rome and South Carolina. He explained the universal significance of the enthronement, and the importance of the connection between the Roman Phalanx and such secular counterparts as Otto Sekuler. And he adduced the fact that some of the clerical Participants in that ceremony were now engaged as *papabili* in the General Consistory under way in Rome.

Signor Giovanni understood the full nature of Gladstone's crisis. "I assume the first order of business is to get you to the Pope before anything untoward happens to him in Russia."

"Exactly right. We cannot acquiesce in the arrangements chosen by the enemies of the Roman papacy. I must make sure His Holiness returns to cleanse his Apostolic House. He may not be the greatest Pope we could hope for, but he is Pope. And, without meaning to be blasphemous, better we have a live ass than a dead lion. So, Signor Giovanni, the trick is for me to get to him without tipping my hand in Rome."

"I'll leave the question of governance to you, Monsignore Christian." Giovanni poured another generous dollop of brandy into Gladstone's glass and his own, and lit up a cigar. "From my point of view—and speaking of live asses and dead lions—we're talking about clandestine flight over international borders, and about logistics."

For the next couple of hours, Lucadamo put his experience to good use. The initial problem he tackled was clandestine flight. First, he said, and even with a Vatican passport, Chris would need visas; but that was something Giovanni could arrange quickly and without difficulty. Second, he advised that commercial travel would be unwise in the circumstances; but here again, it would be no problem to arrange for a private jet to take the Monsignore from one of the smaller airports to his destination. The destination itself, however, was something to consider. Because no one knew what sort of trap Maestroianni and his cabal had arranged for the Pope, or when it would be sprung, Chris's instinct was to head straight for St. Petersburg. But Lucadamo felt such close timing would be the greater risk. Better to gamble that the Pope would make it to Moscow. Chris could be there ahead of him, and lay the whole problem out to him before he started his day.

What clinched the argument in favor of Moscow was the next element that had to be taken care of. Gladstone agreed that his sudden and unexplained disappearance from Rome would be a red flag of warning for Maestroianni and Aureatini. Some plausible cover had to be devised for his absence from the Secretariat, therefore; and less suspicion would be aroused if he attended to that task in person. That meant Chris would have to spend part of Thursday morning at the Vatican. And that in turn meant he wouldn't even get out of Rome until the Holy Father's hectic St. Petersburg schedule was well under way.

With the basic elements of flight and logistics pretty well settled, there remained one terrible possibility Gladstone hadn't addressed in his explanation of the enthronement. A possibility Lucadamo decided to broach straight on.

"I understand the old Pope's weakness at the end of his life, Monsignore. And clearly the September Pope was cut off before he could counter the *rituale* with the full force of an exorcism. But isn't it possible that the Slavic Pope has also been told of the enthronement? That he knows, and has done nothing?"

That question was one among the many Chris had wrestled with at the villa; one among the few to which he had no answer. For all he knew, maybe Carnesecca had gone to the Slavic Pope with the information he had given to his two predecessors. For all he knew, the Pontiff had even made an attempt to find the envelope. Or maybe he had been so bent on his own strange pontifical agenda that he had simply shoved Carnesecca's revelation into the background, exactly as he had done with those reports. And yet, all the maybes in the world didn't change the one thing Gladstone knew for certain. He had to get to the Holy Father.

"I don't know the answer to your question, Signor Giovanni," Christian replied at last. "I may never know. But with your help, I intend to show him the evidence once and for all. Name the names. Confront him. Shock him. Anger him if need be. Use every force at my command to get him to do what should have been done long before now. What happens after that will be up to him. In the end, as in so many other things, the final decision will be his."

"No, Monsignore," Lucadamo reminded the priest. "In the end, the decision will be Christ's."

LII

"ARE YOU MAD, Monsignore Christian? You can't leave Rome!" That was the only explanation Monsignore Taco Manuguerra could see for Gladstone's behavior on this otherwise splendid Thursday morning. Madness.

On second thought, he decided to be fair about it. As Cardinal Maestroianni's secretary, Manuguerra was privy to all of His Eminence's plans. Sometimes he forgot that others—even men as intimately connected with developments as Gladstone—weren't fully in the information loop. "Look, *Reverendo.*" Taco leaned forward and lowered his voice. The hour was early and no one was near; but his years of experience at Maestroianni's side had taught him that a man couldn't be too careful. "Between you and me, His Eminence has important plans for you. You'll be making a big mistake if you leave Rome now."

Christian scrutinized Manuguerra's face. His intention had been to make an early-morning appearance, establish an acceptable cover story to account for his absence from the Secretariat and then be on his way to Moscow. Like all good cover stories, Chris's was simple and not entirely untruthful. An unfinished assignment he had to complete for the Holy Father, he had told Taco, would take him away from the Vatican for a few days. Now, though, the Monsignore's explosive reaction suggested something more might be achieved in this conversation. If he played dumb, who could tell what he might learn?

"I can't tell you how grateful I am for your advice, Monsignore Taco." Chris leaned forward and whispered in his turn. "But I'll only be gone for a couple of days. If all goes well, I'll be back by the time the Pontiff returns on Saturday. What with the Consistory and all, His Eminence won't have time for a *minutante* like me."

That was one of the things Manuguerra had always liked about this American. Unlike some of the other puffed-up staffers around here, he knew his place. "Of course, do what you choose, Monsignore." Taco got up to close the outer door to his office. "But my advice is to stay here. These are stirring times!" The secretary returned to his chair and looked fixedly at some papers on his desk. He was obviously wrestling with a big decision. Finally, he raised his eyes and smiled.

"I know His Eminence has already told you about this being a time of transition from one pontificate to another." The Cardinal's secretary sat back, his eyes glistening. "Of course, I wouldn't breathe a word of this normally. But there's no point in your running off to perform some task for a Pope who will not be returning. Not when you can stay and be present with the rest of us at the creation, if I might say so."

"Not returning?" Chris feigned disbelief. "But the Holy Father's schedule is set. The whole world knows . . ."

What a gratifying response! Manuguerra was so rarely the first to impart significant news, it hardly mattered that his audience was such a lowly Vatican creature. And besides, he had reason to expect Gladstone's status to take an upward turn very soon. It never hurt to look to the future. "Forget what the whole world knows, my dear *Reverendo*. Let me give you the unpublished time lines. Then you'll see where wisdom lies."

Manuguerra had been schooled well in his service to Cardinal Maestroianni. In double-talk that made unthinkable treachery sound like holy scripture, he dealt first with the unpublished time line of the Holy Father's pilgrimage. The Pontiff, he confided pietistically, was "destined for a quiet time of repose and contemplation" with the Hermits of St. Paul who lived in seclusion at Poland's Jasna Gora Monastery in Czestochowa. "For the enrichment of the Church," he confided further, "like Mary in the Gospel account, the Holy Father has chosen the better part."

"He will sign the Resignation Protocol in Russia, then?" Chris was sure his attempted smile was sickly.

"Oh, no." The truth of the matter, as Manuguerra knew, was that neither St. Petersburg nor Moscow was secure from Rome's point of view; that no one wanted to entrust such extraordinary power to a mere watchdog and enforcer like Monsignore Jan Michalik; and that in any case Roman usage and decorum must hold sway, even in situations like this. Speaking of usage and decorum, however, it wouldn't do to come right out and say such things. Far better to keep up the charade of holy intent. "No, no," Manuguerra repeated himself. "His Holiness has initialed the Protocol as an indication of his mind. But he will sign it into law, so to speak, under the benediction of the Holy Icon of the Madonna at Czestochowa. And he will do so, fittingly, in the presence of his own faithful servant Monsignore Vacchi-Khouras, the Holy See's representative in Warsaw."

Chris didn't want to seem overeager for details, but neither could he let this moment pass. "Timing will be everything in such an enterprise."

"What a quick mind you have, *Reverendo!*" No wonder Maestroianni put such stock in this fellow, the secretary thought. "His Eminence's arrangement of the Roman time line has been made difficult by that very question. He had to make allowance for uncertainties in the papal schedule."

Difficult or not, arrangements had been worked out as neatly as a train schedule. The Papal Nuncio would set out from Warsaw, Protocol in hand and ready for signature, the moment he got word from Jasna Gora Monastery in Czestochowa that the Holy Father had arrived. The actual timing would depend on a signal from Monsignore Jan Michalik. But because it would all have to be accomplished by early Saturday morning at the outside, Manuguerra said, the Rome schedule had been keyed to that date.

"At his news conference on this very day, in fact"—Monsignore Taco practically winked at Gladstone—"our good friend Monsignore Buttafuoco will announce a synod to be convened at eight o'clock on Saturday morning. The extraordinary number of bishops in Rome just now have all been summoned to attend, and the press will be invited. At that synod, Cardinal Maestroianni himself will make the Common Mind Vote a matter of public record.

"Now, Monsignore Christian"—Taco thumped his desk with a finger—"Cardinal Maestroianni does not minimize the importance of your work in bringing the CMV to fruition. He wants you to be present when he informs the People of God and the wide world that an overwhelming majority of the Church's bishops has concluded it to be right and just that His Holiness has voluntarily resigned in order that the Holy Spirit choose a new Apostle to lead the Church into the third millennium."

Manuguerra paused to let Gladstone savor the news of such signal preferment in his regard. So stony was the expression on the young American's face, however, that he restated the point in bolder terms. "If your work on the Common Mind Vote doesn't knit you a Cardinal's hat, Monsignore, then I don't know Rome." With a smile, then, and with an eye to his own preferment down the line, he dipped into the Gospels again for suitable inspiration. "Remember me when you come into your kingdom, *Reverendo.*"

"That will be a day of fireworks, Monsignore Taco." Chris did his best to enter into the spirit of things. More than anything else at this moment, he wanted to keep Manuguerra talking.

"Ah, my friend, the synod and the publication of the CMV will just be the prelude to the real fireworks. The most important event of Saturday will take place when the Cardinals meet in a plenary session of the General Consistory at noon. By then, Vacchi-Khouras will have delivered the fully signed and duly sealed Resignation Protocol to Cardinal Secretary of State Graziani. In view of that Protocol, and under His Eminence Maestroianni's guidance as Camerlengo, the Cardinals will realize how closely the papal resignation coheres with the movement of the Holy Spirit among the faithful and the bishops. The Consistory will transform itself into a Conclave.

"In fact"—Manuguerra sat back in his chair—"I happen to know that Cardinal Maestroianni is thinking of inviting you to act as his personal secretary in that historic meeting."

Christian felt as if he had suddenly been weighted down by stones. All of his and Giustino Lucadamo's worries had been confirmed. But Manuguerra had said that events in Rome had been geared to Saturday because of uncertainties in the papal schedule. Clearly, then, whatever move would be made to waylay the Pontiff to Czestochowa could take place at any moment. Perhaps this very day in St. Petersburg. Still, the Protocol itself wouldn't be presented to His Holiness for signature before he reached Czestochowa. Not before Monsignore Vacchi-Khouras reached Czestochowa, in fact. What it came down to, then, was a race between himself and Vacchi-Khouras. A contest to see who could get to the Holy Father first, and a competition to see who would be more persuasive.

"So, Monsignore Christian"—Taco Manuguerra spoke as the very soul of practical reason—"with all these facts at your disposal, is it not clear now where wisdom lies? Is it not clear that you must stay in Rome?"

Taco's question came as a timely reminder. Chris had gotten way ahead of himself. He was still at square one. For the briefest moment, he was tempted by the idea of trying to buy time. He was tempted to leave a note for Maestroianni that would upset the smooth timetable he and his colleagues had worked out. But it was a swiftly passing thought. Nothing, Chris realized, would turn Maestroianni back now. Not even knowledge of the enthronement ceremony. Not even the fact that his closest colleagues had hitched a ride on his agenda for unspeakable reasons. On the contrary, Aureatini and the others were bound to deny any such accusations and to make counteraccusations of their own against him. To make any such move, then, would be worse than fruitless. In all likelihood, it would set Christian himself up as a much more urgent target than Carnesecca had been.

No. What Gladstone needed was what he had come for in the first place. He had to get out of Rome with the blessing of Cardinal Maestroianni in the person of his self-satisfied *secundo*. "Brilliant!" Christian bestowed a look of such admiration on Manuguerra as to make the angels blush. "The plan is positively brilliant, *Reverendo*. And your explanation, even more brilliant. But, my dear fellow"—Gladstone leaned forward again in imitation of Taco's best conspiratorial style—"everything you have confided to me this morning makes my own business outside of Rome even more urgent."

The Italian's mouth dropped open in surprise.

"I knew you'd understand." Christian followed up his advantage with a glad hand. "It's all very hush-hush. But I can say that it's intimately connected with the plans for the Pope's resignation. You can take it for granted that I will do everything in my power to be back here in time for the great events on Saturday. And be assured of this, Monsignore: I will never forget what you have done for me this morning. Thanks to you, everything is so much clearer in my mind. Now, let me have your blessing and I'll be on my way."

"Of course, *Reverendo*. But . . ."

"Clever devils, your colleagues in the Vatican, Monsignore Christian." Giovanni Lucadamo couldn't help but admire the scenario Christian laid out for him at the Raffaele on that same Thursday morning. "Somehow they get the Holy Father to Czestochowa. The Apostolic Nuncio somehow gets him to sign the Resignation Protocol to justify the legality of Rome's moves. The crowd in the Vatican holds a Conclave to elect a successor. And it's all done without a drop of papal blood being spilled, and without a shred of Cardinalitial dignity being torn. Marvelous!"

Gladstone bridled at Lucadamo's professional admiration. There was work to be done and he wanted to get at it. He might have saved himself the anguish, however. Giovanni had his little ways, but he was already turning possible countermoves over in his mind.

"It can't be that difficult, Signor Giovanni," Chris urged. "The same plane that was to take me to Moscow can simply take me to Czestochowa instead."

"If it were as simple as getting you into Poland for a chat with His Holiness, you might be right. But there are other considerations now."

"Like what?"

"Well, let's start with the problem of getting the Holy Father back to Rome—assuming that's what he agrees to do. In Moscow, it would simply have been a matter of using his normal Alitalia transport. But your friend Manuguerra put his finger on the key to their success. The Pope will be isolated in Czestochowa. There'll be no white DC-10 waiting for him there. We'll have to have some alternative way of getting him back to Rome on a fast track. And even to get to that point, we have to get you directly into Czestochowa in a hurry, and without alerting anyone of your movements. That in itself will take some doing. From what you tell me, Maestroianni's man—what's his name again?"

"Michalik, Signor Giovanni. Monsignore Jan Michalik."

"Right. Michalik must trigger the plan, whatever it may be, well before the Pontiff's scheduled departure for Rome on Saturday. Time is the big gamble. Speed and secrecy are the big hurdles. We're going to need help."

"You have a plan in mind?"

"I have people in mind." Lucadamo sat down at his desk and reached for his scrambler phone. "People I can rely on in situations like this. But you'd better pray that whatever ploy they have in mind to waylay the Pope to Czestochowa won't come into play today in St. Petersburg. There's no way to get everything in place that fast. In fact, Monsignore"—

Giovanni dialed through to a private number at the American Embassy in Brussels—"we'll have our hands full even to revise our plans and get things under way at our end by the time the pilgrimage makes Moscow tomorrow. . . .

"Ah!" Lucadamo spoke into the phone now. "Is that you, Appleyard?"

The papal party touched down at Sheremetyevo-2, Moscow's international airport, early on the morning of Friday, May 12. The two planes carrying the accredited press corps landed soon after. No matter how tumultuous the success of His Holiness' visit to Ukraine had been, and no matter how heartwarming and welcoming his daylong stay in St. Petersburg, everyone, including Monsignore Jan Michalik, knew that the tension on this final stop of the pilgrimage would outstrip everything that had come before.

For one thing, the government in Moscow wished to have as little as possible to do with this Pope who had frustrated and angered the American President and his administration at the population conference in Cairo. For another, there had never been anything but bad blood between Rome and Muscovy. And to top it all off, after the Russians had dominated the Slavic nations of Eastern Europe for so long, there were those who considered it an indignity that the very Slav who had done so much to end that domination was coming to Moscow bearing their Holy Icon of Kazan as a gift.

The Holy Father was welcomed there in a purely private capacity as a pilgrim, but certainly not as a head of state, by a second-level member of the Moscow Ministry of Foreign Affairs. That gentleman conveyed his government's cordial good wishes, then handed His Holiness off like hot goods to the Roman Catholic Archbishop of Moscow and the Italian archbishop who served as the Holy See's Ambassador to Moscow.

Within an hour, the members of the papal party had been transported forty-three miles northeast of Moscow to the town of Sergiyev Posad, where they would be quartered at the Troitse-Sergiyeva Lavra founded by St. Sergius in the fourteenth century. There, the Slavic Pope was installed in special apartments once maintained for imperial visitors and more recently for important ecclesiastics of the Russian Orthodox Church.

The formal welcoming for the Holy Father went off without incident. The reception was a quasi-official affair; which was to say that no high-level members of the Moscow administration participated. The same hapless second-string diplomat who had drawn duty at the airport turned up to convey his government's good wishes once again, and this time added his hope that the Pontiff would have a safe return journey to Rome.

"Safe, as in speedy," Damien Slattery said in a stage whisper to Giustino Lucadamo.

Quasi-official though it was, the reception was a signal success. The papal ambassador and the Roman Catholic archbishop were in attendance again, this time with members of their senior staffs. Practically all the Roman Catholics of Moscow were there, as were a number of archbishops from Poland and other nations of Eastern Europe. The arrival of the principal prelates of the Russian Orthodox Church stole the show for a time. The Metropolitan of St. Petersburg and Ladoga, the second-highest-ranking Russian prelate, had followed the Pontiff from St. Petersburg to underscore his reverence for the Roman Pope. And while the mood of Patriarch Kiril of Moscow had less to do with reverence than a desire to keep his eye on everything, his presence added a certain spice to the affair.

"I wonder, Angelo"—Slattery strolled up to Father Gutmacher as he watched the Russian prelates kiss the ring of the Slavic Pope—"how many have already switched allegiance to Rome secretly in their hearts."

Gutmacher's reply was mild, but it came from the fund of firsthand knowledge acquired in his travels for the Holy Father. "I have no doubt that many of them merely await the word from on high telling them to go to Rome."

The arrival of the Pope's longtime correspondent, Mikhail Gorbachev, caused a great stir among guests and journalists alike. Clad now in his new dignity as head of the international Gorbachev Foundation and chief mover and shaker in the increasingly powerful CSCE, he spent a considerable time in sotto voce conversation with the Holy Father. Raisa Gorbachev, meanwhile, chatted with a number of distinguished guests, who remarked, among other things, on the impressive crucifix she had donned for the occasion.

Many who surrounded His Holiness that morning commented on how he had aged since last they had seen him, and noticed a certain subdued quality to his mood. Except for intimates like Slattery and Gutmacher and Lucadamo, however, no one guessed that the dominant emotion he was undergoing was a deep and poignant sadness. For he had come to the last hours of his pilgrimage, and nowhere had the Queen of Heaven sent her sign to him.

"I wonder, then," the Pontiff had said to Slattery prior to the reception. "What was the point of my journey?"

It had been less a question than a comment. But His Holiness had seemed so fretful and tense, as if he half expected some dire blow of misfortune, that in his compassion for the Holy Father's obvious pain and disappointment, Damien felt he had to answer. "Do not worry, Holy Father; Our Lady has everything in hand. For me, the greatest sign—a sign from her hand, I have no doubt about that—is that Your Holiness is preserved in good health. And besides, this journey in her honor has been so signally successful! When Your Holiness presents the Holy Icon of Our Lady of Kazan to His All-Holiness the Patriarch of Moscow this afternoon, that will crown this pilgrimage and honor the Queen of Heaven."

The Pontiff had not replied in words; but the sadness enveloping his heart and soul had been plain to see.

❑ ❑ ❑ ❑

It wasn't until the morning of Friday, May 12, that Gladstone found himself speeding away from Rome toward the Old Appian Way in one of Giovanni Lucadamo's limousines. Sitting beside the troubleshooter who doubled as driver, he couldn't help but think of the leisurely walks he and Aldo Carnesecca had taken along that classical Roman road. The *Regina Viarum,* Aldo had called it; the Queen of Highways.

As his car whizzed past the relics of a dead Roman past—the tombs of the Scipios, of Cecilia Metella, the Arch of Drusus, the ruined Gothic chapel of the Caetanis—Chris fell prey to feelings of regret and loss. For he could not shake the feeling that he was saying goodbye. The Scipios and the Caetanis and the others seemed to be telling him that they, too, had come to Rome; that they, too, had finally said goodbye to the city. An unwilling goodbye.

Some distance beyond the church called *Domine Quo Vadis* where, as tradition tells, Christ turned Peter back in his flight from a fierce imperial persecution to face his martyrdom in Rome—Christian's driver slowed, took a right turn onto a country road and, after a bumpy three-quarters of a mile or so, pulled up at an American-style ranch house.

"This is it, Monsignore." The chauffeur walked Chris to the door of the safe house. "You're clear on the arrangements?"

Yes, Christian said. He was clear.

"*Addio,* then, Monsignore Gladstone." The fellow's handshake was warm and sincere. "Go with God."

Chris watched the car recede; watched it disappear; watched until the clouds of dust it kicked up had faded; watched even then in the profound silence that settled around him as his sole companion. He had never expected to be hiding out, not even for a few hours, in this land that was so famous for art, for heroism, for sanctity, for wine, for love, for beauty. Still, he reflected as he let himself into the lonely house, this land was famous for a few other things as well. For an invincible cruelty, for a mercilessness that lurked among its olive groves and sycamores and oleanders, for the smell of blood that had so often mingled with the scent of lemon blossoms and roses. The perennial violence of Italy was an ancient evil that had sealed the destinies of many, and that continued to strike down the good and the evil, the just and the guilty, the innocent and the damned.

Had he allowed it, Chris might have felt more at sea than he had ever been in his entire life. He certainly was more alone. He glanced at the telephone in the comfortably furnished house. He assumed it was secure; but there was no reason to call Signor Giovanni. As he had said to his driver, he was clear on the arrangements. A couple of hours from now, a helicopter would arrive to transport him to Triforo, a small secondary military airport on the coastal plain about two hundred and fifty miles north of Rome. A private jet would pick him up at Triforo around midday. He should be in Brussels well before nightfall. His brother Paul would pick him up there. After that, his race to reach the Slavic Pope before Vacchi-Khouras reached His Holiness and got him to sign the Protocol would depend on Gibson Appleyard.

The presentation of the Holy Icon of Our Lady of Kazan took place at the monastery of Troitse-Sergiyeva Lavra at two o'clock on Friday afternoon. In a ceremony that lasted a quarter of an hour, the Slavic Pope presented the treasure to Patriarch Kiril of Moscow. "What matters"—the Holy Father concluded his brief remarks to the Archbishop in fluent Russian—"is that this Holy Icon of the Mother of God is back among her people in this land."

For a time, as Pontiff and Patriarch sang the *Magnificat,* Mary's great hymn of praise and thanksgiving to God, all who had come to share this significant moment tasted the remote and yet perceptible joy of fraternal unity. Then, with press cameras flashing and videocams whirring, the Icon was installed in the Monastery Chapel. There it would remain until its original location—a cathedral in Red Square that had been leveled by Bolshevik cannons in 1917—could be rebuilt.

While the guests remained behind to admire the Icon, His Holiness followed Patriarch Kiril out of the Chapel toward a small salon where refreshments had been set out for the papal party. It was at that moment that exhaustion and disappointment caught up with him at last. Dizziness and a slight nausea were the first signs.

Always alert, Monsignore Sadowski and Giustino Lucadamo were at the Pontiff's side immediately, followed almost at once by Damien Slattery and Dr. Fanarote. Sure enough, Monsignore Jan Michalik was right behind them, homing in on his target like a heat-seeking missile. With that much help and a stout heart, it took only a few minutes for the Pontiff to reach his apartment.

The Holy Father's nausea became severe before it subsided. Nevertheless, Dr. Fanarote's lengthy and careful examination revealed nothing more serious than deep fatigue. After four days of continuous preaching and dialogue, rejoicing and frustration, too little sleep and constant performance in the public eye, it was a wonder, the doctor said, that His Holiness hadn't felt the effects of this punishing journey before now. Certainly everyone else had!

"But, Doctor." Michalik wasn't about to accept such a benign diagnosis. With time running out, he couldn't afford to. "Isn't it possible that His Holiness has suffered a slight stroke? An ischemic attack?"

Fanarote turned from the Pontiff's bedside, a thunderous scowl on his face. "Anything is possible, Monsignore. But in my professional opinion . . ."

Michalik was not interested in Fanarote's opinion, professional or otherwise. The possibility was enough for him. Within moments he was in the

Abbot's office putting a telephone call through to the Secretariat of State. A moment more, and he was patched through to the Camerlengo.

"He can travel, I presume?" Maestroianni asked the most salient question at once.

"Yes, Eminence. And I presume our people have made the necessary arrangements for transport?"

What an insolent piece of baggage Michalik was, Maestroianni thought. "We have been ready at every step of the way," he answered testily. "You have allowed the time to grow very short, Monsignore."

"But, Eminence . . ."

"Proceed, Michalik. Let's make an end of it!"

When the line went dead with a click that sounded in his ears like doom, Michalik made tracks back to the papal quarters. He ordered everyone, including Dr. Fanarote, to leave him alone with the Holy Father. Slattery and Lucadamo both stepped forward as if to make short work of Graziani's stooge. At a nod from His Holiness, however, they were left with no choice but to comply. For what seemed to them like an eternity, Slattery, Fanarote, Sadowski and Lucadamo paced in helpless fury outside the door to the Pope's quarters. They could hear the rise and fall of voices—mostly Michalik's—but it was impossible to catch what was being said.

"Is he all right?" Father Angelo Gutmacher's worry was obvious as he hurried down the corridor toward the papal apartment.

"I've managed to quiet things." The papal spokesman Lázaro-Falla came up behind Gutmacher. "But there's a lot of buzzing going on downstairs that something has happened to His Holiness. What's going on?"

As if that question had been a signal, Michalik opened the door and motioned the six men inside. "We have new travel plans, my friends . . ." Terrible though the Holy Father's first words were as his supporters gathered around him, he somehow conveyed the impression of serene control over his situation and his emotions. He seemed so tranquil, in fact—so uplifted in a strange sort of way—that the oldest hands were reminded of the enterprise and quiet eagerness that had marked his first papal journeys years before. "The Monsignore has been in touch with the Secretariat of State." The Pontiff turned a brief glance on Michalik. "We are to leave here in an hour for Czestochowa. The Monsignore has arranged special transport for us . . ."

His Holiness caught the flash in Slattery's eyes and broke off for just a second to smile reassuringly at the giant Irishman, and then at the other five. "The world at large will be informed of my condition at five o'clock Rome time. My Cardinals in consultation with my bishops have made special arrangements to cope with the situation. For the sake of unity, I wish to comply with the first step in those arrangements. You have been my faithful associates. Together now, we will pay a visit to Our Lady of Czestochowa. May the Queen of Poland protect me and the Church."

Lucadamo exchanged a glance with Slattery. Had this been medieval times, those two would long since have torn Michalik limb from limb; and they were mightily tempted to do so now. But, as so often over the past dozen years and more, the trouble was that the Pope himself had acquiesced. Once again—perhaps for the final and fatal time—the Slavic Pope had acquiesced.

At about the time his friend Damien Slattery was contemplating murder, Chris Gladstone's small jet began its approach into the Brussels airport where his brother was waiting for him. Minutes later, as he and Paul sped along the *autostrade* toward the city, the first thing Christian wanted was the latest news about Declan.

"He's come through with flying colors, thanks to you and your friends!" Paul Gladstone flashed a grateful smile at his older brother. "He's still in the hospital. But I'm happy to say that he's not so sure about this spelunking business anymore. He and Régice Bernard have become great friends, and Deckel has decided to go into heavy construction. That way, he says, he'll be able to fly his own helicopter, just like Régice does."

"Some improvement." Chris laughed. "Have you told Mother the news?"

"All of it." Paul nodded as he turned off the highway and made for the American Embassy. "Almost all of it, anyway. I've kept her up to date about Deckel. And I've told her about my confession the night Régice came to our rescue. But I haven't told her about this mad dash of yours. And now that we're on the subject, tell me. How can it happen that a powerful central leader like the Holy Father can be taken over like this by his inferiors? Mustn't he somehow or other have connived at it? I don't mean connived in the bad sense, but . . ."

Christian was surprised that an experienced Eurocrat like his brother should be so puzzled. "It's too complicated to explain much more than I told you on the phone from the Raffaele. As complicated as what went on around Chairman Mao in his declining years, I suppose."

"Not as bloody, I hope." Paul pulled up near the Embassy. "But you're right. It's too complicated to go into in the time we have. Appleyard should be waiting for us by now."

At 3:30 P.M. on Friday, a chartered Trans-Europa jet lifted off from a private government airport south of Sergiyev Posad. Once in the air, and before he joined the Pontiff and the other six in the cabin, Michalik used the cockpit radio to confirm the flight plan to the Vicars-Cardinal in Rome. American monitoring satellites picked up the message. A transcript quickly reached the desk of a U.S. State Department liaison officer at the U.S. Embassy in Brussels. He in turn alerted Gibson Appleyard.

At 4 P.M. local time, the Slavic Pope's personal invitees, together with the journalists waiting in Moscow for news of the Pontiff, were apprised of his sudden departure. Their Rome-bound planes, they were told, would depart from Sheremetyevo-2 international airport at 7 P.M. By the time some of the reporters managed to call their home offices, it was past five, and what they had to say was old news. All of the Holy See's eighty-five diplomatic representatives around the world had already received faxed copies of the Resignation Protocol, together with instructions from the Vatican Secretariat of State to alert local governments at once and to release the news to the national media as of 5 P.M. Rome time.

By the time the Vatican press officer, Archbishop Canizio Buttafuoco, faced the Vatican press conference that had been called for five o'clock Rome time, the grapevine had done its work. Well over six hundred media representatives were there from all over Europe and the Americas and even a few from Asia. The usual Rome-resident correspondents had to fight for their customary front-row seats, and many were beat out by a large contingent of clerics and nuns, media representatives by trade, who had got there first.

Buttafuoco was somewhere between stony-faced and goggle-eyed as he tried to keep things in hand. As of this hour, he said as he handed out a printed communiqué, the Slavic Pope was voluntarily resigning from the papacy. No reason was given. He had already departed Russia for a location to be disclosed later. . . .

That was as far as Buttafuoco managed to get before the rows of journalists were on their feet trying to shout each other down, hurling questions at him like hailstones.

Uncertainty about the Slavic Pope eclipsed all other news. Banner-headline stories in all major newspapers, and a stream of special reports that interrupted normal radio and television programming, carried a few facts and a great deal of speculation around the world with lightning speed. The facts, which were less than sparse, revolved around the Venerable College of Cardinals. Acting now as the temporary government of the Church Universal, Their Eminences would meet at midday on Saturday. Under the leadership of His Eminence Cosimo Maestroianni as Camerlengo, they would take appropriate action in accordance with Canon Law and with the legislation enacted recently by His Holiness. Prior to that meeting, a special synod of the Church's bishops would assemble for an open and democratic discussion of this unprecedented situation.

The speculation, meanwhile, revolved entirely around rumors that His Holiness had suffered a severe setback in his health. A flood tide of tremors ran across whole continents at all levels—governmental, financial and popular. In major countries, special cabinet meetings were called; in major economic capitals, heavyweight board meetings were swiftly convened. Waves of emotions—surprise and fear, exaltation and regret, puzzlement and satisfaction—wracked the world's almost one billion Roman Catholics and their sympathizers.

Such global reaction was inevitable. For over a decade and a half this one individual, the white-robed Slavic Pope, had been seen and heard by over three and a half billion human beings. It was impossible to believe he had suddenly quit the public ken of his contemporaries. Nor was it possible to gauge the void left by the removal of such a universally recognized icon from his well-known niche in the globalist public square.

"The major elements of the situation are clear, Monsignore Christian." Gibson Appleyard wasted no time on preliminaries as he and the two Gladstone brothers settled down in the Embassy office he used in Brussels. "So far, the information Giovanni passed along to me on the phone tracks to a tee."

"They've taken him, then?" Chris's knuckles showed white on the arms of his chair.

Appleyard handed over the transcript of Michalik's in-flight radio transmission to the Vicars-Cardinal in Rome. "The trajectory of the flight is southwest from Moscow. The Holy Father is well on his way to the Pauline Monastery at Czestochowa. In the meantime, the unofficial word is that there's been a major breakdown in the Pope's health, and that those left in charge of the Vatican during his absence have invoked and implemented a legislative document about papal resignation seen and recognized by the Holy Father before he left on his Russian pilgrimage. Now, if that's the case, Monsignore—if he signed such a document . . ."

"No!" Chris cut Gibson short. "I don't know about his health, but I do know about the document. He initialed it, but he refused to sign it. That's why Vacchi-Khouras has to get to him. His job is to make the whole thing legal. And that's why I have to get to him before Vacchi-Khouras."

"Understood." Appleyard accepted Gladstone's confirmation as superior to anything on the diplomatic circuit. "But let me ask you another question. Suppose we're successful in getting you to Czestochowa before the Papal Nuncio can tie things up. And suppose further that our plans are clever enough to get His Holiness out of his present entrapment. Given the tremendous pressures that have been mounting against him recently, I have to ask if you think he'd agree to be rescued."

Christian stared at Appleyard steadily while he turned the question over in his mind. In essence, it was the same issue Paul had raised on the way from the airport. Like his brother, Gibson was asking if the Pontiff hadn't somehow connived at his own removal to Jasna Gora Monastery; but he was taking that question one step further. Was there any point, Gibson wanted to know, in trying to move Heaven and Earth to pull off a complex and potentially unwelcome rescue operation?

"Without some counterstimulus," Gladstone answered, "I think he might accept what amounts to a coup d'état as the will of Heaven. Without a counterstimulus, he might sign that Resignation Protocol."

"And you have a counterstimulus?" Gib wasn't being confrontational.

He was willing to risk a great deal in this venture, but he wanted to reckon the odds.

"In my breast pocket." Gladstone took the double-sealed papal envelope from his jacket, but didn't hand it over.

"You Romans!" Paul spoke for the first time. He was up to his hips in this affair, too, and he hoped to goad his brother into some further explanation. "You always have your secrets!"

"Grubby secrets, at that," Chris acknowledged as he tucked the envelope away. "Apostolic secrets that should speak for themselves when the Holy Father knows them."

"Let's get at it, then." Appleyard turned a questioning eye at the EC's Secretary-General.

"Let's get at it," Paul agreed.

Gib shoved his chair back and crossed his long legs. "Since Giovanni called from the Raffaele about this crisis yesterday morning, Monsignore Christian, I've been in consultation with some of my colleagues. I've been able to persuade them that the best interests of the United States are served by maintenance of the status quo. The principle is this: Palace coups—even coups in the Apostolic Palace—make for unhealthy geopolitics. At this particular juncture, U.S. foreign policy is best served by stability in world events. Hence, certain facilities are at my disposal. I have been able to sign off on the expenditure of time and the use of equipment needed to monitor this situation, and to guide it according to our best interests."

"Excuse me, Gibson." Gladstone wasn't up to diplomatic double-talk. "Will you run that by me again in plain language?"

"In plain language." Appleyard laughed. "I'm sure we can get you from here to Czestochowa. We've got a place for you on a military milk run set to leave Brussels for the Czech Republic in about an hour. It should get you into Prague at half past midnight. It's all been arranged. A colleague of mine will meet you in Prague. You'll be making the run to Czestochowa in a Czech Army helicopter of the HP-C class. It's a good craft. Russian design. At an altitude of about a mile, it makes a standard speed of one hundred sixty miles per hour. With auxiliary tanks it may be a little slower, but it should see you through. If all goes well, you should touch down at the Monastery on Jasna Gora Hill sometime around three tomorrow morning."

Appleyard picked up a small card and passed it to Chris. "This may come in handy. It has the military transport flight number and the captain's name. On the back is the name of your contact in Prague. In case His Holiness chooses to leave with you and return to Rome, we've arranged for the Czech helicopter to make the run to Radomsko aerodrome to refuel and wait there at your disposal."

Christian acknowledged the plans to that point with a nod. But there was still the problem of transport to Rome. As Giovanni Lucadamo had said, there wouldn't be any Alitalia jet waiting for the Holy Father in Poland.

"I've taken care of that part of things, Chris." The younger Gladstone flashed a grin. "I can't let a bunch of ecclesiastical hijackers take over my Church just when I've decided to come back aboard. So I've made a little personal investment, you might say. I've chartered a Belgian passenger jet. It's not as grand as an Alitalia DC-10, but it has other advantages. It's privately owned, and that avoids a lot of complications. We have settled on an appropriate flight name, though. Fisherman One. The Polish government is fully cooperative. Not fully informed, mind you, but cooperative. They've assumed it's official EC business, and I haven't said otherwise. Anyway, we have clearance to fly into Radomsko at about sunrise. It's a military installation, of course, so they were a bit touchy. But we can remain for two hours. God willing, that should be long enough."

"God willing."

"That's the upside in the situation." Appleyard took up now. "The downside is that there won't be a fighter escort. So you'll be on your own until you enter Italian airspace."

"You expect us to be picked up by escorts in Italy?" Chris shot an apprehensive look at both men.

"We realize that will alert the Holy Father's enemies in Rome." Appleyard acknowledged the problem. "We'll delay as long as we can, but since your destination is Rome, we'll have to alert the Defense Ministry. And when we do, we think they'll provide escort. We think they'll insist, in fact. But if everything goes our way—if that counterstimulus you have in your pocket is powerful enough, and if we can delay Vacchi-Khouras long enough—by the time Maestroianni and the others get word of the Pontiff's return, there won't be much they can do about it."

Christian wasn't sure he had heard right. "Delay Monsignore Vacchi-Khouras? Is that what you said, Gibson?"

"Ham radios." Gib smiled. "Poland is full of them."

All that Friday, May 12, heavy squalls enshrouded a wide area of southern Poland. Like a veil of tears shed by Heaven at the climax of the *coup de théâtre* being carried out by the Slavic Pope's mortal enemies, rain fell from Wroclaw in the west to Lublin in the east, and from as far north as Lodz all the way down to Katowice near the Czechoslovak border.

It was only when the chartered Trans-Europa jet carrying the papal party nosed its way down through the bank of dark clouds that the runway lights were switched on and the pilot had a clear view of Radomsko military aerodrome six hundred feet below. The plane touched down and taxied to within fifty yards of an Army helicopter parked a little distance off one side of the runway. Hard by the other side of the runway, two jeeps waited, each manned by a driver and a single uniformed officer. When the jet came to a stop, its body streaked with glistening moisture, its engines were kept idling. At a quick exchange of staccato voice signals, the rotor blades of the helicopter clattered slowly into movement. The two jeeps pulled rapidly to the rear of the plane. The officer in charge climbed down from his seat, checklist in hand. The second officer came up behind and opened his umbrella. Both waited while the rear exit door opened and the access ramp was lowered to the ground.

The first passenger down the ramp was a moderately tall and curiously angular cleric in black cassock and wide-brimmed Roman hat. Jan Michalik returned the officers' salute with a brief greeting in Polish, showed his ID card and took up his post beside the man who held the checklist. Then he beckoned to the other passengers. As each one descended, Michalik nodded to the officer, who dutifully checked off the corresponding number, for his list contained no names. Only numbers.

The three laymen were the first to be accounted for. The Monsignore nodded to the officer as each man stepped down, and then waved each, one by one, to the waiting jeeps. Giustino Lucadamo, his black leather case in hand. The always elegant papal press officer, Miguel Lázaro-Falla. A very unhappy Dr. Fanarote.

Three clerics emerged then. The scars on Father Angelo Gutmacher's drawn and miserable face stood out like the crimson flames that had etched them. Damien Duncan Slattery, his brow set in a black scowl, had to bend head and shoulders to get through the skimpy exit. Monsignore Daniel Sadowski brought up the rear, trying to look impassive as he fought back silent tears. That made six. The officer turned his eyes up toward the exit door, looking for number seven. Yes. There he was. Outlined against the cabin lights. Another cleric, to judge by his Roman hat. But this one was all muffled up in a topcoat, scarf and gloves.

Number seven came down the ramp slowly, as if to savor some sweet, warm sense of return. Finally, as he set foot on the rain-washed tarmac, the figures of Michalik and the two officers seemed to shrivel to pygmy silhouettes for this pilgrim. The wide spaces seemed to open around him on every side all the way to the gray-black horizon. The low ceiling of rain clouds hid no part of this beloved land from the inward man. He could see it all as a tranquil vision bathed in the sun of a special blessing. The streets of Wadowice, where he had been born. The spires of Kraków where he had been bishop and Cardinal. The fields and rivers and the grandiose Carpathian Mountains to the south. And, yes, the graceful towers of Czestochowa's Monastery on Jasna Gora Hill, where the sacred Icon of the Queen of Poland shed the radiant promise of her divine Son down across this land and people.

The officer bestowed the same cursory glance on this seventh anonymous passenger as he had on the other six. He was about to tick off the final number on his checklist when, at a sudden onrush of memories, his eyes opened wide and the color drained from his cheeks. He was frozen momentarily by those memories—a sunny day some years before; the

Slavic Pope standing in an open automobile; the smile; blessings given to the cheering crowds surging around him on Warsaw's Nowy Świat; his slow progress along that royal way of the kings of Poland from Wilanów Palace past the Presidential Palace and on into the new part of metropolitan Warsaw. No one who saw that white-robed figure ever forgot his unmistakable profile, or failed to discover in himself his own yearning for the blessing of the Father.

"Maryjo! Królowo Polski!" The words—the traditional invocation of Poles when faced with danger—were out of the officer's mouth before he could think. "Mary! Queen of Poland!"

Michalik stiffened at this breach in the web of security woven around the transfer of the Slavic Pope into obscurity. Peremptorily, he waved the Pontiff on toward the waiting jeeps. *"To Panski obwazak!"* He hissed the order into the officer's ear. "Do your duty, sir! Check number seven! Immediately!"

With an extreme effort, the officer complied. But not even the baleful stare of Monsignore Michalik could prevent the Holy Father from answering that powerful invocation with the traditional triple response as he set off across the tarmac. *"Jestem przy Tobie! Pamietam! Czuwam!"* "We are with you! We remember! We are on the alert!"

By the time the Pontiff reached the jeep, the triple refrain had been picked up by the officers and both drivers. Michalik, beside himself with fury, took the first officer firmly by the arm and walked him up and down in the pelting rain. His face set in granite, his eyes hooded, his voice a rasp, he explained the harsh penalties for any breach in the security of this mission. When he had finished, he took a sharp salute from the shaken man, strode to the lead jeep, clambered up behind him and barked an order to the driver. In the wake of the jet, already roaring down the runway for takeoff, both vehicles sped to the waiting helicopter.

As the pilgrim party was lifted from the ground in a terrible clatter of motors and whirling blades, the first officer shouted that invocation again at the top of his lungs. *"Maryjo! Królowo Polski!"*

"Jestem przy Tobie!" His three comrades shouted the triple response into the wind and the rain and the noise. "We are with you! We remember! We are on the alert!"

LIII

THOUGH THE FINALE to the drama of the Slavic Pope's meteoric career was even more surprising than his unexpected election over a decade and a half before, those engineering it intended it to be far less tumultuous. Despite his extraordinary recognition profile in the wide world, his transition from public view and papal status into private life was to be executed, so to say, in total seclusion some ten miles to the southwest of Radomsko military aerodrome.

The rolling hills that rise in that region form a natural basin occupied by Czestochowa, an ancient town of some 250,000 souls. On one of those hills, Jasna Gora by name, stands the most revered monastery in all of Poland; a mighty block of rectangular buildings enclosed by high walls and crowned by a tall bell tower.

Since its foundation in 1382 by the monks of St. Paul the Hermit, the Monastery of Jasna Gora has been the spiritual center of the Polish nation, and the military target of that nation's enemies. It has acquired the appearance and strength of a fortress, and the very names of its structures echo Poland's centuries-long battle for survival. At each corner of its surrounding walls stands a solid, square bastion, each named after a glorious moment in Polish history—Potocki; Szaniawski; Morszstun; Lubomirski. Access to the Monastery grounds is doubly guarded by two monumental gates, the Lubomirski and the Jagellonian. The approach to those gates is formed by a huge circular mosaic, two lions rampant around the Tree of Life, embedded in the ground. Two wings of the Monastery are occupied by the monks' cells. But the central portion reflects the complexity of its history: side by side with the Abbots Houses, the Sacristy and a series of magnificent chapels—the Jablonowski, the Denhoff, the Last Supper—there is the Knights Hall, the Arsenal and the Royal Apartments.

But the abiding importance of Jasna Gora Monastery has centered on the Icon that hangs above the High Altar in its Gothic Chapel of Our Lady. For over six centuries, the Black Madonna of Czestochowa has been and remains today the true Queen of Poland. Jasna Gora is her home. And her home is the true capital of the Polish nation.

Shortly after dark on Friday evening, May 12, the Polish Army helicopter transporting the papal party approached the walls of Jasna Gora Monastery and set down on the giant circular mosaic outside Lubomirski Gate. The rain had stopped, but the place appeared deserted. Only when the passengers had passed through the twin gates into the Monastery grounds did Abbot Kordecki and his assistant, Father Kosinski, emerge to welcome their guests. Though Monsignore Jan Michalik strode forward to take firm charge of the situation, the monks seemed not to notice him. They knew their Pope when they saw him—had known him since his youthful, ebullient days as Cardinal Archbishop of Kraków—and they went to him now. Both knelt to kiss his Fisherman's ring as a sign of loyalty to Peter the Apostle; and both kissed the instep of his right foot in the ancient sign of obeisance to Peter's lawful successor.

Michalik had no choice but to wait for the Abbot and Kosinski to rise to their feet. No choice but to wait while the Slavic Pope, his face cruelly ravaged by strain, smiled and spoke a few words to these two old comrades. It pushed his patience to the limit, however, to see the monks turn to the Pope's companions as, one by one, the Holy Father presented them by name. Only Father Angelo Gutmacher needed no introduction. A frequent visitor here on his many missions for the papacy, he was welcomed by Abbot Kordecki and Father Kosinski as a devout and courageous man of God. Indeed, such was the understanding among these battle-scarred veterans of Eastern Europe that it took but a gesture for Kordecki to see that Gutmacher wanted a moment apart with him.

Father Angelo's summary of the events that had brought the Holy Father to Jasna Gora was brief but accurate. Clearly the Holy Father had not come here merely to rest after his pilgrimage.

"Father Abbot!" A moment was too much for Michalik. He was impatient to call the Papal Nuncio in Warsaw, and he made his annoyance plain.

Kordecki turned a bland face to the Monsignore. This Monastery and its monks had survived centuries of siege, war, massacre, hunger and persecution. No man here would quail before such a contemptible excuse for a priest as this.

"Reverend Sir." Abbot Kordecki came to the Pontiff's side again, but his words were addressed to Michalik. "Within these walls, the disposition of all people and all accommodations is under my jurisdiction. I have arranged suitable quarters for His Holiness and his household in the Abbots Houses." He gestured toward the north wing of the complex. "However"—he gestured now toward the extreme south wing—"Your Reverence will surely find the seclusion of the Musicians Houses more agreeable until the Papal Nuncio arrives."

Seclusion? Michalik had to let the word sink in for a second. Surely the Abbot wasn't talking about monastic seclusion! Not now! Not at the very moment he had to make his crucial call to Vacchi-Khouras!

Kordecki met Michalik's objections with restraint. "Please understand, *Reverendo*. It is at Monsignore Vacchi-Khouras' personal instruction that my monks are on solemn spiritual retreat. *Magnum Silentium* is in effect; the Great Silence. That means all meals will be served in your apartment, and there will be no communication with the outside world. Do not be troubled, however. I will make the call to Warsaw."

Michalik's mouth opened and closed more than once as he saw Father Kosinski move toward him the way a bailiff might step toward a prisoner. His precious schedule wasn't merely going awry; it was being taken out of his hands. He had been checkmated.

"Your Holiness will remember." The Abbot spoke quietly as he led the Slavic Pope and his companions to the Abbots Houses, where they would all be quartered. "We have evening prayer at nine o'clock. We ask Your Holiness to come and lead us in our devotions."

"Of course I remember, Father. And of course I will come. We will all come." He turned to look at Sadowski and Slattery; at Lucadamo and Gutmacher and Lázaro-Falla; at poor Dr. Fanarote—each of them silent as they strode along behind. "We have come so far together and have been through so much. Let us have this last evening of prayer before . . ." The Pontiff's thought was so transparent that Kordecki rushed to counter it.

"Please pardon me for saying this, Holy Father. But these Italians—including Polish-Italians like Monsignore Michalik, who should know better—have failed to learn that we cannot be herded like cattle in our own land. The Austrians, the Germans, the Swedes and the Russians have all tried. They're all gone. And we're still here, aren't we?"

The quiet flare of humor in the Pontiff's eyes was sufficient answer. Michalik wasn't gone, alas. But thanks to Father Abbot, at least he would be out of commission for the remaining hours of the night.

Damien Slattery took his time about emptying his hastily packed overnight case. His desperate concern was to come up with some means to open the jaws of the trap that had been sprung on the Slavic Pope. The difficulty he faced, however, was that the trap couldn't have been sprung at all had the Pontiff dug in his heels; and it couldn't be opened without his consent. "There's such a childlike calm and trust in the Holy Father's attitude toward all that's happening," Slattery told himself. "But behind that calm is a mood, a mode of his spirit, that puts him almost beyond reach.

"How do you get to a man, Pope or not, who understands all the arguments we put to him, but who seems to place everything in a different context? No doubt about it, he's always had a mystical side to his nature. But he seems to respond to everything now as if he could see a brighter dimension to all our words. Or as if there were some supernal grandeur to all the dialogue."

Slattery was mired in frustration and getting nowhere, when Father Kosinski tapped gently on his door and asked him to join Abbot Kordecki in his rooms. "Maestro Lucadamo and Father Gutmacher are already with Father Abbot." Kosinski spoke softly as the two clerics made their way up to the third floor.

"And the others?" Slattery took the stairs two at a time.

"Monsignore Sadowski remains with the Holy Father. And Father Abbot thinks it best that Dr. Fanarote and Signor Lázaro-Falla be allowed to rest before chapel."

Apparently *Magnum Silentium* didn't apply inside Kordecki's rooms. He, Lucadamo and Gutmacher were all glued to the Abbot's shortwave radio like limpets to a rock. Damien took his place in the group and listened uneasily to the reports coming through. As the Abbot turned alternately to the BBC, the Voice of America and Polish home broadcasts, it was plain that the papal resignation was prime news everywhere. According to the commentators in Europe and the Americas, the Slavic Pope had resigned from the papacy because of ill health. There were quotations from major government spokesmen and the secretaries of many important Bishops Conferences. Already, too, speculation was abroad about the near-future Conclave and the identity of the next Pope.

By and large, the tone of the commentaries was laudatory. Some commended the Holy Father for his wisdom in resigning. Still, the overall conclusion was that the Slavic Pope now belonged to history. "Henceforward," as Cardinal Maestroianni was quoted as saying, "the former Holy Father will sustain the Church by his prayers and experienced advice."

There were elements of confusion evident in some of the newscasts, however; particularly in the Polish home broadcasts. According to reports, a few major cities abroad were coping with some ugly street demonstrations and the inevitable counterdemonstrations. New York, Paris, Milan and Madrid were all mentioned, and Rome as well. Ultratraditional Roman Catholic groups, meanwhile, had issued statements of varying kinds. Some declared that the Slavic Pope had never been a valid Pope; others, that he had fallen into heresy during his reign and therefore had ceased to be Pope. Neo-Catholic groups, with bishops as their spokesmen, thanked God in public that such a misfit Pope had finally decided to get out of the way of Church development. Moderate Catholic groups, which represented by far the vast majority of Roman Catholics, declared themselves obedient sons and daughters of the Church who would accept whatever decisions were made by Rome. Official Bishops Conferences issued statements calling on everyone to stay calm and pray for the papal succession.

It was the Polish broadcasts, too, that gave the greatest play to rumors still rife about the Slavic Pope. Rumors that he was dead. Rumors that he was lying comatose in a Moscow hospital. That he had retired as a monk to Sergiyev Posad outside Moscow. That he was back in the Vatican. That he was in Castel Gandolfo. That he was being treated for cancer in Germany, or for severe depression in a Swiss clinic. About all such reports Vatican officialdom was tight-lipped, referring inquiries to the press conference that would take place after the midday meeting of Cardinals on Saturday, May 13.

"If we didn't know the truth"—Giustino Lucadamo was the first to unglue himself from the set—"we'd think it was all over."

"Unless you know something I don't," Slattery grumbled, "I'd say it's all over, bar the shoutin'. Once Father Abbot here makes that call to Monsignore Vacchi-Khouras . . ."

"Unless we want to panic the Nuncio into hasty action," Abbot Kordecki acknowledged, "that call will have to be made. But I needn't hurry about it. His Holiness isn't tied to a precise schedule, and delays are easily explained. Besides, Maestro Lucadamo felt that a call to Rome would be more useful from our point of view."

"A call to the Vatican?" What with Maestroianni and Aureatini and the others in charge at the Apostolic Palace now, Damien's cynical surprise was understandable.

"A call to another center of information," Giustino countered. "A call to my uncle at the Raffaele. We're normally discreet about sharing information, but our situation has been anything but normal for some time. And in case you think the Vatican has anything on the Raffaele as a nerve center, Father Damien, let me bring you up to date on a few items. Including news of our friend Monsignore Christian Gladstone. According to my uncle, he's done quite a job of work in our absence."

The first items Lucadamo set out for Slattery had to do with the agenda being followed in Rome. According to Gladstone, a call from Michalik to the Secretariat was to be the signal to the Vicars-Cardinal to accept the Pontiff's virtual resignation as an accomplished fact and to authorize his removal to Jasna Gora. News of the Pope's resignation had been announced to the world during a Vatican news conference at five in the afternoon Rome time. Another call from Michalik—the one he had been so anxious to make on his arrival here—was to be the signal to Monsignore Vacchi-Khouras of the Holy Father's arrival at Czestochowa. The Nuncio would make the drive from Warsaw to present the Resignation Protocol for the Pontiff's signature. Once formally signed, that document would have the force of an Apostolic Constitution. The Vicars-Cardinal would be free to proceed with the next Conclave.

"And what if His Holiness doesn't sign?" Slattery was grasping at straws and he knew it.

By now, all governments would have received copies of the initialed document; the world at large would be impressed at the sight of a peaceful, harmonious, democratic transition from one pontificate to another. Given their long experience with the Slavic Pope, Maestroianni and the others were obviously convinced that His Holiness could be persuaded to sign the Resignation document for the sake of Church unity and for the sake of the papacy's standing as an institution.

Apparently Slattery wasn't the only one grasping at straws, however. Lucadamo replied to his question with news that left the Irishman speechless. As of this moment, Chris Gladstone was on his way to Jasna Gora with data in his possession that he hoped would persuade His Holiness not to sign the Protocol. "In fact," Giustino added, "you wouldn't believe the array of machinery that's been activated to transport the Pontiff back to Rome."

"Does the Holy Father know all this?" Damien found his voice again.

"I've informed him." It was Angelo Gutmacher who answered. "But I'm not sure Chris or anyone else can keep the Pontiff from resigning. We've all known about the intrigue and clerical double-dealing of Maestroianni and his cabal. And we've all known the aim of their policies. I know you won't understand this easily, Father Damien. But His Holiness feels this move by his Cardinals could be taken as the sign he's spoken about. He concedes that it's not the sign he foresaw or expected when he left Rome on his pilgrimage. But he thinks God may want him in retirement. That, in one sense, he might do more for the Church if he were no longer a bone of contention."

"Do more good for the Church!" Slattery's frustration erupted like an explosion in the quiet Monastery. "Rome is now networked by the Church's enemies, and he thinks the solution is to retire to work in peace and solitude?"

"He admits his mistakes have been great." Father Angelo took up the point. "He said as much. In fact, it may be on that very account that he thinks God and the Virgin have done with him as Pope; that perhaps they want him in another capacity. But the truth is he doesn't know. He says that events must be his guide now. He wants to hear what Christian has to say."

"I'd like to hear that myself!"

At that moment, Abbot Kordecki held up his hand for silence. He had kept half an ear tuned to the shortwave as if he was expecting some particular bit of news, and he turned up the volume now to catch a bulletin coming across on the home broadcast.

It seemed that police in various regions of Poland were reporting masses of people on the move. Roads everywhere were becoming clogged with men, women and children traveling on foot, in cars and carts, on bicycles and horses and donkeys. Special Militia units and some Army battalions were being readied in case public safety might be endangered. But everything seemed orderly. Everything seemed organized, in fact, as if some massive signal had called the nation out. Indeed, everyone interviewed seemed to have a single destination in mind: Jasna Gora Hill overlooking the town of Czestochowa. All eyes except Father Kosinski's turned to the Abbot. What did he make of such news?

"We Poles are about to teach an old lesson to your Italian friends in the Vatican." Abbot Kordecki smiled first at Kosinski and then at his guests. "But there. The bell is sounding for chapel. His Holiness will be waiting for me." The Abbot switched the radio off and rose from his chair.

"Father Kosinski will escort you to the Chapel of Our Lady." He paused for a second before hurrying off toward the papal apartment. "Once prayers are over, I think we can safely make that call to the Nuncio in Warsaw."

As the pealing of the bells faded in the evening of May 12, the pews of Our Lady's Chapel at Jasna Gora were already filled with white-robed Pauline monks kneeling in silent prayer, heads bowed before the Tabernacle and before the Icon of the Mother keeping vigil above her divine Son's Presence. At the sound of a quiet pattern of footsteps along the center aisle, an overwhelming sense of privilege and hope swept through the community. Once again robed in white, the Pope walked confidently to the prie-dieu in front of the High Altar. There he stood for one golden moment of silence, his arms crossed on his chest, his face lifted, his eyes fixed on the face of the Mother.

Finally the Holy Father knelt down. His voice resonant, he began the ancient invocations. *"Maryjo! Królowo Polski!"*

"Mary! Queen of Poland!" With one voice and one heart, the kneeling monks repeated the opening words of prayer. Nor did they doubt that their chant was echoed among God's Saints in Heaven, among the Souls in Purgatory, in the voices and hearts of Poland's faithful sons and daughters everywhere on earth.

"Hail Mary! Full of grace . . ." As the sounds from the Chapel wafted into the isolation of his rooms in the Musicians Houses, Monsignore Michalik tried the telephone for the hundredth time. No use. He tried the door again. No use. *"Jestem przy Tobie!"* There was that awful chant again, come back to deepen the Monsignore's misery in this place. "We are with you! We remember! We are on the alert!"

"We'll remember all right, Abbot Kordecki!" Michalik devised his own impious response to the refrain.

"O Lady of Czestochowa . . ." The Monsignore covered his ears, but that was no use either. "O Mary, we ask you. Bless all your children . . ."

Michalik sank into a chair and rocked back and forth in his anguish. "We'll remember, Kordecki. . . ." Over and again he hissed his acrid vow and yearned for silence. "We'll remember. . . . We'll remember. . . ."

"Your Eminence, I'm sure I don't know why it took so long for the call to come through. It was the Abbot himself who telephoned, and we all know how careless of time these cloistered monks can be." After Kordecki had finally confirmed the Slavic Pope's safe arrival at Jasna Gora, His Excellency Alberto Vacchi-Khouras thought it best to check in with Cardinal Maestroianni one last time before setting out from the Apostolic Nunciature on Warsaw's Miodowa Street. This was a unique mission, after all, one that His Eminence had said would long be recorded in the history books, one that would, therefore, guarantee His Excellency's own future career within the Curia of the new Roman Pontiff.

"Yes, Eminence." The Nuncio fiddled with the red folder on his desk. "I have all the documents right here, and I know the appropriate remarks to be made to—er—His Holiness. . . . Yes, Eminence. The beginning of a new era for the Church, I quite agree. . . . No, Eminence. The Abbot's delay should cause no difficulty in our schedule. The road from the capital to Czestochowa is the best highway in Poland. It will take an hour and a half maximum to reach the Monastery. Once I have the Pope's signature on the Protocol, it will be a quick run back to Warsaw's Okecie Airport to catch the special charter flight to Rome. There's plenty of time."

❑ ❑ ❑ ❑

Cardinal Maestroianni frowned as he hung up the phone in his study. It was all very well for Vacchi-Khouras to be so confident. But as Camerlengo, His Eminence was the only one who could appreciate the awesomeness of his position. Only he had charge of all matters concerning the papacy as high office, and the management of the due transference of papal power. In his need to work off a sudden case of nerves, the little Cardinal began to pace about among the stacks of books and monographs piled on the tables. There could be no question of going to bed tonight. Not with such great burdens resting on his shoulders.

To proceed with plans on a straight line, Maestroianni knew, he and his colleagues would have to hew closely to ecclesiastical tradition and Church legislation. Exactitude was the essential characteristic of sacrosanct tradition and detailed legislation. The sole aim of tradition and law alike was to ensure that the man chosen to succeed a former Pope would be unmistakably and manifestly God's choice, the chosen one of the Holy Spirit. Every action was laid out to that end. Each step had to conform to law and tradition. Otherwise, the canonical legality of the whole process could be challenged.

Normally, of course, a new Pope was chosen only when an old Pope had died. The complicating factor this time was that the Church had a Pope who was very much alive. Canonically speaking, therefore, the position taken by the Council of State—the position, that is, of Maestroianni himself, together with Cardinals Palombo, Aureatini, Pensabene, Graziani and a few others—that the living Pope had virtually resigned was of paramount importance.

Maestroianni assured himself that the action under way not only was logical but enjoyed some canonical basis. Any Pope could resign without any obligation to explain why he resigned. Further, the phrasing of the Resignation Protocol created the impression that His Holiness had left it to the Council of State to judge whether he was so incapacitated as to be gently "resigned."

Logically, Maestroianni was on the firmest possible ground. For one thing, the Slavic Pope had actually and openly discussed the possibility of resigning with several among his household; with Cardinal Secretary of State Graziani, for one. More, he had acquiesced in the need to seek the common will of his in-house Cardinals before he undertook his Russia pilgrimage. And now he had even allowed himself and his papal party to be hustled off to the isolated, backwater town Czestochowa. He had not protested. He had not refused to go along. He had not insisted on returning to Rome.

If it was fair to say that success in this entire matter was measured by the acquiescence of the Slavic Pope in the arrangements made by the Council of State, what was the worry? From the beginning of his pontificate, it had been the same story. Except for abortion and contraception, the lesson was clear and consistent. The Slavic Pope had always acquiesced. "And besides . . ." Maestroianni began to mutter aloud to himself as he wandered and pondered among his books on this sleepless night. "When all is said and done in this matter of utmost gravity, we have historical precedent on our side. This case of papal succession is not much different from the case of Pope Celestine V."

With all his reverence for history's footsteps, the little Cardinal had boned up on the dark lessons to be learned from the record in Celestine's regard. Until now, his had been the only other authentic case of papal resignation in the annals of the Church. And while it had taken place as long ago as 1294, there was more than enough evidence to show that Celestine, too, had been the victim of deliberate deception and entrapment by his eventual successor, Cardinal Benedetto Caetani. Curiously, that Pope's enemies also had sought to confine him physically. He, too, had become a virtual prisoner. In fact, he had died of "an infection" in the Tower of Castel Fumone east of Ferentino only a few months into his confinement.

"Beh!" Maestroianni scolded himself as he bustled back to his cluttered writing table. Not that he wavered at the thought of Celestine's fate. But he had wasted enough time on the Slavic Pope. It would be far more fruitful to review plans for the events that were now just hours away and that he would have to manage with as much sanity and dignity as possible.

The most serious item for His Eminence had to do with the Synod of bishops set to convene at eight in the morning. At that meeting, with members of the press attending, Maestroianni aimed to accomplish a three-point agenda. First, he would call for a final vote to clarify—to "globalize" as Pensabene had said—the results of the Common Mind Vote. To that end, Cardinal Aureatini had prepared a splendid array of visuals and graphics to demonstrate that the single most important item of concern for a majority of the Church's bishops was a fear for their internal cohesion and unity around the venerable See of Peter in Rome. There should be no difficulty about this point, Maestroianni told himself, except perhaps to avoid a raucous stampede of assent and acclaim for formal recognition of such a widespread feeling.

Next Maestroianni would call for a vote of gratitude and blessing for the signal services of the Slavic Pope. He had no doubt that a number of bishops would complain that their all-important unity had been rendered fragile during the past papacy. Still, any spontaneous speeches to that effect would only play into Maestroianni's hand. He intended to point out that the difficulty had been the fault of no particular individual; that it had merely been the result of unfavorable conditions arising in the Roman administration and in the various dioceses of the Church. Indeed, it was this very state of affairs—the bishops' worry over failing unity and the inability of the past papacy to remedy the problem—that had led the Holy

Father and the Council of State to agree on a formal papal resignation, to be followed forthwith by a new papal Conclave.

"*Optime,* Cosimo!" Maestroianni congratulated himself as he reviewed his plans to that point. "*Optime!*"

To cover the third element of the agenda, the Cardinal would have to gamble. To bring the Church into line with the forward footsteps of history, the Holy See's backward and often obstructionist influence on the bishops around the world would have to be blunted. A dilution of the central authority of the papacy was essential. It was not enough simply to remove the present Pontiff. The moment had come to prepare the world for a not distant future when Popes would be truly and democratically elected by all the pastors of the Church. The trick for Maestroianni was to inaugurate that decentralizing process and still keep firm control. He intended to throw the floor of the Synod open to let all the bishops have their say. To increase their already increasing appetite for a broad democratization of Church structure, even to the point of urging them to ask direct questions of the principal papal candidates. "Share with us," he intended to say to his Reverend Brothers in a grandiose invitation. "Tell us your hopes, your aspirations, your ideas. Let a thousand flowers blossom!"

Thanks to the heroic labors of Monsignore Christian Gladstone, of course, and thanks to the time the Camerlengo himself had spent with the bishops over the past week, the gamble wasn't as terrible as it might otherwise have been. Those questionnaires Gladstone had worked so hard to complete were nothing less than pastoral and dogmatic position papers for virtually every bishop presently in Rome. And because he himself had spoken with every one of those bishops, Maestroianni felt he knew what to expect.

As he rehearsed the roster of issues he expected to blossom like flowers on the floor of Saturday morning's Synod, Maestroianni's fit of nerves ebbed and flowed by turns. Certainly some of the bishops in the Synod would be hard to handle. Their mood was festive, upbeat and triumphalistic. Their gatherings over the past five days had been filled with unruly speeches and with an infectious current of self-congratulatory happiness. At times, it had almost seemed they were something more than an assembly of individual bishops. Something on the order of a highly organized array of parties and factions who had been talking and networking among themselves to a degree even Maestroianni had neither planned nor expected. The little Cardinal had a remotely queasy feeling that he himself might be out of step. That he might not be able to control the bishops. That he was no longer truly in charge.

"What idiocy!" His Eminence beat back all such demons of doubt with a vengeance. Another rehearsal of his program for Saturday morning's Synod, and for the Consistory to follow at noon, buoyed his gumption again. Instead of queasy misgivings, he began to feel the first stirrings of what he had labored so long to create. He began at last to understand how it felt to be counted among history's chosen few. To be one of the world's master engineers!

Still, somewhere deep inside him there remained a remote sense of unease. It troubled the Cardinal, for example, that Monsignore Christian Gladstone had chosen to leave Rome at such a capital moment. It was a minor thing, of course, surely no more than a temporary lapse of judgment. And there was every likelihood that he would return in time to take part in the monumental events of Saturday, just as Taco Manuguerra had said. Why, then, this disproportionate sense of dissatisfaction concerning Monsignore Christian?

Probably, Maestroianni reasoned, it had less to do with Gladstone than with the venom of Cardinal Aureatini's reaction to the news of the American's abrupt departure. It was unaccountable that Aureatini should have kept repeating his charge that a man like Gladstone could endanger all their plans for Holy Mother Church. Was he to put Aureatini's attack down to jumpy nerves, now that the great operation of changing Popes had actually begun? Was it Aureatini's dislike of Americans? Was it a ploy—an old one—to wreck Gladstone's chances of advancement? Slander, calumny and lies were the ever ready arrows in the quiver of every bureaucrat to dispose of rivals, and Maestroianni had made it plain that he had marked Monsignore Christian out for preferential treatment.

As he examined the puzzle, Maestroianni began to realize that the deeper question here was why he should care at all what Aureatini thought of Christian Gladstone. He began to realize that he truly liked this American. That he had always preferred the Gladstones of this life to the Aureatinis. That all the principal actors and agents in this entire project often palled on him, in fact. That he disliked such an untouchable ecclesiastical cactus as Cardinal Palombo, for instance, whose words always seemed to carry a wound and a sting.

Maestroianni had just begun to rouse himself from such dangerously honest musings when one of those actors and agents—the prickly Noah Palombo himself—rang through on His Eminence's private line to ask if there had been any news yet from Monsignore Vacchi-Khouras.

"Do not trouble yourself, Eminence," the Camerlengo cooed to the cactus. "Well before our historic Consistory opens at noon, we will be in possession of the fully signed and duly sealed Resignation Protocol. His Excellency has everything in hand."

Once his Mercedes-Benz reached Warsaw's suburbs and picked up speed on the highway, His Excellency Alberto Vacchi-Khouras rested his head on the back of the seat and closed his eyes. In his mind's eye, he reviewed the documents in the red folder resting safely on the front seat beside his personal secretary. He went over the appropriate remarks he would make in his interview with the Slavic Pope. He imagined the moment when, his mission fulfilled, he would reach Rome bearing a copy of the legal instrument, *De Successione Papali,* signed and sealed by His Holiness in the presence of His Excellency and one more witness.

As one of the few Palestinian Christians ever to carve out a high-ranking career in the Vatican diplomatic corps, Vacchi-Khouras had never doubted he had a special destiny. Now his every expectation was about to be fulfilled. Of all human beings alive, he had been selected to witness and accept the resignation of a reigning Pope. Imagine! Only once before in two thousand years had such an event taken place.

He was just beginning to imagine the upward pathways that were opening to him when he became aware of the raucous sounds of traffic. Odd, he thought, that there should be so much movement at such an hour. But a lazy glance through the tinted windows explained everything. Just a lot of carts and trucks and such; probably the first early convoys of fresh vegetables heading for the city markets.

The Nuncio roused himself. It never hurt to see that everything was in perfect order. He flicked a button to open the partition and asked his secretary for the red folder. That was when he realized that the car had slowed considerably.

"We're traveling at a snail's pace, man!" Vacchi-Khouras tapped the chauffeur on the shoulder.

"Yes, Excellency. It's the traffic. It's getting thicker as we progress."

"Thicker? Outbound traffic shouldn't be getting thicker; not at this hour."

"Please, Excellency. Look again carefully. This traffic is definitely going our way. And it's definitely getting thicker." The Nuncio zipped the tinted windows down on both sides of his car. Immediately a medley of sounds poured in along with a wash of rain from a sudden squall. Radios blared with music and news. Klaxons sounded. They were surrounded by an amazing array of conveyances.

"Do something useful!" Vacchi-Khouras snapped the order to his secretary as he closed the windows. "Call someone. Find out if we can escape this mess. We're losing valuable time."

"I have roused the substitute on duty at the Nunciature, Excellency." The secretary held up the cellular phone in a helpless bit of show-and-tell. "He says heavy squalls are predicted to continue, and that the highway is crowded."

"I can see that much for myself!" His Excellency turned to the driver again. "There!" Take that exit. Let's make time on the side roads and get back to the highway up ahead."

The maneuver worked. The Mercedes picked up speed over a rough country road. But His Excellency had hardly finished grumbling that he had to do the thinking for everyone when they found themselves engulfed again by a jumble of traffic—automobiles, bicycles, motorbikes, men and women and young boys and girls walking, families riding on drays. It was as if all of Poland were headed for a midnight picnic in the pouring rain.

As his limousine inched back toward the highway, and with not even a signpost in view to tell him where he was, Vacchi-Khouras gave way by turns to a series of fits and to moderately consoling thoughts. This situation was demonstrably not his fault, he told himself on the one hand. It was a temporary setback. He could wait it out. Yet it was unthinkable, he raged on the other hand, that his mission—his entire career—should be at the mercy of a classic gridlock.

"Get me the Ministry of the Interior on the telephone!" Unable to restrain himself, Vacchi-Khouras fairly screamed at his secretary.

After an excruciating delay, His Excellency found himself dealing with a sleepy night watchman at the Ministry of the Interior in Warsaw. No, the fellow said; he could not reach the Minister. The Minister was out of the country. No, he said, he didn't know who the Deputy Minister was. Yes, he could telephone the Air Ministry for His Excellency and ask for an airlift. But where exactly was His Excellency? Where? Somewhere between Warsaw and Czestochowa? Perhaps His Excellency would care to call again when His Excellency knew where His Excellency was. After 10 A.M. would be best. Monday to Friday. . . .

"Yes, Your Eminence." At the sound of Cardinal Maestroianni's voice, the harried young man on Friday-night duty at the Nunciature in Poland thought the phone might turn to ice in his hand. "His Excellency Vacchi-Khouras asked me to relay the message to no one but Your Eminence. . . . Yes, Eminence. He's been in touch with us by cellular phone several times during the evening. Constantly, you might say. . . . No, Your Eminence. His Excellency advises that he is unlikely to make Rome before noon. In fact, he doubts he will get to Czestochowa before midmorning. . . . Yes, Eminence. We have checked the situation. There is an extraordinary flow of traffic jamming the entire one hundred twenty-five miles of the highway between Warsaw and Czestochowa. There is no possibility of his turning back. I'm afraid reports have gotten around that the Holy Father may be overnighting at Czestochowa Monastery, but we haven't confirmed a definite connection between one thing and the other. . . .

"Yes, Eminence, I'll relay the instructions. Yes, I have it word for word. His Excellency is to keep going, no matter how slow his progress. He is to secure the signature of His Holiness before midday. He is to understand that the document's immediate presence in Rome is not essential. The signing is."

The Camerlengo had more than a fit of nerves as he disconnected the call from Warsaw. Gridlock on the main highway to Czestochowa in the wee hours of an ordinary Saturday morning? Was this a normal thing in Poland? Or was it rather the shadow of things to come? Was he going to have to contend with huge popular rallies in favor of the Slavic Pope? And not only in Poland? Maestroianni shuddered at the nightmarish image of a couple of hundred thousand fervent supporters of the Slavic Pope jamming the space between the doors of St. Peter's and the river Tiber. He could practically see all those dreadful charismatics jumping about, shattering the privacy of every room in the Vatican with their screams to the Holy Spirit. Or, worse still, all those dreadful television cameras homing in on the spectacle, recording the triple beat of the thunderous cry: *Papa! Papa! Papa!*

Such was his momentary panic that the Cardinal actually reached for his telephone. But wait. Think about it. What would be the point of disturbing the other members of the Council of State? No doubt Their Eminences were all tucked away in their beds by now. And anyway, there was nothing they could do except natter at him.

"Hang on to your nerves, Cosimo." His Eminence straightened his mind with a quick reality check. "Plans have been well laid. Crowds or no, Vacchi-Khouras will get through. Crowds or no, the Pope isn't going anywhere. He's boxed in. He will sign. Meanwhile, his initials on the Protocol and his unprotesting retirement to Jasna Gora can lead to only one conclusion. He has clearly acquiesced in the Council's decision that his latest physical weakness was an indication of papal incapacity."

The Camerlengo removed his hand from the telephone. "Just hang on to your nerves," he said again. "And remember who's in charge here."

LIV

FOR LONG YEARS after these disturbing times were over, men and women throughout Poland would tell how, suddenly and as if from nowhere, a message had spread to town, to hamlet, to city: "The Slavic Pope is in Czestochowa! Our Holy Father is at Jasna Gora!" They would tell how they had gone to greet him, protect him, support him, show solidarity with him. They would tell how all the lights in all the streets and all the houses in the town of Czestochowa had been turned on to welcome them. They would tell how they had gathered in their thousands and tens of thousands under carpets of clouds that stormy night on Jasna Gora Hill; how the lights on the Monastery walls had shone down on them; how they had sung and prayed and talked and cheered. And they would tell how, throughout it all, there had seemed to be a wordless dialogue between them and the white-robed figure framed in the light of the covered balcony far above them—how he and they had seemed content to be in each other's presence; to rely on one another; to share a communion in faith.

"There must be a million people down there!" Damien Slattery kept his voice low. Looking out on the scene from one of the east-facing windows of the Pontiff's apartment, he and Gutmacher and Lucadamo and the other members of the papal party felt like intruders. It was as if the current of feeling they sensed between the crowds below and the Holy Father standing alone on the nearby balcony was privileged, sacred, private.

"And thousands more will come, my friend." Abbot Kordecki came up beside Damien. "I've seen this happen before, on one of his earliest visits here as Pope. It was the height of his clash with the Stalinist government of Poland, and he was overnighting here. Then, too, the people began to assemble spontaneously around Jasna Gora Hill. Standing on that same balcony, His Holiness never made a formal speech. Every so often he gave his blessing or made some gesture with his hands, much as he's doing now. But he never once lost control of those crowds. That's the way it is with him.

"The Stalinists had never seen anything like it. Few people have. They threw a steel ring around this place. Called in an entire armored division. But still the people came. A million and a half flocked in from all over Poland. They flooded the tanks with their sheer numbers. They lay down in front of them; squatted on top of them; blocked their caterpillar treads; draped flowers on them; poured Holy Water down their gun muzzles; recited the Rosary on their turrets. They nullified them. Rendered them pointless. It was something to see, Father Slattery. The way those bullyboys withdrew, with the crowds jeering and cheering and chanting hymns at them."

As Father Abbot told the story of that now distant day, Damien and his companions began to feel the enormous multitude as a living, breathing organism. The sounds of talking and praying, shouting and singing, chanting and cheering allowed them to hope that this would be the turning point. That the Pontiff would see this manifestation of the faithful as the sign he had been seeking from Heaven. That he would not accept resignation and retirement from the papacy. That he would return to the Holy See and resume its governance, which, anyway, he had not yet formally renounced.

And yet, even as they gazed down on the crowded slopes of Jasna Gora Hill and the vast basin of land farther on, Father Gutmacher and Giustino Lucadamo exchanged a glance of perfect understanding. It was far from certain that anything—even a demonstration like this by his faithful Catholics—would shake the Slavic Pope from his curious, almost mystical mind-set of calm acceptance.

The Czech Army helicopter bearing Christian Gladstone wound in and out along the dark contours of gently rolling hills, until the lights of the town and the Monastery above it came into view. A few minutes more, and the craft dropped down to a landing outside Lubomirski Gate.

"We saw your approach, Father, and we've been expecting you." Abbot Kordecki introduced himself the moment Gladstone cleared the rotor blades. The helicopter revved up and took off for Radomsko aerodrome; but as soon as Kordecki could be heard again, he made his disappointment clear. Hadn't Monsignore Gladstone come to take His Holiness out? Shouldn't the helicopter wait, then?

"No, Father Abbot." Chris followed Kordecki through the double gates. There was no smile or trace of pleasantness in his person. "That's not the plan. They will come back for His Holiness if he chooses. But *he* must choose."

"Holiness." In the corridor where the Pontiff waited to receive him, Gladstone dropped to one knee and kissed the Fisherman's ring. Slattery was the first one to come forward then, followed by Lucadamo and Sadowski and Gutmacher and the others. All were eager for Gladstone's news. But Damien cut the greetings short with a little gesture to his companions as a sign that they should all follow the Abbot's pointed example and withdraw. It would be best to leave Pope and priest alone.

"No, Damien." Though he sought permission from the Pontiff with his eyes, Chris spoke more in command than request. "We have little time left, Holy Father. And I do have to speak with Your Holiness. But we are all of us together on the edge of this abyss. What happens now happens to us all. Either we all win. Or we all lose."

By way of answer, the Pontiff turned his back to the corridor. Without a word, he crossed the living room to the balcony where he could look out toward the lights of Czestochowa and take strength from the still gathering crowds.

"Did you know, Monsignore . . ." The Pope acknowledged Gladstone's presence behind him without turning his head. "Did you know that it was here, in 1966, that over a million people assembled for the consecration of Poland to Mary as the nation's Queen?"

Christian glanced down at the thousands of lights on Jasna Gora Hill, at the thousands of lights in Czestochowa, at the dark basin beyond. He stepped back and glanced at the men waiting in the living room: at Father Gutmacher and Monsignore Sadowski settling down to recite the Rosary together, at Giustino Lucadamo perched on the edge of a large writing table, at Lázaro-Falla and Dr. Fanarote talking quietly, at Damien Slattery standing at the balcony door, his eyebrows knit, his normally ruddy complexion gone ashen-gray with inner pain and apprehension, his eyes fixed on Gladstone. But the one thing Chris did not do was answer the Slavic Pope.

Like Slattery and all the others, he, too, felt the bond between the crowd and their supreme pastor. Yet he entertained no illusions. He knew better than any in that little group of loyalists what bitter discouragement had afflicted the mind and soul of the Pontiff. He had frequented the Slavic Pope's enemies. He had experienced firsthand the hate and disrespect those enemies nourished for the Pontiff; had tasted the unpleasant reality of their desire to end his pontificate. He knew what a relief it would be for the Holy Father to escape that hate, to be free once and for all from the bitterness that had filled the days and nights of his reign. Resignation and retirement promised a release, such a wish for easement.

For all of those reasons and because he knew the news he carried would add a terrible dimension to the bitterness so often spewed at this man, Gladstone wanted Christ's embattled Vicar to take the measure of what was happening. He wanted his Pope to think all the thoughts provoked by this unexpected outpouring of support by a nation of Catholics assembling spontaneously in front of his eyes. This man who was about to renounce the papacy—this man who had been assured he could no longer hold the people of God together as their supreme pastor—had to see that there was an ecclesial as well as a spiritual dimension to this event.

"Shall I be pleased you came, Monsignore?" At last he turned to Gladstone. His Holiness' question made it seem as though he had read the young man's mind.

"Only a quasi-miracle of goodwill for Your Holiness has made my journey possible, Holy Father. Goodwill on the part of strangers and faithful alike has made everything possible."

"To make everything possible would be more than a quasi-miracle, Monsignore Christian." The Pope was being contentious, but he had given Chris the opening he wanted.

"The aim has been to make one thing possible, Holy Father." Gladstone withdrew the double-sealed envelope from his inner pocket and laid it face up on the balcony ledge. "Lucifer has been enthroned within the precincts of the Holy See on Vatican Hill. The documentation is all there. Names. The rites used. All the factual data. Most of it is in microcopy, except for the testimony of Your Holiness' recent predecessor and a brief inscription prepared by Father Aldo Carnesecca."

"Carnesecca!" The Pontiff repeated the name as an exclamation of poignancy and deepest regret. He took the envelope in both hands. Examined the two papal inscriptions on its face. Saw the dates. Read Father Aldo's trenchant hands-off warning. Read the old Pope's letter. "So . . ." He wasn't talking to Gladstone; wasn't looking at him even. "I knew . . . No wonder we couldn't . . ."

The Pope's words were so indistinct against the rising murmur of the crowds that Chris didn't catch them, but he followed every move with his eyes. Watched the Pontiff finger the remaining contents of the envelope; watched his face take on a frightful aspect; watched him retreat a step backward toward the living room.

"You've read all the documentation, Monsignore Christian?"

"All of it, Holy Father. Every word warrants and guarantees what I have said." Gladstone battled a wave of desperation and discouragement that swept over him. The voice of his faith reminded him that this was his Pope, the Pope Christ had willed the Church to have at this point in time; that he had to be faithful to him unto death. But the voice of his logic warned him that this man was on the brink of accepting his fate as a Pope who resigned; that he was within a millimeter of total acquiescence in Satan's fait accompli.

"At this moment in history, Holy Father"—Christian put his case straight out—"only one man stands between us and the summary evil of our ancient Adversary. As Pope, you are the buffer God has placed between us and Lucifer. I know it must make you quail to be told this. But my words are no more than a reminder of the Blessed Virgin's description of your papacy. An echo of her description of you as 'the last Pope of these Catholic times.' " Gladstone knew the Pontiff understood his cryptic reference to a personal revelation made by the Virgin Mother within the context of her famed appearance at Fatima. The Holy Father was a firm believer in the authenticity of that revelation. And yet, at this moment, he seemed unwilling to make the connection between the enthronement and the prophecy.

"Your Holiness is not an ordinary man." Christian drilled that connection home. "Your Holiness is the only official human representative on earth of the King of the Universe. Why else call you, a mere mortal man, our Holy Father, if not because of that sacrosanct and holy office? You personally are supposed to combat the principal Adversary of your King. But now that Adversary, the Prince, has been surreptitiously enthroned in what should be the Holy of Holies on this earth. He has actually been installed in the house in which you reside.

"So I say again, Holy Father. At this moment, you are the one human being on the face of this earth who is guaranteed the personal power of enchaining Lucifer. Of binding him in shackles. Of casting him back into the pit of Hell. And I say this: faced with the brutal effects of the enthronement in the Holy of Holies, it is unacceptable that you should wish to retire. To resign. To make the ultimate act of acquiescence."

"Have I a viable alternative, Monsignore?" The Pontiff dropped his arms to his side.

Gladstone shook his head. "If Your Holiness chooses to remain cooped up here, the answer is no. The Apostolic Nuncio will arrive. When he does, given the forces gathered against Your Holiness—and given the degree to which Your Holiness has already agreed to be co-opted—I do not believe you will be able to refuse your signature on the Resignation Protocol. If Your Holiness remains here at this Monastery, that is surely what will happen."

"I repeat, Monsignore." Still trapped behind the barricade of his mind-set, the Pope merely broadened the scope of his question. "Have I a viable alternative?"

"Is Your Holiness asking if you have a physical means of getting out of here with impunity?"

"That's only part of it . . ."

"Agreed, Holiness. But an important part. And the answer this time is yes. The helicopter that brought me here is waiting at Radomsko aerodrome. In less than an hour, a chartered jetliner will come in from Belgium. As the lawful successor to the Great Fisherman, Your Holiness has been granted a new papal plane. Fisherman One. The pilot has permission to remain on the ground for two hours. If you choose, Holy Father, you can be on that plane before sunrise. Well before the Apostolic Nuncio arrives. Your Holiness can be in Rome before the final blasphemous deception is perpetrated on the Church and the wide world at noon today."

"Wait, Monsignore! Wait, please!" The Pontiff's interruption was not a summary objection. Simply, Gladstone's proposal was too abrupt, too much to assimilate suddenly and on the spot; it called for too violent a departure from that mind-set of his. "You know me, Monsignore. You know how I have proceeded. The most compelling thing for me has always been the unity of the Church. For that reason, I have agreed with my Venerable Brothers, the Cardinals. I have preferred to see in their judgment a sure sign of what the Lord wants of me. I have always sought a sign of God's blessing in the reactions of those nearest me in our service of the Lord. I must ask you, then, Monsignore. Do you take it that your own arrival here and the sudden gathering of Poles around Jasna Gora are supernatural signs of God's will?"

"No, Holiness!" Until now, Gladstone had spoken firmly, but without passion, as if he had come merely to present travel options. Only his eyes had betrayed the cauldron of feeling steaming inside him. But it was too much to hear a question like that in circumstances like this.

"These are not supernatural signs, Holy Father! I and the others who have acted with me have done what we have by our own choice. That we have so far succeeded is a strong indication for us that God has accepted our offer of service and has blessed our plans. But it was our doing by our free choice. And so, too, for the people who have gathered here on this hill. The Poles have been moved by the spirit that possesses them as the people of God. But it is their free choice to gather here around Your Holiness."

By this time, every one of those six men standing in the room behind them was aware that Gladstone was forcing the Slavic Pope away from simple acquiescence. That, one way or the other, the Pontiff would have to make a choice; that he would decide the future of his pontificate; their own future; the future of the Church.

The Pope stepped slowly back toward the balcony rail, where he could, when he chose, glance at the crowds. "These days, Monsignore Christian,

I have meditated long on those words Jesus said to Peter about how, when he became old, others would bind him and lead him where he would not choose to go. . . ."

"Holy Father!" If this was to be a farewell speech all gussied up in more talk of signs from Heaven, Gladstone refused to hear it. He held nothing back now. His entire being—mind, nerves, heart and soul—was strung out along the thinnest edge of survival. "Please do not think of yourself as even remotely included in what the Lord said to Peter on that occasion! Nobody has bound your arms. Nobody has forced you to go where you didn't want to go. You have simply acquiesced in the results of a greater cunning than you can muster. It is true that you are the lawful successor to Peter. That you are Peter in that sense. It's true that Peter once took it into his head to leave Rome. No doubt he thought that best for the good of the Church. If he could escape being killed, the Church would benefit. And we all know the story of how Christ Himself met Peter in his headlong flight from Rome along the Via Appia Antica. Met him. Reproached him. Sent him back to his post. And to his death.

"But please, Holiness. There is no way on the face of God's earth that Your Holiness can compare where you are now to where Peter was that day. This is not the Via Appia Antica, and the men ready to take your place in Peter's chair are not in the line of men like Linus or Clement or Cletus who took Peter's place. This is an obscure little corner of the world chosen by the enemies of Christ's Church. This is the hole in which men like Maestroianni and Palombo and Aureatini intend to bury you and, with you, the papacy itself as an institution.

"No, Holy Father! You have allowed yourself to be persuaded that, for the good of the Church, you should accept the renegade judgment of the Council of State. By your own choice, you have allowed yourself to be taken into seclusion. But if you consent any further—if you wait for the Nuncio—you will complete the abandonment of your post. An abandonment of fifteen years' duration."

"Abandonment, Monsignore?" The Pontiff recoiled. He knew Gladstone was a man of temper; but no one had ever spoken such harsh words to his face. "Abandonment? And fifteen years of it? Surely not!"

"Yes, Holy Father. I must insist you listen to me about this!"

"I am listening, Monsignore! How have I abandoned my faithful?"

"Better than anyone within or outside the Church, you know that every statistic shows that the Catholic Church is going down. Corrupted from within, it is being marginalized, displaced and corroded as a public institution and as a personal religion. Your Holiness knows that. We have made sure you know. We have filled your ears with audio reports and your eyes with video documents. We have piled your desk high with detailed studies. But even without those reports, you knew. As the best-informed man in Christendom, you knew that the vast majority of your Catholics were being led by the nose away from our sacred Catholic traditions. You knew they were being led into a new form of ersatz Christianity that none of your predecessors could recognize as Catholicism. Not Pope Pius XII. Not Pius XI. Not Pius X. Not Pius IX. None of them.

"Yet, what have you done to arrest that deterioration, Holiness? You speak of your search for unity. But you have abandoned your seminarians to heretical teachers. You have abandoned your parish faithful to dissident, yes, to immoral bishops and Cardinals. You have abandoned your schoolchildren to a non-Catholic system and your nuns to a destroying wave of secularizing feminists. You protected none of them. Not even our sacred buildings themselves. You have allowed our very churches and chapels to be denuded of Altar and Tabernacle, of Confessional and Statue. In all of that, you have acquiesced continually. And now you are on the brink of acquiescing in the liquidation of your own pontificate."

Gladstone stopped as abruptly as he had begun. What was the use? He could feel the Pontiff receding into the inner sanctum of his own mind. His words were like dead stones falling on tin; so much sound, and no more.

In the silence that fell between them, the Pontiff's face flushed with color. It wasn't anger he felt, but a deeper emotion only he had known. A terrible consciousness. A sense of standing completely alone. Behind him was the whole people of God for whom he, as Pope, was the Almighty's sole earthly representative. In front of him, the abyss of God's immeasurable being and infinite power.

"Just a simple sign of God's intention." The words came haltingly, gently from the Pontiff's lips. "All along I have waited for a sign of God's holy will."

The effect on Gladstone was devastating. He was staring at failure; and the reality of the situation struck him so cruelly that his face went white. In those two sentences, the Pope had given a summary of his attitude. He had spelled out the rule by which he was judging his present situation, Christian's words, his own next moves.

Chris felt a desperate need to call out for divine help; a desire to pray that was painful in its intensity. The pressure that had been mounting for days threatened to go over the edge of his control into helpless despair. Was this to be the sum total of his achievement? To hear his Pope, the most divinely empowered human individual alive, hold back timorously? In a concrete situation in which the safety and integrity of Christ's Church was at stake, could he elicit no more than a querulous, insistent plea for a sign? Had he come this far only to be witness to a Pope—the man who should be the very pillar of Roman Catholicism's willingness to take on the entire world—reduced to the condition of a hesitant septuagenarian looking for a bargain with the Almighty?

His own resolve almost broken, Chris fought against his emotions. He searched the Pontiff's face with his eyes. He noted all the devastations of time's onrush, the unrelenting depredations of age. Once upon a recent time, he thought, this man had been a rampant lion let loose by providence on the U.S.S.R.; and he had ravaged that colossus into disintegration.

And then, as suddenly as thunder, Chris understood. Compassion, the firstborn of genuine love, poured fresh insight into his soul for this most widely known of twentieth-century Popes. Insight into much more than his undoubted moral virtue and his uncanny geopolitical foresight. Insight into his peculiar destiny. Insight, above all, into his fatal weaknesses.

This Pontiff had won his great victory over Soviet Marxism. And he had enabled millions already born and millions more yet unborn to escape the cruelest tyranny so far realized by evil hearts. But he had achieved that victory in the name of human solidarity. And once he had done that—once this Pope had acted successfully in the name of human solidarity as the indestructible cement of human fraternity; of human identity as a family—he and his papacy had been co-opted into the building of that solidarity. Thus, the essential mission of the Catholic Church had been mongrelized. For, in sacred principle, Pope and papacy are not supposed to act as surrogates for human solidarity, but for the kingdom and the regime of Jesus of Nazareth as Lord of human history. Nevertheless, he as Pope, and his administration as the papacy, were aligned with a purely human goal.

In the empathy of his humanitarian feeling, he never explicitly spoke of that Jesus of Nazareth as the King of nations, but of the solidarity he hoped would be fostered through transnational organizations. He didn't consistently present himself in globalist meetings of the nations as the all-important Vicar of that Jesus. His favorite description of himself was something as disarming—as anodyne—as "I, a son of humanity and Bishop of Rome." Nor did he inculcate the truth of Roman Catholicism as the explicit will of Jesus, but rather as ethical rules; as conditions deduced by human reason for safeguarding the solidarity of the human family.

Still, to say that the Slavic Pope had been co-opted by circumstances was not to say that he did not act on his own choice. On the contrary. Nobody could deny this man's belief in the divine person and role of Jesus of Nazareth and Calvary. No one could cast suspicion on his personal integrity or doubt his innate piety. But it was by choice that he spoke in the language of his contemporaries, not in the well-known accents of Roman Pontiffs, stating that which is true about God. It was by choice that he removed Catholicism's icons from its sacred buildings—removed even the Body and Blood of Christ—in an effort to accommodate alien religious minds and the pagan rites of nonbelievers. It was by choice that he had relegated the panoply of his Catholicism to the background. By choice, he had frequented too much the company of non-Catholic prelates who never shared his Catholic faith, and of un-Catholic theologians who were devoid of Catholic piety.

Now, in the evening of his papacy, it was no longer easy for him to reach beyond the limits of human solidarity to proclaim the ancient message of the traditional papacy. It no longer seemed to occur to him to wield his papacy as a weapon. Hence, the facility with which he could consider resignation and retirement in the face of cunning he could not measure.

That whole tide of understanding rushed in on Gladstone in a matter of seconds. He knew now where this enigmatic Pope stood. And he knew there were only two possible means of turning him around. To persuade him to go back to Rome, if only for the time it would take to undo the enthronement, it would have to be urged on him as a basic duty to that human solidarity he had so signally vindicated, and of which he was now a prisoner. And it would have to be urged on him as a direct consequence of his particularly fervent devotion to Mary, the Mother of Jesus, to whom he had dedicated his pontificate.

"Holiness." Gladstone gathered his courage again. "Holiness, we have no need to request a miraculous sign—Christ appearing in all His glory to you or the sun dancing again in the skies. In a certain true sense, Your Holiness doesn't deserve that. But, more to the point right now, Your Holiness doesn't need that. We are not dealing with the Apocalyptic. Not yet! A minute ago, I mentioned the Virgin's description of you as 'the last Pope of these Catholic times.' If you accept that as authentically Mary's statement—and especially if you see it in the context of the men in Rome who would be Pope—are you not the last one capable of cleansing the Holy Basilica and the Vatican of any trace of Lucifer's enthronement?

"You have insisted that, from the beginning of our salvation by Our Lord Jesus, God has decided to deal with the world through His Blessed Mother. Again and again you have said that you yourself were chosen by God as Pope to be the special servant of His Mother. If you still claim total devotion to her, is it not your duty to trample on that most ancient enemy of the human race? It cannot be, then, Holy Father, that you will turn your back. That you will refuse to exercise the unique power Christ gave you. That you will shilly-shally away from your destiny as the last Pope of these Catholic times. That you will leave Lucifer and his in-house Curial agents free to wreak their blasphemous filth on Altar and Tabernacle and priesthood and papacy.

"Resign if you will, Holiness. But not yet! For the fate of your own soul, you cannot leave us naked and unprotected to face that Fallen Archangel who, in Peter's very words, seeks to devour us all like a ravenous lion. You cannot think that you can leave us in this lurch of evil. You cannot walk away from this papacy knowing you have left that supreme enemy in charge."

Christian had no more to say; no more to give. He was without further resources of energy. As he stood immobile beside the Pope waiting for his decision, his mind began to conjure up freeze-frame images of his earliest conversations with Aldo Carnesecca. Of that simple, greathearted priest who had understood the tactics in the global warfare of spirit that had nearly swallowed Christian whole.

Chris turned away from the Pope, away from the crowd. Turned to look at Angelo Gutmacher, his scarred face bowed in urgent prayer. He thought of that last week he and Father Angelo had spent together a lifetime ago at Windswept House. He saw again all the men and women who had come in such numbers looking for counsel, for comfort, for valid Sacraments they could no longer find elsewhere. He remembered how Gutmacher had come before dawn to the Tower Chapel at Windswept; how he had chided Chris—shamed him, even—for his hesitation in accepting the call to priestly service in Rome. He recalled Gutmacher's words about the dangers in Rome and about what the grace of God can achieve. He remembered how Cessi had embraced him that morning in Old Glad's Tower and, as the true Gladstone she was, had told him that Rome needed a good shaking-up.

He recalled how his own Stateside mission for this Pope had begun with such vibrant hope: how he had believed that the Holy Father really did want to take the measure of abuse in his Church; that he really would take a stand. He remembered how incensed he had been that the fiery-tempered, quick-fisted Michael O'Reilly had been fed to the wolves by weak-willed prelates, while a systematic ecclesiastical cover-up was allowed to flourish. "When the Holy Father does his duty in this diocese," O'Reilly had complained, "then he can put my affairs in order." That hadn't been a lot to ask. Like all the people gathered here on Jasna Gora Hill, O'Reilly wanted what had been promised. A leader. A shepherd who would be with his flock for all days.

Gladstone shifted his glance to Damien Slattery still keeping vigil in the doorway, and thought how he, too, had found his way to Windswept House after his priestly service had been trampled in Rome and then shredded by the apostate Cardinal of Centurycity. How he had rallied his courage nonetheless, and had insisted on doing a good job of work in America for this Slavic Pope. But that big Irishman's face now was so contorted with pain and puzzlement that Chris took the few steps needed to bring him to Slattery's side.

"Chris, what do you think?" Damien spoke in a hoarse whisper. "Is he or is he not going to come? And what do we do if he decides to stay put?"

Gladstone felt a sudden chill in his heart. He had no consoling word for Slattery in his misery. "We go back by ourselves, Damien, and we get crucified. But have we ever really known what drives this man? You know him as well as I do. Has he ever really eased our pain? Hasn't he left us in doubt perpetually? Left us so we can't be sure our priestly ordinations are valid; can't be sure you must be Roman Catholic to be saved? He's left us in severe doubt about so many vital issues; allowed us to be spiked on so many grave doubts.

"I'll keep at him." Chris was speaking through his tears now. "Maybe I can get him to budge. But I don't know, Damien. There are so many of us now, all heading for lifelong disaster. I know only that he has abandoned us piece by piece, in minor things and in major issues. Will this be any different? I don't know. . . ."

Chris moved forward onto the balcony again. He raised his eyes to the silent Pope while searing questions coursed through his mind. Can this be your answer, Holy Father? To Carnesecca? To Slattery and Gutmacher? To all of us? Silence?

Can this be what it all comes down to, Holiness? All your years as Pontiff? All the millions of miles in papal pilgrimages? All the billions of men and women and children who have seen your face and heard your living voice? All the vast rivers of words you've poured out in so many languages; all the cities you've seen; all the world leaders you've visited and who have visited you?

Is it all reduced to this, Holy Father? To your seclusion on a lonely hill in southern Poland at the bidding of Christ's clever enemies? Can this really be the will of Christ for you, His spokesman, His personal Vicar on this earth? Can you think that the God Who came to be crucified for us would give you a sign to justify acquiescence in the petty plots of pygmy men? Or in the darksome will of the nether forces those men serve?

Surely those questions must occur to Your Holiness before you allow the final page of these terrible events to be turned, and Your Holiness' chapter of history to be closed forever. . . .

"Precisely now, Holy Father, is the moment of truth."

Gladstone took another step forward on the balcony of Jasna Gora Monastery. One step closer to the Slavic Pope. "It's not yet dawn, but it's a matter of minutes. Holy Father . . ."

Christian's voice was drowned in a burst of extra-loud cheering from the crowds. A couple of television crews had made it to Czestochowa and had just turned on their searchlights to illuminate the scene.

Still silent, the Slavic Pope lifted his eyes to the morning. The steady drizzle of rain had ceased. The banks of clouds had begun to shift, chased by a bright carpet of stars unrolling behind them.

But Gladstone had said it. There was no trace of dawn yet in the eastern sky.